"Why did you stop?

"I was startin' to like it. Can we try again?" Danny asked.

"No!" Beau walked off.

"I gotta learn sometime. Someday I hope a man will come courtin', and if he wants to kiss, how am I goin' to know what to do?"

His hands on his hips, Beau stood there watching her, a dark eyebrow raised. "I've never met anyone so eager to learn."

"If you don't know how, just say so. I reckon I can learn from someone else."

This time she wasn't going to get away with her statement. The time had come to teach the wildcat a lesson. He leaned down until his lips were on hers. He kissed her passionately, and his hand slid down her flat stomach.

Danny suddenly jurked away. "What are you doin'?" Her breathing had become heavy, and a strange, delicious feeling consumed her body.

"Now you know what kissing can lead to," he said.

Dear Reader:

You are about to become part of an exciting new venture from Harlequin—*historical romances*.

Each month you'll find two new historical romances written by bestselling authors as well as some talented and award-winning newcomers.

Whether you're looking for an adventure, suspense, intrigue or simply the fulfilling passions of day-to-day living, you'll find it in these compelling, sensual love stories. From the American West to the courts of kings, Harlequin's historical romances make the past come alive.

We hope you enjoy our books and we need your input to assure that they're the best they can possibly be. Please send your comments and suggestions to me at the address below.

Karen Solem
Editorial Director
Harlequin Historical Romances
P.O. Box 7372
Grand Central Station
New York, N.Y. 10017

Bittersweet

DeLoras Scott

Harlequin Books

TORONTO • NEW YORK • LONDON
AMSTERDAM • PARIS • SYDNEY • HAMBURG
STOCKHOLM • ATHENS • TOKYO • MILAN

Harlequin Historical first edition December 1988

ISBN 0-373-28612-0

DeLORAS SCOTT

believes her writing is derived from a love for historical novels, a strong dash of humor and an excellent support group. A full-time writer, she enjoys the freedom of being able to create characters and have them come alive in plots of her choosing.

The mother of five grown children, she and her husband have lived and traveled throughout the U.S. A native of California, she now resides in the state of her birth.

Prologue

Territory of New Mexico, 1861

What a mighty fine day, Jed Turner thought as he guided his horse along the bottom of a dry creek bed. The sun shone brightly, and the sky looked as blue as cornflowers. Even the plumage on the cactus was a sight to behold. A broad grin crossed his tanned face. "After forty years," he cried out jubilantly, "by God, I finally hit it big. I got me a silver mine!"

Suddenly, the quiet land exploded with the high shrill of war whoops. Jed jammed his heels into the horse's sides, and the animal lunged up and over the rocky embankment that ran along the old wash. On the flats below, three Apache renegades mounted on painted ponies were circling a lone covered wagon.

"What the hell is a wagon doin' out here in the middle of nowhere?" Jed wondered aloud. His blood ran cold as he watched a woman climb from the wagon and run toward a man lying motionless on the ground. Two feathered arrows crisscrossed the man's back, and his blue shirt was stained with blood. Jed grabbed for his new Henry rifle, but before he could get off a shot, one of the savages impaled the lady with his lance and raised her body in the air like a rag doll. Jed pulled the trigger. The Apache fell from his horse and landed next to the woman's limp body.

Hearing the shot, the other braves turned their horses around and headed angrily toward him. Jed felt his hands start to shake and sweat clouded his vision as he looked down the rifle barrel at the grotesque faces covered with war paint. The two Indians spread apart, their ponies quickly closing the distance. As one savage raised his lance, Jed squeezed the trigger and the brave fell to the ground. Swinging the rifle to the left, Jed shot the other Apache in the chest.

The sudden silence was overwhelming. Everything had happened in a matter of minutes. Jed wiped the sweat from his forehead. Taking a deep breath, he dismounted.

After checking the savages to make sure they were dead, he went to the wagon and tied his horse to the back. He stood there a moment staring at the young couple, then rolled up his gray shirt sleeves. He didn't care about the Indians, but he'd be damned if he'd let the buzzards have their victims. Untying the shovel from the side of the wagon, he walked a short distance away and began digging a grave.

By the time the grisly task had been completed, Jed was hot and thirsty. He returned to the wagon and had just lifted the lid from the water barrel when he heard a noise from inside the wagon. Drawing his six-shooter, he crept to the back and stood listening. The sound came from the far corner, behind a stack of quilts. Jed climbed inside and worked his way toward the unidentifiable noise, then, gun ready, he jerked the quilts aside. A small child stared up at him, fear in her large brown eyes.

Dumbfounded, Jed felt like giving himself a hard kick. With all that had happened, it hadn't even occurred to him that someone might be inside.

"I want my ma," the child whimpered.

"What's your name, honey?" Jed asked in a soft voice.

"Danielle Louise. Where's my ma and pa?"

Jed didn't know what to say. Finally he found his voice. "Danielle Louise, I'm afeared you won't be seein' your ma and pa no more. I'm sorry, little one, but the Injuns done got 'em."

"No!" she screamed as she jumped up and headed toward the back of the wagon.

Jed caught her around the waist. "You're gonna be all right, honey," he crooned, "ain't nothin' gonna hurt you." He gently wrapped his big arms around the child.

The child's small hands balled up into fists and she began beating wildly on his chest as she continued to scream and cry hysterically.

It didn't take long before the little girl's strength was spent. Jed continued to hold her, uttering soothing words to the anguished child. When she fell asleep from exhaustion, he laid her down on a feather bed. He then went through the family trunks and found a diary, a sizable sum of money and various items of jewelry. He wasn't too good at reading, but good enough to know the diary confirmed that Danielle Louise was six years old and had no living relatives. He tucked everything back into the trunks for safekeeping. At least the little tyke would have something when she grew up, he thought as he climbed to the front of the wagon.

Untying the reins, Jed sat down on the driver's seat. He wanted to get as far away from the area as he could before the child woke up. Buzzards were already circling, ready to claim their Indian meal. He flicked the reins across the horses' backs, and the wagon moved forward.

Chapter One

Territory of New Mexico, 1873

Beau Falkner woke with a start as the Overland stagecoach in which he rode came to an abrupt halt. A cloud of dust billowed in through the open windows, and the small, gray-haired woman across from him quickly reached inside her satchel and pulled out a handkerchief to cover her mouth.

"Everyone out!" a voice commanded from outside.

"It's a holdup," said the short, balding banker, already shaking with fear. His thin squeaky voice had grated on Beau's nerves for the past fourteen days.

"I said get out! Now!"

"Guess we'd better do as the man says," Beau stated. He looked at the two passengers seated across from him. Since neither seemed anxious to be the first to leave the sanctuary of the stage, he set his black frock coat to the side and proceeded to exit the coach. Because of his height and broad shoulders, he had to turn sideways to get through the small opening. As soon as his feet were on the ground, he lifted the gray-haired woman down.

Beau glanced at his surroundings. Judging by the abundance of blue spruce and mountain mahogany, they were still in the Sangre de Cristo mountains. The bandits had selected a well-secluded area.

"Well, now, ain't this a useless lookin' group?"

Beau looked at the person talking. My God, it's only a skinny kid, he thought. The boy had a black, silver-trimmed hat pulled down low on his forehead and a red bandanna across his face. Behind the bandanna, a pair of squinting, dark eyes watched him.

"Well, I'll be danged. We got us a real live dandy," the boy said to the second outlaw. "Just look at them fine city clothes."

The big burly man holding a shotgun on the driver let out a grunt. "Let's get busy and get gone," he grumbled through his face covering.

"All right, driver, throw down that strongbox, and make it nice and slow," said the boy, turning his attention to the job at hand. "Don't go tryin' any brave stuff 'cause my pardner's got an anxious trigger finger." He motioned to the passengers. "You three. Step away from the coach."

As he moved, Beau took a closer look at the kid. The boy had the eyes of a hunter. He was cocky as hell, and from the way his guns were tied down on his legs, Beau felt sure the kid knew how to use them. Hearing a loud thud, he glanced over at the strongbox, now lying on the ground next to a rifle and a couple of pistols. He assumed the weapons belonged to the driver and the man riding shotgun.

The kid pointed to the banker. "You!"

"Ye-yes, sir." The banker shook so badly he could hardly speak.

The boy tossed a cloth bag to the ground. "Collect everything of value and put it in there. And don't go tryin' anything 'cause I'm watchin' you."

Damn if this doesn't beat all, Beau thought. Being held up by an old man and a kid who probably considered himself the fastest gun in the West. Slowly he began emptying his pockets into the bag the banker held out to him. He didn't have anything of value on him, so he wasn't concerned.

"Is that the best you can do, city slicker? Let's not be forgettin' that watch you got in that vest pocket," said the young outlaw.

Beau removed the watch and dropped it in the bag. Instinctively, he knew this stumped version of a male wanted to prove he was every bit as much a man as Beau. He'd seen it happen many times before.

"You wouldn't have a gun under those purty clothes, would ya? Naw, I reckon not, they fit too tight to be hidin' anything." The boy broke into laughter and slapped the leg of his dusty trousers. "You Easterners wouldn't know what to do with a gun if you had one."

The gray-haired woman had remained quiet until the banker held the sack out for her valuables. "Please, young man," she called in a pleading voice, "let me keep my wedding ring. It's all I have left to remember my late husband."

"Is it worth anythin'?" the boy asked.

"It is to me."

Beau's temper flared, but his deep voice remained calm. "If you were a gentleman, instead of a wet-nosed kid trying to play grown-up—"

"Who the hell you think you're talkin' to?" demanded the young outlaw as he slowly dismounted the big horse. Though he still didn't draw his guns, his eyes watched the passengers closely.

"You know exactly who I'm speaking to." Beau maintained his nonchalant manner. "Without those guns to play with, you'd be just like any other child."

"Leave him alone," the older man warned the boy. "We got what we come for, send 'em on their way!"

"Hell, no! I don't like any man puttin' me down! Maybe you need a real Western welcomin', mister. You big shots come here from your fancy places and think you know it all till someone teaches you different."

"Danny—"

"Keep quiet. I'm goin' to do purty face a favor and teach him a lesson. Hand me the bag, little man."

Perspiration dripped down the banker's face and onto his black suit despite the cool mountain air. He handed the outlaw the bag and quickly stepped away.

"Now you and the lady get back in the coach," said the boy. The kid kept his eyes on Beau while the two hurriedly did as they were told.

At least he's forgotten the woman's ring, Beau thought.

"All right, driver, take off, and don't come back," the boy ordered.

Needing no encouragement, the bearded driver cracked his whip across the backs of the six lathered horses. The noise sounded like a gunshot. Before the dust settled, the stage had disappeared.

"Surely you're not planning on leaving me here?" asked Beau.

"Gall dang!" the kid said. "Did you hear that, Jed? I thought you talked funny, mister, but I just figured it out. You're one of them prissy English fellers. I met one of your kind in a saloon a couple months back."

"Come on, Danny, we gotta get!" the big man said, showing his irritation. He now had his shotgun aimed at Beau's middle.

"I assume you're going to make me walk," Beau stated.

"Yep, but probably not like you think. I've taken a real likin' to those fine duds you've got on."

Beau's eyes narrowed. "You'll have to grow some for them to fit," he said, with far less English accent.

"Well, now, I'll just have somethin' to look forward to, won't I? Take 'em off!"

"You can't be serious."

With lightning speed, the boy whipped his gun from the holster and shot between Beau's feet. "Oh, I'm real serious. Now get busy, or I'm goin' to lift the barrel of this gun higher. Just for the record, I wasn't goin' to take the widder's ring. If you'd akept your highfalutin nose out of it, I might even of let you get back on the coach. Just 'cause you got some book learning, you think you know it all. Now move! And take it all off, including your johns and boots!"

"I'm not wearing johns. It's too damn hot," said Beau.

"You're not wearin' johns?" the boy asked with contempt. "I never heard of such a thing." Regaining his composure, the young outlaw added, "Well, it don't matter, get on with it."

Beau continued to keep his anger to himself. He knew he could knock the kid flat with one swing of his hand, but with a shotgun and a .45 aimed at him, there was nothing he could do to change the situation. He had to admit, the boy was fast.

After taking off his black vest, Beau slowly began unbuttoning his starched, ruffled white shirt. His eyes were locked with the kid's in a silent duel. When he'd removed the shirt, he loosened his belt, slowly drawing it through the loops as though he wanted to use it on the kid. Then he shrugged and dropped it to the dusty ground. A possible means of escape began to formulate in his mind. It was worth a try.

"Can I sit down and take off my boots?" Beau asked.

"Sure," the young outlaw said magnanimously, "but hurry up."

Sitting on the ground, Beau tugged at a boot. "I can't get it off," he lied. "I'm going to need your help."

The boy hesitated.

"It could be a trick," warned the other outlaw. "Let's just let him go!"

"I said I was goin' to learn him a lesson, and by damn that's what I'm gonna do!" The boy slid his gun in the holster then unbuckled the gun belt and looped it around the pommel of his saddle. "Watch him close, Jed."

"Wait a minute," said the big man, completely disgruntled. He dismounted and walked behind the stranger. Lifting the shotgun, he placed it against Beau's head. "All right, let's get this over with."

At first Beau thought they were going to kill him, until the kid straddled his leg and grabbed hold of the boot. Beau had hoped to use this to his advantage, but with Jed behind him, there was nothing he could do except give the little bastard a good shove. He placed his other foot on the kid's rear and pushed. The boy went flying to the ground, taking the boot with him.

"You ring-necked buzzard!" the youngster yelled as he stood up, dusting himself off.

"Don't try that again!" growled the man with the shotgun.

The kid took hold of the other boot, but this time, remained facing him. The soft leather boot came off with little effort.

"Thought you were bein' smart, didn't you?" asked the boy as he tossed the boot aside. "You'll have time to think again while you're walking under that hot sun. Now get the rest off, and you'd best make it quick. I'm losin' patience real fast."

Beau stood up, unbuttoned his broadcloth pants and let them fall to the ground. Stepping away, he stood straight and proud in his nakedness.

The boy laughed nervously. This wasn't the reaction he'd expected from the stranger. "Well, now, with them fancy duds off, you look just the same as the rest of us. A man needs to learn a little humility in these parts, and I reckon you're fixin' to learn. Start walkin', purty boy. It's not that far to Santa Fe. Folks in town are goin' to have a real good laugh when they see you."

When the stranger was well out of sight, the two outlaws pulled their bandannas down. Danny eagerly removed her gun from the holster still resting on the saddle and shot the lock off the strongbox. Jerking the lid open, she stood there for a moment in a daze.

"It's empty!" she said, kicking the ground in frustration. "We're never goin' to make money this way, Jed."

"That's what I been tryin' to tell you," he answered gruffly. "We're gonna get ourselves killed, that's what we're gonna do. 'Specially if you're plannin' on pulling any more smart stunts like you just did with that stranger. I don't know how the hell I let you talk me into this!" Jed started to get back on his horse then stopped and looked over at his partner. "Why did you do it, Danielle Louise?" he asked, a frown creasing his forehead.

Danny knew Jed was mad. That was the only time he called her by her given name. "Oh, I don't know. I just get tired of his kind lookin' down their nose at us. They're no better'n we are. They just got money, and we gotta work for ours." Danny gave Jed a smile that showed her small, perfect white teeth. "I tell you, though, Jed, he was right good-lookin'."

"Ain't you worried somethin' might happen to him?"

"Naw, he can make it to town when it's dark. He's gonna be a mite red, but he'll be okay."

"What're you gonna do with his things?"

"Just leave 'em here." Danny laughed. "He's right, I'm sure as hell never gonna grow into 'em."

They mounted their horses and took off through the trees. The sun filtered between the branches like shiny silver. When they started climbing toward the cliffs, the trees thinned out.

"I'm not sure you should'a done what you did."

Danny remained silent. She knew she was in the wrong.

"You never know when things like that are gonna come back to haunt you," Jed continued.

"You spook too easy," she chided as she guided her horse around some young spruce trees and over a rocky ledge.

"It ain't that," Jed insisted. "There was just somethin' about him that didn't run true. Somethin' in his eyes. And he weren't afraid."

"That's silly. 'Course he was scared. He just didn't let it show. Any man trembles when he's got a gun pointed at him. He's just some English feller comin' here to check out the stories he's heard. Hell, he probably don't even know what it's like gettin' his hands dirty."

"Could be, but I got an awful funny feelin' about him. He sure was a big feller. Way over six foot, and not a inch of fat on him. I ain't too sure I could even whip him."

Danny looked at him, surprised. Jed always said he could lick anyone, man or beast, and she had seen him prove it more than once. Why would Jed say something like that? The fellow had been taller, but he sure wasn't as big around as Jed. She figured the Englishman to be around thirty, while Jed was fifty-two. But even at that age, Jed's broad shoulders and barrel chest filled out the red and green plaid shirt he wore. He'd gotten a little flabby around the middle but he was still as strong as a bull. Besides, the dandy didn't even have a gun!

The way Jed talked, she began to feel a little uneasy. "You know, Jed, maybe we should move on. We've hit this stage-coach three times, and it's been empty every one of 'em. I think we'd be pushin' our luck to try again. What do you think about us headin' west?"

"Sure sounds good to me. The sooner we get away from this place, the better."

Danny let out a sigh. "Right now, all I can think about is gettin' back to the hideout so I can take this bindin' off. It's too damn hot." Danny always kept her breasts bound unless she and Jed were alone. It was a lot safer to look like a man out in the middle of nowhere. The fact that other men thought she was male, combined with her fast draw, had kept both of them out of a lot of trouble.

As soon as the land began to flatten out and cactus replaced the trees, Beau knocked off pods of a *puntia* with a rock and covered his body with the juice. Digging his fingers into the sandy dirt, he dusted it over the sticky liquid to protect his skin from the sun. When the mixture dried, he looked like a ghost.

Beau was sure he'd stepped on every rock in the narrow, hard-packed stagecoach ruts, and his feet were killing him. They'd become soft during his seven-year stay in England. If he weren't in such a hurry to return home after so long an absence, he'd damn well circle back and hunt the cocky kid down. His full lips twisted into an evil smile.

"I'd better not catch that kid in my part of the country," he vowed for the hundredth time. "If I do, he will pay dearly." There would be no problem recognizing him. The boy had been mounted on a big roan nag, while his partner rode a bald face. He knew the kid and his sidekick were named Danny and Jed, but it was the auburn hair that had curled out from behind the kid's hat that would be the easiest to spot.

In order to make the time pass, Beau thought of the years he had waited to return to the desert. Albeit not in this fashion. The young outlaw had called him a prissy Englishman, and Beau had to admit his English accent had been a little thick. In England he'd learned to hide his heritage under the outward mannerisms of a gentleman, but his heart remained Cheyenne. It was the Indian side of him that wanted to get even with the kid, and the Indian side that could not forgive his father for sending him away. There resided within Beau a strange mixture of love and hate for Gerard Falkner. Though Beau loved his father, he couldn't wait to see the old man and spew out all the words of hatred he'd nurtured for so many years.

Sweat dripped from Beau's hair into his eyes. He'd been walking about two hours when the sun began to dip behind the mountains. As the sun continued its downward course, he felt the heat finally start to subside.

Suddenly he heard a hee-haw and the jangle of pots and pans. Squinting into the rapidly disappearing sunlight, he could just make out a man leading a burro some distance away. Unfortunately, they were headed in the wrong direction. Beau didn't relish the idea of leaving the trail, but he had no choice. He started running, yelling and waving his arms.

The old prospector stopped and shook his head. He couldn't believe his own eyes, and he sure as hell hadn't had that much to drink in town. What was a gray man doing in this godfor-

saken country stark naked? The way the man was acting, he
had to be out of his head, or the sun or Indians had gotten to
him. "Maybe I should just shoot him and take him out of his
misery," he mumbled.

He started to reach for his gun, but couldn't bring himself to
do it. Rubbing his bearded chin, he placed his hand on the hilt
of a knife hanging from his waist and waited to see what the
loco fellow would do next. The man fell and didn't get up.

"What do you think, Maggie?" the prospector asked, turning to the pack animal.

The old burro pricked its shaggy ears forward.

"Yep, you're right. Guess we should take a look. If he's still
alive, it's gonna take a month of Sundays just gettin' all the
cactus thorns out."

The miner reached the still body and leaned down to check
the stranger's breathing. The man's eyelids suddenly snapped
open, and the prospector was staring into a pair of cold blue
eyes. Before he had time to react, the stranger's big hand
snaked around his throat. Next thing he knew, he was on the
ground with the man on top of him.

"I don't wish you any harm, mister, but I want to be damn
sure you feel the same way about me," Beau said.

"Ezekiel."

"What?"

"Name's Ezekiel. Most people call me Zeke."

Beau squatted on his heels and took a good look at the man
beneath him. Zeke had a craggy lined face, and the crow's-feet
around his eyes told of long periods in the sun. Straggly brown
hair, streaked with gray, stuck out from beneath his sweat-
stained floppy hat, which had long since lost any semblance of
color. How the hat had managed to stay on was a mystery to
Beau. The buckskins Zeke wore were equally stained and dirty.

"Did I hurt you?" Beau asked.

"Hell, no, it'd take more than that to hurt an ol' codger like
me."

Beau moved off the man and helped him up. "I saw you put
your hand on your knife, and I wasn't sure what your intentions were," said Beau, still watching the old man closely.

"Well, what would you do if you saw some critter, naked as
a jay, runnin' toward you?" Zeke gave Beau a toothless grin.

"Probably worse." Picturing in his mind what he must have looked like, Beau started laughing.

"I got me a little cabin not too far from here, and you're more than welcome." Zeke scratched his cheek. "Can't understand how you managed to keep from getting any thorn bites." He wanted like hell to ask this man what he was doing out here, but he'd learned a long time ago not to question strangers.

Beau gave the old man a broad, friendly smile. "I'll take you up on that offer. As you can see, I'm certainly not equipped to do much else."

Jed finished a large portion of Danny's stew and let out a sigh of contentment. He sat on the hard-packed earthen floor next to the fire, watching the flames cast eerie shadows across the ancient sandstone walls and pine beams. Their hideout was an old Indian ruin with the entrance well hidden by thick brush. Nearby, a small stream of cool, clear water fed into a large, natural pool. Jed had found the dwellings about two months ago. More than once he'd wondered about the Indians who had lived here. He glanced over at Danny who was busy cleaning her pistols, deep in thought.

Danny sat thinking about her ranch. A prospector named Gus Smith had been going around Dusty Creek to the mine owners, trying to get someone to buy his land. Everyone thought he was loco. She'd been fifteen at the time, and feeling old enough to take care of herself, she'd listened to what the fellow had to say.

Gus had gone to the gold rush in the Arizona territory, and when he made a little money, he'd purchased land, intending to settle down and raise cattle. But he was obsessed with gold fever, and eventually started drifting again, searching for the elusive metal. Ultimately, he ended up in Dusty Creek, sure he'd discovered a rich deposit, but he needed a grub stake.

Danny had always wanted land and a home. Jed had never spent her parents' money, saying it would be there for her when she grew up. So, without consulting Jed, she had bought the land from the prospector. To her way of thinking, this is what her ma and pa would want the money used for, and she would finish what they had started so many years ago. She smiled, remembering how furious Jed had been when he'd discovered what she'd done.

As if Jed's anger wasn't enough, the other miners laughed, saying she'd been suckered. Jed contacted Jose Jackson who, according to local gossip, knew cattle, and hired him to run the ranch. After giving the man a considerable amount of money to file the land in Danny's name and purchase livestock, he'd sent him and his wife on their way to Prescott.

"You're one hell of a cook," Jed said, adjusting his right leg as it rested across a saddle. "Make some man a fine wife."

Deep in thought, Danny was startled by Jed's words. "What did you say?" she asked.

Jed chuckled. "I said, you're a hell of a cook and would make someone a good wife."

"Why would you say something like that?"

"Been sittin' here thinkin'. You ought to be married by now, Danny, with kids hangin' on your apron strings, instead of robbin' stages and havin' a reward on your head. I reckon I ain't done too good a job raisin' you."

"It wasn't your fault that ol' mine was fixin' to play out, and it wasn't your idea to turn to robbin'. And what would've happened if you hadn't come along and saved me when I was little? I would've starved to death, that's what. Are you wantin' to get rid of me, Jed?" she asked playfully.

"You know better than that. You just ain't never learned…woman things. You're mighty comely now, and you got purty sorrel-colored hair, if you'd just let it grow instead of choppin' it off all the time."

"I like it this way. It's a lot cooler."

Jed chose to ignore her comment and continued saying what was on his mind. "The only woman I ever knew was that squaw woman 'fore I met you, and the women I visit in town."

Danny laughed. "You want me to be like them?"

"Hell, no! I'd blister your bottom. What I'm tryin' to say is, I don't know how to teach you any of them female things. You deserve better. Maybe it's time to settle down."

"You mean become respectable."

"Yep, I reckon that's what I'm tryin' to say. We ain't seen that ranch you bought. We don't even know if Jose bought the cattle or whether he ran off with the money."

"Oh, I'm not worried about Jose. You know how happy he was to finally have a permanent place for him and Carlotta to live." Danny sat a moment, thinking. "Jed, all we need is a couple of good holdups and we'd be set."

"You got it in your head that we need more money. Hell, we still got us a pretty good stash after sellin' the mine."

Danny remembered how hard they'd worked to dig out what silver they could.

He picked up a log and tossed it on the fire. "Maybe the Silver J is doin' fine. We ain't gonna know till we see it. We're just no good at this robbin', Danny. This last one was the only one we did right, and there weren't no money in the box."

"But we're gettin' better. Tell you what, let's head west. Who knows, along the way we might pick up a stage or two. You gotta look on the bright side, Jed." Danny gave him a cheery smile.

Well, Jed thought, at least that would get them headed toward Arizona territory and the ranch. "All right. We'll hole up here till we're sure there ain't nobody lookin' for us." He stood up and stretched, ready to call it a night.

"Jed," Danny called, after he'd settled down on his bedroll.

"Yeah?"

"You reckon that English prissy made it safe to town?"

"Why you thinkin' about that now?"

"Oh, I don't know. Jed, I really didn't want nothin' bad to happen to him, I was just so damn mad at what he said and the way he was lookin' at me."

"Well, it's too late to be worryin' over it now."

A picture of the tall, handsome man with black hair and creases in his cheeks flashed through her mind. "You know, it'd be kind of nice wearin' a fancy dress and havin' a man look at me like I was someone special."

Jed rolled over on his side, pleased with Danny's words. He'd tried over the years to get her to wear a dress, but she had stubbornly refused. She said it was easier to handle a gun and ride in men's clothes. As he drifted off to sleep, he reflected on how fast the twelve years had gone by since he'd found her. Seemed like yesterday. He'd grown to think of her as his own daughter, and loved her dearly. Yep, time had come for her to start learning female ways.

Danny went back to cleaning her guns, but her thoughts were on Jed. He was a mighty fine-looking man for being fifty-two, especially when he shaved. His brown eyes were as alert as ever, and his dark hair hadn't changed color during the years. But his bushy beard was streaked with gray and made him look older. Of course he only shaved when he went into town to pay a visit to the ladies, as he would say. It was during one of those visits to Santa Fe that Jed had seen the wanted posters. But when he was duded up, no one would ever recognize him as the man who held up stages. Sometimes Danny felt guilty about Jed having to raise her. If she hadn't been around, maybe he would have found some nice woman and settled down.

Danny slid her guns in the holster, then went outside. She lifted her short hair off the back of her neck, welcoming the cool breeze. It's getting too long, she thought. It needs cutting again.

As she stood on a rock, looking across the moonlit valley below, Danny considered what Jed had said. Was he trying to say she'd end up an old maid? She had to admit even some of the girls at Bonnie May's house of pleasure were younger than she. There had been some fine-looking men in the small town of Dusty Creek, but they'd paid scant attention to Jed's tomboy kid.

She'd tried for a long time to keep her mother and father fresh in her mind, but over the years their images had faded, and Jed had become her family. Her parents' possessions were now safely tucked away at the ranch. Jose and his wife had taken them when they'd left for the Silver J. Now that she was grown, Danielle had a gnawing desire to reacquaint herself with her mother's diary and the items in the trunks. Jed always said they'd be there waiting for her when she decided to settle down.

Maybe someday she would, but for now, all her thoughts were centered on the Silver J and the need to make it a success. It was the only thing she'd ever owned, and she clutched and nursed the knowledge of that ownership to her bosom as dearly as a woman would a babe.

Because of her obsession over the ranch, she had slowly developed the theory that they needed lots more money. It didn't take long for her to come up with the idea of how to secure it. When she'd told Jed of her plan, he'd flatly refused. Knowing how to get her way, she'd informed him that if he didn't want to help her, she'd rob the stages by herself. Just as she had suspected, Jed, afraid something might happen to her, had finally relented. Now she felt bad about forcing him into it. Jed had been right all along. Robbing stagecoaches was the worst idea she'd ever come up with.

Chapter Two

Zeke's shack sat in the middle of nowhere. A rocky-bottomed stream ran close by, and small, low, thorny cacti covered a good portion of the surrounding land.

As Beau paced back and forth in the dirty abode Ezekiel called a cabin, his eyes lazily scanned the now-familiar room. It was a wonder the place remained standing. During the day, light poured in between the old log walls and through the holes in the roof. The single room had an earthen floor and a stone fireplace covering one end. The rough-hewn table and two chairs were the only pieces of furniture, and slats had been nailed up, helter-skelter, for storing food and anything else Zeke chose to throw there. Everything in the cabin was in total disarray. Apparently the old man never threw anything away, including empty food tins.

Walking to the window, Beau pulled back the cracked deer-hide and looked out. Since the cabin was only a short distance from town, Zeke should have already returned. It was getting dark. God, he hoped Ezekiel had found his trunk.

When Beau first arrived at the cabin, Zeke had told him he didn't feel right having a full-grown man going around naked in his house. Beau chuckled softly, remembering what he had gone through before finally convincing Zeke there were problems. Where Beau was broad across the shoulders and chest, Zeke was small. After trying on several shirts, the old man finally agreed that Beau couldn't get his arms into them, let alone his body. Zeke had even admitted he may have gotten a little too carried away by saying Beau was too persnickety.

The pants were an entirely different matter. Beau's waist and hips were narrow while Zeke's were thick. Beau could wear the pants, but had to hold them up with a piece of rope, and the bottom of the pant legs ended almost at his knees. Ezekiel was happy, but Beau wasn't. The old man wasn't the cleanest person who'd ever lived, and the pants had an offensive odor. But during the three days he'd been here, he'd already grown fond of the old codger.

Suddenly Beau saw a weaving figure heading toward the cabin. Then he heard the old man singing. Beau let the hide fall back into place and stepped outside.

"Howdy, Beau," Ezekiel called. "You was right. The stage-coach driver left your trunk in town, all right, but not at the hotel like you thought." The old man laughed, exhaling the sour smell of whiskey. "No sirree. It was at the undertaker's. They figured you wouldn't be comin' around to pick it up."

Beau went over and lifted the trunk from Maggie's back. "Hallelujah," he yelled. "At last, clean clothes that fit."

Zeke started dancing a jig, and Beau laughed at the man's antics.

"Hey, Beau, I brought some good sour mash from town. Care to join me in a drink or two?"

"I'd love to, old man. Can't think of a better way to celebrate."

The next day Zeke took Beau to town. Beau, dressed simply in a pair of gray trousers and a white shirt, could already feel the early morning sun blazing down on him.

Santa Fe, a thriving, bustling, adobe-walled town, sat on a mesa. Large wagons, pulled by long teams of mules and filled with trade goods, could be seen arriving and leaving via the Santa Fe trail. Some of the wagons could haul up to four tons of goods. Narrow streets emanated from the central plaza and led to various businesses, churches and the homes of the wealthy. Everyone seemed intent on completing the morning business.

"Beau, how's about we stop for a little nip?" Zeke asked, licking his lips in anticipation. Ezekiel felt all visits to town should begin at one of the many cantinas.

"You go ahead," Beau said. "I'll meet you there shortly. I want to stop at the bank before I do anything else."

Ezekiel became nervous. What was the boy going to do now? he wondered. "Are you sure you're not still sufferin' from heat, son?" Zeke rubbed the side of his bearded jaw. "Ain't plannin' on robbin' it, are you?"

Beau chuckled. "No, I'm not going to do anything like that. I just need some money to buy a few things."

They turned down one of the streets, but when they passed a saloon, Zeke didn't turn in. He continued to trail after Beau.

"Well, you can't just walk in a bank and ask 'em for money. 'Sides, what you need that I ain't got?"

"A horse and rifle would be a good start."

"I'm tellin' you Beau, you shouldn't go in askin' some banker for money. I don't know what they do in that there place you came from, but out here it's called robbin'!"

They arrived at the bank, and Beau turned toward the old man. "You wait out here, Zeke. I'll be right back."

Beau was about to open the door when the old man grabbed his arm. Ezekiel's eyes peeked out from under bushy, peppered eyebrows and mirrored his concern. "Don't do it, boy. You'll be runnin' the rest of your life. I've thought about doin' it many a time, but it just ain't worth it. They'll lock you up and throw away the key."

"I promise I won't do anything that will cause trouble," Beau said in an equally serious tone, trying to appease Zeke. He removed the old man's hand from his sleeve and entered the bank.

Beau avoided the lines in front of the teller cages and went straight to the rear. A low, highly polished wooden railing surrounded a small area where a blond man sat behind a desk. The man's black suit was spotless, but the silk vest was pulled tight across his ample belly, threatening to pop its buttons. His round face had a reddish hue. Beau pushed open the swinging gate and walked in.

"Are you the manager?" Beau asked.

The banker looked up and over the top of his metal-rimmed spectacles. "As you can see, I'm busy. Please wait outside, and I'll be with you shortly." His tone left little doubt that he resented the intrusion.

"I'll only take a minute of your time, Mr. . . . ." Beau lifted a dark eyebrow, waiting.

"Bicker, Mr. . . . ." In his agitation, the man's face became even redder.

"Falkner. Beau Falkner." Beau waited for the name to penetrate.

Suddenly Mr. Bicker's face lit up. "Oh, I am sorry, Mr. Falkner." He stood up, his chubby hands quickly putting some papers in some semblance of order. "Please, sir, have a seat." The banker indicated the chair behind the desk. "I've been expecting you. I have your money ready. It will only take a minute to bring in the bank records. I wasn't sure just when you would be arriving."

"That's quite all right, Mr. Bicker." Ignoring the banker's gesture, he sat down in a chair facing the desk and stretched out his long legs. "I'm not here to check on the bank. As you know, we have someone who handles that for us."

"If you'll excuse me, I'll be right back with the money." The banker disappeared, but was gone only a few minutes. "Here you are, sir," he said, placing a bag on the desk in front of Beau. He walked behind the small desk and sat back down. "It must feel good to return home after being in England for so long," said the now amiable man.

"Yes, I'm quite anxious to see my family."

"I was expecting you to arrive by coach." The banker gave Beau a friendly smile.

"I would have. Unfortunately there was a holdup—"

"You were on that coach?" Mr. Bicker asked, surprised. "There's a reward out for the Gringo Kid, but so far he's gotten clean away. That's the third time he's held up that stage. Overland decided to stagger their gold shipments, and fortunately the kid has always picked a stage that wasn't carrying anything. Something needs to be done." The banker's eyes suddenly lit up. "You weren't the man that didn't get back on, were you?"

"It's a long story," Beau said, as he stood, ready to leave.

Mr. Bicker immediately stood also. "I know you'll be needing supplies to get you the rest of the way, so if that's not enough, let me know and I'll fix you right up. Prices are a lot higher now than when you were last here."

"This should do just fine," Beau replied.

"If there is anything else I can do while you're in town, Mr. Falkner, be sure and let me know." The two men shook hands. "Please give your sister my regards. I hope she's feeling better than the last time I saw her. But it's been a while, so she's probably overcome her grief by now."

Grief? What was the man talking about, Beau wondered. "When did you last see my sister?" he asked.

"I attended your father's funeral. I know how upset you must have been to hear the news. It's too bad you weren't able to get back in time."

Beau felt a throbbing pain start to twist in his gut, but he maintained a stoic demeanor. He hadn't known of his father's death. "Ah . . . yes, it was. Thank you for your help, Mr. Bicker." Beau longed to ask questions, but refused to let the banker see his turmoil.

As soon as Beau walked out of the bank, Zeke was beside him. "What took you so long? Did you do it? Are we gonna have to make a run for it?"

Why now, Father? I was almost home, Beau thought. He had to be alone.

"I have to leave, old man. I don't know how long I'll be gone. Where can I buy a rifle?" he asked.

"There's a general store on the next street over," Zeke grumbled. He was confused. If Beau hadn't robbed the bank, why was he so anxious to get out of town? The boy never told him nothing!

Thirty minutes later, when they left the store, Beau wore buckskin pants and shirt. A bowie knife and scabbard were attached to his wide belt next to the leather pouch of cartridges. Tucked under his arm was a Winchester rifle.

"Ain't you gonna tell me what you're plannin' on doin'?" Ezekiel asked, still put out at Beau's continued silence.

Beau ignored Zeke's question, his concentration centered on getting out of town. All he needed now was a horse.

The two men had just arrived at the plaza when they heard a woman scream, and everyone began clearing the street. Beau could see dust flying into the air. Through the maze of frantic people, he finally discovered the cause of all the commotion as five scruffy looking riders came into view. Two men rode on each side of a big, snorting black stallion, their ropes pulled taut around its strong neck. They had spaced themselves far enough away to miss the horse's flying hooves. The fifth man rode in back of them carrying a bullwhip. Beau knew the horse had been provided for him. It was a sign.

"Hey, George. What's that you got?" a short, fat man called out.

The man with the bullwhip grinned and pulled his horse over to the side. "He's really something, ain't he, Cecil?"

"Maybe so, but what are you going to do with him?" Cecil asked.

The other four riders stopped near the cottonwood trees in the middle of the square and were having a hard time keeping the ropes pulled tight. The stallion continued to fight, kicking up dust and screaming out his defiance.

"Thought someone might want to buy him," stated George, pulling the wide-brimmed hat down to shade his eyes from the sun's glare. "How about you, Cecil? You got a lot of nice mares."

"He'd probably kill 'em. That horse looks plumb loco. Reminds me of cowboys when they been smoking mescal. Yep, I'd say Mescal is a perfect name for him." Cecil started laughing, and his whole belly shook.

More men began to congregate, asking George questions about the black beast. Beau wasn't listening. His eyes quickly assessed the big stallion. His coat was in bad condition and lathered over his prominent ribs, and places along his neck had been rubbed raw. He stood almost seventeen hands, with a well-proportioned frame and deep chest. Solid muscle rippled his haunches and his head was small and wide between the eyes.

"So I killed me an Injun," George bragged, "and we played hell catching his horse."

"They ain't gonna sell that devil," Ezekiel mumbled. "Nobody's crazy enough to buy the critter!"

Beau had forgotten Zeke was beside him.

"Hey, George!" yelled one of the riders. "We gotta find some place to put this varmint. We're tuckered out."

Beau suddenly let a high, shrill sound. The stallion pricked his ears forward and looked in Beau's direction.

"Who the hell did that?" someone yelled. "Sounded like a damn Indian!"

Zeke didn't know what to think, but he knew it was time for him and Beau to get out of town. "Son—"

Beau shoved the bag of money in Ezekiel's hand. "I want the horse. You pay for him."

Before Zeke could say a word, Beau walked toward the animal.

"You! Stranger!" George called out. He started laughing. "You're gonna get your head bit off."

Beau's steps never faltered. As he neared the animal, he started muttering incomprehensible words. "Hand me the ropes," he ordered the riders.

All four men looked toward George.

"You planning on buying...Mescal, mister?" George hollered at Beau.

"How much?" Beau asked, never taking his eyes off the stallion.

"I figure he's worth a hundred." George snickered.

"Sold. The man over there has the money." Beau motioned his hand in Zeke's direction.

"I gotta see the money first," George insisted.

"Pay him, Ezekiel," Beau called over his shoulder.

Ezekiel was flabbergasted. Obviously Beau knew nothing about horses, and this man George was taking advantage of him. The horse wasn't worth a plugged nickel. He stepped out in the street. "Now, Beau, let's talk about this. You—"

"Pay him!" Beau barked.

Zeke turned to the side so no one could see how much money he had, then counted out the proper amount. Mumbling, he went over and handed it to George.

After George had counted it, his thin lips formed into a big grin, showing his brown, stained teeth. "Well, I reckon he's all yours, mister," he said, and broke out laughing. "Now, what you reckon you're gonna to do with the damn critter?"

The gathered crowd laughed, appreciating the sly horse trading George had pulled on the stranger.

"Easiest money I ever made," George said, proud of himself. "Okay, boys, drop the ropes."

The four men tossed the ropes at Beau's feet, then kneed their mounts in an effort to get away before the enraged stallion charged. Mescal stood there a moment, trembling, ears flattened back and eyes rolling wildly. Beau spoke softly to him in a low voice as he quickly removed three of the ropes and cut off the end of the fourth one. Suddenly the stallion reared up, and when he came down, he headed toward George, his big teeth snapping.

In his haste to escape the charging animal, George fell from his horse. When he landed on the hitching rail, it broke, and George found himself momentarily submerged in the dirty water trough. Beau chuckled in appreciation of the justice rendered.

At the last second, the horse checked his stride and changed direction, ready to take off for freedom. Beau moved quickly. He shifted the rifle to his right hand, and as the mighty stallion bolted forward, Beau grabbed his mane and swung himself up on the racing animal. Everyone stood watching as man and beast disappeared down the street in a cloud of dust.

"Damn fool, you're gonna get killed!" Ezekiel yelled, even though he knew Beau couldn't hear him. Shaking his head in disbelief, Zeke sauntered over to the nearest cantina, bought a bottle of whiskey and left. He wanted to be home in case Beau returned and needed help.

Mescal's long legs stretched out and he arched his tail high. Beau thanked the gods for sending such a worthy steed, and as they headed northwest, he made no effort to change their direction. He knew the animal had been sent to deliver him to a place of worship.

As the miles rushed by beneath Mescal's hooves, Beau was consumed with anger, hurt and grief. There were many things he had needed to confront his father with, but now the opportunity had passed forever.

Beau finally realized the need to slow Mescal down before the stallion was entirely spent. He pulled back on the rope, but the horse refused to slow his pace. Beau tossed his rifle to the ground and leaned down to the left side of the horse's neck. In one fluid movement, he wrapped his right arm under the black neck and swung off the horse. Suspended in air, he threw his left arm around Mescal's muzzle and pulled back, bringing the stallion to a halt.

Beau grabbed the rope as he lowered his feet to the ground and spoke soothing words to calm the high-spirited animal. When the stallion stopped strutting around, he led him back to where he'd dropped the rifle. After discarding his shirt, Beau walked for some time to cool the horse down. Finally he remounted and nudged the animal forward at a slower pace.

For two days they continued on. The land looked flat but was actually cut by gullies and ridges. The sun bore down unmercifully. In the late afternoon of the second day, they entered a small canyon surrounded by fir trees and large granite boulders. Beau knew he had arrived at his place of worship. He turned the horse loose.

Later that night, clouds drifted over the moon, and the night became exceedingly dark. A storm was threatening. The reverberating peals of thunder and the repeated flashes of vivid lightning strengthened Beau's belief that the canyon was a holy place. Here he would perform the rituals.

Slowly, Beau undressed. He accomplished everything in a trancelike state, knowing the mind must be clear and open to communicate with the spirit world. Picking up the buckskin pants, he cut three wide pieces and four long strips. One piece he used to make a breechcloth that went up and over the thin strip he tied above his hips. The other two were placed on his feet and tied with buckskin strips around his ankles. He placed the fourth strip around his forehead and tied it in the back. Everything completed, Beau sat waiting.

When light started creeping up into the heavens, he walked to the boulders and began his ascent. In no time, sweat ran down his body and more than once he started to slide down. Although his body was lean and muscular, he had to stop many times to catch his breath. His dry, painful throat reminded him how long he'd been without water. It was an arduous climb, and took several hours before he reached the highest point, where the spirits could seek him. A huge rock jutted out over the canyon. He climbed up on the flat surface, went out almost to the end and sat cross-legged. His chanting echoed through the canyon. He knew a true vision seldom came quickly.

For four days, Beau performed the rituals, calling to Maheo, the All Father, Grandmother Earth, Sun, Thunder and Moon. Hunger, thirst, sun and cold nights assailed him. He saw visions of his childhood at the ranch. He relived the pain he'd felt when his father had destroyed his medicine pouch and forced him to leave the Colorado Territory; and again when he was placed on a ship bound for England. He enjoyed the laughing and happy times spent with his mother's people, and the raids on the Crow camps. He saw eagles soar through the clouds and joined them in their flight.

When the white buffalo appeared, followed by his tall, blond father, Beau wanted to join them. He had not yet saved his father's soul. He let out a loud, mournful cry.

Grasping the handle of his knife, he raised it to his arms and pierced the inner skin. Slowly he moved it downward. Released from its confinement, his blood flowed freely.

"No, my son. You must not do this," said a soft, warm voice.

The image of Beau's mother suddenly appeared before him and a white glow surrounded her. She was young and beautiful. Long black braids hung over her shoulders and down her beaded, white doeskin tunic. More beads circled her forehead. She smiled the sweet smile Beau remembered so well.

"Why do you stop me, my mother?" he asked, shocked at her statement.

"It is not your way, my son."

"But my father is dead."

"You are a white man. Is this not why you were sent to the land across the great waters? This is the way it was meant to be, my son. One cannot change one's destiny."

"Am I not of *the* People?" Beau asked in an anguished voice. "Have I not a Cheyenne heart though half of me is white?"

"You are of my blood, as you are of your father's blood. You will not forget your Indian teachings, and you will pass this knowledge on to your sons. It was a good life, but will be no more."

"Why do you speak so?"

"The white man will destroy all we hold sacred. They will drive us from our lands. There has been much bloodshed on both sides, but our people and our ways suffer the most. I would not have you be a part of it, on either side. You must live and remain strong. As the years go by, your generations will tell of the glories and life we once had. Go in peace, my son, and remember.''

As if in a cloud she turned, and his father walked up beside her. They joined hands and disappeared into the mist.

When Beau regained consciousness, he had no idea how much time had passed. He was blistered from the sun, his tongue swollen from lack of water and his stomach cramped from going so long without food. The blood on his arm and hand had long since dried. He thought about what his mother had said and considered his position in life.

As a boy, life had not been easy. The children on the ranch had ridiculed him, and he'd grown to hate the word half-breed. Not until years later, when he was tall and strong, did they finally keep their comments to themselves. His complexion was quite light, but he had Indian blood, and that was all that mattered. The only place he had felt free and accepted was with the Cheyenne. Then the time came when he didn't care what they thought, and he began to hate the white man.

England had changed everything. There they had accepted and liked him. Still, he found it difficult to trust anyone, especially women. He had become very popular with the opposite sex in England, and it didn't take him long to realize how conniving they could be. That didn't mean he didn't enjoy their company. Quite the contrary. He just made it clear that marriage was out of the question. The mighty Cheyenne warrior, Roman Nose, believed that women could steal his strength. Maybe he had the right idea. With great difficulty, Beau stood and began his descent.

Although Beau had come to accept his mixed blood, his mother's words made the blending of his two cultures complete. Upon leaving the small canyon, Beau Falkner was finally at peace with himself.

It had been two weeks since Beau had taken off on the loco horse, and Zeke was worried. The boy could be lying somewhere hurt or dead. He was seriously thinking about looking for him when he heard the distant whinny of a horse. Stepping outside, Ezekiel saw an Indian riding toward him. He started to run into the cabin for his gun when he heard the man call his name.

"God Almighty!" he whispered, recognizing Beau.

Beau pulled Mescal to a halt in front of the openmouthed old man.

"Tryin' to give me heart failure?" Zeke asked. "I thought you was an Injun. Why you dressed like that?" Something about Beau had changed. His skin had turned much darker, and his hair had grown longer, but that wasn't it. The fact that he was practically naked had nothing to do with it, either. Zeke couldn't put his finger on it, but for some reason, Beau seemed older.

As Beau slid off Mescal's back, his tall shadow fell across the shorter man.

"How the hell did you ever tame that critter?" Zeke asked, watching Beau turn the stallion loose.

"The Indian way." Beau smiled.

"You tellin' me you're Injun?"

Beau let out a hearty laugh. "And if I did, would you run for your gun?"

"I don't reckon I know what I'd do. Seein' as how I've come to know you, don't reckon I'd do nothin'."

Beau walked into the cabin with Zeke on his heels.

"You don't have to worry, I'm not going to scalp you." Beau chuckled. "Do you have anything to eat?"

"Yep. Sit down and I'll have you somethin' in a jiffy. While I'm gettin' it, you're goin' to do some explainin'?" Zeke dipped some food from the black cauldron hanging in the fireplace onto a tin plate and set it down on the table in front of Beau.

"About what?" Beau asked, taking a bite of food. Exactly what he was eating was questionable, but it was tasty.

"About why you're actin' like you are. Dressin' like an Injun and such. And where you been all this time?" Zeke dragged the other chair out and plopped down, waiting for his questions to be answered. Beau remained silent. "Well, you don't have to say nothin' if you don't want to. I already know what happened. The sun got to you again, didn't it?"

"You could be right."

"Yep! You should'a taken me with you! You people come out west and ain't got no idea how to survive."

Beau laughed.

"Go ahead and laugh, but you been plain lucky so far."

When Beau had finished eating, he leaned back and looked at the old man. "I'll be leaving in the morning, Zeke. Time for me to be heading on."

"Which way you headin'?" the old man asked. He'd taken a real liking to the boy and would miss him.

"West. You're welcome to come along."

"Naw, I'm too old to be gadaboutin'. I'm right happy where I am." A twinkle entered the old man's eyes. "If you think you can get along without me."

Beau chuckled.

"I reckon we've got everythin' ready to leave in the mornin', Danny," said Jed.

Danielle was busy cleaning up after the evening meal. "I'm really lookin' forward to seein' the ranch," she said, looking up from her chores. "I don't plan on ever leavin'."

Jed took paper and a bag of tobacco out of his shirt pocket, rolled a cigarette then lit it with a piece of kindling from the fire. He took a deep breath then exhaled the smoke slowly. "You know, I'm too old to be driftin'. I'm ready to settle down and enjoy the peaceful life."

Danny smiled. She wasn't so sure Jed even knew what living a peaceful life meant.

Chapter Three

Danny and Jed traveled at a leisurely but steady pace. They camped at sunset, and left each morning after daybreak. Close to noon on the fourth day, they followed a steep trail from the upper part of a mesa. Below sat a large meadow.

Several deer were grazing at the outer edge of a sea of tall grass that rippled like rolling waves from the brisk, warm breeze. Tall fir trees surrounded three sides, and the sweet odor of pine resin reached Danny's nostrils.

They sat admiring the peaceful scene when suddenly shots rang out and a flatbed wagon appeared from between the tall firs. The driver crouched low in an effort to keep from being hit by the bullets from the guns of the four masked riders in hot pursuit. He managed to keep a firm hold on the reins and continued to slap them across the horses' backs, encouraging a faster speed. The second man on the wagon seat was turned to face the rear, shooting his rifle in retaliation.

As Danny watched the scene unfolding below, the wagon bounced into the air and something fell off the back. She wanted to help, but knew they'd never reach the meadow in time. One of the masked pursuers fell from his horse, while at the same time the driver of the wagon fell forward. So many shots were being exchanged that Danny couldn't tell which ones hit their targets. Two more outlaws fell. She had to admire the good eye of the man in the wagon.

The last rider suddenly slowed his horse and took off in the opposite direction, apparently giving up the chase. As he rode out of view, slumped low over his saddle, she could see a large red blotch of blood soaking the back of his shirt.

She urged her horse into a gallop, Jed close on her heels. When they reached the meadow, they took off in the direction the wagon had gone. It didn't take long to locate the conveyance, but unfortunately both men were dead. Jed unhitched the horses and turned them loose.

"What you reckon that was all about?" he finally asked.

"You got me," Danny replied, feeling a mite squeamish.

Jed climbed back on his horse. "Let's go and check on them other fellers," he said.

After finding the other men dead, Danny insisted they look for what had fallen off the wagon. The tall grass made the job like looking for a needle in a haystack.

"Hell, Danny," Jed said, showing his aggravation, "let's just give it up."

"Not till we see what it was. I think it was a strongbox. There had to be somethin' important in it, or those men wouldn't of been chasin' the wagon. Keep lookin', Jed."

Mescal hadn't taken too kindly to the saddle, but as the days passed, he'd finally come to accept it. Beau could appreciate the horse's desire to shed the unwanted weight. He felt the same way about his shirt and pants.

He stopped thinking about discomfort when he heard shots some distance up ahead and urged Mescal forward.

Nearing the area the shots had come from, he heard two people talking. The tall pines allowed him ample cover as he circled Mescal around and came up from behind. When he had a good view, he drew back on the reins and sat watching quietly. The pair seemed to be searching for something. The short one wore a black hat trimmed with silver and Beau could see auburn hair sticking out from behind. They were walking slowly, the burly man a short distance ahead of the boy.

The corners of Beau's mouth curved into a smile as he recognized the outlaws. This was a very pleasant turn of events. In front of him stood an opportunity he couldn't refuse. A chance to get even with the kid, and maybe teach him a lesson. Beau pressed his knees to the stallion and let out a war whoop. Mescal bolted forward.

The sound momentarily startled Danny, and by the time she reached for her guns, it was too late. A strong arm whipped around her waist, lifting her upward. A second later, Beau's boot came up under Jed's chin, knocking him to the ground. The stallion was in a full gallop and never slowed down.

Danny screamed, kicked and fought, but the steel band around her waist held firm. She could see the grass passing swiftly beneath her, and some of it hit her in the face. She felt sure the other scavenger had returned to claim his prize, and she became determined to get loose or die in the attempt. Gathering all her strength, she tried to thrust her body backward. As she started to slip, a strong hand grabbed her by the britches and threw her across the horse's neck, the pommel jabbing her side. Still she fought.

Jed shook his head and pushed himself off the ground. It took a few minutes before he could get his thinking going in the right direction. He had no idea how long he'd been knocked out. Danny! Jed ran to his horse and jumped on. Grabbing the reins of Danny's horse, he studied the ground in front of him and took off following the fresh tracks.

Beau traveled a considerable distance before coming to a stop. He'd left a deliberate trail for the kid's partner to follow, and Beau knew it would take the man about three hours to find them. A little less if Jed knew anything about tracking. The length of time wasn't a coincidence. It was a little longer than Beau had spent walking from where the stage had been held up.

"Let me down, you bastard!" Danny yelled. She felt as though she'd been pounded to death. Beau released his hold and she fell to the ground with a thud, the breath momentarily knocked out of her.

Beau dismounted.

Drawing air into her lungs, Danny saw a pair of dusty boots a short distance from where she lay. Her eyes traveled upward along the hard-muscled legs to a broad chest, then the face. "You!" she snarled. "For a minute there, I thought I had somethin' to worry about." She spat on the ground, showing her disgust.

Beau opened his saddlebag and pulled out a hatchet.

Good lord in heaven! Did he plan to use it on her? Danielle automatically reached for her guns. The holsters were empty. Then she tried to stand, but her legs buckled under her. Determined to defend herself, she reached down and snatched a knife from her boot. The man stood watching, an evil grin spreading across his face. It occurred to Danny that, with his black hair and black clothes, he looked like the devil.

"Don't come near me, you English bastard," she threatened. "I'll slice you from one end to the other!" Slowly, never taking her eyes off him, she pulled herself up to a standing position.

Without any apparent concern, Beau went over to a young spruce and began hacking at one of its limbs.

The fact that he showed no fear didn't set well with Danny. "My partner will be here any minute," she jeered. "Then you're in for real trouble!" She heard the man let out a low, soft chuckle.

Danny watched him cut the green limb into four sections. Picking up a rock, he walked a short distance away, kneeled and pounded the pieces of wood into the ground. She knew he watched her out of the corner of his eye.

She started doing some fast thinking. Like Jed had said, there was something about this man that didn't add up. They had traveled for hours and were now in what looked like an old, dry wash. Giant saguaros dotted the rocky land, but there was no apparent means of escape. If she tried to run he'd catch her. The man was big, but she'd seen him move with amazing speed. Even the horse had wandered too far away. Maybe she should throw the knife and hope it landed in his back. On the other hand, she might miss. All her time had been spent practicing a fast draw. A lot of good it did her now! Danny had never killed anyone, but she might not have a choice this time. All she could do was stand her ground and let him come to her.

"What you think you're gonna do?" she asked. The man's continued silence rubbed her already raw nerves. "Ain't you got a tongue? Can't we talk about this?"

Beau went over to Mescal and took a pair of Indian leggings out of the saddlebag. He began unlacing the rawhide strips while watching Danny's every move and expression. The kid would never make a good poker player, Beau thought. His thoughts are mirrored on his face.

When the pieces of rawhide were finally free, Beau took his time soaking them with water from his canteen. The task completed, he stood there a moment studying the young outlaw. He took in the boy's determined stance and his readiness to defend himself. Sweat ran down the kid's cheeks, leaving smudges of dirt, and his damp, auburn hair clung to his neck and forehead. Beau started forward.

"If you're going to do something with that knife, you'd better do it now, Danny!" he said.

The Englishman's face reminded her of solid granite, and his cold blue eyes were piercing. She was frightened, but she stood her ground, knife raised. As soon as he came close enough, she lashed out. With lightning speed, he grabbed her wrist and wrenched the knife free. She tried to bite his hand, but he twisted her arm behind her back and pulled upward. Pain shot through her shoulder.

Suspicion suddenly assailed Beau's mind. The wrist was too small! Then he remembered how soft the boy's body had been when he'd lifted him off the ground. Damn!

Beau released the arm and spun the kid around. The hat had long since fallen off. The face was dirty, but this was definitely not a boy! The discovery made him even angrier. Since she liked to play games, he'd play right along with her.

"You think you're so big, and you haven't even started to shave," he taunted in a disgusted tone. "If you want to act like a man, you should be prepared to die like one!"

"You should talk! You won't even give me a chance to defend myself. Give me a goddamn gun and we'll draw. Or maybe you're afraid of a fair fight!"

Grabbing the girl's arm, Beau swung her toward the stakes. "Lie down!" he ordered.

"Hell, no!"

Beau stuck his boot behind Danny's foot and pushed her backward. She landed hard on the rocky ground. Before she could scramble up he was straddling her waist. She pounded her fists against his hard chest. Grabbing one thrashing wrist, Beau slipped a rawhide noose around it, then did the same with the other one.

"What are you doin', you jackass?"

"As you told me a few weeks ago, a man needs to learn humility in these parts. Now it's your turn." Lying down on top of her, he forced her arms out, deftly tying the ends of the rawhide to the stakes.

Danny fought like a wildcat, trying with every ounce of strength she had left to pull the stakes out. Beau stood, placed his big hand on her kicking leg and squeezed. She went rigid from the pain, then felt her boots being yanked off.

"I want you to feel the rawhide on your flesh," said Beau. If he was going to get even, he might as well do a good job of it.

In what seemed like a matter of seconds, Danny was spread-eagled on the ground. "You're not just goin' to leave me here?" she asked. "Turn me loose, and when my partner comes I'll make sure he lets you go."

Beau went to Mescal, then returned with the canteen. He dripped a small amount of water into her mouth. His smile wasn't pleasant.

"I want you to die slowly, my friend."

Danny's mouth was already dry, her lips parched. She eagerly lapped at the water.

Beau looked down on the prostrate figure. "First the rawhide will begin to shrink. Then the circulation will slowly be cut off to your arms and legs. Your body will stretch until you think you're going to be pulled apart."

His voice was low and soft, and Danny inadvertently shuddered.

"The sun will bake your skin, causing it to blister and crack. Your throat will become dry, and your tongue will swell until you can't swallow. Be careful of the buzzards, because they'll pluck your eyes out. And be very still so the snakes and vermin won't spend too much time on your body. Maybe they'll leave you alone. Your death will be slow, little bandit, and I will stay and watch."

"You bastard, you—"

"Don't waste your breath. You'll need it."

For a moment the stranger disappeared from Danny's view, then she saw him climb on top of a rock and sit, watching her, his face expressionless.

Beau pondered as to the girl's age. Twelve, thirteen? At her age, fast draws were the most dangerous. He was tempted to leave her, but he'd wait. Jed should be here in less than two hours.

The girl had completely fooled him. Never once had he even suspected, and considering all the women he'd known, it seemed unbelievable. His rage had blinded him. The only reason she'd gotten away with it was her youth.

"If I ever get loose, you're a dead man!" Danny yelled at the silent figure on the rock. "I'll hunt you till my dying days! Don't ever turn your back, 'cause one day I'll be behind you."

The words were just a bluff, but she wasn't about to let the bastard know. Danny resented dying. She hadn't been on this earth long enough yet. It wasn't fair! She would never see her beautiful ranch. And all the time she suffered, that devil just sat on that damn rock, never moving and not saying another damn word! Well, at least Jed was safe. She hoped he would remember her lovingly. Jed had been a good father. Now she wished she had asked if he'd mind her calling him Pa.

It had been more than two hours since Beau had staked Danny out, and he couldn't understand why Jed hadn't already arrived, especially after Danny said he could follow a trail. If the girl's partner didn't hurry up, Beau might be forced to turn the kid loose, and that would undo everything. He didn't want the girl to die. If that had been his purpose, he would have done a far better job of staking her out.

Not once had Danny asked for mercy or begged to be released. The sandy soil stuck to her perspiration-soaked clothes, and her red hair and face were almost white from the dust. Beau was tempted, more than once, to go down and wash the girl's mouth out. During the past two hours, Danny had called him every foul word she could think of, and her vocabulary was equal to any seafaring man's.

Finally Beau's ears picked up the sounds he'd been waiting for. The girl would be found. He slipped silently from the rock and disappeared from sight. Mescal followed.

When Danny heard the approaching horses, she turned to laugh at her tormenter, but he was gone.

A few minutes later, Jed rode into view.

"Danny, honey, are you all right?" Jed asked as he cut her loose.

"Water," she whispered.

Jed fetched the water, then held Danny's head while she drank.

Her parched, cracked lips hurt as she bestowed a crooked smile upon the big, gentle man. "Jed, I gotta ask you somethin'. Can I call you Pa?"

Tears formed in Jed's eyes. "You sure can, baby. I'd be right proud if you called me that." He helped her sit up. "Did he do you any other harm?" Concern showed on his face. "I mean, well, I reckon you know what I mean."

"No." Her voice was raspy.

"If I ever catch that bastard, I'll kill him for what he done to you." Jed hit his fist on the ground. Looking at Danny, his face softened. "We'll camp here for the night so you can get some of your strength back. You just sit still and I'll do everythin'."

Later that evening, her thirst and hunger satisfied, Danny rested on her bedroll by a warm fire.

"You feel like telling me why that feller ran off with you?" Jed asked, as he rolled a cigarette.

"I'm ashamed to admit it, but you were right all along. Remember that prissy English feller at the stage?"

"Yep."

"It was the same man. You warned me, but I didn't listen."

"No!" Shocked, Jed started coughing from the sudden intake of smoke.

"I got some news for you. That prissy dude ain't prissy! He's gotta be the coldest and meanest bastard I've ever run across. His blood must be ice. You've never seen anyone as quiet or can ride a horse like he can. I tell you, Pa, he was plumb spooky. I thought I was dead."

Jed shook his head, finding the story hard to believe. "Well, I'll be damned," he said softly.

"He could of killed me any time, but he didn't. Just staked me out, that's what he did," Danny said. She sat thinking for a minute. "He knew you were comin', but that didn't seem to bother him at all. I'm just glad he never found out I was female."

"Me, too, baby."

Danny looked up at the full moon and a shiver ran through her entire body. She felt as though a ghost had just crossed her path. A man's face flashed into her mind. He had black hair and blue eyes. Then the picture was gone. She jerked into a sitting position, suddenly very nervous.

"Are you all right honey?" Jed asked.

Danny looked at her beloved Pa and felt safe again. "I'm okay. Think I've just had a little too much sun. I been thinkin'. After what happened today, I've had enough of this robbin'. I don't think I want to see a stage for some time to come. We don't have as much money as I'd like, but I reckon we can make do." Her amber-brown eyes suddenly lit up. "Jed! Do you think he took what fell off the wagon?"

Jed couldn't believe it. After all she'd been through, Danny still wanted to know what those scavengers were after! "We'll talk about it tomorrow," he grumbled.

Beau rose from his crouch beside the fire and poured himself a cup of black coffee. As he turned away from the camp, the full moon lit his path and he heard Mescal snort a couple of times, acknowledging his presence.

He finally stopped and looked out over the desert. Lavender shadows cast by the full moon painted the eerie but beautiful starkness. He could still smell the heat and dust. He loved this wild, unpredictable land, and knew it well. I should be at the ranch, Beau thought, Andrea's waiting for me. He smiled, thinking of his half-sister. They had always been close, despite the fifteen-year difference in their ages. It was hard to believe she'd soon be forty-three. Yes, he should be heading home, but he couldn't get that damn kid out of his mind! Why couldn't he just say to hell with Danny and get on with his own affairs?

The more he thought about it, the more he was convinced he'd accomplished nothing. If he had, the girl would surely have asked for mercy. No, she knew she would get out of trouble when her partner arrived. A smile creased the corners of his lips. He couldn't help but admire her bravery. He finished off his coffee.

Danny said she would track him down no matter how long it took, and he believed her. There was no doubt about it, she certainly knew how to use her guns. A shot in the back when he least expected it? Was she already near? He doubted it; she'd need a good night's rest after today's episode.

Beau wasn't sure just when the idea began to form in the back of his mind, but it grew with every passing minute. He was seriously considering going back and abducting the girl. Getting even with Danny was one thing, but Jed's influence over the fiery girl continued to prick at Beau's conscience. Jed had to be the lowest kind of a man to use a young girl to help him rob stages! Beau was ready to accept the responsibility for his actions. Jed would follow, but he'd never find them. If he did, Beau would just have to kill him. It might come to that anyway. After all, it wouldn't be the first time he'd taken a human life.

Having a young girl to raise just might be what Andrea needs, he thought. His sister had been barren during her marriage, and her loneliness had grown since her husband's early demise in a carriage accident. Maybe this entire situation could be turned to Andrea's advantage, as well as Danny's. He realized he would have to tame the girl before turning her over to his gentle sister, but Andrea would have the child to raise, and Danny would have a good home.

He raked his fingers through his thick hair. If he never did another selfless deed in his life, at least he could say he'd done one. A grin began to form on his lips, and his eyes sparkled in anticipation. The time had come for him to collect his dues from the wildcat. Beau turned and headed back to camp, his mind made up.

Stripping off his shirt, pants and boots, he replaced them with a breechcloth, leggings and moccasins. After tying the knife scabbard around the bottom part of his leg, he pulled out a couple of blankets, his rifle and cartridges.

The sky was pale blue and the occasional puffs of white clouds did nothing to keep the sun's glare from Danny's unshaded eyes. Among other things, yesterday's experience had left her hatless. She pushed her auburn hair away from her face. Hopefully, when they reached the meadow, she'd at least find her pistols. For now, Jed's gun rested reassuringly in her right holster.

They were riding single file down a loose bank arroyo, with Jed leading the way. Her horse, in a stiff-legged gait, stumbled over yet another rock and Danny had to stifle a moan. Every part of her body ached, all because of that black-headed devil. Fortunately, she'd never set eyes on the bastard again, but with all the discomfort she felt, nothing would please her more than to see him grovel!

Jed turned in the saddle. "Why don't we stop a spell? We ain't in no rush."

"No!" Danny returned to her evil thoughts, enjoying mental pictures of her captor suffering.

Jed shook his head and turned around. He knew Danny was hurting, no matter how hard she tried to hide it. He'd seen the rawhide burns on her ankles and wrists. God only knew what the rest of her body looked like. He'd like nothing more than to get his hands around that no-account Englishman's neck. He'd kill him without a moment's hesitation.

This morning Danny had ignored him when he suggested waiting another day. She had always been stubborn, and he'd long since learned to go along with what she said. It made life a lot easier. When Danny got mad, she could be a real hellion. But he loved her just the way she was, and wouldn't change a thing. Well, not much.

"How much farther to the meadow, Jed?" Danny called.

"Ain't got far now."

"Seems like we've been ridin' all day! Hold up and let me come alongside. I've got somethin' I wanna say." Danny gritted her teeth as her horse moved forward.

"What's on your mind?" Jed asked when she was even with him.

"If somethin' should happen to me again, and you can't find me, I want you to promise you'll get what fell out of that wagon and head straight for the ranch. I got a gut feeling there's somethin' important in that meadow."

"Don't go gettin' your hopes up, Danny, it might be gone. Why are you talkin' like this? You expectin' trouble?"

"Naw, but I wasn't expectin' anything to happen yesterday, either. We've still got a long ride to the ranch, Pa, and anything could go wrong. I'd feel a lot better knowin' you were at the ranch waitin' for me, instead of us traveling all over the country tryin' to find each other."

"That makes sense. Okay, you got a deal, but I want you to do the same if anything should happen to me."

"I promise." Her voice was very serious.

Jed smiled. "Well, one of your worries will soon be over. The meadow's just on the other side of that stand of trees ahead."

Beau was well hidden by trees and resting on a soft burrow of pine needles when he felt horse's hooves vibrating against the earth. A knowing smirk stretched across his features. He knew they'd return for the box he'd found while scouting the area.

As the two riders cleared the trees on the far side of the meadow, Beau sat on Mescal's back with the Winchester resting across his legs. Patiently, he waited.

Danielle eagerly urged her horse through the tall grass at a gallop when she saw the sun shining on metal. Riding straight to the box, she swung to the ground before the horse came to a complete stop.

"It's here! The box is here!" she yelled with joy.

A big grin lit up Jed's face as he joined her. "Well, I'll be damned."

While Danny and Jed were laughing with joy, Beau moved the stallion forward. He raised his rifle when he saw Danny draw her gun to shoot off the lock.

Seeing the sudden movement out of the corner of her eye, Danny twisted around, but Jed had maneuvered his horse forward to look at the box and was now blocking her aim. Watching the rider quickly advancing toward them, Danny gave Jed's horse a hard slap across the rear to get him out of the way. Just as she had a clear view, the .45 was shot out of her hand.

Jed's frightened horse began bucking. It was all the surprised Jed could do to hang on and remain in the saddle. Danny, caught in the animal's path, tried to move away but her boot got caught in the thick underbrush and she fell to the ground just in time to miss the flying hooves. Jed finally managed to get his horse under control, and even though he still didn't know what was going on, he automatically reached for his shotgun.

"Don't do it, or she's dead!" a deep voice called to him.

With his finger curled around the trigger, Jed looked up and froze. An Indian atop a big black horse had a rifle pointed straight at Danny. A chill ran through Jed's body. The Indian's cold eyes told Jed the man was dangerous.

"Give it a good toss," the Indian ordered.

Jed threw the shotgun some distance away.

Danny recognized the horse first and the rider second. "You!" she gasped. Her thoughts jumped in various directions trying to understand why this devil had returned. "You came for the box?" she asked suspiciously.

"I couldn't care less about the box."

"Then what the hell are you here for?"

"I came for you." His voice was soft and deadly.

"Me? Ain't you done enough already?" she hissed, her face flushed with anger. "From the bruises I got, you're more than even for what I did!"

"Take your boots off," Beau commanded. Although his features remained stoic, Beau was enjoying the expressions of fear, anger and confusion that crossed the faces of the pair.

"Why?" she asked.

The realization of who the man was finally reached Jed, and he felt helpless and afraid for Danny. There must be something I can do, he thought. If the man would only turn the muzzle away, I could charge him.

"I don't want you pulling another knife on me," Beau replied.

Danny pulled the knife from her boot and cast it aside. "Satisfied?" she asked angrily.

"What other weapons do you have hidden beneath all those clothes?"

"I swear to God, I've got nothin' else on me," she said nervously. "Look, we ain't gotta have everything in that box, what you say we split it?"

"I don't want to split it."

Finally Jed found his tongue. "We don't need any of it. Take it all and let us go."

"Get up in front of me, Danny," Beau commanded.

"You'll burn in hell before I'll do that. If you're aimin' to kill me, go ahead and do it. There's no way I'm gettin' on that horse!"

"Oh, but you will, little girl." Beau let the words slowly drip from his mouth and watched the shocked look on Danny's face as she realized he had called her a girl. Beau lifted the Winchester and pointed it at Jed.

"If there's going to be any killing, he gets it first," Beau said softly. "I'd just as soon shoot him anyway."

"No!" Danny yelled.

"Then climb up in front of me. Now!"

She stood up. "I can't. The horse is too big," she said, stalling for time while trying to figure a way out of this mess.

"Use my foot."

"You ain't gonna kill him, are you?"

"Not if you do as you're told."

Danny placed her foot on top of his. Grinding the heel of her boot into his moccasin, she tried to knock him off balance. It didn't work. Grasping his arm, she swung her leg over Mescal's neck and quickly positioned herself in front of him. She considered shoving his rifle aside, but the man's hand held the weapon steady at his side, still pointed at Jed.

Beau wrapped his arm around Danny's waist, pinning her arms to her sides. "Don't try anything foolish, or your friend's dead," he warned. As soon as Beau turned Mescal around, the horse surged forward.

Jed leaped to the ground and ran for his shotgun. By the time he'd picked it up, they had already disappeared into the trees. Running to his horse, he mounted and took off after them, but the pair had vanished.

Chapter Four

Territory of Arizona

Danny knew her poor aching body would never be the same. She'd lost all track of time. With the sun glaring in her eyes, she knew they were headed west. Everything else became a haze in her mind. They had walked over and around large boulders, ridden down steep embankments that seemed impassable and over long stretches of flat land. She tried sitting up straight, but as the time dragged by, she found herself leaning more and more against her enemy for support. Was he ever going to stop? She yearned to ask him, but bit her tongue to fight off the impulse. He hadn't said one word since they'd left Jed, and she'd be damned if she was going to break the silence.

Nearing sundown, Beau finally came to a halt. At first all Danny felt was relief; then she heard running water. Glancing around, she discovered they were at the bottom of a deep gorge, with red rock on either side. Her attention, however, was focused on the river. She licked at her dry lips in anticipation.

Beau slid from the horse's back and all thoughts of water ceased. Danny saw her chance to get away. Twisting her hand in the stallion's mane, she kicked the animal in the sides. Instead of taking off, the horse reared, and it was all she could do to keep from sliding down his rump. The man muttered some Indian words and the stallion calmed down. Danny gave him another hard kick but the animal refused to budge.

Frustrated, she watched Beau walk to the water's edge. Cupping his hands, he leaned over and began to drink. Thirsty beyond words, she quickly dismounted and ran toward the waters, but Beau stopped her.

"What the hell are you doin'?" she demanded. "I want a drink!"

Beau knew the time for taming had begun. "For tonight you will drink only if I say so."

"You can't do this, you bastard! I got just as much right to that water as you do." She tried to kick him on the shin, but he moved too quickly for her to connect.

With little effort, Beau swung her to the ground and removed her boots. A quick toss, and they ended up in the middle of the river.

Danny let out a screech as she jumped up and leaped onto his back. "You dirty varmint!" she screamed. Throwing an arm around his neck, she straddled his strong form, simultaneously clawing, biting and hitting. She was as strong as a she cat protecting its young, and Beau had to finally knock her off.

Danny hit the ground and immediately made a dive for the river. An arm circled her waist and she felt herself being carried away from the water she wanted so badly. She tried to wrench loose, but her efforts were useless. When they reached a sycamore tree she was released. There was no fight left in her. The long ride, combined with her battle, had taken its toll. She was sore, exhausted and tired. Within minutes she drifted off into oblivion.

Beau looked down at the sleeping girl and rubbed his back, feeling the teeth marks. What the hell had he let himself in for? He'd made a vow that however long it took, he'd tame her. From all indications, they were going to be in the gorge for some time.

He glanced around the canyon. Jed would never find them, and there was plenty of water and game. His eyes returned to the filthy child presently lying peacefully on the ground. No, he thought, those things are the least of my problems. He turned and walked to the water's edge.

"Here," Beau growled.

At his word, Danny's eyelids fluttered open. She felt as

though she had come up from the dead. Then she saw the big man squatting beside her, his hands cupped and extended. Small drops of water seeped through his fingers and onto the ground. Quickly she sat up. She was too thirsty to even consider knocking his hand away.

"More!" she demanded after drinking the small offering.

Beau suddenly felt sorry for the young tomboy. She had probably never known a real friend or anyone she could trust. He was sure her actions stemmed from fear and a false show of bravery. He suddenly realized this was the answer to everything! He would become the child's friend.

"Not now, little one," he said in a soft friendly tone, "you'll get sick. In a few minutes I'll bring more. How old are you, Danny?"

"How old do you think I am?"

"Taking a guess, about twelve or thirteen. Am I close?"

"You're close," she quickly assured him.

Beau studied the girl sitting in front of him. Doesn't she ever wash her face, let alone her body and clothes?

"Why don't you call me Beau?"

"That's your name? I've never seen an Englishman who looked and dressed like an Injun."

"I want you to know you have nothing to be afraid of. I mean you no harm. If you do as I ask, we'll get along just fine."

"I'm not afraid of nothin', and I'm not goin' to kowtow to no man! Let alone a Injun lover," she hissed.

Danielle had never felt one way or another about Indians. All she knew were stories she had heard. But after what this devil man had put her through, she needed an outlet for her anger. She spat at him. "That's what I think of Injuns! What are you? Some filthy half-breed?" she asked scathingly.

Beau smiled evilly and stood. To hell with friendship! "Maybe you'd prefer calling me Quiet Storm, which is my Indian name. Would you like me to show you what Indians think of white females? Or perhaps what white men do with young girls that hang around old men and rob stagecoaches!"

The fear that leaped into the girl's eyes pleased him. As long as she was afraid, she'd probably be easier to handle. It was still hard for him to believe someone so young could be so strong. He suddenly became curious as to what her face looked like under all that dirt. She had amazingly long, thick eyelashes that surrounded large, beautiful, amber-brown eyes.

"Are you ready for another drink?" His smile was chilling.

"I can get it myself!"

"No! You will drink from my hands. This way you'll learn that it is only by my hands that you live."

As he walked toward the water, Danny knew she should get up and run, but she didn't have the strength. She couldn't even think straight.

It was the smell of food that woke her the next morning. A short distance away, a speared fish lay roasting over a fire, and Beau was nowhere in sight. In a matter of minutes, she had devoured the food, sucking even the smallest pieces of flesh from the bones. Her hunger satisfied, she went over to the water and drank her fill.

To Danny's amazement, Beau still hadn't returned. Would he be gone long enough for her to escape? She studied her prison. On either side of the gorge was a red rock precipice, with large gnarled rock formations halfway up the sides and sheer cliff the rest of the way. On each end the water curved out of sight. Danny vaguely remembered them traveling through the gorge for hours before Beau had stopped.

Not knowing which direction Beau had taken, Danny decided the only safe way to freedom was up. The sheer face of the cliff could pose a problem, but she'd have to handle that when she got there.

She ran over to the large, red boulders and started climbing. She needed to put as much distance behind her as possible before Beau discovered her gone.

For several hours Danny continued to work her way upward with dauntless determination. Not until her breathing became so labored it hurt did she finally stop to rest. As she looked down at the canyon floor below, she felt a deep sense of satisfaction. Then she looked up. Although she'd climbed a considerable distance, it was nothing compared to how far she would have to go to reach the top. It would take her days! Her feet were already badly cut and bleeding. She'd been stupid not to save some of the fish, or find a way to carry water. At that moment she knew she would never make it. All her effort had been in vain. Furious, she stood on a rock shelf and yelled, "You knew I couldn't go anywhere, you bastard!"

Danny's words echoed through the canyon. Beau had been watching her progress for quite a while. He chuckled softly as she began the long, arduous descent. It was going to take hours for her to reach the bottom, so he spent the time familiarizing himself with the area. If Danny got into trouble, he'd hear her.

Danny finally made it down. After she had quenched her thirst, she sat under the welcoming shade of the sycamore. Where was Beau? Her stomach told her it was time to eat.

An hour later, she walked to the water's edge and began tossing pebbles. Why has Beau brought me here? she wondered. After all, his little walk in the sun, naked, was nothing compared to what he's doing to me now! Anger flushed her cheeks. No one had ever treated her like this! Well, she assured herself, Jed will soon find us.

In no time, Danny became bored. What was she supposed to do? Sit around and wait for the great warrior to return? Great warrior indeed! Great at stealing innocent women!

As the time slowly passed, Danny found herself anxiously awaiting Beau's return. When the sun started playing hide-and-seek behind the high peaks, she sang old miners' songs that Jed had taught her. Her voice rang out in an effort to keep away the lonely feeling that had begun to engulf the canyon as the shadows of night crept down.

Beau sat, relaxed, high on a ledge, observing the girl. He had decided to leave her alone, let her stew over her predicament and come to the realization that to fight him was futile. He hoped that, when he returned to camp, her guard would be down.

As Danny's singing reached his ears, Beau found her low, throaty voice appealing. It was a strange voice for one so young. He'd been studying her for some time, and something wasn't right. He couldn't put his finger on it, but there were things about the girl that didn't fit. As he watched her walk to the edge of the water to get a drink, his eyes narrowed. She didn't walk like a child, her reactions were not like a child's, and it took a long time to learn how to handle guns the way she did. She was too knowing. It was hard to tell how she was shaped under those baggy clothes. Could there actually be a woman hidden beneath them? No! Impossible! He couldn't be that blind!

What the hell is the matter with me? Beau sighed, knowing it was going to be a long night. Had he been so long without a woman that he was trying to make this slip of a kid into one? In order to get his mind back in the right direction, he thought about the ranch and how he longed to return home. His father should never have sent him to England. He understood his reasons, but that didn't make it right.

The next day Beau waited until midmorning before riding back into camp. He'd killed and cleaned a couple of rabbits and collected berries and roots. Beau was convinced his plan had worked when the ragamuffin ran toward him, her face alight with joy. Then Danny stopped, and in the next moment her face turned to uncontrolled rage.

"Where the hell you been? Did you leave me here to die, or were you tryin' to teach me a lesson?"

Beau had heard enough. He jumped off Mescal and started toward her.

Danny knew by the look on his face she was in trouble, and his tall muscular body became very intimidating. Not caring what she stepped on, she started running as fast as her feet would go. She hadn't gone far when Beau made a flying leap and caught her around the legs. She fell face down with Beau on top of her.

"I've listened to that mouth of yours for the last time!" he growled. "I'm also tired of smelling your stink. Animals are cleaner than you!" He picked her up, slinging her over his shoulder like a sack of potatoes, then headed straight for the river.

Seeing the direction they were going, Danny screamed. "No, no! You're gonna kill me!"

"I'll kill you if you don't wash yourself and those damn clothes! While I'm at it, I might as well wash your mouth out!"

Beau waded out until he was waist deep in the water, then dropped her. As Danny bobbed up to the surface, she started sputtering and coughing. The moment she realized she could stand, she turned, ready to head for dry land. But Beau stood in her way and wouldn't allow her to go around him.

"Is this how you plan to kill me?" she yelled as she brushed away the water dripping from her hair down into her eyes.

Beau saw the terror on her face, but couldn't suppress his laughter over the way she looked and her ridiculous statement.

"How is water going to kill you, Danny?" he mocked.

"Everyone knows you can die of all kinds of things if you get wet!"

He roared with laughter. "Where the hell did you ever hear that? Water can't hurt you as long as you can stand up. I've bathed every day for years and I'm healthy."

"I don't believe you. Now move so I can get out."

Beau's humor was replaced with pure determination. "No. You're going to scrub your clothes as well as your body. If you don't, I will."

His threat was suddenly more frightening than the water. She had to keep him thinking of her as a young girl! "I'll do it, but I'm not goin' to do it while you're watchin'," she groaned.

"All right, I can understand your need for privacy."

"If you want to kill me, why don't you just shoot me?"

"I don't want you to die. That would take away the joy of teaching you manners. But if you don't do as I say, you'll leave me no choice but to take you back into the water and do the job myself. While you're washing, I'll fix something to eat."

Danny watched him wade out of the water. Still afraid, but even more worried that Beau might decide to watch, she slowly worked her way around an outcropping of rocks. Convinced he could no longer see her, she undressed. Still smoldering with anger, she washed her clothes as best she could, then laid them on the rocks to dry and proceeded to clean herself. The task completed, she rebound her breasts. The binding had slipped considerably, but the johns and baggy shirt had still managed to hide her womanhood. Now a new problem presented itself. The clothes were no longer stiff, and less apt to hide as much. Any close contact with Beau must be avoided. Oh, how she hated him for all this torture he was putting her through. No one should be made to go into the water!

Beau looked up from tending the rabbit and watched Danny walk toward him. Her beautiful face, surrounded by thick, damp, auburn hair, told it all. He knew she wasn't a child. She had made a fool of him again! Having lived with the Cheyenne most of his life, he knew his face didn't mirror the fury he felt over the newfound knowledge. Now it was his turn to get even for all the stunts she'd pulled since their first meeting.

"I'm clean," Danny stated as she joined him, "and I'm ready to eat. Hand me a piece of meat; I'm hungry as hell. You ain't proved to be a very good provider, till today!"

"I'll eat first. From now on, if you want something to eat you'll ask in a proper manner."

"What the hell are you talkin' about?" Her smoky brown eyes challenged him. "I'm ready to eat now!"

"Do you always get what you want?" he asked softly.

"Why shouldn't I?"

"From now on, you'll say please when you want something and you'll eat when I'm finished. I don't want to have to fight you off, so if you can't sit and wait like a good little girl, I can always tie you up." He gave her a devilish grin as his eyes traveled down her shapeless-looking figure. "In fact, I might enjoy wrapping the rope around your body. You may be young...but it's been a long time since I've felt a female beneath me." He stuck a large piece of rabbit in his mouth.

"No! I can wait," Danny said, backing away. Her tongue circled the contour of her lips as she thought about how good the juicy meat must taste.

After consuming several pieces of rabbit, Beau leaned back and looked at Danny. "Tell me, don't you think it would be perfect justice if I made you take your clothes off?"

Danny's eyes became wide circles of shock. "You...you wouldn't do that to a defenseless child." She stepped back a little farther.

"You made me undress," Beau said in an innocent tone.

"But you're a grown man!"

"Perhaps you have a valid point. I'll think on it. Come here," he said softly, holding a piece of meat out to her.

Cautiously Danny moved forward, then reached for the succulent tidbit. He withdrew the morsel.

"I'll feed you."

"I ain't no dog!"

Again Beau extended his hand.

Drooling, Danny moved closer. Putting her mouth over the meat, she sucked on his fingers for a brief moment, enjoying the delicious taste of fat that had dripped down his hand. Stepping away, she chewed and smacked her lips with pure pleasure.

The unexpected sensuality of Danny's action ran through Beau's body like a hot poker. Knowing it would be impossible to hide his aroused manhood beneath a breechcloth, he turned and headed for the water.

"Feed yourself!" he growled over his shoulder.

The reason for his sudden anger completely escaped Danny, but she didn't care. She just wanted to get to the food.

When Beau came out on the opposite bank, he laid down on the warm ground. The cold water had achieved the desired effect, but now he welcomed the sun's heat.

Finally he sat up and watched the woman on the other side devouring the hot meat as fast as she could get her hands on it. What was he going to do with this half animal, half woman? Every time he decided how to handle her, Danny did something that made him back off. He thought he knew everything about women, but he couldn't understand this one. Had she deliberately tried to seduce him? Was she a virgin? On the other hand, if she had been trying to tease him, this he could understand. No, none of that made any sense. She tried too hard to conceal her femininity. She must be a virgin, but if she had fooled him again, he'd damn sure bed her before they left!

Wiping her greasy face on the sleeve of her shirt, Danny reached for another piece of food. Suddenly she felt miserable. Tossing the meat to the ground, she sat down and wrapped her arms around her aching stomach. God, how she wished she could get away!

Absentmindedly she watched Beau reenter the water. As he neared the bank where she sat, water ran down his brown muscular body. He's beautiful, Danny thought with a shock, even if he is a damn Injun. Remembering how white his skin and rump had been at their first meeting, she started laughing. The laughter was quickly cut off when her stomach started rumbling. Jumping up, she ran to the nearest scruffy clump of bushes. When the heaving stopped, anger took over.

Standing up straight, Danny marched to where Beau stood. On the way she stubbed her toe on a small rock, but she didn't care. Her feet were already a mess, what was one more sore spot?

"I just got sick all over the place!" she yelled as she neared him. "And it's your damn fault! You made me go into that water knowin' that would happen, you bastard!"

Beau's jaw became rigid and his blue eyes almost turned black. "I told you never to cuss me again," he hissed furiously. "You have the foulest mouth of any woman it has been my misfortune to come in contact with! You are a spoiled brat, and it's about time you learned the world isn't here for your convenience. You became sick because you gorged yourself like some buzzard! And if you ever cuss me out again, you'll get your butt spanked. While I'm at it, I might as well tell you a few more truths. Number one, you will bathe—"

"It makes me sick! You saw how sick I was," she yelled at him.

"...and wash your clothes every day."

"My clothes'll wear out and I won't have nothin' to put on, you bas—" She saw the muscles in his jaw flex and stopped herself just in time.

"Then I'll kill a buck and you can make a tunic and moccasins from the hide. Which brings me to point number two! It's no wonder you stink. With all those clothes you're wearing, you sweat. So you have a choice. You can wear either your long johns or your shirt and trousers, but not both. I know you're not a child, so there isn't any more need to pretend."

Danny lowered her head. Did he really know she wasn't a young girl, or was he just guessing? "You don't know nothin'," she bluffed, "and you can't make me!"

"Oh, yes, I can, and you know it."

She suddenly realized that when he spoke in that low, soft tone of his, he was the most dangerous.

"I don't know just how far you will go to escape," Beau continued, "but don't try getting rid of me. The cartridges are hidden, and my horse won't let you mount him. If I die, so will you."

"You son—"

"What?"

"Nothin'."

"Number three. From now on, you'll do all the cooking."

"I can't cook," she lied.

"You'd better learn fast. I'm not the only one who's going to eat it." He went to where Mescal stood grazing on some tufts of grass. Mounting the horse, Beau rode out of camp.

You think you're so high and mighty, Danny thought, but there are ways of getting even.

Chapter Five

Jed tried for days to pick up Danny's trail, but finally had to accept defeat. When he returned to the meadow because of his promise, he discovered the strongbox was packed with leather bags of gold dust. His first inclination was to return it, but he didn't know who the gold belonged to. Jed panicked. What if the owners accused him of stealing it? It would be impossible to prove his innocence and he'd likely end up with a noose around his neck. Not knowing what else to do, he stuffed Danny's saddlebags with gold, then packed the remainder in his.

Riding westward, Jed worried that someone might discover what he carried. A man could get himself killed hauling so much gold around, he kept telling himself. Would Danny be waiting for him at the ranch? Had she managed to escape? Was she all right?

Danny sat relaxed in the cool water, enjoying the gentle current as it swirled around her warm, naked body. She'd been there for some time. As the days had passed, she'd lost her fear of getting sick and dying, and actually looked forward to her morning bath. Especially on days like this, when Beau had taken off to explore the area and would be gone for some time. When he stayed in camp, she bathed in the pool hidden behind the boulders.

Her eyes scanned the camp. It had taken on a lived-in look. A gutted buck hung from a tall cottonwood a short distance away, and on some boulders surrounding the river, meat had been laid out to dry. Beau had circled flat rocks around the camp fire, and had collected other rocks for cooking. These sat near the outer edge of the fire. Some were cupped out and held piñon nuts and berries, as well as various herbs collected by Beau. Shortly after they'd arrived, he had discovered wild onions and other fresh vegetables growing in abundance close to camp. But whatever he collected Danny refused to use for cooking.

Danny laughed. Maybe Beau had the upper hand when it came to most things, but she'd gotten even by fixing the worst food a man had ever eaten. Unfortunately, the thought of eating another piece of burnt meat made her gag, and she knew it would have to come to a halt soon.

As she slowly rinsed her body, Danny marveled at how the sun had turned her skin a golden hue. She felt wonderful. Of course, Beau played a big part. Being honest with herself, she couldn't deny the attraction she felt. Seeing him every day, tall and perfect of body, was like being drawn unwillingly into a spider's web.

Having lived in a rough mining town most of her life, Danny knew all about sex, and there wasn't much she hadn't seen. She'd been propositioned by most of the miners; that is, until they found out she belonged to Jed. Nobody wanted to mess with Jed. Bonnie May, who owned one of the brothels in Dusty Creek, had even asked her to be one of her "girls in waiting." Bonnie May told Danielle she could make a hell of a lot more money than Jed's mine would ever bring in. Danny thanked her for the offer, but declined. Danny giggled, remembering Jed's reaction when she told him about the incident.

Danny suddenly realized how much time had slipped by. She would have to hurry if she wanted to wash her clothes and have them dry by the time Beau returned. She stood and had just reached out to fetch the items when Beau rode into camp. She fell back into the shallow water, trying to hide, and ended up bruising her buttocks on the hard rocks.

"Go away," she yelled.

Beau sat there, startled, but not for the same reason. The woman before him had full, firm breasts, a waist he could easily put his hands around and long, shapely legs. How the hell had she managed to hide such a desirable body? he wondered.

All the women he'd known tended to expose more than they hid.

Dismounting, Beau walked to the water's edge and squatted. Danny had her arms wrapped around her body, unsuccessfully trying to conceal her female attributes.

"Go away," she screamed, horrified at this blatant perusal.

Beau chuckled, and a look of pure orneriness leaped into his eyes. Reaching over, he picked up her clothes and found the cloth she'd been using as a binder.

"Well, the full truth finally comes to the surface, doesn't it, little girl!"

"Give those to me," she demanded.

"This is the first time I can honestly say you have nothing to hide. What's wrong, Danny, afraid of being a woman?" he taunted. "Maybe you're right. You certainly wouldn't fit in a woman's world, not with that mouth of yours, let alone your manners." He tossed her the shirt and pants and walked away. She would never see the breast binder again.

Danny grabbed the clothes and made a dive for the rocks.

Beau sat waiting for Danny to return from her morning dip to fix breakfast. Ever since he had discovered her naked in the river, they'd remained at an impasse, which did nothing to improve Beau's disposition. Danny did everything he insisted on, but now she refused to talk.

Beau had also inadvertently created another problem for himself. Danny only wore her pants and shirt now, and the well-worn material clung to her ripe, firm breasts. Especially after her morning bath, when she and the shirt were still damp. The erect nipples were like an invitation that proved difficult not to accept. His present state of awareness grew stronger with each passing day, and he spent more and more time away from camp because of it. They would have to leave soon. He didn't like having to fight desire.

The truth of the matter was quite simple. Beau didn't know what to do with her. He certainly couldn't follow through with his original plan to take her home and let his sister raise her. And, not knowing Jed's whereabouts, he couldn't return Danny to him. Besides, Beau didn't want her holding up any more stagecoaches. Leaving her in town with some money wasn't the answer, either. She'd probably just spend it. Then what?

Beau heard Danny returning and glanced in her direction, his eyes trailing the length of her. With each passing day, she became more beautiful. The thick, auburn hair had taken on a glossy luster, and her skin had a flawless glow to it. She moved with a natural grace, especially if she thought he wasn't watching. Beau tried to convince himself that, next to other beautiful women, he probably wouldn't give Danny a second look. He only noticed her now because he'd been too long without a woman.

"Beau, I wanna talk to you," she announced.

"What about?" he asked suspiciously.

Danny sat down, then placed a couple of venison steaks on the large flat rock sitting in the middle of hot coals. The meat sizzled and popped when it touched the hot surface.

"I wanna know what you aim to do with me. We ain't goin' to be stayin' here forever. I reckon I got a right to know if you're plannin' on turnin' me in for the reward."

"Reward?" Beau feigned innocence.

Danny could have bit off her tongue. He didn't know! It wasn't fair. Hellfire! She and Jed never got anything, so why did someone have to go and put a price on her head?

"Wait a minute," Beau said, placing his fingers to his forehead as if in deep thought. Suddenly his face registered shock. "You're the one they call the dangerous Gringo Kid?" He roared with laughter.

"You wouldn't think it was funny if it was your ass they were after," she said in a huffy tone. "You give me a gun and I'll show you just how dangerous I can be!"

It took a bit before Beau could stop laughing and get himself back under control.

"Are you gonna answer my question or not?" Danny demanded.

Beau studied the petite woman for a moment. She looked him straight in the eye. Her small chin tilted up in defiance, and her amber-brown eyes sparkled with fire.

Beau became serious. "What would you have me do?" he asked. "Turn you loose so you can rob again?"

"I'm not gonna rob no more." Her voice became soft and laced with sincerity.

Beau refused to be taken in, sure Danny was trying to trick him. "Do you really expect me to believe anything you say after all the stunts you've pulled? What are you planning, Danny?"

"I've got a place to go."

Beau eyes narrowed. "Where?"

"A small ranch. That's where we were headin' when you took off with me. All I want to know is what you're aimin' to do."

If only she were telling the truth, he thought. It would be the answer to everything. But how the hell could he believe her? "We're going west," he said, tired of the entire situation. "I'm taking you to my ranch where you can work and make a decent wage. Andrea's not going to like the idea, but it will be up to her to put you to work. Then I wash my hands of this whole bloody mess!"

"Why can't I just go to my own place?"

Beau was angry. "Why do you have to lie? You know as well as I do you don't have a place to go to. I'll be damned if I'm going to turn you loose on this poor, unsuspecting world!"

"You..." Danny stood and marched away. She could get around much better since she had moccasins and her feet had toughened. In fact, she thought, I could leave now!

Beau watched Danny head for the side of the cliff again, knowing she wouldn't get far. He'd deliberately avoided saying anything about the wanted poster, just as he'd never told her about scouting the meadow before they'd arrived or that he'd seen the dead bodies. Studying the tracks, he knew Jed and Danny had come from the opposite direction, and if he hadn't been convinced of their innocence in the killings, his reaction to their arrival would have been entirely different.

It had taken some time, but Beau was now convinced he had to take Danny to the ranch, even if it meant upsetting his sister. He looked at the meat drying in the sun. There wouldn't be enough time to dry more. They would also need fish; it took less time to dry. Now that he'd made up his mind, he wanted to leave as soon as possible. Once on the trail, he didn't plan on stopping except to rest.

Beau suddenly smelled meat burning. Quickly he removed the steaks from the hot rock and transferred them to a cool one. "Damn," he muttered, "burnt again!" No longer hungry, he picked up the spear he'd whittled from a branch and headed for the river.

Danny sat on her high perch for some time and watched Beau. Arm raised and body poised, he waited patiently for a fish to swim by. The sun glistened on his hard-muscled, bronzed body. Nothing moved except his raven black hair, as a warm breeze came down the canyon.

Danny knew, one way or another, she had to escape. In unguarded moments she'd seen the desire in Beau's sky-blue eyes. "I wonder how he'd think of me if I was a lady and wore them purty dresses?" she mumbled wistfully. "He only thinks of me as a way to relieve his man's need!" As she had done so many times before, she thought about Beau informing her she would never fit in with ladies. Oh, hell, I ain't never gonna be one of them fancy women, she thought. Jed's right. I ain't got no learnin', 'cept for readin' and writin'. Now Beau wants to take me to some damn ranch. And who is Andrea? His wife, mistress, housekeeper?

Her eyes lit up, suddenly realizing she had looked at this all wrong. As long as they remained in the canyon, she had no means of escape. Going to Beau's ranch might take her farther from the Silver J, but at least she would finally have a way of getting a gun, a horse and food for her trip. And he did say they would be heading west, and that would take her in the direction of the Silver J.

So far, Beau hadn't made any move toward her. If she could just keep her mouth shut, she'd probably get to his ranch without anything happening. "Yep, that's the answer! Now all I gotta do is get Beau's ass headed toward home!"

Slowly Danny started down. Dirt and sweat from her upward climb covered her clothes, and she already looked forward to going into the cool water and rinsing off.

Engrossed in her thoughts, she didn't hear the first rattling of danger. When the sound finally penetrated her mind, it was too late. The snake struck her in the leg. She screamed and started throwing rocks at the vile creature, who quickly slithered away.

Beau heard the scream and looked up. Seeing Danny hurl the rocks, he guessed what had happened. He ran out of the water and yelled, "Danny, don't move! Do you hear me? Stay right there and don't move!"

As Beau climbed the large boulders, she marveled at what little effort it took on his part. When he was halfway up, she saw him draw his knife from the scabbard. Fear shot through her. She knew what he was going to do. "No! No! I ain't gonna let you cut me!" she hollered.

When Beau reached her, he knew by her stiff-legged stance and chalk-white face that she was in shock. He forced her to sit down. "Danny," he said, shaking her gently. "Listen to me! I have to do it. You know there isn't any other way, or you'll die! Where did the snake bite you?"

Beau's voice finally penetrated her blank mind. Nerves on end, she had difficulty speaking. "My leg," she whispered.

"Which leg?"

"The right one."

Slitting the pant leg, Beau saw the nasty puncture wounds. He pulled off her moccasin and handed it to her. "Wad this up and bite down on it hard."

Gratefully Danny took the hide and placed it between her teeth. Clamping down, she closed her eyes and felt the knife pierce her flesh.

When the crisscross incisions were made, Beau started sucking and spitting, trying to draw out the venom. Convinced he could do no more, he sat back and looked at Danny. Beads of perspiration had broken out on her face. The moccasin lay in her hand and tears rested in the corners of her wide, brown eyes.

"Am I gonna die?" she asked.

"I think I got it all."

Danny heard the worried tone in his voice. "I weren't scared for a minute."

Beau leaned over and gave her a quick, gentle kiss on the lips. "That's for being so brave," he said.

She looked at him questioningly, confusion clouding her mind. She'd had men slobbering over her, trying to get a kiss, but she'd never had a *real* kiss. For some reason she felt disappointed. Maybe he just doesn't know how to do it, she thought. "Is that the best you can do?" she asked innocently.

The question took Beau completely off guard. He chuckled. "Are you asking me to kiss you again?"

"No, I was just thinkin'. You ain't very good at it, are you? But that's all right, I ain't good at it, either."

Beau definitely felt his male pride being pricked. Never had he received a complaint about his kisses; in fact, just the opposite. But this certainly wasn't the time to prove her wrong. Danny's face had already become flushed with fever.

"We'll continue this conversation at a later time. Right now I've got to get you back down." Leaning over, he picked her up in his arms.

"There ain't no need for you carryin' me, I can walk."

"I don't want you walking on that leg."

By the time they reached the campsite, Danny was drifting in and out of consciousness, her clothes damp with perspiration. Beau placed her on a blanket, then quickly stripped off her shirt and pants. After soaking the other blanket in the river, he placed it on top of her to help reduce the fever. Knowing a bird killed and split would absorb the poison, he whistled for Mescal. In the short time it took for him to find a bird and return, Danny's fever had already warmed the blanket. Beau picked it up and headed toward the water.

In her fevered state, Danny saw visions of herself dressed in a beautiful yellow gown. Beau stood beside her, handsome in his large feathered Indian headdress. He smiled then leaned down and kissed her lightly on the lips. Suddenly he disappeared and in his place stood a fat, ugly woman with gray hair that stood straight up.

"You slut," the vision accused. "You've tried to take my husband from me, but you'll never get him, he's mine!"

People gathered. They pointed their fingers at her and laughed. Danny looked down. Instead of the yellow dress, she now had on her filthy long johns. Humiliated, she began crying and tried to run away and hide in the clouds, but the people followed.

Later, Danny dreamed someone was lying beside her and holding her close. "Beau?" she whispered.

"Sh," came the reply, "you can sleep now. The fever broke and you're going to be fine."

She snuggled up to the warm body and drifted into oblivion.

When Danny finally opened her eyes to the bright sunlight, she turned to see if Beau was lying beside her or if it had all been a dream. She was alone. Her next concern centered on her nakedness beneath the blanket.

"How do you feel?"

Danny looked up at the tall man. Next to him she always felt so small.

"Are you thirsty?" he asked.

Beau leaned down, placed his arm under her shoulders and raised her high enough to drink from the hide pouch. Danny held the blanket firmly to her body.

"I feel so weak," she whispered.

"I'm not surprised. You've been wracked with fever for three days."

"Three days? I've never been sick in my whole life!"

He gave her a warm smile and laid her back down. "If that's the case, this bout should be enough for another fifty years of good health. I have some rabbit broth for you. You're going to have to build your strength back up."

"Rabbit broth? Where did you get a kettle?"

"I located some Indians down in the canyon, and they were kind enough to let me have one. I'll be right back."

A lot of questions suddenly assailed her mind. When did she start thinking of Beau as a man instead of a filthy Indian? Why did the fact that he only wore a loincloth seem so natural? How long ago had he undressed her?

Danny sat leaning against the tree, the blanket wound tightly around her. For several days, she'd felt as good as new. She'd enjoyed having Beau feed and take care of her, but now she wanted to get up. She felt dirty after her bout with fever, and seeing Beau enter the cool water proved to be more than she could take.

"Beau, I've had it!" she called out to him. "You know I'm fine! Why can't I go in the water, too?"

Beau chuckled. Danny had changed a great deal since their arrival. "Sounds like a good idea. After all the complaining you've been doing, I'd certainly say you're well enough."

"I don't have any clothes!"

"You haven't had any clothes for over a week. They're washed and dried. When you get out you can put them on." Beau found the conversation amusing.

"Are you expectin' me to get up an' walk naked into the water?"

"Would you feel better if I turned around?" he asked, watching her stand and making sure her legs were steady.

"Hell, yes!" Danny looked longingly at the inviting water. "You won't turn back around, will you?" She heard him chuckle. "What you laughing at?"

"Danny, I've seen naked women before," he teased, "including you."

Danielle found no humor in his words. "Well...I'm not one of those kind of women. I'll go over to the pool!"

"No. If you're going to get in the water, you'll do it here where I'll know you're all right." He turned his back, a big grin still on his face. "I promise not to look, Danny."

Danny made her way to the river, keeping a tight hold on the blanket. When she reached the edge of the water, she knew she couldn't drop it and go in naked. She'd seen men without clothes, but for her to walk around with nothing on in front of someone she didn't even really know was an entirely different matter.

Determined to have her way, she waded into the water with the blanket still wrapped around her. She hadn't gone far when the water-soaked wool became heavy. Glancing at Beau to make sure he still had his back turned, she waded back to the shore, dragging the heavy material behind her.

"What are you doing?" Beau asked, hearing the splashing noise.

"Ain't none of your business. Just keep your eyes turned the other way."

Still determined, and knowing there wasn't any other choice, Danny dropped the blanket and waded in naked. Worried that Beau might turn around, she decided to go out far enough for the water to completely cover her. When it reached her breasts, she continued to inch out even farther.

"I have some news you'll be interested in," Beau said over his shoulder.

"What's your news?"

"I think you're well enough for us to leave the canyon in a couple of days."

Danny glanced toward Beau, but in her excitement, she slipped on a rock and plummeted to the bottom, drifting into deeper water. Terrified, she began thrashing.

When Beau reached her, he had a hard time holding her and fighting the strong current at the same time. Finally, he grabbed her from behind and managed to pull her into his arms. She continued to fight as he quickly worked his way back to the shallow water. Holding her across one strong arm, he slapped her on the back several times. When the glorious air began to fill her lungs, he carried her to the bank.

"Are you all right?" he asked as he stood her on her feet.

She smiled sheepishly. "I reckon I went out too far."

Beau smiled back. "Yep," he said mocking her, "I reckon you did."

They both started laughing, then Danny reached up and kissed him on the lips. "That's for bein' so brave," she said with a twinkle in her eye. "I reckon I'm clean now, can I have my clothes?"

The unexpected act was Beau's undoing. Gathering her in his arms, he leaned down and kissed her. Slowly he pulled away from the soft, closed lips. He had never taken an innocent before, and at this moment, he felt especially protective of the little outlaw. He stepped back and watched her eyes cloud with confusion.

"Why did you stop? I was startin' to like it. Can we try again?"

"No!" He walked off to get her clothes.

Suddenly remembering her nakedness, Danny snatched up the heavy, wet blanket and covered herself. "What you gettin' so mad about? Huh?" she called to Beau. "Come on, Beau, I gotta learn sometime. Some day I hope a man will come courtin', and if he wants to kiss, how am I goin' to know what to do?"

Beau returned with the clothes and handed them to her. She tried to slip her shirt on under the blanket without exposing herself, but wasn't successful.

His hands on his hips, Beau stood there watching her, a dark eyebrow raised. "I've never met anyone so eager to learn. Danny, do you know anything about coupling?"

"Hell, yes, I'm not that dumb."

Beau studied the beautiful face staring up at him. "Is that what you want to learn?"

"I'm not talkin' 'bout that! I just want you to teach me how to kiss!"

"And what if kissing leads to that? Then what?"

"That wouldn't happen 'cause I wouldn't let it. Now come on, Beau, if you don't know how, just say so. I reckon I can learn from someone else."

This time she wasn't going to get away with her statement! The time had come to teach the wildcat a lesson. "Very well, I'll teach you. It's the least I can do for someone so curious." The corners of his lips twitched with humor. "To begin with, you don't keep your lips and teeth closed."

"Why not?"

"Because a man likes to put his tongue in the woman's mouth."

"Why would he want to do that?"

"Shall I demonstrate?"

"I'm ready."

It was all Beau could do to keep from laughing when Danny stood there with her mouth wide open. "You're supposed to close your eyes also."

She shut her eyes tightly.

He leaned down and waited until he saw her tight jaw relax from the tension. Softly he kissed each corner of her mouth, then pulled back, his lips only inches away from hers. "Follow me, Danny."

"All right—"

"And don't talk, just feel," he whispered.

Danny kissed the corners of his mouth, then he kissed her neck and she did the same. His tongue trailed around the contours of her lips, and she repeated the action.

"Can you feel the closeness?" he asked.

"Mm—"

Then his lips were on hers and his tongue caressed the inner portions of her mouth. When she tentatively put her tongue out, he caught it with his teeth and sucked gently. His arms encircled her body, then slid down to her hips and drew her against him. As the blanket fell away, his lips left hers and began to trail kisses down her neck again. When she proceeded to do the same thing while clinging to him, he gently laid her down on the ground. Kissing her passionately, he cupped her firm breast while fingering the already erect nipple. His hand slid down her flat stomach, then slowly up her inner thigh until it came to rest on the furry triangle.

Danny suddenly jerked away and sat up. "What the hell are you doin'?" Her breathing had become heavy, and a strange, delicious feeling consumed her body. "I ain't gonna have no one's bastard child!" She jumped up, grabbed her pants and left.

"Now you know what kissing can lead to," he called after her. He knew she had learned her lesson well. Thank heavens he'd guessed right as to what her reaction would be. She could have so easily been deflowered. Much longer, and he wouldn't have been able to stop.

That night was the worst Danny had ever experienced. Beau had started a flame within her that reached her soul. She hated him for it, but at the same time she wanted to go over and lie beside him. She relived his kisses over and over again, wanting more.

She didn't know Beau had an equally hard time trying to control his sexual drives. Sleep didn't come easy for either of them that night or the following nights.

Three days later, in the wee hours of dawn, Beau woke her. "Get up, we're leaving the canyon."

She couldn't understand why he sounded so harsh. Still tired, she wanted to go back to sleep, but he insisted she get up immediately. Beau already had everything prepared for their departure. After a quick meal, they left.

Chapter Six

An old tree stood near the center of the wide courtyard, majestically bestowing its shade over a large portion of the area. As she did so often lately, Andrea sat on the bench that circled the thick trunk. How much longer before you arrive home, Beau? she wondered wistfully. She smoothed the sides of her blond hair and inhaled deeply. The green bushes and the pleasant odor of nearby flowering plants always helped her to relax.

Hearing the rustle of skirts, Andrea looked up, resenting the intrusion. She studied the petite brunette headed in her direction. Although the neckline of Margaret's dress rose to a respectable height, the bodice had been designed to show off her perfectly proportioned figure. The emerald-green silk matched the color of her eyes, and made her skin look like fine porcelain.

Andrea had long since done away with all the extra skirts and corsets considered so necessary in Europe. They were useless, and too hot in the warm climate.

"Andrea, have you heard anything about Beau?" Margaret's voice was soft and melodic.

"No." Every day Lady Margaret asked the same question. Andrea didn't like Margaret, and although the woman claimed to be a member of the nobility, her English wasn't pure. She had an accent that Andrea couldn't place.

"How much longer am I going to be forced to wait in this godforsaken place?" Margaret asked, taking her frustrations out on Andrea. "I wish I had told Beau I was coming. I'm sure, had he known, he would have been here long before now." She left in a huff.

Andrea made a silent plea to her brother. Dear Beau, will you please hurry home? You just don't know how much I need you.

When Margaret entered her bedroom, she slammed the heavy door. "Sara," she called, "come help me change clothes! I'm going for a ride."

A short, rail-thin woman with a hawk nose and graying hair entered the room. She had accompanied Margaret to England from the States, and had remained in her employment. Although she acted as a maid, she also served as Margaret's confidante and only friend. The two women got along well because they were of a similar disposition. Conniving.

Margaret went to the clothespress and yanked out a blue riding costume.

"Why are you in such a bad mood?" Sara asked as she helped Margaret dress.

"Because nothing is going right," Margaret pouted. "I thought I was being so clever by arriving before Beau. It was supposed to be a delightful surprise for him. But here I am stuck in the middle of nowhere. This place isn't much better than Dad's ranch in Texas!"

"Don't get yourself all worked up," Sara soothed. "He'll be here any time, then everything will be fine. You always get what you want, and this isn't going to be any different."

Margaret considered Sara's words. She had always gotten anything she wanted. Though her parents had been wealthy ranchers, she had never been satisfied. At eighteen she had talked her father into sending her to England, where she met and married Lord Leighton, Earl of Hampton. That he was her senior by many years was of little consequence. She had become a woman of nobility.

Dressed, Margaret went to the mirror and pinned on a small hat, making sure it was tilted at just the right angle. She would enjoy her ride today. The Falkners had magnificent horses.

Beau continued to push Mescal at a steady pace. Danny couldn't understand how man and horse could cover mile after mile without tiring. They only stopped when night fell, and left at the first flicker of dawn. She'd learned to catnap against

Beau's chest while they rode. Still, each night she collapsed into a deep sleep the moment they'd finished eating.

Over the weeks Danny and Mescal had been together, a strong bond had developed between the horse and the young woman. Although she hadn't tried to mount the big stallion, he would now come to her when she called. Other times, he'd unexpectedly walk up and give her a nudge, waiting for her to stroke his muzzle and croon sweet words to him. At first Danny thought Beau would be angry, but he just laughed.

"You have a rare gift," Beau told her one night before they bedded down.

"What do you mean by that?" she asked suspiciously.

"You have a way with horses. Believe me, Indian horses are very selective when it comes to making friends."

As they descended a mountain range, Beau pointed to a large green valley stretched out below.

"That's our final destination," he told Danielle. "It's called the Chino Valley."

A day and a half later, they arrived at one of the largest homes Danny had ever seen. Riding up to the veranda, Beau slipped off Mescal's back while she just sat there staring in awe. It had never occurred to her that Beau's family were rich.

"Beau, you've returned!" an excited man greeted him. "It is so good to have you back. Miss Andrea will be most pleased."

"And this time for good, Armando," Beau replied.

The two men clasped each other in a warm embrace.

"I must tell everyone you have arrived." Armando ran toward the house. "Maria, Miss Andrea, Beau has returned!" he called out.

Beau reached up and helped Danny down. "Well, little one, this is your home now."

A woman came running out of the house, arms extended. "Beau. My darling Beau. You're home!"

Beau grabbed her around the waist and started swinging her in the air. They both laughed with joy.

"It's good to see you, Andrea," he said, gently putting her down.

"I didn't expect you to arrive looking like an Indian, but then I should know better." She smiled fondly. "Your mother will always be with you, and that's the way it should be."

Danny, more than a little surprised, studied the attractive tall blonde. She looked nothing like her vision, except she was much older than Beau!

Beau became sober. "Andrea, in Santa Fe I was told Father is dead."

"Yes," Andrea said sadly. "Father made me promise not to say anything until you came home. With all your traveling, I'm not sure I could have even gotten a message to you. I'd hoped to be the one to inform you of his death, Beau."

"Let me get my horse taken care of, then I'd like a hot bath. We can talk later."

Andrea stood back and took a good look at her brother. "You've grown a few inches since I last saw you. I doubt that any of your old clothes will fit." She laughed. "I swear you're as tall as Father! Oh, Beau, how I've missed you. We have so much catching up to do."

Seeing Beau glance around, Andrea looked in the same direction. She hadn't even noticed the girl. "Who have we here?" she asked.

"It's a long story," Beau said. "I thought you could find her something to do around the house. Danny has nowhere to go and could use the pay. Will you take care of her?"

"Well . . . yes."

"I'll be in just as soon as I put my horse away," Beau said, picking up the reins.

"Why don't you have one of the hands take care of him?"

"No, I have to do it myself. He won't let anyone else handle him."

"Very well. You go on, and I'll see you later. I must tell Maria to prepare a special dinner to celebrate your return."

Beau took off toward the large, well-cared-for barns with Mescal following.

Andrea turned toward Danny, not really sure what to do with her. She knew Beau had just dropped all responsibility for the girl on her shoulders. Why had he even brought her here? "I'm afraid Beau has been amiss in his manners. I'm Andrea Windall. Your name is Danny?"

"Yep, that's my name."

"What a strange name for a girl. How old are you, Danny?"

"I ain't never told Beau, but my real name's Danielle Louise, and I'll be nineteen right soon. I'd be mighty pleased if you didn't pass that information on to Beau."

After hearing her age, Andrea took a second look at the woman standing in front of her. "Why don't we go inside?" she suggested. "Perhaps you would like to take a bath and rest before dinner?" Looking at the filthy girl, Andrea prayed the answer would be yes.

"I'd be right pleased to get this here dirt off."

"Tell me. Where did you meet my brother?" Andrea asked as they started toward the house.

Danny thought she would drop her teeth right then and there. She stopped dead in her tracks and looked at Andrea. "Your brother?" she asked.

Andrea gave her a warm smile. "Why, yes."

"I thought you was his wife... or somethin'." Danny lowered her head, ashamed at what she'd been thinking.

Andrea contained a laugh. She knew exactly what was running through the girl's mind. "No, I'm sorry to say Beau isn't married."

"Well I'll be danged!"

"Did Beau tell you he was married?"

"No, I just figured when he said he was goin' to turn me over to you... Well, it sure never came to mind you're his sister."

"Why don't we get that bath for you, and you can tell me how you happened to be with my brother." As if she didn't have enough trouble with Margaret, now she had another female to contend with. Margaret! Oh, heavens, I didn't tell Beau about Margaret! Andrea thought. Well, he'll find out soon enough.

Inside the house, Danny's head turned from side to side. The beautiful furnishings glistened with wax, and the floor didn't seem to have a speck of dirt on it.

Spying one of the maids, Andrea told her to bring water for a bath.

As they entered a bedroom, Danny couldn't believe her eyes. It was huge! Every bit as big as the entire cabin she and Jed had lived in at the mining camp. She went over to the big four-poster bed and pushed her hands down on the fluffy feather ticking.

"This will be your room, if it pleases you."

"You can't mean it?" Danny said, her eyes slowly traveling from the marble-topped commode to the silk sofa and brocade chairs. "Why, this is the purtiest room I've ever seen. You sure you want me to stay here?"

She started to walk over to the mirror when a series of women began filing into the room. The first one unfolded a large silk screen and set it in the corner. Two other women followed close behind with what looked to Danielle to be a big copper laundry tub, strangely shaped. They left it behind the screen. Other women entered carrying buckets of water.

"Where they puttin' all that?" asked Danielle.

"They're pouring it into the tub," Andrea replied.

"You mean I'm gonna wash my clothes?"

"No. The tub is used to bathe your body in. That's why it's shaped that way."

When the last woman left, Danielle went behind the screen to see what Andrea was talking about. "Well, I'll be a son of a bitch! Ain't nobody gonna believe me when I tell 'em about this!" She stuck her hand in the water. "And it's hot!"

Andrea winced at the girl's language. Contrary to what her father and Beau may have thought, after living on a ranch for twenty-five years, there were few words she hadn't heard. Even her beloved husband, Thomas, had been known to cuss when he became angry. But never had she heard a woman express herself in such a manner.

Danny turned to Andrea, who had followed her. "I ain't never seen nothin' like this. Look, ma'am—"

"Call me Andrea."

"Andrea, I know I ain't the type of guest you're used to havin' in a fine house like this. If you give me a horse, I'll be gettin' out of your hair once and for all."

Now this is an interesting turn of events, Andrea thought. Why hadn't Beau given her a horse instead of planting her here? Questions, questions! "You go ahead and take your bath, and I'll see what I can find for you to wear."

"Oh, that won't be necessary. I can wash my clothes in this here tub. When they're dry, I'll just put 'em back on and leave."

"I won't hear of it. What kind of a person would I be if I didn't have you stay at least one night?"

"I'm tellin' you, it ain't necessary. I got a place to go."

"Nonsense! I simply will not allow it. I'll leave you and be back shortly. There's plenty of soap on the stand by the tub."

After Andrea left, Danielle took off her clothes and dropped them by the corner of the colorful screen. The hot water stung her skin, and it took a few minutes before she could comfortably submerge her entire body. Once in, Danny never wanted to get out. She soaked for some time before she reached over and picked up the soap. Smelling it, she was overcome with delight. God must surely be paying me a visit! she thought.

Danielle scrubbed her hair first, then her body. It felt so good, she did it all over again. Ready to wash her clothes, she reached for them, but they were nowhere in sight.

Beau also sat in a tub, thoroughly delighted with himself. He had met his responsibility; now he could completely wash his hands of Danny. Andrea wasn't going to be pleased with him for dropping the mouthy, man-dressed woman on her hands, but if she complained, he would have to put his foot down. After all, someone had to take care of Danny, and a woman could certainly do a better job than he could.

After dressing, he left his room in search of Andrea. To his amazement, he found Margaret instead. She had her back turned, but he recognized her immediately.

"Margaret?"

"Beau, darling! I didn't hear you come in."

Her green eyes became emeralds of joy. He was so devastatingly handsome. Margaret wanted to rush into his arms and taste his passionate kiss, but she contained herself. She had already decided that the only way to catch Beau would be to let him make the advances.

"This is a pleasant surprise," Beau said with a smile.

"I hoped it might be. Remember, darling? You did invite me to come visit your beautiful ranch."

Beau, delighted with the sight before him, could smell her heady perfume. Always perfection, not a single hair escaped

Margaret's well-groomed brown head. The deep red slippers matched the color of her satin dress exactly. He went to where she stood and pulled her into his arms. "I think you are just what I need," he said in a deep, husky voice.

Margaret almost swooned from his words, then he kissed her, and she felt sure every bone in her body would melt from pleasure.

Suddenly he released her, then calmly walked over to the table and took out a cigar from the box sitting on top. Margaret stood there confused. He acted as though the kiss meant nothing to him. For Beau not to pursue her was indeed strange.

"How long have you been here?" he asked after lighting the cigar.

"Too long. You told me you had several places your father wanted you to go, so I knew I'd arrive before you. I must admit, though, I certainly didn't expect you to take so long." She gave him a pretty smile.

"Have you been comfortable?"

Why is he making small talk, Margaret wondered. "Yes. Who wouldn't be, with your lovely sister for company?"

Beau chuckled. "Oh, come now, Margaret. We both know this is not the type of living you're accustomed to."

Margaret grinned. "Well, it is rather quiet and dull."

"The one thing I like about you is your forthright attitude."

"Much the same as yours?"

"You might not have thought it was so dull when Indians were here a great deal of the time."

"I would have found that interesting. I've never seen one."

Beau laughed openly. "Oh, I think you have." He almost wished he hadn't cut his hair before leaving his room. It would have been amusing to see Margaret's reaction.

"Well, you're wrong. Admittedly, though, I certainly wouldn't want to see one on the warpath. I've been told, however, that some of them are most attractive."

"Yes, I believe I've heard that mentioned also. Why don't we go sit in the courtyard? You can tell me what our mutual friends in New York were doing after I left, and all the gossip you're so fond of. It is good to see you, Margaret, I've missed your...company. It's been a long, lonely trip."

Margaret giggled happily as they left the room.

* * *

When Andrea returned to Danny's room some time later, the girl was nowhere in sight. Tossing the dress she'd brought on the bed, she called, "Danny?" Then she heard water splash. "Do you ever plan on getting out?" she asked playfully.

Danny laughed, a clear, sweet sound that reminded Andrea of bells chiming.

"I've been enjoyin' myself," Danny replied. "Did you take my clothes?"

"One of the servants took them while you were bathing. They're being washed."

Andrea went behind the screen and found Danny standing in the middle of the tub. "You can use this to dry off," she said as she handed the girl a towel.

"Thank you kindly. I saw 'em, but I didn't want to mess 'em up."

My heavens, Andrea thought, the girl is perfect in every way. With her hair combed and styled properly, and the right clothes, she could outshine any woman. Even Margaret.

"I brought one of my dresses for you to wear," Andrea said, as they left the small area. "Maria will be in shortly to make the necessary adjustments."

Danielle ran her fingers down the beautiful flowered material. "I ain't never worn a dress," she said softly.

"Have you ever wanted to?"

"Yep, but I ain't never learned how to ride sidesaddle. Don't reckon I ever wanted to. 'Sides, it's a lot safer lookin' like a man than a woman."

Andrea's curiosity was piqued. "Let's sit down and talk while we're waiting for Maria."

"All right." Danny wrapped the large towel around her and plopped down ungracefully on the rose sofa beside Andrea.

"Tell me, Danny, how did you happen to meet Beau?" Andrea asked, trying to sound casual.

"He run off with me."

"He did what?"

"He come out of nowhere and kidnapped me. I tried tellin' him I had a place to go, but he wouldn't listen."

"Why would he do something like that?"

"Well, you see, he thought I was a boy."

"I beg your pardon? I mean . . . this is all very confusing."

Danny began to fidget. "I did something to make Beau mad, and he took off with me to get even."

"Oh, that's hilarious." Andrea broke out laughing.

Danny glared at the woman. "I don't think this is so funny!" she said irritably.

"I'm sorry, my dear. I'm really not laughing at you. If I'm starting to put the pieces of this whole mess together correctly, I'm laughing at my brother. If you managed to pull the wool over his eyes, it is an absolute first. Why don't you tell me the whole story? I assure you, nothing you say will leave this room. Contrary to what my brother probably thinks, you won't shock me."

Danny studied the woman's kind face. She'd never had a female friend, and she found herself needing someone to confide in. Would Andrea be her friend? She would soon find out. "Well, it all started..." Danny proceeded to tell her story. "And finally we arrived here," she ended.

"You poor dear! And to think he put you through all that! He should be horsewhipped!"

"He wasn't bad to me, except for the time he staked me out. When the snake bit me, he waited on me hand and foot and was as gentle as any person could be."

Andrea didn't miss the dreamy look that came into Danny's eyes. She knew that, like most women, Danny had become enamored with Beau. She liked this totally unrefined woman. "So Beau knows nothing about your ranch or that you've only attempted three holdups?" she asked.

"No, and I don't reckon he'd believe me if I was to tell him."

"Just where is your ranch, my dear?"

"Jed said it's near the Falkner ranch. It's called the Silver J."

"Oh, Lord in heaven!"

"Are you all right?" Danny asked. Andrea's face had suddenly become ashen. "What's the matter?"

"What is your last name?" Andrea's voice came out as a whisper.

"Jameson. Why?"

Andrea stood and walked over to the window. Drawing the lacy curtain back, she looked out with unseeing eyes. Now I know why people refer to the world as being small, she thought. "I know where your ranch is," she finally said.

"You do?" Danny jumped up excitedly. "I reckon I can be leavin' then."

Andrea turned and faced the happy girl. "Before I tell you where it's located, I want you to promise me something."

"What's that?" Danny asked suspiciously.

Andrea took a deep breath. This wasn't going to be easy. "I want you to promise me you'll stay here a month before going to your ranch."

"Why?" The smile had left Danny's face.

"For several reasons. The main one being, I want to become your friend." Andrea secretly hoped this would all work out and that she wasn't making a big mistake.

"What's the other reasons?"

"I'd like you to become familiar with this ranch before leaving."

"Why do I need to do that?"

Andrea searched for the right words. She knew Danny had her guard up. "It might help you run your own ranch."

"I'm mighty anxious to get to my spread."

"Would four weeks make that much difference?"

"That's quite a while." Danny plopped back down on the sofa. "Jed's gotta be awful worried about me."

"Yes, I'm sure your dear friend is very worried. What if I send a message telling him you're all right?"

"I reckon that would do it." Danny couldn't figure out why Andrea didn't just tell her what she wanted to know. "My place must be near if you can send a message."

"Will you promise to stay?"

Maybe Andrea isn't proving to be a friend after all, she thought. "Reckon I ain't got no choice."

"No, I don't suppose you do," Andrea replied, determined to remain firm.

"Then I promise, and I ain't one to go back on my word. Now where's my ranch?"

"Danny, this is the Falkner ranch."

"Who the hell is Falkner?"

"Beau."

"It can't be. You said his name's Windall."

"No. You misunderstood. My name is Windall."

"You tellin' me he owns this ranch?" Danny didn't know whether she felt shock or anger or both.

A knock on the door saved Andrea from having to answer any more questions. Without waiting for a reply, a heavyset woman entered. A big grin creased her pudgy, dark-skinned face. She carried a wicker basket with sewing utensils in her hand, and underwear over her arm.

"Danny, I would like you to meet Maria," Andrea said. "She has been with the family for years, and I don't know what we'd do without her." She smiled fondly. "She's the one who really keeps this house running in proper order."

Danny forgot all about her concern over reaching the ranch when the two women began dressing her. She became giddy with pleasure as the silk stockings were put on, followed by a chemise and pantalets. Next came a heavily starched, ruffled petticoat.

"We gotta do all this just to get dressed?" she asked, as Maria tied the petticoat strings around her tiny waist. The material caused her skin to itch. "Can't we put on some long handles and put the dress on over that?"

The two women laughed, and Danny found herself caught up in their merriment.

When the dress had been altered to fit, Danny went to the long mirror and took a look at herself. She let out a screech of delight, then ran over and gave Andrea and Maria a big hug to show her pleasure. "It's so purty," she exclaimed with pride.

"I have to leave and get dressed for dinner, dear," said Andrea, heading for the door. "Maria will stay and arrange your hair. When she's through, you might want to practice walking." Danny is going to be such a pleasure to have around, Andrea thought, as she left the room. She brightens up the place already.

Danny's hair had grown considerably since the last time she'd chopped it off, so getting the thick, knotted mass combed proved to be no easy task. But Maria managed to style the shiny auburn hair even though the young woman begged her to stop.

Danny was as nervous as a mouse when Andrea arrived to take her to dinner. She'd practiced walking around the room as Andrea suggested, but kept tripping over the dress hem.

"Are you ready?" Andrea asked. She still couldn't believe the transformation. She's beautiful, Andrea thought. Now, if I could only brave the task of teaching her proper English.

"Yep, reckon I am. Ain't Beau gonna be surprised?"

"Oh, I'm sure he will be, in more ways than one." Andrea had talked briefly to Beau before coming to get her, but she hadn't told him the girl would be dining with them. "Before we go, I want you to know we have another guest. Her name is Lady Margaret Leighton."

"What am I supposed to call her? Maggy?"

Andrea laughed. "No, you call her Lady Margaret. She's here to visit Beau." Andrea watched an expression close to jealousy cross Danny's face. Just what Andrea had hoped for!

"Is she purty?" Danny asked.

"Yes, very."

"Oh."

"Also, I want you to do me a favor."

"What's that?"

"Under no circumstances do I want you to let anyone at the ranch know you own the Silver J, or that your name is Jameson," Andrea said in a kindly voice.

"Why not? I ain't ashamed of it!"

"I haven't time to explain, dear, but believe me, it's very important no one finds out. We'll say your last name is...James."

"Anything else you got to tell me?" Danny asked in a huffy tone.

"Believe me, dear, I'm only trying to protect you. Please, trust me on this matter."

"Well, you ain't done wrong by me so far, reckon I gotta start trustin' someone sometime." She smiled. "And I'm gonna try real hard not to embarrass you by cussin'. I know it ain't proper, but sometimes I just say what comes into my head. When I was a kid, Jed used to give my rear a good wallopin' when I said words like the other miners."

Andrea's heart went out to the girl. She's like a beautiful, untamed animal, she thought. The more I'm around her, the fonder I become. Andrea found it refreshing to spend time with someone who had not learned the subtle art of trickery. Unlike Margaret, Danny appeared to be a truthful person.

"Andrea, I been wonderin'. How come you don't look anything like Beau? You got the same color eyes, but that's all."

"I'm his half-sister. I'll tell you about it when we have more time. Now, sometimes it's all right for a beautiful woman to make a late entrance, but on the other hand, I'm not fond of cold food."

Danny laughed as the two women left the room.

Beau stood talking to an attentive Margaret when the ladies entered the salon. Looking in their direction, he watched Danny trip on the hem of her dress and almost fall to the floor before recovering herself. Stunned, he wondered what possible reason Andrea could have for bringing her to dine with them.

"I'm sorry we're late," Andrea apologized. "We didn't mean to keep you waiting. Shall we go straight to dinner?"

Margaret turned, and upon seeing Danny, her eyes narrowed. She hadn't expected another guest, especially not a female.

When they reached the dining room, Danny started to sit at the end of the table.

"No, my dear," Andrea said, taking Danny's elbow and leading her farther down the table. "You can sit by me."

Beau walked around and held the chair for Margaret before taking his place at the end of the table. Danny immediately realized her mistake. She had almost taken Beau's seat.

It suddenly occurred to Danny, that this could be a good opportunity to learn some ladylike ways. In fact, it would probably be her only chance. From this moment on, she vowed, I'll do nothing until I see someone else do it first.

"Beau, darling, I don't believe I've been properly introduced to your guest," Margaret said sweetly.

"Excuse my bad manners, my dear. Lady Margaret, I'd like you to meet Danny. Danny, this is Lady Margaret."

"Danny?" Margaret asked. "Why, my dear, how did you ever end up with a name like that?" She turned to Beau and laughed softly. "It sounds like a man's name, doesn't it, darling?"

"Danny ain't my real name. Name's Danielle Louise."

Beau raised a dark eyebrow. He'd taken it for granted Danny *was* her real name.

Margaret became curious about the obviously illiterate creature sitting almost across from her. At first she thought she might have a little competition, but now she knew she could make mincemeat of the chit. Danny probably came from one of the local ranches. She should have known immediately. Who would be seen dead in that dress? It looked like something Beau's sister would wear.

"Her speech is so quaint. Tell me, Andrea, is she from around here?" Margaret asked.

Andrea saw Beau look in her direction and knew he was waiting to hear her explanation. "No. Danny is a distant relative. She's here on a visit. Actually, I invited her some time ago and I'm so happy she finally accepted my invitation."

Why did Andrea say that? Beau wondered. He definitely needed to have a private talk with his sister. Andrea had something planned, and he wanted to know what.

Danny looked across at Margaret. Though a smile curved the woman's ruby-red lips, her eyes were green daggers. For the first time, Danny felt the claws of jealousy. She could understand how Beau would be attracted to a beautiful woman like Lady Margaret. She had never seen a dress as beautiful as the one Margaret wore. The vivid lavender color made her skin as clear as a babe's. But how Margaret kept from falling out of the low neckline was a mystery. It hardly covered anything! All those diamonds hanging from her ears and around her neck must be worth a fortune, Danny thought. Margaret leaned over and whispered something in Beau's ear. They both laughed. Danny assumed they were laughing at her.

Keeping to her resolve, she watched the bowls of food being passed around and waited patiently until they came to her. Too late, she noticed everyone had taken small portions and she had heaped her plate full. What the hell, she said to herself. They may not be hungry, but I'm starved. Picking up a fork, she began gulping down the delicious food.

Margaret looked at Andrea, smiled, then turned to Beau, placing her hand on his arm. "My heavens," she said, with just the right inflection of shock. "Does she always make so much noise when she eats? You'd think the poor girl has been starved to death!"

Danny stopped eating and looked up. "I ain't had a decent meal in some time. From the way you pick at your food, I reckon you have." She made a supreme effort at keeping her temper down.

"I must admit I have, but even if I hadn't I certainly wouldn't eat like some animal," Margaret said sweetly. "Didn't your father or mother ever take the time to teach you proper manners?"

Danny looked down at her plate and tried to eat with less noise.

Amused, Beau unobtrusively watched the beautiful outlaw. He knew her volatile temper better than anyone, and if Margaret continued to aim her snippety remarks toward Danny, that temper would eventually cause an explosion. In fact, Beau couldn't understand why it hadn't already. Margaret, on the other hand, acted like a bitch. So wrapped up in her own self-importance, she'd let her English accent slip, as well as her assumed ladylike conduct. Beau knew, at the rate things were going, a confrontation loomed.

Although Margaret wasn't aware of it, Beau knew quite a lot about her and her lovers. She'd been a constant gossip item in England. Even though Margaret married into a titled family, she had never been accepted in society.

"Really, Beau," Margaret pouted, "am I expected to sit here and listen to her slop her food? She's completely ruined my appetite." *Why doesn't someone remove this creature and let her eat with her own kind?* Margaret thought angrily.

"Danny—" Beau started to say.

"Danny has every right to eat with us. She is a guest," Andrea spoke up.

"Danny is not a guest," Beau reminded his sister.

"Then what is she, Beau?" Andrea asked in a calm voice. "I really would like to know."

"Look, I ain't here to cause no one trouble. I reckon I'd best go." Danny push her chair back, ready to leave.

Margaret, feeling a smug sense of satisfaction, said, "Well, it's about time. At least you'll allow decent people to eat in peace. Look at the trouble you've already caused."

To Danny, Margaret's words were like a slap in the face. "Listen, you bitch, I didn't start this."

"Wait just a minute!" Beau said in a soft but angry voice, hiding his amusement. "Now I have no idea what is going on here, but it will end right now. I refuse to sit at a table and listen to cats yowling."

Margaret quickly gained control of herself. "You're absolutely right, darling, and I'm completely to blame. My words were totally uncalled for."

The corner of Beau's lips twitched with humor. It was very difficult for him to keep a stern face at Margaret's expected change of attitude. "I'll talk to you later, Margaret," Beau said in a gruff voice.

Furious at being cut off, Margaret placed the blame squarely on the shoulders of the baggage sitting across from her.

"Now, Andrea," Beau continued, "I have no idea what your thinking is in regards to Danny, but I believe we should have our talk in the study an hour from now. In the meantime, if you insist Danny eat with us, I seriously suggest you take the time to improve her manners before she returns to the table. Tell Maria I'll have my meal in the study. Now if you ladies will excuse me, you're welcome to continue your *friendly* conversation."

When Beau left, the three women sat glaring at one another. Andrea started to say something, then changed her mind. That Beau had been exposed to Margaret's true nature pleased her no end. At the same time, she felt sorry for Danny.

Margaret finally spoke. "Well, I hope you're happy, Andrea! This is what you planned, isn't it?"

"I have no idea what you're talking about," Andrea said with deceptive innocence.

Margaret stood up. "How could you bring this tramp to the table, especially with me here?"

Danny jumped up so fast she knocked her chair over. "I've had all I'm goin' to take! I ain't heard you do nothin' but bad mouth. You think you're so high and mighty, and you ain't no better than a jackass roamin' the damn desert!" Danny yelled.

"You have your nerve talking to me like that!" Margaret screeched. "Do you know who I am? No, I don't suppose you do, scum wouldn't be privy to that sort of information!"

"Well, you might call me scum, but at least I don't go around hangin' out of my dress, and I don't act like some bitch in heat lookin' for a cur to mount her!"

"Oh!" Margaret stormed out of the room.

Danielle picked her chair up and sat down. Propping her elbows on the table, she rested her head in her hands. "I'm sorry, Andrea, none of this would'a happened if I weren't here."

"You said what needed to be said, Danny. I'm not the least bit upset. We might need to tackle your vocabulary, however. Now I don't know about you, but I'm not going to let a perfectly good meal go to waste. I still have an hour until I meet with Beau."

"He's gonna be godawful mad."

"You let me handle Beau." Andrea smiled. "May I pass you the potatoes, my dear?"

Danny giggled. "I reckon you can." This time, she placed a small portion on her plate.

"Since I've been delegated to teach you how to eat, I guess it's time for your first lesson. The reason people put smaller amounts of food in their plates is quite simple. They can always take second or third helpings if they're still hungry."

"Well, now, that makes sense! Andrea, you ain't gonna keep me to my promise, are you? Me bein' here isn't gonna cause nothin' but trouble."

"I must have misjudged you, my dear."

"What do you mean?"

Andrea took a bite of the beans nestled on her plate, then dabbed her mouth with the napkin. "I didn't think you were the type of person who would put their tail between their legs and run."

"What do you mean run? I ain't runnin'!"

"Well, what would you call it?" Andrea looked at Danny and smiled. "I know what Margaret would say."

"I reckon I do, too, but she ain't gonna say it where everyone could hear."

Both women broke out laughing.

Margaret entered her room and went directly to the mirrored dressing table. She picked up a brush, then hurled it across the room. The comb followed. "Damn!" she said, her voice trembling with anger. "I'll be so glad when Beau and I can leave this place." She collapsed on the sofa, glad that Sara wasn't in her room waiting. She wanted to be alone. Closing her eyes, she began to reminisce.

Her first encounter with Beau had been in England. She'd seen him at various social gatherings, and had danced with him on several occasions. From their first meeting she wanted Beau, but other than the normal chitchat, he'd shown little interest. At the time, he was involved in a much talked-about affair with Lady Covingham. But Lady Covingham, considered to be the most beautiful woman in all England, had never managed to draw Beau to the altar. Margaret personally thought the woman's beauty highly overrated.

Margaret had done some checking with a few close friends and discovered Lady Covingham hadn't been the only lady to set her cap for the elusive Mr. Falkner. The man proved to be quite notorious for his love affairs, which made Margaret even more attracted.

Before Margaret could pursue the illustrious Mr. Falkner, her husband, Lord Leighton, graciously condescended to die of old age. Although free at last, society dictated she play the part of a grieved widow.

Her trip to the Americas proved far more delightful than expected. Beau Falkner had boarded the same ship. It took virtually no persuasion on her part to get to know him on a personal basis. He proved to be every bit as good a lover as the reputation that preceded him. Never had she experienced such a delightful romp in bed. He was everything she'd ever wanted in a man.

No matter what it took, she planned on marrying Beau. Once married, she could foresee little difficulty in getting him to return to England and civilization. After all, why would he want to stay on at this godforsaken ranch?

Chapter Seven

Exactly one hour later, Andrea entered the study ready for a fight. The wide grin on Beau's face came as a complete surprise.

"Come in, Andrea. I'm not going to bite your head off," he said, moving away from the large mahogany desk. "May I pour you a sherry?"

"Yes. I could use one." Andrea sat and glanced around the familiar, male-oriented room. This had been Gerard Falkner's study. She pushed the memories from her mind as Beau handed her a drink.

After pouring himself a healthy shot of whiskey, Beau sank onto the leather sofa beside her and chuckled.

"Well, dear sister, I'm glad to be home, but my first night wasn't anything like I expected."

"I'm sorry, Beau."

He gave her a sly grin. "No need to be. I found it rather amusing. Now, do you want to tell me why Danny dined with us, and why you made up that story about her being a relative?"

"I like her, Beau. I don't think it's fair to stick her somewhere so she'll be out of the way. You owe her more than that."

"I suppose you're right, but to tell you the truth, I didn't know what to do with her. I take it she's told you everything?"

"As much as she's willing to. Why did you abduct her, Beau?"

"I've asked myself that a hundred times over. Don't laugh, but when I thought she was just a young girl, I considered her as a daughter for you."

"I wouldn't mind having her for a daughter, even now. But I'd settle for her friendship."

"I get the feeling you feel differently about Margaret. You don't like her, do you?"

"That's not a fair question. She's your friend, not mine."

"You have a valid point." Beau finished off his whiskey then became silent. He sat rubbing his forehead in a slow thoughtful manner. "Tell me, Andrea," he finally said, staring into space, "how did Father die?"

Andrea wondered how long it would be before he broached the subject. "He wasn't a young man, Beau," she said quietly. "His illness started slowly, with a slight cough. For about a year the cough continued to worsen. He remained convinced he'd get over it. Near the end, he finally realized he was dying and sent for you. His last words were 'Twana,' then 'Beau.' He loved you both very much."

"He shouldn't have sent me away."

Andrea heard the hurt in his voice. "If it had been your son, wouldn't you have done the same thing? Think of it from his viewpoint for a change. While Twana lived, she kept the balance in you of white man and Indian. But when she died, you became more and more Indian and less and less white man. Then Father found out you were a dog soldier, and knew he would lose you completely if he didn't do something. You had ceased to be a white man, Beau. He needed you. Not just to leave the ranch to, but as his son.

"We talked about you all the time," Andrea continued. "It was his dearest wish that you would find the right woman and settle down, as long as you moved back here to live and raise his grandchildren."

"Why didn't he have me come straight home instead of sending me all over the country looking at cattle to upgrade the stock?" Beau moaned, then tossed his hands up in the air. "Damn him! He cheated me out of saying all the things I've waited for years to tell him!"

"He knew he wouldn't be alive when you arrived, and he wanted you to remember everything you had learned about ranching. Father wanted you to see the country and remember that this is where you were born and raised. Not England. He thought of it as a homecoming.''

Beau stood, poured himself another drink and tossed it down. A soft, spiteful snicker escaped his lips. ''Oh, yes, a gift. The only gift he ever gave me was bitterness. If the great and mighty man loved me so much, why didn't he ask me to come home sooner?''

Even with Beau's back turned, Andrea knew he suffered a deep pain. She tried to pick her words carefully. ''He honestly didn't know death stood looking at him until he wrote the letter. And all your letters stated how happy you were. Never once did *you* ask to come home.''

Slowly Beau turned. ''Oh, God,'' he said, raking his fingers through his thick hair. ''Those letters were all written out of stubborn pride, Andrea! I was mad at Father for sending me away, and I wanted *him* to do the asking. When I first arrived at our uncle's estates, I waited for Father to send for me and looked forward to refusing. Then, as the years passed, I guess I finally grew up. When I did receive his letter, I booked passage on the next ship.''

Andrea walked to where Beau stood and embraced him. ''It's all right now, Beau. You're home, and that's all he ever wanted. He can rest in peace.'' Releasing him, she walked to the desk and withdrew a sealed paper from the top drawer. ''He left this for you,'' she said, holding it out to him.

Beau had just taken the paper when there was a knock on the door. The sound startled both of them.

''Beau, are you in there, darling?'' Margaret called.

''I don't want to see anyone, Andrea,'' he said in a hushed tone. ''I want to be alone for the rest of the evening.''

''I'll take care of it.''

''Do you mind?''

''No, dear.''

Andrea opened the door, then closed it behind her, purposely blocking Margaret's view. ''Beau is asleep and doesn't wish to be disturbed,'' she whispered.

''He'll want to see me,'' Margaret insisted.

Andrea continued to block the doorway. ''Margaret, Beau has been traveling for days, and he wants to be alone! Now if you care for him nearly as much as you would have everyone believe, you'd be wise to honor his request.''

"Well, of course. I only want what's best for him."

"I knew you'd feel that way. Why don't you go into the drawing room? After I check on Danny, we can go for a stroll."

"Yes . . . that would be lovely."

Andrea knew Margaret wasn't happy about having to spend another evening in her company, but the woman had no choice.

Andrea entered Danny's room and found the girl fast asleep. The floral dress had been carefully placed across one of the rose brocade chairs. Andrea smiled at the sleeping figure, wrapped in the sheet like a cocoon and curled into a ball. Beau doesn't know it yet, Andrea thought, but Danny is the woman for him. He needs someone with spark and fire, and this one has it all. Beau would never be happy with anything less.

It certainly wouldn't be easy, considering all Andrea knew, and the others would eventually find out. But something inside her said someday it would happen, and she would do everything in her power to help it along.

In the study, Beau placed the decanter and glass on the desk, then turned up the kerosene lamp. Pushed by an unwanted curiosity, he turned the letter over in his hands several times before taking a seat in the large chair. Slowly he broke the seal and unfolded the missive. Both anger and pain seared through him upon seeing his father's scrawled handwriting. He took a couple of swallows of whiskey and began reading.

February 10, 1872
My son,

When you read this I shall be departed. There are so many things I want to say, but because we haven't been close for many years, I do not know where to start. So try to excuse any rambling I might do.

I know there lies within you a deep seed of hatred and anger. Though I have always felt disinclined to explain my actions to any man, I feel called upon to do so now. I have never been a weak man, but when your beloved mother gave me a son, I thanked God for bestowing upon me a special favor. You were our joy of love. I loved Twana deeply. When she asked that you be raised in her culture as well as mine, I agreed. You see, I could refuse her nothing. Falkner men are known for truly loving only one woman. Our time spent in the territory of Colorado was without a doubt the best part of my life. We had Andrea, a strapping son and each other. What more could a man ask for?

I watched you grow tall and strong, but as the years passed, it bothered me that you preferred being with your mother's people. Although you worked hard on the ranch and knew more than any hired hand, you couldn't wait until summer and your return to the lodges of the Cheyenne. I resented your obvious preference. I wanted a son who would some day take over the empire I'd built, but we seemed to drift farther and farther apart.

As you are aware, when I went with "Uncle Joe" Walker to explore the Arizona Territory, we discovered gold. I claimed thousands of acres, which is the ranch you now own. It was not an easy life. There were constant problems with Indians and the onslaught of men seeking gold. But I persevered. I am not ashamed to say that more than one man died by a bullet from my gun, or from those of the men I hired to help run the ranch. Times were hard, and guns were the only law.

When I returned home, I discovered your mother had died. I will take my grief to my deathbed. Also during my absence, Andrea lost a husband and I lost a son. I had to search for you, and thank God I was friends with the Cheyenne people or I would never have found you. When I did, I discovered you had become a dog soldier, the fiercest and most daring of all the Cheyenne warriors, and were on the warpath against the white man. After Colonel Chivington's massacre at Sand Creek, I could understand your anger over the useless slaughter of Indian women and children, and the loss of your good friend, Chief Black Kettle. But I am a white man, and you are my son. My only son. Was I supposed to let *my* son remain a savage? My God, Beau, you bragged about scalps! You were headed toward certain death.

Beau looked into space. One of the women killed at Sand Creek had been Morning Flower, his childhood playmate. After they were grown, there had been great expectation in the village that he would take Morning Flower as his wife. Although he loved her more as a sister, he'd actually been giving it serious thought. He had seen the look in her doelike black eyes that proclaimed her love. Morning Flower's beauty would have made any brave proud to claim her.

Beau looked at the paper and continued reading.

I saw only one recourse. As you recall, I sold the ranch and moved family and cattle to the land I owned in the Arizona Territory. I know we fought bitterly, and your hatred grew. Not only for what I forced you to do, but also because I represented the white man you had so grown to hate. So, I sent you to England and away from all Indians.

I do not offer this as an excuse for my actions. I would do the same thing again. But in my waning hours, I find myself saddened at the loss of years we could have spent together. I love you, my son. Through you and your children, I shall live on. I pray you will release your pent-up bitterness and continue on to a fruitful life.

Your father

Beau let the paper fall onto the desk. He remained motionless for some time, not sure what his feelings were. Gerard Falkner had been the strongest, most ungiving man he'd ever known. His word was law, and no one questioned what he said; nor was there ever an explanation given. Now, after almost twenty-eight years, Beau saw a side of his father he'd never known. Beau knew it was partly his fault. He'd never taken the time to look beneath that hard exterior and discover the real man. It must have always been there, or his mother could not have loved him so deeply. All Beau could remember was a man who didn't wait for things to happen. Gerard made them happen. "Time wasted," Beau muttered, as tears came to his eyes.

After several more healthy drinks, Beau stood and left the room. With firm steps, he walked through the house and out the front door. When he reached the stables, he let Mescal out of the stall and jumped on the stallion's bare back. He guided the horse with his knees, and they took off at a fast gallop.

Beau didn't bring the horse to a halt until they reached the black iron fence surrounding the ranch's small cemetery. Beau had no problem finding his father's grave. It was marked with a tall granite tombstone, the only indication that a man lay beneath the surface.

"Rest, my father," Beau said in a husky voice. "We are at peace with one another."

The next few days passed quickly. Beau spent most of his time reacquainting himself with the ranch hands and with the status of the ranch.

When he was in the house, if he wasn't in the study discussing business with Andrea, Margaret seemed constantly to be at his side. In a sweet but demanding way, she continuously reminded him that they should return to England. Her excuse was that he had lost all traces of his English accent and sounded like one of the men working for him. Beau really didn't care. It had all started during the months he'd traveled around looking at cattle prior to returning home. After all, he'd lived in this country practically all his life, and speaking as an American was far more natural to him.

Andrea spent most of her time with Danny. She found the girl to be extremely bright. Not unlike the way a sponge absorbs water, Danny quickly absorbed every bit of information she could get hold of. And to Andrea's amazement, the girl didn't forget a single thing. Andrea was especially pleased and surprised that Danny could read and write. She brought Danny books and the girl spent her nights reading. She particularly liked the stories about English knights in shining armor.

Danny had an untiring drive, and practiced over and over again how to walk, talk and eat. Never again will I give Margaret an opportunity to make fun of me, she vowed. She refused to have dinner with the others until she could do everything correctly.

Learning to speak properly took longer. In order to keep from making mistakes, Danny spoke her words slowly. She constantly encouraged Andrea to correct every error, no matter how small. Her vocabulary grew by leaps and bounds.

Danny's quickly becoming a full-fledged woman, Andrea thought one day as she sat in the young woman's bedroom.

Danny was standing on a stool while Maria basted the hem of a yellow dress the girl seemed particularly excited about. Andrea had had the material brought in from Prescott, and Maria, with the help of the maids, worked diligently to create a wardrobe for her.

"Andrea," Danny questioned, tired from having to stand still for so long, "didn't you tell me you are Beau's half-sister?"

"Yes I did. My mother and father were living in England when my mother died."

"How did she die?"

Andrea laughed. "All right, I know what you're leading up to. I'll tell you the whole family history if you'll just stand still and let Maria finish the dress."

Danny giggled.

"My mother and father were both blond and quite tall. Father stood as high as Beau—"

"That's why you and Beau are so tall!"

"Hush and let me tell the story. And yes, to answer your question."

"How tall is Beau? He towers over everyone. Ouch, Maria, you stuck me."

"Then be still, and it won't happen again," Maria gently scolded.

"Beau is six feet five, the same height Father was," Andrea answered. "Now, to continue. When I was thirteen, my mother, Agatha, died of influenza. Father had the misfortune of being the youngest son of Conrad Falkner, the Duke of Wilmington. The only way he could inherit the title would be for his very healthy brother, Andrew, to die. Shortly before Father married Mother, Andrew married, and eventually had three sons. As you can see, the chances of Father becoming titled were almost impossible.

"Mother had been married before, and when her husband died, he'd left her a goodly fortune. So, when she died, her money, coupled with what Father had inherited, left him a very wealthy man."

"Were they in love?"

"I'd like to say yes, but I'm afraid it was a marriage of convenience. Actually, they didn't get along very well."

Andrea sat back in the chair, making herself comfortable, her slender hands folded neatly on her lap. "Somewhere along the way, Father became obsessed with seeing the colonies, and when Mother died, he considered it an excellent time to leave. He wanted to take me, but grandfather finally convinced him of the dangers in the wild colonies.

"During Father's travels in the territory of Colorado, he stayed with a group of Indians called the Cheyenne, and fell madly in love with a chief's daughter. Ultimately they had Beau.

"An exceptional woman, Twana did what very few Cheyenne women would do. She loved Father very deeply, and when Beau became two, she suggested they leave and build a home where I could come and live with them. She knew how much he missed me."

"What was your father's name?"

"Gerard. So," Andrea pressed on, "Father bought some land and started ranching."

"If you had a ranch somewhere else, how come you're here now?" Danny asked.

"After Twana died, Father sold the old ranch and brought his family west. He was taken with the comfort of the Spanish-style homes, and he had this house built in a like manner. All the other homes in the valley and in town are wood."

Maria stood up, holding her back as she stretched. "I'm all finished," she said, letting out a big sigh. "I'll take the dress and have one of the girls stitch the hem properly."

Danny took the dress off and handed it to the large woman. "Thank you," she said with a cheery smile.

Maria left, and Danny curled up in a chair, completely absorbed in Andrea's story.

"When you finally arrived in this country, were you unhappy? Did you like having an Indian for a mother?"

"At first I resented having to leave England and all my friends, but that didn't last long. I had a lot of my father's adventuresome spirit. As for Twana, I loved her dearly, as did most people who knew her. I would say her adjustments were far more difficult than mine. But she never complained, and always seemed happy as long as she had my father beside her."

"What a beautiful story. But that means Beau is a... I mean...."

"I know what you're trying to say, but you're wrong. Father and Twana were married by a minister to make sure Beau was a legal heir in every sense of the word."

"How come you never married? You're a beautiful woman, and I'd think all sorts of men would want to court you."

"I was very happily married, but my husband died in an accident almost nine years ago."

"I'm sorry, Andrea. I didn't mean to bring up sad memories."

"I've gotten over it, so I don't mind talking about it. Now, have I answered all your questions?"

"No, I still have one more."

Andrea laughed. "What else could there possibly be to tell?"

"If Beau only lived with the Indians until he was two, why does he still act like one?"

Andrea refused to tell Danielle everything. "Beau's mother asked that her son spend time with her people so he could come to know the ways of the Indian." She laughed softly. "Now, curious one, are you satisfied?"

"Yes, I suppose."

"Oh, no, you still have something on your mind, so let's get it out and over with."

"I'm curious about one other thing. If Beau lived with the Indians, did he ever scalp anyone?" Danny had become very quiet.

"I don't know, I never asked."

"Do you really think he could be that savage?"

Andrea looked away, trying to think how to answer the question. Finally she looked at the auburn-haired beauty. The question had to be answered, but she didn't want Danny to be frightened.

"Beau is the most gentle and caring man I know, but I wouldn't want him for an enemy."

"So your answer is yes."

"I honestly don't know. In many ways he's much like you. Part of him remains wild and free, while the other part is civilized. It's the two worlds that have made him the man he is today. I don't believe I would want to change that quality in either of you."

Tears appeared in Danny's big amber-brown eyes. She leaned over and hugged her friend. "Thank you, Andrea, that's the nicest thing anyone has ever said to me."

Touched, Andrea had trouble containing her composure. "Well, enough of this serious talk. What would you like to do this afternoon?"

"What I'd really like to do is go for a ride, but I would never be able to handle one of them—those sidesaddles."

"I have just the answer. I've been saving it as a surprise. Wait here."

Andrea soon returned, carrying a white doeskin outfit.

"What's that?" asked Danny.

"The Cheyenne are known for their riding ability, and that includes the women. Twana loved to ride, so my father had these made for her." Andrea held up the outfit. "See, it looks like a skirt, but it's actually pants."

Danny started laughing excitedly. "It's perfect!"

"And here's the top that goes with it. It slips over your head. You and Twana are about the same size. She had a larger waist than you, but as you can see, this rawhide strip goes in and out around the waist and you can tighten it. I also brought her doeskin boots. Would you like to try them on?"

"Oh, yes."

When Andrea and Danny entered the large stable, Danny's eyes became wide with wonder. She'd never seen anything like it. The wonderful odors of fresh hay, leather tack and oil and saddle soap reached her nostrils. Everything looked spotless.

Stalls lined both sides. Some of the horses had their necks extended out the compartment opening and, upon seeing the women, they nickered softly, hoping to get a tasty tidbit.

"Oh, Andrea! I've never seen so many beautiful animals. And they all have their own stalls!"

"This was always Father's pride and joy. He shipped selected stallions and mares over from England, and started a very strict breeding program."

"Well, hello, little Indian princess."

Danny turned and saw Beau. She started to comment on the beautiful animals, but stopped when Margaret walked up behind him. Margaret wore a chocolate-brown riding habit and carried a riding quirt. A perky hat sat on her perfectly groomed head. That's the most ridiculous outfit I've ever seen, Danny thought, almost giggling. On the other hand, Beau looked magnificent in his Spanish pants and white blousy shirt opened almost to his waist.

A horse whinnied. Danny turned and saw Mescal's head stuck out of a stall near the far end. She went to him and stroked his velvet muzzle.

"Hello, my black beauty," she crooned. "Have you missed me?" The big stallion gently pressed his head against her shoulder.

"Beau, darling, you said he was dangerous," Margaret stated.

"He is. Don't go near him." Beau thought about how many times he had seen his mother wear the buckskin outfit Danny had on, and it brought forth good memories.

"He doesn't like strangers, Margaret, don't go near him," Andrea repeated.

"But look at him. He's not the least bit dangerous." Margaret's temper flared. She felt certain she knew more about horses than that bit of baggage! After all, she had ridden the best England had to offer!

"He has a special attachment to Danny," Beau replied offhandedly. His mind wasn't on Margaret. His eyes were busily raking Danny from head to foot, and he liked the view. Even if she had been dressed in the latest fashion, she wouldn't have been as beautiful as she was at this moment. A picture of her naked at the river flashed through his mind and, for some reason he couldn't understand, he felt a yearning deep inside his soul. His thoughts absorbed with Danny, he didn't pay attention to Margaret until it was too late. Both he and Andrea called her name at the same time.

She had marched over to Mescal. The stallion stretched his long neck and snapped his teeth, missing her by inches. Furious, Margaret lifted her quirt and struck the animal across the head.

"This beast needs to be taught a lesson," she yelled, and hit him again.

Mescal let out a terrible scream and lunged hard at the door, breaking the lock. The swinging door knocked Danny to the ground, but Mescal easily jumped over her and headed for the running Margaret. Everything happened in a matter of seconds, but Beau's reactions were quick enough to prevent a disaster. As Margaret fell to the ground, Beau stepped between her and Mescal. "Whoa, boy! Whoa!"

The horse whinnied and strutted, but made no effort to move forward.

"Danny! Are you all right?" Beau called.

"Yes."

"How about you, Andrea?"

"Yes, Beau, I'm fine."

"Beau," Margaret whined, "do—"

"Danny! There's an empty stall near you. Open the door and call Mescal."

Danny jumped to her feet and held the door open. "Come on, pretty baby," she coaxed, "Beau will take you outside shortly, and you can run out all your problems."

Mescal turned on his hind legs and trotted to Danny. She had no trouble getting him inside. Locking the door, she started toward Beau and Andrea, who were helping Margaret up.

"What the hell were you trying to prove?" Beau raged at Margaret. "I told you to stay away from him! You could have been killed!"

Margaret started crying. "Oh, Beau, how can you talk to me like that? He attacked me! He's an evil horse and should be shot. It wasn't my fault. You should be taking it out on him, not me."

Danny and Andrea watched Beau's eyes turn to blue ice. The muscles in his jaw flexed with barely controlled anger.

"Margaret," said Andrea, "why don't I take you back to the house and get you cleaned up? After such a terrifying experience, I'm sure you'll want to rest."

"Yes, you're right," she said, sniffling. Looking up, she saw Beau's back turned to her as he headed for Mescal's stall. "Beau, darling, will you be coming to the house soon?" she asked in a deliberately weak voice.

"No! Danny and I are going for a ride." He didn't even bother turning around.

As Margaret walked to the house, she mentally called Danny every foul word she could think of, and she knew plenty. Her relationship with Beau had moved along so beautifully, but now this had to happen! Only when that bitch showed up did they have any differences!

Andrea's thoughts were just the opposite of Margaret's. A smile creased the corners of her full mouth. Beau's first concern had been over Danny's welfare. Maybe they still had enough time to fall in love before finding out about the trouble between the two ranches. Hopefully, the barbecue would push things along.

When they reached the house, Margaret turned and faced Andrea. "How did Danny get on such friendly terms with Beau's horse?" she demanded.

"They have known each other for some time. They're just like brother and sister."

Margaret smiled. "Oh. I didn't realize."

As Margaret took off for her room, Andrea wondered just when she had become so proficient at lying.

"Beau," Danny said softly, "I'm sorry about what happened." She stood watching Beau check Mescal. She didn't know what to say. "I ain't . . . I mean, I don't have to go riding. I'll just go back to the house, too." She turned, ready to leave.

"Danny, don't go." He chuckled softly, seeing the confused look on her face. "After all, I haven't seen you in days. Andrea's been telling me how hard you've been working. This is the first opportunity I've had to say how proud I am of your accomplishments."

Danny's face lit up with pleasure. "Why, thank you, Beau. Can you really tell a difference?"

"Most decidedly, little one, most decidedly. Have you picked out the horse you want to ride?"

"No. We'd just walked in when you came. Is Mescal all right?"

"He's fine. There might be a particular horse that hits your fancy. Why don't we take a look?"

They started working their way forward, stopping at each stall.

"Oh, Beau, they're all so beautiful. I'm not sure I can make a choice."

At the next compartment, Danny stopped and drew in her breath. The most beautiful mare she had ever seen stood toward the back of the stall. The animal turned her head toward Danny, but her ears were laid back. She was large for a mare, with powerful flanks and long legs that promised great speed. Her white mane and tail set off her glossy chestnut coat. Danny had never seen a horse like her.

"Hello, pretty lady," Danny said. "Won't you come see me?"

The mare shook her head and pawed the ground.

"Oh, now, stop that! I'm not going to hurt you, and you know it. I'll bet if I had a carrot you'd come." Danny turned to Beau, who stood leaning against the wall studying her. "Is something wrong?" she asked.

"No, why should something be wrong?" Standing up straight, he looked in the stall. "This is the one you would pick, isn't it?"

"You sound like the answer is already no. What's wrong with her? Why doesn't she come forward like the other horses?"

"Come here, Sheeka," Beau said softly. The mare immediately came forward and nuzzled him.

Danny laughed. "She's another Mescal, isn't she?"

"I just settled her down yesterday. I've been working with her since the day after we arrived. Finally I took her out for a full day's ride, and now we get along fine."

"Has anyone else ridden her?"

"Yes, at least they've tried. She's a tricky lady. She acts tame, then when the rider least expects it, she bucks him off. No one has gotten out of the compound with her."

"Except you."

"Do you still want to ride her?"

"Beau, I know she's a very special animal. I'll pick another one."

"You didn't answer my question."

"Yes, I would like to ride her, but not today."

"Very well," he said with a smile.

Danny returned his smile. "We'll never be able to go for a ride if we don't get going. Why don't you just pick a horse for me?"

Chapter Eight

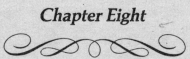

Danny and Beau rode for some time at a full gallop, both enjoying their freedom and the exhilaration of riding fast animals. When they finally slowed down, Danny's cheeks were rosy and her face glowed with pleasure.

"Oh, I didn't realize how much I've missed being out in the open," she said.

Beau laughed. "I know the feeling. Are you happy at the ranch, Danny?"

"Yes." She started to say she would be even happier when she left for the Silver J, but thought better of it.

"Andrea has taken quite a liking to you."

"And I'm very fond of her."

"I'm curious. What made you decide not to ride Sheeka?"

"I want to make friends with her first. Beau, when you took her out yesterday, did you use a saddle and bridle?"

"No. We went Indian style. Don't try it, Danny," Beau warned.

"I don't know what you're talking about."

"You know exactly what I'm talking about. She's a lot different when you take her out than she appears in the stall."

"She's beautiful."

"So are you."

Danny's cheeks turned pink and her heart skipped a beat.

Watching her, Beau laughed. "Well, well. The little robber is blushing. Now I haven't seen that very often. Tell me, Danny, are you going to do that every time a man pays you a compliment at the barbecue?"

"What barbecue?" she asked.

"Andrea's having a barbecue in two weeks to celebrate my return and birthday. Did she tell you she asked me to teach you how to dance?"

"No. Why do I gotta learn how to dance?" It took a moment before Danny realized what she had said. "I mean—"

"It's all right, Danny, I know what you meant. You're going to make mistakes, don't feel bad about it. Think of how much you've accomplished in such a short time."

He's actually talking to me like I'm a lady! Danny thought.

"Every woman should know how to dance, little one, especially beautiful ones. Andrea loves to dance, and she feels you should learn."

"Why can't she teach me?" Danny asked worriedly. *I'm sure if he takes me in his arms I'll swoon,* Danny thought.

"Since you will be dancing with men, don't you think it makes sense for a man to teach you?"

When they returned to the stable, Smoky, the man in charge, took Danny's horse to cool him down while Beau attended to Mescal. The stallion still wouldn't allow anyone except Danny and Beau to touch him.

"Thank you, Beau, for riding with me," said Danny, ready to return to the house.

"Don't you think I deserve a kiss for keeping you company?"

"Why...ah...yes, I guess so."

"Then come here."

She walked the short distance to where Beau stood, and when he leaned down, she kissed him on the cheek.

"Will you be joining us for dinner tonight, Danielle Louise?"

Excitement rushed through her. Beau had never called her by her given name. "Yes. I'm tired of eating alone." She left the stable whistling.

Even after Danny disappeared from view, Beau remained rooted to the floor, deep in thought. In his mind, he could still picture Danny's shiny auburn hair blowing in the wind, her laughter and her wild, carefree pleasure as the horses had stretched out into a full gallop and raced over the land.

He'd thought when they'd left the canyon and Danny had been delivered into Andrea's capable hands that he would be rid of his desire. He knew differently now. The ride had brought back the same feelings. He still wanted to possess Danny and feel her naked body beneath his. He'd been a damn fool in the canyon. He should have taken her then and there and gotten her out of his system, instead of putting himself through so much torment!

Where the hell did I come up with that protective attitude? he wondered. Well, he certainly didn't feel that way now. He felt nothing but pure, unfulfilled desire, and he had every intention of resolving the problem. Danielle was naive when it came to the subtle games played between men and women, but he would teach her the rules. Beau knew that beneath this newly acquired ladylike facade there still lived a full fledged she cat in hibernation who could be awakened with very little provocation. However, he had all the time in the world, and Beau could be very patient when he'd set his mind on something. He chuckled softly. Although Danny didn't know it, the game had begun, and this time he planned on enjoying the victor's reward.

"Come on, Mescal," he said, patting the stallion's neck. "Let's get you rubbed down."

While Beau's thoughts were on Danny, she in turn thought about him. Sitting on the daybed in her room, she relived their ride together. Beau had treated her like a lady! She could hardly believe this was the same man who had staked her out and taken her to the canyon. In her mind, Beau became one of the great English knights she'd read about in the books Andrea had given her. A true knight, pure of heart and incapable of any wrongdoing.

Danny sat wallowing in romantic visions of Beau riding to get her on a white steed when a knock at the door brought her back to the present.

"Come in," she called.

Margaret waltzed into the room, acting as if she owned it. Walking around, she let her fingers glide across the heavy furniture as her eyes took in everything.

"Hello, Margaret, I'm glad to see you're all right after your accident." Danny tried to sound sincere.

"I'm fine, but that horse should be shot. He's a danger to everyone."

Danny's back stiffened at the unfair words. It took pure willpower to calmly say, "Won't you have a seat?"

Margaret gave her a warm smile. "No, thank you, I just dropped in to ask if Beau said anything more about that little incident in the stable."

"No."

"I really made a fool of myself, didn't I?" She laughed softly. "I'm quite embarrassed over the whole matter. I've also done some very uncalled for things to you, my dear, and I want to apologize." She deliberately continued to move around the room, never meeting Danny's eye. "Unfortunately, I suffer from a bad temper. An unforgivable trait, I must admit, but one I can't seem to overcome." Finally looking at Danny for effect, she continued, "I would like us to become friends, Danielle Louise. Andrea told me you and Beau are like brother and sister, and I certainly do not want to alienate someone in the family when I plan to soon become a member."

Danny didn't know what to think, but she knew one thing for sure. She didn't believe a single word this woman had said. "Thank you, Lady Margaret, I know it must be difficult for you to say these things." I'm certainly not going to tell her I'm sorry! she thought.

"Please, call me Margaret. Being an only child, I would like to also look upon you as my little sister, if you don't mind."

"Little sister? How nice."

"You know, darling, you really shouldn't keep yourself hidden away. You should at least join us for supper."

"As a matter of fact, I plan on joining you tonight."

"Wonderful. I'll see you then."

When Margaret left, Danny sat staring at the closed door. Now what is Margaret up to? she wondered. This needed to be discussed with Andrea.

Jed and Jose rode up to the small house and dismounted. Jed could smell the food Carlotta had prepared, and after being out on the range all day, he was hungry as hell.

"What are we going to do, Jed?" Jose asked.

"I gotta think on it," Jed replied. "For now, all I want is something to eat."

The big man and his short, thin companion entered the dilapidated house and went straight to the table, ready to be fed. Carlotta, Jose's wife, shoved two bowls of food in front of them, then settled her broad hips into a rocking chair. As far as Jed was concerned, Carlotta had to be the laziest woman he'd ever come across. If she wasn't preparing food, she sat in the old rocker. The chair's constant squeaking drove him crazy, but because Jose thought the sun rose and set on the big woman, Jed kept his thoughts to himself.

Other than their similar dark hair and dark complexions, the couple were complete opposites. Where Carlotta never remained standing, Jose never sat down, except to talk, eat or ride a horse. Although small, Jose had a wiry build, but Carlotta was just plain fat. Jed judged them to be in their late forties.

Since his arrival, Jed had discovered a lot of problems he hadn't taken into consideration when hiring Jose. Although Jose did know cattle, to Jed's horror, the man knew nothing about running a ranch. The results had been disastrous. However, Jose did have one quality that Jed put a lot of stock in. Loyalty.

"I tell you, Jose," said Jed, his mouth full of stew, "I haven't any idea what we're gonna do unless we declare an all-out war with the Falkners. If we do that, we'd have to hire some guns, an I ain't likin' that idea."

"It's going to be awfully hard convincing young Falkner he can't run his cattle on your land and use your water any more. Especially after his dad did it all those years."

"I know, but it's somethin' he's gotta get used to. You said the boy's been gone a long time. Maybe he'll look at things different than his old man did."

"Are you going to take them up on their offer to buy you out?"

"I ain't seen nobody except that feller who delivered the message about Danny, and I sure haven't heard any offer. All I know is what you've told me. 'Sides, it's not just my decision. It's Danny's, too. I'll be damn glad when she gets here."

"The man didn't tell you where she's staying?"

"Nope. Just said she was all right and she'd be here in a few weeks."

Lifting the chain around her neck, Carlotta pulled out the cross nestled between her heavy bosom and made the sign of the cross. "I hope the bambino really is all right," she said, looking upward as if to the heavens. "She shouldn't be out there all alone. Poor darling. Lord only knows what she's going through."

Jed had to laugh. "It's been years since you've seen her, and she ain't so little no more. Believe me, she's as smart as a whip and can damn well take care of herself."

Danny didn't see Andrea all afternoon; therefore she hadn't been able to discuss Margaret's questionable change of attitude. But Maria told her Andrea knew she would be joining the family for dinner.

For her first outing as a lady, Danny chose to wear the yellow silk dress. The hem finished, Maria had delivered it soon after Margaret left. Fine Italian lace circled the small cap sleeves that hung over her shoulders, leaving her long, slender arms bare. The low neckline and tight-fitted waist were trimmed with the same lace. The skirt hung in soft yellow folds over a single petticoat. Because of the simplicity of the dress, Andrea had said it looked like a French creation, and showed Danny's feminine attributes to the fullest advantage.

Maria took special care in dressing Danny's thick auburn hair. She brushed it until it glistened, then pulled the heavy mass on top of Danny's head and let the ends fall down in soft curls. Wispy tendrils hung around her ears and the nape of her neck, acting as a picture frame for her face. Tickled almost to the point of giddiness over her appearance, Danny left the room.

Beau stood holding a snifter of brandy as Danny entered the salon. She watched his blue eyes travel the length of her and felt a thrill go up her spine.

"Am I early?" she asked nervously.

"No, Andrea and Margaret are late. You look ravishing, my dear."

"Thank you," she whispered.

"May I pour you a glass of wine?"

"Please." The room suddenly seemed very small. Beau's tall frame dominated everything, and Danny felt like a bird caught in a cage. She felt both tongue-tied and breathless. Not wanting to just stand there, she went over and sat on the sofa. She tried to keep looking away, but slowly her eyes were drawn back to Beau. He's magnificent in that gray tailored suit, she thought. The pants fit tightly around his muscled thighs; the jacket showed off his broad shoulders and trim waist; and the pure white ruffled shirt brought out his dark coloring and raven-black hair. He's so beautiful, she thought.

Beau had just handed Danielle her drink and moved to the other side of the room when Margaret came sailing in.

"Darling," said Margaret, as she rushed to him. "I know I'm late, but I wanted to look extra special for you tonight." Standing on tiptoe, she placed her arms around his neck and kissed him seductively.

Danny knew Margaret hadn't seen her, and felt uncomfortable at having to witness their kiss.

"Beau, dearest, you're not still angry with me, are you?" Margaret pouted prettily. "I know I behaved abominably this afternoon, but I promise it will never happen again."

Beau glanced down at the seductress. "I'm not angry," he said, removing her arms from around his neck. "Let's just forget the incident for now."

"Thank you, darling, I've been worried sick all afternoon that you would still be upset."

Margaret, pleased at knowing her actions had produced the right results, turned to sit down and spied Danny. Seeing how beautiful the girl looked momentarily stunned her, but she quickly regained her composure. She was well aware of Beau's roving eye, and had to admit the woman in front of her had the capability of turning any man's head.

"My dear, I didn't see you sitting there," Margaret said, a friendly smile on her face. "I do apologize. I know you are too young to understand, but when two people care as much for one another as Beau and I do, one simply cannot let a silly argument come between them." She sat beside Danny. "How sweet that little dress looks on you, my dear. It's quite becoming, and such a nice color for girls your age."

"Thank you," Danny replied. The nice words belied her true feelings. She would have liked nothing more than to pull the witch's hair out.

Margaret looked at Beau. "Darling, you'll be pleased to know that Danny and I had a nice chat this afternoon, and she's agreed to be my little sister, also. Now we can be one happy family."

"Oh? How interesting." The corner of his lips twitched with humor.

"I'm sorry I'm late," Andrea said, entering the room, "but I've been working on the cattle logs, and the time completely slipped away."

As the two women stood, Margaret took Danny's arm and guided her toward the dining room. "I am ravished," she said. "How about you, my dear?"

Andrea looked questioningly at Beau, not knowing what to think of Margaret's friendliness. All Beau could do was shrug his shoulders. He didn't know what was going on any more than she did.

The meal passed quickly, with Margaret doing most of the talking. She made a point of being pleasant to the other two women. While Margaret chatted away, Beau surreptitiously watched Danny. Her transformation made his desire even stronger.

"As always, Andrea, the dinner was excellent," Beau said when they had finished eating.

"Thank you, dear."

"Andrea, why didn't you tell me about the barbecue?" asked Danny.

Andrea laughed. "Who told you? Beau?" She looked at her brother.

"I plead guilty." He chuckled.

"Beau, darling, you didn't tell me there was going to be a party." Margaret pouted. "Will there be many important dignitaries?"

"This isn't England, Margaret," Beau replied. "It will be mostly ranchers and their families, and of course people from town. Everyone's invited."

"How exciting. What is the occasion, darling?"

"It's to celebrate Beau's birthday and his return home," Andrea informed her.

"Birthday?" Margaret's green eyes took on a sparkle. "I'll have to think of something special for a gift."

"How long were you going to wait before telling me, Andrea?" Danny teased.

"You would have already known if you hadn't kept yourself cooped up all the time."

"And you didn't even tell me you'd asked Beau to teach me to dance."

Andrea looked at Beau. This was the first time she had heard about any dancing lessons.

"Beau, darling, why don't you just hire someone to teach your little sister?" asked Margaret. She didn't want her intended holding *that* woman in his arms!

Beau didn't know why Margaret kept referring to Danny as his sister, but he decided to go along with it. "But what are big brothers for, if not to help their little sisters grow up?" he said smoothly. "Isn't that right, Danny?" He leaned back in his chair, a broad grin on his face.

"Well, ah..." Danny stammered. She didn't like Beau thinking of her as his sister.

"In fact, why not have the dancing lesson tonight?" he asked. "Andrea, would you mind playing the piano for us?"

"It would be my pleasure," Andrea replied. She hadn't missed Beau's glances toward Danny during dinner, nor had she missed how little attention he'd paid Margaret. Elated, Andrea felt better about keeping Danny there. Everything was moving along perfectly.

At first Danny had trouble following the steps. But she was light of foot, and Beau proved to be a good teacher. She caught on quickly. When she learned one set of steps, Andrea changed the tempo of the music and Beau taught her another. Everyone laughed and had a good time except Margaret, who sat in her chair fuming. Soon, Beau was turning Danny in circles as they danced around the room. The kerosene lamps made their shadows look like a kaleidoscope on the wall.

"Beau, stop," begged Danny, "I'm out of breath!" Breathing heavily, she made for the nearest chair and sat down. "Oh, that's a lot of fun, but it sure can wear you out!"

Andrea rose from the piano stool, a broad smile brightening her face. "Well, I hate to end an enjoyable evening, but I have a lot to do tomorrow if I'm to have everything ready for the barbecue. If you'll excuse me, I'll go to my room."

"What can I do to help?" Danny asked as she started to follow Andrea. "Why don't I go with you and you can tell me how you're going to put me to work." She also needed to talk to Andrea about Margaret. Suddenly she stopped and turned toward Beau. "Thank you, I had a wonderful time."

Beau chuckled softly. "My pleasure, little sister, but aren't you going to kiss me for my bravery?"

Danny's eyes became round circles. Her mind flashed back to the canyon and the last time she had kissed him, jokingly, for his bravery. She felt her whole body flush. Had he deliberately said those words to make her remember? No, it must be my mind playing tricks on me, she thought. Walking over, she kissed him on the cheek.

"You're a coward, Danny. Last time it was on the lips."

His words were so soft she was the only one who heard them. She quickly turned and left the room, followed by Andrea.

Margaret hadn't failed to notice the interchange. "What did you say to her?" she asked suspiciously.

"I told her good night. Why do you ask?"

"Her cheeks were flushed and she looked embarrassed."

"From the dancing, I suppose. Would you care for a glass of wine?"

Margaret went to him. "You're all the wine I need, darling." She looked up, her soft, red lips slightly parted.

Beau smiled at the beautiful, voluptuous woman who wanted to give him her favors. Drawing her to him, he leaned down and kissed her passionately. She molded her body to his, in an expression of pleasure and desire. Picking her up in his arms, he headed for her bedroom.

"You're right. Why should we waste our time on wine?" he whispered in her ear.

Margaret moaned with anticipated pleasure.

Beau looked at the woman he'd just placed on the bed. Her eyes glowed with unsuppressed passion, and her arms reached out, inviting him to join her.

An evil smile crossed his face. "Sorry, my dear, but women who take their frustrations out on animals are of no interest to me. Next time you'd be better advised to use your quirt on me. But you're too smart to try that, aren't you, Margaret?"

His words were as chilling as a whisper of snow, and Margaret felt her warmed skin turn cold. "You heartless bastard! You're incapable of loving any woman!" she yelled.

"A point worth remembering, my dear."

Margaret hurled her pillow at the door as it closed behind him, then broke down in tears of frustration. "Damn, damn, damn!" she cried as she pounded her fist on the bed.

Danny blew out the bay-berry candle by the bed and sat on the window seat. The heavy shutters were wide open to allow in any breeze that might find its way to the hot room. She had talked with Andrea about Margaret, and Andrea concurred that she shouldn't trust Margaret or believe a thing she said. Danny hadn't managed to gather up enough courage to ask Andrea about Beau and Margaret's relationship. Did he really plan to marry her?

Danny began sliding her hands up and down her bare arms as her thoughts centered on Beau and how much fun she'd had dancing with him. He acted the perfect gentleman tonight, she thought. And instead of complaining when I stepped on his toes, he merely laughed. His deep, robust laughter was so infectious. I'm sure he was just teasing when he called me a coward, she assured herself.

Danny knew what had caused her embarrassment. It wasn't just what Beau had said. She'd *wanted* him to take her in his arms and kiss her the way he had in the canyon. But a true knight didn't take advantage of a woman, and that's the way it had to be. When she returned to her ranch he'd forget all about her. But she wasn't completely blind in her hero-worship. Even though she thought of him as a knight, in the recess of her mind she felt sure his good looks and charm drew women to him like flies before the rain. Dreams were one thing, reality another.

For the next few days Danny remained busy, helping prepare the house for guests. There were many rooms in the large, one-story house, and much needed to be done. To everyone's amazement, Margaret also pitched in. For some reason that neither Andrea nor Danny understood, Margaret acted different. She'd become quiet and reserved. But even though she said nothing, Margaret made it perfectly clear Beau belonged to her by staying at his side when he returned to the house each evening.

According to Andrea, many of the guests would be staying over, which meant sheets had to be washed in the large tubs and beds made with the fresh linen. Danny soon learned how to supervise the servants and check to be sure they did their work properly. She also took charge of the dusting and the polishing of the furniture. She even supervised the removal of cobwebs.

The kitchen became a beehive of activity as herbs, spices and vegetables were gathered from the large garden. Danny went there often to see how Maria prepared and supervised everything. She loved the savory aroma that filled the large room. Maria always had something special for her to taste or eat.

Danny's pride and joy was a book Andrea had given her, titled *The Young Housekeeper's Friend*, by Mrs. Cornelius. The book not only gave recipes but also had instructions on cleaning, laundry, ironing and so on. Before going to bed each night, she read at least ten pages. With everything she'd learned from Maria and Andrea, plus the book, Danny felt confident she could run her own house capably.

The ranch had numerous outbuildings set well away from the house. These included a bunkhouse and kitchen for the hands, the servant's quarters, a blacksmith's forge and other buildings that were needed to maintain the livelihood of all the people who worked at the huge ranch. There were also many corrals and barns, but the stable that housed the finest horses sat well away from the hubbub of the other areas, and closer to the house.

At least three times a day, Danny went to the stable to see Sheeka, always bringing some treat for the horse to nibble on. By the end of the fourth day, she became overjoyed at seeing the mare's head sticking out of the stall and turned toward the entrance as if waiting for her arrival. Danny had also made friends with Smoky, the head of the stable. She told him she had Beau's permission to ride the mare, but wanted the accomplishment to be a surprise.

By taking Smoky into her confidence, and knowing he couldn't resist a woman, her activities remained a secret. Smoky didn't know—nor did anyone else—that Danny had every intention of entering the horse race at the barbecue. All the ranchers were bringing their finest animals for the competition. If Sheeka could run nearly as fast as she looked capable of, Danny planned to give the ranchers a run for their money.

Chapter Nine

Danny didn't take Sheeka from her stall until Smoky agreed to let her know when Beau was in the area. She walked the mare around on a lead rope, and fortunately the frisky animal didn't rear up or try to pull away. After several days of the same procedure, Danny decided to ride the mare. She had a brief discussion with Smoky, and they agreed to give it a try the next morning.

That night, no one could understand why, shortly after dinner, Danny excused herself, saying she didn't feel well and would like to spend tomorrow alone, resting. On the way to her room, she stopped by the kitchen and commandeered several bunches of carrots.

As the sun peaked over the horizon the next morning, Danny put on her old britches and shirt and sneaked out of the house by way of the bedroom window. She headed for the stable. If luck stood by her, no one would come to her room and check to make sure she was all right.

When she entered the large barn, she saw Smoky at the far end, busily saddling two horses. He reminded her of a bantam rooster—without the plumage—because of his short stature and cocky manner. Smoky considered himself quite a ladies' man, and more than once had insinuated as much to her. Why he should have such a high opinion of himself totally escaped her. He had thin, mousy-colored hair, a red-tipped, bulbous nose, which immediately drew her attention every time she saw him, and a pock-marked face—and he was bowlegged. Only his high-heeled boots made him appear taller than she was.

"Shall I take Sheeka out of the stall?" she asked as she neared the man.

Smoky looked up, shocked. He'd never seen a woman dressed in men's clothes and felt more than a little uncomfortable. Even the woman in the crib houses didn't dress like that! He quickly looked away and said, "Yeah, I'm just about ready to go."

Unobserved, the cohorts rode off, headed for an old corral some distance away. Sheeka followed closely behind Danny's horse, the rope circling her powerful neck held firmly in Danny's gloved hand.

When they arrived at their destination, Danny took Sheeka inside the corral and turned her loose. The sun glistened across her smooth chestnut coat as the mare pranced around the confines, neck arched and white tail held high. Danny spent the morning talking to Sheeka while standing in the middle of the corral. Occasionally she'd hold out a carrot, and upon seeing the delectable offering, the mare headed straight for it. When the mare started nuzzling her and acting playful, she knew it was time to get down to business.

Smoky insisted she use a saddle. "Be easier to stay on the critter's back," he commented.

Danny wasn't too keen on the idea, but common sense prevailed and she went along with his suggestion.

Smoky quickly unsaddled the gelding Danny had ridden and transferred the saddle to the mare's back. Sheeka stood perfectly still while he tightened the cinch and wiggled the saddle back and forth to be sure it was secure. Danny remembered Beau telling her the mare was unpredictable, but as she sat atop the tall animal and easily guided her around the corral in a trot, she began to relax, proud of herself. Without warning, Sheeka flattened her ears and started bucking.

The big mare kicked and bucked on stiff front legs from one side of the corral to the other. Her hooves looked like small flashes of lightning as the sun streaked across the metal shoes. Suddenly she came to a quick stop, and Danny went flying over her neck. Danny had given Sheeka a good ride, and Smoky had waved his hat and cheered her on, but she now found herself flat on the ground.

"Are you all right?" Smoky called as he jumped down from the top of the split-log fence and ran toward her.

"I'm fine!" Danny stood and dusted herself off. She glared at the horse standing quietly nearby. "Get back on the fence, Smoky," she ordered. Grabbing the end of the rope, she climbed back in the saddle.

Smoky could see the determination written on Danny's face. He had to admire her efforts, but he already doubted her victory. He'd seen too many good cowboys try to ride the mare, and they'd all failed, except Mr. Falkner. But what can you expect, he thought, spitting a wad of tobacco juice on the ground. He's an Indian.

He didn't like Beau, and dearly resented having to take orders from a damn half-breed, but the job paid well. Because of his feelings, he'd gone along with Danny's scheme. He knew Beau hadn't given her permission to take the mare out, but secretly he'd hoped the girl could ride Sheeka and show the big man up. He'd thought there might be a chance after seeing how close the horse and girl had become, but as he watched Danny hit the ground for the fourth time, he knew it wasn't going to happen.

Caked with dirt and sweat, Danny again pulled herself off the ground, mad. Slowly she limped over to where Sheeka stood. Although the mare's sides heaved and her coat was lathered, she appeared calm as usual. Grabbing the girth, Danny unbuckled it and slid the saddle to the ground. "Come give me a hand up, Smoky!" she called.

Glancing at the sun, he frowned. "I think it's time to quit," he said, as he walked up beside the girl. "You're going to get yourself killed. Why don't you give it up? Ain't you had enough? You can try again some other time."

"If Beau can ride her, so can I! Now give me a hand!"

Smoky looked down at the ground and kicked at a small clod of dirt. If anything happened to Danny, he'd be the one who'd have to face Falkner. It would be his hide, not hers. He might not like the man, but he sure as hell didn't want to tangle with him. I shouldn't have brought her out here, he told himself. One way or another, I've got to get her back before Falkner discovers what's going on. "We gotta go now," he said in a firm but strained voice. "It won't be much longer till the sun starts going down."

Danny's amber-brown eyes flashed. "I'm not leaving until I accomplish what I came out here to do. If you want to leave, go ahead."

"We have to get back now, before someone discovers we're missing."

"No! I'm not ready to leave. I thought you said Beau wouldn't be coming back until later tonight?"

"Yeah...ah, he might come back earlier than I thought."

"Well, are you going to give me a hand up, or do I have to get on by myself?" she asked impatiently.

Damn, he thought, I could lose my job over this, or even worse, get the hell beat out of me. He became angry at Danny for putting him in this position. "Look, if we don't leave right now, I ain't going to have any choice but to tell the boss where you are," he threatened.

Smoky didn't know Danny well enough to realize he'd said the wrong thing. Her eyes turned almost black. "You say one thing to Beau about any of this, and so help me God, I'll tell him you put me up to it. Who do you think he'll believe, Smoky? Now you climb on your horse and get the hell out of my sight! I never could abide being around a yellow belly."

He knew he wasn't a brave man; wily, yes. But being called a coward to his face, and by a woman, only served to heighten Smoky's anger. It took every ounce of self-control he could muster to keep from slapping her. Hellfire, he thought as he left the arena, I should of stayed a drifter instead of taking the job at the ranch. Women always cause nothing but trouble. Climbing on his horse, he rode off. If she broke her neck, that was her problem.

As Smoky rode out of sight, Danny guided Sheeka over to the side of the corral and climbed up on the fence. Once again she swung herself onto the mare's back.

When Danny finally headed back, she chastised herself for staying gone so long. She knew if Beau found out she'd taken the valuable animal out of the compound, he'd be mad. Suddenly she laughed. She had taken a foolish chance, but even if she did get caught, it had been worth it. She'd ridden Sheeka! She had even ridden her outside the corral.

Nearing dark, Danny returned to the stable. Seeing Mescal's stall still empty, she knew Beau hadn't returned. The weight of her worry started to subside. Never would she take another foolish risk like today. On the way back, she'd decided that from this time on, Sheeka would be ridden at night after everyone had gone to bed. Maybe she wouldn't win the race, but she'd sure give it one hell of a try.

"I'll brush her down," said an angry voice.

Danny whipped around, then let out a sigh of relief upon seeing Smoky standing there. Without saying a word, she handed the rope to him and left by the back way.

Danny had just entered her room and taken off her clothes when she heard a light tap on the door. "Who is it?" she called, as she kicked the filthy garments under the bed and tossed on her robe.

"Maria," came the reply.

"Come in."

When Maria entered the room, she looked thunderstruck. "My heavens, girl. This place smells of horse sweat! And what have you done to yourself? You're filthy."

Danny hadn't even thought about her appearance. "Oh, well . . ." She couldn't think of an answer.

"You been out to the stable?" Maria asked suspiciously.

"Yes!" she blurted out. "Oh, Maria, I'm so embarrassed. I did a very unladylike thing." She lowered her head to give just the right effect. She had learned a lot from watching Margaret. "I wanted to go for a walk unnoticed, so I put on my old clothes and went to the back stable entrance to see the horses. Unfortunately, I didn't look where I was going. I slipped on some horse droppings and fell." She looked up at Maria with what she hoped was a worried expression. "Please don't tell, I would simply die if anyone found out. Especially Margaret."

Maria's expression hardened at the mention of Margaret's name, and Danny knew she'd touched on the magic word. Maria made no secret of her dislike for the woman.

"Don't you give it another thought," Maria assured her. "No one will know, least of all that witch. What did you do with your clothes?"

Danny pulled the smelly garments from beneath the bed and handed them to Maria.

"I'll see they're washed. Now you get busy and get yourself cleaned up. I came to see if you'll be having dinner in your room."

"No, I'm dining with the rest of the family. Would you have some water sent in for my bath? I have to hurry or I'll keep everyone waiting."

Danny quickly finished her toilet and dressed. Taking a final look in the mirror, it was hard to believe she looked normal after all she'd been through. Every bone in her body ached, and she walked stiffly. She'd wanted to remain in the hot tub and soak her sore muscles, but time wouldn't permit it. Smoothing out the skirt of her blue muslin dress, she proceeded to leave the room.

Danny sucked in her breath when she saw Beau standing in the narrow hallway. For him to be waiting, he had to have ridden in shortly after she'd left the stable. Smoky must have done some fast maneuvering. "Hello, Beau," she said, unable to think of anything else.

"I wanted to have a few words with you and escort you to dinner." He took her hand and lifted it to his lips, brushing a soft kiss across her knuckles. His eyes traveled appreciatively over her form. "You look lovely," he whispered.

Feeling his lips on her hand caused a tremor to run through Danny's body, while at the same time she felt apprehensive. Did he know about Sheeka? "What do you want to talk about?" she asked, pulling her hand from his grasp.

"Shall we step outside?" he asked. The large house surrounded a central courtyard, and he opened the French doors leading from the hall.

As she walked into the open area, she could smell the sweet odor of flowers. The stars were shining brightly, and the moon cast a soft glow over the setting. Her hand still tingled from Beau's kiss, and now she was alone with the man of her dreams in a very romantic setting. She took a big breath. Suddenly she felt both afraid and excited. To quell the silly notions forming in her head, she turned and almost bumped into Beau. She hadn't realized he was standing so close. They were only inches apart, and Danny could feel the heat emanating from his body, or why else would she suddenly feel so warm?

As always, he towered over her, and as always, his handsomeness almost stopped her heart from beating. "What did you want to talk about?" she asked breathlessly. He stood there looking down at her, a faint smile on his chiseled lips. She just knew he would kiss her, and her lips automatically parted in response.

Beau was thinking about doing just that. But the place and time were inappropriate. He could see her desire, but he wanted more than just a kiss and knew she wasn't ready to give herself completely to him yet. He purposely strolled away.

"I talked to Andrea this afternoon," he said, "and she seemed to think I haven't accepted you as a member of the family." He turned around and saw a look of disappointment on Danny's face. "I just wanted you to know I'm honestly not adverse to having a little sister." Beau almost choked on his own words, but for the time being it suited his purpose. He had to take it slow. If he made any advances now, Danny would start running scared. Also, he had to get her away from the house and any possibility of interference. Andrea watched over her like a mother hen, while at the same time Margaret seemed to always be in the shadows waiting for him to make an appearance.

"Well, thank you, Beau, I . . . I would like being your sister," Danny said, crushed. She wanted him to think of her as a woman, not a damn sister!

Beau watched the conflicting emotions play on her face and smiled. All he had to do was keep her off guard and play with those emotions, while building her desire. Anticipation could be quite titillating!

He walked to where she stood. "I'm glad you feel that way." Slowly he ran his hands up and down her bare arms, then leaned over and kissed her on the tip of her nose. "Shall we go in?" he murmured.

Through the following days, Danny continued to help with the cleaning, and at night she sneaked Sheeka out for their ride. She found herself sleeping later in the morning, but fortunately, no one appeared to notice. Beau seemed to always be popping in while she worked, and when she least expected him.

He would place an arm around her shoulder and tell her not to work too hard, or plant a kiss on her cheek and tell her what a fine job she was doing. Once he even brought her a rose, saying that when he saw it, it made him think of her. It bothered her to know that everything he did stemmed from brotherly affection. More and more, she found herself watching him and remembering how wonderful it had felt when he'd kissed her in the canyon. It never occurred to her that it was all a deliberate ploy.

Andrea also remained busy. She tried to avoid Margaret as much as possible because the woman, as of late, seemed to always be in a foul mood. She had managed to tell Beau not to mention anything to Danny about their problems with the Silver J ranch, explaining that Danny would want to get involved, and Andrea wanted nothing to interfere with the girl's task of learning to be a lady and run a household. Fortunately, Beau didn't question her reasoning.

Unfortunately, Beau and Danny's relationship didn't seem to be developing at all. Maybe she had misjudged the pair. They treated each other like brother and sister, and Andrea didn't know what to do about it. With time running out, she was forced into accepting the fact that she couldn't make them love each other if those feelings weren't there to begin with.

Margaret, on the other hand, waited impatiently for Beau to get over his anger. He remained courteous and never ignored her, but other than that, nothing. She constantly told herself it couldn't last forever, and when he came to her bed she'd welcome him with open arms.

Beau and two cowhands busily checked the condition of a herd of cow ponies that had been brought in from the pasture. When the men were finished, they left the corral.

"Chuck," Beau said, securing the gate behind them, "go tell Tom we have fifteen horses that need to be shod. Then come back here and help Bobby cull them out and take them over to the forge."

"Okay, boss," Chuck replied.

Beau was fixing to leave when he noticed Armando headed in his direction. Beau studied the man as he approached. Armando was tall and slender, his sun-leathered skin stretched taut across aquiline features. Even though his hair was streaked with gray, his looks did not depict his age. Armando had been Gerard's foreman ever since Beau could remember. He'd helped drive the original Falkner cattle from Colorado Territory. Although of Spanish descent, he once told Beau he'd never been to Mexico and had no desire to go.

"Beau, do you have a minute?" the foreman asked as he drew near.

"Sure, what's on your mind?"

"Joe just rode in from the line shack."

"What's he doing back here?" Beau asked. "I thought he and some of the men were moving a herd."

"He came back to get some supplies and tell about the trouble they've run into. Seems as though they were driving the cattle up to the high grazing land and stopped to let them water at the Silver J. As he tells the story, they heard shots, and the next thing they knew, the cattle started stampeding."

Beau frowned. "Did anyone get hurt?"

"No."

"Are the cattle on high ground now?"

"Yes. He said they finally got them back under control and took them on up."

"Armando, I left explicit instructions that no cattle were to cross onto Silver J land," Beau said angrily.

"I know, Beau, and I passed the word on. But it's hard to make the boys understand. They've been traveling the same route for years, and you know as well as I do, it's a lot shorter distance than to have to go all the way up and around the Jameson land. They did it when your pa was alive and can't understand why you're backing off. Word's going around that you're not the man he was."

"And what are your thoughts on the matter?"

"I've known you a long time, Beau, and I've never seen you back off from a fight if you thought you were in the right. I don't think your stay in England has changed that. You know I'll back you up. Besides, I figure you've got a plan in mind."

Beau shoved his hands in his pockets and leaned against the fence. "You know," he began, "when I traveled around the country looking at cattle, I saw a lot of other interesting things as well. I saw trouble between nesters and cattle ranchers, and

I saw land being fenced off with barbed wire. Open range, as we know it, will one day cease to be. Even though I don't like it, it's a fact."

"You know they got all them creeks and springs that feed down across your land?"

"I'm well aware of our situation. That's why we have to play it their way for the time being. I do not want one single cow of mine on their land. Let them think they've finally won. In the meantime, Armando, make damn sure every cowpuncher on this ranch obeys my orders. If they don't like it, get rid of them. We're going to sit tight for a couple of months, then we'll approach them with an offer to buy."

"Your father tried that, Beau, and it didn't work," Armando informed his boss. "He wanted that land something fierce and offered four times what it's worth. The owner was never there. He looked up the records and found out it's owned by a D.L. Jameson. There's a fellow by the name of Jose Jackson that's been running the place for years, but he'd never tell Gerard where to locate the owner. Gerard even tried to get Jose to send a message telling Jameson he wanted to buy it, but all Jose would say is that Jameson didn't want to sell."

"Well, we'll just try again. If they refuse, we'll see if we can't make some arrangements that will be satisfactory to the both of us. And if that doesn't work, well, we'll handle that problem when we come to it. I'm going to send a message apologizing for this incident and a personal invitation to the barbecue." Beau smiled. "One of the first things an Indian learns is that he has the advantage when his enemy is off guard and unsuspecting."

Armando chuckled at Beau's wisdom.

"Now, if you will excuse me, I need to get dressed for dinner." Beau started to leave then turned. "Armando, I'm going to be gone a day or so. I'm leaving early in the morning to catch me a couple of mountain lions."

"Two?" Armando scratched his jaw. "I thought Fred said he only saw the tracks of one cat."

Beau laughed. "Well now, my friend, there are cats, and there are cats."

Armando smiled as he watched Beau head for the house. He felt better after their conversation. Beau took good care of his men, and he had every right to demand that they obey his orders.

The conversation at dinner centered mainly on the barbecue four days away.

"When will the people start arriving?" Danny asked, trying to appear attentive, when actually her sole interest centered on Saturday's race.

"Friday some of the distant ranchers and their families should start coming in," answered Andrea. "Are all the pits dug, Beau?"

"Yes, Armando is personally attending to it. The mesquite and wood will be lit tomorrow, and as soon as they become coals, he'll put the meat in. The beef and hogs are ready, and a couple of the boys brought in two nice-sized bucks."

From her visits to the kitchen, Danny knew the sauce that would be poured over the meats would soon be simmering in five huge copper pots.

Margaret, having completed her meal, daintily patted her ruby lips with the napkin and placed it on the table. "I imagine you're looking forward to this jamboree, Danny. It will be a wonderful opportunity for you to meet some eligible men." Margaret smiled. "At your age, you're probably looking forward to the day when a man will ask for your hand in marriage. You aren't getting any younger, you know."

Andrea laughed. "That's nonsense. Danny doesn't need to rush into marriage. I'm sure as time goes by she'll have more than her share of suitors."

"Ladies, could we please change the subject?" asked Beau in a gruff voice. "Any decisions regarding Danny's future are strictly up to her." The conversation bothered him. He had his own plans for Danny.

A ray of hope sparked in Andrea's breast. Apparently Beau didn't like discussing the possibility of Danny marrying.

Relaxing, Beau looked at his sister. "Andrea, I'll be leaving in the morning before sunrise and might not make it back in time for dinner."

"Where are you going?"

"A mountain lion's been bothering the cattle up by the ridge. He's already taken off with some calves. The drovers had a couple of shots at him but missed, and they can't track him in the rocks."

"Surely you're not going after him?" Margaret gasped. "You could get hurt! You're a gentleman, Beau, and you have men to do that sort of thing. It's not your duty."

Beau looked at Margaret with cold, unwavering eyes. "I'm well aware of what my duties are, my dear."

Margaret reached over and started fidgeting with her napkin. "Well, of course you do, darling, I was just trying to say—"

"I know what you were trying to say. Nevertheless, I will track the lion myself."

"Don't worry, Margaret," Andrea said, trying to ease the sudden tension, "Beau will be just fine."

"Is it a big cat?" asked Danny, her interest piqued.

"They say they're the biggest tracks they've ever seen. He has to be an old fellow who's not able to catch game any more, so he's taking easy pickings." Beau smiled. "Would you like to go with me?"

Before Danny could say yes, Margaret started talking.

"Why would you want to take Danny with you? I never heard of such a thing!" Margaret spurted out. She didn't trust Beau, and she certainly didn't want the two of them spending a period of time alone! "Darling, you would be endangering her life. Young ladies don't go out into the wild. They stay home and attend to their duties."

Leave it to dear Margaret, Beau thought. Without realizing it, she had said just the right words. "I wasn't serious, Margaret. I have no intention of taking Danny. She'd just be in my way, and she's too inexperienced." He looked over at Danny and watched the fire leap into her amber-brown eyes. "I wouldn't take anyone with me unless she could ride well and knew how to shoot a rifle."

For the first time in weeks, Danny's hackles rose. How could he sit there and say she was inexperienced, plus insinuate she couldn't ride or handle a rifle? Did he think his superior attitude impressed everyone? Through clenched teeth, she said, "I know how to shoot a rifle!"

"I doubt that," Beau said in a friendly offhanded manner.

Danny's hands balled up into fists under the table.

"But it really doesn't matter," he said, "you won't be going with me. You're a lady now. You'd just be underfoot and make me lose valuable time. I once knew a kid—well, that's another story."

That's hitting below the belt! Danny thought.

"What are you talking about, darling?" Margaret laughed, happy now that Danny would remain at the house. "You're not making any sense."

"I guess what I'm trying to say is that women are basically cowards."

That did it! It was all Danny could do to keep from going over and smacking him!

Watching her face flush with anger, Beau knew he'd said enough. The time had come for him to back off. The she cat was no longer in hibernation, and he knew she'd like nothing more than to claw his eyes out.

"Well, I should hope so!" Margaret giggled, feeling quite sure of herself. "It's their softness that appeals to men. I like being a woman. I don't want to go out and buck the odds, as you would say."

Beau chuckled. "A point well taken, Margaret. Well, ladies, I won't be joining you in the salon tonight. I have a long day ahead." He let out a big, deliberate sigh. "I shall have my cigar and go straight to bed. If you'll excuse me, I bid you good night."

Even after Beau left, Danny's fury remained. She wanted to pick something up and throw it. How dare he call me a coward! she raged. There was no doubt in her mind that he'd aimed every word directly at her. How could she have been so stupid? White knight, indeed! This was the same devil she'd come to know before he'd brought her to the ranch. The realization that he'd tricked her into letting her guard down made her twice as angry. Well, she'd teach him not to fool with her!

When she felt she could excuse herself for the night without drawing questioning looks from Andrea and Margaret, she left the salon. She knew what she'd do, and how. While supervising the cleaning of the study, she had seen several rifles and pistols. She also knew there were cartridges and gun belts in the wooden chest on the floor. Unfortunately, she wouldn't be able to take Sheeka out tonight, but proving a point to Mr. Big Chief took precedence.

Danny stood by the corral of horses in her old garb, the boots Andrea had given her and a low-crowned, wide-brimmed hat with a chin strap. A .45 nestled inside the single-holstered gun belt that hugged her hips, and her hand grasped a loaded Winchester rifle. Even though the sun hadn't lifted its head over the horizon, the gray sky afforded enough light to see Beau ride away.

It took her almost ten minutes to find the tack room, and an equal amount of time to catch a horse and saddle it. Shoving the rifle in the leather scabbard hanging from the saddle, she quickly mounted and headed off in the direction Beau had gone.

Beau sat totally relaxed on top of Mescal, his leg looped around the saddle horn. They were on a slight knoll, hidden behind a tree. Danny couldn't see him, but he had no trouble watching her shadowy figure running around in a frenzied manner. Beau chuckled softly when he saw the saddle. Some cowboy was going to be mad as hell when he discovered his saddle missing. A satanic smile formed on his chiseled lips as Danny rode out of the compound. "The lamb finally enters the eagle's nest." He unhooked his leg and placed the pointed toe of his boot in the stirrup. Turning Mescal around, he urged the horse forward in a slow trot. He wanted to be sure Danny had an easy time finding him.

When Beau heard the horse coming from behind, he brought Mescal to a halt and waited until Danny pulled up alongside. Not wanting her to know she'd been tricked, he acted irritated. "What are you doing here?" he asked.

"I'm going with you to hunt the cat," she stated.

"Well, you can just turn around and go back."

Danny's hand dropped to the butt of the pistol. "No man calls me a coward, least of all you! Now if you want, we can settle this right now. But if I go back, so will you!"

Beau knew, by the hard look in her eyes, she meant business. She had that same no-nonsense look he'd seen in her eyes peeking over a bandanna, months ago. "I'm not going to take you up on your challenge, I haven't the time. If anything needs to be settled, it'll have to wait until later." He took off at a gallop, with Danny right behind him.

For the next two hours they continued on at a hard, steady pace. Danny spent most of the time trying to figure out how she could have possibly thought she loved this part man, part savage. She *would* have shot him. Not killed him. A bullet in the arm or leg would have sufficed.

Beau, on the other hand, spent his time laughing to himself. *His* she cat trailed behind him, as planned. But he hadn't forced her. It had been Danny's decision to come with him, instead of remaining safely at the house. Not a particularly wise choice, as she'd eventually find out. If she had half as much fire when he bedded her, he truly had something to look forward to. He vowed to himself that when they returned, Danny would have lost her innocence. Once and for all he would get her out of his system!

It wasn't until they'd topped a big hill that Danny saw the large, grassy plateau. Hundreds of peacefully grazing cattle were stretched out over a wide area.

Beau and Danny hadn't ridden very far when a wrangler broke away from the herd and joined them.

"Howdy, Mr. Falkner." He gave Danny a questioning look, tipped his hat, then turned toward Beau. "Ol' Fred drove in with the supplies last night and told us you was coming."

"Have you seen any more of the cat, Charly?" Beau asked.

"He grabbed off another calf about twilight," replied the tall, lanky man. "He's a crafty one. The herd started getting nervous and bawling, so we knew he was coming. He hides in the grass, and we can't see him. Anyways, we spread out and waited, but still didn't see or hear him until he'd made his kill and was taking off. Took a shot, and I think I got him. I'm not really sure, though. When the sun came up this morning we found a trail of blood, but we didn't know whether it was his or the calf he carried."

"How far did you track him?" Beau asked.

"Not far. We knew you was coming, and we didn't want to leave the herd alone in case he decided to double back on us and start a damn stampede."

"Which way did he go?"

Charly pointed toward the cliffs. "Headed that way, same as before. Follow me, and I'll show you his tracks."

When they arrived at their destination, Beau dismounted. "Okay, Charly," he said to the cowhand, "we'll take it from here."

As the man rode away, Beau walked around studying the ground. Finally he motioned to Danny. "Get down and come here," he called. "I want to show you something."

She dismounted and joined him.

"There's our boy," Beau said, pointing to the ground.

Danny could hardly believe the size of the paw print embedded in a patch of dirt. "He's huge!" she uttered, her anger totally forgotten.

"Do you know anything about cats, Danny?" Beau asked.

"No, not really."

Beau started walking again, and she followed.

"Charly hit him all right. See the blood on the grass?"

"Yes, but Charly said it could be the calf's."

"A cat jumps on its prey's back and breaks its neck immediately. Any bites are usually on the neck or head. There would be a lot of internal bleeding, but very little external blood. We're some distance from where the lion attacked, and the calf wouldn't be bleeding like this. Also, if you pace it out you can see the blood is coming from the cat's right rear leg."

The way Beau pointed it out, it all made sense. She'd never have figured it out on her own.

"Let's mount up, little one. All we have to do now is find the den."

They hadn't traveled far up the mountain when Beau pulled Mescal to a halt.

"There's the kill," Beau said, pointing off to the side. "The old fellow had a feast last night. If we don't find the den, we'll catch him when he returns to continue his meal."

It took a moment before Danny spied the partially covered carcass. "How do you know he's old?" she asked as they moved on.

"A healthy cat attacks deer, horses, sheep and cattle as well as calves," Beau replied. "But this one is living on animals that take little speed or effort to kill."

They continued to climb the rocky mountain, with Danny bringing up the rear. At times, Beau would dismount, look around, then climb back in the saddle. Danny marveled at his tracking ability. It remained a mystery to her how Beau knew which direction they should go. He seemed to be following a trail, but she couldn't see any indication of the cat ever having been here. She wanted to ask Beau questions, but knew she should remain silent in case they were nearing their quarry. Suddenly Beau stopped and looked up. Danny's eyes followed the direction he was looking. There, across a small ravine and some distance up, she could make out the long body of a lion stretched out on a ledge. What looked like the opening to a cave sat directly behind him.

"Is he dead?" she whispered.

"No, probably sleeping. He has a full stomach and is resting his leg. The air's nice and cool up here. He's probably enjoying the sun."

Danny couldn't contain her curiosity any longer. "How did you know he was up there?"

Beau turned and smiled. "I can smell him."

"That's impossible."

"For you, perhaps. I'll have to climb from here. I want you to stay with the horses."

"Why can't I go?" she quietly demanded.

"It's steep. I'm going to climb onto those rocks up there to the right so I can get a clear shot."

"I want to go!" she insisted.

This was not the time for an argument. "Very well," he said in a condescending tone. "We'll be downwind so he won't smell us. But you're going to have to be quiet. Even though he's on the other side, he can still hear us. If he's alerted, I'll probably end up having to go in the den after him."

Danny felt her throat constrict. Common sense told her she should stay put, but she was determined to prove she could do anything he could without getting underfoot.

The climb proved to be far more difficult than she anticipated because she had to watch every step she took, making sure she didn't dislodge any rocks. Plus she had to carry a rifle.

She pushed her hat to the back of her shoulders and concentrated on how good a cool breeze would feel. Salty perspiration dripped down into her eyes, causing them to sting. She had granite dust and dirt all over her, and every time she wiped the sweat from her face, she left a muddy streak. In no time, her clothes were sticking to her damp body. As if she didn't have enough problems, the thin air made breathing difficult.

Farther up the rocky incline, Beau continually looked down to check Danny's progress. He had to admire her dogged determination. Her legs were much shorter than his, which made her task twice as difficult. She had more spirit than any woman he'd ever known. He chuckled at the thought of what Margaret's reaction would be under the same circumstances.

Finally reaching the rocky ledge he wanted, Beau pulled himself up onto it. He rolled over on his stomach and aimed the rifle. The cat still slept peacefully, so he waited for Danny to join him. He'd already decided that, if possible, she could have the kill. She'd earned it.

Several minutes later Danny reached the rock. Beau leaned over and pulled her up with his hand. Exhausted, Danny lay down beside him, trying to catch her breath.

"When your breathing is back to normal, I'm going to let you shoot the cat," Beau said, still keeping his aim on the big animal.

Hearing his words, fresh adrenaline surged through Danny's body. It took a few minutes to get her second breath, but when she did, she rested the rifle on the rock and pressed the butt firmly against her right shoulder. Taking aim, her finger curled around the trigger, then she froze. The big cat reminded her of Jed! From her viewpoint, Danny could see the cat's languorous half-closed eyes. It was the same look Jed had when he relaxed after a good meal, and although they were both past their prime, they maintained a sort of dignity. She laid the rifle back down.

"Are you going to shoot or not?" Beau asked impatiently.

"No."

Beau pulled the trigger. Danny saw the cat's body jerk. Then he lay still, his long tongue hanging out the side of his mouth. As the animal's blood covered the rock, Danny's tears began to fall.

Beau rolled over on his side to ask why she hadn't shot and saw the wet trails down her dirty cheeks. "It had to be done," he said softly.

"Why?" she moaned. "What difference could a few calves mean to you?" She couldn't express the deep feeling she'd had. It was as if someone had shot her pa.

"It wasn't just the calves. Soon he wouldn't be able to forage for himself. Even the calves would outrun him. Would you rather he starved to death? This way there's no suffering, and he died painlessly."

Danny finally managed to get herself under control, realizing how stupid the comparison had been. "Oh, I guess you're right," she said, wiping her tears away.

"You're quite a contradiction, little one." Beau laughed softly. "After all we've been through together, this is the first time I've seen you cry. You'll battle all odds and never blink an eye, but you can't stand to see an animal hurt."

Danny smiled, feeling a bit embarrassed. "Well, that's not exactly true. I've shot a lot of game for food."

"Are you ready to head back?"

She nodded.

"Not too far from here there's a natural rock pool," he said as they started back down. "When you get washed, you'll feel a lot better."

As they started down, Beau mentally reinforced his determination. I *am* going to possess her before we head back to the ranch, he thought. Her sudden vulnerability over the death of the lion almost made me back off. But her unpredictable change of personality is what caused me so much trouble in the canyon, and this time I'm going to finish what I started! I want to see that same fire she has in her eyes when she gets mad turn into a fire of desire. Most of all, I want her out of my thoughts so I can return to Margaret's bed. I prefer a woman who offers her charms, instead of having to plot ways to bed a female who doesn't even desire my sexual favors!

Chapter Ten

Danny enjoyed her bath. She felt like a queen on a throne. The large pool of water sat in the middle of a huge granite rock with a natural deep cup. After Beau had shown it to her, he had returned to the small meadow below to wait his turn.

Feeling lazy after her dip, she dressed slowly. She hesitated about putting her gun belt back on, but decided she should. "Never know when a gun will come in handy," she mumbled as she headed down.

Beau's eyes narrowed as he watched Danny descend the rock. He'd talked to her continuously ever since he'd shot the mountain lion, in order to calm her down. She'd be even more settled when he returned from his bath. If he took it slow and easy, he really didn't anticipate any trouble. Danny's expressions were always mirrored on her face, and he hadn't failed to notice how longingly she looked at him now, or her moon-struck mannerisms.

Seeing the gun still strapped to her side, however, didn't set well with him. He considered grabbing her and removing it, but she'd get angry, and he'd end up seducing her. Before he did that, he wanted to wash.

"All right, Beau," Danny called to him as she drew near. "It's your turn." He sat propped up against a tree, and with his thick, black lashes lowered, she couldn't tell whether he was awake or sleeping.

He finally looked up. "You're so right," he said, standing. "Now it's my turn."

Danny, thinking he referred to his bath, smiled. "The water will make you feel as good as new. Were you napping?" she asked cheerfully.

"As a matter of fact, I did doze off. You might do the same. It's a long ride back. Why don't you lie down and rest? And take off that gun belt. You'll be a lot more comfortable."

Danny watched him go up the rock then disappear. A short nap sounded inviting. She started to remove the belt then decided against it. It wasn't really in the way; she'd just rest on her left side.

When Beau returned, he walked quietly up to the figure resting on its back. He had deliberately stayed away long enough to make sure she would fall asleep. Seeing the gun still at her side, he frowned. "As you said this morning, little one," he said softly, "we're going to get this settled once and for all."

Danny mumbled something in her sleep then rolled over on her right side. Beau had put his pants on, but carried his boots, socks and shirt, which he placed on the ground. He laid down beside her and cuddled her back. Danny unconsciously snuggled against him. Just like she did at the river when her fever broke, Beau thought. Only then, she'd been naked. Slowly he worked one arm under her head, then placed the other around her waist. He intended to remove the gun without waking her, but then his eyes landed on her slender neck and he couldn't resist kissing it. She smelled fresh and clean. His hand began caressing her flat stomach then slid up to cup a firm breast. Even in her sleep, the nipple already stood erect, inviting his fingers to play with it. His tongue traced her ear, then he drew the small lobe into his mouth and nibbled on it.

Danny started drifting out of sleep. She moaned with pleasure, feeling wonderful sensations assaulting her being. She didn't want them to stop. Suddenly she came wide awake, and the realization of what was happening worked as well as cold water thrown in her face.

"What the hell do you think you're doing?" she yelled, struggling to get loose. Beau's arms held her firmly.

"Don't fight me, Danny. I intend to have you before we leave this place. Now, it's up to you. If you relax, I can assure you you'll enjoy it. Besides, you know you want me as much as I want you."

"You dirty son of a bitch! You're no better than all the other men rutting around and thinking of nothing but satisfying their own pleasure!"

At first, Beau was shocked. He'd expected her to put up a fight, if just to save face. But certainly nothing quite like this. The truth of her words hit him right between the eyes. What is it about her that has driven me to this point? he thought. I've *never* forced any woman into my arms! Damn! She's doing it again. I'm already starting to change my mind!

Without realizing it, Beau slackened his hold, and Danny, angered beyond control, saw her opportunity to escape. Bending her knee, she brought her boot straight back and kicked him in the groin. He immediately released her and rolled on the ground, holding himself.

Danny jumped up, and after running a short distance, turned and drew her gun. Enraged past the point of thinking, she stood there, feet spread, waiting. When Beau finally looked up, she was about twenty paces away, her amber-brown eyes smoldering. Ever so slowly, he stood.

Danny spit on the ground. "I told you once you're no better than any other man, and I was right. I should have stuck with my first feelings."

Equally furious, Beau asked in a quiet voice, "What do you plan to do? You didn't play your cards right, Danny. I may have let you go before, but not now. Your only choice is to kill me, because you know you'll never escape any other way. But you can't shoot an unarmed man, can you?" Slowly he started forward, counting each step silently. One, two...

Danny could see his jaw muscles flex, and his eyes were frosty indigo. "The hell I can't," she said, and pulled the trigger. The bullet hit directly between his moving feet. "I warn you, Beau, stop right there!"

Six, seven...

Again Danny pulled the trigger. She missed his right arm by inches, but his expression didn't change.

Nine, ten...

"Stop, Beau, or the next one will be in the chest!" she threatened.

Thirteen, fourteen... A flicker of indecision crossed her face, and at that moment Beau dove for her.

She was thrust backward with so much force that the pistol flew from her hand. When she hit the ground, her entire body jarred. Beau was immediately on top of her. Grabbing her fists, he placed them in one large hand and stretched her arms over her head.

"You wild little thing," he said, then brought his mouth down brutally on hers.

Danny tried moving her head from side to side, but with his free hand, he twisted his fingers in her auburn mane, holding her head still. His mouth hurt and she could taste blood where his teeth had cut her lips. Wanting to die rather than let him assault her, she fought blindly to get free.

Suddenly his kisses became softer, yet strangely more demanding. He nibbled at her lower lip then sucked gently on it, and her efforts to escape began to weaken. His tongue darted in her mouth, caressing the interior. She tried to hold her body stiff, but couldn't. This is what she'd dreamed of, night after lonely night. He was kissing her as he had in the canyon, but this far exceeded any of her memories.

Strange, wonderful sensations were starting to take hold of her. When she felt his swollen manhood against her stomach, a surge of excitement shot through her like a bolt of lightning. She knew instinctively his need was as strong as her desire. She wasn't sure when he released his hold on her hair, but she felt his hand brush across her breast before he proceeded to unbutton her shirt.

"No," she protested out of fear, yet not wanting him to quit.

Beau, almost beside himself, felt her body start to respond. He unbuttoned her shirt and cupped her full breast in his hand. He watched the brown bud come to life. Gently he rotated it back and forth between his fingers, then, unable to wait a moment longer, he lowered his mouth and sucked gently on the delicate flesh. Her body began to move under his, but this time it was a sensual movement. Hearing a soft gasp, he looked up. Her eyes were closed tightly, but the look on her face showed growing desire, and beads of perspiration covered her upper lip.

Slowly he released her hands, but they remained in the same position. Unbuttoning her pants, he let his tongue trail down the valley of her full breasts and onto her stomach as his hand moved up her thigh and rested between her legs. Again he heard her moan, but this time it was from need. He positioned himself so that his swollen member nestled between her legs. Only their pants kept them apart. Gently he moved his hips back and forth.

"Open your eyes, Danny," he said, his voice husky.

He watched her lashes flutter as she slowly raised her lids, and he saw the fire of passion he'd longed for. "Touch me," he whispered.

Lowering her arms, she tentatively let her fingers trail across his chest and felt him shudder. It excited her to know her touch had as much effect on him as his touch had on her. Slowly she moved her hands over his body, enjoying the feel of the hard-muscled chest and arms. When he leaned down and kissed her, she kissed him back, following his example. She pulled on his bottom lip, and her tongue met and intertwined with his. Fire consumed her as his hands worked magic on her heated skin. She wanted more. The delicious throbbing between her legs began to dominate her thoughts, and as his hips moved her hips moved with him. When he rolled away she felt lost.

"Please, Beau," she said with a heavy voice, "don't stop."

"I'm only going to take your clothes off. I want to feel you naked beneath me."

His words made her heart pound.

He raised her up and removed her shirt, then gently laying her back down, pulled off her pants. After shedding his own, he lay down beside her and drew her into his arms. Kissing her, his hand slid down to her hips, pulling her up against him, molding their bodies together as one. A surge of raw flame licked through him as her hips began to undulate. Feeling the need to memorize every inch of her exquisite body, his hands roamed freely. When his hand came to rest on the furry mound, he felt her stiffen. Gently parting the folds, he located the protruding tip he was seeking, and slowly stroked the sensitive area.

Danny gasped with pleasure and pushed her hips forward. "Oh, God!" she panted. "What are you doing to me?"

Beau watched her tongue trace the contours of her lips as he moved his finger down and pressed it inside the warm moist area he so desired. When her passion became all-consuming, he entered her. Upon touching the thin membrane he thrust forward, wanting her to suffer as little pain as possible.

Feeling a ripping sensation, Danny bucked beneath him and screamed. Then the pain left. As he moved himself in and out, she felt a tension building inside, and an uncontrollable need. She met him thrust for thrust, her body drenched in perspiration. Nothing mattered except the pleasure Beau gave her. Then everything exploded, and wave after wave of spiraling bliss took over.

When she yelled out, Beau reached his own heights of gratification. Pleasantly exhausted, he lay down beside Danny, who was already falling asleep. Seeing the smile on her face, he chuckled. The actuality had far exceeded his anticipation.

Later they bathed together in the pool, then Beau made love to her on the rock. This time he was slow and deliberate, not entering her until she pleaded for him to take her to the stars. She wasn't disappointed.

"Beau, I'm sorry I shot at you," Danny said. They had bathed again and were stretched out on the rock letting their bodies dry. A smile flickered at the corners of her lips. "Weren't you even worried? I could have killed you."

"Danny, you're a good shot. If you had wanted to kill me, you would have done it with the first bullet." He chuckled.

Danielle gazed at the declining sun. "Sometimes I let my temper get away with me, and I'm always sorry afterward." She knew she was babbling, but she couldn't think of anything else to say. Just how was a woman supposed to act after making love with a man? Beau certainly didn't help; he'd hardly said two words. Their mutual passion seemed to be the only way they could communicate.

Beau rolled over on his side, his eyes taking in her beauty. Her hair lay spread out like a reddish-brown fan around her head. Everything about her was perfect. "Are you sore?" he asked gently. Surprisingly he felt concern for her, and that protective feeling he'd experienced in the canyon was threatening to take over again.

She looked at him, wanting him to take her in his arms. "Are you?" she whispered.

Beau saw the spark of desire in her amber-brown eyes, and her nipples were erect. He laughed. "You little vixen, you're like a child that's discovered a sweet tidbit and can't get enough of it."

Danny was embarrassed. Her thick feathery lashes lowered. "I'm sorry, Beau. I don't know the rules for this sort of thing."

"Don't ever be sorry," he said, pulling her into his arms. "I wouldn't want it any other way." She snuggled up to him, and he felt his member come alive. "I've branded you, Danny, just as sure as if I'd used an iron. You can't escape me now."

"Why would I want to do that?"

He could feel her warm breath on his chest. Oh, you will, he thought, and you'll probably hate yourself for your weakness, but you'll come to me when I want you. Your bodily needs will dictate. And there is so much I can teach you.

He rolled her over on top of him. "Straddle me." His voice was already husky with desire. "I'm just as insatiable as you are, love."

Danny placed her legs on either side of him; then he lifted her up by the hips and lowered her down on him. Her body became hot from the wonderful sensations as he entered her. He did this several times, and Danny writhed with pleasure.

"If you want something, Danny, never be ashamed to take it," he told her.

Danny began to make the movement without his help, absorbed in her own enjoyment. She started moving faster and faster. This time she made love to him.

During their ride back, Danny finally accepted her fate. She loved Beau. No matter how many different ways she tried to deny it, she couldn't escape the truth. She'd loved him ever since the canyon. Even though she hadn't realized it at the time, her determination to become a lady had been to attract him.

At first, Beau had been pleasantly surprised at Danny's quick response to his lovemaking, but after due thought he understood why. Danny threw herself totally into everything she did, from robbing stagecoaches to becoming a lady. He had a feeling that it would be some time before he tired of her, unless she tried to force him into marriage. But he knew the day would come when he'd seek greener pastures. It had always been that way with women. Why should Danny be any different? Margaret knew of what she spoke when she accused him of being incapable of love. He'd known many women, and had never felt that all-consuming desire to spend the rest of his life with any of them. The love his father had spoken of in his letter was not for Beau. He didn't even like the idea of a woman having that much control over a man.

But for now, however, Danny proved to be exactly what he needed. He'd already given some thought as to when he could be with her again. He might have to wait until after the barbecue, unless he could devise a means of signaling her. Too many people would be around for them to take the chance of being caught, and he didn't want anyone to know what was going on between them. As long as he didn't have to give her up, he would keep her reputation from being sullied.

As they were walking to the house, Beau drew Danny into one of the black shadows of night and kissed her, enjoying the feel of her body melting against his.

"I don't know when we'll be able to see each other again, Danny," he whispered into her ears, "probably not until after everyone leaves. But should an opportunity arise, I'll hoot like an owl twice." He made the sound so she would be able to recognize it. "Will you come to me?"

"Yes, Beau. Try to make it soon."

Beau chuckled. "As soon as possible, love." He kissed her on the nose. "Now go to bed. The next few days are going to be busy."

"Aren't you coming in?" she asked.

"I'm going to enjoy a cigar first. I'll see you tomorrow."

Danny had no trouble falling asleep. All her dreams were about Beau.

Jed reread the note Carlotta had given him, paying scant attention to the rolled cigarette that hung from his mouth until the lit end reached his lips. He grabbed the stubby butt and quickly tossed it to the floor where it joined a dozen or so others. "Damn," he muttered, licking his burnt lips.

"What does the message say?" asked Carlotta. She had moved the rocking chair over by the window, and sat rocking in an effort to stir up a breeze as well as chase away flies.

"For God's sake, Carlotta," Jed barked, "if you gotta keep up that infernal noise, why don't you take the damn rocker out on the porch!"

Jed's words had no effect on the easygoing woman. She'd grown used to his grumpiness. "Just because you're in a foul mood doesn't mean you have to take it out on me, Jed Turner. If you don't want to tell me what the note said, maybe you can tell me if Jose will be back tonight."

"Yes," Jed grumbled, "he should be here any time."

"Well, supper's ready when you are. I'm glad you hired those two men. At least now you and Jose don't have to trade off every other night watching cattle. The work's just too much for the two of you. You must have lost twenty pounds since you came back." She laughed. "I have to say, though, you look a lot better now that you've gotten rid of that roll around your middle."

"You ain't got no room to talk," Jed mumbled, not loud enough for her to hear.

"Planning on hiring any more men?" Carlotta asked.

"Not until we get a place for 'em to sleep. Clancy and Joe are drivin' the cattle over to the south pasture so one man can keep an eye on 'em. I'm taking the buckboard into Prescott tomorrow and pickin' up some wood so we can get started on building a bunkhouse."

"The reason I'm asking is, if you are, you'd better start looking for a cook. I'm certainly not going to work my fingers to the bone cooking for a bunch of wranglers."

"What the hell you gonna do? Sit in that damn squeaky rocker all day?"

Carlotta pushed back a strand of black hair that hung in her face. "You've been good to us, Jed, but you hired Jose on, not me. I don't mind cooking for the two of you, but pretty soon you're going to have a bunch of men working for you, and that's where I draw the line."

Jed grabbed a metal bowl and dipped some food out of the large black caldron. "Maybe you're right," he griped, "at least I'd get somethin' besides stew!" Heavy footsteps pounded on the porch and he looked up just as Jose walked through the open door.

"Howdy, sugar," Jose greeted his wife.

Carlotta giggled.

"Got a note from Falkner," Jed said. Using the back of his arm, he cleared a place on the dirty table so he could put his bowl down.

"An offer to buy the ranch?" asked Jose, as he sat across from Jed.

"Nope. Said he was real sorry about that little incident the other day and that he'd keep his cattle off Silver J land, but he didn't say for how long."

Jose's expression was one of disbelief. "Think he's telling the truth?"

"Hell, I don't know. Seems too good to be true. Reckon we'll have to wait and see. He's also invited us to that there barbecue he's throwin'."

"We going?"

Carlotta waved her cross. "You may be walking into a trap," she said. "I wouldn't trust any of those Falkners."

Finished eating, Jed shoved his bowl to the side and rolled a cigarette. "I was thinkin' the same thing. Damn! Still gonna be another week before Danny gets here. I wish I knew where the hell she was, I'd go get her."

The next morning Danielle felt wonderful. She left her room and almost ran into Andrea, who had her arms piled high with linens.

"Here, let me help you," Danny offered, taking part of the stack.

"Did you have a good sleep?" Andrea asked as they headed toward the storage room.

"Yes. I'm sorry I didn't get up earlier. I know there's still a lot of work to be done."

"There really isn't much left. Beau said he tracked down the mountain lion."

"Andrea, I know I should have left a note telling you where I went."

"Nonsense." Andrea gave her a gentle smile. "As soon as we discovered you weren't in your room, I knew where you had gone. I suspected as much last night. This morning at breakfast, Beau raved at what a trooper you were. He gave us a complete accounting of everything."

I doubt that, Danny thought. "Is Beau still here?"

"Oh, no. He left early this morning. He took Armando with him to check one of the pastures. Margaret insisted on going along."

They reached the large room and placed the linen in the bins.

"And did he take her?" Danny asked.

"Yes."

Danny's good mood disappeared.

"Well, now, that's all taken care of," Andrea said, closing the door behind them. "Why don't we go get you something to eat? You must be starving. According to Beau, you went all day without food."

"That's true." Funny, the thought of food hadn't even entered her mind yesterday!

When they were comfortably situated in the dining room and the food had been brought out, Danny could only pick at it. This is silly, she thought. Why should I let myself get all upset just because Margaret went with Beau? Besides, Armando is with them. Feeling better, her appetite returned, and she devoured everything. Her hunger satiated, she relaxed.

Andrea laughed. "My goodness. You were hungry, weren't you? I'm amazed at how much such a little person can put away."

"Yesterday was a real workout." Realizing what she had said, Danny giggled.

"I wish you could have seen the look on Margaret's face when she found out you had gone with Beau." Remembering, Andrea smiled. "I should be ashamed of myself, but I enjoyed watching her pace back and forth. Actually, I tried to avoid her, but she seemed to find me every time. If she asked once she asked a dozen times, 'When do you think they'll be back?' Of course we all suffered from that sharp tongue of hers, but it was worth it."

Danny was stunned. Never had Andrea expressed her feeling toward Margaret in such a manner.

"And since I'm bending your ear," Andrea continued, "another thing that bothers me is Margaret's maid, Sara. She's always trying to milk information out of Maria." Seeing the surprised expression on Danny's face she quickly added, "I know I shouldn't say things like that, but for the life of me, I can't make myself like Margaret. Lord knows, I've tried."

"What will you do if Beau marries her?" Danny asked. It pained her to even talk about it. On the other hand, she refused to go around with her head completely in the clouds and not consider the possibility.

"I don't believe Beau has any intentions of marrying her. I think it's only in Margaret's mind. But if it happens, I'll simply move to Santa Fe."

"And that wouldn't bother you?"

"Possibly for a short time, but I'm very adaptable." She started laughing. "Oh, get that grim look off your face, Danny. I don't see Beau rushing to the altar. Do you?"

"No, I don't. . . . Not for any woman," Danny replied, her voice soft.

"See? So why worry?" Andrea decided to change the subject. "Are you looking forward to the barbecue?"

Danny's eyes lit up. "Yes. Oh, Andrea, I'm dying to tell someone . . . Promise you'll keep a secret?"

"Of course, dear."

"I'm going to enter the horse race."

"You're what?" Andrea choked.

"Now don't go getting upset with me, I have it all planned."

Andrea let out a half laugh. "I'm not upset, I'm just surprised. Tell me what you have in that pretty little devious mind of yours."

"I'm going to ride Sheeka."

"How?"

Danny told Andrea what she'd been up to.

"Are you angry with me?" she finally asked, her concern written on her face. "I know she's a valuable animal, and it wasn't my place to—"

"Stop right there! The time for concern has long since past. Had I known about this, my worry would have been that you might get hurt." Andrea's full pink lips spread into a broad smile, and her sky-blue eyes twinkled with mischief. "Oh, Danny, that's why I so enjoy having you here. You keep life interesting. Do you really think the mare has a chance of winning?"

"Andrea, she moves like lightning. Of course, I haven't seen any of the horses the ranchers are bringing in, but I think she has a good chance. My biggest concern is Mescal. I've thought about telling Beau, but I'm afraid he'll stop me."

"And you're probably right. Now if I understand this correctly, no one knows you can ride the horse, and Beau knows nothing about any of this. How do you plan on entering the race without him finding out?"

"Smoky said the race would start near the stable, circle the compound, go by the stable again and end at the cattle barn. Is that right?"

"Yes, the boys have already started smoothing out the track."

"All I have to do is slip away, change my clothes, and after Beau has taken Mescal out, I'll mount Sheeka. Just before the gun goes off to start the race, I'll ride up in back of the other horses. I don't think anyone will notice me, all their concentration will be on the starter."

"Why don't you let me help? Smoky may say something to Beau in order to save his own hide, especially if Beau finds you taking the horse out at night. However, if Smoky knows I'm aware of it, he'll probably feel safe. I think we should tell him what you've been doing, and that it's your surprise for Beau's birthday. Are you planning on taking Sheeka out tonight?"

"I'd thought about it."

"Then we'd better attend to it right away. I don't know when we'll get a chance to be alone again. Margaret and Beau could come riding in any time, and tomorrow people will start arriving. So we have to plan everything now."

Seeing Andrea's excitement, Danny had to laugh. "You have a better idea than mine?"

"I can slip away, take your clothes to the stable and stay there while you change. I can also watch for Beau and signal when he's coming. I'll leave with him, and position myself so you can see me from the doorway. When the race is about to start, I'll raise my hand and you can ride out."

"Oh, Andrea, that's a wonderful idea! Andrea, why are you doing this?"

Andrea reached across the table and placed her hand on top of Danny's. "My dear, it's been a long time since I've had so much fun. And I am certainly going to enjoy seeing the shocked look on that stoic Indian face of my brother's. I cannot begin to tell you all the stunts he used to play on me. Now it's my turn."

"Andrea," Danny said in a serious voice, "I know Beau will recognize me, but I can't let anyone else know. Especially Margaret. I don't want people laughing and pointing their finger at me because I dressed in men's clothes."

Andrea remembered what Danny had looked like when Beau first brought her to the ranch. She had worked so hard to become a lady. Andrea could understand the girl's need to not have people laugh at her. "All right," she said, "we'll get a hat that will hide your hair and tie a bandanna around your neck."

Danny giggled. "And a binder for my breasts."

Andrea laughed. "By all means, a binder for your breasts. I can stand halfway between the stable and the finishing line and see who wins. Then I'll rush back and help you change into your dress. Can you think of anything else?"

"No, I think that does it."

"Then let's go for that stroll."

Smoky had an easy job. Two of the blacksmith's sons, Jessy and Adam, were his main helpers. The boys arrived just after dawn, cleaned out the stalls and spread fresh straw. When the horses had been watered and lightly fed with hay, they were let out to exercise. The boys also made sure the saddles and tack were properly cleaned. Smoky simply checked to be sure the mixture of bran and oats was the right consistency and that the boys were doing their work. Even that he did in a haphazard manner. He knew Jessy and Adam did their work well. Of course if any of the Falkners showed up, he made a show of all his supposed accomplishments.

Smoky had just finished checking some of the stalls when the two women entered. "Howdy, Miss Falkner," he said, tipping his hat. "Miss Danny." He greeted Danny with far less enthusiasm. Without thinking, he spat a wad of tobacco juice into a small tin he carried around when in the stable. Mr. Falkner had told him not to spit on the brick floor or in the stalls.

"Hello, Smoky," Andrea said. "We came to see how Sheeka is doing. You are keeping her in top condition, aren't you?"

"Yes, ma'am."

"Smoky, I want to thank you for helping Danny ride Sheeka." Andrea watched a look of confusion cross his face. "Danny has been taking the mare out every night and riding her, unbeknownst to anyone but me. It's a special surprise for my brother's birthday."

What the hell is she talking about, Smoky wondered. At least Danny hadn't snitched about him riding off.

"The reason we're letting you in on our little secret is because the barbecue is in two days, and Danny can't possibly stay out all night. I want you to meet her when she returns, cool the horse down for her and give it a good brushing. It'll only be for two nights."

Smoky, always looking for a chance to better himself in the owners' eyes, quickly agreed.

"I know you'll continue to keep our little secret," Andrea continued. "I would be absolutely furious if Beau were to discover what we're up to."

"You don't have to worry, Miss Falkner, my mouth is sealed. And don't worry about Miss Danny or Sheeka, I'll take good care of them."

Danny and Andrea left the stable. When they were out of hearing distance, they broke out laughing.

Chapter Eleven

Late that afternoon, Andrea and Danny were relaxing in the shade when Margaret and Beau entered the courtyard. Margaret had her arm possessively tucked beneath Beau's and the two were laughing and discussing mutual acquaintances in England.

"Greetings, ladies," Beau said upon seeing the women.

"We had a marvelous time." Margaret's face mirrored her pleasure. "As always, Beau acted the perfect English gentleman and attended to my every need."

Danny wanted to strangle the both of them.

"I'm glad you enjoyed yourself, Margaret," Andrea said, hiding her dislike for the woman.

"I always enjoy myself when I'm with Beau." She removed her arm, and reaching down, shook the dust from her skirt. "Oh, darling, I must look a mess. If you will excuse me, I'm going to my room to bathe and make myself presentable for dinner."

"I have some things I need to attend to also," Beau said, smiling down at Margaret. "I'll escort you to your room." He turned slightly toward Andrea and Danny. With a slight bow, he turned to leave.

"Darling, do you think we can do this again soon?" Margaret asked, her voice coated with honey.

Danny didn't hear Beau's reply. The couple had entered the house.

"Well," Andrea said, trying to be cheerful, "it sounds as though they had a good time."

"Yes, doesn't it." Danny tried to keep the sarcasm out of her voice, but the attempt came off weak. "I think I'll go to my room, Andrea, and read."

Confused, Andrea watched the girl leave. Did Danny get upset because Beau had spent the day with Margaret, or because she simply didn't like the woman? Unfortunately, it was probably the latter. She stood and stretched her shoulders back. I probably made a big mistake by having her promise to stay for a month, she thought. No, that's not true. Danny has changed so much since her arrival, and all for the better. Plus, I've found a good friend. She headed toward the kitchen. "Obviously, my brother is blind!" she muttered.

Danny spent most of the remaining day pacing back and forth in her room. She had tried to read, but was unable to concentrate. Beau had acted as if she weren't even there! It thrilled her no end knowing Beau had treated Margaret like a *perfect English gentleman* should! Well, she thought, he sure as hell didn't treat *me* that way! I may love you, Beau Falkner, but you're a two-timing bastard! If you were trying to make me jealous, it sure as hell worked, but you'll never know it.

Dinner did not improve Danny's state of mind. Again, Beau said less than two words to her. The rest of the time he listened attentively while Margaret expounded on their marvelous day together.

After exercising Sheeka late that night, Danny was both mentally and physically exhausted, but sleep didn't come easily. Pictures of Beau flashed through her mind, and she could almost feel his hands caressing her. Perspiration began to break out all over her body and she became tight with hunger for him. She rolled over on her stomach, but the coarse cotton sheets acted as a stimulus to her already aroused nipples. Quickly she turned on her back, but passion and desire had a firm grip on her senses. She could picture Beau standing naked beside her. Her mind and body were screaming for satisfaction when, in the far reaches of her mind, she thought she heard an owl hoot twice. Had it been her imagination playing tricks on her? Raising her head, she listened and soon heard the sound again. "Oh, thank God," she moaned. She ran to the window and started to climb out, then stopped. Her mind yelled, Go to him, he can fulfill your desires. "No!" she muttered. "I won't let you treat me like I'm nobody, then come running when you beckon, Beau Falkner!'' She slammed the shutters closed and bolted the lock.

Knowing he stood outside waiting for her only served to heighten her need for him. He had made her a complete woman and she'd loved every minute of it. Now she paid the price. Her night was hell.

The next morning, Danny arrived late for breakfast. Beau and Andrea had already completed their meal and were discussing business when she entered the dining room. As usual, Margaret would not be joining them. She always slept late.

"Good morning, dear," Andrea greeted her. "Did you have a good night's sleep?"

Danny pulled out a chair and sat down without answering.

Seeing her pale face and the dark circles under her eyes, Beau chuckled. "I wonder when the weather will cool down?" he commented. "I thought it was exceptionally hot last night."

"Did you?" asked Andrea. "I found it to be pleasant."

"You must have been quite chilly, Danny." A broad grin crossed his face. "I couldn't sleep, so I went for a stroll and happened to see your shutters closed."

Andrea looked questioningly at the girl. "Why in the world would you close the shutters? Didn't you burn up?"

Beau broke out laughing.

"An owl kept hooting, and wouldn't let me sleep, so I closed the shutters to keep out the sound," Danny said through clenched teeth.

"An owl?" Andrea asked excitedly. "How wonderful! When we first moved here there were two owls, and I loved hearing them hoot at one another. They were here for years, then they must have left because I never heard them again. I wonder if one of them has returned or if it's a different one."

"Oh, I'm sure it's a different one," said Beau. "Too many years have passed since you heard the old ones."

Beau watched Danny dip food from the various silver bowls that graced the table. Her eyes never left her plate. At first he'd been angry last night, but the more he thought about it, the more amused he became. She had to have closed the shutters because she couldn't tell him no to his face. And if she couldn't tell him no, then she must have wanted him. He also knew she was angry about Margaret, but he remained firm that no one would learn of their affair. She would have enough of a problem explaining why she wasn't a virgin when she picked a husband. It also served as a buffer, just in case Danny should get any wrong ideas about him wanting to marry her.

"Danny, are you feeling all right?" Andrea asked. "You look worn out."

"I didn't sleep well last night."

"That's because you closed your shutters, love," Beau teased. "I'm sure if you'd left them open, you would have had a most enjoyable night, and felt quite refreshed this morning."

Danny suddenly realized she'd eaten all her food. She couldn't even remember tasting it.

"Maybe you should go back to your room and take a nap," suggested Andrea worriedly. "You'd have more than enough time before our guests start arriving."

"I think Andrea is right." Beau slid his chair back. "Well, I have to check everything to be sure all's ready for tomorrow. Would you like me to escort you to your room, Danny?"

"No!" she blurted out before thinking. "No," she repeated in a softer voice, "I'm certainly capable of walking by myself. If you have nothing for me to do, Andrea, I believe I'll take your suggestion. I'm sure, after I've rested, I'll feel just fine." She stood and quickly left, hearing Beau's laughter trail behind her.

This time Danny had no trouble falling asleep. She welcomed the sweet abyss of nothingness.

By afternoon, Danny felt like her usual self. When distant ranchers and their families started arriving, everyone was in a festive mood, and she joined in the merriment. Rooms were assigned, and in most cases the men, women and children were divided up into groups, thus allowing more sleeping space.

Danny had already agreed to share her room and was delighted with her two roommates. As the girls sat on her big bed in their nightgowns talking, Danny studied her guests.

Beth Watson, nineteen, had a willowy figure, with a beautiful heart-shaped face, blue eyes and a smattering of freckles across her nose. Her thick, silver-blond hair hung to her waist. Jane Morgan, Danny's age, had a well-curved figure and was obviously quite proud of it. She always had a smile on her round face, and her hazel eyes twinkled with humor. She also had long blond hair, but much darker than Beth's.

Both girls were extremely attractive, friendly and talkative. They told Danny they lived on adjacent ranches and had known each other practically from birth. They talked about the ornery stunts they'd pulled as children and laughed uproariously at their antics. The girls never asked why Danny lived on the ranch, because Andrea had conveniently mentioned that she was related to the family. The girls just assumed her to be a rancher's daughter.

The conversation soon turned to what stayed uppermost in Beth and Jane's minds: men. They discussed several men, wondering if they were coming tomorrow—hoping they would. Not knowing any of the men they were referring to, Danny sat quietly and listened.

"Of course," Beth purred, "none of them can compare to Beau. Don't you agree, Danny?"

Taken completely off guard by the question, Danny didn't know how to answer.

"Of course she agrees, silly," Jane said. "There isn't a woman around who wouldn't run to him if he crooked his little finger at her. I'd sure like to get my claws in him."

"Fat chance, with Margaret always hanging on to him. Tell us, Danny, before Jane makes a fool of herself, are they a twosome? Are they planning to get married?"

"Not that I know of. I think it's more in Margaret's head than it is in Beau's," Danny answered, repeating Andrea's words.

Jane rubbed the palms of her hands together. "Oh, I do like to hear that."

"Tell us all about him," Beth encouraged. "He's been in England so long, we really don't know what he's like now. Besides, all I can remember is that he had long black hair and wore buckskins all the time."

"That's not true, Beth," Jane interrupted. "I can remember us talking and you saying you couldn't take your eyes off him." She turned to Danny. "He was so tall, quiet and majestic-looking. We were always wondering what he was thinking."

"Well, I was much younger then," Beth said defensively. "But you're right," she said, dreamy-eyed. "I do remember how I would follow him around when he came to the ranch with his pa."

"And he looks even more interesting now," Jane insisted. "Is he as devilish as he looks?"

Danny laughed. "Yes."

Jane giggled. "Pa said he was a savage when he left. He's curious to see how much Beau's changed. Beth, do you remember how our folks used to talk about him when they thought we weren't listening? The way they talked, you'd think Beau would rise from the ground and kill everyone."

"Oh, that was because of all the trouble they were having with the Apache. And since then, they got to know Beau's dad and completely changed their attitude."

"Well, ladies, we have a big day tomorrow," Danny warned, not liking the turn of the conversation. "I'm ready to call it a night, how about you?"

"Oh, I just know we're going to have barrels of fun," Beth said, sighing.

They blew out the candles, and in no time Danny could hear the others' slow, even breathing. She was still burning over Beau's treatment of her, or lack of treatment, and because of it, the race had taken on an even greater significance to her. She wanted to see Beau eat Sheeka's dust! Checking to be sure the girls were fast asleep, she put on her pants and shirt, climbed out the window and headed for the stable.

Danny had never seen so many people gathered in one place. By noon, they were everywhere, and carriages were still arriving. While the grown-ups caught up on all the news, the children played games; London bridge, run-sheep-run, leapfrog and button, button were the most popular, or chased each other in and around the adults, while screaming and laughing.

The aroma of meat cooking in the pits wafted through the area. Tables had been set up in the courtyard with various punches and lemonade, and bottles of whiskey, rum and other spirits for the men.

Danny spent the morning with Beth and Jane, enjoying their company. The girls seemed to have a knack for knowing who the single men were, and one way or another managed to meet most of them. There were other groups of single women, basically doing the same thing. Jane seemed to find a hundred and one reasons for talking to Beau. Because Danny was a permanent guest, women of all description prodded her with questions about him. It served to prove what she'd suspected all along. He attracted females like dogs attracted fleas.

Shortly after noon, Maria and her crew of women began to bring out the food. The seemingly never-ending array included dove, quail, chicken, fish, vegetables, Mexican dishes, breads, fritters, fruit and a variety of desserts. They set the many bowls and platters on the ten long planks of wood, which rested on barrels placed near the pits and covered with crisp white linen. The food would remain available until dark, at which time the dancing would start.

When the tables were filled to capacity, one of the cowhands assisting with the cooking of the meat started banging a big fork against a metal triangle and calling, "Come and get it."

"At last!" Jane proclaimed. "I'm starved."

"How can you be starved after eating such a big breakfast?" questioned Beth.

"I have to make sure my curves remain curves!"

Danny smiled at the friendly bickering that went on between the two girls.

The food proved to be every bit as good as it looked, and Danny made an honest effort to eat, but very little reached her lips. All she could think about was the race, which wouldn't take place until late afternoon. Before joining the festivities, she had taken her clothes to Andrea's room, so at least that part had been taken care of. While there, Andrea had warned her to be careful. "Everyone starts at the same time, and there will be a lot of riders. Most of them get knocked out of the saddle before they even get started. It's a free-for-all, Danny," Andrea had said.

"Danny! Is your mind riding in the wind?"

"What? I'm sorry, Jane, I guess my mind was somewhere else."

"I asked you three times if you wanted to go over and see the shooting match," Beth kidded her.

"You know why Beth wants to go over there, don't you?" Jane asked, a sly grin creasing her full lips.

"No, not really," Danny replied.

"She's hoping to see Tracy Stuart. He's supposed to be quite good with a pistol. I think Beth's smitten with him."

"Can you blame me?" asked Beth. "I think he's most attractive."

Danny remembered meeting the nice-looking man earlier. He had curly brown hair.

"No, not really," Jane replied. "He's just not my type. He's too young."

"Well, I hope he's not your type. I saw him first. Shall we go? Even if he isn't there, at least it will be interesting to watch."

"It's fine with me," Danny replied.

"All right," Jane agreed, "but what I'm looking forward to is the dancing. That's when the fun begins."

The girls took off. The contest was to be held behind the blacksmith's shed. When they arrived, a large number of people had already started congregating to watch. Danny followed closely behind Jane, who wove in and out of the crowd stopping only when she reached the front. Ten men were lined up single file, each holding a pistol, and targets had been placed some distance in front of them.

"Is that all they have to do? Hit the targets?" Danny asked. "That seems too easy."

"When these ten men are finished, ten more will move up, and so on. When they have taken their six shots, the ones who hit the bull's-eye will have another shoot off. If a winner can't be picked, they'll start shooting at coins until a winner is finally proclaimed."

"That could take all day!"

"No, Danny," said Jane. "Most men are better with a rifle than a pistol."

Danny couldn't understand why they would have a contest over something so simple.

When the last row stepped up, there were only four men. "For the life of me, I fail to see why so many men have missed the center," Danny said.

Jane and Beth looked at her. "Danny," Jane whispered, "it's not as easy as it looks."

"Excuse me, miss. Could you hit that target?"

Danny turned and looked at the man standing to her right. He had blond wavy hair and an extremely handsome face. His clothes were impeccable and he appeared to be in his early thirties.

"I didn't mean to eavesdrop," he continued, "but I've been listening to your comments, and became curious."

Danny blushed.

"Could you hit the target?" he asked again.

"Yes."

The man laughed. "You know, I believe you."

Before Danny realized what he was up to, the man called out, "Just a minute. We have another contestant."

Danny wanted to find the nearest hole and climb in. The on-lookers, seeing who the man referred to, began laughing. She started to turn and leave when her eyes met Beau's. He was standing at the far end, and a broad, I-dare-you grin crossed his face. Her pride took over.

"I haven't a pistol," she stated.

"I do. You're welcome to use it," said the blond man, handing it to her. "It shoots true."

Danny tilted her chin up and joined the four men. She could hear whispers and people snickering behind her.

"I'll take my shots, then I quit," she proclaimed.

"Start any time you like, gentlemen . . . er, and lady," a man announced.

Danny tested the weight of the pistol in her hand, then, lifting it, she shot six times, one right after the other. When she finished, there was a clean hole, dead center, in the target.

Turning, she returned the gun to the stranger and walked away, failing to notice the man's cold eyes watching her. Jane and Beth had to chase after her.

"Danny," Jane called. "Wait a minute."

When well away from the eyes of the crowd, Danny finally slowed down and let her friends catch up.

"My heavens," said Beth, "where are you going? To a cock fight?"

Jane brought up the rear, slightly breathless. "Where did you learn to shoot like that?" she asked admiringly.

"When other girls were playing with dolls, I learned how to shoot a gun." All of a sudden Danny was tired of having to hide her true identity. Even Beau had never taken enough interest to inquire about her last name. She was just Danny, period! Nothing more, nothing less.

"I wish I could shoot like that," said Jane, all smiles. "Why did you rush off?"

"Because I made a fool of myself, and I don't like people laughing at me."

Jane grabbed Danny's arm and pulled her to a stop. "Well, they certainly weren't laughing when you finished. Didn't you hear them showing their appreciation by clapping?"

"No."

"Danny, you remind me of my mother," Beth said. "When she and Pa came here by wagon train, all the women were taught how to shoot. According to her, they had to in order to survive. She was a crack shot, and used to tell stories about how she and Pa had contests. She still claims she can outshoot him."

"Really?" Danny questioned, suddenly feeling better about herself. Beth's mother was small, attractive and very feminine. She would never have dreamed the woman had ever even held a gun, let alone shot it.

Jane giggled. "Pa tried to teach me how to shoot, but after two weeks I still couldn't hit the haystack and he gave up."

"All of a sudden I'm hungry," Danny exclaimed with a smile. "A big piece of pie sounds good."

The three women laughed and took off toward the tables.

A little more than an hour before the race, Danny started feeling nervous. She even began to question her motives for entering the race. Perhaps it wasn't such a good idea after all. Then she saw Beau talking to some woman, and her resolve returned. Damn, she thought, I'll be so glad when it's over! When she finally saw Andrea headed in her direction, she knew the time had arrived.

"Hello, ladies," Andrea said. "Are you having a good time?"

Beth and Jane assured her they were.

"Danny, I hate to bother you, but I need your help for a few minutes. I hope you ladies will excuse us. I promise not to keep her long," she apologized.

"You're not going to miss the race, are you?" Jane asked. "It will be starting shortly."

"If I'm not back, go on over. I'll meet you there." She gave them a big smile, but under her skirts, her knees had started shaking.

"I put your clothes in the tack room," Andrea said when they were out of hearing distance. "Smoky wasn't there. I think he's off having a drink or two. If we hurry, you can change without him knowing."

They started walking faster toward the stable.

"Danny, I thought this was a great idea, but now I'm worried. I didn't realize so many men would enter the race. Dear, you could be seriously hurt. Are you sure you want to go through with this?"

Hearing Andrea mirror her own doubts only served to make Danny more determined. "I'm sure," she replied.

"All right, then, let me tell you some of the things my father used to say. He always said most races, assuming it's a fast horse, are won by the rider."

"Why?"

"Because the rider has the intelligence to guide the horse and stay out of trouble. He also said taking the lead is not always the wisest choice. Inexperienced riders only have one thought in their mind, and that's to get the horse out front as fast as possible and stay there. In most cases, the horse can't stand the pace for that long a distance, and begins to tire and drop back. Now I'm not saying all horses. Some can handle it. You just need to know the animal."

"I never thought of it that way. What you're saying is, hold back, take advantage of the openings, save the horse's strength, then finally let him go?"

"Exactly. Father loved to race his horses, and was very knowledgeable on the subject. I hope what I've said will be of some help."

"Well, it certainly makes a lot of sense."

Smoky had still not returned when they entered the stable. Andrea stood guard while Danny changed clothes in the tack

room. When she had finished, Andrea tucked her hair under
the wide-brimmed hat and pulled the chin strap tight. Then,
mixing some water and dirt, she smeared Danny's cheeks.
Stepping back to take a look at her handiwork, Andrea
laughed.

"What's wrong?" Danny asked.

"Absolutely nothing. Beau may recognize you, but I assure
you, no one else will."

Danny grinned. "Now you know what I looked like when
Beau met me. Except then, I wore long johns."

"No wonder he thought you were a boy!"

Andrea went into the tack room and returned with Danny's
clothes. "We certainly don't want anyone discovering these."
She hastily tucked them away in a safe place. "Now, I think
you should hide. Since Smoky hasn't seen you, we might as well
take advantage of it. He won't know what we're up to until it's
too late. Let's see, where can you hide?"

"In Sheeka's stall. No one will think to look there."

"Wonderful! Are you going to have enough time to get her
saddled?" Andrea asked when Danny was safely hidden.

Danny hadn't told her she wouldn't be using a saddle.
"Yes," she replied. She knew Andrea was worried, and didn't
want to add to her concern.

"Howdy, Miss Falkner."

Andrea felt sure she must have jumped two feet off the
ground at Smoky's words. She was nervous enough without
him scaring her half out of her wits. Deliberately she walked
away from the stall.

"If I'd known you were here, I'd have come back sooner. I
just went to get me something to eat," Smoky said nervously.
Falkner had told him not to have anything to drink until after
the race, but he'd figured a little nip wouldn't hurt. Now he
wished he'd waited.

As usual, Smoky had a big wad of chewing tobacco in his
mouth, causing his cheek to bulge out, but Andrea could still
smell the liquor on his breath.

"Is there something I can do for you?" asked Smoky.

"No, I'm just waiting for Beau. I wanted to wish him luck."

"Seeing as how that horse of his still won't let me touch him, there's nothing I can do to help." Damn, he thought, I shouldn't have drank so much.

At that moment, Beau and Margaret came in.

"Andrea. I didn't expect to see you here," Beau said, pleased at seeing his sister.

"I wanted to wish you luck."

"I'll be out back if you need me for anything, Mr. Falkner." Smoky made a quick exit.

"What's the matter with him?" Beau wondered aloud. "Usually he won't stop talking, and does everything but lick my boots."

Out in front, Andrea could see men leading their horses toward the starting line. "Do you think you'll win?" she teased her brother.

"I don't think there's an animal out there that can beat Mescal. I anticipate an easy run."

"So you'll take him out front and stay there?"

"I don't know why not."

"Beau, darling, I'm going to leave and find a good spot to watch," Margaret purred. "I'll cheer for you all the way. Would you care to join me, Andrea?"

"I would love to, but I promised to join some friends."

"Very well." Margaret reached up and kissed Beau on the cheek. "I'll see you later, darling. Good luck."

Beau watched Margaret leave, wishing it were a permanent departure. He no longer had any interest in the sultry brunette and, as a matter of fact, hadn't for some time. After the barbecue, when everyone had left, he would tell her it was finished between them and send her packing.

"Don't let me stop you, dear," Andrea said. "I know you want to get ready for the race. I'm just going to wait here until the Jacobsons arrive."

Beau walked back to Mescal's stall. Is it just my imagination, he wondered, or are Andrea and Smoky acting peculiar? He shrugged his shoulders. He didn't have time to worry about it now.

When Beau rode out of the stable to join the other contestants, Andrea headed for Sheeka's stall. "Okay, Danny, it's time."

Danny poked her head up. "Is he gone?" she whispered.

"Yes. Now hurry, you haven't much time. They're already starting to line up. I'm going over to the other side. Watch my hand."

Danny had just put the bit in Sheeka's mouth and was getting ready to take her out of the stall when Smoky entered through the back.

"Hey! What you think you're doing with that horse?" he called, not recognizing her.

"It's me, Danny."

Smoky stopped dead in his tracks. "Why are you dressed like that? What you planning on doing with Sheeka?"

"I'm going to race her," Danny said as Sheeka's rump cleared the cubicle.

"Oh, no, you ain't! I'm not going to let you get me in trouble. It's my neck that will be in the wringer!"

Danny tossed a woolen rug over Sheeka's back and led her to the mounting stool.

"Just stop right there, missy!"

"Listen, you jackass! One way or the other, I'm going to be in that race. I know it, Andrea knows it and now you know it! You're not stupid, so you'd better give it a lot of thought before you go trying to stop me!"

Smoky's mind started racing. If Miss Falkner knows what's going on, how can I be blamed? I sure as hell don't want to get on the wrong side of her, he thought. He also took into consideration what he'd heard about Danny in the shooting contest, and from the look in her eyes, he could just picture her coming after him with a gun.

Now seated atop Sheeka, Danny saw Andrea's hand go up in the air. She rode past Smoky and out the door. Just as she approached the other riders, the starting gun went off.

All the horses bolted forward, including Sheeka, but Danny held the reins firm. She'd given a lot of thought about what Andrea had told her, and had decided to run the race as Gerard might have done.

She watched the solid mass of men and horses in front of her. They were knitted so tight together, they bumped each other, and men began to fall off their mounts. She had to pull Sheeka up to avoid running over one of them. It flashed through her mind that they looked like a swarm of bees.

Then some of the riderless horses started veering off to the side, while others moved forward. Her ears drummed with the thunder of hooves and dirt was flying up in all directions from the pounding on the soft ground. Holding the reins in one hand, she reached down and pulled the bandanna up over her nose to keep out the dust.

Finally, she saw a hole and made for it, hoping it wouldn't close. Nudging the mare to go faster, she made her way through without being bumped. Up ahead the riders had spread out. Seeing the next group, she maneuvered her horse around them without too much effort. The mare hadn't reached her full speed, but still Danny kept her in check. She continued to pass other horses.

When they raced by the halfway point, Danny felt she couldn't hold back any longer. Loosening up on the reins, she leaned forward. "Let's go, pretty girl," she said in Sheeka's ear while patting her neck with a gloved hand. She felt the surge of power beneath her as the strong mare stretched out her legs. Through the dust she could barely make out the four leaders. Closer and closer they came. She passed one, then two, then three. All that remained was Mescal.

Hearing the roar of the crowd, Danny knew she was closing in. "Come on, baby, come on," she encouraged Sheeka, and the mare again responded. What seemed like an eternity was only a matter of seconds as they neared the big black stallion. They were almost matched stride for stride when Beau turned and Danny saw the surprised look on his face. The two horses ran neck and neck, each trying to pull away from the other. They were nearing the finish line when Beau leaned down and put his heels to Mescal's sides. The response was immediate, and Mescal pulled ahead, winning the race by a half length.

Seeing the excited crowd start to surround Beau as he slipped off Mescal's back, Danny quickly turned Sheeka around and headed for the stable before they engulfed her.

When she rode inside, Smoky still stood where she'd left him. Sliding off Sheeka's back, she tossed the reins to him. "Cool her down," she ordered.

Andrea came running in, her face flushed with excitement. "Danny, that was as good a race as I've ever seen. You almost beat him!"

Danny removed her gloves and struck them across the side of her leg. "But I didn't win!"

"Well, that's certainly nothing to be ashamed of! You gave it your all, and I don't know anyone who could have done better. Now stop being a sore loser, and let's get you changed before anyone comes."

Andrea grabbed Danny's clothes then hustled her into the tack room. When the door closed, she picked up a rag and soaked it in one of the water pails.

As Danny came out, Andrea took hold of her arm and rushed her toward the back exit. "If you don't want anyone to know you rode that horse, we have to hurry. Smoky," she said just before they walked out, "no one is to know about this. If I hear one leak, I'll know it was you, and you'll no longer have a job. Don't worry about Beau, he already knows."

Once they were away from the stable, Andrea handed Danny the wet rag. "Use this to wipe off your face," she said in a kindly voice. "Oh, Danny, I'm so proud of you."

When Beau finally managed to get away, he headed straight for the stable. Everyone had wanted to know who rode the other horse, but he told them he had no idea.

"Where is she?" Beau demanded as he entered the stable. Smoky had Sheeka on a lead rope and was leading the mare around in a circle to cool her down.

"They left out the back way, Mr. Falkner."

"They? Who is they?"

"Your sister and Miss Danny."

"So the two of them were in on this." Suddenly Beau started laughing, but stopped when he saw Smoky spit tobacco juice on the floor.

"I believe I told you I didn't want to see any of that damn tobacco juice around."

"I'm sorry, Mr. Falkner, sometimes I forget. I'll clean it up as soon as I get the mare cooled down."

Beau's eyes narrowed when, for just a moment, Smoky staggered. "You been drinking?" he asked.

"I had a little nip just after the race to celebrate."

"Beau, darling," Margaret said as she rushed in. "That was a beautiful race."

"I have to take care of Mescal, Margaret," he said in a sharp tone, cutting her off. "You go ahead and I'll see you later."

Margaret, furious at Beau for talking to her in such a manner in front of the hired help, whirled around and left.

As he removed the saddle from Mescal's back, Beau studied Smoky. "Tell me, Smoky, when did Danny start riding Sheeka?"

"Well, ah, I'm not sure. Miss Falkner can tell you all about it."

"But I'm asking you. Are you telling me you didn't know she'd taken the horse out?"

"Not exactly." The side of Smoky's face twitched.

"That's no answer." Beau left Mescal and leaned against the wall. "Stop right there," he said as Smoky came around. "Now. Did you know Danny had taken Sheeka out to ride or not?"

"Only the first time." Smoky knew he couldn't lie about everything because the girl might tell Falkner what happened.

"The first time?"

"She told me you'd given her permission to ride the mare. So we went to that old corral over on the west end."

"And what happened?"

"She got bucked off." Smoky wiped off the perspiration that had formed on his brow.

"Then she rode the horse?"

"No, she got bucked off again."

"Just how many times did she get bucked off?"

"Oh, four or five times, I guess. Honest, Mr. Falkner, I tried to get her to stop, but she wouldn't do it."

"So when did she finally ride her?" Beau was getting mad.

"I don't exactly know. When she wouldn't leave, I rode off."

"You did what?" Beau exploded.

"Well I figured if I left, so would she," Smoky said defensively.

"You're lucky I don't knock your teeth down your throat! She could have been killed. Who the hell do you think runs this place?"

"You do."

"Yet you didn't even bother to tell me about any of this!"

"She said I shouldn't tell you 'cause it was suppose to be a surprise."

"I don't give a damn what anyone tells you. You answer to me, and me alone. Have you got that straight?"

"Yes, sir."

"If Danny comes up with any more notions, you'd damn well better be by her side at all times watching over her and making sure she doesn't get hurt! Anything like this ever happens again, you pick up your boots and head them in my direction."

Beau didn't say another word to Smoky. When he'd finished taking care of Mescal and had put him back in his stall, he left.

"Who the hell does he think he is, talking to a white man like that?" Smoky mumbled. "Someone ought to teach him some manners." He took a bottle of whiskey from between the stacks of hay and proceeded to get drunk.

Chapter Twelve

"Where have you been?" Beth asked, when Danny rejoined them. "Have you been running? You seem out of breath."

"Did you get to see the race?" Jane's face was flushed with excitement.

"Parts of it."

"We saw the beginning and the end," Beth declared.

"It was exciting right to the end! Beau almost lost. No one knows who rode the horse that came in second," Jane finished.

"We think Beau knows," Beth added. "But he won't tell."

"Why do you think that?" Danny asked.

"Because he owns the horse." Jane smiled, pleased at being able to repeat the information. "I overheard Buck Taylor say he'd tried to buy the mare this morning. From the way he talked, he must have offered Beau a huge amount of money. Now he's even more determined to buy her. He laughed and said he thought Beau had deliberately turned him down until after the race so he could get a higher price."

Danny's heart sank. She hated to see Sheeka sold, but after what she'd just pulled, Beau probably wouldn't let her ride the mare again. Beau! She had to go somewhere and calm down. Eventually she'd have to face him, but not now. He's going to be angry as hell, she thought. Good!

She looked at the sky. "It's getting dark. Don't you think we should get ready for the dance?" she asked.

Jane and Beth agreed, and they headed for the house. As they entered the courtyard, Danny felt someone touch her arm. Turning, she saw the blond man who had let her use his pistol.

"You took off so fast," he said, "I didn't have a chance to tell you how impressed I was with your marksmanship."

"Why, thank you," she said, giving him a warm smile. He sure is good looking, she thought.

"Permit me to introduce myself. I'm Garret Beckman. Would it be presumptuous of me to ask your name?"

For a moment, she couldn't remember the name she and Andrea had decided on. "Danny . . . James."

"I'm pleased to meet you, Miss James. I would, however, consider it an honor if you'd save me a dance later."

"I'd be delighted, Mr. Beckman."

He made a slight bow, and Danny continued on into the house, followed closely by her roommates.

"Danny," Jane said when they were in the bedroom. "Do you know who that was?"

"Yes. He let me use his pistol at the shooting match."

"I know that, silly. But do you know he's considered a rather unsavory character?" Jane started getting undressed.

Danny went to the clothespress and pulled out the dress she would be wearing. "Why do you say that?" she asked as she tossed it over the back of a chair.

"He owns a small ranch, but he also owns a saloon and gaming house on Whiskey Row."

"What's wrong with that? He seems to be a gentleman, and a very handsome gentleman."

"Oh, I couldn't agree more. Margaret even gave him the eye during the race. But he's considered quite a rake."

"You're a fine one to talk, Jane," said Beth, letting her dress fall to the floor. "You'd love to have him notice you!"

Jane giggled. "Pa would tan my bottom if I had anything to do with the likes of him, but it sure would be tempting. Have you noticed how his eyes change color? They were almost gray when he talked to Danny."

"Well," Beth spoke up, "he's too experienced for me. Even though Beau is the best-looking man I've ever seen, I feel the same way about him. You'd have to watch out for every single woman in the area, and probably some married ones, too.

That's why I prefer men like Tracy Stuart. You always know where you stand with his type.''

Danny remembered how shy Tracy had acted when Beth talked to him earlier. His head remained lowered, and he'd kept shuffling his feet.

When the girls were down to their chemises and pantalets, they sat on the bed and relaxed. Beth and Jane continued with their discussion of all the qualities they liked and disliked in men. The two opinions differed considerably. Danny had never talked to females her own age, and found their conversation quite enlightening. She came to realize that mentally, she was much older than they were. She preferred the way Jed had raised her to a cloistered life.

When Beau finally left the stable, people again surrounded him, full of praise for his victory and curious over who rode Sheeka. As the compliments flowed, Beau scanned the area for Danny. He didn't see her, but he did see Andrea talking to some merchants from Prescott. Excusing himself, he walked over to her.

"Pardon me, gentlemen, but I need to have a brief word alone with my sister," he said.

When they had moved away, Andrea started laughing. "She almost beat you."

Beau chuckled. "That she did. I understand you took a part in it."

"A small part. It was Danny's idea, I merely helped. After all the tricks you've pulled on me, I finally got to pull one on you, little brother."

Beau broke out in a roar of laughter.

"You're not mad at her, are you?" Andrea asked, a twinkle still in her eyes.

"No. I have to give her credit. She rode that horse better than most men. If it hadn't been for Mescal, she'd have won the race. I think she deserves a reward for her efforts. What do you think?"

"I think it's a wonderful idea. Oh, Beau, she worked so hard to win. She rode that mare practically every night after everyone had gone to bed. She was that determined. She doesn't want anyone to know who rode Sheeka because she's afraid people will ridicule her for dressing like a man. So we can't do anything public.''

"I already know the perfect gift.''

The dancing had already started when the girls entered the large barn. Bright paper streamers had been strung across the beams, and kerosene lamps were strategically hung on nails. The musicians were all men who worked on the ranch. Two played the fiddle, one had a guitar and the fourth man played a harmonica. The music was lively, and even the people that weren't dancing toe-tapped to the music. Clad in their Sunday best, everyone was in a festive mood.

Danny smoothed out her skirt, a little nervous at her low-cut bodice. She'd chosen to wear her peach silk dress with white rosettes embroidered on the full skirt and short puffed sleeves. Her thick auburn hair was pulled up into a full pompadour with a bun twisted in the center. To complete the outfit, she had on the pearl necklace and earrings Andrea had lent her for the occasion.

Within minutes of their arrival, all three girls were on the floor dancing. Unable to avoid Beau, Danny danced with him several times. To her surprise, he made no mention of the race. She refused to believe he didn't know she rode Sheeka. He just smiled and asked if she was enjoying herself, and complimented her on the perfume she was wearing. The rest of the time they whirled around the floor with little opportunity to talk. Even though she was still angry with him for treating her like any other woman, to be cast aside or danced with out of courtesy, her heart pounded rapidly when she was in his arms. His black hair glistened in the light, and she could feel his hard muscles flexing beneath the light brown broadcloth of his jacket.

She also spent a considerable amount of time dancing with Charly, the cowhand who had shown them the mountain-lion tracks. Charly had a keen sense of humor, and she enjoyed his company.

Later in the evening, she was leaving the floor after dancing with an older man who continually stepped on her toes when she saw Garret Beckman waiting with two drinks in his hand.

"I thought you might be thirsty," he said, handing her one of the cups.

"How thoughtful of you, Mr. Beckman."

"Please. Call me Garret."

Danny smiled.

"Would you care to rest a minute before I claim my dance?"

She started to refuse, but changed her mind. Other than dancing with her, Beau continued to ignore her. He hadn't even given her the satisfaction of being angry about the race! All he cared about was having his way with her when he had a need! It felt good to have another handsome man show her consideration.

"Yes," she replied, "I am a little tuckered."

Taking her by the elbow, Garret guided her to a bench and sat down beside her.

Danny lowered her thick lashes so he couldn't see her observing him. Although not as tall as Beau, he certainly towered over her. His thick, wavy blond hair was perfectly groomed and met his collar in the back. Even though rather slender, he appeared to have a wiry build, like a whip when uncoiled. Most of all, she liked his gentlemanly manner and thoughtfulness at bringing her a drink.

"I haven't...would you mind if I called you Danny?" he asked.

"Certainly not."

"As I started to say, I haven't seen you in town and I thought you might be new in this area."

"I am. I'm here on a visit." She took a long, slow drink, her dry throat enjoying the sharp flavor of the lemonade. She liked the way Garret looked at her. It wasn't a blatant perusal, like Beau's. Garret made her feel appreciated, and when he made no effort to hide his interest, she didn't feel offended.

"Will you be coming to town soon? I'd like very much to take you out to dinner."

"Well, I don't know. Andrea may be going into town, I'm just not sure."

Garret smiled, showing even white teeth. "Dare I hope that you would send a message to me at the Glass Slipper? I would be more than happy to dine with two lovely ladies."

"Maybe. It will depend on what all needs to be done in town." Danny finished her drink. He took her cup and set it on the ground.

"Would you care to dance now?" he asked.

Garret proved to be an excellent dancer. He was charming, and Danny enjoyed his company immensely. They laughed and talked about nothing in particular. They danced a lot, and when they weren't dancing they strolled outside or sat down to catch their breath. She'd seen Beau off and on dancing with other women or chatting, and when their eyes met he gave her a hard smile. Did he think she was trying to make him jealous? If only she could!

When some of the local people began leaving, Garret said it was also time for him to go. Danny walked with him to where he'd tethered his horse.

"I hope to be seeing you again soon, Danny," he said in a soft voice. "I've had a most enjoyable time. You are quite a lady. I would like to come calling and take you for a buggy ride, but I don't think the Falkners would appreciate it."

"Why would you say that? Andrea has always welcomed everyone to her home."

Garret laughed ruefully. "I'm not exactly the type of man she would pick to call upon a lady of your breeding, and I'm sure I would be told that in no uncertain terms."

"But that's ridiculous. Just because you own a saloon doesn't make you any less a person."

"It really doesn't bother you, does it?" he asked incredulously.

"No. Should it?"

Garret leaned over and kissed her lightly on the lips. "I'm sure we'll be seeing each other soon."

Danny watched him ride off. Turning, she ran right into Beau's chest. Before she could say a word, he grabbed her by the arm and started dragging her toward the stable. She stumbled and almost fell several times, but he didn't release his hold.

"What the hell are you doing?" she yelled. She let out a moan upon hearing her skirt rip as the toe of her shoe caught the hem.

Still he marched on. When they reached the large complex, Beau shoved her inside. Danny barely managed to keep her footing. The kerosene lamps were low, but she had no trouble seeing the anger in his eyes.

"What am *I* doing?" he asked in a low, deadly tone. "I think I should be the one to pose that question!"

"What are you talking about?" She pushed back the strands of auburn hair that had fallen into her face.

"Did you enjoy your evening hanging on to Garret Beckman?"

Danny saw the muscle in Beau's jaw harden, but other than that, his face remained expressionless. "I didn't hang on to Garret!" she replied. "And even if I did, it's none of your concern what I do. At least he's a gentleman, which is more than I can say for you!"

"A gentleman? That's a laugh. He's gutter trash. He's a damn crook who's out to get anything he can, any way he can."

"So what does that make me, Beau? Do you look on me as gutter trash, too? Remember? I'm the one who robs stages and has a wanted poster in Santa Fe. I'm the Gringo Kid! So as I see it, Garret and I are brethren!"

"You will never see him again. No one takes what's mine, least of all him."

"Yours?" she asked bitterly. "No one owns me, Beau Falkner, least of all you. And that's exactly the way you think of me. A damn possession! Go back to Margaret. I refuse to be one of those women who comes running when you crook your little finger." Danny knew she was yelling, but didn't care.

"Oh, you're mine all right. Fight it all you want, Danny, but you want me, and you know it. I told you once, you're branded."

"Go to hell, Mr. Falkner!"

Beau started walking slowly toward her, and she moved away.

"What's wrong, Danny?" he asked in a voice that sounded like a soft caress. A devil's smile crossed his face. "Why are you backing away from me? Don't you trust yourself?"

Danny's eyes were glued to his, and she wasn't paying attention to where she was going. Suddenly her back met the wall. Placing his hands on either side and trapping her, Beau leaned down and brushed his lips across hers. Danny kept her mouth tightly closed. Then he ran sweet tiny kisses down her neck, and she felt her legs turn to jelly. It isn't fair! she thought. All he has to do is kiss me and there's no fight left. How can I be so furious one minute and want him to make love to me the next?

"Kiss me, damn it," he said in her ear, then placed his lips on hers.

Absorbed in their desire for one another, neither saw Margaret enter the barn. Watching Danny's arms curl around Beau's neck, and the undeniable passion they shared, jealousy consumed the older woman. She watched as the two moved into one of the empty stalls and heard their moans of pleasure. Sara had said all along that Beau had no intention of marrying her, but Margaret had refused to listen. Now she knew the truth. Well, Margaret thought as she left the stable, I'm not going to stay around here any longer than necessary. But before I go, I'll find a way to get even with both of them for making me look the fool.

Smoky also left the stable. He'd awoken from where he'd passed out just as Beau and Danny had entered, and he'd overheard the entire conversation. Walking into his room at the back, he lay down on the cot and deliberated how he could make use of his newfound information.

Most of the guests stayed another three days. Although Danny had become very fond of Jane and Beth, she longed to have her room to herself. Every night since the barbecue, she had heard Beau's owl hoot, and checking to make sure the girls were asleep, sneaked out the window and joined him. She hated herself for her weakness, but when night fell she waited anxiously, afraid he wouldn't come for her.

During the day, Beau paid her scant attention, explaining it was for her own good. He didn't want anyone to find out what they were up to. Danny knew Beau didn't love her, and she wasn't foolish enough to try to convince herself otherwise. All she could do was make the best of what little time they had left.

Finally the day arrived for everyone to leave. As Danny stood, saying farewell to Jane and Beth, Beau strolled up to the veranda, leading Sheeka. Buck Taylor immediately broke away from the friends he'd been talking to and joined Beau.

"So," Buck said, a broad grin on his face, "you knew I wasn't going to up my offer, and you've finally decided to accept?"

Beau smiled back at the big, bearded man. "No, I haven't changed my mind."

"All right. I'll make one last offer—"

"Don't bother. If you want the horse, you'll have to talk to Danny. You see, the mare is hers."

Danny's mouth dropped open, but no words came out. Why had Beau lied to the man?

"I thought the mare belonged to you," Buck said.

"She did, but I'm giving Sheeka to Danny. Besides me, she's the only one who can ride her."

Danny could feel all eyes turning toward her. She wanted to die.

"But that means . . ." Jane didn't finish her sentence.

Andrea tried to intervene, but Beau stopped her with a raised hand.

"You see," Beau continued with a broad grin, "Danny thought you would all look down on her. But I know how much everyone cheered her on as she came from the rear and almost beat me. I also know that all anyone would do is praise her for her magnificent horsemanship."

To Danny's shock, what Beau said proved to be the truth. Everyone became excited, and she could see a new respect in their eyes. The fact that she'd dressed like a man made no difference to them. Beau had also taught her a lesson. Being yourself wasn't all wrong. He stood back and let her enjoy her belated glory.

"Well, little lady," Buck said, "would you be interested in selling the mare?"

Danny looked at Beau. "Is she really mine?"

Beau nodded. "You even have witnesses," he said, smiling.

She looked at Buck. "Nothing could convince me to sell her. A gift is something to be cherished." Her amber-brown eyes sparkled with happiness.

The people laughed and shook their head in agreement. Within a half hour, everyone had left.

As Beau took Sheeka back to her stall, Andrea and Danny turned to go in the house and saw Margaret blocking the doorway.

"Such a touching little scene," Margaret said with a sneer. "What other gifts do you plan on receiving from Beau for being his . . . *little sister*?"

Danny almost stopped breathing. Margaret knows! she thought.

"You've been drinking," Andrea accused.

"Yes." Margaret moved away from the doorway to let the two women enter, and followed them into the salon. "While you were all saying sweet goodbyes, I availed myself of your excellent brandy." She sat down on the sofa.

"I think I'll go thank Beau for giving me the mare," Danny said, edging toward the door.

"Oh, do," Margaret said. "And make sure you do it properly."

"I think you've said enough, Margaret!" Andrea warned.

The three woman looked toward the entrance and saw Beau standing there.

Margaret's snide expression immediately changed to a look of pleasure. "Darling. I do believe I've had too much to drink. I'm not even sure I can make it to my room. Could you please help me?"

Beau walked over and helped her up. When they had left, Danny stomped out of the room and headed for the courtyard, heedless of what Andrea might think. All Margaret has to do is say something, she thought, and Beau comes running!

As they reached the door to her room, Margaret seemed to sober up. Beau watched her green eyes momentarily become sad.

"Beau, would you please come into my room? I think we should have a talk."

"I agree."

Beau opened the door and let her enter first. Sara sat in a chair, her fingers busily embroidering a piece of material circled with a wooden hoop. Her welcoming smile disappeared when Sara saw Beau. Picking up her basket of thread, she silently left the room.

As Margaret sat in the chair smoothing her skirt out in a fashionable manner, Beau made himself comfortable on the sofa, resting one arm across the back.

Finally, Margaret looked up at him. "It's over, isn't it Beau?" she asked.

"It never started."

Margaret winced at his unfeeling words. "Did you ever consider marrying me?"

"You know the relationship we had was never predicated on the possibility of marriage. It was your choice to come here, not—"

"I know, you needn't remind me. Just what is your relationship with Danny?"

"I don't know what you're talking about."

"Don't try to fool someone who's been around the horn, Beau. I saw you in the stable the night of the barbecue."

"So?"

"You are one of the coldest men I have ever met. You sit there after I say I know what's going on, and you don't even bat an eyelash. I found out at the barbecue you're half savage. Many a night I wondered why you were so different from other men. Never having known an Indian before, I can only assume that's what it is." Margaret paused and smiled. "You're not going to answer my question, are you?"

"No."

"Why did you turn to her when you had me, Beau?" Margaret asked bitterly.

"We had our time together, Margaret. Why even bring up such questions? It's over."

"And you want me to leave, don't you?"

"Yes. Staying serves no purpose. I won't be returning to your bed."

A low guttural sound escaped as Margaret jumped up and headed toward Beau, her long nails extended. "You bastard!" she screamed.

Anticipating her action, Beau stood and clenched his hands around her wrists, easily holding her at bay. "Can't you be more original than that, Margaret? You're not the first woman that has used those words, and probably not the last." He turned her loose and watched her fall back into the chair. "Now that we understand each other, I don't believe we have anything more to talk about. You should be packed and ready to leave by Saturday. I'll make arrangements for one of the men to drive you and Sara to Prescott, and see to your transportation back east. I'm fixing to head out to one of the line shacks and will be gone for several days. I'll be back late Friday night so I can see you off Saturday." He left the room.

Beau walked down the narrow hall and saw his sister heading toward the kitchen.

"Andrea."

Andrea stopped and waited for her brother to join her. "Is Margaret feeling all right?" she inquired.

"Yes, she's fine." He smiled down at his sister. "You'll be happy to know Margaret's leaving."

Andrea tried to contain her joy, but failed miserably. "When?"

"Saturday. You might want to send a couple of girls to help her pack."

"I'll take care of it right away."

"Oh, and something else. I'm riding out with Armando and Charly to the line shack at the northeast corner. I won't be back until late Friday night."

"But you can't leave," Andrea blurted out.

"Why not? Is anything wrong?"

"No...I just thought you'd want to spend the time with Margaret." And Danny is leaving Friday morning, she thought.

"I've already said my farewell. Where is Danny?"

"I don't know, she left the salon right after you did. She seemed to be angry about something."

Beau chuckled. "She'll feel better after Margaret's gone. When you see Danny, tell her where I've gone and when I'll be back. All right?"

"Don't you want to tell her yourself?"

"I haven't the time. We're already leaving later than planned. If I don't see you Friday night, I'll see you Saturday." He leaned down and kissed her on the cheek. "Now you be a good girl," he teased.

Andrea watched her tall, broad-shouldered brother leave. After Margaret's departure, she would have to tell Beau the truth about Danny. She wasn't looking forward to his reaction. She let out a tired sigh. Maybe it's a good thing he won't be here when Danny leaves, she told herself.

Danny didn't take the news of Beau's departure well. Why couldn't he have told her personally? At least he owed her that much! Even the news that Margaret was leaving didn't cheer her up.

On the other hand, when Margaret found out Danny would also be going, she broke out laughing. Beau's little bedmate would not be here when he returned, which served him right. She still wanted to pay them back for making a fool of her, but couldn't think of a way to get even.

Early Thursday morning, after Danny and Andrea took off for town, Margaret decided to go for a ride. Sara and two other women were busy finishing the packing, and she had no desire to sit around doing nothing. Smoky was nowhere in sight when she entered the large stable, and Adam saddled a horse for her. When she returned Smoky hurried over to help her down.

"I hear you're leaving," Smoky said after she'd dismounted. "I hate to see you go. You're the only nice person around here. If anyone goes, it should be that redheaded tart!"

Smoky immediately had Margaret's attention. "But she is leaving. Tomorrow, as a matter of fact."

"Good riddance, I say." He spit a wad of juice into a can. "She's already caused me a bundle of trouble."

"You don't like her?"

"No, ma'am. I suppose it's all right to say that now."

Smoky tied the end of the reins to a rail, then removed the sidesaddle.

Margaret followed him to the tack room. "How did she get you in trouble?"

"It was all over that mare. I thought I was doing her a favor, and I ended up getting the blame. That damn half-breed—" Smoky suddenly realized his slip of tongue.

"So! You don't like Beau either."

"Now I didn't say that," Smoky said nervously.

"It's all right. I won't tell anyone what you said. We are of a kindred spirit, Smoky. I would love nothing more than to get even with the both of them."

"You're jokin'."

"No, I'm not." Margaret sat down on an old chair, making herself comfortable. A plan was beginning to formulate in her mind. Straightening her jacket, she let her hands slide seductively over her breasts. She smiled as she saw Smoky's reaction. "I'm sure we can be of great help to one another. You could make yourself a great deal of money, plus . . . other pleasures."

"What is it you want me to do?" Smoky had trouble getting the words out, and his breathing had become heavy.

"I want you to chase Mescal off Friday night after Beau returns."

"What? Falkner would break my neck! I'm not that crazy a fool!"

Margaret unbuttoned the front of her jacket far enough so he could see the beginning of her creamy, firm breasts, and began fanning herself. "My, it's hot in here."

Smoky looked out the door to make sure no one was around. He removed his hat and wiped the sweat from his forehead.

"Maybe I misunderstood," Margaret said as she stood. She now knew exactly how to get Smoky to do what she wanted. "I thought you disliked Beau and Danny as much as I do," she finished in a disgusted tone.

"I don't like either of them, and I don't like no half-breed telling me what to do. But I have to look after my own hide."

"But who would suspect if you left Danny's glove by the stall?" She watched Smoky's eyes light up as he absorbed what she had said.

Margaret decided to add fuel to the fire. "Besides, no one would know the horse was gone until Saturday. With Danny leaving Friday, they'll have no choice but to suspect her."

"Damn, I'd live to get rid of that beast. He's always trying to bite me!"

"I hate the horse as much as you do. Some good lashings is what he needs. If you do the job properly, I'm sure Mescal will never return."

Smoky grinned, thinking of the pleasure he'd receive getting back at the crazy animal as well as Falkner and Danny. "You said you'd pay me plus . . . other rewards?"

"When the job's done, I'll come to your room."

"But you're leaving," he said suspiciously.

"Not until Monday morning," she lied. "That will give us two whole nights together. Believe me, Smoky, you have no idea how pleasurable your nights will be." She watched the look of hunger enter his eyes. "Don't give me an answer now. Think on it. Saturday morning I'll know what you decided."

Margaret left, her step jaunty. I've found the solution to everything, she thought. There's no doubt in my mind that Smoky will drive away Beau's pride and joy, Mescal. I've also managed to take care of that witch Danny. Of course I have no intention of paying Smoky. After all, what can he do about it? If he says anything, he'll be putting his own neck in a noose.

Chapter Thirteen

The bay gelding moved at a crisp pace with Andrea expertly handling the reins. They were following what Danny considered a poor resemblance to a road, but the springs kept the ride relatively smooth. A small smattering of white puffy clouds cast shadows over the land, making it look as though areas had been burned by fire.

They were headed to Prescott to introduce Danny to the town and the local merchants she would soon be doing business with.

As they traveled across the large valley, Andrea gave Danny a brief history of the area, explaining that in 1863 Arizona had officially become a United States territory, with Prescott as its capital. Unfortunately, in 1867 the capital had been moved to Tucson.

"Because of all the miners' lean-tos and shanties that lined Granite Creek, Prescott used to be called Granite City," she continued, wondering if she sounded like a schoolteacher giving a history lesson. "The town was named in honor of William Hickling Prescott, a great historian. Father told the story over and over how in sixty-four, they had a community meeting at Manuel Yseria's store to select a name for the new settlement and lay out the town site. He was so proud to have been a part of that."

"I can certainly understand why. Dusty Creek was the only settlement I ever knew," Danny said, "and that's not much to brag about. When we first rode into Santa Fe I couldn't believe there were such big towns in existence. My head kept turning from one side to the other, afraid I might miss something."

"I've enjoyed watching Prescott grow. It's too bad it's been tarnished by places like Whiskey Row, the cribs and bordellos. Maybe someday those will be gone and we'll have a fine upstanding town we can be proud of."

"All towns have those kinds of places, Andrea. How else are the wranglers going to let off steam? In fact Jed and I have had some fine times in saloons." Because Andrea never acted as judge or jury, over the last couple of days Danny had found herself telling her more and more about her life before coming to the ranch. In fact, Andrea had laughed a great deal at the different fixes she and Jed had gotten themselves into.

"Jed sounds like such an interesting character," Andrea commented, "I'm looking forward to meeting him."

"He's a good man," Danny said, a bit misty-eyed. "I'll be glad to see him tomorrow."

When they reached the town, it was larger than Danny had expected. Carr's Freight Team had just pulled in with a new group of settlers. Andrea parked the buggy in front of the Pioneer drugstore.

The day passed quickly, with Danny meeting merchants and checking out the various goods for sale. Although she didn't remember most of the people, they certainly remembered her. Word had spread quickly, and everyone seemed to know she was the other rider in the horse race. That, coupled with her shooting ability and beauty, had made her a celebrity in the town's eyes. Several store owners said there had even been an article about her in the *Miner*, the town newspaper. The people had definitely taken her to their hearts.

But her biggest shock came from Andrea. Andrea introduced her as Danny Jameson, owner of the Silver J. Danny's heart jumped with joy at finally being able to acknowledge her true identity, but she didn't understand why the proprietors gave her strange looks. She learned just how quickly word travels in a small town when, upon entering C.P. Head and Company, the owner called her Miss Jameson.

They had just returned to the buggy when Danny spied Garret Beckman headed in their direction, a broad smile on his face.

"Ladies," he greeted them. "I heard you were in town."

Andrea's forehead creased into a frown, showing her distaste for the man.

"Before you take off," Garret said, "may I have the pleasure of buying you ladies something to eat, or at least a sarsaparilla?"

"I'm afraid not, Mr. Beckman," Andrea spoke up. "We have a long drive, and need to be heading back." Andrea made a move to get in the buggy, and Garret was immediately by her side helping her in. He walked to the other side and did the same for Danny.

"Perhaps some other time," he said in a pleasant enough voice. "If the gossip is correct," he said to Danny, "I understand you are the elusive owner of the Silver J ranch."

"Yes." She beamed with pride.

"And you're still staying with the Falkners?" he asked, raising an eyebrow.

He's acting strange, too, she thought. "I'm leaving tomorrow," she replied.

"Oh. I'll ride out in a couple of weeks and see how you're getting along, if that's agreeable with you."

"I'm sure she's going to have her hands full for some time to come," Andrea snapped. Lifting the reins, she moved the bay forward.

Garret watched the buggy take off in a cloud of dust. What a strange turn of events, he thought. Did Danny know the Silver J was a thorn in Falkner's side? Considering how close the two women seemed to be, he doubted it. He'd make a point of paying Miss Jameson a visit. Maybe he should even give marriage some consideration. Marrying her could reap all sorts of benefits. He laughed, thinking about the uppity Falkners' reaction to such a union.

As soon as they were out of town, Danny turned crossly to Andrea. "I can't believe you, of all people, treated Garret like that. You have always said everyone is welcome in your home!"

"Danny, in some ways you are so naive. I admit he is very handsome, and suave, but he's also very dishonest. Good looks and gentlemanly manners don't always add up to a good man."

"I can't believe this. You're acting just like Beau. Honestly, Andrea, I never thought you were such a snob. Just because he owns a saloon doesn't—"

"And several bordellos."

"And a ranch."

"And hires paid gunmen to run it."

Danny's anger suddenly disappeared. "Well," she said, still trying to defend the man, "maybe he feels the need to protect his land."

"What land? A few scrubby acres that aren't even good to run stock on? Even if he could, I doubt that he would. Ranching is a lot of hard work, and he prefers to make money the easy way. I understand that in his saloon there is a huge crystal chandelier he had shipped in all the way from San Francisco, and his clothes come from there, as well. There is no question that he has money. The question is, where does he get it? Certainly not from that small saloon he owns."

Danny felt like a fool. "I'm sorry, Andrea, I didn't realize. You certainly know more about him than I do. And I shouldn't have called you a snob."

Andrea reached over and patted her leg. "Don't worry, I'm not mad. All women are susceptible to handsome men, but as you get older you learn to weed the bad from the good."

"But he can't be all bad. Everyone has some redeeming qualities."

"Most people, yes, but I don't think Garret Beckman is one of them. I'm usually a pretty good judge of character, and I believe that man is bad to the core."

They continued on for some distance in silence, both deep in thought. Danny suffered from mixed emotions. She wanted to go to the Silver J and Jed, but she didn't want to leave Beau. She lived for the times he made love to her, but she hated the ability he had to turn her to jelly with just a glance. She could refuse him nothing. The only possible way she could break his spell would be not to see him, at least until she got him out of her blood. The Silver J and Jed would be her salvation.

Andrea finally quit brooding over Garret. Instead, she thought about Danny and the trouble between the two ranches. She was tempted to tell the girl everything, but whatever she said in the Falkners' defense, Danny would take all wrong once she went home and heard Jed's side of the story. No matter what happened, Andrea was determined not to let their friendship fall by the wayside. In a few weeks, she had every intention of paying a visit to her neighbor.

At dinner that night, the two women ate alone, Margaret choosing to have her meal in her room. Their conversation remained light, neither wanting to discuss Danny's departure in the morning. Andrea did however, tell her how to reach her ranch.

Danny's excitement started to build. Suddenly it was all she could think about. She hated leaving all the pretty dresses behind, but felt guilty about taking them with her. It seemed only fair she leave with the clothes she'd arrived in. Not wanting to be barefooted, however, she decided to take the boots, along with a hat, her book, *The Young Housekeeper's Friend*, and Sheeka. After all, she excused herself, I have to have a horse, I can't walk all the way.

As the sky turned from black to gray, she put her clothes on and left her room. A note sat on the dressing table with Andrea's name written on the front of it. Crossing the narrow hall, she opened the French doors and walked out of the house for the last time.

Jessy and Adam were already giving the horses their morning hay, and Danny felt guilty for not allowing Sheeka to finish, but she was in a hurry to leave. She was taking the coward's way out. She didn't want any tearful goodbyes.

"Good morning," Jessy greeted her, showing no surprise at her clothing. "You taking Sheeka out?"

"Yes," Danny replied.

"Wait right here and I'll get a bridle and rug." He laughed. "I don't suppose you want a saddle."

With Jessy's open friendliness, Danny suddenly felt in the best of spirits. She gave him a broad smile. "No, we haven't gotten to that point yet."

As soon as Jessy had the mare ready, Danny placed her foot in his cupped hands and he boosted her up.

"Thank you, Jessy," she said, settling herself on top of the mare. "It's too bad you're not running the stable. You'd do a lot better than that no-account, Smoky."

Danny headed Sheeka toward the door. "See ya, Jessy," she called as she rode out.

"Mother in heaven," Carlotta said, making the sign of the cross. "Are you going to just sit in the house all day, Jed? You don't even know for sure when she's coming."

"She's bound to be here today."

"You said that yesterday."

Jed went to the open front door and squinted his eyes. He looked over the land for some sort of movement that would indicate Danny was on her way, but saw nothing. He wasn't sure if she'd be riding, walking or what. "Damn," he muttered, "I can't just stand around waitin'. I gotta do somethin' to make the time go by faster!"

He crossed the porch and went down the rickety stairs. I'll go see how the boys are coming along with the bunkhouse, he thought.

When she spied the ramshackle abode, it didn't occur to Danny that this was her new home. The place wasn't much larger than a lean-to and seemed to be falling apart, and the several smaller buildings in the rear were in similar condition. A small curl of smoke came from the chimney, so someone had to be living there.

"Is anyone home?" she called as she brought Sheeka to a halt in front of the structure. A sound of shuffling feet came from inside, then a large woman appeared in the doorway.

"Danny?" the woman asked.

"Carlotta?"

"Blessed be the Lord. It is you!" Carlotta started laughing, causing her heavy frame to shake. "Heaven's sake, girl, Jed was right. You are all grown up, and just as pretty as a picture. Jed's going to be so happy to finally have you home!"

Home? Danny wondered. This was not the house she had pictured in her mind.

"Now you get down and come on in. I'll bet you're hungry. I have a fresh batch of stew already made."

Danny slid off the mare's back and tied the reins to the hitching rail. Slowly she climbed the stairs and walked across the porch, making sure she didn't step in the holes.

"Where in the world did you get that horse?" Carlotta asked. "I've never seen anything like her before. Did you steal her?"

"No, she was given to me," Danny answered absentmindedly. As she entered the house, her eyes took in everything, from the dirty floor to the greasy pots hanging from the fireplace. She brushed the food off the seat of the hard-backed chair before sitting down. My God, she thought, is this how we used to live? No. Even their small place at Dusty Creek had been kept cleaner than this!

Carlotta wobbled over, and with her forearm, swept off a space on the table to set a bowl of stew. Some of the metal cups fell to the floor, but she made no effort to pick them up.

"Eat up, *querida*, you need to put some meat on those bones of yours," Carlotta said, sitting across from her.

Danny looked down at what had been placed before her and thought she would be sick. All she could see was grease floating on top of water.

"I'm really not hungry."

She was saved from having to make another comment when Jed came bounding in.

Seeing her beloved pa, she jumped up and ran to him. Jed threw his big arms around her in a crushing hug, but she didn't care. They both had tears in their eyes when they finally pulled apart.

"I thought I'd lost you," Jed said, making no effort to wipe the tears away.

"Well, I'm here to stay, Pa."

"I sure have missed you. I want to hear everythin' that's happened since I last saw you."

They sat down, and for the rest of the morning Danny told her story, with the exception of her relationship with Beau. Jed didn't even notice the creaking chair as Carlotta rocked back and forth.

"Well, I'll be damned," Jed said when she finished. "I ain't never heard of such a thing. All this time you been close, and it was that young Falkner who had you! He'd better never set foot on this land, or I'll break his neck. I been wantin' to do it for a long time anyway. How come that Andrea treated you so nice after you got to the ranch?"

"She's a nice person, Pa, you'd like her."

"She's a Falkner, and I wouldn't put any trust in anything she did!" Carlotta interjected.

Danny found it interesting that for such a big woman, Carlotta had a high-pitched voice and sounded almost like a little girl.

"Did she say anything about the trouble we been havin' with them?" Jed asked.

"No," Danny said, surprised. "What trouble?"

Jed let out a snort. "For years the ol' man ran his cattle across this land, usin' the grass and water. Jose tried to stop him, and I guess at one time they almost exchanged shots. Jose couldn't stand up against all the men the old man had workin' for him, so he had to back off. When I come here, they was still doin' the same thing."

"Why? They have plenty of land."

"Ol' Gerard bought up everything 'ceptin this place." Jed frowned. "His land surrounds us. It was a hell of a lot easier to get from one place to the other by cutting across our land. 'Sides, we got more water, and they want it."

"That old man Falkner." Carlotta pulled out a cross hidden in her blouse. "God rest his soul, he tried every way he could to either run us off or buy your land. He was a mean man, and furious at Jose for bucking him. More than once I thought Falkner was going to do away with my Jose. I never knew when he left of a morning if he'd be back."

"Well, we don't have to worry now, Gerard is dead," Danny said, trying to sound cheerful. She leaned back and stretched her legs, feeling weary from last night's lack of sleep.

Jed pulled a pouch of tobacco and papers from his pocket and rolled himself a cigarette. "Young Falkner sent a note a couple of weeks ago sayin' he wasn't gonna let any more of his cattle on our range, and so far he's stuck to it. But I think he's stallin' for time."

"Why do you say that, Jed?" Danny asked.

"Just a gut feelin' I got."

"How are our cattle doing?"

"What cattle?" Smoke curled from Jed's nostrils.

"Are you telling me we don't have any cattle?" Danny gasped.

"Only about five hundred head, and the only reason we got them is 'cause Jose kept 'em out of reach."

Danny's back became rigid. "They stole our cattle?"

"Not exactly," Jed said, his voice a bit strained. "Seems as the herd grew, Jose wasn't able to brand or round up all the calves."

"Wasn't his fault," Carlotta said in Jose's defense. "A man can only do so much work."

"Why didn't he hire more men?" Danny asked. "You certainly sent him enough money."

"Apparently," Jed replied, "Jose didn't think of that until it was too late. We told him to buy cattle, and by damn that's what he did."

"So what happened to all the cattle he bought?" Danny was confused.

Jed flicked his cigarette butt on the floor and ground it out with the heel of his grubby-looking boot. "Well, when ol' man Falkner's men drove his big herds across the land, our cattle joined in. Next thing Jose knew, our stock was down to nothin'."

Danny shook her head in disbelief. "Are you telling me that all those cattle now belong to the Falkners?"

"That's what I'm tellin' you."

"All right," she said, trying to get over her shock and think rationally. "All we have to do is show them our purchase records and demand the cattle back. It's been too many years to hope for all the calves, but at least we can get what we bought."

"That there's another problem. Jose didn't keep no records."

"What?"

"You're not being fair to Jose," Carlotta said, again jumping to her husband's defense. "How was he supposed to know to keep them bills of sale? He bought the cattle for you, and as far he was concerned, that's who owned them. He didn't know they'd stray off with Falkner's herd."

Danny looked at Carlotta in total disbelief. Then she realized, had she not learned so much by listening to the discussions between Andrea and Beau about cattle, she may have felt the same way. But she'd damn sure have kept the receipts!

"Are the cattle we do have branded?" she asked.

"I hired a couple of hands, and they've taken care of it. We got a bunkhouse started, too. If we hire on more men, they're gonna need a place to stay."

"As I see it," Danny said, tipping her chair back, "the Falkners owe us some cattle."

"And we'll play hell gettin' 'em," Jed said angrily.

"Well, we won't know until we try. Let's give it a month, then I'll pay Beau a visit and ask for what's rightfully ours." Danny glanced around the room. "How are we fixed for money, Jed?"

"We're in good shape. I still got most of the money from the mine. Only bought some wood, a buckboard, plus a couple of plugs to pull it."

"If I remember right, wasn't Jose a good hand with horses, Carlotta?"

"The best there is," Carlotta spoke up. "He knows them better than he knows cattle, and there's not much he don't know about cattle."

Danny winced. From what she'd been hearing about Jose's knowledge of cattle, she wasn't too sure she should put Sheeka in the man's hands.

"What you got on your mind, Danny?"

"I have a mare outside that's led a rather pampered life. For tonight I'll put her in one of those shacks out back, but I want to be sure she's well fed. I thought we might get Jose to look after her."

Carlotta spoke up. "He's always dreamed of having a horse like that."

Danny laughed. "If I don't see him before you do, be sure and tell him not to try and ride her or he'll find himself eating dirt. I want a stall for her and her own paddock. Have those two new hands got a place to sleep?"

"Yep," Jed replied. "They're sleepin' in the part of the bunkhouse we already finished."

"I think we should forget about the bunkhouse for now. With so few cattle, I doubt that we'll be hiring any extra hands soon. What we need to do is fix up this house before it falls to the ground, and put up some barns. Winter is going to be on us before we know it."

"What's wrong with this place," asked Jed, "'sides needing a good cleanin'?"

"Where does everyone sleep?"

"Jose and Carlotta use the back room, and I sleep in here on the floor."

"So now there will be two of us sleeping in here, and there isn't that much room. Believe me, Jed, when I'm finished, you're going to be much happier with the arrangement."

Shortly after midnight, Smoky held the lantern high so he could take a good look around. After making sure there would be no witnesses, he walked toward Mescal's stall. He laughed when the big stallion snorted his dislike, and laughed even harder as the horse leaned out and tried to bite him.

"Oh, how I'm going to enjoy this, my big friend."

Hanging the lantern on a nail, he removed the bullwhip from his shoulder and let it uncoil onto the ground. Raising the handle, he snapped it in the air. A thrill of anticipation shot through him at the loud crack. The other horses in the stable became uneasy and started moving around in their stalls.

"I've waited too long. You've needed this ever since Falkner brought you here." He lifted the whip again and let the frayed end strike Mescal across the head. The big stallion screamed. Smoky repeated the action several more times, not wanting to quit, enjoying his power over the big, helpless animal.

When the horse moved to the back of the stall, trying to escape the lash, Smoky quickly unlatched the door. Stepping back, he grabbed the pitchfork in his left hand and waited. "Come to me," he said, chuckling.

As Mescal bolted out, he struck the stallion with the whip, delighted at seeing blood continue to creep over the satiny black coat. Mescal charged. Laughing wildly, Smoky lifted the pitchfork and jabbed the stallion in the chest, causing the horse to move back. "How did that feel, my lovely?"

"What the hell's goin' on here? You gone nuts?"

Smoky looked toward the entrance where Charly stood. As Mescal bolted toward freedom, the man jumped back, just in time to miss being hit by the stallion as he galloped past out of the stable.

Still feeling the exhilaration of power and danger, Smoky ran forward. When Charly reentered the stable cussing, Smoky raised the whip and let it curl around Charly's neck. With a sharp pull, he jerked the cowhand to the ground.

Sudden fear gripped Smoky as he came to his senses and realized what he'd done. Blood had started to cover the floor, and Charly's head lay twisted on his shoulders. Smoky knew he was dead; the broken neck told it all. Smoky stood there in a daze, suddenly not sure what to do. How would he get rid of the body? Forcing himself to think, he dropped the whip, then grabbed the man by the feet and dragged him outside, just past the brick flooring. After looking to be sure there was no one else around, he hurried inside, picked up the bullwhip and made straight for the lantern. It took only a few minutes to mop up the blood from the floor, and even less time to hide the rags and hang the bullwhip in the tack room. He went outside and lifted the lantern. Upon seeing Mescal's hoof prints beside Charly's body, he chuckled. Everyone would think the horse killed him.

"You damn Indian lover," he said, spitting juice on the ground. "Serves you right."

Smoky started to return to his room when he suddenly remembered what Margaret had given him earlier. Removing Danny's glove from his hip pocket, he placed it by Mescal's stall. Convinced everything looked right, he left the stable.

Chapter Fourteen

Everyone at the ranch attended the funeral. The service was brief, with Beau reading scriptures from the Bible and saying his own personal farewell to Charly.

Smoky paid scant attention to the words. He thought about how he had stayed up most of the night anticipating Margaret's promise of money and favors. He didn't realize he'd been tricked until he found out Margaret had left the ranch early this morning. Ever since their talk, he'd had all kinds of visions of her beneath him, writhing with desire and begging for more. But that would never happen now, and there wasn't a damn thing he could do about it. Well, he thought, trying to look on the brighter side, the damn horse is gone. Everyone thinks Danny turned Mescal loose, and that the horse killed the cowpoke. No one suspects me, and I still have an easy job with good pay.

Andrea returned to her buggy. Waiting for Beau to join her, she sat twisting her hands, deeply worried, and thinking about what had transpired on this worst of days.

She still flinched from the horror she'd felt when Jessy awoke them early this morning with the news of the cowhand's death. Beau had quickly thrown on some pants and rushed out. Not since they'd left Colorado Territory had he looked as frightening as he did when he returned to the house. Then he informed her that Danny's glove had been found by the stall, and Andrea had done everything she could to try to convince him of the girl's innocence. She'd even pointed out how much Danny had cared for Mescal.

"Then why did she take off, and why hasn't she returned?" he quietly demanded.

Andrea hadn't had a chance to explain because Beau had spun away, saying he was going to his room to finish dressing. She didn't see him again until just before the funeral. Beau did, however, send Armando to tell her the burial would be held that afternoon. Andrea had been shocked that the funeral would take place so soon and that there wouldn't be time to bring in a preacher. Armando told her he'd tried to change Beau's mind, but Beau had been adamant.

Beau finally climbed in the buggy. Picking up the reins, he guided the horses away from the cemetery. Not a flicker of emotion showed on his face.

Beau went into the house without saying a word. Andrea followed right behind, desperate to convince him of Danny's innocence.

"Beau! You have to listen to me!" she insisted.

Finally he stopped and faced her. "All right, Andrea," he said in a soft, cold tone, "what do you want to talk about?"

"Could we please sit down?"

"Very well. Let's go to the study. I could use a drink."

When they entered the large room, Beau picked up the whiskey decanter and a glass, then sat behind the big, imposing desk. After pouring himself a healthy shot, he leaned back and looked at her. "What do you want to talk about?"

His eyes were cold. Taking a deep breath, Andrea said, "Beau, Danny is not guilty of this crime! I know this with every fiber of my being. You can't accuse her just because of a glove. Anyone could have placed it there."

"Why did she go, Andrea? You know, so you might as well tell me now, before I leave."

"Leave? Where are you going?"

"To get Mescal."

Even though his eyes were blue ice and his face still expressionless, Andrea's heart went out to him. "Oh, Beau, do you think you should? Can't you let someone else shoot him?"

"I'm not going to kill him, Andrea, I'm going to bring him back home."

"But he's a man killer."

"The horse isn't guilty, it's the person who turned him loose," he said quietly, his eyes never leaving hers. "Now, back to my original question. Why did Danny leave?"

Andrea shifted uncomfortably. She hadn't wanted to tell Beau about Danny under these circumstances, but now she had no choice. "Because her time was up," she whispered.

Beau took a drink of whiskey but said nothing, waiting for his sister to tell him what he wanted to know.

"I have to begin from when you first brought her here." Andrea proceeded to tell him what had taken place. As she revealed Danny's true identity, Andrea expected to see a look of surprise on Beau's face, but not even a muscle twitched. When she finished, Beau continued to sit and stare at her.

"Aren't you going to say anything?" Andrea asked nervously.

"What's there to say?"

"You could at least yell at me or something!" Andrea said frantically. "I don't care what you do, but do something! Beau, you must have feelings about this. Don't just sit there! Don't draw yourself away from your feelings, please," she pleaded. "Don't go back to the person I knew seven years ago. Talk to me, Beau, damn it!"

Still he remained expressionless. "Oh I have feelings, Andrea, but I'm not too sure you would like me to tell you what they are." He stood up. "Are we through talking?"

"Yes," she said meekly.

"I'm not angry with you, Andrea, you did what you thought best. I'll be leaving before dawn, and I don't know how long I'll be gone. There was blood in Mescal's stall and I'm not sure what condition he's in or how long it will take to find him. Don't expect me back until you see me." He left the room.

Tears came to Andrea's eyes. "Oh, please, Beau," she muttered, "don't go back to the cold person you used to be."

"Get up, Smoky."

Smoky woke with a start and jerked to a sitting position. It took a moment for his eyes to adjust to the dark. A tall man dressed only in buckskin pants was standing by the bed, his hard-muscled body depicting great strength. Smoky finally recognized the man.

"Oh, Mr. Falkner. You startled me. What can I do for you? Is something wrong?"

"No, nothing's wrong, I just want you to go somewhere with me."

"Sure, Mr. Falkner, let me just slip my clothes on."

"Let's go, Smoky," Beau said after Smoky had dressed. "I'm in a hurry. We'll go out the back way."

The fresh air brought Smoky fully awake. Though the sun hadn't quite made its appearance yet, he could clearly see the two saddled horses. His first instinct was to run. What am I worried about? he asked himself. Falkner doesn't know anything about what I did. He thinks Danny's guilty.

"Where are we going?" Smoky tried to sound friendly.

"I'm not good at following a trail and I want to find Mescal as soon as possible. Since you know so much about horses, I thought we'd ride out a ways and you could help me try and locate Mescal's tracks."

"I can sure do that," Smoky said, mounting the horse Falkner pointed out to him. "His left hind shoe has a crack in it, and I was planning on telling you to take him to the blacksmith to have it fixed." Actually, it had been Jessy that told him about the shoe. "I'm real good at tracking, and that stallion has a definite hoofprint."

"Good. I'll follow you," Beau said, getting on his horse.

Smoky suppressed the laughter that had started bubbling up inside. If he helped Falkner find the stallion, Falkner would be impressed. It could possibly mean more money in his pay envelope. This had turned out far better than he'd ever anticipated. Turning the horse, he headed off in a southerly direction.

Beau and Smoky were in the flatlands. Cholla cactus, with its spiny cylindrical stems, a frequent pest on cattle land, grew in abundance in the stony earth. Smoky mopped off the sweat that rolled down his face, caused by the relentless sun. He couldn't understand how Falkner remained so cool.

"Looks like he's headed for the river," Smoky said. During the entire trip, Falkner hadn't said two words, and the man's silence was like an itch in the middle of Smoky's back that couldn't be reached. "I'm sure ready for a drink myself!"

In some places cottonwood trees lined the riverbank, and Smoky headed straight for them, welcoming any kind of shade, no matter how small. Looking down at the water, he quickly dismounted. He hadn't taken two steps when a rope suddenly circled his body. Before he could do anything, the rope was looped around him several more times.

"What the hell you doing?" he yelled as Beau knocked him to the ground and rolled him onto his stomach. Feeling his feet being tied and his boots removed, fear leaped into Smoky's soul. The rope burned and cut his arms when they were jerked back and secured.

Beau rolled Smoky over onto his back and sat him up. After removing the lariat, Beau pulled out a knife and deftly cut away the clothes, leaving the man naked.

Smoky, gripped by panic, tried scooting away but felt himself being lifted up, like he was nothing more than a rag doll, and tied to one of the trees. "Have you lost your mind, Falkner?" Smoky hollered. All he received in reply was an unmasked look of loathing.

Smoky tried frantically to get loose, his mind registering nothing but inexpressible fear. Almost mesmerized, he watched Falkner pull a hatchet from his saddlebag and chop off a thick limb. Cutting it in two, he pounded the stakes into the ground, then walked over to where two tall, sturdy saplings stood close together. Using the lariat, he pulled the top of one down and secured it to a stake, then did the same with the second one. Smoky's fear rose in his throat, a hot, bitter taste choking him until he felt as if he'd retch. In the next instant he started vomiting. He knew what was going to happen to him.

By the time Smoky felt himself being untied from the tree, he had the dry heaves. He tried fighting, even though it was useless. Thrown to the ground, he felt his wrists being untied, then each one secured to the end of a sapling. Smoky started screaming, and his heart pounded in his chest. "Oh, God, don't do it!"

Smoky heard the snap of the rope being cut before he felt his body jerked up in the air. Excruciating pain shot through his shoulders as his arms were practically pulled from the sockets. He passed out.

When Smoky came to, the ache in his arms was unbearable. His legs had been spread apart and tied to the saplings. He groaned in agony.

"Did you really think you would get away with it, Smoky?"

Even though the sun's glare was in his eyes, Smoky could see the man standing below him. "I don't know what you're talking about." Because of the pain, he had trouble getting the words out. To admit his crime meant sure death. He had always been a clever man, and if he could convince Falkner of his innocence, he might get out of this.

"Why did you kill Charly, Smoky? Did he catch you beating Mescal?"

"I don't know what you mean," he groaned.

"Did you have to use the bullwhip on Charly, too?"

"Cut me down, Falkner, and let's talk about this. I think you've lost your mind. I had nothing to do with his death! It was that whore you were snuggling up to that did it. I saw you in the stable the night of the barbecue, and she's turned your head. My arms are killing me. Cut me down."

"Oh, no, Smoky, Danny had nothing to do with it. You did it all. You should clean your equipment better. Mescal's blood was still on your whip."

"Think about it, Falkner. Why would I want to do such a thing like that? What did I have to gain?"

"I don't know, but I'm going to find out."

"I'm innocent, damn it! I don't know what makes you think it was me." Sweat dripped off his body.

"I think you should change your brand of chew," Beau said in a cold, clipped voice. "You left your trademark on the ground beside Charly, along with your footprints, which told the whole story."

Even though the heat remained unbearable, Smoky felt a cold chill. All he could do was try to bluff his way out. "Probably because I was out there that afternoon. I'm innocent, I tell you. None of that is proof!"

"You forget, Smoky, I'm half Indian. The sun would have weakened the smell."

"I tell you, I'm an innocent man. No one's going to believe I killed him."

"I do, and that's all that matters."

Beau turned, walked to his horse and climbed onto the saddle. He leaned down and gathered up the reins of Smoky's mount. "How did you know what direction Mescal went, Smoky?"

"Falkner! You can't leave me here to die!" Smoky started panicking and yelling as Beau nudged the horse forward. "You damn Indian bastard . . . you can't leave me here. It was an accident. Your whore Margaret put me up to it!"

"You have been avenged, Charly," Beau whispered as he rode out of sight.

In the two months Danny had been home, great changes had taken place. Everyone went around grumbling, but she remained steadfast in her determination. Jed couldn't understand why he had to shave every day and be constantly reminded not to say ain't. Carlotta didn't like being pushed into helping Danny clean the house; Jose was unhappy because Carlotta complained every night, and Clancy and Joe, the hired hands, felt they should be working cattle instead of building rooms onto the house and repairing it.

As the days passed, the house became spotless inside; the porch looked as good as new, and the outside had a new look. The buildings to the rear of the house had been brought up to proper condition, and Sheeka resided in her own stall. Even the chickens and pigs, which normally ran around the area freely and were always underfoot, had been rounded up and were contained in an area especially made for them.

Danny's energy seemed to be endless. If they hadn't know better, everyone would have sworn there were at least three of her. She appeared to be everywhere at once, checking to see that everything met her specifications. But she always had a smile on her face and a pat on the back for a job well done.

Carlotta couldn't really complain too loudly, because when she did the washing or cleaning, Danny worked right beside her. The washing had to be done in flour barrels. They didn't work as well as the large copper tubs used at the Falkner ranch, but they served the purpose.

She also taught Carlotta how to cook. Some of the receipts from *The Young Housekeeper's Friend* turned out badly, but it didn't bother Danny. She just turned around and tried another one. At least the men were happy with the change of menu.

They all cussed under their breath, sure that Danny was going to be the death of all of them. As if things weren't bad enough, she insisted the men bathe under the well pump and use soap, and their clothes had to be clean. They didn't take her seriously, but after having to go without supper a few times, they decided she meant business. At first Jed had balked, but after a few rounds with her temper, even he fell into line. Their eating habits also underwent a drastic change. Danny proceeded to teach them proper etiquette, and even gave them lessons.

When two of the three new rooms were completed, Danny had Jed bring in all her parents' things. She was anxious to discover more about her family.

Glancing over the items, she was amazed at how much could be carried in a covered wagon. There was practically everything needed to set up a household, including pots and pans, a coffee grinder, china, tableware and furniture.

After she had put everything away and the feather mattresses had been placed outside to air, she tackled the trunks. Opening the four trunks was like having Christmas in summer. Sitting cross-legged on the floor, she removed one thing at a time. The first two trunks contained mostly bedding. She wondered if her mother had sewn the quilts.

All the trunks reeked of camphor gum, which was tied up into small bundles and wrapped with bits of muslin, and of cedar chips. The two trunks of clothes proved to be Danny's favorite. Children's clothes as well as adult clothes were stored inside. It came as a shock when she realized the children's clothes must have been hers. "Oh, Mother," she whispered, "you must have looked forward so to your new life."

Danny examined the other clothes, and decided both her parents must have been small. Her father's shirts fit her quite well, and except for the larger waist, she could even wear the pants. She tried on different shoes, tickled to discover her feet were the same size as her mother's. Her mother's clothes were a bit small around the bust, as well as being too short, but they all had a good hem that could be let out. What really clutched her heart was the wedding dress at the bottom of the chest, wrapped carefully in paper. Feeling especially close to her parent at this moment, she picked up the diary she'd put in a safe place on the floor and tenderly ran her fingers over the rose velvet cover. "I won't read it now, Mother, I'll wait until the bed and dresser are set up, and we can be by ourselves." Tears started trickling down her cheeks.

Late the next morning, Danny was in the process of assembling her parents' bed when Carlotta came into the room. "Danny, Joe came by and said a buggy's headed this way."

Danny stood and brushed off her shirt and pants. They were her father's. She had spent most of yesterday washing and drying everything, happy to at last have a change of clothes. She'd thrown out her old pants and shirt. "Who would be coming here?" she asked.

"How would I know?"

The two women were standing on the front porch when Andrea drove up. "I thought I would pay you a neighborly visit," she said.

Danny didn't know whether to be angry or happy. But as she watched the slender, graceful woman climb down from the vehicle, she suddenly realized how much she'd missed her friend. Running down the stairs, she clasped Andrea in a warm embrace.

"Oh, it's so good to see you, Danny, you just don't know how much I've missed you."

Danny stepped back and started laughing. "Of all people, I certainly didn't expect you. Don't you know you're in enemy territory?"

A warm smile crossed Andrea's lovely face. "Why do you think I waited so long to come?"

"Carlotta, fix Miss Falkner something to drink. After her ride, I'm sure she's thirsty."

Andrea was used to being called Falkner and didn't bother to remind Danny her name was actually Windall.

Discovering who the woman was, Carlotta hackled and made the sign of the cross. "I wouldn't fix a Falkner anything!" She turned and went into the house.

"I'm sorry, Andrea," Danny apologized. "As you can tell, Carlotta isn't too fond of your family."

"It's nothing more than I expected, dear. I want you to know, I have no control over what's been going on between our ranches. My father wouldn't let me interfere, and now Beau's of the same mind. I can do the paperwork, but that's where it stops. Believe me, if I had had the power, I would have stopped this foolishness a long time ago. But whatever happens, I refuse to let it come between us. I don't want us to lose our friendship."

"I didn't realize it until you drove up, but I guess I feel the same way."

"I brought the clothes you left behind, and a special gift. Is there someone who can take it into the house?"

At that moment, Jed came bounding out of the house with a shotgun. Danny knew Carlotta had gone straight out the back door and headed directly for him.

Andrea was more than a bit taken aback at seeing the big man.

"Jed," Danny scolded, "put that gun down. I can assure you, Andrea isn't here to shoot up the place."

"What the hell is she doing here?"

"She came to pay me a visit, and I'm happy to see her! Now set the gun down and come help take the trunk she brought me into the house."

Amazed and amused, Andrea watched Jed set the butt of the shotgun on the porch and lean the barrel against the wall. She found it hard to believe such a little woman had so much control over this mountain of a man. So this is Jed, she thought. Now I can understand all the things Danny has told me about him.

"What trunk," Jed grumbled as he came down from the porch and joined them.

"It's on the back of the buggy," Andrea answered. "Also your surprise is back there, Danny. Come and I'll show you."

Danny screamed with joy the moment she saw the copper bathtub on top of the trunk.

"What's that?" Jed asked, curiosity taking over.

"You know, Jed," Danny replied, "I asked that very same question some time ago. That is a bathtub."

Jed untied the ropes holding the items. "Where am I supposed to put these?"

"In my room. I'll explain later. Come in, Andrea, I have a fresh pot of coffee made."

The moment Jed had put the trunk and tub in Danny's room, he went to the kitchen and sat down at the table with the women. He wasn't about to leave Danny alone with a Falkner, no matter how pretty.

After introducing the two, Danny proudly told Andrea of all the improvements they were making as she poured the coffee.

"Oh, Danny, I'm so pleased everything is going well for you," Andrea said.

"It's not anything like your place, but we're proud of it." She joined the other two at the table.

"The size of a house is of little importance. What matters is happiness. I could be perfectly happy in a house like this."

"I can't picture you wantin' to live in a place like this with all those fancy things you're used to," grumbled Jed.

"Why not?" Andrea came right back at him. "You have everything here, what makes it any different?"

Jed couldn't think of an answer.

"Haven't you kicked her out yet, Jed?"

They all looked at Carlotta standing in the doorway.

"I'll not have you talking to Miss Falkner that way," Danny said angrily. "Andrea has said, more than once, all are welcome in her home, and the same goes here! If you can't be civil to her, Carlotta, then say nothing at all."

"Danny, I didn't come to upset everyone. I should probably leave," Andrea said, starting to rise.

"Please, Andrea, sit down. I don't want to make you uncomfortable, but this needs to be settled right now. Jed, you and Carlotta both know how well Andrea treated me when I stayed at her house. She gave me love and kindness when I needed it the most. She gave me clothes when I had hardly a shirt on my back. Because of that, and if for no other reason, I expect you to show her the same respect."

Dead silence filled the room.

Jed cleared his throat. "I reckon a name don't make all people the same," he said. "But I got somethin' to say, then we'll be done with it. 'Cause of what you did for Danny, you'll always be welcomed at this ranch—" he looked at Carlotta "—and by everyone who works here. But I won't be forgivin' your brother for all the things he's done to my baby. And if I ever meet him face to face I'll beat him to a pulp. Do I make myself clear?''

Andrea looked Jed straight in the eye. "My brother is not the demon you make him out to be, Jed. But I'm sure, were I in your shoes, I would probably feel the same way. I am also sure there is nothing I can say that would change your mind. I guess this is something that will only be worked out in time, and between the two of you.''

Jed nodded his head in agreement. "Well, now that we got that all out into the open, would you care for a shot of whiskey?''

"Jed!'' Danny gasped.

"I was just tryin' to be friendly.''

Andrea laughed. "Yes, Jed, I'd like a drink of whiskey.''

Danny glanced from one to the other, not believing what she was hearing.

When Andrea left, with a promise to return soon, she and Jed were both a bit tipsy, and on the friendliest of terms. Danny didn't have a drink, and had sat listening to the two of them chat as if they were old friends. Jed even took Andrea out and showed her all the improvements they'd made, with Danny trailing behind.

Because she hadn't finished putting her bed together, Danny was forced to spend another night on the floor, a feat she still hadn't gotten used to after living at the Falkners'.

Chapter Fifteen

After Andrea's visit, Danny knew she could no longer put off seeing Beau. She had excused the delay by telling herself too much still needed to be done at the ranch, but the excuse was no longer valid. Since she needed to go to town for supplies, and since the Falkner ranch would be on the way, the time had come to get the confrontation over. Of course, he could be out on the range instead of at the house.

Upon arriving at the house, she climbed down from the buckboard, checked to be sure her white chemise blouse was properly tucked into the waistband of her colorful muslin skirt, squared her shoulders and walked to the door that now seemed terribly ominous. Lifting the heavy clanker, she let it fall several times.

As the door opened, Danny was surprised to see Andrea. Usually one of the servants answered.

"Danny! What a pleasant surprise."

"Hello, Andrea," she said, stepping inside. "I came to see Beau. Is he here?"

"Yes, he is." In fact, Andrea thought, he just rode in last night with Mescal. But there's no need to tell Danny, it would take too much explaining. If Beau wanted her to know, he could tell her himself. "He's out at the stable talking to Jessy. I'll go get him. Shall I tell him what this is about?"

"I want to talk to him about cattle."

"Oh, I see. Why don't you go on into the study, dear? I'm sure he'll be with you shortly. Or would you rather go on out there?"

"No, this is business. I'll wait in the study."

Danny paced back and forth, sure she had worn a trail. What's taking him so long? she wondered. The longer she waited, the more nervous she became, which wasn't at all the way she'd planned it. She wanted to be cool and calm. She glanced at the guns hanging on the wall and easily recognized the rifle and pistol she'd taken with her when she insisted on going with Beau to kill the mountain lion. Oh, she thought, how different everything would be today if I hadn't gone on that fateful trip. Entrenched in her thoughts, she jumped when the door opened.

Seeing Beau enter the room, she realized that in the two months she'd been gone, she'd forgotten just how tall and intimidating he could be. His skin was darker from being in the sun, but that made him all the more attractive. He was still the same handsome man with beautiful, thick black hair and the superbly muscled body she couldn't get out of her dreams.

"Hello, Danny." His words were crisp. "Have a seat. I understand you want to talk about cattle."

"Yes," she said, choosing to remain standing. She watched him relax in the chair behind the desk, his face blank.

"What do you want to discuss? I've kept my cattle off your range."

She started pacing again, trying to get her speech in the right order.

Beau watched the beautiful minx closely. He had half a notion to make love to her right here in the study. During the time he'd spent tracking and healing Mescal, Danny had constantly been on his mind. Especially at night. It's been too long since I've enjoyed her tempestuous lovemaking, he thought. But business is business, and I want the Silver J. Later, I'll find a way to solve the other problem.

"Over the last three years," Danny began, "Jose—he's the man that's been running our place—has been receiving money to stock the ranch. And he did! But your father kept running his cattle over our land, and took our stock with him." She stopped pacing and looked at Beau. "I want those cattle back. They're ours."

"How many are we talking about?"

"I figure you owe us at least five hundred head."

Beau raised a dark eyebrow. "Do you have the bills of sale proving your statement?"

"Well . . . no. Jose didn't keep them."

"And you expect me to just turn over that many cattle because you say you own them? There isn't a cow on my ranch that has your brand."

"I don't care. You have cattle that belong to me!"

"Prove it!"

Danny sank down on the couch. She had no proof. "All right," she said in a much calmer voice. "I have an idea. Why don't you just give me your spring calves and we'll call it even."

"Oh, I imagine you would be more than happy to settle for that. I expect the calves so far outnumber five hundred. However, I have an even better idea. Sell me your ranch."

Danny bounded to her feet. "Sell you my ranch? I'd never sell, to you or anyone else!"

"That's not a very wise attitude. Think about it. I'm willing to pay you twice as much as it's worth."

His words were spoken in that soft, quiet tone she had come to know so well. It meant, beware! But she was getting mad. "And just who sets the value as to what it's worth?" she asked scathingly. "You?"

"With that kind of money, you could buy another stretch of land and all the stock."

"I don't want your damn money. I want *my* ranch, *my* cattle and *my* right to run the ranch as I see fit!"

"How are you going to move your cattle to market, Danny?"

"What?"

"My land surrounds yours. The only way you can move your cattle is to go over my land, and I'm not about to let that happen. I want your place, and one way or another, I intend to have it."

"You bastard!" she raged. "Well, two people can play your game. If I have to, I'll stretch barbed wire around every acre I own. I'll be a thorn that's going to pierce that thick hide of yours, Beau Falkner." She watched his eyes narrow, and knew barbed wire were words he didn't like.

"We'll see," he said.

Beau stood and looked out the window. After a few minutes, he turned around. "Is Jed at the ranch, Danny?"

"Of course he's at the ranch."

"Get rid of him. He's no good, and you sure as hell don't need him. Look at all the trouble he got you into before. His name's not on those wanted posters, just yours."

It suddenly occurred to Danny that Beau really knew nothing about Jed except that they had robbed stagecoaches. In fact, she thought, from the way he's talking, he probably thinks Jed set me up to doing it! Well, Chief Walking Cloud, or whatever your Indian name is, you sure as hell don't know as much as you think you do!

Beau continued to press his point. "I'm telling you this for your own good, Danny. Get rid of Jed."

"Why? Because if you get him out of the way you think it will be easier to run me off?" A bitter smile came to her lips. "Who knows, I might need to go rob a bank or two so I'll have enough money to put up my barbed wire!"

Danny jerked around, ready to leave, but Beau moved faster than she did. He grabbed her arm and swung her around, his steel fingers cutting off the circulation.

"You even think about robbing a bank and I'll have you in jail so fast you won't know what happened," he snarled, releasing his hold. "And don't even consider putting up barbed wire. I'll tear it down faster than you can put it up!"

"I can do anything I want on my land. As for putting me in jail, you'd have to prove it first. Who would ever believe a woman was guilty of such crimes?"

"Don't try it, Danny, or you'll have to deal with me." His voice had become even more threatening.

"Then give me my cattle!"

"No!"

"Then go to hell!"

Beau watched Danny storm out of the room. "Damn!" he said, hitting his fist on the desk. "She's just crazy enough to go rob a bank!"

Danny, still furious when she finally reached town, didn't see Garret standing at the doorway of his saloon.

"My," Garret said aloud, "that's one pretty lady."

Smoky, sitting at a table in the corner in his usual drunken stupor, heard Garret's words. "Who's that?" he slurred.

"Danny Jameson. Too bad I've been busy the last couple of months. I had planned on paying the lady a call."

"You think she's a lady, but she ain't." Smoky poured himself another shot of whiskey from the bottle sitting on the table. "I know the truth!"

"What are you talking about?" Garret asked, half listening as his eyes followed Danny down the street.

"She's got everyone fooled. She's nothing but a stagecoach robber. Used to call herself the Gringo Kid."

"You're drunk, Smoky." Garret left the doorway and headed for his office.

"I know what I'm talking about," Smoky mumbled. "Her and that half-breed are two of a kind."

Smoky sat in the corner so he could keep an eye on the entrance just in case a Falkner ranch hand moseyed in. If one did, he could make a quick exit without being seen. He sure as hell didn't want Falkner to know he wasn't dead. Only through pure luck had he survived. "I'm sure as hell not going to tempt fate." He took a swig of whiskey and almost fell off the chair.

Smoky had suffered a hundred deaths after Falkner left him. For days, he hung there, his skin blistered, watching the water that remained out of his reach, screaming and begging for mercy and fading in and out of consciousness. When he finally regained his senses, he was lying on the floor of a peddler's wagon, covered with a blanket.

As the weeks passed, Smoky grew to hate the peddler, but knew he couldn't get well without him. When he'd discovered the codger was headed for Prescott, he'd panicked. But after due thought, he'd decided Falkner would never suspect him of being in town. After all, Falkner thought he was dead. Smoky could buy a horse and hightail it out of town with Falkner never the wiser. But he needed money.

When Smoky arrived in town, his pockets were lined with the peddler's money, and Smoky headed straight for Whiskey Row. For the past week he'd stayed drunk, trying to drown his memories. When he went to sleep sober, he relived his experience by the river and always jerked awake screaming, his body soaked with sweat.

"Howdy, boss," said a grubby-looking man as Garret entered his office.

A scowl crossed Garret's handsome features. "What are you doing here, Butch? I told you to stay away."

"But you said you wanted to know when we returned, so I hurried on over. No one saw me, I came in through your private entrance."

"How did the job go?"

"As slick as a pretty woman's behind. We was in and out of that bank 'fore they knew what happened."

"Anyone get hurt?"

"Nope."

Garret picked up one of the canvas bags sitting on his desk, testing the weight. "Looks like a good haul." Turning, he leaned down and spun the combination to open the safe, then placed the bags inside.

"You was right about that gold delivery. The men that delivered it to the bank turned right around and left, and we went right in."

"You go back to the ranch," Garret said as he closed the safe. "And make sure no one sees you. We're going to lay low for awhile. People around here are getting nervous. They already know about the other bank jobs and the gold we've taken from the mines."

"But we ain't done nothing around here."

"It doesn't matter, word travels fast. We'll just sit still for awhile, unless I come up with another idea."

"Whatever you say, boss."

When Butch had left, Garret sat down and looked toward the safe. "Just a few more takings, and I'm set for life." A picture of Danny flashed through his mind. Now that he had no pressing business, he should pay the lovely lady a social call.

"Armando," Beau said as the two men headed toward the blacksmith's shed, "I want you to have the men keep a close eye on the Silver J."

"What's up, boss?"

"A couple of days ago Danny came by and threatened to string barbed wire."

Armando shook his head worriedly. "I've heard some bad tales about that stuff and cattle. Cuts them right up, I hear."

"I know, I've heard the same thing. We don't need or want it in the valley. That's why I want the place watched. If she puts it up, I want it torn down." Beau looked at the cloudless sky. "We've been a long time without rain. Got any ideas as to when this heat spell's going to break?"

"Can't say as I do. You're the Indian, Beau. You're supposed to know those things."

Both men laughed.

"The water's getting low, Beau," Armando said, turning serious. "I don't like the looks of it. We need that water sitting on the Silver J, Beau. That's what's helped us through in past years when we had a heat spell like this."

Upon reaching the shed, the two men stopped and looked at each other.

"How bad a shape are we in?" Beau asked.

"Not that bad, yet. But if this keeps up much longer, we're going to be in trouble. The cattle will start dropping like flies. We have a late crop of calves that needs branding, but I've put it off because of the heat. I've got most of the cows and calves on that back range where the water comes down from the Silver J, so they're fine for now."

"Well, keep me posted. As soon as I see how Jessy's coming along, I'm going to the house. I think I'll ride over to the back range in the morning and take a look."

Armando left and Beau entered the hot shed. A fire burned in the forge, and the red-hot coals glowed, making the place feel like an inferno. Shirtless, with a leather apron on, Karl's huge, muscled body glistened with sweat. He stood shaping a horseshoe on the anvil. Jessy, off to the side, had a firm hold on the rope around Mescal's neck. Upon seeing Beau, the horse stretched his neck out to nuzzle him.

"Having any trouble, Jessy?" Beau asked, patting the horse's neck.

"No, sir, Mescal and I are getting along just fine. He hasn't forgotten me. He's looking real good. What did you use to heal him?"

"When we have a day to sit and chat, I'll tell you. Why didn't you tell me before I left that you could handle Mescal?"

"Smoky hated the horse so much, I figured if he found out he'd make life hell for me. Mr. Falkner, I haven't had a chance to thank you for putting me in charge of the stable. I just want you to know, I'll do a good job."

"Have you heard anything about Smoky?" Karl said out the side of his mouth. Lifting Mescal's hoof, he took a nail from between his lips and started hammering the shoe on.

"He'll never be back," Beau replied.

"He'd be dumb if he did, after what he pulled. At least you were smart enough to figure it out. Armando told us all about it while you were searching for this big fellow. I'm glad you ran Smoky off, but it seems a shame he didn't have to pay for what he did."

"Yes. Well, I'm sure he's gone to his just reward. I'll see you later. If anyone comes looking for me, tell them I'll be at the house."

Andrea looked up as Beau entered the small room she called her office. Large ledgers lay open across her desk.

"Have you found anything?" Beau asked.

"We did take on a lot of extra cattle in the past three years, but according to my records, they're listed under strays. Father must have given me that information, so I can't really tell."

Beau let out a half laugh. "And if he knew, he sure wasn't about to tell anyone."

"No, he wouldn't."

Beau sank down in one of the chairs and let out a big sigh. "We may have problems soon, Andrea. Unless the weather breaks, we're going to need water."

"And your thinking is slanted toward the Silver J," Andrea said, almost in a whisper.

"I can't let the cattle die."

"What are you going to do?"

"I don't know. I have several options, but I'll wait a little longer before I do anything."

"And one of those options is to start driving the cattle onto their land." Andrea wasn't asking, she already knew the answer.

"Or I could give them their five hundred head in exchange for letting us move the stock to their water."

"Oh, Beau, that's the perfect answer!"

"Then what happens when we have another hot season, Andrea? Give **the**m another five hundred head? The next time the number will probably be higher."

"I didn't think about that. I'm sure they wouldn't, though."

"When it comes to cattle and money, sister dear, people tend to change. Well, if something doesn't break soon, I'm going to have to make a decision. I know how fond you are of Danny, but I hope you won't try and fight me over whatever I decide."

"I love Danny dearly, Beau, but you are my brother. I would like to see this settled amicably. Peace between the ranches is long past due. But I will stand behind you."

"Jose, you still haven't given me any answers!" Danny said, frustrated.

She, Carlotta and Jose were sitting at the kitchen table while Jed paced the floor, rubbing the back of his head.

"I can't believe you're thinkin' about doing this!" Jed said.

"It wouldn't be rustling, Jed," Danny tried to assure him. "We'd just be getting back what's rightfully ours. We can dam up the water like I first thought about, and we can string barbed wire. But that takes time and money, and I want our cattle now. By the way, Jed, when I came back from town the other day, something occurred to me. Did you go back to that meadow and pick up the box that fell off that wagon like you promised?"

Jed turned away, not wanting Danny to see the look of worry that crossed his face. "I went back, but the box was open and empty," he lied. "Someone else must of got to it first." No one knew the gold lay buried beneath the porch.

"That's too bad. Wonder what was in it? Oh, well, no use crying over spilled milk. Now, Jose, we were talking about stealing cattle." Oh, Beau, she thought, none of this would be necessary if you only loved me as much as I love you.

"All I know is what I've heard. When I was down in Mexico, some of the gringos I knew would run over into Texas and rustle cattle. Let me tell you, a lot of the big ranches started that way. Usually they took them from large ranches that were owned by Easterners."

"So what did these men tell you?" Danny asked anxiously.

"Well, if they were after calves, like you are, sometimes they'd cut the muscles around the eyelids, temporarily blinding the calf, and making it easy to get away with him. But when it heals, the eyelid sags. They called it droops, and it's a telltale sign of stolen cattle."

"Oh, this is goin' too far." Jed stormed out of the room.

Danny's stomach wasn't feeling too good.

Jose, oblivious to Jed and Danny's uneasiness, continued. "Or they'd put hot coals between the hooves of the cow so she'd be too sore to follow."

"Stop!" Danny didn't want to hear any more. "I have no intention of doing any of that. There's got to be a simpler way. When I took Sheeka out the other day, I noticed a herd of cows and calves near our back border. I didn't get too close, but maybe I should have. Early in the morning, I'm going to ride back over there. I can tie Sheeka up and sneak close without anyone seeing me. I'll find out how many cowboys are watching the herd. Then we can formulate a plan."

Beau left the ranch early. As he headed toward the Silver J, he had only one thing in mind. Bedding Danny. He'd had enough problems trying to get her out of his mind, but ever since her visit, she was all he could think about. He'd always enjoyed a woman until he tired of her, and he could take or leave them without a backward glance. Never had any woman stayed on his mind like this she cat, stage robber, hellion, witch, gun-toting... Hell, he thought, I could go on and on. "But I still want her, damn it," he mumbled, urging Mescal to a faster speed. He felt a sense of uneasiness. For some reason, the way he hungered for her seemed different. No matter how he tried to figure it out, he couldn't understand what kind of hold Danny had on him. He dismissed his line of thinking. He'd tire of her sooner or later. But for now, he was going to satisfy his need.

When Danny took off to spy on the cattle, she had no idea she was being watched or followed. She rode for a long distance before deciding to stop and walk the rest of the way. Tying Sheeka to a small shrub, she had walked about a hundred yards when she heard a horse let out a soft nicker. Turning, she saw Mescal standing by Sheeka, riderless. Turning around, ready to start running, she stopped dead. Beau stood not twenty yards in front of her.

"I knew I should have brought my guns," she hissed.

Beau started laughing.

"What's so damn funny?"

"You, my lovely. It's been too long since we've seen each other, Danny."

"We just saw each other a couple of days ago."

"That's not the kind of seeing I'm referring to."

"No!" she gasped, as she started backing up. "I won't let you have your way with me, Beau Falkner. That's done and over. I've gotten you out of my blood once and for all!"

"You're lying."

Seeing he wasn't moving toward her, she stopped backing up. "It's over, Beau," she whispered.

"Come here, Danny."

"No," she replied weakly, already wanting to feel his arms around her.

"You can try fighting it, but you know you want me just as much as I want you."

God help me, she pleaded silently, give me strength to turn around and leave. She squeezed her eyes shut, wanting to block him out of her mind and leave, but her body wouldn't move. So many nights she'd yearned for him to make love to her and satisfy her physical need.

"Come here, Danny."

"No, damn it!" she barked out, trying to get her composure. "I hate your guts and I refuse to be your play toy!"

"Open your eyes and come here, Danny."

His voice was like a caress. When she did look at him, she knew she was fighting a losing battle. His deep blue eyes held hers and she felt like a piece of metal being drawn to a magnet. Without even realizing what she was doing, she slowly moved toward him. When he put his arms around her and drew her to him, she couldn't fight, nor did she want to.

"You're mine, Danny, don't ever forget it," he said, bringing his head down close to hers.

"We're enemies, Beau," she whispered.

"What goes on between our ranches has nothing to do with this." He placed his lips on hers, not wanting her to say any more. He felt her lips open, accepting his tongue and sucking gently on it. God, how he wanted her!

Danny felt the same need and urgency. As Beau started unbuttoning her shirt, she unbuttoned his. She desperately wanted to feel his naked body against hers. Her hunger was deep and all-consuming, and feeling her naked breasts against his bare chest sent her mind spiraling. She wasn't even aware of him laying her down in the high grass. All she knew were the sensations flowing one after another as he sucked on her breasts and his hands seared her body. "Please, Beau," she moaned, "take me now. I can't wait any longer."

They lay side by side for some time before Danny's heart slowed to a normal pace. Now that the throes of desire had subsided, unwanted thoughts started taking over.

"Beau?"

"Yes?" His voice was almost as soft as hers.

"This doesn't change how I feel about our ranches."

"I know."

She leaned on her elbow and looked at his strong, chiseled features. His eyes were closed, and if she didn't know better, she would have thought he was asleep. "Can we talk about it?"

He opened his eyes and studied her. "Danny, we both have to do what we think right, and nothing can change that. When we're together like this, I don't want to talk about the outside world. There's just the two of us, and to hell with everything else. Do you understand what I'm trying to say?"

She thought she saw a moment of sadness in his sky-blue eyes, but then it was gone. She lay down. He was right, nothing had changed. Their two ranches would probably always be at war. He wanted her land, and she refused to sell. He wanted her body, and she didn't have the strength to refuse him. That's what it all boiled down to.

"I have to go," Danny said as she sat up.

Beau reached over and picked up her clothes. "Let me dress you," he said, his voice soft with pleasure.

Their lovemaking had always been wild and all-consuming, but Beau's dressing her was different from anything she had ever experienced. He even put her boots on for her.

"There you are," he said, the job completed. "I want to see you tomorrow night, Danny." His voice had a husky quality.

"How?"

"Listen for my call. You can figure a way to get out of the house."

"Beau, I don't—"

"Hush. Don't say anything. Listen for my call."

When Danny reached the horses, she spent a few minutes stroking Mescal and noticed the scars on his head. "What happened to you, pretty boy?" She made a mental note to ask Beau next time she saw him.

After untying Sheeka, she looped the reins over the mare's neck, then, grabbing a handful of mane, she swung herself upon the mare's back. Without looking back, she rode off, headed toward the house.

Carlotta met Danny as she entered by the back door. "You have a visitor," Carlotta said, her brown eyes lit with pleasure.

"Andrea?"

"No. It's a very handsome man. He said his name was Garret Beckman. Oh, Danny, you have a caller!" Carlotta said excitedly. "And he's such a gentleman, make any woman proud to be seen with him."

Danny frowned. "What's Garret doing here?" she wondered aloud.

"Why, he's come to see you! You look a mess. Your hair even has grass in it. What did you do? Crawl on your stomach to see those cows? Now, you go on into your room and change clothes, and I'll tell him you'll be there in a minute. Don't just stand there, hurry. You don't want to keep a fine man like that waiting forever."

My, my, my, Garret thought as he watched Danny enter the room dressed in a flowered calico dress, her thick auburn hair hanging loose. That's one beautiful woman. He walked over to her. Lifting her hand, he placed a soft kiss across her knuckles. "It's so nice to see you again," he said, escorting her to the sofa. "I must apologize for taking so long to pay you a visit. Are you all settled in now?"

Garret stayed for some time, and Danny found herself enjoying his light conversation and sincere interest in what she had accomplished since her arrival. He had a manner that immediately put her at ease. She invited him to stay for dinner, but he politely declined, saying he needed to return to town.

Chapter Sixteen

About the same time Danny went out again, to spy on Beau's cattle, Garret sat in his office counting the money from the previous night's business. The Glass Slipper did well, but it certainly didn't make the kind of money he needed to set his future. Garret stuck the money in the safe and walked out of the office and into the saloon.

Acknowledging Jake, the bartender, with a nod of his head, he walked to the swinging doors and looked out. He had enjoyed spending yesterday with Danny, and already anticipated the pleasure of taking her to bed. As he stood thinking about the fiery girl, Garret noticed a tall, slender man nailing a poster on the store wall across the street. When the man turned, the sun reflected off the silver star on his chest.

Walking out the doors, Garret purposely strode toward the marshal, who had stopped down the street to nail up another poster.

"Howdy, marshal," he said, in a nonchalant manner. "What's that all about?" He pointing to the piece of parchment.

The marshal turned and gave him a friendly smile. "The Cordhill Mine has put out a reward for the return of a gold shipment taken over in New Mexico territory some months ago."

Garret raised an eyebrow. "You don't say. Have any leads as to who might have done it?"

"Not really, but they think it was the Gringo Kid."

Garret stuck his hands in his pants pockets and studied the poster. The name sounded familiar. "You said the Gringo Kid?"

"Yep. He'd been robbing some stages over there, and they're pretty sure he was in on it. Haven't seen hide nor hair of him since, so he's probably enjoying his take."

"Don't they have any witnesses?"

"The two men delivering the box and three outlaws were found dead. The Kid probably headed west. I doubt we'll ever hear from him again."

Smoky! That's where he'd heard the Kid's name. "Well, marshal, hope you catch your man." Garret headed back to the Glass Slipper.

After poking his head inside and telling Jake he'd be back later, he mounted his horse and headed out of town.

"What brings you back so early?" Butch asked as his boss rode up.

Garret didn't bother getting down. After he found out what he wanted to know, he planned on heading straight back to town. "Butch, I thought you told me the Cordhill Mine recovered the shipment on that job you bungled."

"Like I told you, I didn't bungle the job. What was I supposed to do? That damn fellow with the rifle done shot Billy Joe, Jacob and Stacy, and I took a bullet in my shoulder. I was just damn lucky it went straight through."

"Did you see anyone else?"

"What do you mean?"

"Just what I said." Garret was getting impatient with the slow-witted man. "Did you see anyone else?"

"Hell, no."

"And when you finally went back the box was empty, if I remember correctly."

"That's right, someone from Cordhill must have come got the gold. Why you askin' me all these questions again?"

"I pay you to do what I tell you, not to question me! I want you to ride into town tonight. Come in the back door, and if I'm not there, wait. Make sure no one sees you. I might have a job for you." Garret turned his horse around and headed back the way he'd come.

* * *

"Heaven sakes, girl, where you been all this time?" Carlotta asked. "Thought you'd be back way before now. It's almost supper time."

Danny plopped down on one of the kitchen chairs and rested her elbows on the table. She gave Carlotta a big smile. "I've been watching cattle. I told you where I was going."

"You didn't say you'd be gone all day."

Danny heard Jed's heavy footsteps before he entered the room.

"I saw Sheeka," he announced.

Jose walked in behind him and asked, "What did you find out?"

"It's perfect!" Danny laughed.

"Danny, are you sure you still want to do this?"

"Oh, Jed, get that worried look off your face. There's only one man watching the herd. I've been flat on my belly all day watching him. About every four hours, he checks the cattle, and the rest of the time, he's either practicing his draw, which is godawful, or he just sits around and dozes off. It's a perfect setup!"

"When we going to do it?" asked Jose excitedly.

"Well, it'll have to be at night so he can't see us coming. And it has to be soon."

"Sounds good to me." Jose smiled. "It's going to feel great to finally get back at the Falkners!"

In more ways than one, Danny thought. While watching the cattle, she had given a lot of thought to her relationship with Beau. Somewhere along the line she had to use her backbone. Loving him and knowing he only thought of her as a physical convenience was slowly driving her crazy. Awake she thought of him and at night she dreamed about him. She had determined that when he called to her tonight, she wouldn't go. She'd end it once and for all!

After night had fallen, Smoky came staggering into the Glass Slipper. Garret had spent most of the day searching for him, without any luck, and had become concerned that Smoky may have left town. It never occurred to him Smoky might be hiding out.

Garret went to the bar and motioned for Jake to hand him a bottle of whiskey and a glass, then walked over to where Smoky sat in the corner. Placing the items on the table he pulled out a chair and sat down. When Smoky looked at him questioningly, he said, "It's on the house." After years of playing poker, Garret was very good at masking his thoughts.

"How come?" asked Smoky, more than just a little suspicious.

Garret poured out some whiskey then shoved the glass in front of the small man. "I need your help."

"Can't help no one," Smoky said, gulping down the amber liquid. "I'm getting me a horse in the morning and leaving this hellhole."

"Why are you leaving town?"

"None of your business."

Garret, realizing Smoky wasn't as drunk as he had first appeared, refilled the glass. "All I need is some information. If you're wanting to leave, I'm willing to pay. It would give you some extra spending money."

"It depends on what you want to know."

"I've taken a liking to Danny Jameson, and have even thought about asking her to marry me."

Smoky spit some juice, hitting the spittoon dead center. "You're wasting your time. She's already tied up with that Indian, Falkner."

Garret raised an eyebrow. This he hadn't known about. Does Smoky have his facts straight, he wondered, or is he just blowing at the mouth? "That's why I wanted to talk to you," he said with a friendly smile. "I plan on selling this place eventually and settling down. Naturally, I want a woman who will do me proud. The other day, you made a comment about her being an outlaw. Are you sure your information is correct?"

"Let me see the money first." Smoky wasn't about to be taken again. "And I want it in gold."

"I see you have a good business head on your shoulders. I'll be right back."

Returning, Garret tossed a small bag on the table. Smoky loosened the drawstring and examined the contents. Pleased with the amount, he looked up at Garret. "Okay, what is it you want to know?"

"You said something about Danny being the Gringo Kid the other day. How did you come by this information?"

Without any hesitation, Smoky told Garret what he had seen and heard the night of the barbecue.

When Smoky had finished, Garret sat there for a few minutes, a bit stunned by several revelations. He would never have suspected anything between Danny and Beau, especially since everyone knew the two ranches had always been at war over water. On the other hand, maybe Beau was playing it smart, and using Danny to get his hands on her ranch. Garret found it hard to believe the beautiful slip of a girl could be an outlaw until he remembered how well she could shoot and ride. What really interested him was the gold in her possession.

"How did she get to the ranch?" Garret suddenly asked.

"You got me. All of a sudden she was there. Someone said when Falkner returned home she came with him."

"Well, Smoky, I guess that's all I need to know. Looks like I'm going to have to search for a different bride. I certainly want nothing to do with the likes of her."

"That's a smart move. Any woman who beds an Indian is pure scum!"

Garret pushed the bottle in front of Smoky. "On the house," he said before leaving.

As Garret entered his office, Butch jumped out of the chair. "How long do I have to sit here waiting?" he grumbled.

Garret motioned Butch to the door. "See that man sitting over in the corner?"

"Yeah."

"I want you to take care of him. Make sure you get my bag of gold he's carrying, and anything of value. Make it look like someone killed him for his money. Understand?"

An evil expression covered Butch's normally innocent-looking features. "Oh, I understand." He left by the back door.

When Smoky had consumed the contents of the bottle, he stood, using the table to keep his balance. He knew he needed a good night's sleep before leaving Prescott in the morning. He'd already stuck around too long.

Smoky didn't know, as he staggered out of the saloon, he'd never see daylight again. Butch waited for him, and as Smoky rounded the corner, Butch lifted the shotgun and aimed it at Smoky's face.

Danny lay twisting and turning in bed. A comfortable breeze blew in through the window, but she didn't notice. Her thoughts were jumbled. When will Beau arrive? I don't want him to come. He said he would. Why is he so late? I'm not going out there when he calls. I want him... I can't let him use me... I love him.

At the first owl hoot, Danny's eyes flew open. She could no longer put off a decision. As bad as she wanted to join Beau, her determination remained. Snatching up the pillow, she turned onto her stomach and stuck it over her head, pressing the sides against her ears.

For some time she was motionless. Has he left? she wondered. Just as she decided to lift a corner of the pillow she felt someone climb in bed with her. She started to scream when a large hand covered her mouth and an arm circled her body.

Beau chuckled softly. "Tell me, my little wildcat, are you trying to let your mind rule your desire?" he asked as he removed his hand from her mouth.

"Have you gone insane?" she whispered. "What are you doing in my bedroom?"

"You mean you don't know?"

Danny could hear the laughter in his voice.

"Since you chose not to come to me," Beau teased, "I had no choice but to come to you."

"I want you to leave immediately! What if someone should come in?" She struggled to get loose, but he held her firm.

"Then that's their problem, not mine. Besides, everyone in the house is fast asleep."

"How do you know?"

"Because I checked."

"You mean you have gone through my house?" Danny gasped.

"That's exactly what I mean."

"Beau!"

"Sh." He chuckled. "Someone might hear you."

"This isn't funny!" His hand started moving over her body and she tried brushing it aside. "I have something to say, damn it!"

"Fine. Then say it so we can get on to better things. I have an overwhelming desire to possess you."

"I don't want to see you anymore." There, she thought, I've said it.

"Are you finished?" he asked in a silken tone.

"I mean it, Beau!" She had to stifle a moan as his hand cupped a breast and his fingers toyed with her nipple. "I...I want you to leave right now...and never come back. Beau, stop it!" she persisted as he nibbled her neck, her resistance quickly fading.

"Oh, Danny, you're such a liar," he whispered before capturing her mouth.

Her next words were lost as she fell into the abyss of passion.

The next morning at breakfast, Andrea commented on Beau's good mood as she poured his coffee.

"I am in a good mood. I think we're going to get some rain finally. Why are you dressed for traveling?"

"I'm going to pay Danny a visit and take her some bread and a starter."

"Because of the change of weather, you'll be happy to know the confrontation with the Silver J may be delayed."

"Indefinitely, I hope." Andrea took a seat at the table and helped herself to ham and eggs.

"I know that's what you would like, but one of these days it's going to have to come to a head. I want that land, Andrea. The next time we have a hot spell, the weather may not be so kind to us."

"Honestly, Beau! You're just like Father," Andrea said in a tiff. "If it means so much to you, why don't you just marry Danny!" Andrea spurted out the words without thinking.

Beau's face showed shock. "What?"

"Well, I mean.... Well, why not? It would end all the problems." Andrea started eating.

"End all my problems?" Beau stormed. "It would be the beginning of even more problems!"

"You like her, don't you?" Andrea couldn't look him in the eye, but she crossed her fingers on the hand resting in her lap. If nothing else, maybe she had planted a thought.

"Yes, I like her, but that doesn't mean I have to sacrifice my freedom! Why in the world would I want to get married? Answer me that, Andrea."

"It would get you her ranch, which you covet so dearly."

"Oh, I'll get the ranch," Beau said in a deceptively soft voice. "Now, if you will excuse me, I have work to do in the study." He stomped out of the room.

Andrea pushed her plate away, no longer hungry. There has to be some way to get those two together, she thought. It's the only answer to this entire mess.

Beau stormed into the study, banging the door behind him. What in the world could Andrea be thinking, to come up with such a harebrained notion as marriage? he wondered. Unless Danny put her up to it! Well, if the little she cat thought she could coerce him into marriage, she had another thought coming!

Sinking down on the leather sofa, Beau rubbed his temples and thought about Danny. They'd made love all night, and he hadn't left her room until almost daylight. Without a doubt, she was the most extraordinary woman he'd ever bedded. She more than satisfied his carnal appetites. At least for the present, he couldn't seem to get enough of her, which was a foreign feeling to him. The fact that he had no desire to bed any other woman was another inexperienced feeling. His desire for the vixen seemed to cause all kinds of problems.

At least he had taken care of one problem. When he went to see Danny tonight, he knew she would join him when he called. Now that he'd proved to Danny he wouldn't hesitate to enter her room, she wouldn't be about to take the chance of being caught by the others. He slowly shook his head. Never in his entire life had he pursued a woman with such determination or gone to such extremes to bed her. But that sure as hell doesn't mean I want her for a wife, he thought, or any other woman as far as that goes!

Beau stood and went to the desk, determined to get his mind off the she cat and attend to business.

* * *

Danny went to bed early, needing to recoup her lack of sleep from the previous two nights of heavenly lovemaking with Beau. He had told her he would be gone the next few days and, disgusted at herself, she was already looking forward to his return. Heavy clouds had begun to form in the sky, and dampness could be smelled in the air. Glorious rain would soon arrive.

When the first bolt of lightning lit the heavens, followed shortly by a heavy clap of thunder, she jumped out of bed and threw on her clothes. Running out of the room, she stopped at Jed's bedroom and pounded on the door. "Get up, Jed!"

"What's the matter?" he called.

"Get up and get your clothes on. This is it, Jed! This is how we're going to get the cattle!"

The door flew open and Jed stood there in his long johns. "What the hell you talkin' 'bout?"

"With this storm, we can get the cattle, and the cowhand will think the storm spooked them. Hurry, Jed, wake up the others."

"Danny—"

"If you don't want to do it, I will! Even if I have to get those cattle by myself!"

"All right, I'll be right with you, but I don't like it one damn bit!"

Joe remained with the Silver J cattle, but as soon as Clancy and Jose joined them, Danny quickly explained her plan. When they reached the Falkner herd, they were to start moving the cattle onto Silver J land. Because of the storm, the animals would be nervous and spooked, which would only help the story Danny planned to tell Beau. If her calculations were correct, the lone cowboy would already have his hands full trying to keep the herd settled down, and he would never see them behind the camouflage of heavy rain. She gave a silent prayer that the downpour wouldn't stop. The rain was the only chance they had of pulling this off.

As the four riders came upon the restless cattle, Danny shot her gun in the air during a particularly loud clap of thunder, and the jittery animals started moving. The group had no problem heading them in the right direction, and no one ever saw the cowboy. By the time they herded the cattle in with their own, the lightning and thunder had ceased. Only the rain continued to fall.

"What's going on?" Joe asked, after riding over to join them.

"I haven't got time to explain, Joe," Danny said, excitement pouring through her veins. "It's going to be a long night. Let's head them all toward the barn."

All night they worked, branding as many calves as they could. Danny and Jed drove the calves into a holding pen, while Jose, Clancy and Joe did the branding. They were all bone weary and couldn't even think. They just continued on doing what had to be done as fast as they could do it. Even with oil-skin parkas on, their clothes were soaked. The hard work and Carlotta's constant supply of hot coffee helped to keep their bodies warm.

When light began to streak the sky, Danny called a halt. Some time during the night the rain had stopped, but there were still threatening clouds overhead. "Okay, boys," she called. "Let's head them out. If anyone comes asking questions, don't say anything. Just send everyone to me, and I'll do all the talking."

Once the cattle were in the pasture, Jose stayed with the herd as the rest turned for home. When the bedraggled group reached the house, Carlotta came out to greet them.

"I have breakfast ready if anyone's hungry."

The men went to the house and were already eating by the time Danny came in.

"Come on, baby," Jed said. "Grab you some food."

"I'll eat a couple of flapjacks, then I'm headed straight for bed." Jed moved over so she would have a place to sit. "I don't know when the Falkner men will be arriving, but you can be sure they'll come looking for their cows." Jabbing a couple of pancakes with her fork, she slid them on to her plate. "Carlotta," she said between bites, "what about Jose? I know he must be hungry."

"Don't worry your pretty head about Jose, I'll take him some food when everyone's finished."

Bone tired, Danny finally entered her room. She fell on the bed without even bothering to take off her filthy clothes. Her eyes closed, and she had no trouble drifting off to sleep.

Chapter Seventeen

"Wake up, Danny," Carlotta said. "Clancy rode in and said they're on the way."

"Go away." She pulled the pillow over her head, ready to go back to sleep.

"You have to get up! The Falkner men will be here at any time, and you need to change clothes!"

Suddenly Carlotta's words penetrated her foggy mind. The sun rays coming in through the window were like daggers in her eyes. It took a minute before she could keep them open. "Are they already here?" she finally asked.

"No, but they're on their way. When Clancy saw them, he hightailed it back here to let us know. He said they weren't riding hard, but they had a determined look on their faces, and there were a lot of them." Carlotta pointed to the tub. "I've already put water in it. Knowing you, you'll probably want to take a quick bath."

Danny jumped out of bed and started taking her dirty clothes off. She said a silent prayer as she stepped into the tub.

"Carlotta," she said through the soapsuds, "pull out a clean pair of pants and a shirt, then tell Clancy to get Jose and Joe. I want them to stay out of sight. With that many men, there's no way we can stand up to them."

As Danny finished buttoning her shirt and stepped out the front door, the men came riding up. Beau wasn't with them. Jed stood on the porch, his shotgun tucked under his arm.

"Let me do the talking," she whispered.

Several of the men rode around to the back while the others surrounded the front of the house. Danny looked straight at the foreman. "Hello, Armando. May I ask what you and your men are doing on my land?"

"Miss Danny," Armando acknowledged, tipping his hat. "Seems we're missing some cattle. You wouldn't happen to know anything about it, would you?"

"Are they branded?"

Armando shifted uneasily in his saddle. "The cows are, and I'm sure the calves know who they belong to."

"Well, we know nothing about any cattle. If they're on my land, they came of their own accord. And if that's the case, I would think any animal on my land that isn't branded belongs to me."

Armando lifted his hand, and the fifteen or so men drew their guns. "Drop that shotgun, mister," Armando ordered.

"Do as he says, Jed," Danny said, seeing him hesitate. She looked at Armando. "You can't just come on my land and take what you please! Beau's the one that should settle this, not you. Where is he?"

"He had some other things to take care of. I'm foreman of the ranch, and Beau give me full rein to do what is necessary. If our cattle are on your land, we have every intention of taking them back."

"I suppose you plan on taking my stock, too!"

"We'll only be taking what's ours. Any animal with your brand stays here."

"Do I have your word on that?" Danny asked.

"You have my word," Armando replied.

"Well, I'm going to ride with you to make sure you stand by that word."

"That's fine with me, but the big man goes, too," Armando said, motioning toward Jed. "I'll not have him stirring up trouble. I don't want this to turn into a bloodbath, but if that's what it takes, we're ready."

It only took a quick glance at the other hard faces to know Armando meant every word. Maybe Jed was right all along, Danny thought. I may have bitten off more than I can chew.

"Where are the rest of your hands?" Armando bit out.

"We don't have an army like you! There are only three other men, and they're not about to take a chance of getting their heads blown off. Jed and I'll go get our horses," she said, feeling far less sure of herself.

"And we'll follow." Armando backed his horse up so they could walk down the porch steps.

"Where do you want to look first?" Danny asked when she and Jed were mounted.

"We'll start with your herd," Armando stated.

When they reached the cattle, several of the men dismounted and started checking brands.

"They're ours, all right," one of the men said.

"Okay, boys. Start culling them out," Armando ordered.

The Falkner men went right to work.

Danny waited a while before saying anything. The only way she could possibly come out on top was to bluff. Taking a deep breath, she left Jed and rode over to where Armando sat on his horse, watching the cowhands.

Pulling up beside him, she said in an angry tone of voice, "What's going on here?"

"What are you talking about?" Armando asked impatiently.

"I'll not let you take my cattle! You gave your word! Obviously men on the Falkner ranch can't keep a promise!"

Armando shifted his weight and looked at her. His cold black eyes showed his anger at her statement. "We're not taking your cattle," he said through thin, tight lips.

"The hell you're not. What about all those calves that have my brand on them?"

"You don't know what you're talking about."

"Oh, no? Well, what about that calf right over there!" She pointed to one near the outer edge of the Falkner herd the men had started rounding up.

"What the hell," Armando said. "Tony!" he hollered at a passing cowhand. "Bring that calf over here!"

As soon as Tony delivered the calf, Armando dismounted and checked the brand. When he looked at Danny, fire danced from his eyes.

"This is a fresh brand," he stormed.

"Nevertheless, it's my brand. And you can see for yourself, I didn't put it over a Falkner brand. I have a right to put my mark on any cattle that's unbranded and on my land!"

Armando, hands on hips, looked at the sky, trying to control his fury. She's pulled a fast one, he thought, and there's not a damn thing I can do about it! "All right, men," he shouted, "cull out the calves that have the Silver J brand." He mounted his horse and rode off.

Danny wanted to scream with joy. She'd done it! She actually managed to get some of the Falkner herd, and Beau's men were doing all the work. Containing her laughter, she went back and joined Jed.

For the next few hours, the cowhands were hard put to separate the calves from their mothers. They finally ended up taking the entire Falkner herd to the same holding pens Danny had used for branding, and placing the calves inside. It was almost dark when they left, and not a single man departed in a good mood. Least of all Armando.

Shortly after noon the next day, Garret left his ranch and climbed into the carriage he'd rented.

"Are you ready to leave?" he asked Butch, who had followed him out.

"Yep. The men are waiting for me to join them. I got the sombrero, the jacket with silver buttons and the *roweles*. That should be enough to make me look like the Gringo Kid. I ain't going to put them on until we're ready to hold up the banks in Santa Fe and Tucson."

"And don't forget," Garret added, "before you leave the bank, tell them you're the Gringo Kid."

Butch shifted his feet. "I ain't figured out why you're wanting me to go to all this trouble," he said.

"What difference does it make, as long as you get your cut? I won't expect you back for at least three weeks. Make sure you lose any posse before heading back this way."

"I'll take care of it, boss."

Garret flicked the whip over the nag's back and the buggy took off in a cloud of dust. As he headed toward the Silver J, he felt like patting himself on the back. He had everything in motion. If all went as planned, news about the Gringo Kid's holdups would travel fast. If he guessed right, Danny would want to go into hiding. By getting married, she could change her name and no one would suspect her. Naturally, he would be her mate. He would not only own the Silver J, which he would sell at a healthy profit to Falkner because of the water, he'd also have the gold. He had no intentions of telling Butch his plan. When Butch had finished serving his purpose, Garret would do away with him. Then he could move to San Francisco and lead the life of a respectable man.

After a good night's rest, everyone at the Silver J celebrated. Not only was it Danny's nineteenth birthday, but she had accomplished what they had considered impossible. Plus she'd done it without a single shot being fired.

They were all in the highest spirits, as well as half snookered, by the time Garret drove up. It took several knocks on the door before anyone heard him.

"Well, howdy, there," Jed greeted him. "Come on in."

Garret had planned to take Danny for a ride, but seeing the merry group, he changed his mind. In no time, he knew exactly what had happened the day before. He heard the tale not once, but several times.

Garret drank very little and listened a lot. At different times he asked subtle questions in hopes of getting information. It didn't work. No one mentioned the stage holdups or the gold.

When night fell, Jose passed out, and Jed carried him to bed. Carlotta moved to the porch, sat in her rocking chair and immediately dozed off. Clancy and Joe wobbled out of the house, their arms around each other's shoulders, singing old cowboy songs, and headed for the bunkhouse.

Garret, always the gentleman when necessary, said, "It's getting late. I really should head back for town."

Danny had drank very little, and when Garret had arrived, she had stopped all together. "I'm going to fix some supper," she said. "At least stay and have something to eat before you go."

"I've already overstayed my welcome." He chuckled. "I don't want you shutting the door in my face next time I pay a visit."

"Danny's right," Jed insisted. "You shouldn't be leavin' with a empty stomach."

Garret grinned. "Well, if you insist."

While Danny prepared the meal, the two men discussed cattle and ranching in general. Jed did most of the talking, with Garret proclaiming his lack of knowledge and asking questions.

After supper, the threesome remained sitting at the table, drinking coffee.

"You're a fine cook," Garret complimented Danny.

"Thank you."

"Yep, make someone a fine wife," Jed spoke up.

Garret watched an embarrassed flush come to Danny's cheeks. She started clearing the table.

"Would you care to go outside and have a cigar?" Garret asked Jed.

"Why?" Jed replied. "We can smoke it right here."

Garret pulled two cigars from his pocket and offered Jed one.

"Why, thank you." Jed lit the cigar and took a couple of puffs. "Been awhile since I had a good cigar. Tastes mighty fine," he said, a pleased grin on his face.

"When I rode up this afternoon, I noticed you have added some new buildings." Garret blew a smoke ring.

"Yep," Jed replied. "We're gettin' the place lookin' right good."

"The lumber must have cost you a goodly sum. I'm curious. Where did you get the money? Sell some of your herd?"

Jed became suspicious. On his last visit to town, he'd seen the Cordhill Mine poster. Although he had consumed a lot of liquor, he was far from drunk.

"Had a silver mine. Sold it 'fore Danny and me came here. Danny told me you got some land of your own," Jed said, changing the subject.

"Just a small piece. Nothing compared to the size of the Silver J. I don't even run cattle on it. I make my money on the saloon."

"Ain't you ever plannin' on settlin' down and gettin' married?" Jed asked.

Garret laughed. "I could ask you the same question."

"Well, I tell you, son. I reckon all my wild days are behind me. I wouldn't mind findin' a pretty little filly and gettin' hitched. I'd be mighty content to spend the rest of my days right here."

"Have anyone in mind, Pa?" Danny asked while drying her hands on a cup towel.

"Pa?" Garret almost stuttered from the shock. This could cause more complications than he'd planned on.

Seeing the look on Garret's face, Danny explained. "Jed raised me, so he's the same as a pa."

"You mean you're not actually related?"

"Naw," Jed said. "Sometimes Danny calls me Pa and sometimes Jed. But we're the same as family."

Garret slowly exhaled in relief.

As the three moved into the parlor, none were aware of the man standing in the shadows some distance from the house.

Beau had ridden straight to the Silver J instead of going home first. He'd been too long without the feel of Danny beneath him. When he'd first arrived, he didn't recognize the carriage. It took only minutes of scouting to discover who it belonged to. He became consumed with fury. What the hell is he doing here? he wondered. Probably thinks he can snatch Danny from me. He decided to wait until Garret left before confronting Danny. He didn't want the bastard hanging around!

Knowing it had become late, Garret said the proper amenities and proceeded to leave. Danny walked out with him, passing Carlotta, who still sat in her rocking chair, fast asleep and snoring.

"You'll be coming back to see us, won't you?" Danny asked in a hushed tone.

When they walked down the stairs, Garret turned and took her hands in his. "Danny, I have something to say to you."

"What? You sound serious."

"I am serious. It's hard for me to believe that in the short time I've known you, I've fallen in love."

"Garret...."

"Sh. Let me finish." He raised her hand to his lips and kissed it. "I think it only fair to tell you my intentions. I want you for my wife, Danny, and I have every intention of pursuing that quest. I don't expect an answer until you get to know me, but please give it a chance.''

"But you don't know me," she whispered.

"I don't need to know you. My heart says it all. Nothing about you would change my mind. *Nothing.* I'm not a saint, Danny, and I have been accused of many nefarious dealings. I am willing to set all that behind me and start a new life with you. That includes selling the Glass Slipper.''

Danny wasn't sure what nefarious meant, but she thought it might mean crooked.

"Now that I've bared my heart, will you allow me to come calling?''

"Yes," she said without a moment's hesitation.

"My darling." Garret pulled her into his arms and kissed her longingly.

Watching the scene, Beau wanted to go over and castrate the crook! The only thing that stopped him from doing the man damage was Danny's willingness to be kissed. He watched Garret get into his carriage. Danny stood there for some time before walking onto the porch and waking up the heavy woman sitting in a chair, then went in the house. Beau mounted Mescal and rode off.

When Beau arrived home, everyone had already gone to bed. Grabbing a bottle of whiskey, he went to his room. As soon as he'd closed the door, he took a long drink. Something deep inside had hurt like hell when he watched Garret and Danny embracing each other. "Why should I give a damn?" he said, after taking another drink. "It's time to move on to greener pastures. I don't need the witch.''

As Beau proceeded to get drunk, he mentally searched for reasons to be rid of the auburn-haired beauty. He thought of the barbecue and all the women who had let it be known they wanted him in their bed. The widow Johnson had all but seduced him. Like a fool, though, he'd kept his eyes on Danny. He chuckled, thinking about the attractive widow. He should have taken her into the stable, instead of Danny. At least she wouldn't fight him like the she cat had from the beginning. No, he thought, I don't need Danny.

Knowing how passionate Danny could be, he convinced himself she had already taken Garret to her bed while he was gone. "The little hussy! That damn Jed probably put her up to it!" he muttered before passing out.

Danny went to bed in a state of euphoria. Being proposed to for the first time meant a great deal to her. Garret loved her and cared enough to want her for his bride, which was more than she could say for a certain other individual. True, Garret's kiss had not set her blood on fire as Beau's kisses did, but that would probably come in time. And true, she didn't love Garret, but as time passed and she came to know him better, her love would surely grow. It would be a far more solid foundation than the wild, unreasonable love she felt for Beau.

She fell asleep, a smile on her face. Everything would turn out fine, and she'd be rid of Beau's hold on her once and for all.

"Danny did what?" Beau stormed the next morning.

"What was I supposed to do?" Armando asked. "Did you want me to kill them and end this damn mess once and for all?"

"No, no. You did the right thing," Beau said, relenting.

Beau had been headed toward the stable when Armando caught up with him. The two men stood there, neither looking the other in the eye.

"The men are getting those calves branded, so it sure won't happen again," Armando said.

Beau looked at the foreman. "What's done is done, Armando. Let's face it, the little robber outsmarted us."

Beau wandered over to the corral with Armando beside him. Resting his arms on the top rail, Beau stood staring at the horses that would be used for the cattle drive to the forts. "I've decided to leave with the boys tomorrow and help drive the cattle over to Fort Verde and down to Fort McDowell," he finally said. "When will you be taking off for Fort Whipple and Fort Mahave?"

"In a couple of days." Armando also leaned against the fence, looking at the stock. "Is something bothering you, Beau?" he asked.

"What made you ask that?"

Armando looked at his boss and friend. "You don't seem to be your old self. Anything you want to talk about? I got a good ear for listening."

"No, but thanks for the offer. I just need to get away for awhile."

"Okay, but if you change your mind, let me know. I'll see you when you get back."

Beau watched the foreman leave. Armando's concern had been mirrored by Andrea at breakfast. Beau couldn't answer their questions even if he wanted to. If he couldn't understand why he remained in a foul mood, how could he explain it to someone else? Besides, he wasn't used to confiding in others. Going on the cattle drive would be good for him. Hard work was exactly what he needed.

A couple of days after Beau's departure, Andrea paid a visit to the Silver J, and she and Danny sat in the kitchen exchanging stories over coffee.

"On my next visit, I'll bring some clippings, and we can plant them. You really need some flowers and shrubs to brighten the place up."

"That would be lovely," Danny replied halfheartedly. From the moment Andrea had walked in the door, she started feeling guilty about stealing the calves. Taking them from Beau didn't bother her, but Andrea also lived at the ranch.

"Do you have any particular preference?" Andrea asked.

Danny couldn't stand it another moment. If Andrea wasn't going to broach the subject, she would. "Andrea, are you mad at me?"

"Heavens, no. Why should I be mad at you?"

Danny winced. "For taking the calves." She watched Andrea's expression closely. She certainly didn't expect the smile that came to the lovely woman's full lips.

"I told you some time back, I refuse to let the problems between the ranches come between our friendship. What sort of a person would I be if I quit my resolve at the first sign of trouble?"

Danny shook her head. "Oh, Andrea, you're one in a hundred. I don't know what I've done to deserve such a good friend."

Andrea's smile broadened. "Now I'm not saying everyone at the ranch is of the same mind I am."

"You mean Beau," she stated.

"That I do."

"When Armando came after the cattle, he said Beau had gone to attend to some business." Danny was fishing for news. If Beau had returned home, why hadn't he tried to see her?

"Yes, he went to help round up the cattle to be delivered to the forts."

Danny picked up the coffeepot and refilled Andrea's cup. "When did he get back?" she asked, trying not to sound too interested.

"He came back the next day, but left again on the following day to go on the drive."

"Oh, I see." She felt hurt that he hadn't even made an effort to contact her. Apparently Beau had lost interest, she thought sadly. But isn't this what you wanted? she asked herself.

"Where is Jed?" Andrea asked.

"He's out in the barn helping feed some of the calves. We tried to pick the ones that were ready to be weaned, but in our haste, we got some a little too young, so we're having to feed them."

Andrea stood. "If you don't mind, I think I'll go join him. Maybe I can be of some help."

"No, go right ahead."

Andrea started to leave, then stopped. "You know, Danny, we've all been thrown into a situation and I'm not sure just what the solution is. Father created it years ago, and there doesn't seem to be an answer. Somewhere along the way, someone is going to have to change their thinking, or as sure as I'm standing here, there is going to be blood shed."

"I'm not going to sell the ranch, Andrea, if that's what you're leading up to."

"I know, dear. I know how much this place means to you, and I wouldn't be about to ask you to sell. But I also know how determined Beau is to get the Silver J, and at this point, I don't think there is anything that will change his mind, either. This is a terrible thing to say, but Beau can be ruthless if he wants something bad enough. I don't want to see anyone get hurt. Do you understand what I'm saying Danny?"

"Yes," she whispered. "I know exactly what you're saying."

"I'm not worried about Beau. He can take care of himself, and always seems to comes out on top. It's you and Jed I'm worried about."

"Jed?" she asked, surprised.

"Yes. They have a mutual hate for one another. Beau places the stealing of the cattle squarely on his shoulders. He feels that Jed has done nothing but lead you down the crooked path, so to speak. I tried to explain that Jed's not like that, but Beau cuts me off, saying Jed's pulling the wool over my eyes."

Danny sat in the chair. "And I certainly didn't help matters," she said, exasperated.

"What do you mean?" Andrea asked.

"When I went to see Beau about getting our cattle back, I wanted to get even with him for saying he wouldn't allow any cattle drives across his land. So I told him Jed and I were going to go rob banks in order to get enough money to put up barbed wire."

"Barbed wire?" Andrea gasped. "Oh, heavens, Danny, that would be a terrible thing to do. It would cut up all the cattle. You can't be serious!"

"No, I couldn't do it if I wanted to. I haven't the money. I just wanted to make him worry. But I'm telling you, Andrea, if he starts pushing his cattle onto my range, I'm going to have to do something to protect what's mine."

Andrea released a worried sigh. "Well, who knows what the future is going to bring? I guess all we can do is wait and see. I'm going to go help Jed." She left by the back door, headed toward the barn.

Chapter Eighteen

Garret pushed his courtship with a determination worthy of the best of men. He was always the perfect gentleman, considerate in every way and attentive. Other than an occasional kiss, he *never* made a sexual advance toward Danny. He brought gifts, treated Jed with the utmost respect, complimented Carlotta and talked to Jose as an equal. His ploy worked, and soon everyone was encouraging Danny to marry the fine gentleman.

Although Danny enjoyed Garret's company and attention, the sparks just weren't there. Soon, she found herself trying to find ways to avoid being alone with him.

Danny had deliberately kept the knowledge of Garret's courtship from Andrea, knowing the woman's feelings toward the man. But as often as Andrea came to visit since Beau's departure, she knew the meeting between the two of them was inevitable.

After finishing the excellent noon meal Carlotta had fixed, Andrea, Jed and Danny moved to the front porch. Jed brought out a straight-backed chair to sit on, and Danny chose the porch bench.

Andrea sat in the rocking chair feeling quite content. "Winter is on its way," she said. "I can feel it in the air. I hope we don't have much snow this year."

"I like the snow," Danny said, feeling drowsy.

Jed chuckled. "That's because you've never had to stay out in it and watch over a bunch of cattle."

"You make it sound like you're getting old, Jed," Andrea teased.

"I'm not gettin' any younger, that's for sure."

Andrea saw the horse and rider first. As Garret drew closer, she stood, anger darkening her blue eyes. "Why is he coming here?" she asked.

Jed looked at Danny, waiting for her to say something.

"Oh . . . he comes here quite often," Danny said, trying to sound cheerful. "In fact . . . well, I guess I should tell you . . . I mean—"

"What she's tryin' to say is, Garret has asked for her hand in marriage," Jed said for her. He couldn't understand why Danny wanted to keep the news a secret.

Andrea turned toward her friend. "Oh, Danny! You can't be seriously considering it?"

Garret arrived at the house, and Danny didn't get a chance to answer the question.

"Greetings, everyone." Garret dismounted and tied his horse to the hitching rail. "Miss Falkner," he said, nodding his head toward Andrea as he stepped onto the porch.

Feeling the hostility that had suddenly filled the air, Jed greeted the newcomer with a friendly, "Howdy, Garret."

"Jed," Andrea spoke up, "why don't you take me to see how those calves are coming along?"

"But they're out to pasture now."

"How wonderful. It would be a nice drive. That is, unless you don't want to go."

"No." Jed chuckled. "That's just fine with me."

After helping Andrea into the buggy, Jed climbed in and motioned the horses forward. Danny wasn't pleased at being left alone with Garret, but couldn't think of a tactful way of getting out of it.

"Has she been trying to talk you out of marrying me?" Garret asked.

"No. In fact she knew nothing about it until just before you rode up."

"Were you ashamed to tell her?"

Danny heard the bitterness in his voice. "I haven't told her because I didn't want an argument."

Garret's eyes followed the buggy until it disappeared. "I'm sure she's going to try and fill Jed with a lot of lies," he said, not realizing he'd spoken aloud.

A coldness crept into Garret's voice that she had never detected before. But then he turned toward her, all smiles.

"There's some new gossip running around town," he said, sitting down beside her.

"What is it?" she asked out of politeness.

"Well, it's not exactly gossip. I guess I'd be more accurate to call it fear."

Now he had her interest.

"Seems as though there have been some bank holdups by someone named the Gringo Kid. Everyone is afraid he's going to hit Prescott."

Danny's mouth dropped open. "But... but that's impossible!" she uttered.

"Oh, I agree," Garret said, deliberately misconstruing her statement. "I know of no reason why he'd come to Prescott, either."

Danny found breathing difficult.

Seeing her reaction, Garret wanted to laugh. He'd actually begun to wonder if Smoky had told him the truth. "But enough of that. Obviously the news has frightened you. Let's talk about something more pleasant. I had an offer to buy the Glass Slipper today. This means we can get married sooner than I planned."

"How nice," Danny said unenthusiastically. She wasn't really listening. Her mind ran rampant trying to assimilate the return of the Gringo Kid. She'd hoped to never hear that name again.

"Is something wrong, Danny?" Garret asked innocently.

"No! No, nothing's wrong."

"I thought we could set a wedding date."

A wedding date? The thought of marrying Garret suddenly horrified her. "I can't marry you," she blurted out.

"Why?"

"You know nothing about my past."

Garret laughed. "Well, let's see. Since you are so good at shooting targets, shall I assume you're a notorious gunfighter and have twenty notches on the butt of your pistol?" he teased.

"No. Nothing quite that exciting."

"Look, Danny," Garret said, becoming serious, "I once told you I'm no saint. Unless you go around murdering people, I don't care what your past is. I love you." Garret put his arm around her shoulders and pulled her against him.

Danny stood and moved to the edge of the porch.

"What is it in your past that you don't want to tell me?" he asked.

She turned and leaned against a post. "Why do you think I have something to hide?"

Damn, Garret thought. Getting her to talk is like pulling cows' teeth. "Because you keep referring to your past. And if it bothers you and keeps us from getting married, I want you to just get it out in the open."

She didn't want to hurt him, but she had to be honest. She had to put a stop to this now, before she broke his heart with false hope. "Garret, I have to refuse your proposal."

"You're just all nerves, darling. I know what an important step marriage is, and I'm probably rushing you. Don't make a hasty decision." Garret could hardly contain his anger at her refusal. "I have to go back to town, but before I leave, I want you to promise you'll think about it. I can give you a good life, Danny. I'm certainly not without funds. And I'll make you happy. Even Jed and the others know what a good husband I'd be. Listen to what they're telling you, darling. As my wife," he added for good measure, "no one can ever harm you. You'll be safe."

Garret went to her side and pulled her into his arms. He kissed her tenderly. "I'll be back in two weeks for your answer, my dearest. Please don't disappoint me. I think I'd just die if your answer is no."

"Garret—"

"Sh." He placed his finger over her lips. Always a believer in theatrics, he gave her his endearing look, then left the porch and mounted his horse. "Every night, darling, I'll say my prayers that your answer will be yes."

As Garret rode away, all he could think about was wringing the girl's neck. He'd never doubted his ability to woo her and win her hand in marriage. That she would turn him down hadn't even entered his mind. "Damn," he muttered, "she could ruin everything."

On their way back from seeing the calves, Andrea spent her time trying to convince Jed that Garret would be the worst man Danny could possibly marry. He accused her of listening to gossip.

Exasperated beyond words, Andrea held her tongue. Danny probably won't listen to me either, she thought.

Andrea felt relieved when they returned to the house and Garret's horse was gone. Whether it did any good or not, she planned on trying to talk Danny out of making a foolish commitment to Garret. But her plans changed drastically when Danny came rushing out of the house, her face showing panic.

"Oh, I'm so glad you've returned. A terrible thing has happened!"

"What's the matter, baby?" Jed asked worriedly.

"Someone is holding up banks and claiming to be the Gringo Kid!"

"Where did you hear this?" asked Andrea, completely forgetting her other problems.

"Garret told me. I guess the news is all over town. My God, Jed! What are we going to do?"

"Well, we're sure not goin' to do anythin' foolish," Jed said, upset by the news. "Where's Carlotta?"

"She took the buckboard out to pasture to feed the hands."

"Since there's no one to overhear us, let's go inside and think about this."

When they were seated, Andrea spoke first. "Danny, just what did Garret say?"

"Nothing much, just that some banks have been held up by the Gringo Kid, and the people in town are concerned he'll show up in Prescott."

Andrea sat back in her chair and visibly relaxed. "Well, what do you have to be concerned about?" she asked. "You're not holding up the banks. No one will connect you to any of this. They have no reason to suspect."

"I don't know," Danny said, slowly shaking her head. "Something just isn't right."

"Andrea's right, baby," Jed said. "There's no need to get all worried. Besides, you're wanted in the New Mexico territory, not here."

"But why would someone want to impersonate me unless it's to get me in trouble?"

"Maybe the man just heard the name and is using it to hide his own identity," Andrea said. "Who knows? Whatever the reason, you can't let it worry you. There is no way anyone can connect this with you!"

Unable to remain seated, Danny began pacing the floor. "I just have a funny feeling that something is going on we don't know about yet. But I think it's going to come home to roost on my shoulders. I tell you, Jed, for the first time, I'm really worried."

"But no one knows, except us," Jed reminded her.

She stopped dead in her tracks. "And Beau!"

Andrea tensed. "Surely you don't think Beau would do something like that?" she protested.

"I don't think he would hold up banks, if that's what you're asking. But you said yourself, if Beau wants something bad enough, he can be ruthless."

"But I didn't mean in this way," said Andrea defensively.

"What did you mean then, Andrea?" Danny's amber-brown eyes were a blaze of anger.

"I meant...." Andrea couldn't come up with an answer.

"We all know how badly Beau wants this ranch," Danny said sarcastically.

"Why, that low-down bastard!" Jed raged. "So help me God, if he were at his ranch, I'd go look him up."

Andrea tried again to defend her brother. "You're being unfair. I know Beau wouldn't do anything so underhanded."

"I don't," Danny accused. "What better way to get rid of us than by letting it slip that I'm the Gringo Kid?" she asked bitterly.

"But—"

"No, Andrea," Danny said, cutting her off. "I won't listen to any more. I love you as a sister, but I suggest you take an honest look at your brother. Besides the three of us, who knows? I certainly haven't told anyone, and I know Jed hasn't, and I'm equally sure you haven't. Who does that leave, Andrea?"

Andrea bristled. "I'm not going to sit here and listen to these unfair accusations!"

"Now, Danny," Jed said, "you're not bein' fair to Andrea. It ain't her fault."

Danny put her head down and said in a soft voice, "I know. I'm sorry, Andrea. I value your friendship and don't want to lose it." She looked toward her friend, standing and ready to leave. "But facts are facts, and as I see it, Beau's the only person left who knows about the Gringo Kid. I can understand someone pulling this off in New Mexico, but this is too close to home."

Andrea left without saying another word. As she moved the bay toward home, she suffered mixed emotions, one fighting the other. She loved her brother more than life, and honestly didn't think Beau would do such an underhanded stunt. If he wanted to get rid of Jed and Danny, she could picture him forcefully moving them himself, or just running the cattle onto the Silver J land and daring them to do something about it. That would be more Beau's style. On the other hand, Danny had asked some very valid questions, none of which Andrea knew the answers to. "The only one with the answers is Beau," she whispered, "and he won't be back for a couple of weeks. Maybe longer."

For Andrea, the next two weeks went by at a snail's pace. She missed her friends at the Silver J, but knew she couldn't return, not when they were sure Beau had stirred up all the trouble.

Danny felt just the opposite. The days passed too quickly. Soon Garret would return for his answer. Her head swam with indecision. Carlotta and Jed continued to praise all his qualities and insisted she'd be a fool not to marry him. The pressure was almost more than she could handle. She also worried over the bank holdups and Beau's determination to get her ranch. And, as if that wasn't enough, their funds were quickly dwindling down to nothing.

She finally decided Jed and Carlotta were probably right. Marrying Garret did seem the best route to take. There really wasn't any logical reason to turn Garret down, except she didn't love him. Surely, she told herself, love will grow with time.

Two weeks later Garret arrived at the ranch for Danny's answer. He had prepared all kinds of rebuttals in case she still refused to marry him. The waiting and not knowing had been hell, and more than once he started to go see her to plead his cause.

No one answered the door when he knocked. Circling to the back, he found Danny in the paddock currying Sheeka. After they were married, he had every intention of claiming the mare for himself.

Garret looked through the fence. "Hello, there," he greeted her in a deliberately friendly manner. "Your beauty never ceases to amaze me."

Danny blushed. To Garret's frustration, she went back to work on the horse.

"I suppose you've come for your answer?" she said over her shoulder, not wanting to look at him straight on.

"Yes, I have. Would you like to come out of there and discuss it?"

"No, it's not necessary. I've decided to accept."

A groan of relief escaped Garret's lips. He ran his long fingers through his hair and started laughing with pleasure. "Why don't you come out here and we can seal it with a kiss?" he asked.

"I have work to do. What do you say to our getting married here, in about two weeks?"

Garret didn't know what to think of the way Danny was acting. He shrugged his shoulders. What difference did it make? She'd said yes, and that's all that mattered. "Two weeks sounds fine," he replied. "By then I can have all my business tied up. You won't regret your decision, Danny, I'll make you a good husband."

"I'm sure you will." She knew her voice held no enthusiasm, and convinced herself it was only nerves. Once they were married, everything would be fine. "According to Carlotta, we're not supposed to see each other until the wedding."

Garret chuckled. "Then how are we going to make the arrangements?"

Danny laughed softly. "It does sound foolish, doesn't it?" She walked over and looked at him through the fence. "But Carlotta and Jed are already making plans, and they want everything done right. Jed said he'd come into town tomorrow and discuss it with you."

Garret's lips were set in a broad grin. "Then I'll be looking forward to seeing him." He nodded his head. "Until two weeks, my love."

"Until two weeks," she whispered.

When Beau and the men returned to Prescott they headed straight for Whiskey Row. Beau said the drinks were on him, and the men were ready to relax and have fun.

It was a rowdy group that entered the musty saloon. It wasn't as opulent as the Glass Slipper, but Elmer, the owner, ran an honest poker table and didn't water down the drinks. When everyone lined up at the long oak bar, Beau told Elmer to give the men a drink, and not to let their glasses go dry. Some of the men headed up the stairs with a woman in hand, while others sat at various tables. Beau remained standing at the bar, the toe of his boot hooked over the brass rail.

When Elmer had everyone taken care of, he began cleaning the bar, but stopped when he reached Beau.

"What's new, Beau?" he asked.

"Not much, old friend. How come you're tending bar? Where's Sam?"

"His wife decided to have her baby. You've been gone for a few weeks, I hear."

Beau tossed his drink down. "We had to deliver cattle to the forts before winter sets in," Beau replied as Elmer refilled the glass.

"Then you haven't heard that Garret Beckman is marrying that Jameson girl?"

Sudden rage shot through Beau's veins. "When did all this take place?" he asked in a quiet voice.

"You got me. But he's been going all around town bragging about it. I sure as hell don't know what she sees in that no-account."

Why am I getting so upset? Beau asked himself. If she wants to take up with the likes of him, that's her affair! I'm through, and he's welcome to her!

Elmer, always a talkative person, proceeded to express his feelings. "It might be your chance to finally buy the Silver J."

Beau downed another drink.

"You know Garret as well as I do, and I just can't picture him settling down on some ranch. It's my guess he'll be approaching you to buy it."

"Anything else new while I've been gone?" Beau asked, wanting to change the subject.

"Not much. 'Course everyone's still up in arms about the bank robberies the Gringo Kid's been pulling off."

Beau's eyes narrowed. "What did you say?"

"I said, everyone's still talking about the bank holdups the Gringo Kid's pulled in Tucson and Ash Fork."

"How does everyone know it's the Gringo Kid?"

Beau's voice had become so quiet Elmer almost didn't hear the question. "He dresses something like a Mexican, and on each job he tells the banker his name."

Beau reached in his pocket, pulled out some money and slapped it on the bar. "This should take care of everything," he told the owner. "If it's not enough, I'll catch you later."

"Sure thing, Beau," Elmer called as Beau left the saloon.

Once outside, Beau mounted Mescal and headed out of town. Damn her, he thought. She said she'd do it, but I halfway didn't believe her! Well, I warned her, and she's damn sure not going to get away with it!

Beau headed Mescal toward the Silver J in a full gallop. As the horse ate up the miles, Beau called Jed and Danny every name he could think of.

Chapter Nineteen

As the house came into view, Beau saw Danny ride away on Sheeka at a slow trot. He urged Mescal to a faster speed.

Danny hadn't gone far when she heard the stallion's hooves pounding the ground. It only took a quick glance back to see the angry look on Beau's face, and that he was headed straight for her. She didn't even stop to think. Instinctively she knew trouble followed close behind, and she put her heels to the mare's sides. Sheeka bounded forward, stretching her legs and picking up speed. Danny thought she had a chance of escape until a rope circled her body and jerked her out of the saddle.

Danny hit the ground hard. Catching her breath, she scrambled to her feet and shrugged the lariat off. "What the hell are you trying to do? Kill me?" she yelled furiously.

Beau nudged Mescal forward and slowly gathered in the rope, never taking his eyes off her. "Where's the money, Danny?" he asked, drawing Mescal up beside her.

"You get off my land, you bastard," she said, shaking her fist at him. "I've had all I'm going to take from you! You are the lowest, meanest, most underhanded man I've ever had the misfortune to come across! So help me God, if I had a gun, I'd shoot you right between the eyes!" She stomped the ground in frustration. "Oh, I wish I were a man, I'd beat you to a pulp!"

"Your outrage and indignation won't work, Danny. Now I want to know where the money is!"

"Oh! Now you want me to pay for keeping your mouth shut? Is that it? Well, I don't care! Do you hear me. I don't care! Go ahead and tell everyone, because I'm not going to pay you blood money!''

Beau, thinking she referred to the bank money, said, ''I want it all, not just part of it.''

''I already know that, probably better than anyone,'' she said in a hateful tone, her voice raspy from the anger and yelling. Danny could see dust flying in the air and knew someone was coming to her rescue. When she left the house, Carlotta had been standing in the doorway. She must have seen Beau and gone for help.

Beau saw Danny looking behind him and a smile start to form on her lips. At the same time he heard the drumming of a horse's hooves. Without any hesitation, he pulled his rifle from the scabbard and aimed at the oncoming man.

Frantic that Beau would kill Jed, Danny reached down and grabbed a handful of dirt. Before Beau could pull the trigger, she threw it in his face. A shot rang out, but it missed its target.

As Jed rode up, he leaped from his horse, knocking Beau from the saddle. Jed lifted himself off the ground and snarled at the man he'd waited so long to get his hands on. He picked Beau up by the shirt and socked him square in the jaw.

Having seen Jed's temper and the many men he'd crushed in fights, Danny grabbed Beau's rifle and shot in the air. ''Stop!'' she hollered. ''You're going to kill him, and they'll hang you!'' She watched blood start to trickle out the side of Beau's mouth.

''Get away, Danny. He's got this comin','' Jed practically spit the words out.

Beau shook his head, trying to get rid of the grogginess caused by the blow. Wiping the dirt from his eyes, he looked at the mountain of a man standing over him.

''What's wrong, Jed?'' Beau asked, his hate showing. ''Can you only fight when a man's down with dirt in his eyes, and a woman's backing you up with a rifle?''

Furious, Jed said, ''Go back to the house and wait, Danny.''

''No! I can't let this happen!''

''Damn it, Danny, go back to the house!'' Jed commanded. ''And don't send any of the men out here! This is somethin' that's been needin' to be settled for a long time. I intend to teach this feller a lesson he'll be a long time rememberin'.''

Although Jed seldom barked orders, Danny knew that when he did, there was no changing his mind. She jumped upon Sheeka's back and headed for the house.

"All right, Mister Falkner," Jed said, stepping back, "get up!"

Beau stood and removed his torn shirt. Jed did the same. Each man watched the other closely.

"I'm goin' to make you beg for mercy, and that face of yours ain't never going to be the same," Jed growled. "You're going to be sorry you ever set eyes on me!"

"The feeling's mutual, old man," Beau retorted.

Suddenly Jed charged, but Beau easily sidestepped him. The older man proved to be more agile than Beau gave him credit for. Jed grabbed him from behind in a crushing bear hug. Beau thought sure his ribs were going to crack. Because of the difference in their heights, Jed didn't catch him around the chest. Beau hooked his foot behind Jed's and lunged backward, knocking them to the ground. He landed on top of Jed, but still the man held on and Beau could feel the air being pressed from his lungs. He lifted his elbow and came back with a solid blow to Jed's jaw. As Jed's hold slackened, Beau pulled loose. No sooner had he rolled over onto his hands and knees than Jed socked him in the face with an uppercut. Rising up, Beau socked Jed.

The fight continued on and on. As they exchanged blows each man verbalized all the things he hated about the other and used every cuss word that came to mind. They fought standing as well as on the ground, neither giving an inch. The stench of sweat, blood and dirt permeated the air around them. Each man pulled every dirty trick he knew, trying to win the fight.

Finally, when both men could barely stand without falling over from exhaustion, Beau landed a lucky blow, and knocked Jed out cold. Beau fell on the ground, trying to catch his breath. Never in his life had he had a beating like Jed gave him, and he'd been in a lot of fights. There wasn't a bone or muscle in his body that didn't ache.

"What happened?" Jed asked, as he came to, trying to focus his eyes.

Beau sat up, ready for Jed to charge him, not sure he could even defend himself. Raising a tired fist, Beau watched Jed raise the palm of his hand in the air.

"I've had enough," Jed said, gasping for breath. "This is the first fight I've ever lost, but I sure as hell know when to quit."

Seeing the blood and bruises on the man, Beau couldn't help but wonder what he must look like. All of a sudden, he broke out laughing. He felt mentally cleansed. It had been too long since he'd had a good fight.

"What you laughing at?" Jed grumbled.

"You should take a look at yourself," Beau managed to get out.

Laughter started choking up inside Jed as he said, "You don't look so pretty yourself."

The two huge men lay on the ground and roared with laughter, even though it hurt.

Danny banged the pots and pans as she cleaned them. That they were already clean made little difference. She had to keep herself busy or she'd go crazy with worry. She'd intercepted Jose and Clancy on their way to see what the shots were. After telling them Jed wanted to be alone, she sent them back to work.

"What is taking them so long?" she asked Carlotta, who sat at the table peeling potatoes.

"Everything is going to turn out fine," Carlotta said, trying to reassure Danny. She reached down and touched the rosary resting in her lap. She didn't tell Danny she was silently saying Our Fathers and Hail Marys.

The two men were still lying on the ground.

"Tell me, Jed," Beau said when they'd gotten over their laughing spell, "why did you and Danny have to go rob the banks? Was it to get the barbed wire Danny wanted to string up?"

"What are you talkin' 'bout?" Jed asked, sitting up. "We ain't robbed no banks."

"Damn it, Jed, I'm trying to help. I might be able to get you out of this if you'll just let me return the money and promise it won't happen again. I have considerable influence. No one was killed. But however it turns out, I'm going to make damn sure that money gets back to the bank! I warned Danny not to do this or she'd have me to answer to!''

''I'm tellin' you, we ain't robbed no banks. Hell, we haven't even left the ranch 'cept to go to town. If you don't believe me, ask your sister. She's been over here a lot.''

Beau stood and picked up his shirt. ''Then what's this I hear about the Gringo Kid taking the banks in Tucson and Ash Fork?''

Jed studied the tall man before answering. Because of the fight, Jed had a new respect for Beau. It didn't make sense that a man willing to fight until he dropped would bother to do something as sneaky as Danny suspected. Another thing. With as much power and men as Beau had, why would he even bother? Why didn't he just take over and have done with it? And why would he want to help?

''You going to answer my question, Jed?'' Beau asked.

''You know, Falkner—''

''You might as well call me Beau.''

''All right, Beau. What I started to say is, I got a feelin' we're comin' from two different directions, and neither of us knows what's goin' on in the other's head. When we was fightin', didn't I hear you accuse me of makin' Danny an outlaw?''

''That's right,'' Beau said, wiping the blood from his mouth with the back of his arm.

''Sit back down here and let's talk.''

''I'm not changing my mind, Jed,'' Beau warned.

''And I'm not changin' my story. We didn't rob no banks!''

Beau looked hard at the older man, trying to figure out if he was telling the truth. Finally he sat down.

''What do you want to talk about?'' Beau asked.

''What do you know about Danny and me besides robbin' stages and ownin' the Silver J?''

Beau sat thinking for a minute. ''Actually, nothing.''

''Well, I'm going to tell you a story about a little girl I found whose parents had just been killed by Injuns.''

Danny pounded the bread dough with a vengeance. As usual, flour flew up in puffs, covering anything near. ''I suppose it hasn't entered anyone's head to let me know what's happening! Men!'' She buried her fist in the soft dough. ''Women aren't supposed to interfere! Oh, no! They're supposed to be good little critters and stay home until the mighty men decide to inform them what's going on!''

Another puff of flour went flying into the air.

''For all I know, they could both be lying out there dead!'' She turned to say something to Carlotta, only to discover the woman had left. ''Well, I like that! She's even deserted me.'' She slammed her fist back into the dough.

''So,'' Jed finished, ''that's the whole story. Now you've heard my side, what's yours?'' Jed pulled paper and tobacco from his shirt pocket and offered them to Beau.

''No, thanks, cigars are the only thing I smoke.'' Beau chuckled softly, watching Jed roll his cigarette. ''Never could get the hang of that.''

''Well, you got one on me,'' Jed said. ''I could never sit crossed-legged like that.''

''You get used to it,'' Beau muttered.

Neither man paid much attention to what he was saying. Jed waited for Beau to tell him how he felt, and Beau sat mulling over what he'd learned about Danny.

''Well,'' Beau finally said, ''I guess I've looked at this all wrong.'' He raked his fingers through his black hair, trying to remove some of the caked dirt. Looking at Jed, he said, ''I thought you led a poor little girl astray, and all the time it was her idea. In all fairness, what else could I have thought? I knew nothing of what you've told me. All I could go by was what I had seen. Danny and I never talked about her past. I took it for granted the two of you made a living by robbing stages. Knowing her as I do now, I should have suspected the truth.''

''Yet you took her to your home and gave her a good living,'' Jed commented.

''I can't even take credit for that. Andrea's the one that worked with her.''

Jed drew the smoke into his lungs, then slowly let it out. ''You know, Beau, Danny thinks you're the one who let it out about the Gringo Kid.''

''Why does she think that?''

"She thinks there's somethin' behind all this that ain't come out in the open yet. Figures since there's only four of us that knows about the name, and knowin' me or Andrea ain't gonna say nothin', that leaves only you. She thinks it's your way of gettin' hold of the Silver J. Says it don't make sense for the name to suddenly come out of the woodwork, and 'specially so close to home."

"I make no bones about wanting the Silver J, Jed. But while I've been gone these past few weeks, I spent a lot of time thinking about the problems we've had over the years. I decided that if I couldn't get Danny to sell, I'd see if we couldn't work something out that would be advantageous to the both of us. Range wars can last from generation to generation. I think the time has come for peace in this big valley. If you're agreeable, maybe one of these days soon, we can discuss it."

"I'm not sure I'll have any say in the matter, Beau. When Danny marries Garret, he's the one you'll probably be talkin' to."

Something about the look that momentarily crossed Beau's face sparked a thought in Jed's mind. "You did know she's gettin' married, didn't you?" Jed asked, watching Beau closely.

"I heard the news in town. But she's in for a surprise. She's not going to marry Garret!"

"You don't like the man?" Jed asked.

"No. He's as underhanded a bastard as they come." Beau stood up and looked over the land. "Garret never does anything unless there's something in it for him. Danny's a beautiful woman, but that wouldn't be enough to satisfy him. If he's willing to marry her, it can be for only one reason. He wants the ranch so he can sell it to me for a healthy profit."

"Well, then you ain't got nothin' to worry about. Looks like you'll end up gettin' what you want after all."

Now that Beau knew Jed's and Danny's relationship, he realized Jed would never have put Danny up to sleeping with Garret. "Tell me, Jed, just how close are they?" he asked.

Jed jumped to his feet and tossed the butt of his cigarette to the ground. "If you're implyin' what I think you are, we're fixin' to get into another fight. They ain't even been alone long enough for anything to happen!" Jed thought about the day he had taken Andrea for a buggy ride, but wasn't about to tell Beau.

When Beau didn't reply and remained standing with his back turned to Jed, Jed wasn't sure what to think. Then he remembered the look he'd seen, for just a second, on Beau's face.

"Well," Jed said, "it really don't make no difference. They're goin' to be gettin' married anyhow." Jed waited for Beau's reaction.

Beau spun around and gave Jed a hard look. "I said she's not going to marry the man!"

"How you plannin' on stopping her?"

"If need be, I'll take her to another canyon!"

Jed chuckled. "Tell me, Beau, how long have you been in love with her?"

"What? You don't know what the hell you're talking about!"

"Oh, I know what I'm talking about, but I'm not so sure you know what you're talking about. Seems to me a man that's that willin' to keep a woman around must have some mighty strong feelin's for her."

Beau stood staring at the man, totally dumbfounded. "I suppose the next thing you're going to ask is, when do I plan on marrying her!"

"Yep. That was my next question."

"Why, I wouldn't marry that she cat if she were the last woman...." Beau couldn't finish the sentence. Could I possibly be in love with Danny? he suddenly wondered. Is that why I've been in such a damn foul mood ever since I saw her with Garret?

Jed broke out laughing. "Cheer up, Beau, it happens to the best of men."

Beau refused to believe what was staring him right in the face. There is no truth to it! he told himself. I can't be in love!

As they headed toward their horses, Jed stopped. "Before we go back," he said, turning serious, "there's somethin' I think I should tell you. I figure you to be an honest man, and what I'm fixin' to say I ain't told another livin' soul."

Beau made no comment and waited to hear what Jed had to say.

"You remember that box that was in the meadow when you rode up on us?"

Beau nodded his head.

Danny was sweeping the porch when the two men rode up. Although their faces were cut and bruised and they each had a black eye, neither man seemed to be seriously hurt. "Well," she raged, "it's so nice that you two finally decided to let me know you weren't dead!" She threw the broom down and marched into the house.

Jed shook his head. "I'm not going in there to face her," he said. "Not when her temper's up." Turning his horse around, he headed for the barn.

As Beau sat staring at the doorway, his eyes narrowed and the muscles in his jaw began to flex. Slowly he dismounted. Without any hesitation, he stepped up on the porch and entered the house. Danny was nowhere in sight, so he headed straight for her bedroom. He grabbed the handle of the closed door and tried to open it, but it was blocked.

"Open the door, Danny," he called.

No answer.

"Either you open this door, or I'm going to break it down."

"Don't try it, Beau, or you'll be facing a .45!"

Beau lifted his foot and kicked. The door flew open with a loud bang, and the chair she'd placed beneath the handle went flying. True to her word, Danny stood by the bed pointing the gun at him.

"I want to talk to you," Beau said in a quiet voice, "and I sure as hell can't do it looking down the barrel of a .45."

"Whatever you have to say, be quick about it then leave." She didn't lower the gun.

"I have told no one about the Gringo Kid, Danny."

"I don't believe you!"

"I also have the solution to all your problems."

"What? Turn myself in and hope to God I don't end up with a noose around my neck?"

"No. I think we should get married. As my wife, no one would dare question your background."

"Marry you?" Danny let out a bitter laugh. "Nothing could make me marry you! You'll try anything, won't you, Beau? The only reason you would want to marry me is to get this ranch. Well, it won't work. I'm marrying Garret, and that's final!'' She watched Beau's features turn to granite and his blue eyes darken. Without realizing it, her hand started to shake.

"I'll kill him first," Beau said in a deadly quiet voice. "The minute you say 'I do,' he's a dead man. Since you seem to care so much about him, you'd better keep that in mind. It's not an idle threat!" He turned and left the room.

Danny let the gun fall to the floor, and tears gathered in her eyes. It was some time before her crying ceased. But by the time she'd dried her eyes, she had made up her mind. No one on the ranch would be happy with her decision, but she had no other choice.

Andrea was shocked at Beau's battered condition when he arrived at the ranch. "What happened?" she asked worriedly.

"Jed and I got into a fight." Beau was still furious about the forthcoming wedding.

"Is Jed all right?"

"He's fine," Beau snapped at her. "I'm going to my room and get cleaned up."

Andrea stamped her foot. "Are you just going to leave me here worrying? Don't you think I deserve to know what happened?"

"I'm sorry, Andrea," Beau said in a softer tone. "As soon as I'm finished, we can talk."

Not knowing what to do to make the time fly by faster, Andrea ended up at the piano. She paid little attention to her selection of music.

Beau returned some time later and announced his arrival by saying, "You must be in a bad frame of mind if that violent music you're playing is any indication."

"Oh, Beau," Andrea said, jumping up from the seat, "I have so much to tell you! And I want to hear what happened with you and Jed."

"I could use a shot of whiskey. Let's go into the study."

"Sounds like a good idea. I'll have a small one, too."

Beau raised a dark eyebrow but made no comment.

Once they were in the study, Andrea collapsed into one of the large leather chairs. Seeing the unladylike posture, Beau knew his sister was upset.

"Don't worry, Andrea," he said, "everything is going to turn out fine." Unfortunately, Beau didn't believe his own words.

"But you don't know what all has happened!"

"If you're referring to Danny and Garret's proposed marriage," Beau said as he poured their drinks, "or that Danny blames me for telling about the Gringo Kid, I already know all about it. What will you have to drink?"

"Whatever you're having will do fine."

"Andrea, I—"

"I'm certainly old enough to drink, Beau!"

He handed Andrea her drink, then leaned against the desk.

Andrea tipped the glass to her lips and took a stiff belt. She felt the strong liquid burn her throat and chest as it went down. Tears formed in her eyes and she had difficulty catching her breath. "What is this?" she finally gasped.

Beau chuckled. "Something I brought back from the fort. They call it white lightning. From the hollowed look beneath your eyes I'd say you needed something to warm your blood. I didn't expect you to take such a big drink."

"You know, it's not too bad once it settles."

Beau leaned over and removed the glass from her hand. "I think you've had enough, sister dear." A wide grin spread across his chiseled lips as he sat the glass on the desk.

Andrea started wringing her hands. "Oh, Beau, I've been so worried. What are we going to do? Danny can't marry Garret!"

"You can stop fussing. There will be no marriage."

"That's marvelous! I feel better already. What made her change her mind?"

Beau finished off his drink. "I did," he said, hiding the turmoil within him.

"How?"

"I told her if she married Garret, I'd kill him."

"What?" Andrea bounded out of the chair. "Beau, you can't be serious! You couldn't kill a man in cold blood!"

"You're wrong."

Andrea saw an undisguised look of cold hatred cross Beau's handsome features.

"She's mine, and no man is going to take her away from me," he said in a quiet voice.

"My God! You love her!"

"Yes." Beau went over and refilled his glass. "And I'm not too happy about it. All of a sudden here I am, in love with a wildcat and jealous as hell because she wants to marry someone else!"

"But this is wonderful!" Andrea started laughing.

Beau looked at her as if she'd lost her senses. "How can you be so happy? Danny hates me."

"That doesn't bother me a smidgen." Andrea tried to be serious. "Beau, she loves you. She's never said as much, but I know she does. The only problem I can see is Jed."

"Jed and I have settled our differences," he said in a grumpy tone. "I think he'd be more than happy to see me take Danny off his hands. No, Jed isn't the problem."

"How long have you been in love with her?" Andrea whispered.

With the sudden realization of his love and with everything that had happened, Beau hadn't even had time to think it all out. "I don't know," he answered honestly. "I think it was something that grabbed me from behind when I wasn't looking. Who knows? Maybe it's been there for a long time, and I was just too blind or stubborn to see it."

"You have a lot of our father in you, Beau, and he wouldn't be about to let another man get the woman he loved. But killing Garret isn't the answer, nor is forcing Danny to abide by your will. I know women have always been an easy conquest for you, but this time you're going to have to work to gain the woman's love and trust. Too much was happened, and Danny has a mind of her own. I doubt very seriously she'll come running into your arms just because you beckon."

"She has before," he said.

The knowing grin on Beau's face told Andrea that things had been going on that she was unaware of. "I could be wrong, but I don't think she will this time."

Chapter Twenty

Danny's eyes took in everything as she sat atop Sheeka. The mare's head stretched down as Sheeka enjoyed a drink from the creek. The air was crisp, and Danny shivered. She pulled her wool poncho closer around her body. It's much cooler than when Beau first brought me to this valley last spring, she reflected. The late November sun shone bright, but the air felt damp and a line of dark clouds was moving in. Danny pulled the mare's head up, and they continued on at a slow pace. Danny always enjoyed riding across the open land, feeling a deep sense of freedom. The fact that it was her land made it even more satisfying. She loved the smell of the grass and fresh air, as well as the pines that dotted the land. For a few minutes, a bee buzzed around her, but she didn't even mind that.

Danny looked out across the land toward the distant mountains that surrounded the large valley. "This is where I planned to spend the rest of my life," she whispered. "I'll never forget it for as long as I live." Tears gathered in her eyes. "Enough torture!" She leaned forward and patted the mare's shiny neck. "Let's go home, girl."

Carlotta stood in the kitchen making tortillas when she heard the click of Danny's heels on the wooden floor. "You've been gone a long time," Carlotta said, as Danny entered the room.

Danny removed her hat and gloves and tossed them on the table. "Where's Jed?"

"He's unloading hay in the barn, getting ready for winter. We've been lucky this year. Usually winter is already here by now."

Danny went out the back door. She thought about the change
ı Carlotta over the months. The woman hardly sat in her
ɔcker anymore, and she kept the house spotless, a transfor-
ıation Danny thought she'd never live to see.

As she neared the barn, pride swelled in Danny's chest for
vhat Jed had accomplished. It was a huge structure with am-
le room, its height dominating all the other buildings. Enter-
ıg the big room, she inhaled the musty odor of hay mixed with
ıe aroma of fresh wood. At the far end, Jed stood on the
uckboard with his back turned toward her, pitching hay up to
ose in the loft. A wet streak ran down the center of his blue
hirt, serving as a testimonial to the hard labor.

"Hello, there," she called as she neared the buckboard.
'How's it going?"

Jed turned, a big smile on his face. Jamming the pitchfork
ıto the hay, he wiped the sweat from his forehead. "We just
bout got it licked," he said as he jumped to the ground. He
valked over to a large wooden water barrel and drew out some
vater. "Why don't you come on down?" he called to Jose, af-
er taking several drinks.

Jose immediately scrambled down the ladder and accepted
he dipper Jed handed him.

"Mind if Jose takes a break?" Danny asked Jed. "I have
omething I want to say in private."

"Course not."

Danny smiled at the short, wiry man. "Carlotta has a fresh
►atch of tortillas made, if you're interested."

"Now that's an offer I can't refuse," Jose said.

"What's up, baby?" Jed asked when Jose had left.

"Pa, I've made some decisions I don't think you're going to
ike."

Jed could see the concern on Danny's face. "Sounds seri-
ɔus. Why don't we go sit down? I could use the rest."

When they'd made themselves comfortable on a large pile of
ıay, Jed turned to Danny and said in a soothing voice, "All
ight, tell me what's botherin' you, baby."

Picking up a piece of straw, Danny placed the end in her
nouth and nibbled on it. "It would be easier if you asked me
vhat's right," she finally said. "I don't know how to tell you

this, so I guess I might as well just spit out the words." Danny hesitated a moment. "I've decided to sell the ranch to Beau."

Stunned, Jed waited to hear Danny's reason.

Danny rushed on with her words, needing to get everything said. "But first I'll make him agree to keep everyone on. I don't want to see anyone kicked out on their ear without work. Second, I'm not going to marry Garret. I'm riding into town tomorrow to tell him. I know he's not going to be happy. In fact he'll probably be mad as hell. Can't say as I'd blame him."

"Why are you doing all this, Danny?" Jed asked.

"I guess you could say I'm tired of fighting. The odds are all against me, Pa. You can only bluff your way so long, and eventually someone is going to call your hand."

"What does that mean?"

"It all means Beau. There are some things I haven't told you." Danny lay back on the cushiony hay and looked at the beams on the high ceiling. "When I went to see him about getting our stock back, he told me I'd never be able to take them to market because he wouldn't allow our cattle to be driven across his land. We both know he's got enough hands to keep that promise. And no one at Fort Whipple is going to do anything 'cause he's personal friends with the officers. He also told me that if I marry Garret, he'd kill him. Oh, I could go on and on, but there's no reason to." She looked at Jed. "Don't you see? No matter what I try to do, he has my hands tied. One way or another, he'll eventually drive us out of the valley. Why wait until then and only get a third of what this place is worth?"

Deeply affected by her words, Jed reached over and took her hand in his. "Are you in love with Garret?" he asked.

"What difference does it make? It doesn't change anything."

"Because I want to know. I don't like seein' you hurt this way."

Danny gently pulled her hand away and stood. She walked over to the buckboard, keeping her back turned to her beloved pa. "I don't think I even know what love is." At one time I thought I did, she said to herself, but it was all fairy tales like I used to read about in Andrea's books. "Everyone thought I should marry Garret," she continued. "I figured after we married, I'd grow to love him. I know now that would never have happened. I was only letting everyone make my mind up for me."

"We didn't mean you any harm," Jed said, suddenly feeling guilty. He should have talked to Danny about her feelings. He'd just taken it for granted she loved Garret.

Danny turned and faced him. "Don't go blaming yourself, Pa. It's just as much my fault. I should have stopped him from coming over at the beginning. I let a little flattery and attention go to my head. I've never had a man treat me the way he has. Andrea once told me good-looking men weren't always what they appear. Maybe she's right about Garret. I don't know. But I do know I would only be miserable in the end."

"So you're going to go see Beau and tell him your decision?"

"I'm going to stop by the ranch on my way back from town. If Beau isn't there, I'll leave word that I want to see him."

Jed absentmindedly brushed hay from his trouser legs. "Did you know he's in love with you?"

"Did he tell you that?" she asked angrily.

"Well . . . no, not exactly."

"Because if he did, he's lying! Don't you know by now that he wears two faces and uses the one that fits the occasion?" She let out a bitter laugh. "I think I know him better than you do, and believe me, Beau always gets what he wants, one way or another."

A hard look came on Jed's face. "Are you trying to tell me something, Danny?"

"Yes," she said staring him in the eye. "Beau had his way with me. Now what do you think of the upstanding Mr. Falkner? I'm not going to say he forced himself on me. Oh, no. He's too clever for that! No, I walked right into his web, willingly, just like every other woman he's probably known. I should have seen that from the way he treated Margaret." Tears flooded her amber-brown eyes. "Now do you know why I'm bitter?"

Jed went over and pulled her into his arms. "I didn't know, baby. Do you really hate him that much?"

"More than you know," she whispered into his chest.

"Then we'll sell the place and leave."

Danny pulled back and looked at Jed, love showing in her eyes. "No, Pa. It's time I took off on my own. You have a good life here. Maybe when I get settled, I'll come back and see you, or you can come see me."

"Where will you go?" Jed fought to hold back his own tears.

"Some place where there *ain't* no *Injuns*!" She started laughing, a pure, sweet laugh that sounded like bells ringing.

Jed smiled. "I think you're gonna be all right, little one," he said, his voice husky with emotion.

"I do too, Pa."

The buckskin mare bucked, weaved and kicked around the corral, trying desperately to throw Beau from her back. Beau could feel the ton of muscle and sinew beneath him start to slow down as the mare began to tire. When the buckskin trotted around the corral without bucking, Beau dismounted and tossed the rope to a cowhand. The mare was taken out of the compound and the last horse was brought in. And so it had gone for most of the day, as Beau and the men broke the wild colts that had been brought in from the pasture.

Removing his leather chaparajos, Beau left the area. When he reached the well pump, he moved the handle up and down several times, and as the water started pouring out, he leaned over and stuck his head beneath the nozzle. Straightening up, he shook his black hair, and rivulets of water flew in all directions. He stood there a moment, hands on his lean hips, paying scant attention to the water that dripped down his neck and inside his shirt. As usual, his thoughts immediately drifted to Danny.

He'd gotten virtually no sleep last night. Over and over, he relived all their time together with the sickening realization of how unfairly he'd treated her. Now that he'd acknowledged how deeply he loved her, that's all he could think about.

Beau slowly headed toward the house, his mind still on the auburn-haired girl. He loved her as a lady, but it was the wild, stubborn she cat he loved the most. That's why he had forced her back into the role when they went looking for the mountain lion.

When Beau entered the courtyard, he saw Andrea sitting on the bench beneath the ancient tree, deep in thought. He stopped in front of her and chuckled. "I'd join you, but I don't think you'd appreciate the smell," he said teasingly.

Andrea looked up. "I didn't hear you walk up."

"You look tired. Are you sitting there trying to figure out how you can cure the hurts of the world?"

She smiled at her tall, handsome brother. "No, not really. I've been sitting here thinking about you and Danny, and I came to some realizations of my own."

"Like what?"

"Well, since this seems to be our period for soul baring, I guess I should tell you I find Jed extremely attractive." She watched an expression of surprise cross Beau's face. A fly landed on her hand, and she shooed it away. "Maybe that's our problem," she said.

"What?"

Andrea smiled. "Maybe the flies are spreading some kind of love potion around and we've caught the disease."

"Well, we make a fine pair, don't we? But remember sister dear, you're a Falkner, too. I'm sure you'll figure out a way to handle it." He left the courtyard laughing.

As Beau sat in the tub soaking his sore muscles, he thought about what Andrea had said. He really didn't think she would have any trouble convincing Jed to see things her way. After he'd come to know Jed, Beau liked the man. He found him to be an honest, warmhearted person, and wasn't at all adverse to Andrea's selection.

Reaching over, he picked up the towel lying on the small table and stood up. "The question is," he mumbled, "how am I going to convince Danny to marry me?"

The biggest question is, does she love Garret? he thought as he pulled his clothes from the clothespress. Even if I don't win her love, I can't let her marry that no-good bastard. She may hate me the rest of her life, but she'd be even more miserable married to him.

The first thing I have to do is pay Garret a visit and put an end to this whole mess, he thought. Then I need to return the gold to Cordhill Mines. I'm sure when Bill Tucker hears the story and his gold is returned, he'll be more than happy to let the matter drop. As for the *Gringo Kid*, I'm not sure what to do. I'll have to devise some kind of plan. Then, when all the loose ends are tied up, I'm going after Danny. I don't know how I'm going to win her over, but there has to be a way. Damn it, he thought, I've never had to woo a woman before! He left the room. Tomorrow he'd ride over to the Silver J, talk to Jed, then head to town and take care of Garret once and for all.

Because he had to settle a fight between two of his ranch hands, Beau left for the Silver J later than he'd planned. He didn't know Danny had passed by in the buckboard not thirty minutes earlier. As Beau rode up to Danny's house, Jed sat on the porch stairs, looking as though his world had come to an end. Beau wasn't prepared for the mean look the older man give him.

"What the hell you doin' here, Falkner?" Jed asked, standing. "Ain't you done enough?"

Beau slowly dismounted, not bothering to tie Mescal to the hitching rail. "You've had a quick change of attitude, Jed. Last time I saw you I thought we parted friends."

Beau placed one foot on the bottom step.

"That's 'fore I found out about what you've been doing to my baby."

Beau knew exactly what Jed was talking about by the hard look on the older man's face. "I didn't force her into anything, Jed."

"I know," Jed growled, "she told me. You're a grown man, Falkner, you could of kept it from happenin'."

"No, I don't think I could have," Beau said, his voice soft. "In my entire life, I never wanted any woman as badly as I wanted her. And I would have done anything to accomplish that goal." He stuck his hands in his pockets then glanced over the land. After shifting his weight, he looked at Jed. "You see, although I didn't realize it at the time, I love her."

Jed's eyes bored into Beau's. "Are you tellin' me the truth, boy?"

"Yes." Not used to expressing his feelings to another person, Beau had difficulty getting the words out, but he knew they had to be said in order to convince Jed of his intentions. "I'm not sure it's the wisest thing that has ever happened to me, and I'm not sure how it's going to end, but I'm very much in love with Danny."

Jed walked to the side of the porch, scratching the back of his head. "Hell, I don't know who to believe!" he grumbled. "Still don't make what you did right. On the other hand, I can understand where you're coming from, if you're tellin' the truth."

"What do I have to gain by lying?" Beau felt anger starting to rise inside him. "Believe me, it's not easy standing here telling some bullheaded man my gut feelings!"

Jed broke out in laughter. "No, I don't reckon it is. Don't think I'd feel too comfortable in your boots."

"Then what the hell is going on?" Beau demanded. "Are you wanting to see me eat crow? Because if you are, you're going to have a mighty long wait!"

"Calm down, Beau," Jed said, walking back to the steps. "I ain't wantin' that; wouldn't ask that of any man. It's just that I keep hearin' two different stories, and I'm confused as hell. Let's take a walk and see if we can't straighten this whole damn mess out."

When Garret opened the door to the office, his eyes feasted on the lovely vision standing in the room. A blue wool dress adorned her desirable figure. The traveling hat perched on her head and tied with a large bow beneath her chin acted as a frame for her lovely face, while the thick dark lashes made her amber-brown eyes look huge. His eyes stopped at the full lips he longed to crush under his.

"What a pleasant surprise," he said, unable to hide the husky tone of desire.

"Hello, Garret."

Danny's voice was cool and aloof, which made Garret want her even more. "I thought we weren't supposed to see each other until the wedding?" he tried to tease.

She looked at the floor. "I'm sorry, Garret, but there will be no wedding."

Garret could see she was dead serious and that she'd probably given this decision a lot of thought. He doubted he'd be able to change her mind this time. Pure panic streaked through him. "You can't be serious! The wedding is only two days away. I've made all the arrangements, and I've sold the saloon. You can't all of a sudden change your mind!"

"I know, and I'm sorry for everything. I don't want to break your heart, but I don't love you."

"Is it Falkner?" Garret bit out.

Danny's head snapped up. "Why should you ask that?"

Garret knew he'd made a grave error. He needed time to think. He walked behind the desk and sat down, trying to regain his composure. "I just thought that since all the women seem so attracted to him, you might feel that way, too."

"Well, you're wrong!"

"I guess I'm just jealous, and the thought of you becoming attracted to another man is more than I can bear." He forced a smile. "Well, darling, I can see your mind is made up, and I'm not going to give you a bad time over it, or try to change your decision." He saw a look of gratitude on her face. "But some day you might have a change of mind. If you do, I want you to promise you'll come back. I'll be waiting. I doubt very seriously I'll find someone to take your place."

After escorting her out, Garret returned to his office and paced the floor. "She can't do this to me," he growled. "Everyone in town will be laughing!" He sat in the chair. I have to think of something, he thought. She may keep me from getting hold of the ranch, but one way or another I have to get my hands on that gold. He leaned over and placed his elbows on the desk. There has to be a way, he thought as he rubbed his fingers up and down his forehead. Suddenly he sat up straight. A plan started taking shape in his mind.

As soon as the supplies had been loaded in the buckboard, Danny left town and drove straight to the Falkner home. She needed to get the sale of the ranch settled before her determination weakened and she tried to delay the inevitable. A servant answered her knock on the door.

"Is Mr. Falkner home?" she asked.

"He's not here," the girl replied, surprised at Danny using his formal name. "Would you care to come in?"

"No, just say I came by and that I need to talk to him."

Andrea had just entered the hall when she recognized the voice. "Danny?" she called, walking to the door. "It is you. Oh, dear, please come in, if just for a moment."

Having felt guilty ever since their last conversation, and missing her friend's visits, Danny stepped inside. "Well, I can't stay long," she said sheepishly.

"I'm going to sell the Silver J to Beau, Andrea." She watched the startled expression on her friend's face. "I'm leaving the valley."

"You can't be serious! This is your home! You haven't talked to Beau yet, have you? And what about your marriage to Garret? Oh, I can't seem to stop asking questions."

Danny smiled, suddenly feeling older than Andrea. "I just came from town. I went there to tell Garret I wouldn't marry him. As for selling the ranch, I'm tired of staying in one place," she lied. "It's time for me to be moving on. I'm sure Beau will be quite happy with my decision."

As Danny headed home, a spark of happiness dwelled within her. She had stayed longer than planned, but at least she had renewed her friendship with Andrea. She loved the woman dearly, and didn't want to leave the valley knowing there was bitterness between them.

Danny was surprised to see Mescal in front of the house when she drove up. When Beau and Jed walked out the front door, they were both smiling from ear to ear. It infuriated her to know Beau had used his charm to win Jed to his side.

"How did you get here so quick, Beau?" she asked after getting down from the wagon. She marched straight into the house without waiting for a reply.

The two men followed.

"I wouldn't call it quick," Jed spoke up. "He's been here for some time."

Danny turned around so fast Jed almost ran into her. "Then I take it Andrea didn't give you my message?"

"No," Beau replied. He remained standing just inside the door, his hands resting in the front pockets of his dark gray pants. "How did Garret take it when you told him the marriage was off?"

Danny glanced at Jed, then back at Beau. "I don't think that's any of your business." Her words were deliberately cutting. If Jed had told Beau about Garret, then Jed must have told Beau she was ready to sell the ranch. Why doesn't he sit down? she thought. His height always makes me feel at a disadvantage. "I'm going to change clothes. You will stay a little longer, won't you, Beau? After all, I'm about to give you what you've always wanted."

"I'll wait."

"Good. The sooner we finish this, the better." Danny left the room, her back rigid.

When she closed the bedroom door, Danny collapsed on the bed. This wasn't going to be as easy as she'd thought. Knowing that in less than an hour she'd no longer be the owner of the Silver J was the same as having a knife thrust in her stomach. And even though her heart had become callous, seeing Beau, handsome and tall, wearing a red shirt that set off his black hair and sun-browned complexion, didn't help. She would probably spend the rest of her life loving the good-for-nothing man! "God must have truly put him on this earth to show women how foolish and weak they are," she muttered. "Well, no sense delaying this." She rose from the bed and changed clothes.

"Did Jed run off?" she asked bitterly as she entered the room wearing her usual pants and a green and blue checked shirt.

"Yes," Beau replied. His eyes traveled the length of her. Oh, how I love this woman, he thought. One way or another I'm going to make her marry me. At least Garret's out of the way.

"Well, we might as well get down to business," she snapped. "Let's go sit at the table. I could use a cup of coffee."

When they entered the kitchen, Beau pulled out a chair and sat down.

"Want a cup?" Danny asked as she opened the cupboard door and pulled out two cups.

"Yes." Beau tipped the chair back on the rear legs. "Black." He watched Danny remove the pot sitting on top of the woodburning stove and pour the black, steaming substance in the cups. He wanted to crush her in his arms and prove his love, but he instinctively knew that it would be to his disadvantage at this time.

She set the cups on the table, wondering where Carlotta had disappeared to. "I suppose Jed has told you everything," she stated, taking a chair across from him.

"I'd rather hear it from you."

Danny tilted her chin up, ready for battle. "Very well. I am willing to sell you the Silver J." She let out a short, spiteful laugh. "You've won, but there are terms."

She waited for Beau to make some kind of reply, but none was forthcoming. He sipped his coffee, his blue eyes studying her.

Not able to stare him down, Danny looked at the table. Absentmindedly, she began drawing lines on the white tablecloth with her fingernail. "You are to keep Jose, Clancy and Joe on, and of course Jed. I want to be sure Jed will have this house and a place to stay until his dying days. And I want it all in writing."

"Are you planning to stay?" Beau asked.

"You don't have to worry about me being in the way. I'm leaving."

"Where will you go?"

Beau's quiet voice alerted her, and she glanced up at him. He wasn't reacting the way she'd expected. Why wasn't he gloating? "That's none of your business, either."

"You can just take off without a backward glance and leave the man that raised you?"

Beau's eyes had turned cold, but she didn't care what he thought. "What difference does it make, as long as you get what you've wanted all along?" she asked defensively.

Beau leaned forward, the front legs of the chair banging on the floor. "How do you know what I want?" he asked, his words clipped. "You haven't even taken the time to find out."

"Oh! Next I suppose you're going to say you don't want the ranch, and expect me to believe it!" She took a deep breath then said in a calmer tone, "I'm not going to fight with you, Beau. Do you want the ranch or not? I will sell the Silver J. If you don't want the ranch, I'm sure Garret will be kind enough to take it off my hands."

Beau was instantly in a state of rage. "You'd sell it to that bastard?" he stormed.

"You have no right to call him names!" she yelled, needing to vent her hurt. "He is a true gentleman, a word you've never known the meaning of. You're nothing but a half-breed, and that's all you'll ever be!" Danny was shocked at what she'd said. Once again she'd let her anger and frustration override common sense. Seeing his face suddenly turn to stone, she wanted to apologize, but knew she wouldn't. It was better this way. The cord had been cut forever.

"I'll buy your ranch, Danny," Beau said in a cool tone. "The money will be delivered tomorrow afternoon." He stood, walked through the house and outside.

"Beau!" she called from the doorway as he mounted Mescal. "Don't forget! I want it in writing that Jed keeps the house and he and the others will stay on working."

Without answering, Beau kicked Mescal in the ribs, wanting to get away as fast as possible before he did something he might regret. While Mescal's hooves swiftly moved over the land, Beau paid scant attention. His anger continued to consume him. He felt his gut knotting up on him. Not since his younger years did being called a half-breed have such a profound effect on him. An evil smile formed on his lips. Danny would marry him, even if they spent the rest of their lives in hell. She would see just how ungentlemanly a half-breed could be! He knew exactly how to force her into marrying him. If Danny truly cared for Jed, she wouldn't want him hanged for robbing the Cordhill Mine shipment.

Danny bit her bottom lip to keep from crying. It's over, she thought. As of tomorrow there will never be a ranch called the Silver J again. In years to come, no one will even know this place existed. Reverting to an old habit, she started to run her fingers through her hair, but the chenille covering her chignon stopped her. Momentarily, she'd forgotten her hair wasn't short any longer. "Think I'll cut it off!" she grumbled as she watched small flakes of snow start to fall. She was just going to look for Jed when he came walking up.

"Well, did you and Beau get everythin' straightened out?" he asked, a broad smile on his face.

"Yes," she answered flippantly, hiding her true feelings. "He'll be delivering the money tomorrow afternoon."

The grin disappeared. "But didn't he tell you what was on his mind?"

"I didn't give him a chance to say anything. You would be well advised to do the same when he's around!"

"You needn't take that temper of yours out on me, young lady!" Jed said. "There ain't no reason for you to leave. He was willin' to marry you."

"Oh? And am I supposed to get down on my knees and thank him for sacrificing himself?"

"I didn't mean it that way, Danny. You're twistin' everything around and making it come out the way you want to hear it!"

She gasped. "You think I want to sell the ranch?"

"Now, I didn't say that, either!"

Danny turned and went to her bedroom. "Why is everyone acting as if all this is my fault?" she groaned before running into her room and slamming the door behind her.

Butch had spent most of the night shivering and pacing in an effort to keep warm. He waited until it was almost dawn before he cautiously approached Danny's bedroom window. He wanted to be sure everyone was fast asleep before making his move. Not wanting to awaken her, it took several minutes to open the window wide enough for him to crawl through. He heard a soft moan and headed toward the sound. Because the clouds hid the moon, everything was pitch black. Not being familiar with the room, he reached the bed before realizing it, and his knees hit the side.

"What's going on!" Danny demanded, sitting up. She was ready for battle, thinking Beau had entered.

Butch's eyes finally adjusted to the dark, and before the girl could yell and wake everyone, his fist came down on her jaw. She immediately slumped on the bed, out cold. Quickly he wrapped her up in the quilted comforter and slung her over his shoulder. Butch discovered it was no easy task climbing out the window with his captive.

"Danny still ain't up?" Jed asked Carlotta. He'd already done most of his early-morning chores and had returned for breakfast. Jose was already seated at the table.

"No," Carlotta said, setting a large platter of eggs, bacon and steak on the table. That was followed by a plate of hot biscuits, a big bowl of gravy, butter and steaming hot coffee.

Jed sat down just as Clancy and Joe came wandering in.

"I could smell that good food all the way outside," Joe said, taking his place at the table.

Carlotta's ample chest swelled with pride. Danny had shown her how to cook, and she experimented on her own. She now received a lot of compliments on her cooking.

"Maybe you should go wake her up, Carlotta," Jed said, dishing food onto his plate. "She's gettin' too thin. She ain't got no business goin' without food the way she's been doin'."

"Are we all going to be looking for work, Jed?" Clancy asked, expressing the concern that had been on everyone's mind. They all knew Danny was planning to sell the Silver J. "It'll be almost impossible to get on at any ranch this time of year."

Carlotta waited to hear Jed's answer.

"I ain't had a chance to ask what's goin' on, but I know she don't plan on sellin' unless we're all guaranteed a job. I told you that. She ain't one to go back on her word. She'll look after all of you."

"What about you?" Jose asked.

"She said she was goin' to make sure I keep this house." Jed didn't want any of them to know how concerned he was over Danny's future. "I ain't goin' to mind livin' here one damn bit. I'm sure Beau will take care of all of us."

"Huh!" Carlotta said. "What makes you think he'll stand by his word after he's got this place?"

Jed laid his fork down and gave her a hard look. "I've always considered myself a good judge of men," he said in a gruff voice, "and I not only like but I also trust Beau Falkner. I don't want to be hearin' any more of that kind of talk. I want the lot of you to remember one thing. You'll soon be workin' for the man, and you'd damn well better start changin' your way of thinkin', or you ain't gonna have a job for long." He picked his fork up. "Enough said. Go wake up Danny, Carlotta."

When Carlotta came rushing into the kitchen, Jed knew something was wrong. The woman never rushed, and she had a perplexed look on her face. Jed stood, knocking over his chair.

"What's wrong?" he asked.

"Danny's not in her room," Carlotta said, breathing heavily.

Jed let out a sigh of relief and straightened the chair up. "At first I thought something had happened to her," he said, sitting down. "She's probably gone for a ride."

"No! Something's not right."

Jed slowly stood up again. "What you talkin' about?"

"The window is wide open and her bed isn't made. She always makes her bed. And the comforter's gone. I know she didn't pack and leave because the trunk's still sitting there, and her clothes are in the clothespress."

"Are you sayin' someone's took off with her?" Jed growled. He headed out of the kitchen toward Danny's room.

"That's what it looks like," Carlotta said, following him.

Jed entered the room and after a quick look left again. "Jose!" he barked. "Go see if Sheeka is in her stall!" Everyone followed Jed out the back door and around to Danny's window. The boot prints in the snow clearly showed a man had been there. Jed stood there confused as to why anyone would want to take off with Danny, and the first person that came to mind was Beau.

"Sheeka's in her stall," Jose reported, out of breath.

"Clancy, I want you to ride hell-bent for leather to Falkner's place," Jed ordered. "Tell him I want to see him. And if he ain't there, tell his sister what's happened. Then ride back as fast as you can and let me know what you found out. I'm sure they'll lend you a horse to ride back."

"Sure thing, Jed." Clancy took off at a run. A few minutes later, he rode out of the barn at a hard gallop. He hadn't even bothered putting a saddle on the horse.

"Don't you think we should start tracking him?" Joe asked.

"We could, and I reckon we'd find him as long as he left tracks in the snow," Jed answered. "But what if he goes into the rocks or heads up Granite Creek? You good at trackin', Joe?"

"Well, ah, not really."

"How about you, Jose?" Jed asked.

Jose shook his head.

Jed said nothing to the others, but he knew if Beau had Danny, they'd never find them. Jed also knew that if Beau hadn't taken off with Danny, he might be the only man who could find her.

"We can't just stand around and do nothing!" declared Carlotta, tugging at her cross. "Lord only knows what could be happening to the poor child."

"We'll wait until Clancy returns," Jed stated. "I don't want anyone walkin' around and messin' up the tracks." He walked toward the house. "No sense standing around in the cold," he mumbled.

Time seemed to drag by. Jed smoked one cigarette after another, drank coffee and paced the floor. When they heard a horse arriving out front, everyone rushed to the door. Jed, being the closest, was the first one out.

Looking to his right, he saw Beau riding his black stallion; some distance behind was Clancy, and even farther back, a buggy, pulled by a bay, moved at top speed.

Beau leaped off Mescal's back before the horse had time to slow down.

"What's all this about?" Beau demanded. "Clancy said Danny is missing."

Andrea drove up, her face red from the cold air. "Is Danny all right?"

"I don't know what's goin' on," Jed replied worriedly. He looked at Beau. "Someone's taken off with her, and none of us are good at tracking."

"Are you sure she hasn't just decided to leave?" Beau asked.

"Positive. I got something to show you." Jed took off to the side of the house with Beau following.

"Don't worry, Jed," Beau said quietly, after studying the fresh trail. "I'll find her."

Chapter Twenty-One

When Danny awoke the second time, a sharp pain shot through her jaw where the man had planted his fist, and her limbs were stiff. She had to have been lying in the same cramped position for some time. Although the comforter still covered her face, she no longer felt the rope around her. She didn't know whether it was safe to move.

She thought about what had happened, not understanding why. After being knocked out, she'd come to her senses only to discover she was bound and draped over a moving horse. For what seemed like an eternity, she'd traveled in that uncomfortable position until finally, and much to her relief, the horse had been brought to a halt. She could see nothing, but she could smell a rank odor of dirty bodies and hear men speaking in Spanish. Then, with no pretense of gentleness, she was yanked down, carried a short distance and dumped unceremoniously on what felt like a cot. She could hear muffled voices, but as far as she knew, no one came near her. Exhausted beyond words, she'd finally fallen asleep.

Her mind jerked back to the present. Unable to remain in her cramped position a moment longer, she slowly stretched out her arms and legs, waiting for someone to yell at her. Having accomplished that with no apparent problems, she lifted the corner of the comforter from her face, just enough to peek out. Although the window openings were covered with hide and the room was relatively dark, she could see bright sunlight creeping in around the window edges. Moving her head slightly, she saw a fireplace, but no fire was lit and cold air had already begun to penetrate beneath the comforter, which was loosely tossed over her.

Feeling a little more sure of herself, she again moved her head to look around the rest of the dirty shanty when her eyes stopped their progress. In the corner, sitting on a chair propped against the wall, was the most ferocious-looking man she'd ever seen. He was about Jed's size, except his stomach hung partially over a large silver belt buckle. A sombrero sat on top of his head and black, greasy hair hung down to his shoulders. The ends of a mustache reached his chin. The ammunition belts crisscrossing his chest over a dirty shirt and short jacket proclaimed him a Mexican *bandido*. Danny's eyes darted down when he moved his feet and the *rowels* attached to the heels of his muddy boots made a chinging noise. She glanced back up at his face, and he smiled, his black mustache unable to hide the brown, decayed or missing teeth.

Sitting up in the middle of the army cot, Danny wrapped the comforter securely around her. Still confused as to the purpose of all this, she managed to ask, "Why am I here?"

"No comprendo Ingles," he replied.

She didn't speak Spanish, and obviously he didn't speak her language. She turned away and stared into space, choosing not to look at the man. Other than changing her position off and on, she remained glued to the same spot.

There seemed to be only three men, none of whom she recognized. One was another *bandido* who looked remarkably like the first one. She did hear the man with the evil grin called Mateo.

The third man entered the shanty only once. He was of medium height, cleaner dress, with average looks, and not Spanish. He reminded her of a young boy, but the crow's-feet around his eyes showed he was older than he first appeared. She asked, "Mister, why have I been brought here?"

"Name's Butch. You'll get all your answers when the boss arrives," he replied in a friendly enough voice. He turned, said something in Spanish to Mateo, who was again taking his turn watching her, and left.

After what seemed like hours, Danny's stomach rumbled with fear, anger and hunger. Plus, she needed to go relieve herself, something none of the men seemed to have taken into consideration!

Someone knocked and Danny assumed they were fixing to change guards again. She watched Mateo go over to the log door and peek through the small chiseled-out slit. Seemingly satisfied, he lifted the wood bar that blocked anyone from entering. Welcomed sunlight streamed in through the opened door. Danny stifled a shriek of joy when she saw Garret walk in behind Butch. Have they captured Garret, too? she wondered. Maybe they would both be safer if she didn't show any recognition. Butch said something to Mateo, and the two men left the shanty.

"What's going on?" she whispered as Garret moved the wooden chair over to the cot. With the back turned toward her, he straddled the seat, facing her and resting his arms on the top rung. Slowly Danny stretched her legs and arms, trying to get feeling back into them. "Do you know why we've been brought here?" she asked.

Garret maintained a somber look. "They're holding you for ransom," he answered.

Realizing the comforter had spread apart and her gown was hiked up, she quickly covered her bare legs. "Well," she finally said, "I wish them luck. I certainly have no money." She glanced up. "Oh, Garret! Surely they don't expect you to pay it?"

"No."

"Thank God. Then they're in for a big disappointment. When they realize that, maybe they'll let us go. From what Butch said, I think the big boss should be arriving anytime."

"I took my life in my hands by coming out here, Danny." Garret managed a deep sigh of frustration. "I always knew you were hiding something," he said in a hurt tone. "Why didn't you tell me you're the Gringo Kid? It might have saved us both a lot of trouble."

She sucked in her breath.

"Do you intend to deny it?" he asked. "Our lives are at stake, Danny!"

Slowly she expelled the air in her lungs. "No," she said weakly. "Do you know how they found out?"

"Apparently someone by the name of Smoky told them."

The piece of information startled her. "How did he know?"

Garret stood, trying to decide how much he should tell her. "I have no idea," he replied. "But that isn't the issue. The issue is the gold you stole from the Cordhill Mine. They want it!"

"Gold? I have no gold. I don't know anything about the Cordhill Mine."

"Danny, this is no time to pull an innocent act! If you give them the shipment, they promise to let us go free."

"And you believe them? Honest, Garret, I don't know what they're talking about!"

The sincere look on her face made him stop and think. It suddenly occurred to him just how much he'd taken for granted. There was no proof whatsoever that the Gringo Kid had taken off with the gold. Anyone could have done it! He ran his fingers through his blond hair. What a fool I've been! He sat down, watching Danny's face closely.

"This is the way they explained it to me," he said, trying to hide his anger. "There was a wagon carrying a box of gold. Butch was one of the men who tried to rob it, but he got hit in the shoulder with a bullet and rode off. The rest of the men were killed." Even in the dim room, Garret saw the flicker of light that came into her eyes. Could he have been right all along? In his eagerness, he shoved the chair a little closer toward her. "It was in a meadow in the territory of New Mexico," he said softly.

Danny was shocked, and didn't try to hide it. She scooted back until her spine met the wall.

"You know what they're talking about, don't you?" he pursued. "You have to tell me, Danny, I'm the only one who can save us!"

"Yes. We saw the whole thing when we were riding down from the mesa."

"We?"

"Jed and I." Her voice had become raspy. "But we didn't take the box. We didn't even know what was in it."

"I told you, this is no time to be making up stories!" Garret barked out, losing his patience fast. The gold was practically in his hands!

"Damn it! I'm not lying! We left, and Jed went back later, ut he said the box was...." Her eyes became round amber-rown saucers. Had Jed told her the truth?

"The box was what?" Garret demanded.

Danny forced her face to look like stone. "He said the box vas gone. And I know he told me the truth, because we trav-led on to Arizona Territory." She couldn't tell him what really appened. "If he found anything, he'd have taken it with us."

Garret's lips curled into an evil grin. "Why did he go back to he meadow?"

"I'd lost one of my guns. Which, by the way, he didn't find, ither! Why are you asking me all these questions? You'd think ou're the one who wants that shipment."

Garret knew he had to calm down. Danny was already get-ing suspicious. If he showed his hand, he'd never get the in-ormation out of her. "I believe you, Danny," he said. "The uestion is, will those men outside believe you? I'll go and see f I can talk some sense to them."

Before Garret reached the door, it flew open, the leather inges allowing it to bang against the wall. He hadn't replaced he wooden bar. Butch stood in the doorway with the two *andidos* behind him.

"So that's what all this has been about!" Butch said, a faint rin on his face. "I've been standing by the window listening o you two."

"I'll talk to you later," Garret said.

"Oh, no, we're gonna talk right now," Butch said as he en-ered the room. He spit out some Spanish to the other men, and hey stayed outside. "You weren't planning on telling me any-hing about this, were you?" Butch accused. "You was going o take it all yourself and hightail it out of town. Was you also planning to take my share of money in the safe, too?"

"Shut up! You don't know what you're talking about. We'll ettle this outside!" Garret ordered.

Danny realized she'd stopped breathing and quickly inhaled air. She started scooting toward the end of the cot, but when the other end lifted off the ground she fell on the dirt floor. Fran-ically she tried to figure some way of getting out of this mess, out nothing was forthcoming.

"We ain't leaving this room until little missy gives us some answers," Butch said vehemently. "You've been too gentle with her, boss. A good slapping around should get some answers And if that don't work.... Well, me and the others wouldn' mind sharing her."

The word boss rang through Danny's head. It suddenly occurred to her just how stupid she'd been. Why hadn't she listened to what Andrea had told her?

"Don't you put a hand on her!" Garret threatened.

"You don't seem to understand, boss. You ain't got no say since you tried milking me out of my share. I'm taking over now," Butch growled. "Keep your nose out of this and I might let you out of here alive. After all, you sure as hell can't tell anyone without hanging yourself."

"Damn it, keep your mouth shut, Butch!"

"You keep yours shut, or so help me, I'll shoot you dead here and now. I don't cotton to being swindled out of what's rightfully mine!"

Danny sat stunned. If she thought she'd been afraid before she was doubly afraid now. There had to be a way out of this mess, but her mind seemed unable to function. She felt sure she would wet her gown. At that moment, sure she had no future to look forward to, she heard an owl hoot twice. It had to be Beau calling to tell her he was near!

She took a deep breath to calm herself. "How did you know I was the Gringo Kid, Garret?" she asked, trying to stall for time.

Garret gave her an almost childish look, as if she should forgive him. "Smoky told me," he said, his voice weak. "He heard you and Falkner talking at the ranch the night of the barbecue. Surely, being an outlaw yourself, you must realize had no choice? If you'd only married me! We could have been sitting on top of the world together in California."

She suddenly saw Garret as a pathetic man. Unable to wield power, he was falling apart.

"That's why I had Butch hold up the banks and say he was the Gringo Kid. I thought it would force you into marrying me. Damn it," he suddenly stormed, "I was good to you! I didn't treat you like the other women I knew."

Danny felt sick to her stomach. She'd come so close to marrying this man.

"Enough talk!" stated Butch. "You got a choice, missy. You don't strike me as dumb, so you know me and the boys are going to enjoy ourselves with you. Fight all you like, it makes even better. After that, you can either die slow or fast, it don't matter to me." He smiled, seeing Danny shudder. "One way or another, you're going to tell us where you've hidden the gold!"

"I don't know where the gold is!" she yelled at him, suddenly getting mad. Where the hell are you, Beau? her mind cried out.

Butch walked over and gave her a wicked slap across the face, knocking her flat on the ground. "That's just a little sample as to what you can look forward to, missy." He leaned down and jerked the comforter away. Butch was so absorbed in his pleasure he didn't see Garret charge until too late. Garret knocked him away and went for his gun. He wasn't fast enough. Butch's draw proved to be faster, and he shot Garret in the head. Hearing a scuffling noise outside, Butch swung around and aimed his gun at the doorway. With his back turned to her, Danny managed to reach over and pick up Garret's pistol.

"Drop it," she ordered, "or you're a dead man!"

Butch lowered his gun and turned slowly around. "I doubt you could hit the broad side of a barn," he declared, and started raising the deadly weapon.

Danny pulled the trigger.

When Beau came rushing inside, the first thing he saw was Danny sitting on the floor in her nightdress and a pistol in her hand with smoke curling out the end of the barrel. He quickly checked the two men on the floor. They were both dead.

"What took you so damn long?" she raged. After what she'd just been through, her hands were shaking. "I could've been killed!"

Even though her face was red and swollen and her eye almost closed, he knew she was all right. He had been sick with worry when he heard her scream, and when the two shots rang out he had almost gone over the edge. But there sat his woman, giving him hell for taking so long. He started laughing out of sheer relief.

"What are you laughing at?"

Beau raised a dark eyebrow as he watched her. His lips we spread in a wide grin. "I can't think of a better way to greeted."

Danny hurled the gun at him, which he easily dodge "Where are the two other men?" she asked, covering herse with the comforter.

Beau chuckled. "They won't be bothering us." He watche Danny stand and march out of the house as though she we royalty, the comforter acting as a train.

The bright sun was a welcome sight, though the ground fe cold beneath her bare feet. Finally able to relieve herself, Dann headed straight for the rocks.

When she returned, feeling considerably better, she sa Mateo strung up in a tree, quite alive and with no means of e cape. The black circles beneath his eyes showed he'd met wit a strong fist. The other bandit was nowhere in sight, and Dann wasn't about to ask what had happened to him. She walke over to where the outlaws' horses were tethered, mounted or and rode off.

The shanty had long since disappeared behind the hills whe Beau rode up beside her. They continued on a short distanc before she asked, "What are you going to do about the man the tree?"

"Send the soldiers from Fort Whipple after him," Beau a swered. "What went on in there?"

She didn't want to talk about it just yet. It was all too fres in her mind. But there was one piece of information Bea should know. "The other white man is the one who posed the Gringo Kid."

"Well, I guess it's a good thing I didn't kill the last *bandide* He can testify, and that will put an end once and for all to th notorious outlaw."

Danny sighed. "Yes, I suppose it will." It took her a m ment before she could utter the words she knew needed to said. "Thank you for saving my life," she practically whi pered, finding it difficult to get the words out.

"What?" Beau asked, teasing. He'd heard her.

"I said thank you for saving my life!" she yelled at him f riously.

"You know, Danny, the only way I can see to keep you out of trouble is to let you marry me."

"That'll be a cold day in hell!" she snapped. "I'm never going to get married, especially to a man who doesn't even know how to treat a lady!" She kicked her heels into the horse's sides, but before the animal could take off Beau leaned forward and grabbed the reins, bringing the animal to a halt.

"What the hell do you think you're doing?" she yelled at him.

Beau slid off Mescal still holding onto the reins of the nag Danny rode. With one swoop of his powerful arm around her waist, he lifted her down and carried her toward a stand of pine trees like a sack of potatoes resting on his hip. Even though it hurt to move, she fought and screamed. Finally he stopped and stood her gently on her feet. Danny balled her fists up and tried socking him in the jaw, but as usual he was too quick for her to connect.

Beau wrapped his arm around the feisty woman, pinning her arms to her sides. "You know what I think?" he asked, his voice soft with pleasure at having her in his arms again.

"I couldn't care less!"

He chuckled. "I'm going to tell you anyway. I think you're in love with me."

"You have really lost your mind!" She couldn't look him in the face. His nearness was already starting to affect her. Yes, I love you! she screamed silently.

"I've given this a lot of thought over the past few days," he said in a nonchalant manner, "and I've decided you would never have given yourself to me so readily if you weren't already in love with me."

"I think I should remind you I didn't exactly throw myself at you. In fact, as I recall, I shot at you!"

He lifted his free hand and pushed the tangled auburn hair out of her face. With the back of his hand he gently stroked her bruised and swollen cheek. "Their deaths should have been slow and painful for what they did to you," he whispered.

Never having heard him speak in such a manner, Danny looked up and saw the unmasked love in his blue eyes. She couldn't say anything, afraid her voice would betray the emotions she was feeling because of his words and gentleness. Did she dare believe what she was seeing and hearing?

"I do know how to treat a lady, little one," he teased.

"Beau—are you trying to say you love me?" she asked breathlessly.

He smiled. "Oh. Did I forget to mention that?"

She clenched her teeth. "You are impossible!" she said, stomping her heel down on top of his soft leather boot. When he released her she headed back to the horses.

She had one foot in the stirrup when she heard him say, "Yes, Danielle Louise Jameson. I am so damn in love with you it hurts!"

She whirled around and saw the big grin on Beau's face. One hand rested on his hip.

"And you'd damn well better be in love with me," he continued, "or we're both going to be in big trouble, because I'm not about to let you leave the valley."

"Are you proposing marriage?" she asked suspiciously.

"You're damn right I am."

Danny's spirits soared. He had to be telling the truth. There was nothing to gain from lying now. She broke out in laughter, even though it hurt her jaw. "From all the books I've read, when a man declares his love and offers marriage, he gets down on his knee."

Beau chuckled. "Not this half-breed. You've been reading the wrong books. God, you're a beautiful sight," he said in a husky voice.

Danny suddenly noticed her state of dress. She brazenly mocked him by placing her hand on her hip. "And you're the *purtiest* man I ever did see."

Slowly he started walking forward, wanting to kiss her. Knowing how much it would hurt her sore mouth, and all she'd just gone through, he kept himself in check. "When you get well, I may never let you out of bed," he said, stopping in front of her.

Danny started to remind him there was nothing wrong with her body, but changed her mind. She liked seeing the concern in his eyes, and it certainly wouldn't hurt him to wait. After all, she told herself, look how long I've waited for him. I might even make him woo me before I agree to marry him. She gave him a smile that would melt the coldest heart. "I'll be looking forward to it," she whispered.

He lifted her up, sat her on the nag, then handed her the comforter, which had fallen on the ground. Jumping on Mescal, he looked over at the woman he loved and said, "Let's go home, Danny."

As they rode away, Beau made a vow to himself. Before returning the gold to Cordhill Mine, he'd hear his she cat say "I do" in front of a preacher.

* * * * *

COMING NEXT MONTH

CHINA STAR—Karen Keast

Famed actress Trinity Lee burned to avenge a murder. She
would sabotage Madison Brecker's railroad, then take the
scarred marauder's life as cold-bloodedly as she believed
her mother was slain. But neither the ruthless Breck nor
the Eurasian beauty had counted on the magnetic passion
that made her veins run hot with anything but revenge....

SILVER NOOSE—Patricia Gardner Evans

Falsely accused Jesse McClintock faced the likely prospect
of a quick hanging—until a sporting judge offered him a
year as foreman on a ranch in Apache country near the
wild Mexican border. But Jesse's plans for an easy
escape were soon waylaid when he met his new jailer:
Miranda Hart.

AVAILABLE NOW:

DAWN'S EARLY LIGHT
Caryn Cameron

BITTERSWEET
DeLoras Scott

Harlequin Temptation dares to be different!

Once in a while, we Temptation editors spot a romance that's truly innovative. To make sure *you* don't miss any one of these outstanding selections, we'll mark them for you.

EDITOR'S
CHOICE

When the ''Editors' Choice'' fold-back appears on a Temptation cover, you'll know we've found that extra-special page-turner!

THE

Temptation

EDITORS

TEARS IN THE RAIN

STARRING
CHRISTOPHER CAVZENOVE AND
SHARON STONE

BASED ON A NOVEL BY
PAMELA WALLACE

PREMIERING IN NOVEMBER

TITR-1

Exclusively on
SHOWTIME®

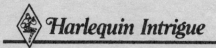

BIRDS OF CALIFORNIA

309. Sage Grouse

Centrocercus urophasianus

BIRDS OF CALIFORNIA

AN INTRODUCTION

TO MORE THAN THREE HUNDRED COMMON BIRDS OF THE STATE AND ADJACENT ISLANDS

WITH A SUPPLEMENTARY LIST OF RARE MIGRANTS, ACCIDENTAL
VISITANTS, AND HYPOTHETICAL SUBSPECIES

BY

IRENE GROSVENOR WHEELOCK

AUTHOR OF "NESTLINGS OF FOREST AND MARSH"

WITH TEN FULL-PAGE PLATES AND SEVENTY-EIGHT DRAWINGS
IN THE TEXT BY BRUCE HORSFALL

CHICAGO
A. C. McCLURG & CO.

1904

THE UNIVERSITY PRESS
CAMBRIDGE · U.S.A.

TO

MY MOTHER

NOTE OF ACKNOWLEDGMENT

WHILE, in the preparation of this work, I have met with universal kindness from the ever-hospitable Californians, my especial thanks are due to members of the Cooper Club and to Dr. David Starr Jordan, of Leland Stanford University, for many courtesies extended and kindly encouragement given. For advice and assistance I am also indebted to Mr. Chas. F. Lummis, Mr. Leverett M. Loomis, Mr. John Muir, Mr. Joseph Grinnell, Mr. H. R. Taylor, and the late Chester A. Barlow. But it is to my fellow-student and co-laborer, my husband, Mr. Harry B. Wheelock, that I owe most. With untiring patience he has read manuscript, checked lists, and corrected errors, thereby making it possible for me to go on in the face of many obstacles.

I. G. W.

INTRODUCTORY

CALIFORNIA is the land of sunshine, flowers, and bird song. In the great sweep of country from Mexico on the south to Oregon on the north are found climatic conditions ranging from the Arctic circle to the tropics. The valleys blossom with roses, while the mountains are crowned with perpetual snow. Hence we find a flora and fauna as unique as the climate. It is the paradise of the bird-lover as well as of the tourist. Birds of the Torrid Zone come here; birds of Alaska winter here; birds from the mountains come down into the valleys. There is a constant movement north and south, a lesser one vertically from the warm lowlands to the colder altitudes, or vice versa.

To live among these fascinating feathered folk and not long to know them, one must have eyes that see not and ears deaf to Nature's music. Yet the bird-lover who wishes to enjoy an acquaintance with them without scientific study finds his road beset with difficulties. From the scientific works that seem to him hopelessly abstruse he turns to the " popular " bird book, which is delightful but does not help him to identify his "bird neighbors." It is in the hope of meeting this need and affording an introduction to the birds more commonly found in California that this non-technical work is offered. Keys have been avoided and a simple classification, according to habitat or color, substituted, following the excellent plan used by Neltje Blantjan, which has never been excelled for easy identification.

In selecting these three hundred from the five hundred varieties listed as occurring within the confines of the State and adjacent islands, no arbitrary rule has been followed, the author being guided by her own experience in field work among them. During a test study in 1902, the ground covered was from Mexico to Oregon, and from the islands off the coast to the eastern slope of the Sierra Nevada; and in this, two hundred and forty odd species were *commonly* met with, while the others were by no means rare. The observations were made in the desert region along the California side of the Colorado River, and at Tia Juana, San Diego, Riverside, Redlands, Pasadena, San Pedro, Santa Catalina, in the Santa Cruz Mountains, Monterey, Pacific Grove, Palo Alto, Alviso, San Francisco Bay region, Martinez, the Farallones, Mt. Tamalpais, Mt. Shasta, Sacramento, Slippery Ford, Lake Tahoe, Fallen Leaf Lake, Eagle Lake, and Lake Tulare. This list is given for the benefit of bird-loving tourists who may wish to do likewise.

Of the birds occurring in the State and not mentioned in this volume forty are ducks and geese, the rest being either rare migrants or subspecies, confusing to the observer and usually *impossible to differentiate without a gun.* The seabirds, usually omitted from non-technical bird books in the East, are so conspicuous a part of California Avifauna that no work on the subject would be complete without them.

Field notes begun in 1894, and made with the aid of powerful binoculars, form the basis of the following pages. The books used for reference, wherever the author's personal observations were unsatisfactory, are " Ridgway's Manual of North American Birds, " Bendire's " Life Histories, " Loomis's " Water Birds of California," Mrs. Bailey's " Manual of Birds of the Western United States," Davie's ." Nests and Eggs of North American Birds," " The Condor, " " The Auk, " " The Nidologist," Nelson's " Report of Birds of Alaska," and Mr. Grinnell's " Check-list of California Birds." The check-list numbers and nomenclature of the American Ornithologist Union have been strictly adhered to.

No originality is claimed for the technical descriptions of the birds, as on this point the author has drawn freely from standard authorities, oftentimes verbatim, when a personal examination of specimens was impossible.

It has been a difficult matter to collect facts for the breeding range and season because there is no published data on the subject; but the work has been conscientiously done, and every precaution taken to prevent possible errors. The dates given include the earliest and latest at which eggs or newly hatched young are usually found. It will be seen from this that especial attention has been given to the habits of each species during the reproduction period, including nest-building, incubation, care of the young, etc., all of which, unless otherwise accredited, has been taken from the author's own notes.

Long and careful study of the feeding habits of young birds in California and the Eastern United States has led the author to make some statements which may incur the criticism of ornithologists who have not given especial attention to the subject. For instance, — that the young of all macrochires, woodpeckers, perching birds, cuckoos, kingfishers, most birds of prey, and many seabirds *are fed by regurgitation from the time of hatching through a period varying in extent from three days to four weeks, according to the species.* Furthermore, that birds eating animal flesh or *large* insects give fresh (unregurgitated) food to their young at a correspondingly earlier stage of development than do those varieties which subsist on small insects or seeds. Also, that exclusive seed eaters are usually fed by regurgitation so long as they remain in the nest. Out of one hundred and eighty cases recorded by the author, in every instance where the young were hatched in a naked or semi-naked condition they were fed in this manner for at least three days. In some instances the food was digested, wholly or in part; in others it was probably swallowed merely for convenience in carrying, and was regurgitated in an undigested condition. There seemed to be no definite relation between the duration of the period of regurgitative feeding and the length of time required for the full development of the fledgeling. Young vultures were fed in this way for ten days, and stayed in the nest nine weeks. Young robins received their food by this process three, occasionally four, days, and usually took flight on the fifteenth day. Humming-birds, swallows, and a few others are fed by regurgitation so long as they remain in the nest. Goldfinches, waxwings, and others are nourished in this way, with an occasional meal of raw food, until they are ready to fly. The list is a long one, and as most if not all of these instances are mentioned in their individual biographies, given in this volume, they need not be cited here. Scientists have long known that pigeons, doves, and humming-birds feed their young in this manner, and the discovery that most species do likewise need cause no surprise.

IRENE GROSVENOR WHEELOCK.

CHICAGO, January 1, 1904.

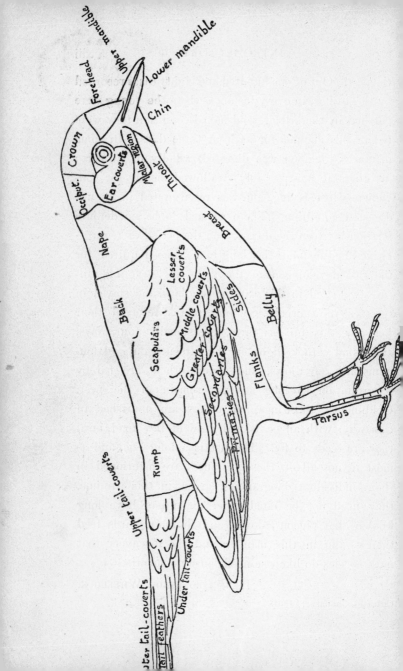

IDENTIFICATION

THE accompanying chart of a bird will explain the terms used in the descriptions. "Upper parts" refers to the entire upper surface of the body of the bird from the bill to the tail. In the same manner, "Under parts" refers to the under surface.

In identifying, decide first into which class the bird you are observing is likely to belong, — that is, whether land or water birds. If water, whether it is found on the open sea, or near shore, or in bayous or marshes, and whether it is a swimmer or a wader, and then look for it in the list where you think it may belong. Always ascertain as near as you can the bird's *length*, and remember, in judging length, that a bird usually *looks* smaller than he actually *measures*. If the bird is among the land birds, and is neither a game bird nor a bird of prey, trace it down in the color classification.

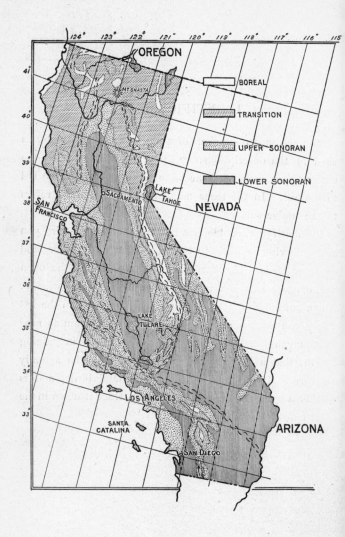

USE OF THE MAP

THE four Life Zones indicated on the accompanying map are those mentioned in the data given under the headings Geographical Distribution and Breeding Range. They represent climatic conditions of temperature in the regions indicated. The "Boreal" extends from the treeless, snowclad summits, far above the timber-line down through the coniferous forests. Next in coldness is the "Transition," which begins at the Yellowpines, overlapping the Boreal a little, and containing some species of oaks, buckbrush, manzanita, and some sagebrush. Lying between the Transition and the almost tropical heat of the "Lower Sonoran" is the "Upper Sonoran," where we find the juniper, oaks, piñon pines, and sagebrush. Last of all, the "Lower Sonoran" is the warmest. In it lie the hot valleys and desert regions of California, and here flourish the live oaks and mesquites. Many California birds migrate from one to another of these zones during the breeding season, as the birds of the Eastern United States migrate north and south. This changing from lower to higher altitude, or the reverse, is termed vertical migration.

CONTENTS

PART I.—WATER BIRDS

BIRDS OF THE OPEN SEA

BIRDS FOUND NEAR THE SHORE OR IN BAYS

BIRDS FOUND ALONG THE BEACHES

BIRDS FOUND IN BAYOUS AND MARSHES

PART II. — LAND BIRDS

I. — UPLAND GAME BIRDS

II. — BIRDS OF PREY

III. — COMMON LAND BIRDS IN COLOR GROUPS

With Brown Predominating in Plumage

With Dusky, Gray, and Slate-Colored Plumage

Plumage Conspicuously Black and White

Plumage Black or Iridescent Black

CONTENTS

CONTENTS

LIST OF ILLUSTRATIONS

PART I
WATER BIRDS

BIRDS OF CALIFORNIA

PART I

WATER BIRDS

BIRDS OF THE OPEN SEA

12. TUFTED PUFFIN. — *Lunda cirrhata.*

FAMILY : The Auks, Murres, and Puffins.

Length : 15.00.

Adults in Summer : Top of head, wings, back, and tail uniform blackish brown ; throat, breast, and belly dark grayish brown ; cheeks, forehead, and chin white ; a long silky tuft of yellow feathers, curved like horns, hanging down and back from each side of the crown, just back of the eyes. End of the bill bright red, base greenish yellow ; feet bright red.

Adults in Winter : Tufts wanting ; sides of head dusky ; feet and bill duller ; horny covering at base of bill replaced by brown skin.

Downy Young : Uniform dark gray or black.

Geographical Distribution : Coasts and islands of the North Pacific from Southern California to Alaska.

Breeding Range : From the Farallone Islands north to Behring Sea.

Breeding Season : Approximately, June 1 to August 1.

Nest : Usually in crevice in rock ; sometimes a burrow is excavated in the shale ; bare, or lined with coarse weeds.

Eggs : 1 ; ranging from white to yellowish buff, variously marked with lilac dots at both ends ; or, irregular, indistinct tan-color spots over entire surface ; or, having nondescript zigzag markings. Size 2.81 × 1.89.

THE name " sea parrot " is applied to all puffins on account of their curious parrot-like bill. The Tufted

Puffin breeds extensively on the Farallone Islands and, to a limited extent, on Santa Barbara and San Clementi and Point Reyes Islands. Its single egg is laid in the barest semblance of a nest at the end of a burrow, or in a crevice among the rocks, or often under the shelter of a boulder. Wherever the nest may be it is always valiantly defended, and only in the rare absence of both parents will the collector rob it. The only child receives all the attention proverbially given to only children, for the nest is never left unguarded and the parents make a fierce fight if molested. The young puffin is an odd-looking baby, for it inherits the family bill. Otherwise

12. TUFTED PUFFIN.
"*As a puppy enjoys a bone.*"

it looks like a gray rat crouched at the entrance to its home run. Both adults and young are noisy, constantly growling from their burrows, and croaking when outside ; this with their odd bill, white face-mask, and drooping yellow ear-tufts, makes them eerie creatures of the sea. Their food consists of fish, mollusks, and crustacea, which they obtain by diving, using both wings and feet to propel themselves under water. This top-heavy bird is exceedingly awkward on land, and especially so when alighting with a fish in its beak, as with a swinging motion it drops its feet very wide apart. In feeding, the parent holds the fish or crustacean firmly in its beak, and the young tear bits from it with snarling whines, somewhat as a puppy enjoys a bone.

The young bird dives or is shoved off from the rocks to the water, both parents assisting at the rather startling début and, apparently, breaking the force of the fall by flying under the little one. One would expect a bird so uncouth and helpless in walking to be particularly graceful on the water, but this is not the case with the puffins, for they swim in such a horizontal position as to seem even more ungraceful than on land.

15. RHINOCEROS AUKLET. — *Cerorhinca monocerata.*

FAMILY : The Auks, Murres, and Puffins.

Length : 15.00.

Adults : Upper parts uniform grayish black ; sides of head, neck, upper neck, and sides dull gray ; lower breast and belly white, washed with gray ; a row of narrow, pointed white feathers along each side of occiput ; another row from base of bill across cheek to ear.

Nuptial Plumage : Base of upper mandible surmounted by a compressed upright horn, the base of which clasps the mandible as a saddle, down to and inclosing the nostrils. In winter this is replaced by leathery skin.

Downy Young : Soft gray-brown.

Geographical Distribution : Coast and islands of the North Pacific from Behring Sea south to Lower California (resident).

Breeding Range : From Washington northward on islands near the coast.

Breeding Season : Approximately, June 1 to August 20.

Nest : In crevice or at end of burrow, 2 to 4 feet from entrance, sometimes lined with refuse, but oftener bare.

Eggs : 1 ; chalky white, with faint gray markings. Size 2.70 × 1.82.

THE Rhinoceros Auklet is an odd-looking bird, having a short chunky body, with head set so close to its shoulders as to leave no neck at all, and legs so short as to be practically invisible. Floating on the water it seems to have fallen over on its face and to be unable to right itself, so that it looks much more like a bit of wood than a bird. You glance at it carelessly, never dreaming that it may be alive, when suddenly it dives, leaving no trace. In a moment it reappears at some distance away, only to dive again the instant you turn in its direction. It is perfectly at home on or in the water, although so helpless on land, and can swim a long distance submerged.

Largely nocturnal in habits, migrating and feeding at night; it hides from the sun in burrows or behind rocks during the day, and if brought into the strong light it blinks like an owl. At night it flies swiftly in flocks, with peculiar, plaintive cries, after the manner of the swift. In winter it is found on most of the islands along the coast from Tia Juana and San Diego north. Migrates in flocks about May 1. Is recorded from Santa Catalina.

16. CASSIN AUKLET. — *Ptychoramphus aleuticus.*

FAMILY: The Auks, Murres, and Puffins.

Length: 8.75.

Adults: Above, dark slate-color, merging into ashy on sides of head and neck ; upper breast and sides slate ; lower breast and belly white ; a white spot on lower eyelids.

Downy Young: Soft brownish gray.

Geographical Distribution: Pacific coast of North America from Alaska to Lower California.

Breeding Range: From San Benito Islands northward.

Breeding Season: Approximately, April 1 to September 1.

Nest: In crevices of rocks, under edge of boulders, or in shallow burrow ; unlined.

Eggs: 1 ; greenish white. Size 1.81 × 1.33.

LIKE the rhinoceros auklet, Cassin's Auklet is nocturnal in habit, hiding in its burrow by day and coming out in the twilight to feed and fly. Both species are expert swimmers and divers, obtaining in this manner the crustacea which form their chief diet. On stormy nights they may be heard calling to each other above the thunder of the surf and the fury of the gale. On clear or moonlight nights they flit like huge beetles over the shore, with continual high-keyed notes. With the screams of the gulls by day and the calls of the auklets by night, the rocky islands of the Pacific coast are never silent.

The Cassin Auklets are resident in small numbers off the coast of Southern California and on the islands of Santa Catalina, Santa Barbara, and Santa Cruz, breeding locally northward along their range. On the Farallones they breed in great numbers, and are also found nesting abundantly on the Netarte Islands and along the rocky coast of British Columbia. Each pair will usually raise three broods, of a single bird each, every season. The young remain in the nest until fully feathered, when they are able to fly, swim, and dive with the ease of adult birds.

21. ANCIENT MURRELET. — *Synthliboramphus antiquus.*

FAMILY : The Auks, Murres, and Puffins.

Length: 10.00.

Breeding Plumage: Head and throat black ; sides of neck, line on each side of crown to nape, white ; upper back gray, streaked laterally with white ; back, wings, and tail brownish gray, blackish on primaries ; sides sooty brown ; breast and belly white.

Winter Plumage: Throat white; upper parts uniform dark gray; under parts white.

Downy Young: Above, soft dark gray; lower parts and throat white.

Geographical Distribution: Coasts of the Northern Pacific from Monterey northward to arctic circle.

Breeding Range: From Sitka northward.

Breeding Season: June and July.

Nest: Unlined, in holes in a bank or shallow burrow.

Eggs: 2; deep buff, with fine markings of light purplish brown. Size 2.32 × 1.47.

IN "California Water Birds," No. II., Mr. Leverett M. Loomis says concerning the occurrence of the Ancient Murrelet at Monterey in midwinter: "About five hundred yards from the surf a belt of drift kelp extending from Seaside Laboratory around Point Pinos (Pacific Grove, Cal.) had gained an anchorage. The nar-

21. ANCIENT MURRELET.

"If a white-cap developed near them, they would always escape it by diving."

row strip between this and the beach was the favorite resort of Ancient Murrelets. A good many were also found near the surf in the little coves in the direction of Monterey, and some were seen several miles out from the land. They were great divers and swimmers under water, and voracious in their pursuit of small fry. Unlike marbled murrelets they did not seek safety in flight when pursued. Neither did they dive as soon or remain as long under water when keeping out of the way of the boat. If a whitecap developed near them they would always escape it by diving. That this little Auk leaves its summer home in the land of icebergs and comes south in considerable numbers in winter to California has not been generally known to ornithologists."

In April it starts north again, and by May 20 has reached the breeding ground in Alaska. Here it selects a nesting place, either a deep crevice in the rock, the abandoned burrow of a rabbit, or under the heavily matted grass. Under the grass it burrows its way for two or three feet, and there scratches out a small cavity, lining it carefully with dry grass from the outside. Here two buff eggs are laid. These are brooded by one bird during the day, while the other feeds out at sea. At night they change places. The only account of their nesting habits has been given by Mr. Littlejohn, who spent some time with them on an Alaskan island. He describes the squeaky noises made by the nocturnal birds, murrelets, auklets, and petrels, as effectually banishing sleep. "As if not satisfied with the constant babble of their neighbors, the murrelets took especial delight in alighting at the foot of the A-shaped tent, toe-nailing it up to the ridgepole, resting there a moment, and then sliding down the other side."

23. MARBLED MURRELET. — *Brachyramphus marmoratus.*

FAMILY : The Auks, Murres, and Puffins.

Length : 9.75.

Adults in Summer : Above dusky, barred with rusty brown ; under parts white, each feather tipped with umber, producing a mottled effect.

Adults in Winter : Above slate-gray with white band across nape ; scapulars mixed with white, and feathers of back tipped with brownish; lower parts white, more or less mottled with gray.

Young : Above uniform dark gray, with light band on nape more or less distinct. Lower parts white, mottled with gray.

Geographical Distribution : Pacific coast of North America from Southern California to Alaska.

Breeding Range : From Oregon coast northward.

Nest : In burrow in ground, or hole in bank, or crevice in cliff.

Eggs : 1 ; buffy, marked with purple-brown. Size 2.14 × 1.42.

THE Marbled Murrelet is found only in the Pacific Ocean, and breeds in such inaccessible places that little is known of its habits. The adult birds and young are found in numbers about Vancouver Island, but its nesting sites are difficult to find. It is more common along the coast of British Columbia than farther south. The best authorities seem to agree that the nesting habits of this species are like those of the ancient murrelet and their usual breeding grounds only a little farther south. In California they are common near the coast all winter as far south as San Diego. At Monterey we found them exceedingly timid, diving at the slightest alarm and impossible to approach. Their food consists of small invertebrates, which they pick from the rocks at some distance under water.

25. XANTUS MURRELET. — *Brachyramphus hypoleucus.*

FAMILY : The Auks, Murres, and Puffins.

Length : 10.00.
Adults : Upper parts plain slaty gray ; under parts, including cheeks and throat, uniform clear white ; lining of wing white ; head without ornamental feathers or spines.
Downy Young : Uniform dusky color above, light gray beneath.
Geographical Distribution : Southern California to Cape St. Lucas.
Breeding Range : From San Diego southward on coast of Southern California and on Coronado Islands.
Breeding Season : Approximately, March 1 to June 1.
Nest : In crevices of cliffs ; usually lined with coarse grass.
Eggs : 1 ; light buffy, with gray-brown markings. Size 2.05 × 1.50.

THE Xantus Murrelet is a common resident along the coast of Southern California as far north as Monterey. Little is known concerning its breeding habits, although it nests on the coast from San Diego south, more abundantly south of the Mexican border. It is numerous out in the open sea south of Coronado Islands during the breeding season, and is said to nest on the Island of San Clementi as well as Coronado. It is found in the Santa Barbara Channel at all seasons of the year, and without doubt a few nest on the Santa Barbara Islands at present, though the breeding ground there is reported as deserted for some years. The nesting habits are probably not unlike those of its Alaskan cousins except as to season.

29. PIGEON GUILLEMOT.— *Cepphus columba*.

FAMILY : The Auks, Murres, and Puffins.

Length : 13.50.

Adults in Summer : Uniform blackish except wings, where black basal half runs to point, making a black wedge between two white patches ; feet red ; bill black and slender.

Adults in Winter : White, varied on upper parts with black ; wings and tail as in summer.

Young : Similar to winter plumage of adult.

Downy Young : Uniform black above, under parts gray.

Geographical Distribution : Coasts and islands of the North Pacific from Behring Strait to Southern California.

Breeding Range : From San Nicholas Island northward.

Breeding Season : Approximately, May 1 to August 1.

Nest : Behind or under boulders or in dark places, as near the water as possible.

Eggs : 2 ; light green-blue, thickly marked with lilac, mostly at larger end. Size 2.43 × 1.62.

THE Pigeon Guillemot, "so like a guillemot and so like a pigeon," is very abundant on the Farallones. It is a pretty, graceful bird, first cousin to the murre, which it somewhat resembles, being of a soft, dark brown color. Two points impress you at first, — its conspicuous scarlet feet, and the broad white band on the wing. Like many sea birds, it stands with the body in a vertical position, supported by the long foot, after the manner of a penguin. Its curious nest is made of pebbles, carried one by one in its bill and deposited in a

29. "THE BABY GUILLEMOT"

circle in dark crannies of the rocks or hidden under boulders. They seem to serve chiefly as a rim to keep the eggs from rolling away. The breeding ground of the Pigeon Guillemot is that also occupied by the gulls, on the lower part of the islands, often near the water's edge. Yet surrounded on every side by the nests of the gulls and living near neighbors with them, they seem to be the only birds which these brigands of the sea do not commonly molest. Probably pigeon eggs are not to their taste. The baby Guillemot when first hatched is covered with thin blackish down on the head, neck, and back, shading to dark gray on the under parts. There is no conspicuous coloring to betray him in the dark nesting place, for even his feet are dull olive rather than red like those of his father. As with our own land pigeons, the family always consists of twins, theoretically a male and a female. Like the land pigeons, also, they are fed by regurgitation ; but here the resemblance ends, for they learn to dive and swim almost as soon as the down is fairly dry, and become expert in paddling swiftly with their heads submerged, in a unique and very amusing fashion.

30a. CALIFORNIA MURRE— *Uria troile Californica.*

Family : The Auks, Murres, and Puffins.

Length : 17.50.

Adults in Summer : Upper parts uniform grayish brown ; browner on neck and sides of head ; under parts white.

Adults in Winter : Upper parts same as in summer ; under parts white ; throat and sides of head more or less washed with brownish ; sides tinged with darker.

Downy Young : Upper parts grayish brown, the head and neck finely streaked with pearl-gray. Under parts white.

Geographical Distribution : Coasts and islands of North Pacific.

Breeding Range: From Farallones to Alaska.
Breeding Season : Approximately, May to August.
Nest: A bare flat place on cliffs, no lining, no protection.
Eggs: 1 ; pear-shaped ; varying from white to buffy, amber, and pale
    green. May be either unmarked or streaked with brown. In size
    they vary from 3.50 × 1.90 to 2.05 × 1.45.

THE great Murre rookery of the California coast is
on the Farallone Islands; until the last few years
their eggs were a common product in the markets of
San Francisco. According to figures furnished by Mr.
Leverett M. Loomis, the collection of Murre's eggs at
the Farallones in 1896 amounted to 7,645 dozen, all
of these being shipped to California markets. Mr.
Loomis also says: " In 1885 three hundred thousand
eggs were gathered. The market became glutted, one
cargo being dumped into San Francisco Bay and another
abandoned on the island." According to another authority, five hundred thousand eggs were sold in less
than two months, — all collected in one limited portion
of South Farallone Island, and, " in the opinion of the
eggers, not more than one egg in six was gathered."
Fortunately the Government has now forbidden the
collection of eggs and the molesting of the birds on
any portion of these islands, and no one is allowed to
land except by permission of the Government Light
House Inspector.

Besides being robbed by human enemies, the unfortunate Murres have to wage continual war against the
Western gulls, who steal their eggs the moment their
backs are turned, or even snatch them from under the
mother bird. Possibly for this reason they often choose

a narrow ledge just wide enough for them to squat upon when brooding the egg, where they will have only one side to defend. Since they brood in an almost upright position, the egg resting between the feet, it is difficult to tell a brooding bird.

Most ludicrous is their habit of ducking their heads as if in salute, and when this is done by hundreds, one after another, the effect is grotesque indeed. I had thought this the result of excitement at the presence of an enemy, but it continued when I fancied myself well concealed and no one else in sight. It is usually followed by the departure of a number, who dive with incredible swiftness from the steep rocks to the sea, either from hunger or alarm. Although so awkward and helpless on land, they are at home on or under the water, swimming submerged with great ease and swiftness.

The nesting date of the California Murres differs with different authorities, Mr. Loomis placing it in April, and Mr. Emerson from the middle of May to late in August; my own date is June. This discrepancy is accounted for by the fact that they rear several broods in a year if accident befall the earliest. And as the Western gulls consider the young Murre a delicious morsel, the life of any nestling is precarious. When the gulls press too closely, the wise Murres push their one baby off the rock into the water below, darting beneath it with incredible swiftness, and the young Murre, although not ready for the dive, is yet born with its swimming-suit on, and bobs up serenely after a dizzy fall.

37. PARASITIC JAEGER. — *Stercorarius parasiticus*.

FAMILY : The Skuas and Jaegers.

Length: 17.00.

Light Phase of Adults: Top of head and lores dark grayish brown ; rest of head and back of neck straw-color, merging into white on throat ; breast and belly white, washed on sides with grayish ; back, wings, and tail slaty gray ; middle tail-feathers narrow, pointed, and 3.00 longer than the others ; tarsi black.

Dark Phase of Adults: Entire plumage dark brownish slate-color, darker on head and lighter on under parts.

Light Phase of Young: Head and neck buffy, streaked with dark ; upper parts dark grayish brown, the feathers tipped with buffy ; under parts buffy, barred with dark.

Dark Phase of Young: Dark grayish brown, darker on wings and tail ; neck, belly, and sides streaked with buffy.

Downy Young: Soft grayish brown above, under parts lighter.

Geographical Distribution: Entire northern hemisphere ; south in winter to equator.

Breeding Range: Chiefly within the arctic circle.

Breeding Season: Approximately, June 5 to July 15.

Nest: A mere depression in the ground, rudely lined with grass, dry leaves, or moss ; situated on dry upland or rocks near the water.

Eggs: 2 to 4 ; pale greenish brown, spotted thickly with umber at larger end and somewhat over entire surface. Size 2.23 × 1.62.

THE Parasitic Jaeger occurs commonly as a migrant on the coast of California, though a few remain all winter. Mr. Grinnell reports one taken at Santa Monica, and Dr. Jeffries tells me they are numerous at Santa Catalina in November. They are winter residents in small numbers, also in Oregon, Washington, and British Columbia, and wherever found in sufficient numbers they render life miserable for terns and gulls by snatching their fish from them. At the end of a month's persecution the bodies of the terns become much emaciated from lack of food, as nearly every capture is seized by the rapacious Jaegers as soon as raised from the water. Like most bullies, the Jaeger never bothers a gull of its own size, but chooses its victim from the smaller varieties. In the northern regions it destroys eggs and nests of other water-fowl, rarely fishing for itself, but living by thievery.

81. BLACK–FOOTED ALBATROSS. — *Diomedea nigripes.*

FAMILY : The Albatrosses.

Length : 28.50–36.00.

Adults : Upper parts dark brownish gray ; under parts uniform grayish ; tail-coverts and anterior portions of head white ; bill dusky brown ; feet black.

Young : Similar, but upper tail-coverts dark gray, and little or no white on head.

Geographical Distribution : North Pacific, including west coast of North America.

Breeding Range : Islands of the Pacific near the equator.

Nest : A depression in the guano, lined or edged with a little seaweed.

Eggs : 1 ; white.

VERY little is known of the nesting habits of this rover of the high seas. I have been able to find only one record of any nest discovered or any egg taken. It is said to breed on the islands in the middle of the Pacific Ocean toward the equator, in January and February. Its cries are said to resemble cat-calls and to have a particularly doleful sound heard in the roar of a tempest. Of untiring flight, it visits the land only to nest, and is seldom seen near the coast, preferring the free, bold life on the open sea.

It has been nicknamed "Gonie" by the fishermen, in supposed allusion to a peculiar croaking noise it makes when feeding.

82. SHORT–TAILED ALBATROSS. — *Diomedea albatrus.*

FAMILY : The Albatrosses.

Length : 33.00–37.00.
Adults : White, merging to straw-yellow on head and neck ; tail-feathers brownish, primaries having yellow shafts.
Young : Uniform dark brownish gray, merging to blackish on head and neck ; shafts of primaries straw-yellow ; bill and feet light brown.
Geographical Distribution : North Pacific ; in America from California to Alaska.
Breeding Range : Islands of the Sandwich group and northward to Aleutian Islands.
Nest : The bare ground.
Eggs : 1 ; elliptical ; white. Size 4.20 × 2.60.

THE Short-tailed Albatross is found on the Pacific Ocean, following the whaling ships to feed on the refuse. Mr. Davie says : " It is easily caught with hook and line, and when taken on board is unable to rise from the deck, as it requires a long range of surface on which to flap its wings."

It is occasionally seen in the Bay of Monterey in December and January, following the whales that frequently come into the harbor, and it is remarkably fearless. A young bird of this species shot by Mr. Loomis was very ferocious, screaming with rage, and trying to bite its wounded wing. When approached by the collector who had shot it, the bird turned its fury upon him. The Chinese fishermen regard these monarchs of the high seas with superstitious awe, feeding them and propitiating them with choice bits, in hope of averting danger and winning good luck in their fishing. According to their belief, the whales drive the sardines into the bay to help the Chinese, but the albatross drives the whales.

86 b. PACIFIC FULMAR. — *Fulmarus glacialis glupischa.*

FAMILY: The Fulmars and Shearwaters.

Length: 17.00–19.00.

Light Phase: Head, neck, and under parts white ; upper parts ashy gray ; primaries and secondaries dark gray-brown.

Dark Phase: Uniform dusky gray above, ashy gray below.

Geographical Distribution: North Pacific, south on the American coast to Mexico.

Breeding Range: Islands of the Pacific from the coast of British Columbia to Behring Sea.

Breeding Season: June and July.

Nest: In colonies on ledges and in crevices of steep promontories rising perpendicularly from the sea.

Eggs: 1 ; chalky white. Size 2.85 × 1.90.

LIKE all the Fulmars, this species is found on the open sea and rarely lands upon the coast. It has been recorded at Monterey, and occurs at most of the islands along the coast of California, Washington, Oregon, and British Columbia. It is very abundant at Santa Catalina in the fall and winter.

Its common names are Goose, Gonie, Gluttonbird, Giant Petrel. Of these " Gluttonbird " seems to apply to this vulture of the sea. Its food consists of dead flesh, fish, or fowl, as the case may be, upon which it gorges until unable to fly. It is eminently a bird of the open sea, visiting the land seldom except in the breeding season, and usually not flying nearer the coast than five or ten miles.

All the Fulmars may be distinguished from the gulls in flight by their characteristic wing motions. The wings of the gulls rise and fall rapidly in wide sweeps, and are held more or less at an angle in soaring; the Fulmar wing stroke is slower and apparently (though not really) less powerful.

The Pacific Fulmar feeds its newly hatched young by regurgitation of an amber-colored ill-smelling oil. It is said by some authorities to eject this as a protection against enemies, also; certainly the odor is sufficiently offensive to prevent any but the most enthusiastic ornithologist from meddling with its domestic affairs.

93. BLACK–VENTED SHEARWATER. — *Puffinus opisthomelas.*

FAMILY: The Fulmars and Shearwaters.

Length : 12.00–15.00.
Adults : Upper parts dark slate-color, merging to gray on head and neck ; under parts white, except lower tail-coverts, which are blackish gray.
Downy Young : Upper parts dark ashy gray ; under parts smoky white.
Geographical Distribution : Pacific Ocean, chiefly the southward coast of Lower California, north to Santa Cruz, California.
Breeding Range : Islands of the South Pacific, north to Lower California.

RECORDS are claimed of this species as far north as the coast of Oregon. Little is known concerning its nesting habits. Mr. Anthony found adults and young on San Benito Islands in July, and writes that they nest in caves there. ("The Condor," Vol. II. page 29.)

Mr. A. W. Anthony in "The Auk," Vol. XIII., has given a full description of the occurrence of these Shearwaters off the coast of Southern and Lower California. Here flocks of several thousand birds may be frequently seen hovering over the vast schools of herring that for some reason come near the shore. Mr. Anthony mentions one flock that numbered at least fifty thousand. The presence or absence of the Shearwater near shore is governed by the abundance or scarcity of fish; during late July, August, and September the maximum is reached.

The Black-vented Shearwater is supposed to breed during the winter months, south of the equator, and the summer flocks usually contain numbers of young birds.

95. DARK-BODIED SHEARWATER — *Puffinus griseus.*

FAMILY: The Fulmars and Shearwaters.

Adults: Plumage uniform sooty gray; lighter, sometimes whitish, on chin and throat; under wing-coverts white, transversely mottled with gray at tips; bill blackish.

Geographical Distribution: South Pacific, north on the American coast, to Queen Charlotte Islands, British Columbia.

Breeding Range: Islands of the South Pacific.

Nest: A rude structure of twigs, dead leaves, and peat at the end of a burrow three or four feet long, in side of a bank.

Eggs: 1; chalky white. Size 2.25 × 1.45.

THIS Shearwater occurs in great numbers at Monterey and Santa Cruz, California. I have seen a black cloud fully a mile long composed of thousands of dark-bodied Shearwaters, a few brandt cormorants, and many gulls hovering over the sardines in the Bay of Monterey in June. So numerous were they that the surface of the water was black with them in continual motion as they dropped for a catch, or rose each with a fish in its beak, or settled to the water to eat. In this multitude the dark-bodied Shearwaters outnumbered both gulls and cormorants, and the combined noise was indescribable. Mr. Loomis, in his work on the migration of sea birds, as observed at Monterey, proves inferentially that the dark-bodied Shearwaters breed in the south temperate zone during the winter months, coming north as soon as the breeding season is over, and remaining until September. In New Zealand, where this bird breeds abundantly, it excavates a burrow in a bank almost exactly like that made by a kingfisher. At the end of this is placed a lining of small sticks, and occasionally a few leaves, or a little moss, and here the one chalky egg is laid.

105.2. KAEDING PETREL. — *Oceanodroma Kaedingi.*

FAMILY : The Fulmars and Shearwaters.

Length : 7.25–8.50.
Adults : Sooty gray, lighter on under parts ; upper tail-coverts white ; tail-feathers shading to gray at base ; tail forked ; bill and feet black.
Geographical Distribution : North Pacific, south to Southern California.
Breeding Range : Islands of the Pacific Coast.
Breeding Season : March to September.
Nest : In burrow, or more commonly in crevices of loose rock ; rudely lined with dried grasses.
Eggs : 1 ; cream white, with wreath of fine purple dots about larger end. Size, 1.34 × 1.00.

According to Mrs. Bailey the Leach petrels reported on the coast of California were really the species known as Kaeding petrels. There is little to distinguish the two except size, the latter being slightly smaller and darker than the Eastern species. In breeding habits the two are probably identical. Male and female take part in sitting upon the single egg — sometimes one of the pair, sometimes both together. The newly hatched young are fed by regurgitation of a brownish oily fluid. Like the forked-tailed petrel, this species ejects the oil from its throat and stomach if molested. The odor clings to nest, eggs and young.

107. BLACK PETREL. — *Oceanodroma melania.*

FAMILY : The Fulmars and Shearwaters.

Length : 8.00–9.00.
Adult : Dusky blackish, lighter on under parts ; greater wing-coverts and outer webs of tertials light ash-color.
Geographical Distribution : South Pacific, northward to Los Angeles County, California.
Breeding Range : Islands off the coast of Southern California and southward to the equator.
Breeding Season : July.
Nest : Bare ground, or burrow one to three feet in depth.
Eggs : 1 ; pure white ; elliptical oval.   Size 1.44 × 1.08.

THE Black Petrel, while less common than the ashy, is yet a resident on the ocean adjacent to Southern California. Mr. Grinnell reports it as far north as Santa Barbara, and as breeding on Los Coronados Islands, off San Diego. Like all its family, it comes to land only to nest, and any acquaintance with it must be made from a boat, or during the breeding season at the islands. It is nocturnal in habits, feeding and flying only after darkness has settled over the sea, and enjoying a storm as the robin enjoys the sun. Its notes are a high plaintive call or a queer, low, purring coo. The latter is heard only during the nesting season. The name "Petrel" means *Little Peter*, and has been given this bird because of its curious habit of skimming over the surface of the water with feet just touching it in a quick, pattering motion, as if trying to walk upon the waves. All the time it flutters its wings like a huge butterfly.

108. ASHY PETREL. — *Oceanodroma homochroa.*

FAMILY : The Fulmars and Shearwaters.

Length : 8.00–9.00.
Adult : Grayish slate-color, merging to lighter on wing-coverts ; quills and tail blackish, merging to ashy slate-color on rump and upper tail-coverts.
Geographical Distribution : Coast of California.
Breeding Range : Islands off the coast of California, including the Farallones and Santa Barbara.
Breeding Season : June and July.
Nest : In crevices under rocks, under driftwood, in stone walls, in burrows.
Eggs : Creamy white, sometimes faintly spotted about the large end. Size 1.19 × 0.93.

THE Ashy Petrels were breeding abundantly on the South Farallone Islands at the time of a recent visit I made to the spot, but few of the birds were in evidence during the daylight hours. The nests were well hidden under loose rocks, in crevices and in all sorts of crannies ; they were betrayed only by their disagreeable odor. In common with other petrels these feed their newly hatched young upon the dark oily fluid which they eject through their bills into the throats of the fledgelings, and this is undoubtedly the cause of the unpleasant smell that ever clings to their plumage. The male petrel takes a full share of the labors of incubation, and some authorities aver that, like the phalarope, he does it all. As soon as he is able to fly, the young petrel takes to the sea,

108. ASHY PETREL.

" The playmate of the grim old sea."

never to come ashore until, a year or two later, he wants a wife and a burrow of his own. Think of it — day after day, week after week, eating, sleeping, resting on the boundless water! His only refuge from the storm is to fly above or beyond it; his only food is the drift he may pick up. Dancing on the crest of the wave, dashing through the salt spray, he is the ocean's own darling, the playmate of the grim old sea.

128. MAN–O'–WAR BIRD. — *Fregata aquila.*

FAMILY : The Man-o'-War Birds.

Length : 39.00.

Adult Male : Uniform iridescent black, with green and reddish purple reflections ; wings very long ; tail forked for more than half its length.

Adult Female : Upper parts rusty black ; under parts white ; wings with gray patch.

Young : Head, neck, and under parts white ; rest of plumage dull blackish.

Downy Young : Uniform white.

Geographical Distribution : Tropical and subtropical coasts generally ; in America north to Florida and Texas, casually through interior along Mississippi River and along Pacific coast to Humboldt Bay, California.

Breeding Range : Gulf of Mexico and islands off coast of Lower California.

Breeding Season : January to March.

Nest : A slight platform of twigs upon the branches of the mangrove trees at edge of lagoon.

Eggs : 1 ; dull white, unspotted. Size 2.70 × 1.84.

FRIGATE BIRD, Frigate Pelican, Man-o'-War Bird, and Hurricane Bird are the common names applied to *Fregata aquila* by sailors and fishermen. It is regarded by seamen as a weather prophet, always flying higher in clear weather and low before a storm. The name "Man-o'-War Bird" doubtless obtains from its resemblance to a black ship as it hangs motionless in midair. Mr. Chapman writes of these birds : "They have a greater expanse of wing in proportion to the weight of their body than any other bird. They rarely alight on the water, but, facing the wind, pass hours resting motionless on outstretched wings, sometimes ascending to great heights and calmly soaring far above storms. It is when feeding that their marvellous aerial powers are displayed to the best advantage. By swift, indescribably graceful darts they secure fish which are near the surface, or capture those which have leaped from the water to escape some enemy below. They also pursue gulls and terns, and, forcing them to disgorge their prey, catch it in midair."

Although rare in California north of Monterey, they are more or less common throughout the coast from that point southward. They are high-handed plunderers of the gulls, meting out to them some punishment for their constant thieving. But it is to the unfortunate fish-hawk that these pirates are most terrible. Reports are given on good authority of the terror exhibited by fish-hawks at the approach of their enemy, who forces them to fish hour by hour until exhausted, and seizes every fish as soon as it is brought up from the water. This frequently results in the death of the hawk by exhaustion and drowning.

BIRDS FOUND NEAR THE SHORE OR IN BAYS

7. LOON. — *Gavia imber.*

FAMILY: The Loons.

Length: 32.00.

Adults in Summer: Head and neck glossy greenish black ; upper parts, wings, and tail iridescent black ; throat and sides of neck crossed by transverse streaks of white ; back and wings spotted or speckled with white ; breast and belly white ; sides black, spotted with white ; bill black.

Adults in Winter, and Young: Plumage of upper parts without white; under parts and throat white.

Downy Young: Uniform blackish ; belly nearly white.

Geographical Distribution: Northern part of northern hemisphere.

Breeding Range: Northern United States and throughout Canada to the arctic circle.

Breeding Season: Approximately, June 1 to August 15.

Nest: A slight hollow in the sand near the water ; sometimes roughly lined with dry reeds, sticks, or marsh grass.

Eggs: 2, rarely 3 ; olive, spotted with umber ; elliptical. Size 3.50 × 2.20.

ON the loneliest lakes of California the common Loon, known as *Gavia imber,* is a regular winter visitant, but he shuns the coast whenever he can. Is this because he likes the taste of fresh-water fish better than that of sea fish ? Who knows ? Like those of all diving birds, the Loon's stout legs are set well back, and propel its heavy body with equal rapidity and ease on or under the water. Its speed in submarine swimming has been estimated to reach eight miles an hour and to continue indefinitely with only the bill exposed. In this he uses only his feet, the wings being folded tightly. All its fish are caught by diving. Awkward and helpless on land, where it uses wings to assist in locomotion, it leaves the water only to nest. Its two greenish gray eggs are laid upon a thin mat of grass in a slightly hollowed place on the ground, and, in order to be as far as possible removed from neighbors, the site chosen is usually a small grass-covered islet. The young Loons are oval balls of blackish down and are occasionally taken into the water on the back of the adult bird. Their first attempts at diving are very funny, and with all their efforts they are able to submerge no more than their heads and necks, so that they seem to be standing on their heads and paddling their feet in the air. They soon become expert swimmers and divers. Yet under the water as on it, lurk the Loon's enemies. The large pickerel are fond of catching him by the feet, and great mud-turtles wait for a delicious piece of Loon meat. If he floats serenely on the surface, hawks and gulls are ever ready to swoop down upon him. Fortunate it is for the poor mother that she has but two to guard.

The peculiar cry of the Loon has been well described by Mr. J. H.

7. LOON.

" The young loons are taken into the water."

Langille : " Beginning on the fifth note of the scale, the voice slides through the eighth to the third of the scale above in loud, clear, sonorous tones, which on a dismal evening before a thunderstorm — the lightning already playing along the inky sky — are anything but musical. He has also another rather soft and pleasing utterance, sounding like *who-who-who-who*, the syllables being so rapidly pronounced as to sound almost like a shake of the voice — a sort of weird laughter.

"Only on a lonely lake in the heart of the woods do you get the startling thrill of the Loon's wild cry — one clear, piercing note, or a long, quavering, demoniacal laugh that to the timid suggests a herd of screaming panthers."

10. PACIFIC LOON. — *Gavia pacifica.*

FAMILY : The Loons.

Length : 27.00.

Adults in Summer : Upper part of head and nape pale gray, nearly white ; sides of head, throat, and fore-neck black, glossed with metallic purple and green ; wings and tail blackish ; breast and belly white ; sides of neck, wing-coverts, and back black, spotted and streaked with white ; sides of belly sometimes finely streaked with black.

Adults in Winter, and Young : Similar to *Gavia imber.*

Downy Young : Dark sooty gray.

Geographical Distribution : Western United States, east to Rocky Mountains, south to Cape St. Lucas, north to arctic circle, east to Hudson Bay.

Breeding Range : From Northern United States to Alaska.

Breeding Season : Approximately, June 1 to August 1.

Nest : Of water grasses, rushes, or decayed vegetation at edge of water.

Eggs : 2 ; varying in color from brown-olive to pale greenish gray. Size 3.00 × 1.85.

THIS species of the Pacific coast Black-throated Loon corresponds to the Black-throated Loon of Eastern United States, being a trifle paler in coloring but identical in habits. It is the most expert of all divers; I have seen one remain under water three minutes by a watch, meanwhile covering a distance of a hundred yards in his submarine swimming. They are very abundant in Monterey Bay all the winter, and I have found a few there as late as June 10, although the regular breeding season had begun and they were long since due in Canada. The nest of the Pacific Loon is usually a mass of wet, decaying vegetation at the very edge of the water, or sometimes floating among the rushes. Occasionally it is lined with feathers. The bird follows the grebe's fashion of covering the eggs during her absence, but does not remain away all day as do the grebes. The Loons are most devoted parents, carrying the little ones pick-a-back as soon as hatched, and, in case of attack by hunters, often rising with a great splash between the hunter and their brood, to cover the retreat of the young. The food of all Loons consists largely of fish, although they occasionally relish frogs, and to the newly hatched young the mother brings the larvæ of water insects obtained by diving. These she lays on the surface for the brood to pick up, instead of placing them in the bills of the little ones.

11. RED–THROATED LOON. — *Gavia lumme.*

FAMILY : The Loons.

Length : 25.50.

Adults in Summer : Sides of head and neck light brownish gray ; throat gray ; a triangular patch of rich chestnut on fore-neck ; crown and broad stripe down back of neck finely streaked brownish black and white ; back, wings, and tail dark grayish brown, finely specked with white ; breast and belly white.

Adults in Winter, and Young : Throat and fore-neck white ; upper parts blackish, spotted with white.

Downy Young : Upper parts blackish slate ; under parts dark gray.

Geographical Distribution : Entire northern hemisphere, south in winter as far as latitude 30°.

Breeding Range : The arctic regions.

Breeding Season : June 1 to August 1.

Nest: A slight hollow on ground, close to water ; unlined and unprotected.
Eggs: 2 ; brown or olive, spotted with umber. Size 2.50 × 1.81.

THIS is the smallest and handsomest of the loons.
It occurs in California from November to late in April,
being the last to arrive from the North and the first to
leave. In habits it is nearly identical with *Gavia
imber*, but is a more northern variety, being more abundant in Canada than in the United States. It has been
found breeding in British Columbia fifty miles north of
Vancouver. Unlike the common loon, however, it frequents the salt rather than the fresh water, and during
the winter months is common along the California coast
from Oregon to Mexico. It is the " gray loon " of the
fishermen, and its long, wild call as it rises against a
breeze and circles under a cloudy sky is always a signal
for the boats to seek shelter, for the storm will break
and not " blow over."

44. GLAUCOUS–WINGED GULL. — *Larus glaucescens.*

FAMILY : The Gulls and Terns.

Length: 25.75.
Adults in Summer: Head, neck, lower parts, and tail uniform white ;
mantle dark pearl-gray ; feet and legs black.
Adults in Winter: Plumage similar to that of summer, but with head
and neck finely mottled or washed with sooty gray.
Young: Dark ash-gray, with mantle mixed with pearl-gray ; head and
neck indistinctly streaked with buffy ; under parts mixed with white.
Downy Young: Dull whitish gray above, white below ; head, neck, and
upper parts marked irregularly with dark gray.
Geographical Distribution: Pacific coast of North America from Alaska
and Behring Sea ; south in winter to Southern California.
Breeding Range: Islands of the Pacific coast from Washington northward.

Breeding Season : Approximately, May 1 to August 1.
Nest : A bare slight depression in the ground near shore, or a rude
affair of seaweeds and grass on shelving rocks or cliffs.
Eggs : 2 to 4 ; from dark olive to white, spotted with light brown and
umber.   Size 2.88 × 2.03.

THE Glaucous-winged Gull is one of the most numerous birds on the California coast.   Mr. Leverett M.
Loomis writes of it at Monterey in midwinter as follows :

"Whales frequently came into the bay.   Often they
would be attended by a great train of gulls and pelicans
'feeding upon the slop-over' . . . In Carmel Valley
near the ocean I found them [the Glaucous-winged
Gulls] in company with Western gulls following the
plough as robins do in the spring in South Carolina.
The tameness and familiarity of the water birds on this
coast strikingly contrast with the wariness of those of
the North Atlantic."

This gull may be known from the others by the long
wing-quills of slate-gray tipped with white.   Its winter
range does not extend so far south as that of some of
its congeners, but it is reported all along the California
coast from Monterey northward.   In nesting habits the
Glaucous-winged Gulls resemble the Western gulls ; the
newly hatched Glaucous-winged are the softest, downiest
nestlings imaginable.   They are fed upon small fish, refuse
from salmon canneries, — which the parents fly miles to
obtain, — and small mollusks.

49. WESTERN GULL. — *Larus occidentalis.*

FAMILY : The Gulls and Terns.

Length : 25.50.

Adults in Summer : Head, neck, lower parts, rump, and tail white ; mantle dark slaty gray ; wing-quills black, with large spots of white. Angle of lower mandible very conspicuous ; depth of bill through mandible greater than at base.

Adults in Winter : Plumage similar to that of summer, except that top of head and nape are streaked with dark gray-brown.

Young : Upper parts brownish gray mottled with white ; quills and tail-feathers black, tipped with white ; under parts grayish ; sides mottled with white.

Downy Young : Ashy white ; head mottled with distinct black patches ; upper parts more or less mottled with dark ash.

Geographical Distribution : Pacific coast of North America from Lower California to British Columbia.

Breeding Range : From Coronado Islands to British Columbia ; at Santa Catalina, Santa Barbara, and San Clementi.

Breeding Season : Approximately, May 1 to August 1.

Nest : Of weeds ; on rocky ledges.

Eggs : 2 to 3 ; light olive, spotted with umber. Size 2.76 × 1.94.

MOST conspicuous because everywhere present, most interesting because of his very wickedness, is the variety of gull found on the Farallones, and everywhere on the California coast. He is known as *Larus occidentalis,* and is the only species that breeds on those islands. The pretty herring gulls of our harbors are quite different in habit from this voracious plunderer.

Larus occidentalis is a degenerate. Too lazy to fish for himself, he steals from whomsoever he can. If the victim be a diving bird who has come to the surface with a struggling fish in his beak, the Western Gull will hover over him, compelling him to dive again and again, until, exhausted, he abandons the food he has had no time to swallow; then the victor, seizing it quickly, flies away to devour it. Fish brought to the nest of other birds as food for mate or young is stolen by the Western Gulls as soon as laid down, and so expert on the wing are they that but once have I seen punishment overtake them. In this case the bird tried to snatch a fish that had been thrown to a baby seal. Quicker than thought, the seal mother caught the bird by the feet and drew it under the water. In a few moments she rose with the lifeless body, shook it viciously, and tossed it con-

49. WESTERN GULL.
The young gull is taught to fish.

temptuously away. This occurred at Avalon, Santa Catalina, and was witnessed by many spectators at 6 A. M. one May morning. But seals are not usually the victims of these tyrants. Cormorant and murre eggs and young, and even young rabbits, are its favorite bill of fare. Eggs they will steal in spite of all precautions; a lighthouse keeper tells about covering a pile of eggs closely with a sail-cloth, only to have the gulls work their way under it and carry off every one.

But in spite of all his faults, the Western Gull is devoted to his mate and nestlings, feeding and guarding them with constant care. Early in May he begins to repair his old nest, stealing material from the cormorants if he can, bringing it himself if he must. The nest is a large, soft, and warm affair made of dried Farallone weed and occasionally lined with a few feathers. It is also scrupulously clean. No fish scales, fish bones, or other debris is allowed to remain near it. The young gulls, usually three in number, are beauties, covered with grayish buff down and spotted all over with dots of darker. At three weeks old they are mottled black and light ashy. They show no fear, and will allow a person to handle them, only looking surprise from their bright little eyes. One would never believe that such innocent-looking babies could ever become thieves and cannibals. They stay in the nest longer than most of the young sea birds, not leaving it until their wings are fully feathered and strong. Even then they are not like the parents, for, until a year old, all young gulls are mottled brown and white. The brownish-looking gulls flying with the others on our harbors and rivers are not a different species, but are the immature.

The young gull learns to fish in a unique way. He also learns to steal, but that is another story. He scrambles with fluttering wings down to the water, accompanied by the rest of his family. As soon as he is fairly launched, one of the adult birds brings a small fish, and showing it to him, lets it float on the surface. If the youngster is an apt pupil, he snaps at it and usually gets it. If not, it is snatched up by some adult, for might is right in the sea-bird world. If after losing several in this way he becomes discouraged, he is fed, taken ashore for a sun-bath, and in an hour is back for another lesson. In the meantime he watches his parents filching food from nestlings around him, and as soon as he dares, or can find a bird more helpless than himself, he tries the plan. He finds it much easier than catching a bobbing sardine in the water, and from that time his career in crime begins.

51. HERRING GULL. — *Larus argentatus.*

FAMILY : The Gulls and Terns.

Length : 23.25.

Adults in Summer: Head, throat, and under parts white ; mantle pearl-gray ; white tip of first primary separated from large white spot farther up by blotch of black half an inch wide extending to the tip ; eyelids yellow ; feet pale flesh-color.

Adults in Winter : Similar, but mottled with ash-color on head and neck.

Young : Grayish brown, streaked or mottled on head, neck, and upper parts with dull whitish ; quill-coverts and tail-feathers rusty black.

Downy Young : Soiled white ; head irregularly spotted with black ; back, wings, and tail washed with ashy.

Geographical Distribution : North America in general ; in summer from latitude 40° northward ; south in winter to Cuba and Lower California.

Breeding Range : Inland lakes from latitude 43° to the Upper Yukon, Alaska.

Breeding Season : Approximately, May 15 to August 1.

Nest : A slight depression in the ground, lined thinly with grasses ; near water.

Eggs : 3 ; varying from blue-white to yellow-brown, blotched with light and dark brown. Size 2.80 × 1.75.

THIS is a common gull throughout its range, and differs from other species in its abundance around rivers and harbors. It is the gull seen following the ferry-boats on San Francisco Bay, perching on the anchored fishing craft in Monterey harbor, and sitting on the buoys at San Diego, and tormenting the seals at Santa

Catalina. It is the species best known East and West, following the coastwise vessels as well as those of the Great Lakes, and feeding on the refuse thrown out.

Its name of Herring Gull is probably derived from its habit of following a school of herring, and gorging itself upon them as it flies. To see the countless numbers of gulls and shearwaters hovering over a school of herrings in Monterey Bay is an experience worth a trip across the continent. No words can describe their multitude or their clamor. A compact cloud of them two miles long and half a mile wide, seeming almost like a solid mass of wings, is a common sight in that harbor.

By a curious adaptation of its natural nesting-habits to necessity for self-protection, in localities where its nests have been continually robbed, it has learned to build in trees sixty and seventy feet from the ground. In these cases the nest is a compact structure somewhat resembling a crow's nest, but more often plastered with a small amount of mud and lined with grasses and moss. In fact, it adapts itself to local conditions in placing and constructing its home : guided by some instinctive law, it lays its eggs on the bare ground in one region ; it elaborately lines and carefully conceals its nest in another; and, wherever necessary for self-preservation, it chooses a tall tree.

The young gulls are fascinatingly fat babies covered with fluffy down, and even prettier than ducklings. When hatched in ground nests, they soon learn to run about, and they are taken to the water when a few weeks old. It is possible that when the nest is seventy-five feet up in a tree the nestlings, like those of the wood ducks, are carried down by one of the adults.

53. CALIFORNIA GULL. — *Larus californicus.*

FAMILY : The Gulls and Terns.

Length : 21.50.
Adults : Head, neck, and under parts white ; mantle dark slate-gray ; the yellow bill marked with red spot, touching or encircling a black spot near end of lower mandible ; iris bright brown ; feet light green.
Young : Head, neck, and lower parts white, washed with brownish gray ; upper parts mottled gray and buffy ; quills and tail-feathers rusty black.
Downy Young : Light ash-gray, marked with black spots on head and washed with dark gray on back, wings, and tail.
Geographical Distribution : Western North America, chiefly in the interior from Alaska to Mexico.
Breeding Range : Inland lakes of Oregon, Washington, British Columbia, and Utah.
Breeding Season : Approximately, May 15 to August 15.
Nest : Of sticks and grasses, lined with feathers ; on ground, on rocks, or in low sagebrush near water.
Eggs : 3 to 5 ; from blue-white to gray-brown. Size 2.50 × 1.65.

THE California Gull is a regular winter visitant on the coast, but disappears usually about May 1. It breeds abundantly on Lake Malheur, Oregon, on Great Salt Lake, Utah, and as far north as Great Slave Lake. It may easily be distinguished from the other species by its smaller size. Mr. Loomis reports it as abundant at Monterey, where it is found in company with the western and glaucous-winged. During the winter it is common on all the fresh-water marshes as well as the coast, throughout Southern California. Mrs. Bailey says, " At

Pescadero in the low fields near the ocean, hundreds have been seen following the plough." A similar statement has been made of two other varieties, the ringbilled and the short-billed.

54. RING–BILLED GULL. — *Larus delawarensis.*

FAMILY : The Gulls and Terns.

Length : 19.00.

Adults in Summer : Head, neck, lower parts, and tail white ; mantle pearl-gray ; first primary black, with white patch near tip ; rest of primaries gray, washed with black on outer web and tipped with white ; iris pale yellow ; eyelids red ; bill greenish yellow, banded near end with black and tipped with orange ; feet yellowish green.

Adults in Winter : Similar, but with ashy streaks on head and nape.

Young : Upper parts dark ashy, mottled with buff ; outer primaries black ; upper half of tail-feathers pearl-gray, meeting a broad band of black which extends to a narrow white tip ; bill yellowish at base, shading into black at tip.

Downy Young : Dull gray-white ; head spotted with black ; back washed with dusky.

Geographical Distribution : Entire North America ; south in winter to Cuba and Mexico.

Breeding Range : Northern portions of the United States, and inland lakes of Oregon, Washington, and British Columbia.

Breeding Season : Approximately, May 1 to August 1.

Nest : Of coarse grass ; on ground, near water.

Eggs : 2 to 3 ; buffy gray, spotted with chocolate. Size 2.77 × 1.67.

ALTHOUGH the Ring-billed Gull is a more or less locally common species in every part of the United States, it is more abundant on the Atlantic than on the Pacific coast. In habits it is like the herring gull, but may be distinguished by its smaller size, yellowish green feet, and banded bill. Quite un-sea-bird-like, it relishes the larvæ of marsh insects as well as the adult forms, and during fall migrations it catches them on the wing, as do swallows. In some localities it has been seen feeding among the freshly turned furrows of a ploughed field. There is reason to believe that, unlike some members of its family, it never robs other birds either of food, eggs, or young, but is content with the small fish and insects it can pick up on inland marshes and meadows.

57. HEERMANN GULL. — *Larus heermanni.*

FAMILY : The Gulls and Terns.

Length : 18.75.

Adults in Summer : Upper parts dark slate-color ; head and neck white ; under parts dusky gray; wings and tail black, the latter tipped with white ; bill scarlet.

Adults in Winter : Similar, but head very dark, nearly black.

Downy Young : Dark ash-color, the feathers of upper parts edged with buffy ; head mottled.

Immature (Second Year?) : Entire plumage uniform dark ash ; tail black.

Geographical Distribution : Pacific coast of North America from British Columbia south to Panama.

Breeding Range : From Coronado Islands northward ; does not breed at the Farallones.

Breeding Season : Approximately, May 20 to August 1.

Nest : On ground near water, or on cliffs ; scantily lined with coarse grass or moss.

Eggs : 2 to 3 ; greenish gray, marked with lilac and brown. Size 2.45 × 1.50.

THE Heermann Gull may be readily distinguished from any other species by its darker plumage. It is a curious sight to see these handsome birds at San Diego Bay and La Jolla following an unlucky pelican who has a fine pouchful of fish. They fly over and around him, darting down to peck at him with their bills until he is forced to disgorge his catch. The dignified and methodical pelican is no match for these swift flyers, and soon yields to the inevitable. I have seen the same pelican robbed three times in succession, leave the vicinity with a flock of several gulls following. A close watch failed to discover any other species of gulls at this sport, and I believe the persecutors are invariably the *Larus heermanni*, although the Western gull is much more apt to commit such atrocities. In this locality, however, the Heermann Gulls outnumber the Western three to one. Mr. Grinnell says this is the case also at Los Angeles, while at Monterey Mr. Loomis reports them as varying in proportion at different times during migration.

60. BONAPARTE GULL. — *Larus philadelphia.*

FAMILY : The Gulls and Terns.

Length : 13.00.

Adults in Summer : Head and throat dark slate, nearly black ; mantle pearly gray ; under parts, tail, nape, and sides of head white ; wings white, shading to pearl-gray ; first primary tipped and edged on outer web with black ; other primaries with broad black transverse spots, forming a bar ; feet and legs orange ; bill black.

Adults in Winter : Similar, but head and throat white, back and sides of head gray.

Young : Head white, top and nape washed with gray ; under parts and tail white, the tail banded with black near end ; back and wing-coverts ashy ; primaries bluish gray, narrowly tipped with black.

Geographical Distribution : Whole of North America.

Breeding Range : Northern parts of the United States northward.

Breeding Season : Approximately, June 1 to August 1.

Nest : Of sticks and grasses ; lined with fibre ; always elevated from the ground in bushes, trees, or high stumps.

Eggs : From greenish to olive-brown, spotted with brown and light purple, chiefly at larger end. Size 1.95 × 1.34.

THE distinguishing feature of the Bonaparte Gull is its slate-gray hood in summer, all the other Pacific gulls having light-colored or white heads. Its appearance as it flies toward you may have suggested its name, for it is not unlike the black cocked hat and white expanse of bosom so characteristic of the portraits of that monarch.

It is found throughout North America, being rather more abundant on the Atlantic than the Pacific coast. Its food is small fish, which it procures by diving from the air to the surface of the water, not beneath it. Swift and graceful in flight, of small and elegant form, it seems rather to belong to the terns than to the gulls. Its breeding grounds are in the far north, through the wooded districts of Alaska and as far south as Manitoba. In November and May these gulls pass through California as migrants, a few remaining at San Diego Bay throughout December and returning there in March.

65. ROYAL TERN. — *Sterna maxima.*

FAMILY : The Gulls and Terns.

Length : 18.21.

Adults in Spring : Top of head and nape glossy black, feathers lengthened to form a crest ; upper parts pearl-gray, merging to white on tail and at back of neck ; under parts, including throat and sides of neck, pure white ; bill bright orange ; feet black.

Adults after Breeding Season and in Winter : Similar, but black on head and crest mixed with white ; bill pale orange.

Young : Similar to winter adults, but upper parts more or less mottled with dusky brown ; tail dusky near tip ; crest slightly developed ; top of head dusky, mixed with white.

Downy Young : Like downy young of *S. caspia.*

Geographical Distribution : Tropical America and warmer parts of North America, to latitude 40°, casually northward to Massachusetts and the Great Lakes. Common coastwise in California at all seasons.

Breeding Range : On Atlantic coast from New Jersey southward ; on Gulf coast from Texas to Florida ; at San Miguel Island on the Pacific coast.

Nest: A shallow depression scooped in the sand of a beach.
Eggs: 2 to 4 ; narrower and more pointed than those of Caspian tern ;
grayish, spotted with brown and purple. Size 2.67 × 1.70.

CONCERNING the Royal Tern, Mr. Frank M. Chapman writes : " It is a strong, active bird on the wing, and a reckless, dashing diver, frequently disappearing beneath the surface in catching its prey. The slow-flying pelican are at its mercy, and it often deftly robs them of their well-earned gains.

" All the terns are to be known from the gulls by the very different manner in which they hold their bills. A tern points its bill directly downward and looks, as Coues says, like a big mosquito, while a gull's bill points forward in the plane of its body."

69. FORSTER TERN. — *Sterna forsteri.*

FAMILY : The Gulls and Terns.

Length: 15.10.
Adults in Summer: Top of head and nape jet black ; upper parts pearl-
gray ; under parts, including throat and sides of neck, uniform
white ; bill dull orange, tipped with dusky ; feet deep orange.
Adults in Winter: Similar, but head white, tinged with gray on nape,
and white dusky patch around eyes and ear-coverts ; bill brownish,
merging to black at tip ; feet brownish.
Young: Similar to winter adults, but with top of head, nape, back, and
wings washed with dark umber ; distinctly darker at end of tail ;
sides of head dusky brownish.
Downy Young: Upper parts pale buffy brown, coarsely mottled with
black ; under parts, except throat, white.
Geographical Distribution: North America generally ; south in winter
to Brazil.
Breeding Range: On Pacific coast from Washington to Lower California ;
common at Lake Tahoe, Eagle and Elsinore Lakes, California.
Breeding Season: Approximately, May 1 to July 20.

Nest : Made of flags or marsh vegetation ; lined with weeds ; in wet marshy place, or floating among rushes.

Eggs : 2 or 3 ; from pure white to pale green or brown-gray, irregularly spotted with several shades of brown and purple. Size 1.85 × 1.35.

DR. BREWER calls this species " pre-eminently a *marsh* tern," and says that its monotonous cry closely resembles the call note of a loggerhead shrike. It is found nesting in colonies in company with gull-billed terns and Bonáparte gulls in suitable localities throughout its breeding range, but chiefly on large lakes in the interior. Its food consists of minnows, insects, and refuse floating on the water.

74. LEAST TERN. — *Sterna antillarum.*

FAMILY : The Gulls and Terns.

Length : 8.50–9.75.

Adults in Summer : Upper parts pearl-gray ; under parts white ; forehead white ; crown, lores, and nape jet black; bill yellow, usually tipped with black ; feet orange.

Adults in Winter : Similar, but lores and crown white ; nape black ; bill black.

Young : Similar to winter adults, but upper parts mottled with blackish and buffy.

Downy Young : Upper parts pale buffy gray, finely mottled with dusky; head distinctly marked with irregular black speckles ; under parts white.

Geographical Distribution : Northern South America, north to California, Minnesota, New England, and casually to Labrador.

Breeding Range : Breeds locally nearly throughout its range. In California as far north as Ballona Beach, Los Angeles County.

Breeding Season : Approximately, May 1 to July 15.

Nest : Scarcely perceptible hollow in the bare sand of the beach ; unlined.

Eggs : 2 or 3 ; greenish gray, spotted with light and dark brown, and light purple. Occasionally these markings form a wreath at the larger end. Size 1.25 × 0.95.

SEA SWALLOW and Little Striker are the common names applied to this little tern, although sea swallow is used of all terns. The Least Tern is said to feed upon insects, and has the peculiar darting, skimming flight of swallows; hence the appellation "sea swallow" is particularly appropriate to it. Its call note is a high-keyed squeal or squeak, and it utters this note almost continuously while on the wing.

Throughout the coast of Southern California these Terns are found nesting on the narrow strip of beach between the tide marsh and the sea. Along the old sea drive, a few miles southward from Coronado Beach, it is not uncommon to find their eggs laid on the bare sand, at the edge of the salt marsh, well out of reach of the tide; but so perfectly do they harmonize with their environment that the searcher may, and usually does, pass them by, unless the distress of the parent bird or the flushing of the mother from the nest betrays its location. Even more difficult to find are the newly hatched young, which are little balls of down scarcely larger than a walnut, and seem to melt into the color of the sand even after you have discovered them. Crouched motionless among the pebbles, they do not even wink until your hand almost closes over them, when, *presto!* they scud off with most surprising speed.

77. AMERICAN BLACK TERN. — *Hydrochelidon nigra surinamensis.*

FAMILY: The Gulls and Terns.

Length: 9.00–10.00.
Adults in Summer: Head, neck, and under parts black; upper parts uniform slate-gray; bill and feet black.

Adults in Winter: Head, neck, and under parts white; upper parts deep pearl-gray.

Young: Similar to winter adults, but feathers of back tipped with brownish, and sides washed with slaty.

Downy Young: Upper parts dull dark brown, coarsely mottled with black; top of head, throat, and breast plain blackish brown; side of head dull whitish; belly white, washed with dark gray.

Geographical Distribution: Temperate and tropical America, from Alaska to Brazil and Chili.

Breeding Range: Interior of United States from latitude 39° northward. On Pacific coast breeds abundantly in Oregon and California.

Breeding Season: Approximately, from May 10 to August 1.

Nest: The eggs are laid on a mat of reeds and decaying vegetation floating among rushes of a marsh, in shallow water; or occasionally on bare ground of a mud flat.

Eggs: 2 or 3; brownish green, thickly spotted with dark and light brown and light purple, mostly about the larger end. Size 1.35 × 0.98.

THE Black Tern has long wings and a short tail which, with its dark coloring, renders it easily dis-

77. AMERICAN BLACK TERN.

" As it picks dragon-flies from the low rushes."

tinguishable from the other species occurring on the Pacific coast. Like *Sterna antillarum,* it is a fly-catcher among the terns, feeding almost entirely on aquatic insects and dragonflies. It darts and skims over the marshes with the

grace and agility of a swallow, scarcely pausing in its
flight, as it picks dragon-flies from the low rushes or
catches them in midair. Fish proper it scorns. Crayfish forms some part of its diet, though possibly only a
small part. It is found circling over a marshy meadow
as well as above the more open water of the lakes, and
its nesting site is not infrequently an almost dry pool.
The choice of these often seems to be a mere matter of
whim, but probably is determined by the abundance of
insect life in the locality.

120 c. FARALLONE CORMORANT. — *Phalacrocorax dilophus albociliatus.*

FAMILY : The Cormorants.

Length : 25.00–31.00.

Adults : Greenish black merging to grayish brown on back and wings.
All the feathers of these parts bordered with black, producing a
scaled effect.

Nuptial Plumage : On each side of head behind the eye there is a small
tuft of long, curved, whitish feathers ; gular sac bright orange.

Young : Head and neck brownish gray shading to light on chin, and
dark on top of head; under parts brownish, darker on sides; gular
sac yellow.

Geographical Distribution : California, south to Cape St. Lucas and the
Revilla Gigedo Islands.

Breeding Range : Farallone Islands.

Breeding Season : May and June.

Nest : A loosely constructed mat of kelp, seaweed, and sometimes twigs.

Eggs : From 4 to 5 ; light greenish, covered with chalky film. Size
2.40 × 1.54.

THE Farallone Cormorant may be recognized from the
other species on the Farallone Islands by the long white
tufts over the eyes. In nesting habits it is identical with
Brandt's cormorant, nor can the eggs of the two species

be distinguished by an expert. Both nest in colonies on the South Farallone, and Mr. Corydon Chamberlin, in the "Nidologist," 1895, reports a rookery at Clear Lake, California. Early in May it constructs a shallow nest, about a foot in diameter, lined with Farallone weed and kelp. Occasionally one attempts to carry a long, bulky-looking string of the latter, which trails behind him as he flies, making him look like a winged polliwog. They mould these nests to a roundness by sitting on them, turning awkwardly about and working the kelp into place with feet and bill, but with none of the fluttering movements of wings and tail apparent in the nest-building of land birds. After the nest is begun, one or the other of the parent birds is constantly present, and even then it is a hard struggle to keep the Western gulls from stealing the nesting material as fast as it is brought. The newly hatched Cormorants lack the down of most young sea-birds and are not handsome babies, their fat bodies and grotesque long necks being covered with a leathery-looking black skin. My observations convince me that they are fed by regurgitation for the first twenty-four hours or longer; this is, if possible, a more ludicrous process of "pumping" than in the case of young herons.[1] After this regurgitation period comes a time when live fish is brought to the nest and torn or chewed by the adults before being given to the nestlings. As soon as the latter are able to manage live fish, small carp are popped into their throats head first, and swallowed with curious gulpings. Each meal is followed by a rest time,

[1] See Brandt Cormorant.

when the half-grown Cormorant sits shrugged up into a discouraged-looking bunch, or lolls listlessly against his fellow nestlings. Around (and beneath the nest if in a tree) are bits of fish and other debris, showing that the supply often exceeds the demand.

122. BRANDT CORMORANT. — *Phalacrocorax penicillatus.*

FAMILY : The Cormorants.

Length : 35.00.

Adults : Head and neck iridescent black, with a patch of whitish surrounding base of gular sac; under parts iridescent dark green; scapulars and wing-coverts dark green, edged with black.

Nuptial Plumage : Uppermost scapulars and sides of neck ornamented with long stiff white filaments; gular sac blue.

Young : Head, neck, and rump dark brown; rest of upper parts paler brown; under parts dusky brown, paler on throat.

Geographical Distribution : Pacific coast of North America from Cape St. Lucas to Washington.

Breeding Range : Islands of the Pacific from Lower California to Washington.

Breeding Season : Approximately, May 1 to July 20.

Nest and Eggs : Identical in appearance with those of Farallone cormorant. Size 2.40 × 1.50.

THIS is the most common cormorant of the California coast, and may be distinguished by its stiff white feathers on sides of neck and by its blue gular sac. Rookeries are found on seal rocks near Cypress Point, Monterey, at Santa Cruz, and on the Farallones. These birds nest in colonies on the steepest crags and ledges of those islands. About the middle of May they may be seen carrying seaweed and kelp to their chosen site. There they fashion a new shallow, bowl-shaped nest, which becomes cemented with guano ; or perhaps they redecorate an old one

122. BRANDT CORMORANT
Phalacrocorax penicillatus

with fresh sea moss. From the amount of guano used, and the solidity with which most of these structures had become cemented to the rock, — indeed, they seemed a part of the rock itself, — I judged that they had been handed down from one cormorant generation to another, for many years. Yet each season sees them carefully redecorated on the outside with new, bright-colored seaweed. This weed is seldom picked up on the rocks, but is freshly pulled from the bed of the ocean near shore, the birds diving in some places more than fifty feet. Upon timing one, I found it was under water two and one half minutes; it then reappeared with a bill full of scarlet algæ. Here again the mischievous gulls are in evidence, and the poor Cormorant must guard his gayly trimmed nest, or every bit of his hard-earned moss will be stolen. After the five chalky green eggs are laid his vigilance must never relax, for cormorant eggs and cormorant babies are the most delicious morsels in a sea gull's menu. So the great awkward birds are ever craning their long necks this way and that, — watching before, behind, on every side, for the white-winged robbers. The effect is that, from any point of view, a cormorant rookery is a weird sight. As the days go by, the pretty nests blossom one by one with newly hatched Cormorants, the very homeliest of all created things. Their ungainly bodies are encased in a naked, greasy black skin, and their preternaturally long necks end in immense mouths, so that they resemble huge polliwogs. Like polliwogs, also, they are ever wriggling. For the first few days the young Cormorants are fed by regurgitation — a curious process, always alarming to the observer. The mother squats at the side of the nest, and immediately four or five long black necks are stretched up like fingers of a black kid glove split at the end. These wave helplessly about, until she selects one and thrusts her bill far down the split, which is the throat of the young. She then violently shakes the baby, thereby emptying the food from her mouth into his. Later on small fish are torn and given them.[1]

123 b. BAIRD CORMORANT. — *Phalacrocorax pelagicus resplendens.*

FAMILY : The Cormorants.

Length : 34.00–40.00.

Adults : Feathers of forehead advancing to base of culmen ; gular sac and naked lores dull coral-red or reddish brown ; head and neck glossy violet-black, more purplish toward head, changing gradually through green-blue to glossy bronze-green on under parts ; scapulars and wing-coverts dark green, tinged with bronze. Back dark green.

Nuptial Plumage : Neck and rump ornamented with narrow white filament-like feathers; flanks with a large patch of pure white.

Young : Uniform brownish dusky, merging to grayish on head ; the upper parts darker, with glossy greenish reflections.

Downy Young : Covered with down of a uniform dark sooty gray (Ridgeway).

Geographical Distribution : Pacific coast of North America from Washington south to Cape St. Lucas, and Mazatlan, Mexico.

Breeding Range : Islands near the coast of California and Washington.

Breeding Season : Approximately, June 1 to July 15.

Nest : Of rock moss or kelp on ledges of perpendicular rock.

Eggs : 4 ; pale bluish green, with lime deposit on surface. Size 2.19 × 1.44.

THE Baird Cormorants are less common and more timid than either of the foregoing species. They may

---

[1] See Farallone Cormorants.

be recognized by a white patch on each flank. They breed in very small rookeries of ten or a dozen pairs, — instead of several hundred as is the case with Brandt cormorants, — and are frequently found nesting alone. Their site is usually the most inaccessible rocks in the vicinity. Frequently, so narrow is the ledge chosen that the young are crowded off and are killed by the fall to the water or rocks below. Each season the old nests are used, being repaired with kelp or relined with fresh sea moss. Baird Cormorants, though so retiring, are particularly courageous in defence of their nests and young, and are either so devoted to the former or so stupid that they will return after being robbed and brood upon the empty nest. Their nests are constructed with greater care than those of the other species mentioned, and are lined with the more delicate varieties of sea moss as well as the coarse kelp. They become cemented into a more or less solid mass and also glued to the rock with guano. Some of them are so solid as to warrant the opinion that they have been in use many years. The feeding habits of this species are like those of the Brandt and Farallone cormorants.

125. AMERICAN WHITE PELICAN. — *Pelecanus erythrorhynchos.*

FAMILY : The Pelicans.

Length : 4½–6 feet.

Adult Nuptial Plumage : Entirely white, quills black, whitish at base; a pendant crest of pale yellow feathers, and a horny protuberance on top of bill ; pouch and bill reddish ; feet bright red.

Adults in Winter: Similar to above, but lacking the crest and the horny
protuberance on bill.   Pouch, bill, and feet lemon-yellow.
Young: Plumage white, merging to brownish gray on top of head;
bill, pouch, and feet pale lemon.
Geographical Distribution: Temperate North America, south in winter
to Mexico ; common on the coast of California.
Breeding Range: Southeastern Oregon, Red River valley in British Columbia; lakes of the interior west of Mississippi River, and from Utah
northward.
Breeding Season: Approximately, April 15 to August.
Nest: A pile of sand heaped up about 8 inches high and 14 inches
in diameter, sometimes lined with sticks and slightly hollowed out
on top.   Usually on dry sandy beach of an island.
Eggs: 2, rarely 4 ; chalky white. Size 3.45 × 2.30.

THE American White Pelican has become a comparatively rare bird east of the Mississippi River, but
is abundant throughout the coast of Southern and Central California and on Santa Barbara Island.   Mr.
Grinnell reports it breeding at Eagle Lake.   It feeds
while on or in the water, scooping the fish in its bill
when swimming or wading, seldom diving for them
from the air, and always tossing the catch until it can
be swallowed head first.   Crustacea are rarely if ever
eaten by this species, and they will travel many miles
for fish rather than eat frogs.

"Often a flock will band together and, by beating
their wings, drive a school of fishes into the shallows,
where they gather up large numbers at every scoop of
their big bag.   The water taken is allowed to drain out
of the corners, and the fish are swallowed.   If the bird
is fishing to feed her young, she still does the same,
and afterwards disgorges the fish ; for she could not
fly if her pouch were filled with fishes."[1]

[1] Mrs. Eckstrom, in "The Bird Book."

It is the White Pelican that the gulls torment so by stealing his hard-earned catch time after time. And the Pelican, always of dignified and care-burdened mien, looks comically disconsolate over losing his dinner in this fashion. Yet he makes no attempt to defend himself, for he has no chance; the quick gulls have seized the booty and fled before his slow brain and slower body can move to resent the robbery.

127. CALIFORNIA BROWN PELICAN. — *Pelecanus californicus.*

FAMILY: The Pelicans.

Length: 4½–5 feet.

Nuptial Plumage: Head and chin white, the top of head tinged with straw-yellow; a chestnut patch more or less lengthened to crest on back of head; neck chestnut, merging to seal-brown; upper parts, including wings and tail, silver gray, more or less streaked with seal-brown; under parts dark brownish, streaked with white; pouch and feet red.

Adults in Winter: Similar, but entire head and neck white, somewhat tinged with straw-color; pouch and feet dull olive.

Young: Head, neck, and upper parts light-brownish gray, tipped with paler; under parts white, washed with brownish gray on sides.

Geographical Distribution: Pacific coast from British Columbia to the Galapagos.

Breeding Range: Islands off coast of Lower California and Mexico.

Breeding Season: May and June.

Nest: Usually on the ground, sometimes in the mangrove trees; a loosely constructed, rather bulky mass of sticks and weed-stalks; lined with grass.

Eggs: 2 to 5; chalky white. Size 3.00 × 2.01.

THE California Brown Pelican is abundant throughout California, especially from Santa Cruz southward. At almost any time of the day during the fall, winter, and early spring, a flock of them may be seen lazily flying along the coast over the water in pelican fashion, one behind another. Their flight is characteristic, being five or six wing-strokes taken by all simultaneously, followed by a soaring, which lasts until the leader gives the signal for more wing-strokes. Back and forth up and down the coast, always in pelican single file, the line broken only when one dives to the water for an especially tempting fish. At the inlet on the west side of the isthmus of Santa Catalina, the early morning hours are vocal with the noise of their fishing. Plunk! plunk! — they dive one by one from various heights, striking the water with a heavy splash that can be heard several hundred feet. Mr. Gosse says that these Pelicans invariably turn a somersault under the surface of the water; for they descend diagonally, and the head emerges in the opposite direction.

Although shown a young Brown Pelican which the owner said he had taken from the nest on Santa Catalina Islands, I found that the fishermen there agreed with Mr. Grinnell that no pelicans nested nearer than Los Coronados Islands. As they return to the same breeding ground year after year, the rookery would certainly have been discovered, no matter how inaccessible.

180. WHISTLING SWAN. — *Olor columbianus.*

FAMILY: The Ducks, Geese, and Swans.

Length: About 4½ feet.
Adults: Uniform white; basal portion of bill white, with lores black, the latter usually with a small yellow spot.
Young: Light grayish; bill pinkish; feet light.

Geographical Distribution: Whole of North America.
Breeding Range: Arctic regions.
Breeding Season: June, July, and possibly May.
Nest: "The eggs are usually laid on a tussock surrounded with water,
    and so near it that the female sometimes sits with her feet in the
    water." [1]
Eggs: 3 to 6 ; grayish white, stained with rusty.   Size 4.19 × 2.72.

THIS beautiful bird is found in the United States only
in winter and while migrating in spring and fall. It is
rare in California, but a few remain through the winter
in the interior of the northern part of the State. The
peculiar call note is kept up while the birds are migrating; it resembles the "honk" of wild geese, but is
shriller and more metallic in tone. Heard overhead in
a small valley shut in by mountains, it has a weird,
vibrant quality.

181. TRUMPETER SWAN. — *Olor buccinator.*
FAMILY : The Ducks, Geese, and Swans.

Length: 5–5½ feet.
Adults: Plumage uniform white ; bill and lores jet black.
Young: Grayish brown, browner on head and neck.
Geographical Distribution: Interior of North America, west to the Pacific
    coast ; rare or casual on the Atlantic.
Breeding Range: Interior of the Northern United States northward.
Breeding Season: May and June.
Nest: On high ground; of grasses and moss ; lined with down and feathers.
Eggs: 2 to 6 ; white.   Size 4.30 × 2.60.

A NOT uncommon bird in California during the winter
and early spring. It is found somewhat back from
the coast in the fresh-water sloughs. According to
Mr. Shields, the cry of the Trumpeter Swan resembles
the tones of the French horn. Certainly it is a different

[1] Davie.

sound from the shrill notes of the preceding species, being deeper and more mellow. It is a more common bird in Southern California, and may be heard, as well as seen, in large flocks migrating during the early spring and late fall. It trumpets, however, at dusk and daybreak, for an hour at a time without ceasing, and is particularly noisy at nesting time when feeding its young; the united clamor carries the news of its presence at the nest to listeners a mile or two away. Although the arctic regions are the breeding ground of this bird, a few pairs are said by Mr. Lockhart to breed on the Saskatchewan River in British Columbia.

BIRDS FOUND ALONG THE BEACHES

224. WILSON PHALAROPE. — *Steganopus tricolor.*

FAMILY: The Phalaropes.

Length: Female, 10.00 ; male, 9.00, a little smaller than a robin.

Male in Breeding Plumage: Upper parts grayish brown, brownest on crown and merging to reddish brown on sides of neck in a more or less distinct stripe ; line over eye and under parts white, tinged with buff on throat and breast.

Female in Breeding Plumage: Back and crown slaty gray ; a black stripe on sides of head and neck merging to red-brown on shoulders ; line over eye and under parts white, tinged with light brown on chest and lower part of throat.

Adults in Winter: Upper parts dusky gray ; under parts white, washed with grayish on chest and sides.

Downy Young: Light cinnamon-brown above, paler below, merging to white on under parts. Line of black through crown and nape to back of neck. Three black stripes on lower back.

Geographical Distribution : From British Columbia, south in winter to Brazil.
Breeding Range : Breeds locally throughout the United States from latitude 35° northward.   At Lake Tahoe and other points in California.
Breeding Season : May 20 to July 15.
Nest : A slight depression in the ground ; lined with grass.
Eggs : 3 or 4 ; buffy, marked with umber.   Size 1.30 × 1.60.

WILSON PHALAROPES present some unique features of bird life.   The female is an inch or more longer than the male and larger in proportion.   She is more conspicuously marked, and is the handsomer of the two, — a condition rarely found among avifauna.   Although so trim and

224. WILSON PHALAROPE.

"Picking up their own food before they were ten hours old."

dainty, she is naturally, perhaps, somewhat overbearing in her domestic relations, refusing to consider her master in anything.   She does all the wooing, and woe to the unfortunate male if two females place their choice upon him.   No voice will he have in the matter, for the more persistent or the stronger will win, and he must follow her.   To do him justice, he seems to admire her fully as much because she is aggressive. Once the choice is made his daily life is cut out for him. He must make the nest in which madam condescends to lay three or four buff eggs spotted with dark brown. After that the entire care of incubation and rearing the brood devolves upon him.   In one instance at least, I am positive that the mother was not near the nest at any time after the eggs were laid. The male brooded continually, leaving only when necessary to obtain food. Almost as soon as the down was dry on the chicks they ran out of the nest like little sandpipers, and followed him about up and down the beach, picking up their own food, before they were ten hours old, and the second day they were swimming in the shallow water as gayly as any of the adult birds.

The Phalaropes are not rare along the eastern part of California, and doubtless nest in other marshes than those bordering some parts of Lake Tahoe. They breed there quite abundantly, and their sandpiper-like cries mingle with the plaintive notes of the killdeer whenever anyone enters the nesting place. Like the killdeer, also, the Phalarope will fly restlessly back and forth over its home, revealing by its very anxiety what it is most anxious to conceal. Wilson Phalarope is exclusively an American species, and is less common on the coasts than in the interior.

225. AMERICAN AVOCET. — *Recurvirostra americana*.

FAMILY: The Avocets and Stilts.

Length: 17.00.

Adults in Summer: Head, neck, shoulders, and chest uniform light reddish brown, merging to buff at base of bill; rump, wing-patches, and belly white; scapulars and primaries black; bill long, black, and curved upward; feet and legs grayish blue.

Adults in Winter: Head, neck, and chest grayish white; otherwise as in summer.

Downy Young: Upper parts grayish, mottled with darker; under parts lighter, nearly white on throat and chest; dark, almost black, splatches on the rump and shoulders.

Geographical Distribution : Western United States in general from lati-
tude 30° to the Canadian border ; south in winter to Guatemala and
West Indies.
Breeding Range : The plains of the Dakotas, Montana, Wyoming, Colo-
rado, Utah, and interior of California.
Breeding Season : June to July 15.
Nest : Of grass stems matted together ; placed in tall grass near water.
Eggs : 2 or 3; light olive, spotted with brown.   Size 1.90 × 1.35.

THE American Avocet is a conspicuous bird under any
circumstances, for its long, curved-up bill, intensely black
and white plumage, and long blue legs are sure to attract
attention.   In some localities its blue legs have given
it the nickname of "blue-stocking."   In writing of these
birds, Mr. Frank Chapman says : "They frequent shores
and shallow pools, and in searching for shells, crustaceans, etc., their peculiar recurved bill is used in a most
interesting manner.   Dropping it beneath the surface
of the water until its convexity touches the bottom, they
move rapidly forward, and with every step swing their
bill from side to side as a mower does his scythe.   In
this way they secure food which the muddy water would
prevent them from seeing."

They may occasionally be found swimming in small
companies, but never in exposed or very open water, and
usually as near shore as possible.   The nest is made in
a wet meadow, and is not unlike that of a king rail, except for size.   The young, like the young rails, are taken
to the edge of a meadow, and, until they are two or
three days old, do not go into the water.   They pick
up bugs for themselves from the damp ground and
run to cover at the call of the mother, after the manner
of killdeer.   Their note is seldom heard until nightfall

when, during nesting season, it adds much to the weird-ness of the marsh music. The alarm call is something between a croak and a whistle, but usually the retreat is made with no sound but the soft flutter of wings as the birds take refuge in the tall marsh grass.

226. BLACK–NECKED STILT. — *Himantopus mexicanus.*

FAMILY: The Avocets and Stilts.

Length: 14.50–15.00.

Adult Male: Back of head and neck, upper back, and wings iridescent greenish black ; tail grayish ; forehead, throat, and under parts white ; white spots above and below each eye ; bill black ; feet and legs flesh-color.

Adult Female: Similar to male, except back, which is grayish brown.

Downy Young: Upper parts light grayish, mottled with dark ; large black patch on back and rump ; crown light grayish, with median line of black ; under parts white.

Geographical Distribution: United States, chiefly west of the Great Lakes ; south in winter to Brazil.

Breeding Range: From Southern States to Oregon. In California, breeds in Los Angeles County and in various localities in interior of State north to Sutter County, west of the Sierra Nevada ; east of the Sierra Nevada it breeds as far north as Rhett Lake.

Breeding Season: May 1 to June 16.

Nest: A shallow depression in ground ; lined with grass and occasionally rimmed with rootlets ; usually in grass on edge of lake.

Eggs: 3 to 4 ; light olive-brown, thickly and irregularly marked with purplish brown. Size 1.72 × 1.20.

THIS bird with the extraordinarily long legs is rare east of the Mississippi River, but throughout the West it is abundant. It is a common summer visitant in California, where it breeds in colonies. Formerly it was found in numbers in Los Angeles County, but of late years it seems to prefer more northern nesting grounds, although a few pairs still breed there every year. It is a picturesque graceful bird, well proportioned in spite of the stilt-like legs which give it its name. In flight it is not unlike the cranes, but when alighting it drops its feet and raises its wings, poising a moment, as do the gulls. It feeds upon small fresh-water crustaceans, mollusks, and larvæ of insects, not scorning earthworms, and picks its way daintily through the marsh grass in search of favorite tidbits, with a charming air of quiet grace. Surprised, it springs into flight, trailing its long legs behind it. During the breeding season it is quite noisy, uttering its hoarse croaks continually, until the whereabouts of its nesting place may be known by any who will investigate. A large part of this noise occurs when the food is brought to the mate on the nest, where it receives a joyous, if unmusical, welcome. The nestlings look like balls of down perched upon toothpicks, but neither their legs nor their bills are developed at all in proportion to those of the adults. They are spry, like the young of most ground birds, and in a marvellously short time become self-supporting.

232. LONG–BILLED   DOWITCHER. — *Macrorhamphus scolopaceus.*

Family : The Snipes and Sandpipers.

Length : 11.00–12.50.

Adults in Summer : Upper parts black, mottled with buff and light red-brown ; rump mottled black and white, and tail barred black and white ; a light line over eye, and a dark one from eye to bill ; under parts mottled on throat, breast, and belly with red-brown and blackish ; sides and lower tail-coverts barred with same colors.

Adults in Winter : Plumage uniform dusky gray ; line over eye and the lower belly white.

Young: Similar, but belly and chest tinged with uniform light red-
brown.

Geographical Distribution: Mississippi valley and Western North America from Mexico to Alaska. In California it is found as a common
winter visitant in the interior valleys.

Breeding Range: The Yukon valley and arctic regions.

Breeding Season: May 28 to July 1.

Nest: A shallow depression in Alaskan moss ; placed on dry hill-tops.

Eggs: 3 or 4 ; dirty grayish buff, marked with blackish brown. Size
1.80 × 1.20.

IN California, the Long-billed Dowitchers occur only
in the winter, when cold drives them southward from
their chosen haunts among the frozen regions of Alaska.
They come in October, flying in little companies along
the coast region or through the interior valleys, feeding
wherever there is a suitable marshy place. About San
Francisco Bay and Alviso they may occasionally be seen
on migration, but as soon as possible they find winter
quarters in the more sheltered valleys. Their flight is
strong and swift, though rather low. When resting, the
Dowitchers huddle together in the tall grass, and are
either so confiding or so stupid that they are easy victims
to the hunter. To know them one must watch them in
their nesting grounds in the Yukon valley. Here, according to Mr. Nelson, their noisy wooing can be heard
morning and evening, the love song being a clear " pee-
ter-wee-too ; wee-too ! pee-ter-wee-too ; wee-too," sung
as the pair hover in midair, twenty yards above the
earth.

The unlined nest is usually in a clump of Alaskan
moss or dry grass, and not very near the water. The
young are covered with brownish gray down, so protective in coloring as to render their discovery difficult.

If disturbed, the mother flies a short distance with a shrill cry and, hiding behind a tussock, watches the intruder but makes no attempt to defend.

By September 1 the adults are in winter plumage and ready for their trip south.

242. LEAST SANDPIPER, OR MEADOW OXEYE.
Tringa minutilla.

FAMILY: The Snipes and Sandpipers.

Length: 5.00–7.00.

Adults in Summer: Upper parts dusky, nearly black ; feathers edged with light red-brown ; middle tail-feathers black, outer ones gray ; upper throat, belly, and sides white ; neck and breast yellowish white, streaked with dusky.

Adults in Winter: Upper parts lighter than in summer, and clouded with dusky ; under parts light gray, finely streaked with darker.

Young: Similar, but with heavy black streak through crown and middle of back.

Geographical Distribution: North America, wintering from the Gulf States southward.

Breeding Range: From Canada to arctic regions.

Breeding Season: May 15 to June 15.

Nest: A slight depression in the dry ground near water; usually lined with leaves and grasses.

Eggs: 3 or 4; light gray, speckled with cinnamon and lavender. Size 1.15 × 0.85.

THESE tiny little Sandpipers are commonly found in flocks, alone or in company with the semipalmated sandpipers, along the shores of the bays and lakes of California during the fall, winter, and spring. They trip lightly along the beaches, just at the edge of the water, with a dainty bobbing walk, scurrying out of the reach of a wave, picking up bugs and water insects, and so absorbed in the fun that they forget to be afraid. Mr.

Bailey describes them as quick to take alarm, but I
have had them pick up food almost under my feet.
Their habit of frequenting the meadows in the vicinity
of water and hiding in the long grass has given them
the name of "Meadow Oxeye." On account of their
small size, they escape the covetous eye of sportsmen
and plume-hunters, and are in little danger of being
decimated by the gun. When newly hatched, the young
are not larger than a man's thumb, and they begin immediately to run about on their spry little legs.

243 a. RED–BACKED SANDPIPER, OR OX BIRD.
Tringa alpina pacifica.

(Common names : American Dunlin ; Lead Back ; Black
Breast.)

FAMILY : The Snipes and Sandpipers.

Length : 7.50–8.00.

Adults in Summer : Upper parts bright reddish-brown, more or less
mottled and streaked with black ; breast whitish, streaked with
dark gray ; centre of belly black ; sides and lower belly white.

Adults in Winter : Upper parts brownish gray, streaked with dark
gray ; breast ashy, streaked indistinctly with darker ; rump, throat,
and belly white.

Young : Similar to winter adults, but with upper parts streaked with
black and buffy.

Geographical Distribution : North America ; south in winter to South
America.

Breeding Range : Arctic regions.

Nest : A slight hollow ; lined with grass.

Eggs : 3 or 4 ; grayish buffy or greenish white, dotted with shades of
brown. Size 1.43 × 1.01.

THIS species may be known in any plumage by its
curved bill. It is common along the coast of California

in the winter, and is found in the interior in spring and
fall. Early in May it leaves for its breeding grounds
in the arctic regions, returning in October. It is seen
usually in large flocks, and, being less active than most
shore birds, is oftener a victim to the surf of the winter
storms. Walking along the beach after a blustering
night or day, one occasionally may find the lifeless
bodies of these little birds half buried in the sand, not
in the same numbers as the more venturesome waders,
but enough to sadden a morning tramp.

247. WESTERN SANDPIPER. — *Ereunetes occidentalis.*

FAMILY : The Snipes and Sandpipers.

Length : 7.00 or 8.00.

Adults in Summer : Upper parts black or dusky, conspicuously mottled
with buffy and red-brown ; breast and sides streaked with blackish ;
rest of under parts white.

Adults in Winter : Upper parts dull brownish gray, indistinctly streaked
with dusky ; under parts white, with faint dusky spots on breast and
sides.

Downy Young : Upper parts bright rusty buff, spotted with black ; a
black line through crown and middle of back ; hair-like feathers
among the down, tipped with yellow ; under parts cream-white.

Geographical Distribution : Western North America ; south in winter to
Central America.

Breeding Range : Alaska and British America.

Breeding Season : June 1 to July 1.

Nest : A hollow in the ground, with scanty lining of grasses.

Eggs : 4 ; clay-colored, thickly speckled with reddish brown.   Size
1.20 × 0.87.

THE Western Sandpiper is abundant on the Pacific
coast during the spring and fall migrations. In its
nesting grounds it is said by Mr. Nelson to be fearless,
and conspicuously devoted to its young. He gives an

instance in which a bird returned to her eggs across a man's outstretched arms. During migrations the Western Sandpiper rests occasionally for two or three days in one locality. It is less timid than most of its family.

248. SANDERLING. — *Calidris arenaria.*

(Common names : Surf Snipe ; Ruddy Plover ; Beach Bird.)

FAMILY : The Snipes and Sandpipers.

Length : 7.00–9.00.

Adults in Summer : Upper parts mottled white, gray, and black ; darker through crown and middle of back ; wing-bar and entire under parts white.

Adults in Winter : Upper parts ashy gray ; bend of wing blackish ; under parts uniform clear white.

Young : Upper parts pale gray, spotted with black and white ; under parts white.

Geographical Distribution : " Nearly cosmopolitan." In America a few winter in Texas and California, and from there southward to Patagonia.

Breeding Range : Arctic and subarctic regions.

Breeding Season : June 15 to July 15.

Nest : A slight depression in ground ; lined with grasses.

Eggs : 3 or 4 ; greenish buffy, speckled with brown. Size 1.41 × 0.91.

THE Sanderling inhabits the entire American continent, and may be found during spring and fall migrations picking up its food on nearly every salt-water beach. It follows closely in the wake of each receding wave, scampering out of the way of the returning water with swiftness and dainty grace. This game of tag with the ocean would seem to be as much for fun as for food, for I have often watched them as they ran back and forth after the waves for several minutes without picking up anything.   In California the Sanderling frequently remains all winter and adds to the delights

248. SANDERLING.

"A game of tag with the ocean."

of a stroll along the beach.   Not especially shy, it will permit one to come within twenty feet of it, and it pays no attention to any observer seated on the sand.

254. GREATER YELLOW–LEGS. — *Totanus melanoleucus.*

FAMILY : The Snipes and Sandpipers.

Length : 12.00–15.00.

Adults in Summer : Upper parts black, streaked and spotted with white and gray ; tail and upper tail-coverts white, barred with black ; middle of belly white ; rest of under parts white, spotted or barred with black ; throat streaked light and dark gray.

Adults in Winter : Similar, but upper parts dark gray, mottled with white ; under parts white, finely speckled with gray on throat and upper breast.

Young : Similar to winter adults, but white of plumage tinged with buffy.

Geographical Distribution : North America ; south in winter to South America.

Breeding Range : From latitude 40° northward.

Nest : A shallow, grass-lined depression in the ground.

Eggs : 3 or 4 ; muddy buff, marked with dark brown.   Size 1.43 × 1.20.

THE Greater Yellow-legs is an abundant migrant throughout California, some remaining in the southern portion near the coast throughout the winter, and, doubt-less, a few breed in the more northern Sierra Nevada district, though I am unable to find any authoritative breeding record. My own record shows that none were seen by me after May 9, although a search and lookout were maintained. They are conspicuous birds, and not easily mistaken for others of their family. The white tail and rump are distinguishing marks, particularly in flight. This bird is the sentinel of the game-birds, giving warning of the approach of the hunter in loud, whistling notes repeated rapidly; hence its names "Tell-tale" and "Long-legged Tattler." Mr. Chapman writes of it delightfully as follows:

"Few birds are flying; lulled by the lap, lap of the water, I have almost fallen asleep, when from far up in the gray sky comes a soft *wheu, wheu, wheu.* I respond quickly, and lying on my back, look eagerly upward. Not a bird can be seen, but the questioning call grows stronger, and is repeated more frequently. Finally I distinguish five or six black points sailing in narrow circles so high that I can scarcely believe they are the birds I hear. But no bar or shoal breaks the sound-waves. The birds grow larger, and widening circles sweep earthward. Their soft whistle has a plaintive tone; their long bills turn inquiringly from side to side. The stolid decoys give no response, they repel rather than encourage; but the whistling continues, and with murmured notes of interrogation, the deluded birds wheel over them, to find too late that they have blundered."

259. WANDERING TATTLER. — *Heteractitis incanus.*

FAMILY: The Snipes and Sandpipers.

Length: 10.50–11.50.

Adults in Summer: Upper parts uniform slate-color ; under parts barred with dark gray and white ; throat white, spotted with dusky ; lower belly white.

Adults in Winter: Upper parts, sides, and breast gray ; middle of belly and throat white.

Young: Similar to winter adults, but feathers of wings and back marked with pure white.

Geographical Distribution: Pacific coast of North America from Alaska to Lower California, west to Hawaiian Islands and Kamtchatka.

Breeding Range: From Vancouver Island northward to valley of Yukon River.

" *Nest* and *Eggs* apparently not recorded : but young birds taken by Macoun on west coast of Vancouver Island " (F. M. Bailey).

THE Wandering Tattler is well named, for it remains in one locality only during the nesting season, which is from May 20 to July 1 in Alaska. Its food consists of mollusks and crustaceans, and for that reason it is seldom found at any great distance from the shore. Its note is a clear, flute-like whistle, not unlike that of the greater yellow-legs, and is translated by one observer as " tu-tu-tu-tu." Like its larger relative, it is a stately little bird, graceful whether on land or in the air. It is said to give warning of the approach of danger by a shriller whistle than its customary sweet call, and consequently is berated by sportsmen.

263. SPOTTED SANDPIPER. — *Actitis macularia.*

(Common names : Teeter; Tip-up; Sandlark.)

FAMILY : The Snipes and Sandpipers.

Length : 7.00–8.00.

Adults in Summer : Upper parts gray, with an olive or greenish bronze sheen ; head and neck faintly streaked with black ; back barred with black ; under parts white, spotted with black ; a white wing-bar conspicuous in flight.

Adults in Winter : Under parts uniform white, without spots or markings.

Downy Young : Upper parts buffy gray, with black line from bill through and down back, crossed transversely at shoulders by two short black lines in form of Greek cross ; under parts white.

Young : Similar to winter adults, but finely mottled or barred with buff on back.

Geographical Distribution : North America to Hudson Bay ; in winter to South America.

Breeding Range : Breeds locally wherever found. In California breeds on shores of lakes in the Sierra Nevada.

Breeding Season : June.

Nest : A depression in the sand a little way back on a beach, usually under a tuft of grass ; unlined, or scantily lined with dry grass.

Eggs : 4 ; light buff, thickly spotted with lilac, light brown, and umber. Size 1.34 × 0.92.

FOUND along almost every beach and river and lake of California, this small Sandpiper is the most abundant and most commonly observed of all our shore birds. Its dainty, dipping motion while standing by the shore has given it the nickname of " Teeter," and that name alone would help to identify it. It is the only one of its family that nests commonly in California, and is a member well worth studying. It may be found in the same locality day after day, picking up its food at the edge of the water, or venturing out on the lily pads in search of some particularly tempting morsel. The young leave the nest as soon as the down is dry, but so protective is their coloring that they might crouch unnoticed at your feet. I have found them sleeping huddled together at night in a hole made by a cow's foot in the grassy meadow bordering a lake, and though they were so openly exposed, I should never have discovered them but for the anxiety of the parent birds. They are about the size of a walnut, quaint little balls of down, perched on toothpick-like legs, and have the same odd habit of bobbing as the adults. Instead of opening their mouths to be fed, after the manner of most young birds, they will pick up the food found for them by the parents, and in a day's time they have learned to hunt it along the shore. They are independent youngsters, wise in tricks of hiding motionless on the sand or in the grass, and in keeping together. Their low, sweet, peeping notes are like those of young chickens, and they seem to care more for each other than for the brooding of the parent birds. The call note of the adults is a sharp "peet-weet" uttered on the wing.

264. LONG–BILLED CURLEW, OR SICKLE–BILLED CURLEW. — *Numenius longirostris.*

FAMILY : The Snipes and Sandpipers.

Length : 20.00–26.00.

Adults : Head, neck, and upper parts streaked and mottled grayish buff and black ; under parts brownish buff, more or less streaked and barred with black ; bill very long, slender, and curved.

Downy Young : Upper parts deep buff, mottled with black ; under parts sulphur-yellow ; bill straight.

Geographical Distribution : Entire temperate North America ; south in winter to West Indies.

Breeding Range: North of latitude 35° to latitude 50°. In California breeds in northwestern portion of the State, in the Pitt River valley.
Breeding Season : May and June.
Nest : A shallow depression in the ground; lined with dry grasses; placed near water.
Eggs: 3 or 4 ; buffy, spotted with purple and umber. Size 2.52 × 1.85.

THE Sickle-billed Curlew is a conspicuous bird wherever it occurs on the beaches. In California it is common on the coast and valleys west of the Sierra Nevada during the winter months, appearing early in October and remaining until the last of April or the middle of May. These Curlews fly in wedge-shaped flocks of from fifty to a hundred, the movement of migration being continuous when started, and mostly by daylight; they rest and feed late in the afternoon. A flock of them alighting is suggestive of a multitude of gigantic butterflies, as they touch the earth with feet down and wings raised over their backs.

Their long bills are used to probe in the earth for their food, which consists of worms, small snails, crabs, crayfish, the larvæ of beetles, and adult insects of all kinds. Their note is a prolonged whistle as heard from high in the air, or a clear rich call as you flush them from the ground. If disturbed in their breeding ground, they unite, as do the jays, to drive the intruder away with harsh cries and a succession of shrill notes that one observer calls laughter. Failing in this, they circle about as near as they dare, and occasionally one, more daring than the rest, comes too near for comfort. The mother, finding defence useless, tries the old feint of a broken wing, while the others watch her with anxious cries.

The young bird has a well-developed but straight bill more than an inch long when hatched; he runs about on strong legs within an hour of his emancipation from the shell.

265. HUDSONIAN CURLEW, OR JACK CURLEW.
Numenius hudsonicus.

FAMILY: The Snipes and Sandpipers.

Length: 16.50–18.00.

Adults: Upper parts mottled and barred with pale cinnamon-brown and blackish; line through the crown buffy, bordered with two brown stripes; under parts buff, narrowly streaked with blackish.

Downy Young: Buffy brown above, merging to lemon-yellow below; upper parts indistinctly mottled with dusky.

Geographical Distribution: Nearly the whole of North and South America; south in winter.

Breeding Range: Arctic regions.

Breeding Season: June 15 to July 15.

Nest: A slight hollow, scantily lined with grasses.

Eggs: 4; pear-shaped, grayish yellow, coarsely scrawled with chocolate and brown. Size 2.27 × 1.57.

265. HUDSONIAN CURLEW.

" When alighting."

THE Hudsonian Curlew occurs throughout North America, breeding at the ponds and lakes of the arctic regions and in all parts of Alaska. In California it is abundant as a spring and fall migrant, and is found on the coast in company with the long-billed curlew and the jack-snipe. Like the others, it is a conspicuous bird on the beach or flying in triangular flocks over the edge of the water; like the long-billed curlew, it drops its feet and raises its wings in a peculiar butterfly fashion when alighting. It is not so commonly found in the interior as other members of its family, and probes in the sand of the beach for its food rather than in the salt meadows; its favorite food is small snails, water-spiders, and crayfish.

270. BLACK–BELLIED PLOVER. — *Squatarola.*

(Common names: Beetle-head; Oxeye; Whistling Field Plover; Bull-head Plover; Swiss Plover.)

FAMILY : The Plovers.

Length : 11.00.
Adults in Summer : Sides of head and neck and under parts black ; lower belly and under tail-coverts white; upper parts mottled black and white ; tail white, barred with black.
Adults in Winter : Upper parts brownish gray, mottled with lighter, and under parts white, streaked with gray.
Young : Similar to winter adults, but spotted on upper parts with buff.
Geographical Distribution : Nearly cosmopolitan.
Breeding Range : Arctic regions.
Breeding Season : July.
Nest : A mere depression in the soil, lined with dry grass.
Eggs : 4 ; light buffy olive, heavily marked with brown or black. Size 2.04 × 1.43.

THE Black-bellied, or Beetle-head Plover is a common migrant on the California coast. Each spring and fall flocks may be seen flying in lines or wedge-shaped ranks after the manner of geese, and their mellow three-noted whistle sounds clearly above the roar of the surf. These birds run along the beach at the edge of the water, snatching up the sea food left by the receding tide, and when the turn sets in they retreat to the higher sand banks to be out of the way of a wetting. The species is nearly cosmopolitan, being found in Asia, Africa, Australia, the West Indies, North America, Central America, and South America on migrations; in the breeding season it is found in Russia, Siberia, Alaska, Franklin Bay, and the Barren Lands. In each locality it has a different common name.

273. KILLDEER. — *Ægialitis vocifera.*

FAMILY : The Plovers.

Length : 10.50.

Adults : Forehead, throat, collar, and under parts white ; front of the crown, lores, ring around the neck, band on the breast, black ; back olive-brown ; rump and sides of the tail dark buffy.

Downy Young : Upper parts olive-brown ; under parts white ; collar and bands across the chest, and across lores black, like adults.

Geographical Distribution : North America ; south in winter from latitude 30° to South America.

Breeding Range : Breeds locally wherever found. In California breeds throughout the State, but in large numbers at Lake Tahoe.

Breeding Season : May and June.

Nest : A slight depression in the earth ; unlined.

Eggs : 3 or 4 ; buffy, marked with dark brown and blackish. Size 1.50 × 1.10.

WHEREVER seen, this pretty plover announces its name in plaintive cries of " kildee, kildee." Often in the night, as if troubled by bad dreams, it sounds this anxious cry. It is abundant everywhere, and is known to every country boy. Its nest is on the bare ground in the edge of an upland meadow ; but the eggs are so protectively colored that you might pass it without notice, did not the old bird by her great anxiety proclaim the hiding place. An hour later you may find every shell broken and the little ones gone, for they run about in the grass as soon as free. No other bird will make more frantic efforts than the Killdeer to lead you away in order that the young may escape: she feigns broken wings, falls over and over on the ground, moaning as if with pain, and begging you to capture her. But the whole performance is only a feint, for when you come up to her, she will fly away on swift, strong wings. The favorite nesting ground is more or less stony, and the little Killdeers, crouching motionless to hide, so resemble the stones as to render discovery difficult. They are very like the adults in form and markings, the characteristic black bands across the upper breast proclaiming the kinship were other sign wanting.

278. SNOWY PLOVER. — *Ægialitis nivosa.*

FAMILY: The Plovers.

Length: 6.00–7.00.

Adults in Summer: Upper parts pale buff-gray ; forehead, cheeks, and under parts white ; bar across forehead, patch at back of cheeks, and patch at the side of chest black.

Adults in Winter: Black, replaced by grayish.

Young: Like winter adults, but feathers of the upper parts distinctly tipped with white.

Downy Young: Upper parts pale grayish buff, mottled with black ; white collar across neck ; under parts white.

Geographical Distribution: Western United States ; south in winter to Chili.

Breeding Range: Breeds wherever found in the United States ; throughout California as far north as Pescadero.

Breeding Season: April and May.

Nest: A slight hollow in the sand ; unlined.

Eggs: 3 ; pale grayish buff, spotted with umber and black. Size 1.20 × 0.90.

THE Snowy Plover is resident all the year round in the southern part of California near the coast, and occurs as far north as Cape Mendocino. It is abundant at Long Beach, San Pedro, and all along the sandy coast near Los Angeles. These Plovers are pretty, plump little birds, and trip unconcernedly at the water's edge, picking up the food left by the retreating waves. If one is disturbed, it crouches flat on the sand, in a hollow if possible, trusting to protective coloring to escape notice. A nest found near San Diego in April, contained, when discovered, three clay-covered eggs. When it was visited three hours later, two little ones had broken the shell and were crouched down like small gray stones. The third egg was sterile. The young were about the size of large walnuts and were the prettiest creatures imaginable. The next morning the nest was deserted, only the particles of eggshells scattered about told where it had been; but the mother bird was discovered with both chicks hiding behind a tuft of grass. No other nest was found nearer than two hundred feet, and it is doubtful whether the one found at that distance was really the nest of a Snowy Plover.

This species has none of the dipping motions of the sandpiper, and is much plumper-looking, though not less trim than the sandpipers. Its call is a whistled "pleep, pleep," somewhat between the note of a spotted sandpiper and that of a golden plover.

284. BLACK TURNSTONE. — *Arenaria melanocephala.*

FAMILY : The Surf Birds and Turnstones.

Length : 9.00.

Adults in Summer: Forehead, sides of head, neck, throat, and chest black, more or less spotted with white, a small white patch in front of the eye ; crown and back iridescent greenish black ; belly and sides white.

Adults in Winter: Similar, but without white spots on head and neck.

Young: Plumage like winter plumage of adults, but black is replaced by grayish, and feathers of the upper parts are tipped with white or buff.

Geographical Distribution: Pacific coast of North America, from Point Barrow to Lower California.

Breeding Range: From British Columbia northward.

Breeding Season: June and July.

Nest: A slight depression in the ground, near beach.

Eggs: 4 ; grayish green, thickly spotted with brown. Size 1.62 × 1.12.

THE Black Turnstone is common along the coast district of California throughout all the year. Mr. Grinnell says that although a few individuals remain all summer, they are not known to breed within the confines of the State. They are seen most frequently along the exposed ocean beaches, where their curious habit of poking under small stones for food has given them their name. They may be known by their short, sharp, tip-tilted bill, black head, and white rump. There are but four species in the family, three of which occur in the United States. Of these the Black Turnstone is the only one met with frequently in California, although the Ruddy Turnstone occurs as a migrant throughout the coast district. All the species are strictly maritime birds, living on the outer beaches and shunning the interior.

287. BLACK OYSTER–CATCHER. — *Hœmatopus bachmani.*

FAMILY : The Oyster-catchers.

Length: 17.00.

Adults: Head and neck bluish black, rest of plumage rusty black ; bill chisel-shaped and red ; feet and legs red.

Young: General color more brownish.

Downy Young: Head, neck, and upper parts sooty brown ; the down tipped with rusty ; under parts black.

Geographical Distribution: Pacific coast of North America from Lower California to the Aleutian Islands.

Breeding Range: Breeds nearly throughout its habitat.

Breeding Season: June.

Nest: The bare ground of the beach or the shale.

Eggs: 1 to 3 ; olive, spotted with umber and purplish gray.   Size 2.20 × 1.52.

THE Oyster-catcher family includes ten species, mostly found in the tropics ; but three species are found in North America, and two occur in California.   While found all along the coast of California, they are especially partial to rocky portions and islands, and are not usually seen on the sand beaches.   Their feeding grounds are the outer bars, beaches, and rocks, where they search for clams, muscles, and oysters exposed by the fall of the tide.   The strong shells of these mollusks the birds pry open with their bills.   Oyster-catchers are abundant along the rocky coast at La Jolla, but I have never found any breeding there.   Mr. Anthony found them breeding on the rocky islands close to the coast, the eggs having been laid on the bare rocks, usually but a few feet above high water, and close to the edge.   All about them were empty shells of limpets brought there by the mate of the nesting bird. In no case was there any attempt at nest-building.

When watching this bird stride over the rocks with a queer stilted motion, one is impressed with the idea that its odd gait is the effect of self-consciousness. So shy is it that it keeps up a constant nervous turning of its head in search of danger, and takes alarm at the least unusual sight in the distance. The call note is a low, rather musical whistle.

BIRDS FOUND IN BAYOUS AND MARSHES

1. WESTERN GREBE. — *Æchmophorus occidentalis*.

FAMILY: The Grebes.

Length: 27.50.

Adult Plumage: Top of head and stripe down back of neck black; rest of upper parts brownish gray; lower parts, including sides of head and all of neck except stripe down back, glossy white; bill long and yellowish white, with black stripe down upper mandible from base to tip.

Downy Young: Above uniform light brownish gray; under parts white.

Geographical Distribution: Western North America from Lower California to British Columbia; east to Manitoba.

Breeding Range: Breeds locally nearly throughout its habitat.

Breeding Season: Approximately, May 15 to July 1.

Nest: A mass of floating vegetation on the surface of the water in a slough or marsh, and usually fastened to surrounding rushes.

Eggs: 2 to 5; soiled bluish green. Size 2.50 × 1.40.

Æchmophorus occidentalis is the largest of all the North American grebes, but not the most common. It is found in the marshy portions of the inland lakes on the Pacific coast and throughout the Western States. Gregarious, like all the grebes, it nests in colonies sometimes numbering a hundred. A marshy place where there is water from two to four feet deep is chosen, so that safety from storm may be secured for the nest among the strong rushes, and escape from pursuit may be found for parent and young by diving directly from the nest into the water. Knowing their helplessness on land, the wise grebes avoid all travel on it for themselves and their broods. The nest platform of rushes is made by pulling the reeds down one by one until they lie criss-cross on the surface of the water. Upon this foundation is placed decaying vegetation of all sorts, picked out of the water, — apparently the wetter the better. The eggs when first laid are a pale blue-green, but soon become a dirty brownish color from contact with the slime of the nest.

Naturalists assert that all grebes cover their eggs during absence both for purposes of concealment and to assist incubation. I believe, however, that this is less the practice of Western Grebes than of any other variety, for out of many nests I visited only one was covered, while I have never found the nest of either a pied-billed grebe or an American eared grebe where there had not been at least an attempt at covering. The eggs of the Western species also are invariably less stained than those of either of the others, a fact which may support the theory that they are not so fully covered.

Eggs of the American eared grebe are often found in the nest of a Western Grebe, but never, to my knowledge, *vice versa*. I believe this is to be accounted for by the more exposed position and looser construction of the nests of the American eared grebe, which results in their destruction by storm. When this occurs, the homeless bird nearly always invades another nest, and usually the better made one of his larger neighbor. Frequently, this results in a battle to the death for the possession of the nest, but never, so far as I have observed, in a victory for the smaller bird.

4. AMERICAN EARED GREBE. — *Colymbus nigricollis californicus.*

FAMILY: The Grebes.

Length: 13.00.

Adults in Nuptial Plumage: Head, neck, and chest black; sides of head behind eyes with tuft-like patches of small buffy brown feathers; under parts silky white, washed with dusky on sides; inner quills dusky; eyes scarlet; eyelids orange.

Downy Young: Top of head dusky, with white markings; upper parts light brownish gray; under parts white.

Geographical Distribution: Western North America from Guatemala to Great Slave Lake. East to Mississippi valley.

Breeding Range: Locally throughout above territory.

Breeding Season: Approximately, May 15 to August 1.

Nest: A mass of floating vegetation more or less matted together and woven to surrounding rushes; in more open situations than that of the western grebe.

Eggs: 3 to 7; elliptical in shape; bluish white, more or less soiled by dampness of nest. Size 1.75 × 1.19.

THIS little Grebe breeds commonly in the inland lakes, grassy ponds, and sloughs of California, Washington, Oregon, and Lower Canada. Dr. Jeffries tells me that it also breeds somewhat sparingly in the slough across the isthmus at Santa Catalina Islands, and I found several individuals there, in nuptial plumage, in

May. This species follows the habits of all grebes in covering the nest with wet vegetation and debris during its absence, leaving the sun to continue the work of incubation. Like other grebes also, it secures its food by diving, and then pursuing its prey under the water.

The Grebe babies are fat, roly-poly youngsters, who tumble into the water almost from the egg-shell, diving and swimming like experts when a day old. They seem to pick up their own food from the water, but the parents also assist with larvæ of water-bugs and tiny minnows. The young Grebe

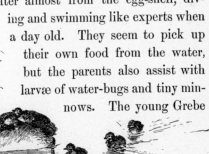

4. AMERICAN EARED GREBE.

When tired, they are given a ride on the mother's back.

is seldom fed by having the food placed in its bill, but by a curious wisdom he is taught to help himself. Sometimes the bug is tossed into the group, and the smartest youngster gets the prize. Oftener it is laid on the water for a little one to pick up. The whole process is very like the way a hen places food in front of her chicks.

The mother's watchful eye detects the first sign of weariness in the tiny swimmers, and gently diving beneath them she gathers them on her back.

These habits in the care of the young characterize all species of grebes, for in no birds are the family traits more prominent than among these queer divers. To the shame of all plumage-hunters be it said, the love of the grebes for their young is one cause of the rapid diminution of their number, for so expert are the grebes in diving at the flash of the gun that, but for the mother love which impels them to protect their helpless little ones, they could easily escape. But they are mercilessly shot while defending their nests, and the young are left to starve, while the silvery breast of the mother bird adorns the hat of a thoughtless woman.

6. PIED–BILLED GREBE. — *Podilymbus podiceps.*

(Common names: Hell Diver; Water Witch; Dabchick.)
Family: The Grebes.

Length: 13.50.

Adults in Summer: Upper parts glossy blackish brown; sides of head and entire neck soft gray-brown; throat black; upper breast and sides of belly light gray-brown, indistinctly mottled with dusky; belly and lower breast glossy white; bill light, crossed by black band.

Winter Plumage: Throat changed from black to dull white; head browner; lower parts whiter, with no dusky spots; white bill replaced by brown without black band.

Young: Similar to winter adults, but sides of head striped with brown.

Downy Young: Head and neck black and white with rufous spot on crown; upper parts blackish, with stripes of white.

Geographical Distribution: The whole of North America from Mexico to Hudson Bay.

Breeding Range: Breeds locally throughout its habitat.

Breeding Season: Approximately, May 15 to July 1.

Nest: A more or less solid structure of mud, marsh grass, and wet weeds; fastened to growing plants. Sometimes built entirely up from the bottom of the slough, and sometimes laid on the rushes pulled over to support it. It is fastened securely, and usually rises several inches above the surface of the water.

Eggs: 5 to 10 ; soiled greenish white.   Size 1.70 × 1.18.

THIS, the most abundant of the grebes, is the one usually shot for its plumage. It breeds commonly in Los Angeles County, California, and about San Francisco Bay. Its common names express well its marvellous powers of diving and remaining for a long time under water, where it swims easily and rapidly with just the tip of its bill exposed. On land it is, like all grebes, awkward and helpless, and, as one author says, looks more like a tiny kangaroo than a bird. Possibly on account of its helplessness when on the nest, it has formed the habit of covering the eggs with decaying vegetation during the daytime and leaving them to be cherished by the artificial heat, and of returning to brood them during the night. Certainly these little Grebes are never found on their nests during sunny days, and in California June days are always sunny. In Oregon, on dark cold days, they are close sitters, and it is an odd sight to see them jump into the water at any distance and disappear with scarcely a ripple. They breed abundantly throughout California in the more sheltered ponds and inland lakes, requiring only that there shall be tule, rushes, or flags to form a platform for the slimy structure called a nest. The young Grebes attempt to dive as soon as hatched, but rarely succeed in submerging their entire bodies at the first trial ; and their plumage, like that of the adults, seems to be waterproof, for never a wet feather do they show on emerging. The Pied-billed Grebe is a much shyer bird than either the Western or the eared grebe, and is less noisy, its call being only a plaintive note quite in contrast to the hoarse croaking cries of the larger species. It is also less gregarious; a pair may sometimes be found nesting in a marsh unfrequented by any other of their species.

187. WHITE–FACED GLOSSY IBIS.—*Plegadis guarauna*.

FAMILY : The Ibises.

Length : 22.50.

Adults : Head, neck, and lower parts reddish brown ; feathers around base of bill white ; lores pink ; upper parts iridescent green and purple.

Young : Upper parts as in adults, except head and neck streaked with white and dark ashy gray ; under parts plain gray-brown.

Downy Young : Entirely black.

Geographical Distribution : Tropical America, south to Argentine Republic and Chili ; north from Texas and Lower California to Oregon.

Breeding Range : Texas and the Gulf States, and, to a limited degree, in the Ballona marshes, as well as various San Diegan points.

Breeding Season : April, May, and June.

Nest : Of reeds woven in among the rushes ; shaped similar to the red-winged blackbird's nest, but much larger.

Eggs : 3 to 5 ; deep bluish green. Size 1.95 × 1.35.

IN the wet meadows and marshes of California there are frequently seen queer black birds which might be taken for large crows but for their long legs and long, curved, curlew-like bills. They wade about probing in the mud for crayfish or snails, or stand motionless on one leg in heronesque attitudes, watching for minnows in the shallow water. In habits they seem to resemble the bitterns, nesting in the rushes and feeding upon frogs, fresh-water crustaceans, or small snakes, trusting to protective coloring for safety except when forced to take flight. At dusk and at dawn, large companies of them may sometimes be seen circling slowly over a marsh as if to find a suitable feeding ground, or flying in long lines as do the pelicans. But after the nesting season is ended, they become more solitary and are less frequently seen on the wing. Look for them

at that time in the tall tule m a r s h e s. They are there, though you may not f i n d them, for they are the shyest

187. WHITE-FACED GLOSSY IBIS.

"*Watching for minnows in the shallow water.*"

of water birds. At night, they roost in trees in certain chosen localities, returning to the s a m e tree year after year. Their cry is not often heard; it has a peculiar guttural quality not unlike that of a bittern.

190. AMERICAN BITTERN. — *Botaurus lentiginosus.*

(Common names: Marsh Hen; Stake-driver; Thunder Pump.)

FAMILY: The Herons, Egrets, and Bitterns.

Length: 29.00.

Adults: Crown and nape slate-color, more or less tinged with light brown; a black stripe on either side of the neck; back irregularly mottled chestnut, blackish, and light brown; quills and coverts gray, tipped with chestnut; under parts light brown to pale buffy-white on throat, striped with darker.

Young: Similar to adults.

Geographical Distribution: Temperate North America, south to Guatemala.

Breeding Range: From the Middle States northward. In California in limited numbers.

Breeding Season: May and June.

Nest: A loose mat of marsh vegetation or grasses; on the ground in swampy places.

Eggs: 3 to 5; light olive. Size 1.90 × 1.50.

THIS much-scorned bird, for whom neither sportsman nor ornithologist has much regard, is common in nearly every marsh and slough throughout the United States at some season of the year. It is called "Fly up the creek," "Stake-driver," "Bog-bull," and other names too unpleasant to mention. Most of them bear some reference to its peculiar love song, called commonly "pumping." The sound is somewhat like the noise of a distant piledriver, and is at once recognized as soon as heard. The birds may be both heard and seen in the marshes at Alviso and in Los Angeles County, California. Only two things are required by the observer, — patience and leisure. Twilight and dawn are the hours at which they may be most frequently heard. They are solitary birds, each pair nesting alone. Their food consists largely of frogs and small fish, which they obtain by still fishing, standing motionless for almost any length of time in shallow water among rushes.

The newly hatched Bitterns are particularly homely nestlings, with their disproportionately long necks and bills. They are fed by regurgitation for at least forty-eight hours after hatching. The Bittern's attempts at love-making and brooding are rendered pitifully grotesque by the ungainly body of the bird and his queer contortions. Even in flight he is slovenly and loose-jointed, as if his legs were likely to be shaken off from the efforts his wings are making. In fishing he sits motionless for hours with head drawn back to the shoulders, the very picture of discomfort. In fact, under no circumstances does he seem joyous or even moderately happy.

191. LEAST BITTERN. — *Ardetta exilis.*

FAMILY : The Herons, Egrets, and Bitterns.

Length : 13.00.

Adult Male : Top of head, back, rump, and tail glossy black ; sides of head and neck light buff, deepening to chestnut on nape ; throat and fore-neck white, striped with pale straw-color. Under parts pale buff ; a dark patch on either side of the breast.

Adult Female : Similar, with brown in place of black on upper parts.

Young : Similar to adult female, but coloring more buffy on upper parts.

Geographical Distribution : Temperate North America, north to the British provinces, south to the West Indies and Brazil ; less common west of the Rocky Mountains. On the Pacific coast north to Oregon.

Breeding Range : Breeds locally wherever found.

Breeding Season : May to August.

Nest : A platform of marsh grass or rushes ; placed on a floating bog or
   slough.
Eggs : 3 to 5 ; light olive.   Size 1.23 × 0.93.

THE Least Bittern, or Little Green Heron, as it is
sometimes called, is a smaller and much shyer bird than
the American bittern.   It is found nesting in small
colonies in the edge of swamps ; its nest is a mere
crushed-down platform of rushes, and itself so exact an
imitation of its surroundings as to be practically invisible
to the naked eye.   On the approach of danger it becomes
rigid, with head and bill extended straight up, in mimicry of a reed, thus rendering its discovery much more
difficult.   If discovered and flushed from the water-side,
it straddles off through the weeds by grasping them on
either side with its feet, producing a comical effect of
walking on stilts.   It looks back often to see whether
it is being pursued.   If approached from the land side,
it takes wing with loud squawks of terror, and flies low
but swiftly through the open channels of the marsh to a
tree if there be one near.   It is frequently found roosting
in trees in the early morning or evening, in groups of
six or more, after the breeding season is over.   During
the breeding season its call is a soft dove-like note,
repeated over and over in a sort of undertone, as if it
were intended for the ear of its mate alone.

94. GREAT BLUE HERON, OR BLUE CRANE. —
Ardea herodias.

FAMILY: The Herons, Egrets, and Bitterns.

Length: 45.50.

Adults: Crown and throat white ; sides and back of head white ; feathers lengthened to form a crest ; upper parts bluish gray ; under parts broadly striped black and white ; legs and feet black.

Young: Top of head sooty slate ; throat white ; neck ashy, washed with light brown ; under parts streaked buff, slate, and white, with some black.

Geographical Distribution: North America from arctic regions southward to the northern parts of South America.

Breeding Range: Breeds locally in colonies wherever found.

Breeding Season: April and May.

Nest: A platform of coarse sticks ; placed high up in the tree ; always in colonies.

Eggs: 3 to 4 ; pale bluish gray. Size 2.50 × 1.50.

THE Great Blue Heron is a common species throughout California, and nests in almost every locality where it is found. At Muir Station, California, there is a large heronry in sycamore trees on the property of Mr. John Muir, and the noise of the young birds at feeding time can be heard half a mile away. The birds return to their heronry in February, and the young are hatched in April, though fresh eggs have been found as late as June 1. The young are fed by regurgitation, which in this case is a more than usually ludicrous performance. So violent is the shaking which each young heron undergoes in the process of receiving his food that he seems in imminent danger of being jerked out of the nest and hurled to the ground fifty feet below.

These herons fly miles to obtain fish for food, and one or the other parent is *en route* during all the daylight hours. After having been fed, the young heron draws back his head until it lies upon his shoulders, and sits there a sleepy, solemn-looking hunchback until next feeding-time.

196. AMERICAN EGRET. — *Ardea egretta.*

FAMILY : The Herons, Egrets, and Bitterns.

Length : 39.00.

Adults in Nuptial Plumage : Snowy white ; the interscapular plumes straight, filamentous, very long, reaching below the end of the tail ; head without crest ; bill yellow ; lores orange.

Young, and Adults after Breeding Season : Same, but lacking the interscapular plumage.

Geographical Distribution : Temperate and tropical America, on the Pacific coast from Oregon to Patagonia.

Breeding Range : As far north as Oregon on the Pacific coast.

Breeding Season : April, May, and June.

Nest : A loose platform of coarse twigs ; in colonies in trees near water.

Eggs : 2 to 4 ; light bluish. Size 2.35 × 1.65.

THE story of the American Egret is one more tragedy in the annals of ornithology, and is " a startling evidence of man's power in the animal world. At his word a species is almost immediately wiped out of existence." These beautiful birds are exterminated in Florida, and the devastation has begun on the Western coast ; already they are listed as " rare " where they once bred in abundance. The " nuptial plumage " only is salable, since it alone contains the pretty " aigrette " plumes ; and so, at a time when the true sportsman is bound by an unwritten law to protect the nesting birds, the plume-hunter shoots them mercilessly for commercial purposes.

197. SNOWY HERON. — *Ardea candidissima.*

FAMILY : The Herons, Egrets, and Bitterns.

Length : 23.50.

Adults : Plumage always pure white.

Nuptial Plumage : Pure white ; "aigrette" plumes hang like a white fringe from interscapular region to beyond the end of the tail ; similar plumes on lower neck and forming an occipital crest ; bill black, yellow at base ; legs black ; feet yellow.

Young : Like adults after breeding season ; that is, white, with no interscapular plumes.

Geographical Distribution : Temperate and tropical America ; on the Pacific coast from Oregon to Buenos Ayres.

Breeding Range : As far north as Oregon.

Breeding Season : April 15 to June 15.

Nest : A loosely built platform of sticks ; placed in trees or bushes near swamps.

Eggs : 2 to 5 ; light bluish. Size 1.80 × 1.20.

BEAUTY has proved a fatal dower to this exquisite bird, which has become nearly extinct through the ravages of the plume-hunters. "The delicate aigrettes which it donned as a nuptial dress were its death warrant. Woman demanded from the bird its wedding plumes, and man has supplied the demand." The saddest part of the whole sad story is the fact, not sentiment, that the killing must be done during the nesting season ; consequently the young, bereft of both parents, starve in the nest. For every dainty aigrette in hair or bonnet, a brood of baby herons has suffered excruciating, long-continued torture, and death. In California this heron is a summer visitant to the interior valleys, but is by no means common at any season of the year.

201b. ANTHONY GREEN HERON. — *Ardea virescens anthonyi.*

FAMILY : The Herons, Egrets, and Bitterns.

Length : 15.00–22.00.

Adults : Crown, crest, tail, and wings green ; sides of neck yellow-brown ; belly light grayish brown.

Geographical Distribution : Southwestern United States ; south in winter.

Breeding Range : Breeds locally wherever found, along the rivers of the interior.

Breeding Season : April.

Nest : On branches of trees and bushes ; a loose platform of sticks; lined with leaves.

Eggs : 3 to 5 ; light greenish buff or olive.

THIS is a subspecies of the Green Heron, and is found resident only in the southern part of California. Mr. Grinnell lists it as a common migrant, and says it breeds along the larger streams of the interior valleys. It is largely nocturnal in habit, and not unlike the American bittern in its guttural alarm note.

This species is found less often in the marshes, and more often along the banks of shallow streams and small lakes, where it sits for hours motionless in a dead tree or concealed stump, seeming to doze through the daylight hours. Early in the morning or late in the evening, however, the heronry awakes to great activity ; for the hungry young clamor harshly for food, and the adults hurry to and fro in pursuit of it. This noise continues far into the night and begins anew with daylight. Frogs, small snakes, fish, and lizards are the prey this Heron seeks, but it occasionally contents itself with insects and field mice.

202. BLACK–CROWNED NIGHT HERON. — *Nycticorax nycticorax nævius.*

FAMILY: The Herons, Egrets, and Bitterns.

Length: 24.50.

Adults: Crown, scapulars, and back iridescent black, with greenish reflections ; forehead, sides of head, throat, and under parts cream white ; sides ashy ; sides and back of neck light brownish gray ; wings, rump, and tail dusky brownish gray ; head ornamented with a few very long, narrow, white occipital feathers.

Young: Upper parts grayish brown, each feather marked with a wedge-shaped streak of white ; the quills with white at tips ; tail brownish gray ; under parts striped dark ash-brown and white.

Geographical Distribution: Nearly all America, except the arctic regions.

Breeding Range: From Manitoba to South America.

Breeding Season: April and May.

Nest: A platform of sticks, bulky ; placed in high trees ; in colonies of 2 to 5 in a single tree, and thousands in the close vicinity.

Eggs: 4 to 6 ; pale greenish. Size 2.15 × 1.55.

THE Black-crowned Night Heron is an abundant resident in all parts of California, breeding in suitable localities. Although these herons prefer a nest in a tree, they frequently build in tule swamps, following the habits of the bitterns. They are gregarious at all times, nesting in large colonies. Except when there are young in the nest, these birds are nocturnal feeders, beginning at dusk. Their food consists largely of frogs. During incubation, one bird remains on the nest constantly, and is fed by the other, who also shares in the sitting. As soon as the young are hatched the fact is made known by the constant foraging for food during the day and carrying it to the nest. It is, however, partly digested and fed to them by regurgitation until they are a week or ten days old. I have never seen anything but frogs, minnows, and small snakes brought to the nest, and these are carefully killed before being given to the young. The cry of the Black-crowned Night Heron is a harsh guttural squawk or croak, and the noise made when the rookery is full of young birds screaming for food is indescribable. Each brood discern their own parent flying toward the nest, and, although the nestlings have sat in unbroken silence until then, at sight of him the hungry cries begin.

206. SANDHILL CRANE. — *Grus mexicana.*

FAMILY: The Cranes.

Length: 44.00.

Adults: Bluish gray, varying to brownish gray; paler on throat and sides of head, darker on primaries; crown nearly bare, covered with reddish membrane and a scant growth of black hairs.

Young: Crown feathered; plumage rusty brown.

Geographical Distribution: United States from the Mississippi valley west to Pacific coast, south to Mexico, east along the Gulf coast to Florida.

Breeding Range: In mild localities throughout its habitat.

Breeding Season: February, March, and April.

Nest: A platform of weeds and grass, on the water line, in a marshy lagoon.

Eggs: 2; grayish yellow, spotted with cinnamon and gray. Size 3.98 × 2.44.

THE habits of the Sandhill Crane and those of the whooping crane are very similar. "During courtship and the early breeding season their actions and antics at times are ludicrous in the extreme, bowing and leaping high in the air, hopping, skipping, and circling about, with drooping wings and croaking whoop, — an almost indescribable dance and din, in which the females join, all working themselves up into a fever of excitement equalled only by an Indian war dance; and, like the same, it stops only when the last one is exhausted." [1]

The alarm call of this species is a long clear note like a bugle blast; it may be heard nearly a mile away. It is repeated over and over, as the birds fly in flocks, like the *honk* of wild geese.

210. CALIFORNIA CLAPPER RAIL. — *Rallus obsoletus.*

FAMILY: The Rails, Gallinules, and Coots.

Length: 17.50.

Adults: Upper parts greenish gray, indistinctly but broadly streaked with blackish brown; under parts red-brown, washed with gray on neck and sides.

Downy Young: Uniform black.

Geographical Distribution: Salt-water marshes of the Pacific coast from Lower California to Oregon.

Breeding Range: In sloughs and salt-water marshes, throughout California and Oregon.

Breeding Season: April, May, and June.

Nest: A loose mat of dry grass; placed among rushes in marsh.

Eggs: 8; buff, marked with cinnamon and lilac. Size 1.71 × 1.24.

THIS species is abundant on the salt-water marshes in the vicinity of San Francisco and Oakland, and particularly in the south end of the bay near Alviso. They are either tame or exceedingly stupid birds — I believe the latter, for they may be captured alive during the early spring and late fall, as they trust to protective coloring and do not try to escape until too late. During the breeding season they are somewhat more shy, but even then it is nearly impossible to flush them because they

[1] Goss.

skulk or dive rather than fly, and refuse to desert the nest. About the middle of April they commence to make a nest of marsh grass on a tussock, and from that time on are devoted to it. Eight or nine eggs are laid, and incubation lasts nineteen to twenty-three days. The young Rails run about within an hour after hatching, and look much like tiny black chickens with overgrown legs and bills. If discovered on a mud flat, they crouch motionless like so many small black lumps of dirt or stones, and though one may know where to search, it is hard to find them. The immature rails are as stupid as the adults, and will often allow themselves to be picked up without trying to get away. Their food consists largely of the larvæ of marsh insects which they pick up in the shallow water and along shore, and mature insects of all sorts, as well as small crustaceans. As is well known, certain varieties of marsh birds build several nests, using but one. The "dummy" sometimes serves as a shelter for the adult male; sometimes the making of it seems to have been a mere pastime; and, occasionally, as in the case of the clapper rail, it forms a convenient platform or nursery on which the young can scramble for a sun-bath when weary with their first swimming lessons. These unused nests are commonly placed close to the one occupied by the brood and closely resemble it. My own observations in this matter, made at Alviso, tally with those of Mr. Adams at San Francisco Bay and Mr. Shields at Los Angeles.

212. VIRGINIA RAIL. — *Rallus virginianus.*

FAMILY: The Rails, Gallinules, and Coots.

Length: 9.30.

Adults: Upper parts brownish olive, striped with sooty ; breast and wing-coverts light chestnut ; wings and tail dark olive-brown ; cheeks gray ; throat white ; under parts light chestnut ; sides barred with white.

Downy Young : Uniform black.

Geographical Distribution : North America, from the British provinces south to Guatemala.

Breeding Range : Wherever resident.

Breeding Season : April, May, and June.

Nest : A mat of grasses ; placed on a hummock in a marsh.

Eggs : 7 to 12 ; buffy, marked with chestnut. Size 1.24 × 0.94.

THE Virginia Rail, although more common east of the Rockies, is by no means rare throughout California. He is an odd-looking bird with voice and manners in keeping with his appearance. In the early morning and at twilight his call is a curious combination of grunt and squeal. The love song, however, is quite different ; it is described as " a guttural *cut, cutta-cutta-cutta* oft repeated for hours in succession." You have only to visit a marsh lake in the afternoon or early in the morning and listen,

212. VIRGINIA RAIL.

" Picking his way cautiously between the tules."

to discover whether or not he is nesting there. But the marsh birds are shy and very wary, and the long marsh grass guards them well. It is far easier to hear them than to see them. If your patience endures long enough, you may catch a glimpse of a Rail picking his way cautiously between the tules, with a curious bobbing motion. If you are so fortunate as to find a mother bird on her eggs, she will become rigid with terror, her red eye dilating and her long neck stretched up not unlike a water snake. In this position you may easily mistake her for a stick or a dry rush. If flushed, her small powers of flight suffice to carry her only a short distance, when she will disappear in the rushes and no patient waiting will give you another glimpse of her. My own experience goes to prove that the nest is always deserted by her after the first forced flight from it.

Mr. Brewster says: " The female, when anxious about her eggs or young, calls *ki-ki-ki-ki* in low tones, and *kiu* much like a flicker. The young of both sexes in autumn give, when startled, a short explosive *kep* or *kik*, closely similar to that of the Carolina rail."

214. SORA, OR CAROLINA RAIL. — *Porzana carolina.*

FAMILY : The Rails, Gallinules, and Coots.

Length : 8.60.

Adults : Feathers about base of bill black ; a broad black line through crown and extending down the back of the neck ; throat, breast, and cheeks gray ; upper parts grayish brown, streaked with black and white ; belly white ; flanks barred with blackish slate-color.

Young : Similar, but no black at base of bill ; upper parts darker.

Downy Young : Uniform black ; a tuft of orange-colored, hair-like feathers on throat.

Geographical Distribution: North America ; south in winter to northern parts of South America.
Breeding Range: Northern United States, northward, including California and Oregon.
Breeding Season: May and June.
Nest: Of grass ; on the ground, in a marshy place.
Eggs: 7 to 14 ; cream-color, marked with cinnamon and lilac. Size 1.26 × 0.90.

THE Sora Rail breeds commonly in California in swamps about Los Angeles and other suitable localities. Unlike the clapper rail, it prefers fresh-water sloughs, where it hides among the tall rushes. The baby Rails are fluffy little black chicks with absurdly large feet, and necks too long for their fat little bodies. Almost as soon as hatched they run about among the grass of the drier parts, sometimes being taken away from the water to an adjacent meadow, where they soon learn to snap up bugs and small grasshoppers. Like all the rail family, the Soras are most musical at dawn and dusk, when their queer weird notes make the marshland seem an uncanny spot. In the South this species is sold as a game bird under the name of ortolan, and is much liked by epicures, though its thin little body has, not without reason, given rise to the saying "As thin as a rail." It is abundant on migrations, flying at night and resting wherever it happens to be during the day, even in the noisy streets of Chicago. In these circumstances it seems stupid and confused. I have captured it without difficulty while it was resting, as it squats on the ground, making absolutely no effort to escape.

Mr. Frank Chapman writes of this species : "The Sora's summer home is in fresh-water marshes, where, if it were not for their notes, the reeds and grasses would long keep the secret of their presence. . . . They will greet you late in the afternoon with a clear whistled *keewee* which soon comes from dozens of invisible birds about you, and long after night has fallen it continues like a spring-time chorus of piping hylas. Now and again it is interrupted by a high-voiced rolling *whinny* which, like a call of alarm, is taken up and repeated by different birds all over the marsh. They seem so absorbed in their musical devotions even when calling continuously, it requires endless patience and keen eyes to see the dull-colored, motionless forms in places where one would not suppose there was sufficient growth to conceal them."

216. BLACK RAIL. — *Porzana jamaicensis.*

FAMILY : The Rails, Gallinules, and Coots.

Length : 5.00–6.00.
Adults : Crown blackish slate ; upper parts dark red-brown, speckled with white ; under parts, neck, and sides of head slate-color; belly sooty brown.
Downy Young : Uniform black.
Geographical Distribution : From northern boundary of the United States south to Chili.
Breeding Range : For the Pacific slope, Oregon and California ; east of the Rockies, through the United States.
Breeding Season : June.
Nest : Of grasses ; on ground ; in wet meadows or marshes.
Eggs : 7 to 10 ; white, thinly spotted with cinnamon. Size 1.05 × 0.80.

MOST of us are quite willing to agree with the man who said that this bird is "about as difficult to observe as a field mouse." It is its shyness and small size that render it so little known to local ornithologists, who content themselves with pronouncing it rare. Its nest is a cup-shaped depression lined with fine grasses, usually in a wet meadow; it may be mistaken for that of a meadow lark, but is nearly an inch less in diameter and *never arched over*. The Black Rail nests in the marshes at Alviso, California, and, I have no doubt, elsewhere throughout the State. The young are tiny black balls of down, apparently less than one inch in diameter; they leave the nest the moment the down is dry, and run about with the agility of sandpipers. Although so tiny, they have the instinct of self-preservation to a marked degree; whenever danger threatens they stiffen into unwinking puff-balls, with only their beady black eyes to betray life.

219. FLORIDA GALLINULE, OR RED–BILLED MUD–HEN. — *Gallinula galeata*.

FAMILY : The Rails, Gallinules, and Coots.

Length : 13.25.

Adults : Dark slate-color, sometimes tinged with brown on back and whitish on belly ; edge of wing and a patch on flank white ; bill and frontal shield red, tipped with greenish ; legs and feet greenish.

Downy Young : Uniform black, a few white hairs among the down on throat and cheeks.

Geographical Distribution : Tropical and temperate North America, north to British provinces.

Breeding Range : For the Pacific slope, from Oregon southward.

Breeding Season : April, May, and June.

Nest : A mat of rushes bent over and more or less woven together, over water.

Eggs : 8 to 10 ; cream-buff, finely marked with reddish brown and chocolate. Size 1.87 × 1.25.

IN form so like a sleek bantam hen, in habits so like a coot, the Florida Gallinule is a most interesting study.

It has a large vocabulary of calls ranging from harsh squawks to pathetic complaining cries not unlike the skirl of a bagpipe. It is a common resident on the fresh-water marshes of California, where it can be heard much oftener than seen; for it is exceedingly shy, and its dusky plumage renders it inconspicuous among the rushes. In swimming it has a rather awkward way of sitting up very straight and bobbing its head with every stroke of its feet. Feeding on the mud-flats, it dips daintily, as it picks its way through the tangled reeds after the manner of the king rail. Its nest is of dried tule or marsh grass, lined with softer grass of the meadow, the latter being brought there from a distance. All about the rim of the structure the rushes are broken to form a guard for the eggs, for although usually about three inches deep the nests are sometimes only a shallow platform. The young run about like tiny black chicks, and pick up a living from the water, almost as soon as they are hatched. It would be impossible to distinguish them from young clapper rails except for the sprinkling of white hairs among the black down. They are quite unlike little chickens in one thing: at the warning call of the parent they disappear noiselessly, as if by magic, or are meta-morphosed into dark stones; feathered barnyard babies, on the other hand, run to the mother with cries of fear.

221. AMERICAN COOT. — *Fulica americana.*

(Common names: Mud-hen; Blue Peter.)

FAMILY: The Rails, Gallinules, and Coots.

Length: 15.25.

Adults: Dark bluish slate, nearly black on head and neck; under parts paler; edge of wing white; bill white; frontal plate, and spots on bill near end, brown; legs and feet greenish; toes with scalloped flaps.

Downy Young: Upper parts rusty black; under parts white; head and neck with orange-colored hair-like feathers, and upper parts with pale yellow hair-like feathers among the down; bill red, tipped with black.

Geographical Distribution: North America.

Breeding Range: Breeds locally through the United States, British Columbia, and Canada.

Breeding Season: April, May, and June.

Nest: Of grass and reeds; among the flags or tall marsh grass.

Eggs: 8 to 16; cream-colored, speckled with dark chocolate. Size 1.89 × 1.42.

ALTHOUGH so closely resembling the Florida gallinule in appearance, the Coots may be easily distinguished from them by their white bills. They are much more social and are better swimmers than the gallinules, gathering in companies morning and evening in the shallow water at the edge of a marsh, to feed upon the larvæ of water insects and small crustaceans, which they obtain by diving. They like best, however, to pick up their food from the slime at the border of a mud flat or low marshy place, and here they take their newly hatched bantlings. The young are covered with down of a rusty black color above and white beneath, with pale yellow hair-like feathers sprinkled through it. Their bills, unlike those of the parents, are red. They sometimes stray near a farmyard and may be picked up easily, as they seem stupefied with fear.

The adult Coots are very noisy birds, constantly calling, screaming, or complaining. Just after nightfall and before dawn, most California marshes are vocal with their varied cries. But, like the gallinules, they are more easily heard than seen, for they are exceedingly shy. If surprised and forced to flight, they rise with much splattering, fly rapidly a short distance, and fall back into the marsh. They are worthless as game birds, as their flesh is tough and rank in taste; for this reason the real sportsman shuns them.

Part II
LAND BIRDS

LAND BIRDS

I. — UPLAND GAME BIRDS

230. WILSON SNIPE. — *Gallinago delicata.*

(Common names: Jack Snipe; English Snipe.)

FAMILY: The Snipes and Sandpipers.

Length: 10.85.

Adults: Crown buff; upper parts black, bordered and mottled with buff; neck and breast mottled and streaked buffy and blackish brown; sides barred black and white; belly white.

Downy Young: Upper parts dusky, more or less mottled with light brown; under parts whitish.

Geographical Distribution: North America; south in winter to Brazil.

Breeding Range: From latitude 45° to the arctic circle. In California, the valleys of the northern Sierra Nevada.

Breeding Season: In California, June 15 to July 15.

Nest: A slight depression on open, marshy ground; sometimes lined with grass, usually unlined.

Eggs: 3 or 4; olive, streaked with black and chocolate. Size 1.55 × 1.07.

THE species known as Jack Snipe, or English Snipe, is a prime favorite with sportsmen and epicures. Breeding so far north, they are commonly hunted as migrants, and so are more or less protected during their nesting season. They usually migrate in small companies. During the breeding season solitary birds are frequently seen, which spring from the marsh grass with a harsh cry and zigzag swiftly out of sight in a way most tantalizing to the sportsman. Only an expert can hope to bag them. The Jack Snipe frequents low wet places, obtaining food after the manner of a woodcock, by probing with its long slender bill, which, although not prehensile to the extent of a woodcock's, is yet very sensitive at the tip, and readily detects the choice morsels of food down in the damp earth.

Their capricious selection of feeding ground seems to be governed by some occult knowledge as to the conditions of the soil, for they are here to-day, gone to-morrow, and often the only places which seem most likely to be their haunt will not be visited by them at all.

Mr. Bailey writes of the Jack Snipe: " He is a common bird wherever there are marshes to his taste. . . . On warm summer evenings or cloudy days before a storm, he mounts high in the air and with rapidly vibrating wings produces a prolonged whirr that increases to a diminutive roar, and repeats it every two or three minutes for sometimes half an hour. At other times he flies low over the grass uttering a guttural *chuck-chuck-chuck-chuck-chuck,* and then drops out of sight. His common all-round-the-year note is a nasal *squawk.*"

281. MOUNTAIN PLOVER. — *Ægialitis montana.*

FAMILY : The Plovers.

Length : 8.00–9.00.

Adults in Summer : Upper parts grayish brown ; under parts buffy ; a white band across forehead and over the eye ; front of crown and lores black.

Adults in Winter : Without distinct black or white on head.

Young : Similar to winter adults, but general tone light yellowish brown or buffy.

Geographical Distribution : United States bordering the Pacific ; in winter as far south as Santa Ana.

Breeding Range : Interior of the United States from Texas to Montana.

Breeding Season : June and July.

Nest : Anywhere on the open prairie ; a depression in the ground, thinly lined with grass.

Eggs : 3 ; light buffy olive, thickly speckled with lavender, brown, and black. Size 1.45 × 1.11.

THROUGHOUT the interior plains of California west of the Sierra Nevada the Mountain Plover is a common winter resident. It can be easily recognized by its large size, and by the absence of rings on throat and breast. Mountain Plover is one of the many misnomers, for although called by this name, the bird loves the prairies and treeless plains, and is never found at great altitudes. Unlike most plovers, it seems to shun the water; even in California it is not found along the beaches where its relatives feed, but hunts grasshoppers and terrestrial insects in the drier inland meadows. Its nest consists of a few grasses scratched together in a spot exposed to wind and weather; and here the female broods for nineteen days. As soon as the down is dry on the chicks, they scramble off at their mother's heels, and in twenty-four hours are catching bugs for themselves.

292. MOUNTAIN PARTRIDGE. — *Oreortyx pictus.*

FAMILY : The Grouse, Partridges, Quails, etc.

Length: 10.00–11.12.

Adult Male: Crest black ; back and upper parts olive-brown, striped on sides of back with light brown ; top of head and entire breast slate-color ; throat and sides dark red-brown ; sides barred with black and white.

Adult Female : Crest shorter, otherwise like male.

Young : Upper parts grayish brown, speckled with white ; breast gray, with wedge-shaped white spots ; a whitish line over the ear ; belly white; sides washed with chestnut.

Geographical Distribution : Humid transition zone of Pacific coast region, from about latitude 35° to Southern Washington.

Breeding Range : Nearly coincident with its habitat.

Breeding Season : April and May.

Nest : A slight depression in the ground, lined sparingly with dry leaves ; placed beside or under a fallen tree or a bush.

Eggs : 8 to 13 ; plain light buff. Size 1.36 × 1.02.

THE Mountain Partridge of the coast belt is so nearly like the plumed partridge of the Sierra Nevada in habits and coloring as scarcely to need a separate description. Both are designated as "mountain quail" in the common parlance, and it is about as difficult to obtain a satisfactory view of one as of the other. The plumed partridge is said to measure a trifle less than this species, but in the field the only distinguishing marks are the grayer tone of the back and the bluish nape, all of which makes it difficult to differentiate the species. The Range is possibly the best guide for an amateur in identifying the species.

(For habits see " Plumed Quail.")

292 a. PLUMED PARTRIDGE. — *Oreortyx pictus plumiferus.*

FAMILY : The Grouse, Partridges, Quails, etc.

Length : 10.50–11.50.

Adult Male : Crest black ; forehead whitish ; upper parts grayish olive, striped on sides of back with light brown ; top of head, hind-neck, and breast bluish slate-color ; throat and sides dark red-brown ; sides barred with black and white.

Adult Female : Crest shorter ; otherwise plumage the same.

Young : Upper parts grayish brown, speckled with white ; breast gray with triangular white spots ; a whitish line over the ear ; belly white ; sides washed with chestnut.

Downy Young : Head and neck buffy ; broad chestnut stripe down the middle of back and rump, bordered along each side by dusky ; breast and belly dull whitish.

Geographical Distribution : Arid transition zone of Pacific coast district, from Lower California northward through Oregon.

Breeding Range : Along both sides of the Sierra Nevada and the southern ranges.

Breeding Season : April and May.

Nest : On the ground ; on bed of dead leaves ; concealed under a bush, or weeds, or log.

Eggs : Usually 8 to 14 ; uniform buff. Size 1.36 × 1.02.

Food : Insects, berries, and bugs.

ONE bright morning in early June, on the way from Fyffe to Slippery Ford on the Lake Tahoe stage route, we flushed a Plumed Partridge from the roadside, and my companion remarked that he had flushed a partridge from that place two days before. A search for a nest began among the manzanita bushes and " mountain misery," which latter was thick, nearly ten inches high. After a short hunt we discovered the treasure hidden well at the base of a tall cedar and guarded by the pretty white blossoms and green leaves of Chamæbatia.

It was made of leaves and stems of this plant and lined
with feathers, and in it lay ten eggs of the Plumed
Partridge. They were nearly ready to hatch, — how
ready I did not guess, — and with a hope that no one
would molest them in the meantime, we departed, resolving to come back the next day. But I reckoned
without my host, for having eaten luncheon and rested,
I stole back alone for a last peep at them, and two had
pipped the shells while a third was cuddled down in
the split halves of his erstwhile covering. The distress
of the mother was pitiful, and I had not the heart to
torture the beautiful creature needlessly ; so going off a
little way, I lay down flat along the " misery," regardless
of the discomfort, and awaited developments. Before I
could focus my glasses she was on the nest, her anxious
little eyes still regarding me suspiciously. In less time
than it takes to tell it, the two were out and the mother
cuddled them in her fluffed-out feathers. This was too
interesting to be left. Even at the risk of being too late
to reach my destination, I must see the outcome. Two
hours later every egg had hatched and a row of tiny
heads poked out from beneath the mother's breast. I
started toward her and she flew almost into my face, so
closely did she pass me. Then by many wiles she tried in
vain to coax me to go another way. I was curious and
therefore merciless. Moreover, I had come all the way
from the East for just such hours as this. But once more
a surprise awaited me. There was the nest, there were
the broken shells ; but where were the young partridges ?
Only one of all that ten could I find. For so closely did

they blend in coloring with the shadows on the pine needles under the leaves of the " misery " that although I knew they were there, and dared not step for fear of crushing them, I was not sharp enough to discover them. No doubt a thorough search would have been successful, but this a dread of injuring them forbade me to make.

So picking up the one which had crouched motionless beside a leaf and which was really not much larger than my thumb, I contented myself with trying to solve the mystery of how so much bird ever grew in that small shell, half of which would scarcely cover his head. Once fairly in my hand, he cuddled down perfectly contented to let me fit the empty shell to his fat little body, as if he knew he was out of that for good. He was a funny little ball of fluffy down, with a dark stripe down his back and a lesser one on each side of that. Meanwhile the adult bird had disappeared, and there was no choice but to put the youngster back in the nest and go on my way. But I had learned two things, — that affairs move rapidly in the partridge household, and that human eyes are seldom a match for a bird's instinct.

Most interesting of the many characteristics of the Plumed Partridge is the habit of migration into the valleys by the first of September each year, and back to the elevations in the early spring. Scarcity of food does not drive them to more fertile foraging grounds, for in the spring they return while yet there is snow. Unlike their relatives, these birds do not band together in large flocks, and seldom more than two broods are to be found in the same cover. Mr. Edwyn Sandys says : " The call of the male is suggestive of the crowing of a young bantam, while the rallying cry of scattered birds is not unlike the yelping of young wild turkeys."

294. CALIFORNIA PARTRIDGE. — *Lophortyx californicus.*

FAMILY : The Grouse, Partridges, Quails, etc.

Length : 9.50.

Adult Male : Crest black ; nape dusky brown, bordered by black and white lines ; upper parts dusky brown, striped with chestnut along the sides of the back ; throat black, bordered by white ; breast slate-color ; belly, except chestnut patch, scaled ; sides dusky brown, streaked with white.

Adult Female : Head plain, with no black and white ; plumage uniform dusky brown ; belly scaled ; no chestnut on under parts ; sides streaked with white.

Young : Upper parts gray-brown ; feathers of back and wing-coverts edged with dark gray and white ; under parts white and gray.

Geographical Distribution : Pacific coast region from Monterey to Oregon.

Breeding Range : Nearly coincident with the *Geographical Distribution.*

Breeding Season : April and May.

Nest : A hollow near a rock or at foot of a tree trunk ; scantily lined with grass ; sometimes under hedge, bush, or brush-heap.

Eggs : 8 to 10 ; buffy, thickly spotted with shades of brown. Size 1.33 × 0.97.

THE crest of the California Partridge is a little longer than that of the valley partridge, and tips forward in the same way.

This handsome little partridge is unfortunately a favorite game bird, and, as such, has become not only somewhat scarce but exceedingly shy. It haunts the cañons and slopes covered with underbrush, as well as the sagebrush and stubble, and has learned to run to cover rather than to flush when pursued. In this way it offers a difficult mark for the true sportsman, and is less in danger from him than from the pitiless trapper.

It differs from the valley partridge in being darker-colored and of a more northern range, but is often mistaken for it, as the habits and call are exactly alike. It is quite unlike the mountain partridge, — an inch smaller, and with more of a blue tinge to the slate-color of the plumage. Moreover the crest is shorter and tips forward like a pompon, while the mountain partridge usually carries his long crest floating backward.

Unlike the nest of the mountain partridge, too, the nest of *californicus* is rarely concealed, the eggs being laid on a mat of leaves or grass on the open ground

294. CALIFORNIA PARTRIDGE.
"*It haunts the cañons and slopes.*"

beside a stump or under a bush, and they are sometimes found in the nest of the Oregon towhee. Doubtless the protective coloring helps to prevent their discovery during the three weeks required for incubation. In this task, unlike our Eastern "Bob White," the male does not assist, but frequently stands guard at a short distance and warns of danger by a sharp short call. The chicks are out of the nest almost as soon as out of the shell, and are as skilful as their parents at running to cover. When a day or two old they learn to find their own food, picking up the bugs and even jumping for them when they themselves are not much larger than a good-sized beetle. Although so capable and independent, they are constantly attended by both parents until the down has merged into fully developed feathers. Then the gregarious habits of the grouse blood assert themselves, and by September 1 all the broods of that district band together to the number of several hundred individuals, and remain so throughout the fall and winter. This is the harvest time of the hunters and the season of unrest for the birds. In the early autumn mornings in the stubble of the field and the underbrush of the cañons, you may hear their plaintive whistle, " who-are-you," questioning whether friend or foe is astir.

294 a. VALLEY PARTRIDGE. — *Lophortyx californicus vallicola.*

FAMILY : The Grouse, Partridges, Quails, etc.

Length : 9.50.

Adults : Similar to the California partridge ; upper parts grayish ; sides olive ; crest short and tipped forward.

Young : Breast gray, marked with wedge-shaped black spots; belly faintly barred dark and light gray; upper parts striped brown and white.

Downy Young : Upper parts white, washed with rusty and mottled with dark brown ; under parts plain dull whitish.

Geographical Distribution : Pacific coast region from Southern California to Oregon ; through upper and lower Sonoran zones.

Breeding Range : The interior valleys between the humid coast belt and the Sierra Nevada.

Breeding Season : April and May.

Nest : A slight depression in ground, under hedge, bush, or brush-heap.

Eggs : Generally 10 to 12 ; buffy, thickly spotted with shades of brown. Size 1.23 × 0.94.

So closely allied are the California partridge and the Valley Partridge that only by direct comparison of the two species may the lighter coloring of the latter be distinguished. In habits they are alike, but in range they differ, the former being a coast bird and found from Monterey northward, while the latter occurs in the interior and southern valleys. In spite of being dubbed the Valley Partridge, it is found on the mountains of Lower California sometimes at an elevation of eight thousand feet.

It breeds throughout suitable localities in Southern California, and is hunted wherever resident, though not so extensively as formerly, when it was the favorite game bird of that region.

The eggs are laid on a mat of leaves or grass, or on the bare ground either in underbrush or in the farmer's door-yard. Incubation requires three weeks, and usually the hen alone broods the eggs. After the young are hatched they are kept in the underbrush or heavy stubble and can rarely be discovered, so expert at hiding are they. Like the California partridge they run to cover rather than fly, and they are so swift-footed that it is almost impossible to flush them. When the young are feeding, the adult males constantly call them, either to keep the covey together or to give warning of danger, and they answer each call with a faint piping note. This is not unlike the scatter call of the Eastern Bob White, but consists of two syllables in one tone, or one longer note. It is not unusual to come upon a covey of these when driving through the foothills and valleys of Southern California, but the sensation is simply of something scampering into the brush rather than a definite sight of any bird, unless the cock comes out into view for a moment to sound his warning and draw your attention from the brood to his handsome self.

295. GAMBEL PARTRIDGE. — *Lophortyx gambelii.*

FAMILY : The Grouse, Partridges, Quails, etc.

Length : 9.00–10.00.

Adult Male : Crest black ; forehead and throat black, edged with white ; crown chestnut ; upper parts slate-color ; breast gray ; belly buff, with black patches ; sides bright chestnut, streaked with white lines.

Adult Female : Similar to male, but plainer; belly without black patches, and sides without white stripes.

Young : Upper parts brownish gray, finely mottled black and white ; belly uniform white ; breast gray, striped with white.

Geographical Distribution : Lower Sonoran zone from Western Texas to Southeastern California, and from Southern Utah to Mexico.

Breeding Range : The desert region of California southeast of the Sierra Nevada.

Breeding Season : April 15 to July 1.

Nest : A slight depression in the ground, under a bunch of tall grass ; usually without lining.

Eggs : 10 to 12 ; buffy, marked with brown and blotched with light purple.   Size 1.27 × 0.98.

EARLY in the morning during the months of March and April, the love note of the Gambel Partridge may be heard from the underbrush of the valleys and foothills of Southeastern California.   So handsome, so confident in his wooing is he that he sounds it over and over, alike in the warm spring sunshine and the soft spring rain. And it is always answered by a demure little hen that comes stealing noiselessly through the mesquite to peep coyly at her lordly wooer.   She admires him.   Who would not, as he swells and struts before her, lowering his pretty crest, assuming such loverlike airs ?   And the protection he seems to offer is not all a mockery, for, although he scorns to take part in the feminine task of brooding those buffy eggs, he will stand on guard ready to warn, and will expose his trim body to the hunter for the sake of his mate and young. The brooding time is twenty-eight days, but the little brown mother has endless patience and cannot be induced to desert. If meddled with, she will in some way remove the eggs to another hollow in the ground, and brood as before. This has been done in four instances that I have recorded, and however much it may be disputed, is true. Most of the nests are hard to find, being usually well concealed in a hollow under a log, or mesquite clump, or cacti. The nestlings resemble those of the Bob White in appearance as well as habit, only they are grayer and with less white down on under parts. They run about the moment the cracking of the shell sets them free, and right spry little balls of down they are, hiding instantly at their father's warning " quit," cuddling under their mother each night, and snapping up bugs for their own breakfasts each day. Fortunately for them, according to Mr. Sandys, although so " beautiful, hardy, and prolific," they have some habits which lead a sportsman a hard, wild chase if he gets them at all. They run rather than fly, keeping under the thickest, thorniest cover ; they fly down into cañons only to climb up the other side among the stiffest underbrush ; they lie low when the foe is searching close beside them, and they " scoot " when least expected. " Only a Christian of the sternest stripe is fit to be trusted on the trail of this nimble-footed little rascal."

297 a. SOOTY GROUSE. — *Dendragapus obscurus fuliginosus.*

FAMILY: The Grouse, Partridges, Quails, etc.

Length: Adult male 20.00–23.00; adult female 16.00–19.00.

Adult Male: Upper parts blackish slate-color, finely mottled with gray and brown; tail black, with or without gray border on end; under parts very dark slate-color.

Adult Female: Similar to male, but much smaller; upper parts washed with dark rusty, and indistinctly barred with sooty brown.

Young: Upper parts rusty brown, mottled with sooty and buff; under parts gray, more or less spotted with black.

Downy Young: Above, brown, white, and black mixed, forming irregular stripes on the back and head; under parts grayish white or light buffy gray.

Geographical Distribution: The Coast Range from Alaska through California in the timbered Transition and Boreal zone.

Breeding Range: Nearly coincident with *Geographical Distribution.*

Breeding Season: May and June.

Nest: A hollow under the side of a log or bush, scantily lined with grass.

Eggs: 7 to 10; cream, thickly spotted with shades of brown. Size 1.78 × 1.33.

THE Sooty Grouse is one of the largest and handsomest of its family. It haunts the coniferous forests of the Sierra Nevada, and rears its brood in security in timber too dense for the hunter. Well it knows that in silence and statuesque rigidity lies its safety, and when pursued it takes to a tree, where its sooty plumage makes it seem like a bump on a branch, rather than a bird. Let it guess, however, that its presence is discovered and like a flash it is gone, cackling like a frightened hen and "whirring" like a small cyclone, down into the cover of the underbrush.

" The love-making of the male is marked by all the

pomp and vanity of the strutting gobbler ; indeed, in his actions he might pass for a turkey bantam, but he has one marked peculiarity. It is his habit to perch in some thick-growing tree, and by filling the sacs upon his neck with air and abruptly expelling it to produce a low booming whistle, which has an extraordinary carrying and ventriloquial power. This booming, or 'booing' as some Westerners term it, seldom fails to puzzle sorely a tenderfoot, the baffling feature of it being that it does not appear to gain volume or distinctness when the bird is closely approached." [1]

In May or June, according to location, the wooing begins, and soon the mother is brooding on her eight buffy eggs in the shade of a fern tangle, near a log, or in a clump of manzanita. No part does the father take in the three weeks of patient incubation, but the mother can seldom be surprised away from the nest. It would be far easier to discover the eggs were she not covering them, for so protective is her coloring that you may be looking directly at her and never suspect it, although at that very moment you are searching for a nest. Her food is all about her, — buds, berries, and insects. If she leaves the eggs, it is only to stretch her tired little legs and pick up a few dainties close by. But once the little mottled puff-balls are out of the shell and dry, away she goes, proud as a peacock, with them at her heels. And now the father is introduced to family cares, and he scratches for bugs, calling the young with imperative little chucks to come. He is the drill-master of the

[1] Upland Game Birds.

little flock, teaching them with infinite patience all that they need to know of wood lore. He stands on guard at every suspicious noise, and whistles his warning when danger threatens. When their wing-feathers have developed and they can flutter up to a low branch in the bush, they roost there instead of cuddling under the mother's broad wings at night. But they remain with the parents and evidently under discipline throughout the first six or eight months of their existence. In the wintry weather, when their mountain homes are covered deep with snow, they often sleep huddled together deep in a drift, waking to feed upon the buds of the coniferous trees, but seldom seeking a lower level. They are the hardy mountaineers, the children of the forest ranges.

300 c. OREGON RUFFED GROUSE. — *Bonasa umbellus sabini.*

FAMILY : The Grouse, Partridges, Quails, etc.

Length : 15.00–19.00.

Adult Male : Rough iridescent black, upper parts mottled dark brown and black, tail rusty dark brown ; under parts heavily barred with black and brown.

Adult Female : Similar to male, and with neck tufts less developed.

Young : Similar to adult female, but browner, and neck tufts entirely wanting.

Downy Young : Upper parts chestnut-brown ; deeper on under wings and rump ; under parts buff ; a conspicuous black line from corner of eye through ear tufts.

Geographical Distribution : Humid transition and boreal zones and the coast ranges from Humboldt County, California, to the northern limits of Washington.

California Breeding Range : The humid coast boreal from Cape Mendocino northward.

Nest : On ground in the woods, usually under fallen trees.
Eggs : 6 to 12 ; buffy, sometimes slightly stained or speckled with brown.
Size 1.56 × 1.16.

THIS is a fairly common resident in the coast district of Northern California. Its habits of "drumming," etc. are like those of the Eastern grouse. The cocks leave their mates as soon as sitting begins, and do not usually return until fall, when the broods get together for the winter. The young are to be found with the mother in the vicinity of the nesting place for ten days or two weeks, and then are taken to a thicket-bordered stream. Their food consists of grasshoppers, insects, young leaves of plants, berries, and a few varieties of seed, such as the wild sunflower.

309. SAGE GROUSE. — *Centrocercus urophasianus.*

FAMILY : The Grouse, Partridges, Quails, etc.

Length : Male 26.00–30.00 ; female 21.00–23.00.
Adult Male : Upper parts mottled and barred gray, buff, and black ; cheeks, chin, and throat spotted black and white ; a white crescent on each side of throat reaching to eye ; fore-neck black, merging to dull gray on the chest ; the feathers with very stiff black shafts ; belly uniform black ; chest white after breeding season. In breeding season, tufts of wiry black feathers mixed with white down on the shoulders ; air sacs on sides of throat yellow.
Adult Female : Chin and throat white ; fore-neck speckled gray in ruffs ; air sacs or shoulder plumes.
Young : Similar to female, but browner ; markings of lower parts indistinct.
Downy Young : Upper parts brownish gray mottled with blackish.
Geographical Distribution : Sagebrush plains of the Rocky Mountain plateau, southwest to California, north to British Columbia.
Breeding Range : In California the arid Great Basin region, east of the Sierra Nevada.
Breeding Season : April and May.

Nest: A slight depression in the ground ; usually unlined, and under a sagebush.

Eggs: 8 to 12; olive-yellow, spotted with dark brown.   Size 2.16 × 1.50.

As its name implies, the Sage Grouse loves the barren alkali plains, "sun-parched in summer and swept by icy blasts and wolf-voiced blizzards during the winter," where no green thing can grow save the sagebrush and the cacti. Here, of necessity, his chief diet is sage leaves, insects, and the pulp of the cactus fruit ; his drink the strong alkali water of the desert.   The storms of winter drive him through the timber belt to the stunted vegetation under the snow, and he lives for weeks at a time in the warm shelter of a deep drift, eating the young green shoots that he scratches from their wintry cover, five or six feet below the level.   With the spring comes a revival of life to the big Grouse.   A restless hunting for something takes possession of him, and he wanders through the brush, fighting every male grouse that he meets.   In March he encounters his fate in the form of a tiny gray hen, before whom he struts and salaams, sliding along on his breast until he wears a bare place among his fine feathers.   What greater proof of his infatuation could he give than this ?   "Then the big air sacs are filled to their fullest capacity, the spiny feathers about them bristle out like thorns, the long tail is spread and the wings trailed.   One familiar with the noise of other grouse naturally would expect from this great fellow a thunderous booming, but the fact is the sounds produced amount to nothing more than a broken, indistinct croaking."   It is all done with an air of desperate earnestness, comical to a disinterested observer, but very pleasing to madam, who, feigning indifference, is not too easily won. Finally, when his much salaaming has scoured his breast nearly bare, you may, if you are sharp enough, discover a nest with greenish-buff eggs in it, hidden snugly under a sagebush. When the mother is brooding, — and during the twenty-two days required for incubation she is rarely away from the nest, — you will find the search difficult if not futile. So protective is her coloring, and so perfectly does she blend with the alkali dust and the shadows of the sage, that it is impossible to distinguish her so long as she remains motionless. She will sit in unwinking stillness until you are about to step on her, and then, with a blinding " whirr " she scoots through the brush, cackling angrily, to return before you are fifty yards away.

When sitting begins, the erstwhile ardent wooer deserts his mate, and the entire care of the little ones falls upon her. Like all grouse nestlings, they run about as soon as the down is dry, which is about fifteen minutes after the shell breaks. They pick up food at her scratching all day, and at night they nestle on the ground under her wings, only a row of little heads being visible. As soon as their own feathers are developed, they sleep every night in a circle about her, each one with head pointed to the outside as before, and always on the ground; for the Sage-Grouse never trees. It is not difficult to come upon a brood sleeping this way on a moonlight night; but the only satisfaction will be to hear the sharp alarm of the mother, a whirr as she runs by you, and a knowledge that though the young are hiding on the dust at

your feet, you could not find them were your eyes ten-
fold sharper. I have groped carefully on hands and
knees among them, and actually touched one before I saw
it at all. For the desert hides its secrets well, and the
little grouse have learned to trust to it for safety.

These broods unite with others in the same locality,
forming coveys of a hundred or more individuals, and as
cold weather advances, they retreat to their snow shel-
ters at the timber edge. This is the time the hunters
go forth to seek them, for the flesh of the young is not
yet tainted with the bitterness of sage diet, and in that
barren region game is scarce.

312. BAND-TAILED PIGEON. — *Columba fasciata.*

FAMILY : The Pigeons, or Doves.

Length : 15.00–16.00.

Adult Male : Upper parts grayish brown, browner on the back, bluer on
the rump, high neck bronzy green, crossed by narrow collar of white ;
head and under parts metallic purplish, becoming pink on belly and
gray on the sides ; belly whitish ; end of tail crossed by broad band
of pearl-gray, bordered by black on the upper edge ; wing-coverts
narrowly edged with white.

Adult Female : Similar to male, but duller and grayer.

Young : Without white on nape ; upper parts paler ; under parts gray,
washed with brown.

Geographical Distribution : Western United States from Rocky Mountains to the Pacific, south through Mexico to Guatemala, through
the Transition zone.

California Breeding Range : Mountains of Southern California.

Breeding Season : May, June, July, and August.

Nest : A thin platform of sticks, in trees or bushes near water ; sometimes on the ground.

Eggs : 2 ; white. Size 1.50 × 1.20.

THE Band-tailed, or White-collared, Pigeon is irregularly distributed from the Rocky Mountains to the

Pacific. It breeds in small numbers at several points in the Coast Range between Santa Cruz and San Diego, laying its two white eggs on the ground near the bank of a pond or river in some localities. In other places it prefers to construct a shallow platform of twigs in a tree or bush. Incubation lasts from fourteen to sixteen days. In shape the newly hatched young are like miniature geese, and their yellow skin is covered with the sparse, cottony, white down. They are fed on a thin milky fluid, by regurgitation, for twenty days. The adult deserts its nest, eggs, or young on the slightest provocation ; it is exceedingly timid, so that any attempt to study its nesting habits, should one be so fortunate as to discover a nest, would prove disastrous to the brood, unless very cautiously done. They are said to have no breeding season in California, but to raise their young during any month except December. From April to September is their usual time. Deep in the recesses of a cañon you may come upon a company of these gregarious birds in the tree-tops. Unless you see the bird, you will fancy you have discovered a new owl, so hoot-like is their "coo." It has been described as "a short, hard hoot and a long coo." In the large aviary on the grounds of Mrs. Sefton at San Diego, a pair of these pigeons taken at Bear Valley have been kept some time ; their note has become modified, I presume by confinement with other birds, for it is much less expulsive and more purring in quality than when heard in the mountains. They breed in the aviary, laying their eggs on the ground behind a bush in one corner and also in compartments for the purpose, like domestic pigeons. The eggs are glistering white, equally round at both ends and very beautiful to look at. The birds themselves are remarkably handsome, and seen coming like rockets through the air down the side of the mountain, are startling to the ear as well as to the eye. The noise is produced by the rapid vibration of the wings, and resembles the roar of escaping steam. In flying upward or on a level, the sound is less loud but quite as characteristic, and, when a large flock are startled into flight, the vibratory effect is not unlike that of a small cyclone.

316. MOURNING DOVE. — *Zenaidura macroura.*

FAMILY : The Pigeons, or Doves.

Length: 11.00–13.00.

Adult Male: Upper parts soft brownish ; head and neck iridescent grayish pink ; a black spot on sides of the head ; sides of neck, chest, and breast changeable metallic purple-pink, changing to buff on the belly.

Adult Female: Similar to male, but paler, and metallic gloss less distinct.

Young: Duller than female, and without black spot on the head.

Geographical Distribution: Temperate North America, north to Canada, south to Panama.

Breeding Range: Breeds throughout its habitat.

Breeding Season: March to October.

Nest: A platform of sticks, in a bush or tree.

Eggs: 2 ; white. Size 1.12 × 0.82.

FOR a land bird, the Mourning Dove is strikingly fond of the water and usually tries to build within sight of it. At intervals all day, the parent birds fly back and forth between it and their nest, if brooding, and I have reason to believe that the male brings the female water as well as food in his own throat. Both adults feed their young by regurgitation for twenty days, and undoubtedly give them water in the same way until they learn to drink, in true pigeon fashion, by suction. The newly hatched Mourning Doves are unique among young birds, for they are daintily formed miniature goslings with goose bill and all. This bill ends in a pearly tip, and the young doves are covered with short, cottony, white down, through which the yellow skin is apparent. The mother birds are both shy and stupid, for they will invariably betray their nest by flying off when, if they remained quiet, it might not be noticed. I know of no birds who desert their eggs and young so readily. The mother bird is also a slack housekeeper, and so loosely is the nest built that the eggs may nearly always be seen from below. In two instances Mr. P. W. Smith, of Greenville, Illinois, found these birds occupying old robins' nests, and once he discovered two of their eggs in the home of a thrasher, which also contained one thrasher egg.

316. MOURNING DOVE.
"*A platform of sticks.*"

In spite of these well-authenticated instances, and the fact that I have found Mourning Doves brooding their young in a kingbird's old nest *thickly lined with sheep's wool,* I believe such cases are uncommon; the bird usually builds her own home, and returns to it two years in succession, if not molested.

II.—BIRDS OF PREY

324. CALIFORNIA VULTURE, OR CONDOR.
Gymnogyps californianus.

FAMILY : The Vultures.

Length: 44.00–55.00 ; extent 8½ feet to nearly 11 feet.

Adults: Head and neck covered with a warty orange skin ; bill pale yellow ; plumage black ; wing-coverts tipped with white ; under wing-coverts pure white.

Young : Like adults, but naked skin and bill black ; more or less covered with sooty gray down.

Downy Young: Covered with white cottony down ; bill yellow.

Geographical Distribution : Coast ranges of Southern California from Monterey County to Mexico.

Breeding Range : Breeds in the mountainous districts throughout its habitat.

Breeding Season : Eggs have been taken in April and May.

Nest : The bare floor of a cave or recess among the rocks, or in a hollow stump.

Eggs : 1 or 2 ; plain grayish green or dull greenish white. Size 4.46 × 2.48.

THE California Condor is, so far as known, the largest bird that flies, except its cousin the Condor of the Andes, and was formerly abundant throughout the coast ranges of Southern California. It has become comparatively rare through various causes, chief among them the feeding upon poisoned flesh put out by stockmen to kill wild animals. For a long time the species was on the verge of extermination, but through the efforts of the Cooper

324. CALIFORNIA VULTURE, OR CONDOR

Gymnogyps californianus

Club it has been protected, and according to latest reports it is increasing in numbers.

On his first trip to California, the Eastern bird-lover expects to see these birds soaring majestically over every mountain, and is disappointed when he has remained a year, or two, or three, with never a glimpse of one, although right in the Condor range. The truth is the Condors keep well back in the hidden and inaccessible parts of the mountains, and if you would see one, you must go where they are and *see the sun rise*, — as they do; for the Condor seeks his prey as soon as the sunlight has reached the valleys and before the world is fairly astir. Then you may see him on glorious wings, circling, circling, with scarcely a movement save of his head, which, stretched out before him, turns this way and that. He is magnificent to look at, — nearly eleven feet from tip of wing to tip of wing, — but in some ways he is very stupid. *All* vultures are stupid. Although so keen of vision that you can never hope to conceal your presence from him, yet he will betray his nest and make no effort to lead you from it by the wise feints of smaller birds. Thus in the animal world nature compensates for great strength and ferocity by giving the quicker instincts to the hunted, not to the hunters. The Condor's senses are keen to show him where to obtain food, and his wings are strong; but, in danger from no creature, he has not been trained to protect himself. He gorges, is satisfied, and sleeps with no need of precaution for self or young, because, unless his food be poisoned, what has he to fear? The young Condor reared by Mr.

Holmes of Berryessa developed some remarkable habits, but I believe these were due to artificial conditions.

Solomon puzzled over "the way of an eagle in the air" and left the mystery unsolved, and bird-lovers have been studying it ever since. When I have been able to watch the nesting habits of the Condor, as I have done those of some more accessible birds, I may recall the epithet "stupid," for in the training of their young some otherwise dull birds show wonderful sagacity. Whether sagacious or stupid, the Condor is one of the glories of a glorious State, and deserves the protection of all loyal citizens.

325. TURKEY VULTURE. — *Cathartes aura.*

FAMILY : The Vultures.

Length : 26.00–32.00.

Adults : Head covered with bare, red, warty skin ; bill white ; upper parts iridescent black ; under parts dull black, shafts of quills and tail-feathers dirty white.

Young : Similar to adults, but bill blackish and naked skin of head and neck livid dusky.

Downy Young : Covered with a white cottony down, naked head covered with a sallow skin.

Geographical Distribution : Temperate North America.

Breeding Range : North to latitude 40°.

Breeding Season : April 1 to June 15.

Nest : Frequently built in a tree, or a slight depression under a ledge or a cliff.

Eggs : 2 ; greenish buffy or white, more or less spotted with brown and light purple. Size 2.73 × 1.87.

Food : Carrion.

THE Turkey Vulture, or Turkey Buzzard, is a common bird East and West, an industrious scavenger, and a self-appointed " Board of Health." In the warmer portions of the United States its offices are necessary and are valued greatly by the farmers and ranchmen. Long before the owner has missed the sheep or known that it is dead, the quick eye of the Vulture has discovered the carrion and he has called his family to the feast. Unlike most birds of prey, the Vulture feeds upon the ground where the carcass is found, and for this reason his foot has become modified for walking rather than for grasping. He is usually silent, except for hisses and guttural growls, uttered when feeding, which remind one of a hyena. Recent successful attempts have been made to prove that he discovers his food by the sense of smell as well as by keen sight. Carrion has been hidden under a dense growth of brush where it could not be seen, and the Vultures have found it quite as readily as when exposed to view.

The nesting season of this Vulture in California begins about April 15, the eggs being laid in a depression in the ground under a ledge, or on a steep hillside, or in the cavity of a tall stump, or in a tree. The young are fed by regurgitation, and remain in the nest nine weeks. Except at nesting season, this Vulture is gregarious, flying and feeding in company and roosting in great numbers in favorite groves. On the wing it is graceful and impressive, moving in great circles apparently without effort and without fatigue. One can scarcely look up to the hills without seeing it, and it comes to be as much a part of California scenery as the mountains or the sea.

328. WHITE–TAILED KITE. — *Elanus leucurus.*

FAMILY : The Falcons, Hawks, Eagles, etc.

Length : 15.50–17.00.

Adults : Upper parts slate-color ; top of head and tail white ; a patch of black on each shoulder and around each eye ; under parts uniform pure white.

Young : Similar to adults, but tinged with rusty, and more or less streaked with dark gray ; wing-feathers tipped with white ; under parts streaked with yellow-brown ; tail with a dusky band.

Geographical Distribution : Tropical America north to San Francisco on the Pacific coast ; on the Atlantic coast to latitude 37°.

Breeding Range : The central portions of California, west of the Sierra Nevada.

Breeding Season : April 1 to June 1.

Nest : Placed high in a tree ; a platform of sticks, lined with straw and grasses.

Eggs : 3 to 5 ; dull buffy white, spotted and tinged with chestnut over the entire surface. Size 1.72 × 1.30.

THE White-tailed Kite is a fairly common resident of the interior valleys of California west of the Sierra Nevada, north to Red Bluff and south as far as Los Angeles. Its nest is always placed just as far from the ground as possible, in a sycamore or oak or maple tree, and is a loosely constructed platform of sticks, occasionally lined with straw. In Santa Clara valley the birds are not at all uncommon ; they nest in the oak groves from April 1 to May 1. They remain paired all the year, and may be seen hunting together over the fresh and salt water marshes. Mr. W. K. Fisher records them as preying upon the field mice in the vicinity of San Francisco Bay. They are common at Alviso in the early morning, hovering over the marshes, as kingfishers do over water, before plunging downward for a strike. Graceful and easy

on the wing, they have a steadiness of flight unlike the
bullet-like dash of some of the hawks, and more closely
resembling the flight of the gulls.
Their call is a high-keyed whistle,
which falls three tones in a plaintive
minor key. Besides this, they utter a
sharp, short squeak when darting down
to seize their prey. Aside from the fact
of his beauty and grace, the food of
the White-tail is such as to
render him beneficial to farmers,
and he should be protected by
law fully as much as the game
and song birds. Lizards, frogs,
snakes, grasshoppers, and
beetles are his bill of fare, and
these he consumes in great numbers. Small birds do not fear
him as they do the bird-eating

328. WHITE-TAILED KITE.
"*Preying upon the field mice.*"

species, and this alone is proof that he does not molest
them.

331. MARSH HAWK. — *Circus hudsonius.*

FAMILY: The Falcons, Hawks, Eagles, etc.

Length: 19.50–24.00.
Adult Male: Slate-color streaked with white; under parts and rump
   pure white; breast and sides lightly speckled with reddish brown;
   tail with alternate bands of brown and black, six or seven in number;
   tips of wings black.
Adult Female, and Young: Rusty, more or less streaked with black.
Downy Young: Rusty buff above, more or less washed with gray, and
   merging to whitish on lower parts.

Geographical Distribution: North America from southern border of Alaska, south in winter from latitude 40° to Cuba.

Breeding Range: In California breeds on the interior marshes as far south as San Diego and north to Oregon.

Breeding Season: April, May, and June.

Nest: On the ground, among the marsh grass ; made of grass and sticks, and lined with feathers.

Eggs: 4 to 6; dull bluish white, sometimes spotted with light and dark brown. Size 1.80 × 1.38.

To most bird-lovers the sight of an old gray Marsh Hawk soaring gracefully over the broad stretch of wet meadows in the early spring suggests but one thing, — an immediate tramp in his direction. All sorts of fascinating things are hiding in that grass, and who knows it so well as he ? A sudden swoop downward, a slow, circling rise, with a small dark object in those strong claws, and an alighting on the nearest tree to dine. What is the menu ? Perhaps a pretty field mouse that, unconscious of the sharp eyes overhead, ran through his burrow ; or a gopher, or possibly a lizard. He has little choice between these and frogs, snakes, young ground-squirrels, and insects. In that he never molests the chicken yard but rids the meadow of insects and small animals, he is the *protégé* of the intelligent farmer. A few there are to whom a hawk is simply a hawk, to be destroyed without mercy or discrimination, but such persons become fewer every year as the economic value of certain varieties of these birds becomes better known.

In a clump of stiff marsh grass or a bunch of weeds, you may find the nest of this " soft-winged still-hunter." It is simply a thick mat of coarse sticks and straw, lined slightly with feathers, and usually measuring about thirteen to fifteen inches at its largest diameter. In it are laid four or five dull light-green eggs, either plain or sparsely spotted with brown. Here the adults brood by turns, the free one bringing food in its claws and dropping it from the air to its mate on the nest below, as if by accident ; for these handsome Hawks are wise and very, very wary. I have seen them bring sticks for nesting materials and drop them in the same way to the other bird in the grass. You will rarely discover the nest by seeing them alight near it. When the time for a change of labor has come, one of the birds circles over and over, without dropping food, and finally alights in a tree, if there be one there. Before you know it another Hawk, his counterpart except for size, is circling in his place while he still sits in the tree. By and by he is gone from the tree, but in most instances you have not seen him go, you have been so intently watching the gyrations of his mate in the air.

In eighteen to twenty days the young Hawks break their hard shells, *one each day*, and cuddle down among the feathers and straw of the crude nest. From the day the first little ball of down appears, one or the other of the adults may be seen constantly on the wing over that meadow. The same tactics are pursued as before, for the food is dropped to the parent on the nest, who, after the first few days, holds it fast in her beak while the nestlings tear off bits from it for themselves. In this way the muscles of bill and neck are developed. Later on the food is simply dropped to them, both parents being off on the hunt, and the little fellows grasp it in their sharp claws and tear from it with a right good-will. It is comparatively easy, with a large amount of patience, a good blind, and a field glass, to watch the brood develop day by day; for although so wild, the Marsh Hawks will not desert their nestlings, and if you can so arrange as to be inconspicuous they have little fear of you.

332. SHARP-SHINNED HAWK. — *Accipiter velox.*

FAMILY : The Falcons, Hawks, Eagles, etc.

Length: Male 10.00–11.50 ; female 12.50–14.00.
Adult Male: Upper parts slate-color ; under parts white, heavily barred and spotted with chestnut ; tail with three or four narrow black bands and a white tip.
Adult Female: Similar, but with markings less pronounced.
Young: Dusky brown above, buffy below, striped with brown or dusky.
Geographical Distribution: North America to arctic circle ; south in winter from 40° to Guatemala.
Breeding Season: April, May, and June.
Breeding Range: Throughout the United States and north to Alaska.
Nest: Of small sticks, lined with fibre of leaves, placed from 10 feet to 60 feet high in a tree.
Eggs: 4 or 5; dull greenish white or grayish green, irregularly marked with brown. Size 1.46 × 1.20.

EQUALLY at home in the dense shadows of the forest, on the treeless plains, or on the pine-covered mountain tops, the little Sharp-shinned Hawk requires but two things, — plenty of food and good water. Alas, that the food should preferably be small song birds ! He is a dainty eater, also, stripping all feathers from his victim and refusing to swallow a bit of fur or a bone. This is the only good thing which can be said of him, for a bird more baleful to other feathered creatures, large and small, can nowhere be found. All laws protecting native birds should offer a bounty on his head and that of his relatives, the big Cooper hawk and the goshawk. Fortunately the last two are not numerous in the Land of Sunshine.

The Sharp-shinned is a fierce defender of his home in the top of a pine or spruce. And this nest he has very likely seized by force from its owners, the magpies or squirrels or crows; for might is always right in the forest world, and whatever this brigand wants he takes. His nestlings receive such constant care and strong food that, by the time they are feathered and ready to leave the nest, they are noticeably larger than the parents. It is worth while to note, also, that the female is larger and fiercer than the male, consequently more rapacious. The note of the Sharp-shinned is in accord with his nature, a high-keyed shrill whistle or shriek, and is uttered when in triumph he dashes into a terrorized flock of small birds or down into a barnyard full of poultry. For he is no coward, and will attack a hen many times his own weight even though she be surrounded by her kin. As one writer says of him, " He is the boldest fellow for his inches that wears feathers." Certainly he is the most destructive desperado, without fear and without mercy.

333. COOPER HAWK. — *Accipiter cooperii.*

FAMILY : The Falcons, Hawks, Eagles, etc.

Length : Male 14.00–17.00 ; female 18.00–20.00.

Adult Male: Upper parts slate-color, top of head black; under parts white, heavily barred with chestnut ; tail rounded at end, barred with black, and tipped with white.

Adult Female: Upper parts duller, top of head rusty black.

Young: Upper parts dark brown ; under parts streaked, not barred.
Downy Young: Uniform pure white.
Geographical Distribution: The entire United States and southern British
　　Provinces, south in winter to Mexico.
Breeding Range: Throughout California.
Breeding Season: April and May.
Nest: Usually in high trees ; often a remodelled crow's nest.
Eggs: 4 or 5 ; pale greenish white, plain or dimly marked with light
　　brown.　Size 1.97 × 1.42.

LIKE the sharp-shinned, the Cooper Hawk is the bane
alike of the farmer and the bird-lover.　He is known
throughout the United States by the name of Chicken
Hawk, and so daring is he that he will come down into
the farmyard for poultry in the face of the farmer.
There are several records of weasels that have been
seized by this hawk, sucking its blood at the throat and
causing its death.　One skeleton specimen was found
with the teeth of the weasel so locked in the bone of the
hawk that it could not be removed.　But unfortunately,
although chickens, weasels, snakes, lizards, and small
quadrupeds are doubtless upon his bill of fare, song birds
are too often his victims, and the ornithologist who is
patiently studying the development of some rare brood
has good cause to dislike him.

The nest of the Cooper Hawk is placed in tall trees,
and being added to and occupied year after year, it becomes an exceedingly bulky structure.　April to May is
the usual date, in California, at which nesting begins,
and incubation lasts thirty-one days.　The young remain
in the nest six to eight weeks, and are fed upon the
small live mammals, never upon dead flesh.　Small wonder they learn to pounce upon and tear anything that
moves in the grass or among the trees.

355. PRAIRIE FALCON. — *Falco mexicanus.*

Family : The Falcons, Hawks, Eagles, etc.

Length : Male 17.00–18.00 ; female 18.50–20.00.

Adult Male : Upper parts light yellow-brown ; indistinctly barred with buffy on the head and neck, and with slate-color on lower back and tail ; sides of the head with dark patches ; under parts and nuchal collar white ; belly lightly streaked or spotted with dusky, and flanks heavily spotted with same.

Adult Female : Upper parts same as male, but duller ; palest toward the tail ; tail tipped with white on the outer edges of the feathers.

Young : Upper parts grayish brown ; under parts grayish buff with broad dusky streaks.

Geographical Distribution : Western United States from the plains to the Pacific.

Breeding Range : Throughout the United States.

Breeding Season : May.

Nest : Of sticks, with a lining of grasses ; usually on cliffs, sometimes in cavities in trees, always in inaccessible places.

Eggs : 2 to 5 ; deep cream-buff, covered with fine specks of cinnamon, rufous, and light chestnut. Size 2.10 × 1.64.

ALTHOUGH not a large hawk and apparently built for swift flight rather than for strength, the trim Prairie Falcon has the courage of an eagle and does not hesitate to attack prey of twice its own weight. Poultry it seizes only when other food is scarce, but a good-sized jack-rabbit is often a victim, and is carried to the nearest low perch to be devoured ; — this by a bird the size of the American crow, but with sinews of steel and a heart that absolutely knows no fear. With an audacity worthy of a better cause it pursues marsh hawks, compelling them to relinquish the fish they have caught ; and not even the bald eagle can strike such terror to a flock of grouse. Their eyrie is a crevice or ledge on the perpendicular face of a cliff where none but the most daring can

10

climb. Of one such exploit Mr. O. W. Howard writes in "The Condor," May, 1902, as follows :

"April 18, I secured one hundred feet of inch-and-a-quarter rope, and we again made our way to the cliff. On reaching the top of the ridge we made our way down to the edge of the cliff where a bunch of oak trees were growing. We tied the rope to oaks, and I slid down it thirty feet to a shelf-like projection. I was then standing just above the nesting cavity where the cliff overhung considerably. About four feet to one side was a crevice in the rock, and by jerking the rope over a point above me I could let myself down it, which I did to a point opposite the nest. It was rather a risky undertaking as I made my way along the face of the cliff, and I held the rope in one hand and the sharp points of rock in the other, at the same time using my feet to steady myself. By keeping my hand-hold I could lean over just far enough to see that the nest contained eggs, and some-how managed to squeeze into the cavity head first. The nest was about four feet from the entrance in a depression in the solid rock, with no nesting material except a few feathers of the old bird and small

355. PRAIRIE FALCON.

"*Not even the bald eagle can strike such terror to a flock of grouse.*"

bones and hair of the smaller quadrupeds; also a number of pellets ejected by the old birds. I am certain that both birds occupy the nesting cavity at night, for there was a depression in the end of the cavity which showed signs of being occupied by one of the birds.

"The nest contained five eggs, rather light in color for this species. They have a yellowish brown appearance, the color being almost solid but darker about the larger ends."

It is a matter of regret that Mr. Howard gives us no record of how the adults conducted themselves during the time they were being robbed; also, that he did not make a study of the feeding and nesting habits of the birds with regard to incubation and care of the young, as this is a field open for just such daring observers and one where good work is needed.

337 b. WESTERN RED–TAILED HAWK. — *Buteo borealis calurus.*

FAMILY: The Falcons, Hawks, Eagles, etc.

Length: Male 19.00–22.50 ; female 23.00–25.00.

Adults: Varying from light grayish brown to uniform dark sooty brown ; under parts white or buffy, with broad brown streaks on throat, belly, and sides ; tail bright reddish brown in any phase, crossed by one or more black bars. In the dark extreme the entire plumage except the red tail is a dark sooty brown.

Young: Darker throughout, and more heavily spotted ; tail grayish brown, barred with black bands.

Geographical Distribution: Western North America, east to Rocky Mountains, south to Mexico.

Breeding Range : Almost throughout the State of California.

Breeding Season: March, April, and May.

Nest: Of sticks ; lined with roots or fibre, placed in trees or ledges of cliffs from 25 to 50 feet high.

Eggs: 2 or 3 ; dull whitish, plain or marked with shades of brown. Size 2.36 × 1.80.

THE Western Red-tail is common, though not very abundant, throughout the wooded mountainous districts of the central portion of the State. On the road from Tallac to Lake Valley several were seen, and one nest was found in a coniferous tree thirty feet from the ground. The climber sent up to investigate shouted back that there were four young nearly ready to fly. Being told to bring one down, he picked one out of the nest, but it bit his finger, and angrily he hurled it out into the air. Fluttering, turning over and over, down it came ; but the fall did not hurt it much, and as soon as it could catch its breath it fought like a little fury. It was a handsome bird, nearly feathered, and in a week more would have flown of its own accord. It fluttered about on the grass, and after resting a time managed to scramble into a low bush, where it felt more secure though it was really much more exposed. In the meantime the adults had circled wildly about with discordant screams, and the mother still remained near. Curious to see how she would manage to get that unlucky youngster back into his nest, we moved off fifty yards and watched through the glasses. Both parents swooped down and looked at him, from on the wing, again and again, screaming when away, but silent whenever near him or the nest. At length a more sudden swoop and a momentary flutter, as a butterfly flutters over a flower. Then she rose carefully and slowly, with the young in her claws, and carried him to the nest. It was impossible to see whether she was holding him between them or grasping him by them. Five days later the nest was deserted and the young hawks were nowhere to be found. The adults still appeared in the vicinity, but the young were safely hidden from prying eyes in the heavy foliage.

339 b. RED–BELLIED HAWK. — *Buteo lineatus elegans.*

FAMILY : The Falcons, Hawks, Eagles, etc.

Length : Male 17.00–19.00 ; female 18.50–21.00.

Adults : Upper parts dark brown, streaked with buffy or white ; shoulders bright red-brown ; under parts chestnut, barred with white on belly and sides ; wings and tail barred with white.

Young : Under parts dusky ; wing-quills spotted with buffy.

Downy Young : Dull grayish white.

Geographical Distribution : Pacific coast of the United States, south to Mexico, east to Texas.

Breeding Range : In California, chiefly in the interior valleys from latitude 33° to 41°.

Nest : Of twigs ; lined with vegetable fibre, feathers, and leaves ; on limbs of trees, usually in the neighborhood of water.

Eggs : 2 to 5 ; grayish white, marked with brown and lilac. Size 2.40 × 1.77.

THIS is the Western race of the red-shouldered hawk. It is one that should receive all protection from the law. Mr. Lyman Beldings records a pair that for three seasons nested near a poultry yard, and whose post mortem proved their food to have been exclusively lizards, tree-frogs, and insects. Mrs. Bailey says that their food is " sometimes small birds," but this is doubtless in treeless regions, where their favorite food is less easily obtained. In most parts of California where they breed, the records show them to have eschewed everything with feathers, and to have dined upon small snakes, lizards, frogs, insects, and crawfish. Fur and feathers are caught only as a last resort, when there are hungry young in the nest.

The Red-bellied Hawk is exceptionally fond of bathing, and in California it usually builds within a hundred yards of water. Both adults indulge in a daily bath, returning to the same place at about the same hour for it. The nest is placed in a tree or giant cactus; it is composed of twigs with leaves and usually lined with leaves and feathers. This hawk utters a shrill, high scream when molested, but does not offer to fight unless the intruder be a bird or snake. Incubation lasts thirty-one days.

342. SWAINSON HAWK. — *Buteo swainsoni.*

FAMILY : The Falcons, Hawks, Eagles, etc.

Length : Male 12.50–20.00 ; female 21.00–22.00.

Adult Male : Upper parts dark grayish brown ; forehead, chin, throat, and under parts white, except a sharply defined reddish brown chest band ; belly often barred or spotted with brownish ; tail a brownish gray, crossed by 9 or 10 narrow dusky bands.

Adult Female : Similar to male, but chest band grayish brown instead of reddish brown.

Melanistic Phase : Both sexes uniform rusty black ; many gradations are found between this black phase and the normal plumage.

Young : Tail as in adult ; upper parts sooty brown, varied with yellow-brown ; under parts and head streaked brown and black.

Geographical Distribution : From the arctic regions to South America, from the Pacific to the Eastern States.

California Breeding Range : San Joaquin and Sacramento valleys, and the San Diegan district.

Breeding Season : May.

Nest: Made of sticks, sagebrush, and leaves; lined with green leaves and plant fibre; from 20 to 50 feet high in trees, sometimes in bushes, sometimes on the ground, sometimes on ledges of rocky cliffs.

Eggs: 1 to 4; pale greenish buffy, lightly spotted with shades of brown. Size 2.21 × 1.70.

THROUGHOUT the interior valleys of California, Swainson's Hawk is a common spring and summer visitant, and one whose full value is not yet so well known as it should be. Pocket gophers, ground squirrels, insects, and grasshoppers are its sole diet in this district, and no one can compute the benefit that accrues to the farmer from the breeding of these hawks on or near their land. Particularly is this true of a sandy barren soil where gopher burrows are numerous. Dozens of the hawks fly down to the gopher colony, just at dusk, and take up their stand at the entrances of the bur-

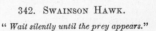

342. SWAINSON HAWK.

" Wait silently until the prey appears."

rows, where they wait patiently and silently until the prey appears. It never escapes them. If there are young hawks in the nest, the victim will be carried to them; if not, it will usually be eaten at the perch nearest to the hunting ground. In either case, back comes the hawk for a

second and a third course in surprisingly few minutes.
Anyone who cares to watch will probably find that sixty
gophers to each dozen hawks each day, besides countless
insects and grasshoppers, is a fair estimate. Small birds
they do not harm. If any proof of this were needed, the
song birds themselves furnish it every season by building
their nests fearlessly in the same tree, and not seldom
within ten inches of that of the hawk. Arkansas kingbirds, shrikes, and bullock orioles have all been found, by
Captain Bendire, rearing their young close to the young
hawks, and a veritably happy family they are.

The hawk's nest is large and slovenly, a mere platform
of sticks, placed indiscriminately in a low bush or a tall
tree, and lined with green leaves and corn husks.
Equally indifferent is he as to the location; for he is
content on a grassy prairie where there are few trees, or
in the timbered districts. The only requirements for his
home seem to be food and water, — the last for bathing
as well as drinking, for, like all birds of prey, Swainson's Hawk is an enthusiastic splasher. Early every
morning he flies down to his favorite pond or stream, and
sends a shower of sparkling drops in every direction.
It is a very wet, bedraggled-looking bird that, a few
moments later, flies up to a sunny perch to shake himself and preen his feathers.

His hunting is mostly done on the ground; after his
young are fledged, you may see them jumping with raised
wings through the grass in brisk pursuit of crickets and
grasshoppers. This they learn to do by imitating the parent, and it is probably their first lesson in pursuing prey.

In the nest, they are fed upon small mammals and, even before their down has changed to feathers, they will tear their food with all the ferocity of a young puppy.

The adults arrive from the South about the middle of March; by the middle of April they have constructed their nest and are brooding their two or three eggs. Incubation requires twenty to twenty-two days, and the young remain in the nest from four to five weeks. One authority says eight, but this is a longer time than any of my own records show, and is, I believe, unusual.

In flight, *swainsoni* seems a trifle clumsy as he rises from the ground with a good-sized gopher in his claws; but, as he swings into full headway, you realize that, like all his family, he is both swift and graceful on the wing.

348. FERRUGINOUS ROUGH–LEG. — *Archibuteo ferrugineus*.

FAMILY : The Falcons, Hawks, Eagles, etc.

Length: Male 22.50 ; female 24.00.

Adults, Normal Phase: Upper parts and flanks bright rufous ; under parts white, lightly streaked with brown ; tail white, tinged with rufous and sometimes banded with dark.

Adult, Melanistic Phase: Upper parts dark brown marked with rusty; under parts dull rufous.

Young: Upper parts grayish brown, feathers edged with rusty ; tail white at upper third ; rest brownish, banded with dark.

Geographical Distribution: From Dakota and Texas to Pacific.

Breeding Range: In California, the interior, west of the Sierra Nevada from Sacramento to San Diego.

Breeding Season: April and May.

Nest: Of sticks ; lined with leaves, grass, and rootlets.

Eggs: 2 to 5; greenish buffy, marked with shades of brown and purple. Size 2.43 × 1.91.

THIS species is variously known as " Rough-legged Buzzard," " California Squirrel-Hawk," or " Prairie

Eagle." It frequents the prairies and desert plains, and, unlike others of its family, cares little to be near water. Its food is small mammals and reptiles, seldom birds, and it is one of the few species that the law should protect. In hunting, it flies low over the fields, carrying its food to a low perch to devour at its leisure. Late in the afternoon it may be seen circling gracefully high in the air; at such times it appears not unlike the golden eagle, which doubtless accounts for its nickname, Prairie Eagle. It makes no attempt to defend its nest when molested by men, but flies away with scarcely a protest.

Incubation is complete in twenty-eight days, the young remaining in the nest six to eight weeks. This difference in time is the difference between a cold and a warm climate, the young of the former maturing less rapidly.

349. GOLDEN EAGLE. — *Aquila chrysaëtos.*

FAMILY : The Falcons, Hawks, Eagles, etc.

Length: Male 30.00–35.00 ; female 35.00–40.00.
Adults: Entire plumage dark brown ; the lanceolate feathers of high neck and the feathers of tarsus golden brown ; tail blackish, irregularly barred with dark gray.
Young: Similar to adult, but upper half of the tail plain white.
Downy Young: Grayish white, grayer beneath.
Geographical Distribution: Northern portions of the northern hemisphere, chiefly in mountainous regions.
Breeding Range: Throughout its habitat, the mountainous regions of California.
Breeding Season: February, March, and April.
Nest: Bulky, sometimes 4 feet deep and 5 feet in diameter ; of sticks, lined with straw, leaves, hair, or feathers ; usually placed in trees on a steep mountain side.

Eggs: 2 or 3 : whitish, marked with heavy blotches, spots, and specks of brown, lilac, and gray, most abundant at the longer end. Size 2.96 × 2.27.

THE Golden Eagle is by no means a rare bird in California. He breeds in the mountains of Santa Cruz County and at many other localities throughout the State. Fortunately, the nest is usually placed in such an inaccessible location as seldom to fall a victim to collectors. It is a large structure, nearly five feet in diameter and several feet deep, lined with stubble, grass, and leafy twigs, and placed in the top of a sycamore, pine, or oak, overhanging a rocky cañon. The two eggs vary from unmarked white to heavily marked with red, brown, and purple. Three and a half weeks are required for incubation, and the young remain in the nest nearly six weeks after they are hatched, so that, although the eggs may be laid in March, the first of June often finds young in the nest. A pair whose record I have, began sitting March 26, and the young were newly hatched April 22. On June 14 they were still in the nest, but June 16 both had left. This nest was in a live-oak on the crest of a ridge in Santa Clara County, and had been built new that year. Rabbits, grouse, and many small quadrupeds were carried to the nest, as well as several good-sized snakes. I saw no lambs, fawns, or fish, but several times the male brought what looked to be young foxes or coyotes. Meal-time came twice or three times a day, never oftener. This pair hunted together, leaving the young unguarded hour after hour, but I believe they were always kept in range of the mother's keen eye, however far away she seemed to be. Early in the morning both plunged into the brook for a bath, and emerged with every feather limp and dripping, to shake violently and preen for half an hour. Then the plumage shone with a tinge of tawny-gold in the sunlight, and the glorious bird seemed worthy his name.

352. BALD EAGLE. — *Haliæëtus leucocephalus.*

FAMILY : The Falcons, Hawks, Eagles, etc.

Length : Male 30.00–35.00 ; female 34.00–43.00 ; extent 7 feet.
Adults : Head, neck, rump, and tail white ; rest of plumage sooty brown.
Young : First year, black ; second and third years, mixed black and white, gray and brown ; head and neck black.
Downy Young : Uniform sooty gray.
Geographical Distribution : United States and Mexico.
California Breeding Range : Among the Santa Barbara Islands and locally along the coast.
Breeding Season : December to April.
Nest : Very bulky ; made of sticks and lined with rootlets, or rock moss ; in trees from 20 to 90 feet up, or on cliffs. Same nest is occupied year after year.
Eggs : 2 ; ivory white, unmarked except by nest stain. Size 2.51 × 1.94.

" ' HERE he is again. Here 's Old White-head robbing the fish hawk.' I started from the fire and ran out to look. The hawk had risen from the lake with a big fish, and was doing his best to get away to his nest, where his young ones were clamoring. Over him soared the eagle, still as fate, and as sure, now dropping to flap a wing in his face or touch him gently with his great talons, as if to say, ' Do you feel that ? If I grip once, it will be the end of you and your fish together. Better drop him peacefully ; you can catch another.

Drop him, I say!' Up to that moment the eagle had merely bothered the big hawk's flight with a gentle reminder that he wanted the fish, which he could not catch himself. Now there was a change, a flash of the kingly temper. With a roar of wings he whirled round the hawk like a tempest. But the hawk knew when to stop. With a cry of rage he dropped his fish. On the instant the eagle whirled and bent his head sharply. I had seen him fold wings and drop before, and had held my breath at the speed. But dropping was of no use now, for the fish fell faster. Instead, he swooped downward, adding to the weight of his fall the push of his strong wings, and glancing down like a bolt to catch the fish ere it struck the water, then rising again in a great curve — up and away, steadily, evenly, as the king should fly, to his own little ones far away on the mountain. . . . One day, when I came to the little thicket on the cliff where I used to lie and watch the nest through my glass, I found that one of the young eaglets was gone. The other stood on the edge of the nest, looking down fearfully into the abyss whither, no doubt, his bolder nest-mate had flown, and calling disconsolately from time to time. His whole attitude showed plainly that he was hungry, cross, and lonesome. Presently the mother eagle came swiftly up from the valley, and there was food in her talons. She came to the edge of the nest, hovered over it a moment, so as to give the hungry eaglet a sight and smell of food, then went slowly down to the valley taking the food with her, telling the little one in her own way to come and he should have it. He

called after her loudly and spread his wings a dozen
times to follow. But the plunge was too awful; he
settled back in the nest, pulled his head down into his
shoulders, shut his eyes, and tried to forget he was
hungry. The meaning was plain enough. She was trying to teach him to fly, but he was afraid." [1]

356. DUCK HAWK. — *Falco peregrinus anatum.*

FAMILY : The Falcons, Hawks, Eagles, etc.

Length : Male 15.50–18.00 ; female 18.00–20.00.

Adults : Top of head sooty black, sides of head and neck blackish, in
    sharp contrast to white throat ; rest of upper parts slate-color ;
    lighter on the rump, dimly barred with blackish ; under parts except
    throat and breast deep buff, spotted or barred with blackish ; tail
    black, barred with light gray and tipped with white.

Young : Upper parts blackish, feathers edged with rusty ; under parts
    chestnut, heavily streaked with dark.

Geographical Distribution : America, south to Chili. In California,
    occurs coastwise.

California Breeding Range : Breeds locally in the mountainous regions
    as far south as latitude 36°.

Breeding Season : March and April.

Nest : On a narrow edge of a cliff ; a few sticks to keep the eggs from
    rolling off.

Eggs : 3 or 4 ; creamy, tinged with brown, spotted and blotched with
    shades of brown.   Size 2.10 × 1.68.

"THIS species," says Mr. F. M. Chapman, "is the
noble peregrine of falconry. It would be difficult to
imagine a bird more highly endowed with the qualities
which make the ideal bird of prey. Its strength of wing
and talon is equalled by its courage. No bird flies more
swiftly than the Duck Hawk. Even teal, those winged
bullets, cannot escape it. No bird is more daring. I

---

[1] W. J. Long in "School of the Woods."

have had Duck Hawks dart down to rob me of wounded snipe lying almost at my feet, nor did my ineffectual shots prevent them from returning."

There is little to be said in favor of this relentless persecutor of water-fowl, shore birds, and song birds. Solitary in habit except at the breeding season, it fears no bird of its kind except the marsh hawk and the prairie falcon. These two wage unceasing warfare on it when it becomes conspicuous about their hunting grounds, which it never does willingly. Its nest is made on an inaccessible cliff, or in a high tree away from all its kind. From the hour they emerge from the shell, the young are taught to devour anything in feathers brought to them ; and when they hunt for themselves, feathered game is the only food they know. When the first wave of migration starts southward in the fall, the Duck Hawks are close behind, easily overtaking any stragglers or weak ones, and, if necessary, pursuing the swift, strong fliers of twice their size and weight. So every flock of coastwise migrating birds, particularly those classed as water-fowl, has one or more of these fierce birds of prey in its wake, and its numbers are constantly decimated to furnish food for its pursuers.

357. PIGEON HAWK. — *Falco columbarius.*

FAMILY : The Falcons, Hawks, Eagles, etc.

Length : Male 10.00–11.00 ; female 12.50–13.25.
Adult Male : Upper parts slate-color, streaked with black ; wing-quills black, inner web spotted ; under parts and hind-neck buffy, nearly white on throat ; streaked on breast, sides, and belly with dark ; middle tail-feathers barred with blackish and light gray.

Adult Female: Top and sides of the head streaked black and brown ; back, wing, and tail brownish ; under parts whitish or buffy.

Young: Like female, but darker ; tail brown, with three or four white bands.

Geographical Distribution: Whole of North America, chiefly north of the United States ; south in winter to Northern South America.

Breeding Range: From Mackenzie River region down to Washington and Oregon.

Breeding Season: May.

Nest: On ledges of cliffs or in hollow trees ; made of sticks or grass, and lined with feathers.

Eggs: 4 or 5 ; ground color cinnamon, covered with large indistinct rust-colored blotches.   Size 1.59 × 1.24.

THE Pigeon Hawk is one of the trimmest and handsomest of its family, and is tolerated in spite of its bird-eating habits.   It is not at all shy, and may be seen feeding in the open country or on the edge of timber land or along the shores.   Its food consists of small birds, pigeons, flickers, blackbirds, orioles, mice, and gophers.   Like the duck hawk, it follows birds in migration to eat stragglers.   Its favorite victims are gallinaceous birds, but it also devours many of our familiar friends among the song birds.   This may be one cause for the habit of migrating at night.

It nests largely north of latitude 40°, and in Northern California it begins to build early in April.   The nest is only a rude platform of sticks, scantily lined with feathers, and placed in the crevices of a cliff, or in a hollow tree, or high among branches of trees ; one observer has found it occupying a space between the rafters of a deserted miner's cabin.   It is most common throughout California in the winter months, when it comes into the interior valleys from the colder districts and remains until the early spring.

360 a. DESERT SPARROW HAWK. — *Falco sparverius deserticola.*

FAMILY : The Falcons, Hawks, Eagles, etc.

Length: Male 9.00–11.00 ; female 10.00–12.50.

Adults: Top of head pale grayish brown, usually with rufous crown-patch ; back light reddish brown, with or without black spots ; wings all grayish brown ; tail reddish brown, with dark band ; under parts whitish to buff, with or without brownish spots.

Young: Similar to adults, but colors more blended.

Geographical Distribution: Western United States and British Columbia, south to Guatemala.

Breeding Range: Wherever resident throughout the State of California.

Breeding Season: April.

Nest: In holes, usually in dead trees.

Eggs: 2 to 5 ; white, marked with shades of brown.   Size 1.36 × 1.12.

NEXT to the marsh hawk, the handsome little Sparrow Hawk is the one oftenest met with in California.   From his lookout on a dead tree at the edge of the meadow, he watches for his prey.   A slight movement in the grass, and out he flies, poises over the spot like a king-fisher over the water or a humming-bird at a flower tube, then swiftly he drops with feet extended, strikes the moving object, and rises with it in his talons.   If he has neither mate nor young in the nest, he carries the tidbit to his dead-tree perch and eats it himself.   But when his home, in an old stump near by, is filled with hungry nestlings, he flies directly to it with every morsel he picks up.   Sometimes it is a field mouse, sometimes grasshoppers, lizards, or frogs, and sometimes, alas ! small birds.

Although so small, he has the courage of his race, and often captures prey at least twice his own weight, managing in some way to convey it to a perch before eating. Of man he has little fear, building his nest in a tree near to human habitation, and paying little attention to anything but his own hunting.

His call is a sharp, high " killy-killy-killy," uttered as he flies over his prey, and has given him the nickname of " Killy Hawk." He is also called " Mouse Hawk " in some sections, from his habit of preying upon field mice.

Early in April the Sparrow Hawk looks about for a place in which to set up housekeeping. Sometimes it is an old magpie's nest that pleases him best, sometimes a kingfisher's hole in the bank of a river, sometimes a snug crevice in a wall of rock, but usually he chooses the deserted excavation of a woodpecker, or a natural cavity in a sycamore tree. No nest is made, but on the unlined surface of the cavity the four or five speckled eggs are laid. Incubation lasts twenty-three to twenty-six days, and the young remain six weeks in the nest.

For the first week the nestlings are fed exclusively on insects ; after that, insects predominate in the nursery menu, although mice are brought several times a day. After leaving the nest they are fed in the tree, for a week or so, before they try to hunt for themselves. The first lesson is very interesting to watch. One of the adults brings a bit of food to the youngster, who is sitting on the perch where for several days he has been fed, and instead of giving it to him, lets it fall in full view, at the same time calling " killy-killy-killy." In nearly every case the young hawk springs after it without hesitation the first time this is tried, and he often gets it. The mother is beside, over, and under him as he drops for it, encouraging him with her calls, and he soon responds with a little cry of unmistakable triumph. But he is not allowed to eat it on the ground, as he would like to do. An imperative call from the adult makes the young hunter exert his strength and follow to the nearest low perch before he tastes it. You watch and wonder at the instinct that prompts such skilful training, and the longer you watch the more there is to see.

364. FISH HAWK, OR AMERICAN OSPREY. — *Pandion haliaëtus carolinensis.*

FAMILY : The Falcons, Hawks, Eagles, etc.

Length : 20.75–25.00.

Adult Male : Head, neck, and under parts white ; a broad black line from bill through eye ; top of head, and nape sometimes streaked with blackish ; a few light brown spots on the breast ; back of wings and tail dark gray-brown, the latter banded with black and tipped with white.

Adult Female : Similar, but upper breast distinctly spotted with brown.

Young : Upper parts dusky brown, each feather tipped with white or buffy ; rest of plumage like that of adults.

Downy Young : Dull sooty grayish above, with broad white stripe down the middle of the back, and a dark stripe on the sides of the head ; crown striped white and dark ; under parts whitish, washed with brown on the chest.

Geographical Distribution : Temperate and tropical America, north to Hudson Bay and Alaska.

Breeding Range : Santa Barbara Islands, and locally along the entire sea-coast and on some of the inland lakes.

Breeding Season : April and May.

Nest : Bulky ; of sticks ; on trees near water.

Eggs : 2 to 4 ; buffy white or deep buff, spotted with shades of brown and purplish gray. Size 2.44 × 1.81.

WHEREVER there are fish there are pretty sure to be fishermen and Fish Hawks. Right good comrades are these two, neither one grudging the other his fine catch, and the more skilful the fishing the greater the admiration for the fisher, be he man or bird. On bold, free wings the Osprey comes swinging over the lake in the cool of the morning, and his clear whistle gives you "Good hunting" before he fairly comes into sight. Down he dives with wings folded. There is a splash of silver spray and he rises triumphant, with a fish held lengthwise in his talons, and flies swiftly back to his nest. It is quite likely to be in that tall tree across the lake that has been his home for years. It is said that each fall, before leaving it, he carefully repairs it with fresh sticks, so that spring finds it ready for him. To make it in the first place was an arduous task, for it is a bulky platform of strong sticks, surmounted and interwoven with smaller ones and carefully lined with leaves, moss, or soft vegetable fibre. Now the Osprey never alights on the ground when it is possible to avoid doing so ; his method of obtaining these sticks is similar, though on a larger scale, to that by which the little chimney-swift gets his, — that is, by breaking them from the tree. But the Osprey does this with his feet, while the swift uses his bill. The former swoops down upon a dead twig with such force as to snap it off, sometimes with a loud crack, and flies with it to the chosen nesting-site. Some of these twigs are four feet long, and several efforts are necessary to break them. If he has the misfortune to drop one *en route*, he will not pick it up again, but with renewed energy will break off another. Hundreds of these twigs must be brought to fashion his strong nest, and it is small wonder he uses it year after year. As in the building of a home, so in the choice of a mate, the Osprey acts once for all; the pair remain together throughout the years, together making the long trip south, as do the loons. When the leaves on the trees are the size of a mouse's ear, the Fish Hawk lays her three characteristic eggs and begins to brood. In a little more than two weeks downy nestlings stretch up their pretty heads for food, and both parents are kept busy supplying the demand. Small fish are carried constantly to the nest, the heads, bones, and fins being thrown to the ground and the soft parts given to the young. As the young emerge from the downy state to the dignity of feathers, they begin to sit up cautiously on the edge of the nest and call with short, sharp, impatient whistles for their food. This the parent answers with a clear, cheery whistle, as he rises from the water, and when he nears the nest the calls of both grow very quick and excited. It is a charming bit of home life, well worth some discomfort to watch.

When the young are fully feathered and strong, — at about four weeks old, — their training in fishing begins. They are taken to the water and, by repeated trials, learn to dive and strike their fish. Sometimes it is learned the first day, and sometimes several lessons must be given, but the end is the same, — the nestling is forced to catch his own dinner, or go hungry.

Among the twigs of the large nest small birds frequently make their home unmolested. I have known wrens to do this, and there are other well-authenticated records of purple grackle, jays, and tree swallows nesting beneath the bulky platform, thus attesting their faith in the friendly attitude of their carnivorous neighbor.

365. AMERICAN BARN OWL. — *Strix pratincola.*

FAMILY : The Barn Owls.

Length : 18.00.

Adults : Upper parts mottled gray and tawny, finely streaked with black and white ; face white to light brown ; under parts white to tawny, with triangular spots of black or dark brown ; wings and tail tawny, barred with black.

Geographical Distribution : United States generally, south to Mexico.

California Breeding Range : Suitable localities in the latitude of the State of Sonora, in the northwest of Mexico.

Breeding Season : April 1 to June 30.

Nest : In holes in the ground, holes in river banks, hollow trees, old crow's nests, barns, belfry towers, etc. The nests are scantily made, with a few sticks, straw, bones, and other refuse.

Eggs : 5 to 8 ; plain, dead white. Size 1.72 × 1.35.

WHEN the sun sinks behind the oak trees and the shadows creep over the valleys, the Barn Owl hurries to the nearest meadow or marsh land on a hunting trip. If it has young at home in the nest, its flight will be swift and noiseless, as it crosses the intervening fields at short intervals, carrying mice, gophers, and ground squirrels. Nine mice form a meal for the brood, and sixteen mice have been carried to the nest in twenty-five minutes, besides three gophers, a squirrel, and a good-sized rat.

Early in April the Barn Owl begins its nesting, laying one white egg every other day until there are from five to ten or eleven hidden in an old crow's nest, or in a hollow tree, or even in a hole in a bank. The cares of incubation are shared by both birds, and last from three to three and a half weeks. Mr. Bendire says it is not unusual for the last eggs to hatch two weeks after the first. The young owls are covered with a whitish gray or brown cottony down, and have the hooked bill and talons of the adults. They stay in the nest until seven weeks old. At four weeks old, a young Barn Owl will tear a gopher as fiercely as an adult, swallowing it fur and all. The noise of a family of these hungry young birds in a tree can be compared to nothing, for it is like nothing else. As soon as they discover, by some occult sense, that the adult is on the way home with supper, the hissing and shrieking begin, and are kept up all night long.

When the nestlings are seven or eight weeks old, the first lesson in hunting is given early in the evening, and the young owls flit about with the adults on noiseless wings like roly-poly bats.

They soon learn to imitate the ludicrous attitude of the parent as, bolt upright, with half-closed eyelids, it blinks at the daylight, looking as wise as a sage and as comical as a monkey.

Except in the breeding season these owls are gregarious, and an old belfry is often the home of from ten to twenty inhabitants. Besides its screech, the Barn Owl has a nasal snore.

366. AMERICAN LONG–EARED OWL. — *Asio wilsonianus.*

FAMILY : The Horned Owls and Hoot Owls.

Length : 14.80.

Adults : Conspicuous brown ear-tufts an inch or more in length ; face tawny ; upper parts mottled tawny, black, and ashy ; wings and tail barred ; under parts mottled buffy and white, the breast broadly streaked, the sides and belly irregularly barred with brown ; flanks tawny unspotted.

Geographical Distribution : Temperate North America.

California Breeding Range : Suitable localities in the interior valleys.

Breeding Season : In California, from February 15 to May 15.

Nest : Occasionally an old magpie's nest ; sometimes in hollow trees, cavities in rocks, old crow's or hawk's nests.

Eggs : 3 to 6 ; white. Size 1.62 × 1.32.

THE American Long-eared Owl breeds in the interior valleys and foot-hills, haunting the lower range of coniferous timber. Unlike the short-eared owl, it never hunts in the daytime ; it is rarely found in the open, but hides through the sunny hours in the shade of the thick woods.

It is not shy, and trusts to protective coloring rather than to flight. When discovered, " it sits upright, draws the feathers close to the body, and erects the ear-tufts, resembling in appearance a piece of weather-beaten bark more than a bird." In flight it is swift and noiseless, and flits about on moonlight nights like a huge black shadow. It has a habit of always flying to the same tree to devour its food, of taking a nap afterwards, and on awakening, of ejecting the undigested portions of food in little wads, which may be found in heaps under the tree. This is a curious performance ; the bird yawns once or twice, and then shakes its head violently sidewise till the pellet is dislodged from its throat.

During the nesting season the male bird is exceedingly devoted to his mate, frequently occupying the nest with her or sitting on a branch of the same tree in close proximity. The incubation requires three weeks; the young stay in the nest about five weeks and afterwards hide in the trees, not catching their own food until eight or nine weeks old.

Major Bendire describes the nest of a pair of these owls less than two feet above an excavation occupied by a family of flickers. The owls were late in nesting, it being a second or third brood, and the families were reared at the same time, neither apparently paying any attention to the other. As the young of these owls keep up a constant calling for food all night long, this brood doubtless disturbed the slumbers of the young flickers. Their note is a low, not unmusical, whistling call, but during the breeding season they hoot like screech owls.

367. SHORT-EARED OWL. — *Asio accipitrinus.*

FAMILY : The Horned Owls and Hoot Owls.

Length: 15.50.

Adults: Ear-tufts conspicuous ; a blackening around the eye, and conspicuous white eyebrow ; plumage tawny to buff, heavily streaked with dark brown ; wings and tail broadly and irregularly barred with dark brown and tawny.

Young: Above dark brown ; under parts grayish buffy ; face brownish black.

Geographical Distribution: Western hemisphere ; common winter visitant in California, some remaining through the summer.

Breeding Range: In California, breeds sparingly on certain coast marshes.

Breeding Season: March 15 to May 15.

Nest: A few sticks ; lined with grasses and feathers ; placed on the ground in the long grass of the meadow, or at the foot of a bush, or beside a log, or in a rabbit burrow.

Eggs: 4 to 6 ; white. Size 1.56 × 1.19.

THE habits of the Short-eared Owl differ so greatly from those of the rest of its family that it is sometimes called the Marsh Owl. It is rarely seen in a tree, and never in the dense woods. On bright days it sits concealed in the long grass of a marsh ; but at dusk or in cloudy weather it can be found hunting its food over the low, wet meadows. In California it breeds on the coast marshes and islands, making its nest on the ground and lining it with feathers from its own body. Incubation lasts nearly four weeks.

The young are more fully feathered when hatched than most young owls. They soon flutter about in the grass with their parents, sitting patiently beside a marsh rat's run, or chasing grasshoppers with awkward fluttering hops. The adult, although it usually flies low over the marshes, may be seen during the breeding season flying quite high in the air and uttering a shrill, high, yelping call.

The food of these owls consists mostly of mice and quadrupeds, but they are very fond of terns, which they pursue through the open, and which, being the better fliers, usually make good their escape. They are eminently gregarious, remaining in flocks and colonies of several hundred.

373 c. CALIFORNIA SCREECH OWL. — *Megascops asio bendirei.*

FAMILY : The Horned Owls and Hoot Owls.

Length : 10.00.
Adults : Ear-tufts conspicuous, about an inch in length ; upper parts brownish gray, heavily streaked with black or dusky ; under parts grayish, with heavy streaks and indistinct cross lines of black.
Young : Plumage barred grayish and whitish.
Downy Young : Covered with a pure white cottony down.
Geographical Distribution : Throughout California.
Breeding Range : In wooded districts throughout the State.
Breeding Season : March to June.
Nest : A cavity in a tree, usually oak or cottonwood.
Eggs : 3 or 4 ; white.   Size 1.40 × 1.17.

THIS bird may be known by its small size and conspicuous ear-tufts.   It breeds commonly throughout California.   On June 15 one was seen going into a red-shafted flicker excavation, eighteen feet from the ground, in an old stump near Santa Cruz.   An investigation showed five eggs, three of which were the flicker's. The Owl had evidently driven off the flicker and taken possession of the nest, and was brooding all the eggs indiscriminately.   Curious to know how it would come out, I hired a boy to watch it.   On June 17 the flicker eggs evidently had hatched, for every trace of their contents had disappeared, but the Owl's eggs were still there. Seven days later they hatched, and two funny Owlets thickly covered with white down were the result.   In order to look at them it was necessary to drive the mother from the cavity by rapping on the tree with a heavy rod, and even then she would not readily go.   All the feeding of the young was done at night, and each morning witnessed a fresh heap of debris under the nesthole, as well as in the nest itself. This habit of leaving all the remains of undigested food heaped just outside the burrow seems to me particularly stupid, but I have found it the case with burrowing owls also. Most birds are careful to remove all trace from the vicinity, in order not to betray the nesting place, as well as for cleanliness.

The parent Owls were remarkably silent when at the nest tree, uttering no sound beyond an occasional odd chuck when one arrived with food for the young before the other had left it. After careful observation, we decided that the young were fed upon insects at first, and afterwards upon mice. The adults came and went every half-hour during the evening, and our presence so near did not seem to bother them in the least. One of them usually sat on the stump, pending the absence of the other, but not infrequently both left at the same time. The young Owls remained in the nest tree eight weeks, and then, one day, were seen sitting side by side among the thick foliage of a neighboring oak.

This species is strictly nocturnal in habits, and is one of the most important aids to the farmer in ridding him of mice and insects, though song birds and sparrows are also among its victims. Like most birds of prey, it is fond of bathing, and may be found just at dusk or dawn in a quiet corner of a small brook or pond, splashing and ducking energetically with evident enjoyment. I have watched one shake himself after such a bath until his mandibles rattled like castanets, and a funnier sight I never saw. Then every feather was carefully combed out with the point of the bill until it felt comfortable and lay well in its place. For birds so untidy in the care of their nest, these Owls are surprisingly particular about their own toilet.

375 a. PACIFIC HORNED OWL. — *Bubo virginianus pacificus.*

FAMILY : The Horned Owls and Hoot Owls.

Length : About 16.00 to 18.00.
Adults : Upper parts grayish, mottled with buff and darker ; under parts heavily mottled light and dark grayish.
Geographical Distribution : The wood regions west and south of the humid coast belt, almost throughout the State.
Breeding Range : Same as *Geographical Distribution.*
Breeding Season : February, March, and April.
Nest : In hollow trees ; 30 to 50 feet from the ground.
Eggs : 3 ; white.

AMONG the tall redwood timber about Rowardennan, the hooting of a chorus of Horned Owls at dusk is a weird, ghostly sound. The theory has been advanced that the call of the owl is a means of terrifying the small animals, which, by their excitement, would reveal their presence to the keen ears of the soft-winged hunter. But this is not always the case, for those six or eight Horned Owls which congregated each night in the trees close together, and made the moonlight hours vocal with their uncanny notes, evidently did so from the mere joy of too-hooing. The effect in itself was bad enough, but when one thought of the timid little wood creatures trembling in their nests from terror at the sound, one longed to wring the necks of the ghostly choir and end their music forever. Yet, when a friend offered the same result with a gun, the relief was declined. The next day when we found many despoiled nests and I was told that these same Owls were the ravagers, I regretted my clemency.

This species breeds more or less abundantly throughout the redwood district and in most of the mountainous regions of the State. So early in the year do they commence their cares that January sometimes finds young in the nest. The only pair with whose domestic arrangements I ever attempted to interfere had domiciled themselves in a hollow tree, where, although at a distance of thirty or more feet from the ground, it was accessible from a ledge near by. All dreams of watching the young develop were rudely dispelled the first time an attempt was made to pry into the nest hole. The prier escaped with one finger badly damaged and nerves somewhat shaken, never again to meddle with that *Bubo* household.

The incubation lasted four weeks, and then we knew by the squeaking cries and hisses that issued from the nest, as well as by seeing the adults carry food, that the young were hatched. From that time on for nearly eleven weeks the devoted parents foraged for the brood, bringing food constantly, and never once did those small Owls venture to peep out of the hole in the daytime. Just at dusk we could hear them scrambling about and practising little " too-hoos," and fancied that we could see a head or two in the doorway. The adults roosted outside during the day, bringing food by sunshine or moonlight as it happened.

In Santa Cruz County the food of this species consists, I am sorry to say, oftener of poultry and song birds than of mammals, though squirrels, chipmunks, and lizards are among its victims. In other parts of the State, under different conditions, it is said to prefer rodents and to be of value to the farmers.

378. BURROWING OWL. — *Speotyto cunicularia hypogæa.*

FAMILY : The Horned Owls and Hoot Owls.

Length : 9.00–11.00.
Adults : Upper parts brownish, mottled with white and tawny ; under parts tawny to buff, barred with brown.
Young : Upper parts uniform brown, except darker bars on wing and tail ; under parts plain tawny.
Geographical Distribution : From the Pacific, east to Dakota and Texas.
Breeding Range : Same as *Geographical Distribution.*
Breeding Season : In California, April to June.
Nest : In a burrow of prairie dog, or rabbit, or badger, or gopher.
Eggs : 6 to 11 ; glossy white. Size 1.24 × 1.03.

ONE of the commonest sights throughout California is a pair of these little Owls sitting side by side at the entrance to their burrow, sunning themselves, or perched on a fence post or low stump, blinking wisely at the passer-by. They are numerous on the drive from San Diego to Tia Juana, and are scarcely less interesting to the Easterner than is the far-famed road-runner. In vicinities where the prairie dog abounds, many fairy stories are told of how he shares his home with the owls and with the rattlesnakes, but I believe there is no grain

of truth in them. The owls hunt among the burrows
for young mammals, and the offspring of the "dogs" are
doubtless a choice tidbit; the snakes crawl from hole to
hole for the same purpose, but include owl eggs and
nestlings in their menu. So far as I have been able to
observe, the "dogs" are in terror from both, but the

378. BURROWING OWL.

" They converse in soft love notes."

sudden advent of a human intruder causes the three
enemies to pop suddenly down the same hole with
surprising unanimity.

Usually one may find the Owls sitting at the doorway
of their own nest-burrow, which may be the excavation
of some badger or prairie dog whose claim they have
"jumped." If the young Owls are old enough, they will
be there also in the family circle, but at sight of a

human visitor they will scramble into the hole and hide, leaving the adults to fool him by flying away. If, however, only the adult birds are outside and there are eggs or young in the nest, the result is quite different. Their antics as they watch a person approaching from a distance of, say, fifty yards, are comical enough. They straighten up and duck excitedly, exactly as a tiny chicken makes a show of his fighting powers, bending so low that the head nearly touches the ground. Then straightening up again, they turn their wise-looking heads slowly from side to side, as if to see the effect, and duck again. Finally one, presumably the male, decides to fly and the other pops into the burrow. It is of no use to try to coax or drive the mother out. She will seize and bite a stick thrust into the nest, but out she will not come, and the only way to see her is to dig for her. All about the door are heaps of cow or horse dung and wads of hair and bones, and I believe the same usually continues to the end of the burrow. It did in the only one I ever excavated.

Incubation begins any time in March, April, or May, and lasts three weeks. Both parents assist, and frequently both brood at the same time at the end of the burrow, which is from four to ten feet long. Usually, however, one acts as sentinel at the door.

While the courtship of these queer birds lacks the grotesqueness of that of the sage grouse, it has some features no less amusing ; after watching a pair, you will conclude, as I did, that the sofa-pillow caricatures are not far from the truth. Sitting as close together as

possible on top of their chosen burrow, they converse
in soft love notes not unlike a far-away " kow-kow-kow"
of a cuckoo; at the same time caressing with head rub-
bings and billings.

Although the Burrowing Owl is more or less shy, it
is not at all difficult to study its habits, and none of the
owls are better worth while.   Only one thing is needful,
patience, — patience to lie flat on your face in the broil-
ing sun with field glass glued to your eyes, hour after
hour, and, if you are a woman, thoughts of possible
lizards or rattlers tormenting your inner consciousness.
But the game is worth the candle, as always in nature
study.   On the Tulare plains you may watch them at
any hour of the day hunting grasshoppers, crickets, mice,
gophers, squirrels, lizards, and shore larks.   You may
even see them kill bull snakes that are crawling too near
their nest.   This war they wage on bull snakes has
doubtless given them the reputation of killing rattlers,
but I know they are afraid of the latter and scramble
away with queer sidewise hops, breaking into flight at
the near approach of one.

379. PYGMY OWL. — *Glaucidium gnoma.*

FAMILY : The Owls.

Length: 6.50–7.50.

Adults: Upper parts grayish brown or reddish brown or drab ; top of
head speckled with white ; under parts white, thickly streaked with
dark brown ; tail barred with white and blackish ; face encircled by a
dusky border.

Young: Similar, with head not speckled.

Downy Young: Gray, merging to white.

Geographical Distribution: Western North America through the timbered
  regions, from British Columbia to Mexico ; not in the humid coast
  district.
Breeding Range: Throughout its habitat.
Breeding Season: April 20 to June 15.
Nest: In deserted woodpeckers' holes.
Eggs: 4 ; white.

THE Pygmy Owl is a tenant of old woodpeckers'
holes all through the San Bernardino Mountains. Early
in May it may be seen sitting close beside its mate near
the trunk of a pine tree, looking somewhat like a huge
pine cone wrong end up. It is a very love-sick wooer,
and the indifference of petite Madame Owl is, we are all
convinced, only feigned. All the soft, purring love notes
may come from the throat of the male, but after lying
concealed and listening for hours at different times, I
felt certain that it was a conversation in which both took
part. The home of this pair was in a charred tree-trunk
next to the pine in which they used to sit morning and
evening. They were so chubby that it seemed to me the
doorway must be too small ; but evidently it suited, for
on May 20 there were four white eggs in it, and from
that time on Madame Owl was a devoted mother. I
watched closely but never saw the male go to the nest
between 7 A. M. and 5 P. M. As soon as the sun's
brightest rays were gone, he would call softly from the
pine, and soon a small brown head appeared in the
round doorway. After a moment of sleepy winking and
blinking at the great sun sinking behind the trees, the
head would come farther out of the nest hole, followed
by the plump brown body, and the next instant there
were two in that old pine tree. It was comical to watch

her stretch each little leg in its pantalette of feathers and give a few preliminary wing flaps, as if so relieved to be out of that dark hole and into the free air once more. But she is hungry, and soon flits down through the low shrubs to hunt grasshoppers or small lizards, while her mate goes into the nest to brood. He does not always do this, I am told, but in the case of one brood I watched the male took his turn on the eggs each night and morning. I judged him to be a male bird from his trimmer appearance and long absence from home during the daylight hours, which he spent largely in eating. Often he would perch on the top of the nest shrub and fluff out all his feathers in a sun-bath, until he looked like a miniature porcupine. This was his favorite place to breakfast also, but I never saw him eat there during the brightest hours of the day. These he spent in the shady depths of the old pine tree.

When the young were hatched, — eighteen days after the first eggs were laid, — they were covered with a cottony down of a soft mouse-color, merging to whitish on under parts, the funniest little puff-ball nestlings imaginable, in size not larger than a walnut. Grasshoppers and various kinds of insects were carried to them by both parents throughout the day. At night the mother remained in the nest while the male hid in the thick foliage of the pine, but with the sun's first ray both were astir hunting breakfast for the hungry babies.

385.   ROAD-RUNNER

Geococcyx californianus

III. — COMMON LAND BIRDS IN COLOR GROUPS

WITH BROWN PREDOMINATING IN PLUMAGE

385.   ROAD–RUNNER. — *Geococcyx californianus.*

(Common names: Chaparral Cock; Ground Cuckoo; Lizard Bird.)

FAMILY: The Road-runners, Anis, and Cuckoos.

Length: 20.00–24.00.

Adults: Upper parts iridescent blue-black on head, neck, and shoulders; metallic greenish brown on lower back, tail, and wings; feathers broadly edged with white; tail-feathers blue-black, broadly tipped with white; under parts whitish, and throat streaked dull buff and blackish; naked skin in front of the eye, blue and orange; feathers of the head and neck stiff and bristly; tail long and graduated; four white thumb marks on the under tail-feathers.

Geographical Distribution: Texas, New Mexico, Southern California, west through California, south into Mexico.

Breeding Range: Throughout its habitat.

Breeding Season: March 15 to July 1.

Nest: A platform of twigs; lined with cowhair, leaves, or feathers, or nearly unlined; variously placed in bushes or trees, from 3 to 8 feet from the ground.

Eggs: 2 to 12; buffy white.   Size 1.56 × 1.23.

THE "Road-runner" is well named.   No matter how long one has lived in California or how familiar one may be with Western birds, the novelty of seeing one of these birds dart out of the chaparral and race down the road ahead of one never loses its charm.   "It takes a right smart horse to keep up with him."   Do not expect to overtake him or to win the race.   A brisk trot merely keeps you the same distance behind him, and a faster gait only sends him scudding along more rapidly.   When

tired, or if he sees that you are gaining on him, he
dodges into the roadside thicket, stopping so suddenly
as to go heels (or rather *tail*) over head. It is a unique
performance, and one never becomes quite used to it.

Few birds are more interesting to study, or better
repay observation. The Road-runners are common residents of the valleys and desert regions of California,
from the Mexican border north to Sacramento valley.
In the southern part of the State and in Mexico they
are occasionally found at an altitude of five thousand
feet, but they prefer the lower range of the cactus-
covered plains and foot-hills.

Their food consists of insects, land crustacea, small
reptiles of all varieties, young birds, and field-mice.
They are popularly believed to destroy rattlesnakes, but
Mr. Bendire denies this. At the same time he reports
having found a garter-snake twenty inches long in the
crop of one of them. A Road-runner killed by Mr.
Anthony had just swallowed a large lizard. Undoubtedly its fondness for lizard diet has given it one of
its many nicknames.

In habits, the Road-runners are shy, suspicious, and
unsocial. Except during the breeding season, I have
rarely seen more than one in a neighborhood. Just
before rearing their brood, and for some time after, they
feed and roost in pairs. In the choice of nesting site
and material they are capricious. Of several nests examined, no two were alike. One found in May was in
a manzanita bush about four feet from the ground, was
lined with rootlets and a few feathers, and contained

five eggs. Another in an oak, eight feet from the
ground, looked as if it might have been built originally
by a jay and relined with a few dried leaves. Several
were in clumps of cactus; and one was within a foot of
the ground, on a broken part of a log, well sheltered by
bushes, — the bird perhaps having fancied that the log
was part of the bush. This nest was quite elaborately
constructed of twigs and lined with cow-hair, snake-
skin, and feathers interwoven with rootlets. It contained, June 3, five young birds, covered with quills.
Twenty-four hours later, every feather on three of them
had burst its sheath, and they were apparently ready for
their début; but they clung desperately to the nest with
their strong feet when an attempt was made to lift them
from it. The noise made by the young resembled the
click of two pieces of wood — not metal — striking
sharply together, and did not fail to bring both parents
to the scene. They were very angry, and presented a
ludicrous though more or less formidable defence, with
bills snapping sharply, wings and head bristling, and
long tail wagging. But they preferred discretion to
valor, and on being pursued slunk away swiftly after the
manner of cuckoos.

In Southern California the Road-runners begin nesting
in March, and eggs are found late in June; hence we
may infer that in some instances even three broods are
raised in a single season. I believe, however, that this
is true only when an accident destroys the eggs or young
of the earlier broods. The Mexicans insist that the
pairs remain united throughout the entire year; but I

doubt if there is good scientific authority for such a statement, and, like the rattlesnake story, it should be taken with a grain of allowance.

Although so shy, these birds are very inquisitive, often coming close to human habitations for apparently no other reason than to satisfy their curiosity. A ranchman told me about a Road-runner that carried off a bright red ribbon half a yard long, which he had picked up in the road, running as fast as his swift legs could carry him with the ribbon fluttering behind him like a flag. Nor do I doubt this, after having seen a very amusing comedy played by one of these birds. The sole actor was a handsome cock, who was jumping backward and forward over a clump of sagebrush at least eight times in succession, each time leaping higher than before. At first I thought it was some sort of love-dance; but no female was in sight. Then I fancied he might be killing some enemy, he seemed so excited. But the passage of a horseman startled him, and away he ran on a merry race, with nothing in his beak. There was no trace of anything on the ground by the time I could cross the thirty yards' distance to investigate.

The usual note of the Road-runner is a modification of the "kow-kow-kow" of the yellow-billed cuckoo into a softer "coo-coo-coo," which some one has likened to the "coo" of a mourning dove; but this is varied by the chuckling notes I have heard a crow utter when talking to himself, and it occasionally degenerates into a cackle.

387 a. CALIFORNIA CUCKOO. — *Coccyzus americanus occidentalis.*

FAMILY : The Road-runners and Cuckoos.

Length : 13.00.

Adults : Upper parts grayish brown, slightly glossed with greenish ;
under parts white, tinged with gray on chest ; lower mandible yellow ;
tail with broad white thumb-marks on the tips ; middle tail-feathers
brown, tipped with black ; remainder iridescent blue-black.

Young : Similar to adults, but duller.

Geographical Distribution : Western United States and Lower California.

Breeding Range : In California the breeding range seems to be confined
to the willow bottoms.

Breeding Season : May, June, July, and August.

Nest : A loose platform of sticks ; sometimes lined with leaves and
catkins.

Eggs : 3 or 4 ; glossy light bluish green ; paler in the incubated than in
the fresh laid. Size 1.27 × 0.89.

THE California Cuckoo, or Western Yellow-billed
Cuckoo, breeds extensively along the willow bottoms of
the interior valleys of the State. Mrs. Eckstrom says :
" As a nest-builder the cuckoo is no genius ; or, if a
genius, he belongs to the impressionist school. The
nest is but a raft of sticks flung into the fork of a
bough." Indeed so frail and so loosely put together is
it that one may see the eggs from underneath. Occasionally an individual will be found who aims at better
things and has made some slight attempt to line her
cradle with grass. Most of these twig platforms are so
shallow that an effort to peep into them will result in
spilling the contents, and a windstorm often scatters the
eggs over the ground in spite of the mother's care.
When this happens, or when the eggs have been stolen,

a second set is laid in another nest, and for this the unfortunate bird sometimes occupies the abandoned nests of other birds. There is no authentic record of her having left her own eggs to be brooded by another, however, and the accusation of parasitic parenthood is, in her case, unjust. It belongs rather to the European species.

Always shy haunters of the willow thickets, cuckoos are most apt to be heard during the mating season, which varies from May, in San Bernardino County, where they are more or less scarce, to the last of August in Sacramento valley, although a brood of the latter date, as noted by Major Bendire, undoubtedly was a belated one.

The only brood of the Western Yellow-billed Cuckoo that I have watched develop was housed in a willow clump in Santa Clara valley. The last of three pale green eggs was laid May 30, and incubation began the next day. For eighteen days the slim brown mother brooded; and when, at the end of that time, three wriggling, naked birdlings filled the nest, her watchful care was doubled. Noiselessly as a shadow she would slip through the low bushes with a cricket in her bill, and during the early hours of the morning one or the other of the parents was *en route* continually with food for the hungry but silent nestlings. These were fed by regurgitation at first, and they grew surprisingly as the days went by. At the end of twenty days they were covered with pinfeathers and looked like tiny porcupines. Suddenly, on the twenty-first day, these sheaths burst, and the young Cuckoos were arrayed in all the glory of real plumage. The next day the three left the nest and I was unable to find them again.

During this period of brooding and caring for the young the adult Cuckoos, though at first suspicious, became somewhat reconciled to my visits; at any rate, they neither moved the eggs — as cuckoos have been thought to do when disturbed — nor deserted them. At my approach the mother would ruffle her feathers until the usually sleek, slender bird seemed to be bristling with rage, her head extended on a level with her body and her long tail slightly elevated. But though her eye followed me with unwinking intensity, she would not desert her post, nor did I ever force her to do so.

The clear " kow-kow-kow " of the father-bird could be heard far into the night, if the moon

B.H.

387 a. CALIFORNIA CUCKOO.

" He was busy feasting where the tent caterpillars nested."

lighted the lowlands, and during the day it floated through the wood like a wandering voice. It was difficult to tell by the sound just how far away he was, but I knew that he was busy feasting where the tent caterpillars nested. In my heart I blessed him for his choice of food, for he is the only bird that will touch these pests, and even he clips off the hairs before he swallows the morsel.

413. RED-SHAFTED FLICKER. — *Colaptes cafer collaris.*

FAMILY : The Woodpeckers.

Length : 12.75–14.00.

Adult Male : General color of body and head brownish, becoming noticeably grayer on back of neck ; rump white ; back narrowly barred with black ; tail black ; nuchal band and mustache red ; a black crescent on chest ; under side of wings and tail red ; under parts thickly spotted with round black dots.

Adult Female : Like male, but malar stripe usually buffy.

Young : Like adults, but with no mustache.

Geographical Distribution : Western United States from Rocky Mountains to the Pacific coast ; north to Sitka, south to Mexico.

California Breeding Range : In suitable localities throughout the State.

Breeding Season : May and June.

Nest : In trees or stumps, from 2 to 70 feet from the ground ; and also in sides of banks.

Eggs : 5 to 10 ; white.   Size 1.12 × 0.86.

THE Eastern flicker, known as " yellow-hammer," " high-holer," or " golden-shafted woodpecker," is represented in California by the Red-shafted Flicker, a bird similar in everything except his red malar stripe and the under surface of the wing-quills and tail-feathers, which in his case are rose-color or soft scarlet instead of yellow. In call-notes, nesting habits, and food the Western is

identical with the Eastern species. The nest is a hole
eighteen or twenty inches deep and four inches wide at
the bottom, with an entrance two inches in diameter at
the top. It is made in old stumps or dead trees, gate-
posts, nooks and crannies in deserted buildings, and
sometimes in banks of earth. Both male and female
birds share in the excavation, working in turns of about
twenty minutes each. The site having been chosen, the
male clings to the surface and marks with his bill a more
or less regular circle in a series of dots, then begins excavating inside this area, using his bill, not with a sidewise twist, as do many of the woodpecker family, but
striking downwards and prying off the chips as with
a pickaxe. When his mate has rested and wishes to
share in the labor, she calls from a near-by tree and he
instantly quits his task. In a few moments, before one
has realized how or whence she came, the female has
taken his place and the chips are flying merrily. As
a rule, the birds work only early in the morning and late
in the afternoon, taking from ten to fourteen days to
finish the excavation. By the middle of May there have
been laid seven or eight beautiful, glossy-white eggs,
having a pearly lustre, and so transparent that when
fresh the yolks show through the shell. As incubation
advances, the shells become more opaque, until, when
ready to hatch, they have a limy ring around the middle,
showing where the shell will part. In fifteen days
appear the most grotesque of all bird babies, unless it be
those of the pileated woodpecker or of the cormorant.
Their bodies are the shape, size, and color of a pink rub-

ber ball, such as children use for playing "jacks." Two
worm-like appendages, for embryo wings, dangle helplessly, and two long, sprawly, weak legs are set far back
on the ball-like body. An extremely long neck waves
aimlessly, ending in a camel-like head, the lower mandible of the wide mouth projecting beyond the upper;
there are black, skinny knobs for eyes and curious, large
ear-holes. If placed on a level surface, these animated
balls roll about helplessly, the only way of steadying
themselves apparently being by bracing and pushing with
their heads. As they are fed by regurgitation they will
swallow two inches of one's finger and hold on so tightly
that they may be lifted up by it. Having been unable
to complete my observations at Lake Tahoe, I once took
two of these ungainly but interesting pets, when three
days old, from California to Chicago, on the "Overland,"
feeding them with hard-boiled yolk of egg mixed with
water, potato, and grated carrot. They were remarkably well behaved, and excepting an occasional clatter-
ing noise, somewhat between a mowing-machine and
a nestful of bees, they were silent and throve well. In
feeding, I first gave them the food and then allowed
them to suck a finger, shaking them by moving it, as I
had seen the parents do, as otherwise they would have
been unable to swallow. As they grew older they were
given mocking-bird food, composed largely of ants' eggs
and resembling their natural diet.

When left to the parent, however, they are brought up
in a much more hygienic fashion. For nearly three weeks
they are fed by regurgitation, and after that time the in-

sects brought are masticated by the parents. The adult, coming with food, lights on the tree at one side of the nest-hole, and instantly the small doorway blossoms with two or three grotesque heads, mouths wide open and ready. Meanwhile all the infants are joining in the buzzing chorus that announces their hunger in language plainer than speech. The parent inserts his bill into the throat of each one in turn, shaking the nestling back and forth vigorously. When all have been fed, he retires behind the tree trunk out of sight, to wait until the hub-bub subsides and to determine whether any of the young-sters are still hungry or are only crying from habit.

After they are old enough to leave the nursery, they follow their parents about for nearly two weeks, begging to be fed and gradually learning to hunt for themselves. This lesson is wisely taught by the parents, who place the food under a crevice in the bark, in full sight of the young, who must pick it out or go hungry. The baby cocks his head wisely, looks at it, and proceeds to pull it out and dine.

Flickers are essentially ant-eating woodpeckers, and consequently are seen upon the ground oftener than any other variety. They run their long bills down into the ant-hills, and, extending their spiny, sticky tongues still farther, withdraw them covered with eggs and larvæ. Their call-note is a shrill " wicker-wicker-wick-wick-wick," and sometimes, when angry, a high, screaming " hii-k-ha." The wooing of a pair of these birds is the most ludicrous performance that can be imagined, and well worth watching.

418 b. DUSKY POORWILL, OR CALIFORNIA POOR-WILL. — *Phalænoptilus nuttalli californicus.*

FAMILY: The Goatsuckers.

Length : 7.00–8.00.

Adult Male : Upper parts blackish or dark brown, with a velvety moth-like surface, barred with finely mottled grayish brown and distinct black arrow-shaped markings ; middle of crown black ; tail-feathers, except the middle ones, tipped with white ; sides of head and chin black ; white throat-patch bordered with black ; under-tail coverts buffy ; rest of under parts barred.

Adult Female : Like male, but tail-feathers tipped with a narrower band of white.

Young : Upper parts grayish, finely mixed with brown ; markings less distinct.

Geographical Distribution : From the foot-hill regions west of the Sierra Nevada to the coast and south to Lower California.

California Breeding Range : Latitude of Upper Sonora, west of the Sierra Nevada.

Breeding Season : May.

Nest : No nest, eggs being laid on the ground.

Eggs : 2 ; glossy white, with a faint pinkish tint. Size 1.00 × 0.76.

THROUGHOUT the coast region of California I believe the Dusky Poorwill is a rather common summer visitant, if not a summer resident. It is a haunter of cañons and deep woody places, never of the open. I found the eggs of a bird of this species on the bare ground at the foot of a tree in Marin County. The mother was brooding ; she flushed from literally under my feet, brushing me as she took flight and hid in the deep wood, and I found the eggs scarcely a foot from where I was standing. Marking the tree and leaving for several hours, I returned to find her on the eggs again, and this time watched her through my glass, not going nearer than fifteen feet. So far as I could judge in that way, she corresponded perfectly to the mounted specimen of the Dusky Poorwill which I had seen, but it was my first experience with the live bird. Three days later, when I went to the spot, there were two downy young ones in the nest, looking so much like the shadows on the pine needles that at first I could not see them and, but for the mother's antics, would have given up the search. She flopped about on the ground, feigning a broken wing, wallowing among the leaves, and whining like a young puppy. I picked up one of the fuzzy babies, looked it over carefully, and replacing it, withdrew to hide and watch. For two hours she did nothing but brood them, but thereafter I was rewarded by seeing her lug one off to a distance of half a rod and drop down with it in a fern tangle. In a moment she came back for the other and repeated the performance.

During the early evening hours of my watching she left the nest and came again, but apparently brought nothing in her bill, and if she fed them then it was by regurgitation. In all this time I saw nothing of the other parent either in the wood or near the nest, and do not think he paid any attention to the cares of the family.

The Poorwills are nocturnal and crepuscular in habits, feeding upon night-moths, beetles, grasshoppers, and gnats, and ejecting the indigestible parts in the same manner as do the owls. Like owls also, they are absolutely noiseless and bat-like in flight. Their note is the well-known soft, two-syllabled call, so imperfectly represented by letters, and rapidly repeated with scarcely a pause for breath throughout the evening hours.

Although it may never have been heard before by the watcher, it may be instantly and instinctively recognized as it floats out of the deep ravine or from the darkness of the woods.

420. NIGHTHAWK. — *Chordeiles virginianus.*

(Common names: Bull Bat; Mosquito Hawk; Will-o'-the-Wisp.)

FAMILY: The Goatsuckers.

Length: About 9.00.

Adult Male: Upper parts black, mottled with gray and buffy; a white or buffy patch on the wing; tail, except the middle feathers, banded with white near the tip; throat white; chest black; belly barred black and white.

Adult Female: No white on tail; otherwise like male.

Downy Young: Covered with thin yellowish brown down mottled with darker.

Young: Markings less distinct than on adults.

Geographical Distribution: In California, the Transition and Boreal zones of the northern end of the State, and south through the Sierra Nevada; recorded during migration through the western valleys; south in winter to the tropics.

California Breeding Range: Wooded districts of northern part of the State.

Breeding Season: May 15 to June 15.

Nest: None; eggs laid on the bare ground.

Eggs: 2; vary from pale olive-buff to buffy and grayish white; thickly mottled and dashed with varied tints of darker gray, olive, or even blackish, marbled, and clouded with lavender. Size 1.25 × 0.85.

WITH the exception of the Texan nighthawk the sub-species of nighthawks occurring in California resemble each other so closely that it is impossible to distinguish them without shooting, and their ranges overlap in such a way as to make locality an uncertain guide. Therefore only one species, *Chordeiles virginianus,* of which the

others are subspecies, will be here recorded. The characteristics of this species may be regarded as belonging
to all.

Although called "Nighthawk," it really hunts almost
as much by day, and may be seen late in the afternoon or
early in the morning, skimming over the water or low
wet ground with graceful swallow-like flight. Its food
consists of the insects found in the air and near the
water, swarms of small gnats, small night-moths and
flies. These it catches in its capacious mouth in the
same manner that a fisherman uses a scoop net, the
"whiskers" helping to trap the prey. It may easily be
distinguished from the poorwill, which it closely resembles, by the conspicuous white patches on its wings, which,
when seen from beneath in flight, look like holes. It is
known also by its diurnal habits, as it seldom flies after
the sun has set. The poorwill, on the contrary, unless
flushed, never flies by daylight, but hides through the
sunny hours in the shadows of the deep wood, usually crouching on the ground or on a well-shaded log.
Nighthawks spend the middle of the day squatting
lengthwise on a limb, their feet, like those of the poorwills, being too weak to perch. Here they sleep, trusting for safety to protective coloring, and refuse to move
unless startled into flight.

They make no nest, but lay their two speckled eggs
on the bare ground usually in plain view of the passer-by,
and not infrequently on the flat gravel roofs of buildings.
Always a well-drained, rather sunny place is selected,
and the eggs are less frequently found than one would

suppose, because their color usually blends so well with that of their surroundings.

Incubation lasts sixteen days, and it is a question how far the male shares in it. In some cases he does; but as a rule he prefers to watch from a limb overhead so long as there are eggs only. So soon as these become animated bits of bird life, his interest is aroused, and he is quite as ready to guard them as is the mother. The newly hatched young are little balls of rusty down, mottled slightly with dusky, and have the characteristic

420. NIGHTHAWK.

"*Crept back as often as she was driven away.*"

large head, wide mouth, and short thick neck of the adults, so that you know at once to what family they belong. They are carefully guarded by one of the parents continually, and if molested they will likely be removed to another hiding-place; but the nighthawks remove their young less frequently than the poorwills.

The feeding of the nestlings is accomplished by a modified regurgitation, the small insects being brought in the gular pouch or cheeks of the parent. A female that we found on the nest would not leave the young until flushed, and then she crept back as often as she was driven away, all the time spitting like a cat and ruffling her feathers like an angry owl. I believe this was due to her courage in defending her young and not to any stupidity. The next day she had removed them, and we did not find them again. Other cases of as great courage on the part of both adults of this species I have noticed, and am sure that the Nighthawks are more devoted to their nests and young than any other birds I have studied.

On the wing, Nighthawks are very sociable, circling in flocks and twittering after the manner of chimney-swifts, to which they are closely related, and uttering their characteristic " boom " which has given them the name of " night jar." They seem always to be having a good time together, — a jolly good fellowship, as it were, — that fits in well with the joy of morning or the glory of evening.

421. TEXAN NIGHTHAWK. — *Chordeiles acutipennis texensis.*

FAMILY : The Goatsuckers.

Length : 8.00–9.00.

Adult Male : Upper parts dull mottled gray, streaked with rusty black ; chest and under parts barred black and light brown ; throat white ; a white band-like patch crossing wing ; wing-coverts spotted and mottled with brown.

Adult Female : Similar, but wing-patch buffy.

Young : Finely mottled above ; under parts washed with pale red-brown.

Geographical Distribution : Southern border of United States from Texas to Southern California, north to Utah, south to Cape St. Lucas.

Breeding Range : In California, the southeastern portion of the State.

Breeding Season: April and May.

Nest: None ; eggs laid on the bare ground.

Eggs: 2; clay-colored, dotted, mottled, or marbled with brown and obscure lilac. Size 1.07 × 0.77.

MR. GRINNELL says the Texan Nighthawk is a common summer visitant throughout the Lower Sonoran zone, and occurs as far north as Stanislaus and San Benito counties. Mr. Bendire records it at San Joaquin County, and Mr. Merriam found it breeding in Inyo County.

It is the smallest of all the nighthawks found in the United States. Like the other varieties, it is gregarious while feeding ; it skims over the water like a swallow, and scoops the tiny gnats in its wide mouth. It is said not to make the peculiar booming of the Eastern nighthawk, but to utter a peculiar humming sound while on the wing.

Dr. Merrill writes of it : " The eggs are usually deposited in exposed situations, among sparse chaparral, on ground baked almost as hard as brick by the intense heat of the sun. One set of eggs was placed on a small piece of tin within a foot or two of a frequented path. The female sits close, and when flushed flies a few feet and speedily returns to its eggs. They make no attempt to drive an intruder away. I have ridden up to within five feet of a female on her eggs, dismounted, tied my horse and put my hand on the bird before she would move. . . . The notes are a mewing call and a very curious call that is with difficulty described. It is somewhat like the distant and very rapid tapping of a large woodpecker, accompanied by a humming sound, and it is almost impossible to tell in what direction or what distance the bird is that makes the noise. Both these notes are uttered on the wing or on the ground, and by both sexes.

457. SAY PHŒBE. — *Sayornis saya.*

FAMILY: The Flycatchers.

Length : 7.50–8.05.
Adult : Upper parts dark brownish gray; tail black ; belly light cinnamon, merging to light brownish gray on breast.
Young : Similar to adults, but wing-coverts tipped with brown.
Geographical Distribution : Western United States, north to arctic circle, south to Mexico.
California Breeding Range : East of the Sierra Nevada to Lower California.
Breeding Season : March 10 to June 20.
Nest : Of weed stems, dry grasses, moss, plant fibre, wool, spider webs, hair, and sometimes of mud ; the lining generally composed of wool or hair ; placed on projecting ledges, protected by overhanging walls, in old tunnels, about barns, or under bridges.
Eggs : 3 to 6 ; white.   Size 0.75 × 0.61.

SOMEWHAT larger than the Eastern phœbe is the Western representative of the family. It has a wide geographical distribution, breeding from the arctic circle to the southern limit of the United States. In habits and general characteristics it resembles the Eastern phœbe, returning among the earliest spring migrants to its old home, whether that be just inside the borders of Southern California or in frosty Alaska. For in whatever spot the Say Phœbe has reared its first brood it will continue to nest year after year.

This species is found in greatest numbers in the open country, seldom or never frequenting the deep forests.

Originally, all phœbes built on sheltered ledges of cliffs,
or shelves in caves, or on any jutting bit of rock secured
from storm by an overhanging roof. But all this is
changed, now that men have conquered the wilderness
and caused it to blossom like the rose. These birds
were among the first to recognize the advantage of
human friendship and to seek its protection. Without
a question they preëmpted the beams of barns together
with the swallows, encroaching more and more upon the
new-found territory, until now they build their nests as
close to human dwellings as the owners will permit.
Beams of piazzas, window-ledges behind blinds, and
summer book-shelves nailed to the wall of the veranda
are among their chosen sites. Unlike her Eastern representative, *Sayornis saya* rarely uses mud in the construction of her home, making quite a flat structure of weed
stems, dry grasses, moss, wool, hair, spider webs, and
silky material from cocoons or plant down. Usually it
is smoothly lined with this silky fibre or wool, or sometimes hair. Four or five pearly eggs are laid, one each
day, and the day after the set is completed the mother
begins her cares. Incubation lasts two weeks, and
although the male does not brood he sits all day long
on a lookout near by. The newly hatched young are
naked except for a slight gray fuzz on their saffron skin.
Until six days old their eyes are closed by a skinny
membrane, and during this time they are fed by regurgitation. They mature very rapidly, and in two weeks
have their feathers well in order for their first attempts
to fly. Up to this time the father bird has diligently

fed and guarded both them and the mother, coming to the nest every two or three minutes with butterflies in his bill. But as soon as they are ready to try their wings, he assumes full charge, teaching them to fly and to catch insects on the wing in true flycatcher fashion.

Two, and occasionally three, broods are raised in a season. No sooner has the father fairly launched the young on the world than the industrious little mother repairs the nest, and in it lays a second set of pretty w h i t e eggs. Again she broods for fourteen d a y s, now seldom or never fed by her m a t e; but, since the days grow warmer, leaving oftener and for longer intervals to forage for herself. W h e n the second family is ready to fly, she takes charge of it unless the

457. Say Phœbe.

" The industrious little mother repairs the nest."

necessity of rearing a third brood should compel her to desert them; and then, from somewhere, the hitherto unnoticed male appears, to assume care of them. It is a mooted question whether any bird rears three broods in one year, and this is the only species for which I make the claim. While the same pairs usually return each year to the same locality to nest, some instances

of very unusual choice of sites have been recorded:
"in an old robin's nest placed in a bush four feet from
the ground "; in old tunnels and mining shafts, in prospect holes, in an old embankment, in burrows of the
bank swallows, etc. But always the nests are lined with
some soft warm material, such as wool or short hair.

The ordinary call-note of the Say Phœbe is a plaintive "phee-er," always accompanied by a twitch of the
tail and the raising and lowering of the crest. Besides
this note, during the mating season it utters a short low
warble.

462. WESTERN WOOD PEWEE. — *Contopus richardsonii.*

FAMILY : The Flycatchers.

Length : 6.20–6.75.

Adults : Upper parts dark grayish brown ; under parts washed with dark
gray ; belly and under tail-coverts whitish or tinged with yellow.

Young : Similar to adults with brownish wing-bars.

Geographical Distribution : Western North America, north to British
Columbia, east to Great Plains, south in winter to Mexico and South
America.

California Breeding Range : In Transition zone throughout the State.

Breeding Season : June and July.

Nest : Of plant fibre, rootlets, down, sage, and grass tops ; sometimes
covered with lichens or spider webs ; in trees, from 5 to 40 feet from
the ground.

Eggs : 2 to 4 ; irregularly spotted with brown and purple at the
larger end.

IN general characteristics the Western Wood Pewee
does not differ much from the common wood pewee of
the East. Its call-note is, however, harsher and more
emphatic, lacking the plaintive quality of the " peeah-
wee " heard morning and evening in the Eastern woods.
It is variously described as " pee-ee," " pee-eer," " pee-ah,"

" tweer," or " deer." It ranges from the valleys to the
higher Sierra Nevada, building its nest indiscriminately
in pine, cottonwood, aspen, oak, ash, or fruit trees, but
always near water. In habits it is essentially a flycatcher, darting out from a favorite perch to seize its
prey in the air. Mr. Lawrence advances the theory that
it feeds high among the tree-tops during the early morning and late evening, because the sunlight sets the insects
stirring there before it does those of the undergrowth.

The nests of this species are deeper and more solid
than those of the Eastern pewee, in whose shallow
structures the bare foundation branch sometimes shows
through the scanty lining. Fine dry grasses, vegetable
fibre, shredded inner bark and plant down, woven well
together and bound with web from spider or cocoon,
form the walls. A lining of softer material, with occasionally a few feathers, completes the cradle which, about
the middle of June, will contain two or three small eggs.
Both parents share in the building of the home, though
the male usually prefers to bring the material and the
female to weave the walls to her own liking. She alone
broods on the nest, but her little lover sits on a twig
near by, calling her "dear " in sweetest tones, and if he
makes two syllables of it, the meaning is just as clear.
At the end of two weeks his cocky airs tell you there
are babies in the wee nest, and that upon him falls the
tremendous responsibility of guarding and feeding them.
Small butterflies, gnats, all sorts of small winged insects
are the orthodox food for infant flycatchers, and are
swallowed at the rate of one every two minutes. Nor

does the supply ever quite equal the demand, for every visit of the devoted father is welcomed with wide-open mouths and quivering wings. At first all this feeding must be by regurgitation, the adult swallowing the insect first and partially digesting it in some cases, and in others merely moistening it with the saliva. After four or five days most of the food is given to the young in a fresh state.

474 a. PALLID HORNED LARK, OR DESERT HORNED LARK. — *Otocoris alpestris leucolæma.*

FAMILY: The Larks.

Length: Male 7.50–8.00.

Adult Male in Breeding Plumage: Fore part of crown, cheeks, horn-like tufts, and patch on the breast black; white stripe across forehead, extending back over the eyes; throat and sides of neck white, sometimes washed with yellow; sides of breast, nape, and upper parts pale cinnamon; the back more or less distinctly streaked with darker; belly white.

Adult Male in Fall and Winter: Plumage generally softer and colors more blended; black markings more or less obscured; chest often streaked or washed with gray.

Adult Female: Similar to male, but decidedly smaller; black on the head replaced by brownish or buffy; the back reddish, and the plumage streaked.

Young: Upper parts brownish, white parts washed with buffy; throat and sides of the head spotted.

Geographical Distribution: Great Plains and Great Basin of the United States; migrating in winter to Mexico.

California Breeding Range: In deserts of southeastern region.

Breeding Season: May 16 to July 21.

Nest: On the ground; well built of grass, roots, and bark; lined with hair and old cocoons.

Eggs: 3 to 4; grayish, irregularly marked with brown. Size 0.86 × 0.60.

IN every suitable locality throughout the great State of California some form of the Horned Lark is found.

From the Sierra Nevada to the coast, and from San Diego north to the vicinity of San Francisco, it is called the " Mexican Horned Lark " ; in the upper Sacramento valley we find the " Ruddy" and south through the interior to San José and Santa Barbara the " Streaked." In the northeastern corner, east of the Sierra Nevada, the species is known as the " Dusky," and that found on Santa Barbara Island is designated as the " Island Horned Lark." The distinction between these forms is one of size and color of plumage rather than structure or habits ; and while all are listed for purposes of identification, the description here given of the habits of the " Pallid " or " Desert " Horned Lark is true of all.

This is an abundant resident in the deserts of Southeastern California, east of the Sierra Nevada and through the Great Plains and Great Basin of the United States. It is characteristically terrestrial in all its ways, nesting and feeding on the ground, and is never found in heavily wooded districts. As its name implies, the arid, sandy regions where only stunted growth is found are the favorite haunts of this species. The others of its family, while equally terrestrial, prefer fallow fields, prairies, meadows, or edges of wet lowlands. The name of Horned Lark has been given them on account of the erectile tufts of black feathers on either side of the head, which, in anger, surprise, or the ardor of wooing, stand erect like tiny black horns. By this you may know them at first sight and love them ever after. Except during the breeding season, these birds are found in flocks ; but as soon as the spring rains are over they

separate, each pair preëmpting a quarter section of land
and setting up a homestead claim. Anywhere in the
open, sometimes close to a clump of sage, sometimes
almost in the travelled wagon road, the little nests are
made in a saucer-like hollow in the ground. The only
material used is dry buffalo grass or fine vegetation, a
small quantity of which usually lines the nest for the
earliest brood. In the second brood, however, whether
because of the warmer season or the carelessness of cus-
tom, the eggs are often laid on the bare ground, with
no attempt at nest-building.

While the mother prepares the cradle, the father
indulges in aerial concerts. You may hear the sweet,
tinkling music while yet he is a mere speck in the blue,
tumbling and turning with the rapture of his song. He
calls to his mate; she hears, you may be sure, and in
a moment she too is frolicking through the sunny air
as if life held no such word as care. But when the
snug little nest holds eggs, she foregoes the fun of a chase
over the fields and sits patiently for nine days, in heat
so intense that she gasps with open bill. It has seemed
to me the eggs would be cooked if left too long exposed
to the hot desert sun, and that her brooding was fully as
much to shield them from his fiery rays as to preserve
them from the cool night air with her body. If surprised on her eggs, the mother runs a few yards and
begins feeding as unconcernedly as possible; but if there
are young in the nest, both parents exhibit great distress. Back and forth over the field they fly, crying
"tseet, tseet!" in pitifully appealing tones, and trying

to muster courage sufficient to come down and defend their little ones.

The young larks leave the nest usually on the ninth day after hatching, although one brood certainly were gone on the fourth day, and one remained until the tenth. They are beautiful babies, of soft mottled light and dark brown and cream buffy; they are fed by both parents until fairly well grown, when the male takes entire charge, and the female scratches out another nest in the stubbly grass or sand. The education of the family thus depends entirely on the father bird, who may be found any sunny afternoon, initiating them into the mysteries of a dust bath, or standing beside them under a sagebush, panting in the terrible heat that beats down from the cloudless sky and up from the blistering sand. In the early morning you can watch them feeding on the insects and seeds on the ground. A little later in the season, if you are an early riser, you may witness their first singing lesson. With wide-eyed amazement and dawning envy they have watched their father rise twittering through the clear air ; and, one by one, they learn to do it too. The first I ever saw start gave a little bound, uttered a weak "tweet, tweet," and fluttered up about ten feet only to sink back again. But he was full of triumph and, unable to contain himself any longer, soon attempted a second flight. The method is very like that of the bobolink, though the result is far less brilliant. Yet so full of irrepressible joy in living is the Horned Lark that as you listen you are glad, like him, just to be alive.

474 e. MEXICAN HORNED LARK. — *Otocoris alpestris*
chrysolæma.

FAMILY : The Larks.

Length : Male 6.75–7.25 ; female 6.50–7.00.
Adults : Upper parts reddish, more brownish in female , nape, shoulders,
    and rump light reddish brown, in contrast to back ; breast pure white
    in both sexes.
Geographical Distribution : Coast district of California and south to
    Lower California.
Breeding Range : West of Sierra Nevada from San Diego to Marin
    County.
Breeding Season : April 15 to June 15.
Nest : On the ground ; of dried grasses ; similar to that of pallid horned
    lark.
Eggs : 2 to 4 ; resemble those of the pallid horned lark. Size 0.82 × 0.60.

474 f. RUDDY HORNED LARK. — *Otocoris alpestris*
rubea.

FAMILY : The Larks.

Length : Male 6.50–7.00 ; female 6.00–6.50.
Adults : Similar to the Mexican horned lark, but smaller and brighter
    colored ; hind neck, shoulders, and rump tawny cinnamon ; forehead,
    superciliary, and throat yellowish ; sides marked with reddish brown.
Geographical Distribution : California, in Sacramento and San Joaquin
    valleys.
California Breeding Range : Upper Sacramento valley.
Breeding Season : May to June 10.
Nest : Usually placed in a depression on the ground under a small bush,
    a tuft of grass, vines by the side of a clod of earth, or a small rock ;
    sometimes in a cultivated field ; composed of fine straw and grasses ;
    lined with horsehair.
Eggs : 2 to 4 ; pale olive buff, finely sprinkled with rusty gray. Size
    0.82 × 0.54.

474 g. STREAKED HORNED LARK. — *Otocoris alpestris strigata.*

FAMILY : The Larks.

Length: Male 6.75–7.25 ; female 6.25–6.50.

Adult Male: Upper parts dull olive-brown ; back broadly and conspicuously streaked with black ; nape and rump ruddy ; under parts generally pale yellow.

Adult Female: Similar, but upper parts more olivaceous and more distinctly streaked.

Geographical Distribution: Coast districts of Oregon, Washington, and British Columbia, west of the Cascade Mountains, south in winter to Southern California.

Breeding Range: Coast region of British Columbia, Washington, Oregon, and possibly the northwestern corner of California.

Breeding Season : May.

Nest : On the ground, in a depression ; of grass stems, and lined with cattle hair.

Eggs: 3 or 4 ; grayish or pale greenish tint. Size 0.83 × 0.56.

524. GRAY–CROWNED LEUCOSTICTE. — *Leucosticte tephrocotis.*

FAMILY : The Finches, Sparrows, etc.

Length: 5.75–6.85.

Adult Male: General plumage deep cinnamon-brown ; forehead and fore part of crown black ; rest of head gray, but not spreading down over ear-coverts ; bill black ; back, rump, and belly streaked with blackish ; upper tail-coverts, wings, and tail more or less tinged with pink ; winter plumage edged with whitish ; black crown smaller ; bill yellow, tipped with black.

Adult Female: Similar to male, but colors paler and duller; same change in winter.

Young : General plumage brownish, without the characteristic markings of the male.

Geographical Distribution: Along the crests of the Rocky Mountains and the Sierra Nevada and the highest peaks of the Cascades, from British America south to Mexico.

California Breeding Range: Locally in the upper Boreal along the Sierra Nevada from Mt. Shasta south to Mt. Whitney.

Breeding Season: June.

Nest: Carelessly arranged on a ledge of a bluff, or in a small crevice; composed of wild parsnip stalks, coarse grass stems, and lined with finer grasses.

Eggs: 4 or 5; white. Size 0.97 × 0.67.

WHERE the range of the Pipilo ends that of the Leucosticte begins. Far above the timber line, amid a wilderness of snow-clad peaks these Alpine dwellers have their home. Only the severest storms of winter are able to drive them to the shelter of the forest. Flying high over the topmost peak of the range, searching in the snow for beetles and bugs that a kind Providence sends there for their special nourishment, they lead charmed lives. Even bumblebees and butterflies are on their menu, coming as mysteriously as do the birds themselves. When storms swirl over the summit, they crowd together in the shelter of a rock or a snowbank. When the sun comes out again, they are off for a frolic over the chasms and gulches, or a dip in the icy water of the glacial lake. They are constantly in motion, and their clear, low "churr" is the embodiment of gayety. Somewhat shy during the breeding season, as soon

524. GRAY-CROWNED LEUCOSTICTE.

"Searching in the snow for beetles and bugs."

as the family cares are over they become as friendly as possible with the few who invade their haunts.

The nest is snugly hidden in a cleft in the rock underneath a crag, where the fury of the storm will pass it by. It is not an elaborate affair, but composed of weed stalks, and lined with deer moss and occasionally a few feathers. Late in June incubation begins, and it continues fourteen days. The newly hatched young are only thinly sprinkled with hair-like gray down and look not unlike baby juncos. They remain in the nest fully three weeks, and by the middle of August are able to fly nearly as well as the adults. In September the broods of the vicinity unite in bands of one or two families, frolicking and chattering about the summit as if it were midsummer, and braving the snowstorms until the cold dark November days drive them to the firs for shelter at night. Even then the adults fly back to the crests during the sunny hours, as if homesick for the bare, bleak crags and the broad vista of snowy peaks. By December they are well within the forest, whirling from place to place in masses like juncos, and sleeping huddled together in the heavy firs, sometimes almost buried in the snow but always sure of a joyous resurrection in the morning.

533. PINE SISKIN, OR PINE FINCH. — *Spinus pinus.*

FAMILY : The Finches, Sparrows, etc.

Length : 4.50–5.25.

Adults : Upper parts grayish or brownish ; under parts whitish ; whole body finely streaked with brown ; sulphur-yellow patches on wings and tail.

Young: Upper parts bright greenish yellow, tinged with brownish yellow ; feathers streaked, except on belly ; wing-bands and patches brown.

Geographical Distribution : Northern North America, west to the Pacific, south in winter to Gulf States and Mexico.

California Breeding Range : In Boreal and Transition zones, along the Sierra Nevada forests, south through the San Bernardino mountains ; also in Santa Cruz mountains.

Breeding Season : May and June.

Nest : Usually a rather flat compact structure of fine twigs, pine needles, grasses, rootlets, and plant fibres ; lined with fine rootlets and hair ; placed generally in pine or cedar trees, from 20 to 35 feet from the ground.

Eggs : 3 or 4 ; pale greenish blue, spotted with various shades of brown, especially at the larger end. Size 0.67 × 0.48.

HIGH up in the mountains the tramper will find these fascinating little birds flitting through the pines, flashing a glint of yellow from wings and tails as they dash from tree to tree.

Wherever a pine cone offers its seeds, or a clump of weeds hangs full of brown pods, a banquet is spread for the Siskins. With a merry note, strikingly like the " per-chic-o-ree " of the goldfinches, they settle down to the feast, only to rise and fly farther on as the whim seizes them. The flight also is of the graceful, undulating character, as the flight of the goldfinch, as if the birds were playing with the air rather than trying to go somewhere. Yet they can fly with speed and strength, and in the breeding season they indulge in dizzy aerial gymnastics, accompanied by their own merry music. Their song is a wheezy little tune in the ascending scale, — a kind of crescendo, — which sounds as if it were produced by inhalation rather than by exhalation, but so bubbling over with gladness as to be enchanting.

The nest of these charming feathered romps is high in a pine tree on the steep side of a cañon, so inaccessible that never have I looked into one. After the broods are reared and able to look out for themselves, the Pine Siskins band together in small flocks. So long as every bit of food is not covered with snow too deep for shaking off, they feast and frolic among the scrubby pines of the mountains until storms drive them to the foot-hills.

540 a. WESTERN VESPER SPARROW. — *Poœcetes gramineus confinis.*

FAMILY : The Finches, Sparrows, etc.

Length : 6.00–6.75.

Adults : Upper parts brownish gray, everywhere streaked with dusky ; bend of wing reddish brown ; outer tail-feathers mostly white ; under parts pale buffy white ; streaked along sides of throat and across chest with dark grayish brown.

Young : Similar to adult; but markings less distinct.

Geographical Distribution : Western North America, north to British America, east to Manitoba, south to Lower California and Mexico.

California Breeding Range : In the valleys east of the Sierra Nevada.

Breeding Season : May and June.

Nest : On the ground ; of dried grass.

Eggs : 3 to 6 ; pale buffy, or dull whitish, often blotched and streaked with reddish brown and lavender.   Size 0.80 × 0.60.

THE hall marks of this dull-colored haunter of grassy upland meadows and roadside thickets are its pale redbrown shoulders and white outer tail-feathers, shown as it flies low over the ground ahead of you. Rarely does it venture higher than the top of a fence post, or the low branch of a scrub pine, to sing its quaint melodious vesper hymn. As the sun sinks behind the dark trees it begins its chant, to end only when all the world is asleep, and when its music alone breaks the silence of the forest.

Hidden deep in the grass of the meadow is its nest, woven of grass and rootlets, and roofed with leaning green spears. Here, rendered doubly safe by her protective coloring, the pretty brown mother broods for twelve days, and though you may locate the spot you will find her difficult to discover. I have actually put my hand down within a few inches of the nest without noticing it, even when I was looking for it. The young are born without feathers and are blind, like most young birds; but they soon don coats of soft brown, indistinctly streaked with darker, and, did not their open mouths stretched up for food betray them, they would, I am sure, never be discovered. The feeding is by regurgitation for the first four days. In eight to ten days they are feathered, and leave the nest, though unable to fly. Like the meadowlarks, they remain hidden in the long grass, fed by both parents, and gradually becoming expert in picking up bugs for themselves.

In the fall the broods flock together in small companies, and leaving the high altitude of the breeding grounds, gradually work down to the brush-covered foot-hills for winter food and shelter.

542 b. WESTERN SAVANNA SPARROW. — *Ammodramus sandwichensis alaudinus.*

FAMILY : The Finches, Sparrows, etc.

Length : 4.75–5.90.
Adults : Upper parts brownish gray, streaked with black ; the streaks in
sharp contrast to feather-edgings of whitish, grayish, or buffy ; crown
stripe and superciliary usually yellow, sometimes white.
Young : Similar to adults, but light markings more buffy ; under parts
less distinctly marked ; superciliary stripe usually without yellow,
and finely streaked.
Geographical Distribution : Western North America, from Alaska south
in winter to Guatemala.
California Breeding Range : In valleys east of the Sierra Nevada recorded from Owens Lake.
Breeding Season : May and June.
Nest : On the ground, in meadows or other grassy places.
Eggs : 3 to 6 ; pale brownish, varying to dull whitish or greenish white,
spotted with brown. Size 0.75 × 0.55.

WHEN on a tramp through salt marsh or upland
meadow you flush a sparrow-like bird, with more white
in its plumage than most sparrows, and with yellow
about the eye and on the band of the wing, you may
write it down tentatively as a Western Savanna Sparrow.
If, a little later, you find it swinging on a grass stem,
uttering its "weak little insect-like trill," you may be
sure of its identity. He is one of the hardest of all the
sparrow tribe to observe, and the one least apt to be discovered by the bird-lover, because the moment he becomes aware of your presence he drops into the grass
and refuses to come into view. Even when flushed, his
flight is merely a short zigzag to the nearest cover. Yet
although you find so few, there are doubtless a large

number hidden in the weed patches and nesting in the wiry marsh grass. His song at best is so weak and low as to seem like the note of an insect, to one who has never heard it, and is not likely to attract attention unless the listener is very near.

In nesting habits the Savanna resembles the field sparrow described elsewhere.

542 c. BRYANT MARSH SPARROW. — *Ammodramus sandwichensis bryanti.*

FAMILY: The Finches, Sparrows, etc.

Length: 4.78–5.30.

Adults: Similar to the Western savanna sparrow, but darker and browner, with sides and breast usually more heavily streaked; the whole head often tinged with yellow.

Geographical Distribution: Salt marshes about San Francisco Bay, south in winter along the coast to the San Diegan district.

California Breeding Range: On marshes of San Francisco and Monterey Bays.

Breeding Season: May.

Nest: Placed on the ground, usually in a slight depression.

Eggs: 4 or 5; grayish white, irregularly blotched with shades of brown and marked with light purple. Size 0.73 × 0.57.

AMONG the thick rushes of the San Francisco Bay marshes the Bryant Marsh Sparrow makes its home. There you may find it swinging on a tule or warbling a short sweet song, as it flies out over the tangled sedges. Its nest is made on the ground among the coarse meadow grass at a safe distance from the edge of the marsh, to escape high tides. Here in the thickest tussock, or perhaps in a hollow in the soil, a thin mat of grass is scratched together and serves as a nursery. It is always more or less damp, but this does not to any marked degree interfere with the hatching. When near their nests these birds skulk through the rushes in the same manner as a rail, straddling along with one foot on one tule and the other on a second. In the shadow of the rushes one might easily mistake them for little black rails. After the four weeks of this constant brushing through the rushes to and from the nest, both parents present a decidedly threadbare appearance, and their tails are often almost as stringy as a rat's. Incubation lasts thirteen days, and the young remain in the nest ten days longer. They are fed mostly upon insects picked up in the damp grass or at the edge of the water.

543. BELDING MARSH SPARROW. — *Ammodramus beldingi.*

FAMILY : The Finches, Sparrows, etc.

Length : 5.00–5.25.

Adults : Upper parts olive-brown, with broad black streaks on back ; superciliary and median crown-stripe very indistinct or wanting ; fore-part of superciliary stripe greenish yellow ; sides of head and neck darker ; under parts more thickly and heavily marked with black ; under tail-coverts with concealed streaks.

Young : Similar to adults, but upper parts more buffy ; superciliary finely streaked and usually without yellow ; under parts less distinctly streaked.

Geographical Distribution : Salt marshes of Southern California south to Lower California and Todos Santos Island.

California Breeding Range : On southern coast marshes from Port Harford to National City.

Breeding Season : May.

Nest : Placed ın salt marsh mud, raised about 6 inches from the
  ground ; made of weed stalks, grass, horsehair, or feathers.
Eggs : 3 ; light blue, marked with lavender specks ; reddish brown
  blotches principally at the larger end.   Size 0.78 × 0.58.

THE Belding Marsh Sparrow is abundant on the
salt marshes near the coast of Southern California from
Santa Barbara south to Lower California.   It replaces
the Bryant marsh sparrow of the San Francisco Bay
region.   Like the latter, its nest is a thin mat of grass
on the ground as near the edge of the marsh as the tide
will allow.   In the vicinity of National City, San Diego
County, the nests outnumber those of any other sparrow.
Many of them are placed on tussocks of grass, which
raise them several inches above the ground.   Even then
they are usually quite damp, and we might expect to
find the eggs addled, which they doubtless would be
were not the water salt.   In May, or early June, the
newly hatched, naked, pinky grayish nestlings are to be
found wriggling their wrinkled necks and opening their
tiny mouths for food.   This consists of the insects picked
up from the wet vegetation, and the seeds of marsh
plants given at first by regurgitation.   By June 20 the
young sparrows are looking out for themselves, secure
in their protective coloring in the long grass.

544.   LARGE–BILLED SPARROW. — *Ammodramus*
rostratus.

FAMILY : The Finches, Sparrows, etc.

Length : 5.30.
Adults : Upper parts light grayish brown, indistinctly streaked with
  darker : under parts streaked with rusty brown : bill long and
  swollen and regularly curved from the base.

Geographical Distribution: Coast of Southern and Lower California; south in winter to Cape St. Lucas and Mexico.

California Breeding Range: Along the salt marshes of the coast from the San Diegan district north to Santa Barbara.

Nest and Eggs: Similar to those of the Belding marsh sparrow.

THE Large-billed Sparrow is found in the winter along the seacoast of Southern California from Santa Barbara to San Diego, usually close to the water; at San Pedro it might be called the Harbor Sparrow, as, according to Mr. Grinnell, it frequents the decks of vessels and haunts the wharves and breakwaters. Its breeding habits are so similar to those of the Belding marsh sparrow that no separate description is necessary. It may be known from all its kinsfolk by its large bill and the uniform pale brown of its upper parts.

544. LARGE-BILLED SPARROW.

"*It haunts the wharves and breakwaters.*"

546 a. WESTERN GRASSHOPPER SPARROW. — *Ammodramus savannarum bimaculatus.*

FAMILY: The Finches, Sparrows, etc.

Length: 5.00–5.50.

Adults: Upper parts reddish brown, black, gray, and buffy; feathers of back spotted with black and brown; median crown-stripe buffy, bordered on each side with blackish stripes; nuchal patch dull gray, marked with reddish brown ; edge of wings yellow ; under parts plain buffy on throat and sides ; belly white.

Young : Similar to adults, but with little or no reddish brown on upper parts, feathers being more conspicuously bordered with pale buffy and whitish ; median crown-stripe more ashy ; under parts dull buffy-whitish ; chest distinctly streaked with dusky.

Geographical Distribution : Western United States east to Great Plains, from British Columbia to Southern California and Arizona.

California Breeding Range : West of the Sierra Nevada, in valleys north to Sacramento, south to San Diego.

Breeding Season : April, May, and June.

Nest : On ground ; rather bulky and deep ; sometimes partially arched over ; made of dried grasses.

Eggs : 3 to 5 ; white, spotted with reddish brown, mixed with a few markings of black and lilac, mostly at the larger end. Size 0.75 × 0.57.

As its name implies, this tiny brown bird hides away in the grass and low shrubbery, like a wee brown mouse or a big brown grasshopper. Its weak, shrill "zee-ee-ee," so like the song of an insect, is readily passed by as belonging to such in the medley of meadow music, unless the listener is close to the little musician. It is even better known as the " Yellow-winged Sparrow " on account of the bright lemon-color at the bend of the wing. It is so shy that one seldom catches a glimpse of it, and "none but the grazing cattle know how many nests and birds are hidden in their pastures." Instead of flying up when alarmed, it runs deeper into the grass, and is seldom flushed. If driven to desperation by close quarters it may dart out in a short zigzag flight of a few yards and seek the first concealment that offers. Unlike most sparrows, it feeds mostly upon insects, and is of incalculable benefit to the farmer. Its nest is hidden in the meadow grass, and differs from that of most other ground birds in being deep and arched over.

552 a. WESTERN LARK SPARROW. — *Chondestes grammacus strigatus.*

FAMILY : The Finches, Sparrows, etc.

Length : 6.50–7.25.

Adults : Upper parts brownish or brownish gray, the back streaked with blackish ; crown and ear-coverts chestnut with median stripe white or buffy ; black and white streaks on side of head, bordering the chestnut patch, also a black streak along each side of throat ; a small black spot on middle of chest ; tail dark brown, all but middle feathers tipped with white ; under parts white, with a small black spot on breast.

Young : Upper parts buffy ; head without chestnut crown or patches or black and white streaks ; chest streaked with dusky.

Geographical Distribution : Western United States east to Great Plains and Middle Texas, south to Mexico, north to British Columbia.

California Breeding Range : Upper Sonoran zone, chiefly in interior valleys west of the Sierra Nevada.

Breeding Season : May and June.

Nest : Of dried grasses, plant stems, and fibres ; placed on the ground, or in bushes and trees.

Eggs : 3 to 6 ; white or pale bluish or brownish, speckled and lined, chiefly on the larger end, with black and brown. Size 0.50 × 0.60.

THE Lark Sparrow is one of the sweetest singers, as well as one of the most abundant of the Western sparrows.   Walking along the country roadside at any hour of the day during April, May, or June, one is likely to hear " a gush of silvery notes accompanied by a metallic tremolo," and find the singer swinging on a weed

552 a. WESTERN LARK SPARROW.

" *The singer.*"

stalk or on a low bush, ruffling his little throat with a continuous flow of music. Or he may be caught dancing before his demure brown sweetheart, ecstatically pouring out melody. It is difficult to go anywhere in the interior valleys of California and not see him. His striped head and white-bordered tail and sweet song are the characteristics by which you may identify him.

His nest is usually well hidden, either on the ground or in low bushes, and in going to it he skulks through the intervening foliage in a secretive fashion hard to follow. The young are like those of his kind, naked, except for thin down, and blind for the first few days, during which they are fed by regurgitation. They are well feathered on the tenth day, and at this stage scramble out of the nest at the approach of danger. Like young meadowlarks they spend their babyhood days in the concealment afforded by the grass and thickets, and not until able to fly do they follow the adults to the more conspicuous feeding grounds.

554. WHITE–CROWNED SPARROW. — *Zonotrichia leucophrys.*

FAMILY : The Finches, Sparrows, etc.

Length : 6.50–7.50.

Adults : Upper parts grayish brown, back streaked with brown or black ; crown with median white stripe, having lateral deep black stripe ; a broad white superciliary stripe, below which is a narrower black stripe behind the eye ; edge of wing white ; under parts plain gray.

Young : Similar to adults, but head striped brown and buffy instead of black and white ; under parts very light brown ; breast, sides of throat, and sides of belly streaked.

Geographical Distribution : United States and Canada, north to Lab-

rador ; in winter migrates stragglingly over the whole of the United
States and south into Mexico.

California Breeding Range: In the higher Sierra Nevada as far south
as Mt. Whitney.

Breeding Season: June and July.

Nest: Composed of fine twigs, weed stalks, and coarse material ; lined
with fine grasses and hair ; placed on the ground or in low bushes.

Eggs: 3 to 5 ; pale greenish blue, speckled with light reddish brown,
more thickly at the large end.   Size 0.89 × 0.63.

As the snow disappears from the sides of the Sierra
Nevada, the White-crowned Sparrow follows in its wake,
higher and higher, until it reaches the extreme limit of
the willows.   Among the dense thickets that border the
upper edge of the timber line it is most abundant, and
during June, July, and August its song rings constantly,
fine and clear.   During the breeding season it haunts the
willows along the mountain meadows, placing its nest
on the ground, or, more commonly, in the lower branches.
Its nest and young can with difficulty be told from those
of the song sparrow ; and as it scratches among the dry
leaves of the underbrush for insects with which to feed
the nestlings, its manner distinctly suggests the latter.
But here the resemblance ends ; the White-crowned
Sparrow is distinguished by its white crown and plain
gray breast, as well as by its large handsome form.

When there are eggs or young in the nest, the male
sings early and late, often piping his clear whistle when
all the world is silent.   I have heard him at intervals
until long past midnight, as if the joy of parenthood
forced him to waken and give to his sleepy mate and
little brood below the assurance that " All 's well."   Evidently the singer needs little rest, for with the earliest

dawn the whole thicket rings with his melody, rousing
the more drowsy willow-dwellers to rejoice with him.
"The ballad singer of the mountains," some one has
called him.

His is a vertical as well as longitudinal migration, for
when the September snow-flurries threaten, the various
broods form a straggling flock that retreat slowly before
the cold, until in October they have reached the valleys
of Southern California, and pass on farther south.

554 a. GAMBEL SPARROW, OR INTERMEDIATE SPARROW. — *Zonotrichia leucophrys gambelii.*

FAMILY: The Finches, Sparrows, etc.

Length: 5.75–6.75.

Adults: Similar to the white-crowned sparrow, but edge of wing pale yellow instead of white, and lores white or buffy instead of black, and white superciliary stripe extending to bill.

Geographical Distribution: Coast ranges of California and north to British Columbia, straggling east as far as Iowa, and south to Mexico.

Breeding Range: From Alaska and Montana to Eastern Oregon.

Breeding Season: June 15 to July 15.

Nest: Similar to that of the white-crowned sparrow, but placed in bushes, trees, and thick clumps of weeds.

Eggs: Similar to those of the white-crowned sparrow, but tinged with rusty brown.

IN form, coloring, and habits the Gambel Sparrow,
or Intermediate Sparrow, closely resembles the white-
crowned, of which it is a subspecies. It breeds in the
far north, returning to California in October, and is an
abundant winter visitant throughout the State. For
nesting habits, see "White-crowned Sparrow."

554 b. NUTTALL SPARROW. — *Zonotrichia leucophrys nuttalli.*

FAMILY : The Finches, Sparrows, etc.

Length : 6.00–7.00.

Adults : Like the white-crowned sparrow, but white superciliary stripe extending to bill ; lores white, and general coloration brown.

Geographical Distribution : British Columbia to Southern California, south in winter to Lower California.

California Breeding Range : Humid coast belt from Oregon south to Point Sur.

Breeding Season : March 15 to May 1.

Nest : Bulky ; of weed stems, and lined with grasses ; placed in thick clumps of weeds or low trees or bushes.

Eggs : 3 to 5 ; pale greenish blue, spotted with pale rusty. Size 0.87 × 0.64.

LIKE the intermediate sparrow, the Nuttall Sparrow is also a subspecies of the white-crowned, and similar in habits. It is a resident of the coast belt in the vicinity of Santa Cruz, and straggles as far south as Los Angeles in winter.

557. GOLDEN–CROWNED SPARROW. — *Zonotrichia coronata.*

FAMILY : The Finches, Sparrows, etc.

Length : 7.00–8.00.

Adults : Upper parts olive-brown, streaked on the back with rusty black ; two white wing-bars ; middle of crown yellow, between two black lines, the yellow merging to gray for the last third ; under parts gray, tinged with brown on sides.

Young : Similar, with forehead suffused with yellow, and black crown-stripes streaked with brown ; under parts soiled white.

Geographical Distribution : Pacific Coast, Southern California to Alaska, straggling to the Rocky Mountains and Wisconsin.

Breeding Range : Alaska.

Breeding Season : June.

Nest : Of weed stems ; lined with grasses ; placed in alder bushes.
Eggs : 4 to 5 ; pale greenish blue, heavily spotted with pale reddish
   brown.   Size 0.90 × 0.66.

Like the Gambel sparrow, the Golden-crowned Sparrow is found in California during the winter months only. He occurs at this season throughout the length of the State west of the Sierra Nevada, and is oftenest found near the haunts of men. City parks and dooryards are not infre-

557.   Golden-crowned Sparrow.

" Their food is chiefly weed seeds and winter berries."

quently his banquet hall, and he regards human friends almost as trustfully as do his less welcome English cousins in the East. Along the foot-hills the Golden-crowned frequents the thickets, keeping *on* rather than *in* the bushes. Other varieties, especially white crowned and *gambeli*, are often found in a flock of the Goldens, and are evidently received into the freemasonry of good-fellowship. Their food is chiefly weed seeds and winter berries, but insects are also eaten, and occasionally caterpillars.

560 a. WESTERN CHIPPING SPARROW. — *Spizella socialis arizonæ.*

FAMILY : The Finches, Sparrows, etc.

Length : 5.00–6.00.
Adults : Back light brown, narrowly streaked with black ; rump and tail gray ; top of head reddish brown, sometimes streaked with ashy and dark ; forehead black, with short white median line ; superciliary line white ; narrow line through the eye black ; sides of head gray ; under parts gray, whiter on chest, and throat unstreaked ; bill black.
Young : Top of head streaked brown and black ; breast streaked.
Geographical Distribution : Western North America, east to Rocky Mountains, north to beyond latitude 60° in summer ; south in winter to Southern Mexico.
California Breeding Range : Upper Sonoran to Boreal zone, nearly throughout the State.
Breeding Season : May and June.
Nest : Of fine grasses ; lined smoothly with horsehair ; placed in bushes or small trees.
Eggs : 3 to 5 ; light greenish blue, speckled around the larger end with black and brown.

THE Chipping Sparrow, or Hair Bird, is the universal favorite of the sparrow family. No other is so confiding, so trustful, building his nest in the fruit tree near the dooryard, or in the evergreen on the lawn, or even in a large rosebush. I have found him weaving his dainty hair-lined cradle in the same bush in which a thrasher was rearing his brood. The wee sparrow mother had dauntless courage, and allowed me to touch her before she could be induced to leave her nest, when the speckled eggs were laid. She was a fluffy, fascinating bit of soft grayish brown and buffy, with sparkling eyes that flashed indignant protest at my intrusion. After ten days, when those small eggs had hatched into nestlings, the life of both parents was full of care. The nestlings were fed by regurgitation for the first few days. After that insects of many sorts, and seed, were brought to the nest at surprisingly short intervals, yet those young Chippies were never satisfied; and long after they were well feathered and out of the nest they followed the parents about, begging constantly for food. They were exquisitely proportioned little creatures, from the time the thin fuzz began to show on their bald heads until they were clothed in soft brown feathers, like the adults.

The call note of this bird is a thin, shrill "chip, chip," which has given it its name. The fact that, wherever placed, the nest is always beautifully lined with horsehair, has won for it the nickname of "Hair Bird" in the East, and this name is equally applicable to the Western variety, though less frequently applied to it.

562. BREWER SPARROW. — *Spizella breweri.*

FAMILY : The Finches, Sparrows, etc.

Length : 5.00–5.60.

Adults : Entire upper parts grayish brown, streaked with blackish, less distinct on head and ear-coverts ; under parts soiled grayish ; winter plumage more buffy.

Young : Similar to adult, but chest and sides streaked with dusky ; upper parts less distinctly streaked ; wings with two distinct bands.

Geographical Distribution : Western United States east to Rocky Mountains, south to Mexico, north to British Columbia.

California Breeding Range : Arid foot-hill regions of the interior, chiefly along the southern Sierra Nevada.

Breeding Season : May and June.

Nest : Of dry grasses and rootlets ; lined with hair ; placed generally in sagebushes a few feet from the ground.

Eggs : Usually 4 ; light greenish blue, with reddish brown markings, chiefly at the larger end.   Size 0.69 × 0.53.

WHEREVER in California there is sagebrush there are Brewer Sparrows, be it in the arid deserts of the southern district, or among the foot-hills, or on the mountains. As Mrs. Bailey says, 8,400 feet high on the snowy crests of the sierras, " morning and evening the curious little tinkling song comes up from all over the brush, and it seems as if we had come upon a marsh full of singing though subdued, marsh wrens."

In appearance this sparrow is much like the clay-colored sparrow, but is paler and duller, being almost ashy on the under parts, and harmonizing well with the tones of its arid nesting ground. The nests are usually in sagebushes a foot or two from the ground, and, unlike those of most sparrows, are lined with hair. In this and in other habits it resembles the chipping sparrow, and the eggs are so like those of the latter as to be distinguishable from them with difficulty. It is sometimes called the "Sagebrush Chippie." The newly hatched young complete the family resemblance, being the same daintily proportioned little creatures that we find in the nests of the Eastern chipping sparrow or hair bird. As soon as they are able to fly, they care for themselves, and the parents turn their attention to another brood. In

the winter these birds wander to the coast and the San
Diegan district and south through the table-lands of
Mexico.

565. BLACK–CHINNED SPARROW. — *Spizella atrigularis.*

FAMILY : The Finches, Sparrows, etc.

Length: 5.50–5.75.

Adults: Upper parts rusty brownish, narrowly streaked with black ;
head, neck, and under parts gray, becoming white on belly and under
tail-coverts ; chin and upper throat black ; bill pinkish.

Young: Similar to adults, but chin and throat gray instead of black ;
chest indistinctly streaked.

Geographical Distribution: Arizona south to the southern border of the
United States and Lower California.

California Breeding Range: Arid foot-hill regions of the southern Sierra
Nevada and desert ranges.

Breeding Season: April and May.

Nest: Of grasses, on a foundation of leaves ; lined with hair ; usually
placed in low bushes.

Eggs: 3 to 5 ; light greenish blue.　Size 0.68 × 0.50.

THE Black-chinned is a common summer visitant in
the foot-hills of Southern California, and occasionally
wanders as far as Alameda and Monterey counties. It
haunts the grassy fields and low thickets on the edges of
meadows, where the clear, low trill is heard through
sunny hours. The nest is very like that of the Eastern
field sparrow in construction, but is placed in bushes
rather than on the ground.

Incubation lasts twelve days, and the young remain in
the nest ten days longer, being fed by one parent while
the other anxiously tries to attract the attention of the
intruder to himself. Rather than betray the hiding place

of the little brood, the adult will flit restlessly about for an hour with a bug in his bill, which he himself absolutely refuses to eat. Finally he compromises by alighting in the grass at some distance from the nest, and running under cover to the bush where it is located.

This species has the red bill of the field sparrow and is said to resemble it in song.

567 c. THURBER JUNCO, OR SIERRA JUNCO.

Junco hyemalis thurberi.

Family : The Finches, Sparrows, etc.

Length : 5.60–6.20.

Adults : Similar to the Oregon junco, but wings and tail longer ; head, throat, and breast black, sharply defined against light brown of back and white of under parts ; sides buffy.

Young : Similar to the young of the Oregon junco, only upper parts lighter.

Geographical Distribution : Sierra Nevada, the desert, and the southern coast ranges of California from Oregon to latitude 32°.

California Breeding Range : Transition and Boreal zones along the whole length of the Sierra Nevada.

Breeding Season : April to July 23.

Nest : Of dry grasses and bits of moss ; lined with finer materials of the same ; placed on the ground, usually under a bush.

Eggs : 4 or 5 ; bluish white, spotted with chestnut, red, and lavender, forming a ring around the larger end ; a few spots scattered over the smaller end. Size 0.71 × 0.58.

Before the snows had left the sides of Mt. Tallac, I found a nest of the Thurber Junco among the pines at its foot. Hidden snugly under the edge of a log and close by a clump of scarlet snowflower, it might have been secure from all detection had not the calls of the parents attracted my eager prying eyes. When I peeped in, the four nestlings were cuddled down on a bed of red-brown pine needles, so exactly matching their own striped plumage that at first I saw nothing. They were too old to be fooled into opening their bills for food, but crouched flat in fear, only their beady eyes telling me they were alive. As I put down my hand to take one, the four popped out of the nest with one accord so swiftly that I could not see what happened. Then ensued a search, long and painstaking, before I found even one. During all this time the excited father and mother were following me just overhead in the lowest branches, the "seep, seep" seeming to my strained imagination like "Don't, don't," but not once had they come to the ground. The instant I espied the youngster sitting placidly on the ground, they seemed intuitively to know it. With redoubled cries they flew down to him, evidently coaxing him to make some effort to escape. And he did try, but I had never photographed a Junco baby and this chance was too good to lose, so I caught him. Soon after I found two of the others. Once caught, they seemed to lose

B.H.

567 c. THURBER JUNCO.

"They protested with plaintive calls."

fear and ate readily while sitting contentedly on my hand. There was no difficulty in inducing them to sit for their pictures, nor did the parents interfere. From a near perch they protested with plaintive calls, but ceased to fly down as they had done when the little ones were first discovered.

On the same day that this brood were found, I flushed a mother from her nest on the lawn of the Hotel Tallac, not a hundred feet from the main entrance. In this case the nest was a little hollow in the ground, lined with dried grasses and entirely concealed by the green grass of the lawn. It was not near any tree or other protection, and, when built, must have been quite exposed to view before the grass had grown tall enough to cover it. Four eggs nearly ready to hatch were its precious contents, which I left as speedily as possible, trusting that no careless foot or knife of the mower would ruin the pretty home. Before I was twenty feet away the mother had returned to them and the father had ceased his anxious cries.

In this and subsequent broods in the same locality I noticed the same fondness for bathing as in the case of the Point Piños juncos at Monterey. No water was too icy for their plunge, but they usually chose an hour soon after noon when the sun was high, and sat in his rays to preen their little brown coats.

Their food was whatever could be picked up, whether crumbs scattered for them or weed seeds or fruit, and quite as often insects caught by hopping up from the grass or gathered from the trees. The green worms found on evergreen trees they ate with impunity, though I feel certain the same variety has killed other birds in the East.

567 d. POINT PINOS JUNCO. — *Junco hyemalis pinosus.*

FAMILY : The Finches, Sparrows, etc.

Length: 5.25–5.75.

Adults: Similar to the Thurber Junco, but the black on sides of head and throat replaced by slaty.

Young: Similar to the young of the Thurber Junco, but under parts more strongly tinged with buff.

Geographical Distribution: Vicinity of Monterey, California, north through San Mateo County, east through Santa Clara County, south to Point Sur.

California Breeding Range: Santa Cruz district south to Point Sur, north as far as King Mountain.

Breeding Season: May to August.

Nest: Of leaves ; lined with dead grasses and hair ; placed in a hollow at a clump of grass.

WHETHER seen in the beautiful grounds of Del Monte or in the pine forests of the Sierra Nevada, the Juncos are the same friendly little birds that we have known and loved as the " snow-birds " of the East. Some one has called them gray-robed monks and nuns, and the description fits them well. During the fall, winter, and early spring they are found in flocks of from ten to twenty, feeding on the ground, flying up at the approach of an intruder, only to alight again farther on. If you sit quietly they will hop quite near you, particularly the Point Pinos Juncos found at Monterey, who are accustomed to the presence of strangers in their haunts and have become as fearless as the English sparrows of the

East, hopping close to the benches and picking up food at your feet. They have a not unmusical call-note and a soft, sweet, twittering song. When the birds are about to begin housekeeping in the spring, this musical effort is heard at intervals all day long and is very pleasing. Both sexes coöperate at the preparation of the nest, which they build in a hollow under the roots of a tree, or, at Del Monte, under the heavy evergreens and low-growing shrubbery. It is a simple affair of pine needles or fine grass, and so nearly matches the bird in coloring as to render her practically invisible when sitting. The little Juncos, although born naked, soon don a pretty habit of striped light and dark brown, and are even more invisible than the adults among the reddish pine needles. They remain in the nest about ten days, when they are fully feathered and able to fly. They are fed by regurgitation for several days, and then with raw insects brought by both parents. For some time after making their début from the nest, the hungry youngsters follow the adults about, begging with quivering wings for food.

They are fond of bathing, and run into the spray of the lawn hose or splatter in the puddles made by it with utter disregard of the presence of gardener or guest. I have seen them pick up crumbs scattered for them by a Chinese helper within two feet of where he lay under a tree eating his own dinner. Evidently the most perfect camaraderie existed between the man and the birds, for when the feast was spread he called them by a peculiar squeaking noise and was instantly surrounded by several pairs. This was late in May, and they were housekeeping; but both male and female responded to the call, leaving the nest unguarded.

All these Juncos found at Del Monte or Monterey and vicinity are of the variety known as Point Pinos, a subspecies of the gray-headed or common junco of the Eastern States. In habits and song the species are closely identified.

574. BELL SPARROW. — *Amphispiza belli.*

FAMILY : The Finches, Sparrows, etc.

Length: 5.50–5.75.

Adults: Upper parts brownish gray, grayer on head and neck ; the back generally without distinct streaks ; orbital ring, spot over the eye, broad malar stripe, chin, throat, and under parts white ; black spot on middle of chest ; throat marked on sides with a continuous stripe of blackish ; wing-coverts edged with buffy ; edge of wing yellowish ; tail-feathers black, indistinctly marked with lighter.

Young: Upper parts light grayish brown, streaked with dusky ; under parts buffy ; chest distinctly streaked with dark gray ; wings with two rather distinct pale buff bands.

Geographical Distribution: West of the Sierra Nevada and San Bernardino mountains from Marin County to Lower California.

California Breeding Range: In upper Sonoran zone locally, west of the Sierra Nevada from latitude 38° southward.

Breeding Season: May and June.

Nest: Of grass stems and vegetable fibre ; lined with hair ; placed in low bushes.

Eggs: 3 or 4 ; pale greenish blue, finely dotted and speckled with dark reddish brown. Size 0.74 × 0.60.

THE Bell Sparrow is abundant on the bush-covered plains of Southern California as well as in the foot-hills. It is a thicket-dweller, darting from the cover of one clump to another with rapid flight as if uneasy in the open. Its nest is in the thickest of the bushes, but the anxious chirp of the male sparrow is sure to reveal his secret to the intruder. His song is a clear, monotonous twitter, not unmusical and full of enthusiasm. Only early in the breeding season does he attempt as much as this, usually preferring to flit silently through the thick foliage. His food consists of both insects and seeds, the latter predominating.

574 a. SAGE SPARROW. — *Amphispiza belli nevadensis.*

FAMILY: The Finches, Sparrows, etc.

Length: 6.00–7.00.

Adults: Upper parts light ashy brown, tinged with ash-gray, the back usually distinctly streaked with dusky; sides of throat marked with a series of narrow blackish streaks; under parts whitish, with black spot on chest; sides and flanks faintly tinged with light brown; outer web of lateral tail-feather white.

Young: Similar to adults, but upper parts and chest streaked; wings with two buffy bands.

Geographical Distribution: Sagebrush region of Western United States, north to Southern Idaho and Montana, east to Colorado and New Mexico, south to interior of Southern California and Western Mexico, west to Los Angeles.

California Breeding Range: In arid upper Sonoran and Transition zones, east of the Sierra Nevada. Arid desert region of Southeastern California.

Breeding Season: April and May.

Nest: Of shredded sagebrush bark, dry grasses, etc.; in a hollow in the ground, or lower branches of the sage or other bushes.

Eggs: 3 or 4; light greenish or dull grayish white, speckled all over with reddish brown and a few blotches of darker brown at the larger end. Size 0.80 × 0.60.

TRULY well named is the little gray bird called the Sage Sparrow. Everywhere in the sagebrush district his metallic call may be heard; and during the sunny spring days when the enthusiasm of nesting time inspires him to music, his sweet, ringing song is a delight to the ear. Little cares he for that. Swinging carelessly on the highest twig of the nest bush, he sings to his mate, not to you; and, the song finished, he disappears earthward in the gray-green foliage.

His nest is either hidden in a low crotch of a bush or on the ground underneath it, and so formed of sage-bark and leaves and dried grasses as to seem a part of its surroundings. Unless the nestlings are hungry and stretch up wide-open bills for food, you will be almost certain to overlook the nest. When on it the mother bird becomes practically invisible, so well does her soft coloring blend with the lights and shadows of the earth and leaves.

574 a. Sage Sparrow.

"*He sings to his mate, not to you.*"

The buds of the sage-brush form at least a part of their diet, but I am inclined to believe that insects form the larger half.

Mrs. Bailey says: "The absence of a continuous stripe on the side of the throat is enough to distinguish the Sage Sparrow from the Bell," and "his long black tail and its gently tilting motion are good long-range recognition marks."

580. RUFOUS–CROWNED SPARROW. — *Aimophila*
ruficeps.

FAMILY : The Finches, Sparrows, etc.

Length : 5.50–5.75.

Adults : Upper parts grayish or grayish brown ; back broadly streaked
   with reddish brown ; crown reddish brown ; under parts light brown,
   palest on throat and belly ; a distinct black stripe on each side of
   throat ; a rusty streak extending back from eye ; edge of wing dull
   white or grayish.

Young : Similar to adults, but upper parts dull brownish ; streaked
   with deeper ; under parts dull buffy, chest and sides streaked with
   dusky.

Geographical Distribution : California coast from about latitude 40°,
   south to Cape St. Lucas.

California Breeding Range : In upper Sonoran zone west of the Sierra
   Nevada from San Diego to Marin County.

Breeding Season : April to August.

Nest : Of coarse grass and weed stalks ; lined with a few hairs ; placed
   on the ground in a hollow.

Eggs : 3 to 5 ; plain white or bluish white. Size 0.89 × 0.65.

BRUSH-COVERED hillsides are the favorite haunts of
the Rufous-crowned Sparrow. Here, on the ground
under thick low bushes, its nest is hidden so securely
that only accidental discovery is possible.

The only way possible to observe these birds is to sit
motionless among the sparse growth of bushes on the
side of a hill and wait their coming with endless patience.
Their bright chestnut upper parts will serve to identify
them. A short, rather sweet song is sung morning and
evening during the nesting season, and occasionally in
their winter haunts in the interior valleys. Their food
is mainly seeds and fleshy seed-pods, such as haws.

581 a.   DESERT SONG SPARROW. — *Melospiza melodia*
fallax.

FAMILY : The Finches, Sparrows, etc.

Length : 6.10–6.50.
Adults : Upper parts light gray; back streaked with rusty, usually
without blackish shaft-line ; under parts brownish buffy; chest
streaked with chestnut.
Young : Upper parts dull brown ; back streaked with brown ; under
parts buffy white ; chest streaked.
Geographical Distribution : New Mexico, Arizona, Southern Nevada,
Utah, Southern and Lower California.
California Breeding Range : In extreme southeastern portion, along the
lower Colorado River.
Breeding Season : April and May.
Nest : Of grasses, weeds, and leaves ; lined with fine grass stems, roots,
and sometimes hair ; placed in low bushes, or in tufts of grass on the
ground.
Eggs : 4 ; light greenish or bluish white, more or less spotted with
brown.   Size 0.75 × 0.55.

THE Song Sparrow is a bird with a name that fits.
Every day in the month, every month in the year, you
may hear his ecstatic song.   In rain or shine, in heat or
cold, whether in Maine or California, he is the same
jolly fellow, singing his glad little roundelay, a "plain,
every-day home song with the heart left in."   And he
may be found everywhere.   No State in the Union lacks
the cheer of his sunny presence.   To be sure, he has
various prefixes to his name, — as in California he is
dubbed "Desert Song Sparrow," "Mountain Song Sparrow," "Heerman Song Sparrow," "Samuels," "Rusty,"
"Santa Barbara," "San Clementa," and "Merrill" Song
Sparrow, — each name indicating some variation of plumage due to environment.   In the extreme northern por-

tions he wears dark brown, while on the sands of the extreme south border he is almost clay-color. But the habits and song remain unchanged. Thoreau declares the Massachusetts maidens hear him say, " Maids, maids, maids, hang on your tea-kettle, tea-kettle, ettle-ettle," and this is exactly the advice he gives to campers in the sierras when the first rays of the sun strike the tops of the pine trees. Day has begun for bird and bird-lover. Then if you rise quickly and steal down to the edge of a mountain brook you may catch him at his bath. Whatever the locality or the subspecies, do not expect to see him at any great distance from water, for he is an inveterate splasher. I have seen him dip into a puddle whose edges were crusted with ice

581 a. DESERT SONG SPARROW.

" *In rain or shine, he is the same jolly fellow.*"

and apparently enjoy it as well as a bath in the heat of a July day.

When alarmed, his first impulse is to dart downward into the friendly shelter of bushes, pumping his expressive tail vigorously as he flies. But in rising from the

16

ground he hops from twig to twig and seldom, if ever, flies in any direction but downward or straight ahead.

Unlike some of the sparrow family, these birds do not travel in compact flocks. If several individuals are together, they are usually part of a scattered band that is working its way to or from the nesting ground.

The nests and nesting habits of all the various subspecies are so alike that one description will apply to all. The structure is usually near the ground, and often on it, with very little effort at concealment. Incubation lasts twelve days, and is shared by the male to a limited extent; but as soon as the little ones emerge from the shell the greater part of the labor of caring for them falls upon him. In ten days they are fully feathered and ready to leave the home shelter and follow him. As soon as this family are launched into the green forest, the busy mother prepares a new nest for a second brood. The male soon leaves the first to shift for themselves, and returns valiantly to his post of duty, guarding and feeding the next instalment with the same zealous care he had given the first.

581 b. MOUNTAIN SONG SPARROW. — *Melospiza melodia montana.*

FAMILY: The Finches, Sparrows, etc.

Length : 6.25–7.00.

Adults : Upper parts grayish, with narrow streaks of black and brown ; wings and tail brown ; under parts white ; chest and sides streaked with brown.

Young : Similar to adults, but upper parts paler and less tawny ; under parts whitish and streaks narrower.

Geographical Distribution: Rocky Mountain district, west to Nevada, Oregon, and Washington, and extending to Western Texas.

California Breeding Range: Eastern slope of the Sierra Nevada from Mt. Shasta to Mono Lake.

Breeding Season: May and June.

Nest and Eggs: Similar to those of the desert song sparrow.

581 c. HEERMAN SONG SPARROW. — *Melospiza melodia heermanni.*

FAMILY: The Finches, Sparrows, etc.

Length: 6.25–6.50.

Adults: Plumage brown or olive; upper and under parts streaked; flanks light grayish brown; spots on chest separate and distinct from one another.

Young: Similar to adults, but under parts tinged with brownish buff, having broad streaks.

Geographical Distribution: Interior districts of California, including eastern side of Sierra Nevada.

California Breeding Range: Along streams of the San Joaquin-Sacramento basin.

Breeding Season: March, April, and May.

Nest: Of grasses, weeds, and leaves; lined with finer grasses and sometimes hair; placed in bushes from 2 to 6 feet from the ground.

Eggs: Usually 4; bluish gray, spotted and blotched over most of the surface, with dark brown, the spots becoming more confluent at the larger end. Size 0.87 × 0.64.

581 d. SAMUELS SONG SPARROW. — *Melospiza melodia samuelis.*

FAMILY: The Finches, Sparrows, etc.

Length: 4.70–5.75.

Adults: Very similar to the Heerman song sparrow, only smaller.

Geographical Distribution: Coast of California.

California Breeding Range: Along the coast belt from Santa Cruz north to latitude 40°.

Breeding Season: March to June.

Nest: Of coarse dry grasses and weed stems; lined with finer kinds of the same ; placed on the ground beneath tufts of grass, in salt weeds, or low shrubs on the sand drifts.

Eggs: 3 or 4 ; bluish gray, spotted and blotched over the entire surface with reddish brown. Size 0.75 × 0.59.

581 e. RUSTY SONG SPARROW. — *Melospiza melodia morphna.*

FAMILY : The Finches, Sparrows, etc.

Length : 6.00–7.00.

Adults: Upper parts rusty brown, almost obscuring the black streaks ; chest with heavy dark brown markings ; flanks greenish olive.

Young : Upper parts dark brown, back streaked with blackish ; under parts buffy grayish ; chest and sides light brown, streaked with darker brown.

Geographical Distribution : Pacific coast district, Washington, Oregon, and Alaska ; south in winter to Southern California.

Breeding Range : Pacific coast region, from Northern California northward through Washington and Oregon.

Breeding Season : May and June.

Nest and Eggs : Very similar to those of the desert sparrow.

583. LINCOLN SPARROW. — *Melospiza lincolnii.*

FAMILY : The Finches, Sparrows, etc.

Length : 5.25–6.00.

Adults: Upper parts dark brown and olive, sharply streaked with black ; crown sharply streaked with black and divided by a median grayish line ; malar stripe, chest, and sides buffy ; sides and chest narrowly streaked with black.

Young : Similar to adults, but colors and streaks less sharply defined.

Geographical Distribution : Whole of North America south of Hudson Bay region.

California Breeding Range : Breeds sparingly along the high Sierra Nevada from Mt. Shasta south to near Mt. Whitney.

Breeding Season : June and July.

Nest : Of grasses ; placed on the ground.

Eggs : 3 ; light greenish white, heavily marked with chestnut and lavender gray, chiefly at the larger end. Size 0.79 × 0.58.

A SHY bird, skulking through the tangle of grass and bushes in the swampy borders of a marsh, is the Lincoln Sparrow. About the edges of a mountain meadow as well as in the wet lowlands, he flits in and out of the willows, giving the observer as little opportunity to see him as he can, and never so absorbed in his insect-hunting as to forget the presence of a stranger. His song is rarely heard, yet he has a happy little lay not unlike that of a song sparrow but inferior in quality.

His nest is deftly concealed on the ground, and he approaches it by a circuitous route, dodging through the grass and never by any chance revealing its whereabouts. Only by catching a glimpse of him with food in his bill one may be able to guess at its location, and that there are young to be fed.

585 a.   TOWNSEND SPARROW. — *Passerella iliaca unalaschcensis.*

FAMILY : The Finches, Sparrows, etc.

Length : 7.00–7.50.

Adults : Upper parts bright chestnut, mixed with gray ; wings, upper tail-coverts, and tail rusty brownish ; under parts white, with dark brown markings on chest.

Young : Similar to adults.

Geographical Distribution : Pacific coast region from Alaska south in winter to California.

Breeding Range : From British Columbia north through Alaska.

Breeding Season : May and June.

Nest : Of grasses, moss, and vegetable fibres, closely woven together ; placed near the ground, in dense thickets.

Eggs : 3 to 5 ; pale bluish green, spotted and blotched with reddish brown and lilac. Size 0.90 × 0.66.

THE Townsend Sparrow is one of the largest and reddest of all our fox sparrows, and in his musical efforts is surpassed by few of that family. In the quiet woodlands of his summer home, he sits on the topmost bough of the dusky thicket and pours out his joy in a song of exquisite melody, clear and pure as that of a thrush, yet lacking the spiritual quality of the latter. The song has a wonderful carrying power withal, that renders it peculiarly attractive.

But it is as a scratcher that he excels all his kind. Among the dead leaves under a thicket, he may be

585 a. TOWNSEND SPARROW.

"*The way he digs for his supper.*"

heard rivalling a towhee in the vigor with which he makes the dirt fly. A few steps forward, and a sudden kick out with both feet, then a thorough searching of the ground laid bare, is the way he digs for his supper. With the same energy that characterizes his scratching, he wooes his chestnut mate by alternate scoldings and songs, treating her with the lordly airs of a successful suitor, and fairly compelling her to accept him. To his credit be it said that he does his share of the nest building, such as it is, and though a tyrant, he is a brave guardian of his brood. When, after twelve days of patient brooding, the eggs are transformed into naked nestlings, he is ready to scratch enthusiastically all day for their sustenance. And this is really just what he is compelled to do so long as they remain in the nest and for at least two weeks afterwards. Then his fine song is hushed and only the metallic "tseep" of his call note is heard. Until the nestlings are three or four days old they are fed by regurgitation, and after that upon insect food.

Usually the Townsend Sparrows fly and feed in small flocks, often along the roadside thickets, and occasionally they stray into the city parks in the winter season. In the great State of California, with its varied climate, which produces variations of form and coloring, the fox sparrows have been divided into several subspecies. These are all so much alike in habits that the description of one applies to all, with a few modifications to be noted in the different subspecies.

585 b. THICK–BILLED SPARROW. — *Passerella iliaca megarhyncha.*

FAMILY : The Finches, Sparrows, etc.

Length : 7.00–7.75.
Adults : Bill thick ; upper parts plain brownish gray, becoming rusty brownish on wings, upper tail-coverts, and tail ; under parts white, with small dark brown spots on chest.
Young : Similar to adults.
Geographical Distribution : Mountains of California, including eastern slope of the Sierra Nevada. South in winter to Los Angeles County.
California Breeding Range : From Mt. Shasta south to Mt. Whitney, in Boreal and Transition zones.
Breeding Season : June.
Nest : Of plant fibre and willow bark ; lined with grasses and horsehair ; placed on or near the ground, in thickets.
Eggs : 3 or 4 ; pale bluish green, spotted with dark brown. Size 0.86 × 0.64.

THE Thick-billed Sparrow inhabits the forests of the Transition and Boreal zones, breeding among the evergreens. His big bill serves to identify him, and during the warm June days his loud clear song rings out from all the thickets early and late. In the winter this sub-species migrates southward to the San Diegan district.

585 d. STEPHENS SPARROW. — *Passerella iliaca stephensi.*

FAMILY: The Finches, Sparrows, etc.

Length: 7.10–7.90.

Adults: Similar to thick-billed sparrow, but averaging somewhat larger, with much larger bill.

Geographical Distribution: Mountains of California.

California Breeding Range: In Boreal zone on southern Sierra Nevada.

Breeding Season: April and May.

Nest and Eggs: Similar to those of the thick-billed sparrow.

591 b. CALIFORNIAN TOWHEE. — *Pipilo fuscus crissalis.*

FAMILY: The Finches, Sparrows, etc.

Length: 8.50–9.00.

Adults: Upper parts uniform grayish brown, darker on head; throat pale rusty, marked with dusky; belly whitish, washed on sides with grayish brown.

Young: Similar to adults, but browner; under parts buffy white; throat and belly rusty; throat streaked with darker.

Geographical Distribution: California, west of the Sierra Nevada from Shasta County, south to Santa Barbara County.

California Breeding Range: Upper Sonoran zone, west of the Sierra Nevada, south to latitude 35°, north to Shasta valley.

Breeding Season: April and May.

Nest: In trees or bushes, usually from 3 to 5 feet from the ground; occasionally in hollow trunks of trees, or in crevices of vine-covered rocks of cañons; made of twigs, bark, and grass; lined with rootlets.

Eggs: 4 or 5; bluish, marked with various shades of dark and light purple and black. Size 0.92 × 0.73.

THE Californian Towhee is the brown chippie, or long-tailed chippie, of common parlance throughout most of

California west of the Sierra Nevada. Unlike the shy
chewink of the Eastern States, it comes to village dooryards not only in winter but often to rear its brood.
Mr. Grinnell called my attention to a nest in a bush not
twenty feet from the house at Palo Alto, and remarked
that at Pasadena the Towhees usually nested upon the
ground, while at Palo Alto they were oftener found in
bushes. Mr. Shields records nests of the Californian
Towhee in crevices of vine-covered rocks, in hollow
trunks of trees, and in thickets five feet from the ground.
These Towhees are most devoted parents, resembling the
catbird in their piteous protests against any molesting
of their treasures. Early and late they scratch under the
dead leaves or in the rich garden soil for insects, or pick
up scattered grain in the barnyard, or crumbs at the
door. I have seen bits of muffin fed to the nestlings
with impunity, but their orthodox diet is small insects
and seeds, the former predominating while the parents
feed them. They are fed by regurgitation at first, but in
a few days they receive fresh food. As soon as able to
fly well, they take to the trees and spend only enough
time on the ground to satisfy their hunger.

The characteristic song, like the tinkle of a silver bell,
is heard oftenest at this time when, late in the afternoon, the little brood are safely housed in the sheltering
branches of an oak tree, and in the earliest dawn the
same clear notes come up from the copse on the edge
of the brook. For, unlike most birds, the Towhee sings
after his family cares are over as joyously as he did in
the full tide of his wooing. Mr. Frank Chapman's

happy description of some characteristics of the Eastern variety is applicable also to that called the Californian. He says:

"There is a vigorousness about the Towhee's notes and actions which suggests both a bursting, energetic disposition and a good constitution. He entirely dominates the thicket or bushy undergrowth in which he makes his home. The dead leaves fly before his attack; his white-tipped tail-feathers flash in the gloom of his haunts. He greets all passers with a brisk, inquiring *chewink, towhee;* and, if you pause to reply, with a *fluff, fluff* of his short, rounded wings he flies to a near-by limb better to inspect you.

"It is only when singing that the Towhee is fully at rest. Then a change comes over him; he is in love, and, mounting a low branch, he gives voice to his passion in song. I have long tried to express the Towhee song in words, but never succeeded as well as Ernest Thompson when he wrote it *chuck-burr, pill-a-willa-will-a.*"

591 c. ANTHONY TOWHEE. — *Pipilo fuscus senicula.*

FAMILY: The Finches, Sparrows, etc.

Length: 8.20–8.30.
Adults: Similar to Californian towhee, but smaller, darker, and grayer.
Geographical Distribution: Southern California.
California Breeding Range: Below Transition zone in the San Diegan district.
Breeding Season: March, April, and May.
Nest and Eggs: Similar to those of the Californian towhee.

THE Anthony Towhee chooses more southern breeding grounds than any of its Californian kinsfolk. This is the species commonly met with in the San Diegan district, and from there north to the valleys about Pasadena. Unless you have the two birds in hand, you are likely to mistake it for the Californian towhee, so similar is it in form and habits.

The song of the Anthony Towhee is less liquid and more metallic in quality. It is most effective in the twilight, when one singer after another takes up the short refrain, tossing it from bush to bush like the echo of fairy bells.

592.1. GREEN–TAILED TOWHEE. — *Oreospiza chlorura.*

FAMILY: The Finches, Sparrows, etc.

Length : 6.35–7.20.
Adults : Crown bright chestnut ; upper parts grayish olive, merging to bright olive-green on wings and tail ; throat, malar stripe, and middle of belly white ; edge of wing and under wing-coverts yellow.
Young : Grayish olive above, streaked with dark gray ; under parts whitish, streaked with dark.
Geographical Distribution : Rocky Mountains to the coast, north to Mt. Shasta, south to Lower California.
California Breeding Range : Higher Sierra Nevada and desert ranges from Mt. Shasta to San Bernardino mountains.
Breeding Season : June.
Nest : On or near the ground, in cactus, sagebrush, or chaparral; of twigs and weed stems ; lined with grass.
Eggs : 3 or 4 ; whitish, speckled with chestnut.

IN the higher Sierra Nevada, where the solitaire and leucosticte form the mountain chorus, look for the Green-tailed Towhee. Among all the mountain songsters he has few rivals. Whether perched on top of a clump of chaparral pouring out his rich bell-like music in the half-light of evening, or dodging among the dense brush, or running swiftly across the open spaces from bush to bush on the arid mountain sides, the Green-tailed Towhee has a manner distinctly his own. You may know him by his semi-erectile chestnut crown, white throat, and green tail.

His alarm note is a cat-like mew, lacking the harshness of the note of the catbird, and the insistent force of that of the spurred towhee. It is a polite protest against your intrusion. His song has somewhat of a thrush-like quality, but is more varied, possessing a vigor and enthusiasm not found in that of the more quiet singer.

His nest is hidden in, or under, one of the stunted bushes with which the rocky ground is covered, and, brooding there day after day, his olive mate is safe in her protective coloring. Newly hatched Towhees are the same naked nestlings, whether cuddled in a chaparral-sheltered nest of the mountains or rocked in a garden rosebush; dark bluish gray in color, with yellow bills, they are covered with a thin whitish down. They feather rapidly, and leave the nest when from ten to twelve days old, those of the warmer localities maturing somewhat sooner than those born on the edge of the Boreal zone. They follow the adults for several weeks, learning to jump forward and kick out backward, in scratching for their food, just as the

592.1. GREEN-TAILED TOWHEE.

"*A manner distinctly his own.*"

parents do. But this is only a small part of the hunting, for the Green-tail uses his bill more and his heels less in procuring his food than do others of his kind. Insects and seeds of all sorts are his chief diet.

596. BLACK–HEADED GROSBEAK. — *Zamelodia melanocephala.*

FAMILY : The Finches, Sparrows, etc.

Length: 7.50–8.90.

Adult Male: Upper parts mostly black ; rump and collar light chestnut ; wings and tail black ; two white wing-bars ; under parts buffy cinnamon, changing to lemon-yellow on belly and under wing-coverts.

Adult Female: Upper parts blackish brown, streaked with buffy ; collar and under parts buffy ; sides streaked ; belly pale yellowish ; under wing-coverts lemon-yellow.

Young: Similar to adult female, but without yellow on belly ; and back mottled, not streaked.

Geographical Distribution: Western United States, east to Great Plains, south to Mexico.

California Breeding Range: Upper Sonoran and Transition zones throughout the State.

Breeding Season: April, May, and June.

Nest: In trees or bushes, usually 5 to 20 feet from the ground ; made of twigs, weed stems, grass, and rootlets.

Eggs: 2 or 3 ; bluish white, speckled and blotched with rusty brown. Size 0.92 × 0.69.

AMONG the alders that border small streams in the valley, in the cherry orchards at cherry time, in the potato field when bugs are rife, in the oaks and evergreens of the lower Sierra Nevada, one may hear the metallic " eek, eek," of the Black-headed Grosbeak. But do not judge his vocal powers by this squeaky call-note, for he is a delightful musician. Unlike most woodland singers, he chooses the sunny hours of the midday for his best efforts. Then from high in an oak or pine he will whistle a rhapsody, so tender, so pure, so full of joy that it seems a floodtide of love let loose in music. But alas for sentiment! No sooner is one round finished than the singer turns his attention to feeding on the young buds nearest to him, sometimes even interrupting his song to seize an especially tempting morsel. And so it is throughout the long bright day, — he stops eating to break into singing, and pauses in his finest carol to finish a meal, flitting from tree to tree and daintily feasting upon the tender terminal buds. No doubt this may be a disadvantage to the tree, but when we see him industriously clearing a potato field of the pest known as " potato bug," and singing gayly as he works, we forgive him all the harm he has done to our pet fruit tree. It is impossible to watch him for one hour without becoming his loyal defender. Although a rather clumsy looking bird, his attitudes are always pleasing. He leans forward to reach a sprig beneath him much as a crossbill feeds on a cone, or he stands erect

596. BLACK-HEADED
GROSBEAK.

" *His little brown throat
swelling with music.*"

with the sunlight bringing out the strong contrasts in his plumage, and his little brown throat swelling with music; or, in masculine awkwardness, he tries to cover the eggs while his mate is enjoying a vacation. Nearly half of the daylight hours he takes her place, but at night it is the mother who broods. Often when the female has been gone a long time he calls her, coaxingly, querulously, and at last imperatively, but I have never seen him leave until she had returned. This constant care enables the Grosbeaks to defend their brood from the feathered kidnappers; and it is very necessary, for the nests are exposed to view from above. After a rest, when the mother has come to the nest again and settled herself comfortably with much turning and fluffing of feathers, she often indulges in a sweet, warbling soliloquy, — a faint imitation of her mate's brilliant song, but so low as to be inaudible at any great distance from the tree.

The little Grosbeaks look like over-sized sparrow babies, covered at first only with a sparse hair-like down on crown and shoulders and afterwards feathering out in soft shades of brown. The bill is wide, rather than swollen, and both it and the tottery legs are pale straw color.

From watching the adults gather insects for the young, I am confident that so long as they remain in the nest, they are fed upon an animal diet, and for the first few days by regurgitation. In a little less than two weeks they hop out onto the small branches, and by instinct are soon pecking at every green thing in sight. For some time they seem to keep with the adults, being fed and guarded tenderly by them.

Notwithstanding the assertion sometimes made that young birds do not sing, I know positively that young Grosbeaks sing when eight weeks old, though, of course, their song is only a low warble as compared with the finished song of the adult.

612. CLIFF SWALLOW. — *Petrochelidon lunifrons.*

FAMILY: The Swallows.

Length: 5.00–6.00.

Adults: Forehead white or brown ; crown, back, and patch on chest glossy blue-black ; rump cinnamon-buff ; throat and collar chestnut ; sides and flanks brown ; remainder of under parts white.

Young: Similar to adults, but colors duller and not sharply outlined ; chin and throat and often other parts of the head spotted with white ; tertials and tail-coverts margined with brown ; chestnut of head partly or wholly wanting ; upper parts dull blackish.

Geographical Distribution: Whole of North America ; migrating in winter to Central and South America.

California Breeding Range: Locally throughout the State.

Breeding Season: June and July.

Nest: Generally a round or retort-shaped structure, made of pellets of mud mixed with a few straws ; lined with feathers ; attached to cliffs or buildings.

Eggs: 3 to 5 ; white, speckled or spotted with brown and lilac. Size 0.82 × 0.56.

CLIFF SWALLOWS present a curious example of the adaptation of a species to its environment. Formerly these little masons were all cliff-dwellers, their adobe nests being hung on the side of a cliff; but the advent of man into the wilderness has brought many changes, and now it is not unusual to find a colony snugly ensconced beneath the eaves of the farmer's barn.

In 1902 these birds were nesting under the projecting tiles of the roofs covering one side of the quadrangle of Leland Stanford University. Students passed constantly just below them, but they showed no fear.

Unlike the retort-shaped nests of most Cliff Swallows, the majority of these nests were open at the top like a wall pocket. The material was sticky clay, and was gathered outside the quadrangle. The Swallows flew down to this in small companies, and there were always one or two on the way going or coming. They seemed to pick up as much as their mouths would hold, but whether they also filled their throats, as some aver, seemed doubtful. The only support I have found for this view is the shape and size of each pellet as seen in an old nest. Also, some of the nests were so much harder than others that it would seem there might have been a difference in the saliva of the builders.

In the case of these nests, the foundations were laid in a semi-circle, and on this were placed the pellets of mud, like bricks on a wall, thus building out and up at the same time. No straw or hair or other material than clay was used in the walls of these nests, but after they were completed a lining of feathers and fine grass was placed in them. We also found these Swallows building in the ruins of the patio of the old mission of San Juan Capistrano. Upon the quaint fresco designs of the chapel, the nests were plastered as abundantly as under the eaves of a barn. "Yesterday a great mission; to-day a nesting place for owls and swallows." Here, as at Palo Alto, in some of the nests housekeeping had begun, and the pretty head of the mother bird peered over the adobe rim when we rapped on the wall.

17

The young or Cliff Swallows are fed by regurgitation of small insects. These are caught, scoop-net fashion, by the adults in flying through swarms of the gnats and other small winged insects that hover in the air morning and evening, or that dance in the sunshine of mid-day. Once every ten or fifteen minutes is the usual time for a meal, but the intervals are shorter early in the morning after the night's fast, and late in the afternoon.

617. ROUGH-WINGED SWALLOW. — *Stelgidopteryx serripennis.*

FAMILY : The Swallows.

Length : 5.00–5.75.

Adults : Upper parts dull grayish brown, darker on wings and tail ; tertials usually margined with grayish ; under parts plain brownish gray ; belly and under tail-coverts white.

Young : Similar to adults, but plumage more or less tinged with brown ; wings with broad cinnamon tips and margins.

Geographical Distribution : United States, from Atlantic to Pacific, and adjoining British Provinces ; migrates to Guatemala.

California Breeding Range : Below Transition zone, east and south of humid coast belt.

Breeding Season : May and June.

Nest : In crevices of stone walls and bridges, and in holes in banks ; made of grasses and straws ; lined with a few feathers.

Eggs : 3 to 6 ; white. Size 0.75 × 0.53.

ALTHOUGH sometimes confounded with the bank swallow, the Rough-winged is slightly larger, lacks the sooty chest-band and clear white under parts, and has in addition the distinguishing serrated outer web of the outer primary. Both this variety and the bank swallow differ from the other members of their family in their lustreless sooty-gray plumage and entire absence of metallic coloring.

In habits the two are very much alike, nesting in banks and congregating in flocks for migration. The Rough-winged are, however, found in small colonies, — seldom more than two or three pairs in a bank, — and are more apt to choose a gravelly soil than are the bank swallows. They are somewhat less timid also, and sometimes make their nests about buildings. The one essential seems to be running water, and crevices in the abutments of bridges are often filled with their nests. The hooked edge of the wings, which has given them their name, seems to be slightly less prominent in the present species than in specimens collected fifty years ago, and it is possible that this characteristic will become modified as their environment changes.

619. CEDAR WAXWING. — *Ampelis cedrorum.*

FAMILY: The Waxwings and Phaïnopeplas.

Length : 6.50–7.50.

Adults : Crest, head, and under parts soft fawn-color, changing to olive-yellow on flanks ; streak through eye velvety black ; upper parts plain olive-gray, becoming blackish on wing-quills and tail ; the latter tipped with yellow ; both tail and wings sometimes tipped with red wax-like appendages.

Young : Similar, but colors duller, and under parts strongly, upper parts lightly, streaked.

Geographical Distribution : Whole temperate North America, from Atlantic to Pacific ; south in winter to Guatemala and West Indies.

Pacific Coast Breeding Range : In the humid Transition zone of Oregon, Washington, and British Columbia. No breeding record for California (Grinnell).

Breeding Season : June, July, and August.

Nest: Rather bulky; composed of bark, leaves, roots, twigs, weeds, paper, etc.; lined with finer grasses, hair, and wool; placed usually in cedar bushes or orchard trees, from 4 to 18 feet from the ground.
Eggs: 3 to 5; bluish or light slate-color, tinged with olive, spotted with brown and dark purple. Size 0.84 × 0.61

THE Cedar Waxwing has kept his individuality so unchanged in the transit from east to west that the California ornithologists have not been able to make a Western subspecies of him. In the coniferous forests of the Sierra Nevada they are the same handsome, gentle birds that we have known and loved in other parts of the United States. When other birds are absorbed with the cares of nest building, the Waxwings are leisurely flying in small companies low over the level tree-tops, or sunning themselves on the highest twig of the pines. After most of the forest nestlings are out of their cradles and foraging for themselves, the quiet Waxwings look about for a nesting site and commence building. Only the goldfinches are late enough to keep them company. Both male and female Waxwings bring material and fashion the nest, though the former does most of the work. It is a coarse affair to be the home of such dainty, satiny birds, and is often in or near a tree bearing berries or small fruit. Both sexes share in the incubation also, brooding by turns of from thirty to sixty minutes at a time; but it is the mother who sleeps there at night while the father perches in the same tree.

When large enough to leave the nest, the young Waxwings look like their parents, but lack the red waxy tips on the wing-feathers. They are very confiding little creatures, and I have repeatedly called them to me in the wood, when they would answer every call, coming nearer and nearer until they lit on a branch of hawthorn berries I was carrying and began to eat as I walked along. I know of no other birds who will endure so much meddling with their domestic affairs with no show of resentment or deserting the nest. They will suffer all sorts of indignities and disturbance of nesting site and environment without seeming to be disconcerted. This is due to the remarkable devotion of the adults to their brood, which induces them to care for the young at whatever cost to themselves. Most of the feeding is done by regurgitation, and often the gular pouches of the adult will be noticeably swollen as he comes to the nest with it full of food, which he transfers to the throats of his brood. It is less easy to tell what that food is by looking at the crops of young birds fed by regurgitation than of those fed with the raw food, yet it is often quite possible to do so with unfeathered nestlings. In the case of the young Waxwings the remains of insects were plainly visible through the semi-transparent skin; and about as soon as the feathers appeared the regurgitation was supplanted by feeding at first hand with large insects. The food of the adults consists of insects, seeds, berries of trees, and any small fruits except strawberries.

The Cedar Waxwings have no varied song, but they have a soft, conversational, whistling chirp and a plaintive call-note like "pee-eet, pee-eet" which they keep up most of the time.

They occur in California during the fall, winter, and spring, departing in June for their northern breeding grounds.

697. AMERICAN PIPIT. — *Anthus pensilvanicus.*

FAMILY : The Wagtails.

Length : 6.00–7.00.

Adults in Summer : Upper parts brownish gray, more or less indistinctly streaked ; wings dusky, with two buffy wing-bars and light edgings ; tail dusky ; inner web of outside feathers white, second feather buffy ; chin light cream-buff ; under parts buff, streaked with dusky on chest.

Adults in Winter : Upper parts decidedly browner ; under parts lighter, streaks on breast usually broader.

Young : Upper parts dull brownish gray ; under parts dull brownish white ; chest spotted or broadly streaked with blackish.

Geographical Distribution : Whole of North America ; migrates in winter to Gulf States and California.

Breeding Range : From about the timber line in the Colorado mountains, north to the Arctic coast.

Nest : Bulky and rather compact ; composed of dried mosses, grasses, etc. ; lined with hair, feathers, etc. ; placed on the ground.

Eggs : 4 to 6 ; dark chocolate-color, surface nearly covered with grayish brown specks and streaks. Size 0.76 × 0.56.

DURING migration and in the winter the American Pipit occurs in flocks on the large open stretches of country along the coast and interior valleys of California. Wherever fire has swept over the grass, or the ploughman has turned the sod, these dull-colored little birds alight in numbers and walk about picking up food with dainty teetering of head and tail. If alarmed, they rise with one accord high into the air, but, instead of flying away to another meadow, they usually come back to finish their feast as if it were only a foolish fright after all. Their plaintive note is a softer edition of the loud "kill-dee" of the plover, and is uttered constantly as the birds circle over their feeding ground or fly from one locality to another.

Early in the spring the Pipits start on their journey to the Boreal zone, either in the far north or above the timber line in the mountains.

Up to the very highest peaks they wander, where snow reigns forever and the fierce heat of the lowlands never comes, there to build "half-way houses on the road to heaven." And although unmusical in the lowlands, as soon as he reaches the solitude of the silent mountains the Pipit rises on graceful wings, a hundred feet in the air, and breaks into song with a melodious crescendo, ending the flight and the song in a precipitous drop back to earth.

In form, color, and tail-wagging, the Pipit is so like the water thrush as to be readily confused with it but for one thing, — the thrush is found alone, or in pairs, and dodges about among the alders low over the surface of a brook; while the Pipit flies high in the air, in flocks, for a

697. AMERICAN PIPIT.

"Up to the very highest peaks they wander."

short distance, wheeling like the killdeer and alighting near the starting point. This species is a common winter visitant and migrant throughout Southern California, while the water thrush is listed by Mr. Grinnell as rare.

701. WATER OUZEL, OR AMERICAN DIPPER.
Cinclus mexicanus.

FAMILY: The Wrens, Thrashers, etc.

Length : 7.00–8.50.

Adults in Summer : Entire plumage uniform slate-gray, more brownish on head and neck; bill black.

Adults in Winter : Similar, with feathers of wings and under parts tipped with white.

Young : Plumage similar to that of adults in winter, but under parts more or less mixed with white and tinged with rusty.

Geographical Distribution : Mountainous districts of Western North America, north to Alaska, south to Costa Rica.

California Breeding Range : Along mountain streams throughout the State.

Breeding Season : May to June 15.

Nest : A very bulky, oven-shaped structure ; composed of green mosses; the entrance on one side; lined with fine rootlets ; placed among rocks, close to running water or behind a waterfall.

Eggs : 3 to 5; white. Size 1.01 × 0.70.

"AMONG all the countless waterfalls in the Sierra Nevada, whether of the icy peaks or warm foot-hills, or in the profound Yosemitic cañons of the middle region, not one was found without its Ouzel. No cañon is too cold for this little bird, none too lonely, provided it be rich in falling water.

"During the golden days of Indian summer, after most of the snow has been melted, and the mountain streams have become feeble, — then the song of the Ouzel is at its lowest ebb. But as soon as the winter clouds have bloomed and the mountain treasuries are once more replenished with snow, the voices of the streams and of the Ouzels increase in strength and

701. Water Ouzel, or American Dipper

Cinclus mexicanus

richness until the flood season of the early summer. Then the torrents chant their noblest anthems, and then is the flood-tide of our songster's melody. As for weather, dark days and sun days are alike to him. No need of spring sunshine to thaw *his* song, for it never freezes. Never shall you hear anything wintry from *his* warm breast, no pinched cheeping, no wavering notes between sorrow and joy; his mellow fluty voice is ever tuned to downright gladness, as free from dejection as cock-crowing. . . . The more striking strains are perfect arabesques of melody, composed of a few full, round, mellow notes, embroidered with delicate trills which fade and melt in long slender cadences. In a general way his music is that of the streams refined and spiritualized. The deep booming notes of the falls are in it, the trills of rapids, the gurgling of margin eddies, the low whispering of level reaches and the sweet tinkle of separate drops oozing from the ends of mosses and falling into tranquil pools." [1]

After this exquisite description gleaned from Mr. Muir's essay on the Water Ouzel, one scarcely dares attempt anything original on the subject. And yet the thrill of discovering my first Ouzel's nest will never be forgotten. Often had I watched the bird fly through the waterfalls, dart into the swirling rapids, or courtesy daintily on a rock that rose in the middle of a white torrent; often heard his clear song rising above the wild tumult of the water; often seen the ball of moss on a slender shelf of rock wet by the spray, and been told that it was the nest

[1] John Muir, in "The Mountains of California."

of a Water Ouzel. But to find one in the middle of a pine-fringed mountain stream, where it seemed to belong just to the bird and me, — ah, that was a different matter.

It was located on a smooth granite boulder that rose from the white foam of the American River in the Sierra Nevada. Resting half on the rock and half in the stream was a fallen tree trunk, and under the shelter of this on the slippery rock the Ouzel had woven his little moss nest, kept fresh and green by the spray that dashed over it. As the mother approached the nest, she paused just a breath on a projecting point of the old trunk, and I distinctly saw that she carried the larva of some water insect in her beak. The babies in the nest knew it also, and the small doorway, where a dainty fern nodded its green plumes, instantly blossomed with four little heads. Four hungry mouths opened wide to receive the morsel. How would she apportion it among so many? After a moment of indecision, she tucked it deftly into one of the four gaping yellow bills; then, as if afraid of a wail of protest from those still unfilled, she darted hastily into the water and was lost to view. In exactly three minutes she appeared on the tree trunk again with another of the queer-looking larvæ, and again the four nestlings stretched hungry little beaks to be filled. This time she was joined by the male, who, though he came last, managed to deliver his load first, and perching on a smaller stone near by, where the spray dashed over him as he sang, he poured out his joy in sweetest music. How I longed to have the river keep silence for one moment that I might hear the wonderful song! The twitter of the young was clearly audible from where I sat, twenty feet away, and the melody of the father bird's rhapsody rang clearly over the noise of the rapids, but there must have been half tones lost in the tumult that were even sweeter than the notes that reached my ears. His song ended, into the water he plunged where the current was swiftest and where a strong man could not venture and live. Yet the bird flew upstream against it as easily as if in the air alone.

In feeding the young, both adults hovered just below the entrance to the nest, as a humming-bird beneath a flower, darting up with a little bound to deliver the food. The queer-looking larvæ were evidently picked up on the bottom of the river, but did not, I am sure, belong to any species of mosquito, for each was an inch and a half long and seemed to have many legs, like a scorpion. These constituted fully half of the food brought, and the rest was too small to be accurately identified. One or the other of the adults came to the nest as often as every ten minutes during the week that I watched them, and at times the intervals were much shorter. They invariably approached the nest in the same way, alighting first on a smaller rock whose top just broke the surface into foam, dipping and winking awhile on it, and hopping to the projecting splinter on the trunk, whence, after more dipping and winking, they fluttered over to the nest. The little Ouzels never appeared in the doorway until the parent had come to the tree trunk, and I think some signal note was uttered by the latter which told the nestlings that dinner was ready.

Later on, in another locality, I witnessed the début of one of these interesting water-babies. He was a comical counterpart of the adults, wink and all, except for the touch of white on his feathers and his absurdly short tail, rendered more absurd by his continual bobbing dip. This dipping on the part of young and old Water Ouzels is a distressingly undecided performance, as if the bird could not quite make up his mind whether or not to sit down, and stood continually in the valley of indecision. This young Ouzel remained all day on a ledge at the foot of the wall of rock which held his former nursery, and was fed by the male as devotedly as though still in the nest. So long as it was light enough to see, he was there, and at my last glimpse of him he stood winking and dipping in the same funny way. The other nestlings were still in the oven-like ball of green moss wherein they had been hatched, and their heads filled the doorway in eager petitioning for food. It never came often enough or in sufficient quantities to satisfy them, and one could only wonder when the overworked parents found time to supply their own needs.

702. SAGE THRASHER. — *Oroscoptes montanus.*

FAMILY : The Wrens, Thrashers, etc.

Length : 8.00–9.00.
Adults : Upper parts brownish gray, indistinctly streaked ; two narrow white wing-bars ; inner webs of two to four outer tail-feathers broadly tipped with white ; under parts whitish, tinged with buffy on flanks

and under tail-coverts ; the chest, breast, and sides thickly marked with wedge-shaped longitudinal spots and streaks of dusky.

Young: Similar to adult, but upper parts indistinctly streaked with darker, and streaks on under parts less sharply defined.

Geographical Distribution: Sagebrush plains of Western United States, from Montana south in winter to Mexico.

California Breeding Range: In upper Sonoran zone southeast of the Sierra Nevada.

Breeding Season: March to July.

Nest: A loose, bulky structure ; made of bark strips, small twigs, dry sage shreds ; lined with fine stems and rootlets, and sometimes hair ; placed generally in sagebrush from 10 inches to 3 feet from the ground.

Eggs: 3 to 5 ; rich greenish blue, spotted with bright reddish brown. Size 0.95 × 0.70.

EVEN amid the sands and barrenness of the sage-brush district, you may hear the full, sweet song of the Thrasher and dream that you are in a shady nook of New England with a babbling brook at your feet and the thick green canopy of vines overhead, — that is, if you close your eyes and forget the glare of the desert sunshine. What a medley of music he pours from that full throat ! It is a sort of " rag-time," and unconsciously you interpret it in words as mixed as the tune. Who else can do it but the brown thrasher of the East ? It is somewhat of a shock to open your eyes and see the grayish bird singing in the top of the low sage-bush with, maybe, not a tree in sight. But his drooping tail and raised bill proclaim him a true thrasher for all his queer environment. Somewhere in the sage-brush his mate is patiently brooding on the four or five blue eggs. For fourteen days she keeps to her appointed task, and then her busy life begins anew. There are naked nestlings to be fed, and all the food must be swallowed by the adult before the delicate baby throats

can receive it.   At first the young Thrashers seem to be
all legs and bills, but on the second day the down grows
more perceptible on head and back.   On the fifth day
the eyes are open, the feathers show well, and the food
is given to them in a fresh state.   Worms and insects
of all sorts form the Thrasher's menu, and these he obtains mostly on the ground under the bushes, working
hard early and late to supply the hungry brood with
food.   It is not an easy task to raise nestlings in such
surroundings.   In some localities lizards and snakes rifle
the nests of eggs and young, while in others hungry
owls make havoc.   My observations go to prove that
the destruction from various causes outside of human
agency is greater among Thrashers than among almost
any other wild birds.

710.   CALIFORNIAN THRASHER. — *Toxostoma*
redivivum.

Family : The Wrens, Thrashers, etc.

Length : 11.50–13.00.
Adults : Upper parts deep grayish brown, the tail darker and browner ;
    under parts dull buffy, darker on chest ; under tail-coverts tawny ;
    ear-coverts dusky, with distinct whitish shaft-streaks.
Geographical Distribution : Coast district of California, south to Lower
    California (F. M. Bailey).
California Breeding Range : Coast region of California north of lat-
    itude 35°.
Breeding Season : March to August.
Nest : A coarse, rudely constructed platform of sticky, coarse grass and
    mosses ; placed in bushes.
Eggs : 3 or 4 ; light greenish blue, spotted with chestnut.   Size 1.18 ×
    0.85.

To the bird-loving tourist or new-comer, accustomed
to the one brown thrasher of the East, the five or six

species of thrasher found in California are a little puz-
zling. Of them all, the Californian Thrasher is the most
widely distributed and best known. In form, habit, and
song he is very like the Eastern bird, except that his
tones have a metallic quality entirely lacking in that of
the brown thrasher.

The young Thrashers leave the nest when twelve to
fourteen days old, but are fed by the adults for some
time after. I have found the male caring for a fully
fledged brood, while his mate was sitting on a nestful
of eggs; and after this second series were hatched, he at
once began to feed them as faithfully as he had fed the
first. Even with all this, he one day managed to sing a
very short, low monologue which had in it the suggestion of all his old-time ardor.

Both sexes assist in the construction of the bulky
nest, and both brood on the eggs. In fourteen days the
naked pink young emerge from the shells and are fed
by regurgitation for four days, or until their eyes open.
By *regurgitation,* in such cases, I mean that the food is
swallowed by the adults first, though it may or may
not be partially digested by them. I believe it is not
digested, but is swallowed for the purpose of softening
and moistening it. After the fourth or fifth day, however, large insects are given to the young, having been
first carefully denuded of wings, legs, etc. Young
Thrashers, while less voracious than young robins, yet
require their meals at short intervals, and long after they
are out of the nest the overgrown fledglings follow the
adults about begging for food. But they soon learn to

swing their long bills sickle-fashion through the dead leaves, and to pick up the insects uncovered by it or to probe in the soft mould for worms.

In describing the song of the Californian Thrasher Mr. Williams says that mingled with its own peculiar notes are various imitative sounds, as the " quare, quare, quare" of the jay, the "kwee-kwee-kuk" of the Western robin, the piping call of the valley quail, and the harsh cackle of the flicker.

710 a. PASADENA THRASHER. — *Toxostoma redivivum pasadenense.*

FAMILY : The Wrens, Thrashers, etc.

Length : About 12.00.
Adults : Similar to the Californian thrasher, but colors duller, chest-band darker ; throat white.
Geographical Distribution : Interior of Southern California.
California Breeding Range : Below Transition zone in the San Diegan district.
Breeding Season : December to May.

THE Pasadena Thrasher is a local subspecies of the Californian thrasher. There is one authentic record of eggs laid by this bird on December 16, and from this a very pretty story, entitled "A California Christmas Carol," has been woven in "The Sunset," January, 1903, which describes the affair as if it were the ordinary habit of this bird to rear his brood at Christmas tide. The usual nesting season begins late in January and extends to the middle of May, though nests have occasionally been found later.

The song of the Pasadena Thrasher is at its best during the late winter, and is a jolly rollicking roundelay, as full of fun and mimicry as that of the Californian. The nesting habits are very similar, modified only by its more southern range.

711. LECONTE THRASHER. — *Toxostoma lecontei.*

FAMILY : The Wrens, Thrashers, etc.

Length : 10.50–11.00.

Adults : Upper parts light grayish brown ; tail dusky and tipped with lighter ; under parts dove-color, becoming white on throat and belly ; the under tail-coverts bright tawny buff, in marked contrast ; ear-coverts light brownish gray ; a distinct malar stripe of whitish, narrowly barred with dusky ; a distinct dusky streak along each side of throat.

Young : Similar to adults, but upper tail-coverts more rusty, and under tail-coverts paler.

Geographical Distribution : Lower Sonoran zone in the desert region from Southwestern Utah to Southern California and south to Mexico.

California Breeding Range : Desert region of Southeastern California.

Breeding Season : February to May.

Nest : Large and bulky ; made of twigs, grasses, and weeds ; lined with feathers ; placed in cactus bushes or mesquite trees from 1 to 7 feet from the ground.

Eggs : 3 or 4 ; pale bluish green, faintly speckled, chiefly at the larger end, with yellowish brown and lavender. Size 1.07 × 0.76.

THE Leconte Thrasher loves the barren desert as a petrel loves the sea ; and so many generations have its hot suns beaten down upon his race that the characteristic light brown of the family has faded to dull grayish tinged with brown, and his breast has taken on the ashy hues of the alkali dust. Wastes of sand with sparse patches of sagebrush, cactus, and perhaps mesquite are

18

his favorite haunts, and from the top of this stunted, grayish green vegetation, he peals out the earliest greeting to the day. So loud and so enthusiastic is his song that it can be heard nearly half a mile away. As the sun rises and the air grows hotter his music ceases, and he skulks among the sagebrush until evening, when he sings again, sometimes far into the night. If you have camped in this dreary waste with the marvellously bright stars overhead and the silence of the desert around you like a tomb, the song of the Leconte Thrasher, breaking the mysterious stillness, has seemed the sweetest music ever heard by mortal ears.

711. Leconte Thrasher.

"*He loves the barrenness of the desert.*"

712. CRISSAL THRASHER. — *Toxostoma crissalis.*

Family : The Wrens, Thrashers, etc.

Length : 11.40–12.60.

Adults : Bill long, sharply curved ; upper parts plain grayish brown, the tail darker and faintly tipped with rufous ; under parts dark fawn or grayish ; the chin and throat nearly white ; under tail-coverts chestnut ; malar stripe white, with dusky streak under same on each side of throat.

Young : Similar to adults, but more rusty on upper parts, especially on rump and tips of tail-feathers; lower parts more fulvous.

Geographical Distribution : Southern California and Northern Lower California, New Mexico, Arizona, and Utah, east to Western Texas.

California Breeding Range : Locally in desert regions along lower Colorado River, from Fort Yuma, northwest to Palm Springs.

Breeding Season : February to July.

Nest : Large and conspicuous ; made of coarse twigs ; lined with strips of plant bark ; placed in bushes.

Eggs : 3 or 4 ; pale greenish blue. Size 1.08 × 0.75.

LOOK for the Crissal Thrasher in the low, bushy underbrush of the valleys where a clear brook winds its way or a pond hides in a fringe of alders. Rarely will you find him nesting at any great distance from water, and one of the first lessons he gives his brood is to take a morning splash. It is well worth while rising at four A. M. to see him plunge so eagerly into the cold water and splash it in a shower of sparkling drops. The bath over, he flies up to the top of a tall bush to preen his wet feathers and fill the air with melody. His song is unlike that of any other thrasher in its smoothness of execution and richness of tone. Every note is sweet, true, and perfect, but the whole lacks the spasmodic brilliancy we are accustomed to expect in his family. It has a more spiritual quality but less dash. From February until late in April this Thrasher sings his sweetest, for then is his springtime of love and joy. From that time on through July, when the second brood is fledged, he sings less enthusiastically, and soon he ceases altogether. Late in the autumn he sometimes is heard again in the valleys, but the full sweetness is withheld until the mating season comes again, in February.

After the breeding season, and often for his second brood, the Crissal Thrasher ranges high up into the oak-covered foot-hills, returning to the valleys with the first fall days.

The young Thrashers hatch in fourteen days. They are naked, except for the faintest suggestion of down on head and back, and are fed by regurgitation until four days old. On the ninth day the young are feathered all but the wings and tail, which still wear their sheaths, and the featherless tracts which are on all young birds. The iris of the eye is white at this time, but gradually becomes straw-color like that of the adult.

Unless startled into an earlier exit, the Thrasher nestlings do not leave the cradle until eleven or twelve days old, and even then they hide in the bushes for many ensuing days, helplessly waiting to be fed by the adult.

Mr. Mearns tells in "The Auk" of shooting a female Crissal Thrasher and, on going back the next day after the nest, he found the male patiently brooding on the two eggs. Surely such devotion in a bird deserves a better end than the collector's basket.

713. CACTUS WREN. — *Heleodytes brunneicapillus*.

FAMILY : The Wrens, Thrashers, etc.

Length : 8.00–8.75.

Adults : Upper parts brown, back streaked with white and black ; wings spotted with pale grayish brown and whitish on a dusky ground ; tail black, except for brownish gray middle feathers, which are spotted with black, and the outside feathers barred with white ; conspicuous white superciliary stripe, bordered beneath by a dusky line; throat and chest white, heavily spotted with black, in contrast to buffy brown belly, which is sparsely marked with brown.

Young: Similar to adults, but streaks on back less distinct, spots on under parts smaller, and colors more suffused.

Geographical Distribution: Southwestern border of United States from Southern Texas to coast of Southern California, south into Mexico, north to Utah.

California Breeding Range: Lower Sonoran zone in Southern California, on both sides of the Sierra Nevada.

Breeding Season: April 15 to August 1.

Nest: Placed in cactus or thorny bushes; flask-shaped, with an entrance at one end; made of little twigs and grasses; lined with feathers.

Eggs: 4 to 7; white or creamy white, thickly covered with reddish brown spots. Size 0.97 × 0.65.

UNLESS you have heard the Cactus Wren sing, you will wonder at the science that classes him with the wrens. But when you listen to the rich, ringing, wren-like song, and come upon the singer sitting on a thorny twig in the exact attitude of the thrashers, with lifted bill and tail curved downward, you are satisfied to leave his name among the wren family. He sings constantly as well as sweetly. His clear notes are the first to waken the weary camper in the morning, and oftentimes they alone break the death-like hush of evening. The Leconte thrasher runs him a close race in this, but, I believe, is always a little short of winning. A spirit brave enough to *sing* in all the dreary waste and scorching heat wins your honest admiration, and you try to imagine what the parched and silent desert would be without these two birds.

In places it seems as if every other cactus contained a nest of this species, so common is it. A long, purse-shaped affair, it is laid flat in the fork of a cactus and having a doorway at the small end whereby the busy brown mother may enter. Another wren-like trait of this bird is the building of dummy nests. I can find no authority for this statement other than my own observation. but am positive investigation will prove it to be true. The male sometimes, if not invariably, sleeps in one of these "dummies."

By cutting a slit in the roof of a nest containing young, it was possible to watch the brood develop.

713. Cactus Wren.
"*A long, purse-shaped affair.*"

This slit was closed and fastened after each examination. At first they were the usual naked, pinkish nestlings, with a sparse sprinkling of whitish down on crown and back, but they soon took on the soft brown and white plumage of young wrens, and were remarkably enterprising. While very young they were fed by regurgitation, but on the fifth day, when their eyes had opened, the parents carried insects in their beaks when they entered the nest, and then the crops of the young plainly indicated a stronger diet. By regurgitation in a case like this, I mean that the adults masticated the food and carried it in their own gular pouch, or crop, to the young. During the last few days that the young Wrens spent in the nest the doorway was full of little brown heads most of the time, and the mother no longer went inside to feed them. She still slept in the nest with them, however, and each night there was a struggle for supremacy between the nestlings who wished to look out and the mother who tried to get in. Finally, one morning when she emerged, it seemed as if the cork had popped from a bottle allowing the contents to escape, for two of the youngsters darted out close behind her, and two more peeped from the doorway. Except for smaller, plumper form and softer coloring, they were exact counterparts of the adults, and they possessed the nervous activity of their family.

715. ROCK WREN. — *Salpinctes obsoletus.*

FAMILY : The Wrens, Thrashers, etc.

Length : 5.12–6.35.

Adults : Upper parts grayish brown, more or less speckled with dusky and white dots ; rump light brown; tail tipped with buffy brown and with subterminal band of black ; middle dusky ; under parts dull whitish ; flank tinged with pale cinnamon; chest usually finely speckled ; under tail-coverts barred with blackish.

Young : Upper parts plain rusty-gray ; under parts whitish on throat and breast, brownish on flanks and under tail-coverts.

Geographical Distribution : Arid regions of Western United States, east to the Great Plains, south to Mexico, north to British Columbia.

California Breeding Range : Locally throughout the State, chiefly east of the humid coast belt. Recorded from the Farallones.

Breeding Season : March and April.

Nest : Usually placed in a rift of rocks or on the ground under a projecting rock, sometimes in hollow stumps or about buildings ; composed
of sticks, bark strips, weeds, grasses, moss, etc.

Eggs : 7 to 9 ; pure glossy white, finely speckled with a few reddish
brown spots, chiefly at the larger end. Size 0.72 × 0.54.

AFTER finding this Wren, the only land bird among
the thousands of sea fowl on the Farallone Islands, one
is inclined to believe that he is well named, since all he
asks for in a home are bare bleak rocks in which to
hide.

In the deserted rocky cañons, where even sparse vegetation refuses to grow, he may be seen busily hunting
insects in the crevices of the rocks, dodging in and out
among the boulders, picking up spiders and worms, and
uttering his crisp, loud note. If you startle him he will
fly a few feet to the top of a small rock and, facing you,
sway from side to side, scolding and bobbing in comical
excitement. It may be that his nest is close by in one
of the dark crannies, but, as a rule, only the master and
mistress of the household can pass through the narrow
doorway. About the entrance is a curious conglomeration of treasures, evidently carried there by the bird.
Bits of glass, pebbles, shells, and anything else that
strikes his fancy, are carefully collected in his dooryard.
On the Farallones, mussel shells, small bones, and small
pieces of coal form the usual collection. The nest itself
is lined with feathers and hair or wool, or any available
soft substance. While you are searching for it, the gay
little Rock Wren is doing his best to lead you astray.
As Mr. Keyser so aptly says, " He will leap upon a rock

and send forth his bell-like peal as if he were saying 'Right here, right here, here is our nest,' but when you go to the spot he flits off to another rock and sounds the same challenge." If perchance you find the treasure, the anxiety of the tiny brown householder manifests itself in ludicrous tail-waggings and excited bobbings, together with energetic scolding protests. The half-fledged nestlings are soft brown balls of feathers with only a promise of the perky little tail of the adults. Apparently they have all the nervous activity of their race, for even in the nest they wriggle and fuss.

The Rock Wren's song, which Mrs. Bailey calls the "most unbird-like of machine-made tinklings," is peculiar to himself, and once heard will be recognized instantly ever afterwards.

717 a. CAÑON WREN. — *Catherpes mexicanus conspersus.*

FAMILY : The Wrens, Thrashers, etc.

Length : 5.50–5.75.
Adults : Plumage conspicuously brown, except for white throat and breast ; upper parts varying from dull brown to cinnamon-grayish and speckled with white and blackish ; the wings cinnamon-rusty and barred with dusky tail light reddish brown with narrow black bars ; belly dull reddish brown.
Young : Similar to adults, but without white spots on upper and posterior under parts, which are instead mottled more or less with dusky.
Geographical Distribution : Southwestern United States, north to Wyoming, east to Texas and Rocky Mountains, south to Lower California and Mexico.
California Breeding Range : Desert ranges southeast of the Sierra Nevada.
Breeding Season : April, May, and June.
Nest : Generally placed in some deserted tunnel or cave, or in holes in

bluffs or about buildings; made of twigs, stalks, bits of leaves;
covered with moss, and lined with down and feathers.

Eggs : 3 to 5 ; speckled chiefly at the larger end with reddish brown and
lavender gray.   Size 0.72 × 0.53.

THE Cañon Wren is found in the southeastern portion
of California among the mountains of the desert range.
In habits he is like the dotted cañon wren, though
much less often seen than the latter, because less common.   Wherever he occurs in California he is a resident,
remaining practically in the same portion of the same
cañon all his life.

717 b. DOTTED CAÑON WREN. — *Catherpes   mexicanus
punctulatus.*

FAMILY : The Wrens, Thrashers, etc.

Similar to cañon wren (*C. m. conspersus*), but smaller, bill shorter, and
spots on back more numerous and more conspicuous.

Geographical Distribution : Oregon and California west of the Cascades
and Sierra Nevada, as far south as Lower California.

California Breeding Range : Local in Transition zone on west slope of
the Sierra Nevada.   Rarely in Coast Range north to Mt. St. Helen's.

Breeding Season : April.

Nest : In crevices of rocks or on ledges of cliffs ; made of green moss.

Eggs : 3 to 5 ; white, speckled with rusty-brown and purple.

THE Dotted Cañon Wren is a fairly common resident
in certain parts of the Sierra Nevada, chiefly along the
west slope.   He may be seen darting in and out on the
steep sides of rocky cañons, and, but for his white throat,
looking much like a big brown bug.   A nearer view
with field glasses reveals the tiny black and white polka-
dots of his brown coat.   He is a handsome little fellow
and a fine singer, making the cool depths of the cañon

ring with his jubilant song. "The Bugler" some one
has called him, and one thinks of the name whenever
listening to the song. He is a rather shy bird, creeping
in and out among the rocks, pausing a moment to eye
the intruder curiously, tilt his tail, and scurry off again.
The busy search in every crack of the hard stone for
possible insects so absorbs him that he has no time to
speculate on what business the intruder may have there.
Enough for him if he can place a boulder between himself and observing eyes while he gathers food for his
mate or his brood. His long bill probes every moss-
covered crevice and tiny hole, and often you may see
him jerk a worm out of its hiding place and scramble up
the cañon wall to his nest with it. A tiny hole is the
entrance to his nesting site, sometimes under a boulder,
sometimes far up the face of a cliff. He will fly down
from it, or rather drop down with closed wings like a
stone, but I have never seen him fly all the way up to
it. Sometimes he ascends by a series of short flights, but
oftener by hops and fluttering scrambles. He loves those
bare bleak rocks and sits upon them to sing, rather than
upon any vegetation there may be, hiding behind them
or on them, much as the lizards do.

The only nest of this variety I have ever seen resembled that of a pewee in material and construction,
but was much larger and more loosely put together.
The moss of the outside was fresh and green, in exquisite contrast with the lining of silver plant-down
and with the gray stone cliff. In it were five diminutive Wrens, the brightest, perkiest bird-babies imaginable.

The effect was irresistibly funny when one ventured out to the edge of the nest and tilted its comically small tail in exact imitation of its elders. Unfortunately, as soon as our presence was discovered, fear spoiled the picture, for the nestling crouched a moment and then scampered back into the dark nesting place. As the nest was discovered on a one day's trip, I do not know how old the nestlings were nor how much longer they remained in the nest. At this stage they were fully feathered, but the dots were much less distinct, shading into the general coloring. Otherwise they were like the adults. The coloring was so exactly in harmony with the rocks in which the nest was placed that the young birds were practically invisible at a distance of ten feet.

719 a. VIGORS WREN. — *Thryomanes bewickii spilurus.*

FAMILY : The Wrens, Thrashers, etc.

Length : 5.00–5.50.

Adults : Upper parts dark brown, with a conspicuous white superciliary stripe ; middle tail-feathers more grayish brown and barred ; outer feathers blackish, spotted and barred ; under parts gray, flanks brownish.

Young : Similar to adults.

Geographical Distribution : California west of the Sierra Nevada to the coast.

California Breeding Range : Humid coast belt from Monterey to Mendocino County, including San Francisco Bay region.

Breeding Season : May.

Nest : Placed in boxes, holes, fence posts, brush heaps, stumps, etc. ; made largely of sticks and grasses ; lined with feathers.

Eggs : 5 to 7 ; white, finely speckled with reddish brown and lilac. Size 0.64 × 0.50.

THE Vigors Wren is a subspecies of the Bewick wren of the Central United States, and combines the characteris-

tics of this species with those of the Pacific house wren.
In the neighborhood of towns this bird prefers to nest
about houses, choosing all sorts of queer places in which
to rear its brood; but throughout Western California, in
open districts as far south as Pasadena (although there
Mr. Grinnell calls it the San Joaquin Wren), it is found
building among brush heaps and in hollow trees. For
breeding habits see Parkman Wren, also called Pacific
House Wren.

721 a. PARKMAN WREN, OR PACIFIC HOUSE WREN. — *Troglodytes aëdon parkmanii.*

FAMILY : The Wrens, Thrashers, etc.

Length: 4.25–5.20.
> Upper parts grayish brown barred with blackish, except head; tail
> barred with black and pale ashy; under parts indistinctly barred
> with ashy and brownish.

Geographical Distribution: Pacific Coast from British Columbia south to
California.

California Breeding Range: West of the Sierra Nevada nearly throughout the State.

Breeding Season: May.

Nest: In cavities in trees, or about buildings; of twigs; lined with mass
of feathers.

Eggs: 5 to 7 ; flesh-color, thickly speckled with pale brownish purple and
rusty.

THE Parkman Wren is the house wren of the Pacific
Coast and is a common summer visitant west of the
Sierra Nevada. His gay canary-like song rings from barn,
house, or cabin, wherever there is a crevice for him to
nest in. From morning until night the bubbling notes
"tumble over each other, they are poured out so fast,"
and you wonder when he takes any breath, yet he is as

full of enthusiasm at the day's close as he was at its beginning. He is very friendly and sociable, allowing you to watch him, and watching you with equal interest.

When nest-building commences it absorbs the attention of both sexes, though the master of the household still sings between loads. Such a mass of material they manage to gather! Shreds of bark, twigs, feathers galore, straw, and often bits of plant-down, such as cotton. The cavity is stuffed to its fullest capacity, and in the top of the mass madam shapes a shallow cup to hold the eggs. But these Wrens are capricious folk, and after the nest is all ready they will often take a vacation and pay no further attention to it for several days, or even a week. Then, one day, you may see the female slipping slyly into the nest hole while her mate sings louder than ever near by, and you conclude rightly that the first egg has been laid. She may lay another the next day or she may wait a day or two, but as soon as there are five or six, she will commence to brood. Fourteen days are necessary for the incubation of those small eggs, and, at the end of that time, a peep into the nest will reveal tiny, naked nestlings, a trifle less than one inch long, with knobs for eyes and little more than mere slits for beaks. Their wingbones are about one-sixth of an inch in length, and their legs are not much longer. But they double their weight every twenty-four hours, and at the end of four days they have down on heads and along the feather tracts, and look much more like birds. The beak also has taken shape and is more or less firmly cartilaginous. On the fifth day the eyes open. Up to this time they have been fed by regurgitation (see Foreword) at intervals averaging every half-hour throughout the day, the periods being longer from 8 to 10 A. M. and 12 to 3 P. M., but now fresh food is given them. The young Wrens feather more slowly than some young birds, and usually remain in the nest until sixteen days old; one brood could neither be coaxed nor starved into flying until the twenty-first day. The location of the nest seems to affect the time of their departure, and, in cases where it is high up, with no near perch, the little ones seem to be afraid to venture. For some time after leaving home they are fed by both adults, and sometimes return to the nest at night either alone or with the mother bird.

722 a. WESTERN WINTER WREN. — *Olbiorchilus hiemalis pacificus.*

FAMILY : The Wrens, Thrashers, etc.

Length: 3.60–4.25.

Adults: Tail very short ; upper parts dark cinnamon-brown, brightest on rump ; wings, tail, and sometimes back finely barred with black ; line over eye, throat, and breast rust color ; rest of under parts darker and barred with dark.

Geographical Distribution: Pacific coast from Alaska to Southern California ; south in winter to Mexico.

California Breeding Range: In the humid coast belt (Transition), south to Point Sur.

Breeding Season: April and May.

Nest: In crevices of stumps or logs ; a mass of moss, with hollow lined with feathers.

Eggs: 5 to 7 ; cream-white, thinly speckled with rusty. Size 0.60 × 0.48.

J. N. BOWLES says of this bird : " The stillness was suddenly broken by the beautiful bell-like warble of the

Western Winter Wren, and I knew that within half a mile must be his nest. I walked to the edge of the brook, and after travelling a short distance along it, the way was blocked by a giant fir that, in falling years before, had split in the middle. From deep in this split appeared suspicious looking twigs, but past experience had taught me not to expect the real nest within a hundred yards of a singing Winter Wren. Nor was I mistaken, for it proved to be nothing more than a well-built decoy, about which the bird had made a very natural 'bluff' of anxiety. . . . I continued up the brook, finding two more decoy nests of the Wrens in the roots of fallen trees. . . . A half-uprooted fir tree, some two hundred yards from where the Wren was heard singing, gave me a thrill of interest. The opening under the roots extended in about ten feet, and was only three feet high at the entrance, so there was nothing for it but to imitate the serpent. The Wren had left me long since, and nothing stirred when I shook the roots, therefore my hopes were high, as these Wrens are never seen near their eggs. After crawling in as far as possible, I turned over on my back and waited for my eyes to become accustomed to the darkness. As things gradually took shape, almost the first thing I saw was the much-hoped-for nest, all of twigs and green moss, directly over my head. It was wedged in among the earth and roots, and a feather protruding from the entrance told me that my search had revealed a satisfactory end — the decoy nests are never lined. The set consisted of six partially incubated eggs, and only one

725a. TULE WREN

Cistothorus palustris paludicola

more decoy was found a short distance further on in a long-deserted placer mine."

Unfortunately Mr. Bowles's excellent description — a part of which I have quoted here from "The Condor," Vol. III. No. 1 — does not record the rearing of the brood or the manner of feeding the young, and these I supply from my own notebook.

One particular pair which my notes record nested in the crevice of an old stump, which, when the young were five days old, I broke open slightly to obtain a better view. This did not in the least deter the dauntless parents from caring for the nestlings, though it doubtless caused them much anxiety. The young of this Wren resemble the young of tule wrens when first hatched, and are rather slow in feathering. They are fed by regurgitation for several days after hatching, the menu being chiefly small grubs which the busy little parents pick out of the bark of the coniferous trees. They are fed on insects and worms also. After the sixth day the food is mostly given in the fresh condition. The Wren nestlings leave the nest between the seventeenth and twenty-first days.

725 a. TULE WREN. — *Cistothorus palustris paludicola.*

FAMILY : The Wrens, Thrashers, etc.

Length : 4.50–5.75.
  Top of head black ; crown brown ; middle of back with triangular black patch, streaked with white ; rest of upper parts buffy brown ; tail-coverts and middle-tail feathers barred with black ; under parts buffy white, browner on sides.
Geographical Distribution : Pacific coast from British Columbia to Mexico.

California Breeding Range: West of the Sierra Nevada, in suitable
  localities.
Breeding Season: June and July.
Nest: Large oval ball, attached to tule stems ; composed of wet tules,
  marsh grass, and pond weed matted together ; lined with tule pith and
  dry algæ. Entrance at one side.
Eggs: 3 to 5 ; pinkish brown, clouded with darker.

To know the Tule Wren you must go to the tall reeds
of a lowland marsh and live for hours each day with him.
He will protest with all the force of his little throat
against your intrusion and will call all his neighbors to
the scene. Clinging to the slender tule, with much tail-
bobbing and attitudinizing, he challenges you angrily and,
were he as big as he is brave, you would never venture
further. His nests are many, all dummy save one, but
you will not be able to guess which that one may be. I
have examined thirty in one day and found but one occupied, and that was the oldest, most tumble-down of the
lot. With undiminished vigor he sings and works, carrying wet marsh vegetation and weaving it among the
rushes into a ball many times the size of his industrious
little self. His mate is already brooding in one of those
nests which he made last year, but that is no reason,
according to his way of thinking, why he should not
keep busy making more. So, resting only long enough
to satisfy his hunger, he keeps on with his self-appointed
task from morning until night, singing as he goes the
merriest, maddest medley of banjo-like notes.

Each nest is lined with pith of the tules, which is
exactly like cat-tail down of the East, but the one containing the purplish brown eggs is padded very carefully
with this material. These nests are conspicuous objects

among the thin-stemmed tule-rushes, and on this account are much more easily watched than are the nests of the long-billed marsh wrens, which live in heavier marshes. It is steaming hot inside the thick-walled ball, and the eggs feel like little hot pebbles to your fingers. Twelve days are required for incubation, and even during this short period the mother is not a close sitter. I have known her to leave the nest for two hours in the middle of the day, trusting to the intense heat of the sun to perform her task for her; and but for the thick, moist walls of the cradle, this same sun would have been fatal to the bird life within the shells.

As soon as the eggs hatched in the nest I was watching, I cut a slit in the top of it to look at the young. They were naked, light pink in color, with tiny heads, mere knobs for eyes and buds for wings; each nestling measured one inch in length. After this examination I tied up the slit, and before I was a yard away the mother entered the nest again. Four days later the eyes of the young Wrens had begun to open, and looked like tiny slits, while a thin buffy down covered the top of their heads and was scattered sparsely over their bodies. As in the young of the long-billed marsh wrens, the ear openings were conspicuously large. Bill and legs had changed from pink to light burnt-orange in color. They were fed by regurgitation for the first four days and doubled in weight every twenty-four hours. (See Foreword.) When a week old they were commencing to feather, and in three days more were nearly ready to leave the nest. They were now fed on larvæ of water insects, slugs, and dragonflies, besides other insects, and meals were served four times an hour during most of the day.

When the young Wrens were twelve days old, my attempt to peep into the nest for the last time resulted in a sudden discharge of all its contents, one by one, into the green rushes, where they sat breathless clinging to the thin stems in desperate efforts to keep right side up. They were entirely feathered and able to pick up food for themselves, but for two weeks more their pretty coaxing chirps induced the adult Wrens to supply them with marsh tidbits even more frequently than before they left the nest.

725 c. INTERIOR TULE WREN, OR WESTERN MARSH WREN. — *Cistothorus palustris plesius.*

FAMILY : The Wrens, Thrashers, etc.

Length : About 4.50–5.75.
   Top of head and patch dark brown ; middle of crown light brown ; upper parts buffy brown ; tail heavily and sharply barred with dark ; under parts pale ashy gray.
Geographical Distribution : From British Columbia south to Mexico, from east side of the Sierra Nevada to Rocky Mountains.
California Breeding Range : East of the Sierra Nevada at various localities. Mr. Grinnell mentions Eagle Lake.
Nest and Eggs : Like those of tule wren (*C. p. paludicola*).

THE Western Marsh Wren is the Western representative of the long-billed marsh wren of the East, and is identical in habits with that bird. (See " Nestlings of Forest and Marsh.")

726 c. CALIFORNIAN CREEPER. — *Certhia familiaris occidentalis.*

FAMILY : The Creepers.

Length : About 5.00 or 6.00.
Upper parts bright brown, reddest on rump ; line over eye, streaks on head, and back yellowish brown.
Geographical Distribution : Pacific coast of North America from Alaska to Santa Cruz mountains, California.
California Breeding Range : Humid coast of Transition zone, south as far as Santa Cruz mountains.
Breeding Season : May.
Nest : Under loosened bark of redwood or cedar, within 5 feet of ground ; made of finely shredded cedar bark ; lined with plant down or feathers.

THE Californian Creeper is the Western representative of the brown creeper. It is so like the sierra creeper in form and habits that no separate description is necessary. Its shrill, wiry note is heard in the redwoods of the humid coast district, but the bird itself is so protectively colored as to look like a large brown bug against the red-brown trunks. Only a few nests have been recorded from the Santa Cruz mountains, but the Creeper undoubtedly breeds there quite commonly.

726 d. SIERRA CREEPER. — *Certhia familiaris zelotes.*

FAMILY : The Creepers.

Length : About 5.00 or 6.00.
Adults : Upper parts dark grayish brown, becoming tawny brown on rump ; line over eye, streaks on shoulders, and spot on wing white ; under parts white, washed with brown on sides.
Geographical Distribution : Cascade Mountains of Oregon and the Sierra Nevada, west to valleys in winter.

Breeding Range: Transition and lower Boreal zones along whole length
   of the Sierra Nevada.
Breeding Season: June.
Nest: Described by Mr. Barlow as under the bark of dead pines, about
   20 feet up ; made of cedar bark and a few feathers.
Eggs: 5; white, spotted and blotched with reddish brown and pale
   lavender.

THE quaint little bird called the Sierra Creeper is a
summer resident of the pine forests, and so perfectly
does his striped brown back blend with the bark that
he becomes practically invisible the moment he alights
on it. His habits are so exactly like those of the brown
creeper of the East that Mr. Chapman's delightful description of that bird fits him perfectly. He says :

" The facts in the case will doubtless show that the
patient plodding brown creeper is searching for the
insects, eggs, and larvæ which are hidden in crevices
in the bark ; but after watching him for several minutes
one becomes impressed with the thought that he has
lost the only thing in the world he cared for, and that
his one object in life is to find it. Ignoring you completely, with scarcely a pause, he finds his way in a
preoccupied, near-sighted manner up a tree trunk. Having finally reached the top of his spiral staircase, one
might suppose he would rest long enough to survey his
surroundings, but like a bit of loosened bark he drops
off to the base of the nearest tree and resumes his never-
ending task. He has no time to waste in words, but
occasionally, without stopping in his rounds, he utters a
few *screeping* squeaky notes, which are about as likely
to attract attention as he is himself. As for song, one
would say it was quite out of the question ; but in its

summer home among the northern spruces and firs it
has an exquisitely pure, tender song of four notes, dying away in an indescribably plaintive cadence, like
the soft sigh of the wind among the pine boughs."

At all times an unsocial bird, the Creeper
is seldom, even at nesting time, seen in company with another of his kind either male or
female. Apparently too busy for any lover's
nonsense, he yet does indulge in it upon occasion and, like all drudges, when he wishes
to be sentimental he succeeds only in being
serio-comic. With utmost gravity he offers
his sweetheart a fat grub, cocking his head
sidewise as he sees it disappear down her
throat. She puts up her bill for more,
which he pretends to give, necessarily at
long range on account of the slender curve
of his beak. Then he goes on with
his task of hunting, while she tags close
behind teasing for more after
the manner of a hungry nestling. This does not last long.
The business of house-building begins. His little home
is hidden snugly behind the
bark of a dead pine tree high
up from the ground, but higher

726 d. SIERRA CREEPER.

"*He offers his sweetheart a fat
grub.*"

still from the same tree he warbles his queer little love
song, when the glorious dawn of a June morning moves
even his plodding soul to music.

Only nine days are required to hatch the small eggs, and the naked nestlings squirm and wriggle like so many pink mice in the cosy nest. They are slow in feathering, not being fully covered until fifteen days old, and even then the down shows through the feathers in hair-like patches. According to the best of my observations with a powerful field glass, they are fed by regurgitation until four days old. After that a visible supply of insect food is given them. Their first journey from home is a creeping about on the bark of the nest tree, to which they cling desperately, aided by their sharp little tails. Instinctively they pick at every crevice in the bark, and soon become so business-like about it that they are quite independent of the adults and of each other.

742. PALLID WREN–TIT. — *Chamæa fasciata.*

FAMILY : The Nuthatches and Tits.

Length: About 6.00–6.50.
Adults: Upper parts gray, washed with olive on rump and tail; tail long ; under parts fawn-color, indistinctly streaked with dusky.
Geographical Distribution: California, from Shasta County southward to San Diego.
California Breeding Range: Upper Sonoran zone, west of the Sierra Nevada, except humid coast belt, from San Diego northward to lower McCloud River.
Breeding Season: April and May.
Nest: In thickets or low bushes ; compactly made of twigs, bark strips, and grasses ; lined with feathers and cow hair.
Eggs: 2 to 5 ; uniform turquoise blue. Size 0.73 × 0.56.

SOME California birds, such as the phainopepla, wren-tit, and others, are like the California big trees, — *sui generis.* There is nothing like them east of the one-hundredth meridian and they are well worth a long journey to study.

The Wren-tit is a unique combination, as his name implies. Exceedingly difficult to watch, he slips along the ground under the chaparral and through fields of dead mustard stalks, eluding observation as well as pursuit by scooting into the thickest patches of weeds, until the patience of the student is exhausted and he drops down to rest in a shady corner. This is really the best thing to do, for if one keeps still long enough the bird is sure to come into view, and often, impelled by curiosity, will approach within a watchable distance. With tail atilt over its back, like a wren, it sidles up the dry stalks, searching diligently for insects, but with one eye on its visitor. A slight movement on your part will send it diving into the thick tangle out of sight again, and only its harsh, scolding notes will betray its whereabouts. Its long tail is the Wren-tit's most expressive feature, for it wags up and down in excitement or anger, and it shakes when the bird sings, as if it had some part in helping on the music. The song is described as a " clear ringing voice running down the scale slowly, distinctly, ' keep, keep, keep, keep-it, keep-it,' ending in a trill." At other times it is a slow, monotonous singing note like " pee-pee-pee-peep," and again a varied succession of whistles. In the early spring the Wren-tits wander in pairs, keeping up a constant call and answer, somewhat like a quick " pit-pit, prrrrt."

Mrs. Bailey accuses this bird of breaking up the nest of a pair of gnatcatchers and one of lazuli buntings, although both parents were present. It is probably the habit of Wren-tits to steal eggs or nestlings; for, wherever found, they seem to be a terror to smaller birds, and their approach is attended with as much consternation as that of a shrike.

743 a. CALIFORNIAN BUSH-TIT. — *Psaltriparus minimus californicus.*

FAMILY: The Nuthatches and Tits.

Length: 4.00–4.50.

Adults: Top of head light brown; upper parts ashy gray; under parts dull brownish gray.

Geographical Distribution: California, except northern coast district.

California Breeding Range: Oak regions below Boreal zone, west of the Sierra Nevada.

Breeding Season: April and May.

Nest: Bulky; pensile; gourd-shaped; entrance a small hole near the top; made of moss, fibre, plant down, oak blossoms, and lichens; lined with feathers.

Eggs: 5 to 9; plain white. Size 0.34 × 0.42.

THROUGHOUT California west of the Sierra Nevada, the tiny gray birds known as Bush-tits are numerous, though so small are they and so protectively colored, one may easily overlook them. At Elysian Park, Los Angeles, they build each year in the circle of evergreens near the pool, and usually there are several nests in the live-oak at the foot of the slope near by. One busy pair were finishing their nest when I discovered them, May 2. They were belated, for in the next tree swung

743a. CALIFORNIAN BUSH-TIT

Psaltriparus minimus californicus

another gray pocket containing young nearly ready to fly. The pair which were building worked together, bringing moss, tiny leaves, lichens, and bits of paper, which they tucked dexterously into the outer walls. At first one could see through the structure, so loosely was it woven, but little by little the weaving and lining filled the interstices until it was of the proper solidity and thickness. Then began the carrying of feathers to the pretty cradle, and for a whole day one or the other of the wee builders, neither one of which was larger than a man's thumb, brought feathers. Often, with his bill so full of these that the bird was very little larger than his load, the tiny male would dart in through the little round doorway, followed closely by the female with her portion; and both would fly out again almost instantly. Usually, however, only one feather at a time was carried. The nearest chicken yard was at least one hundred yards distant, and from the frequency of the trips to the nest and the distance the feathers were brought, the birds must have been constantly on the wing.

When all was finished to their satisfaction, the female disappeared into the depths of the swinging cradle and was seen by me no more for twelve days. Her mate brought her food at short intervals during the warm hours of the day, always alighting near and calling before he ventured to the nest. He never went inside while I was watching, but leaned down to her until only the tip of his tail could be seen in the doorway. On the fourteenth day after incubation had begun, a slit was carefully cut in one side of the nest and a cautious peep taken. A wriggling mass of pinkish heads, wings, and legs lay cuddled in the downiest of feather beds. They seemed even smaller than the young humming-birds, and were certainly less than an inch long. Each little head was triangular in shape, with a mere yellow ridge at the point for a bill, and skin-covered knobs for eyes. The slit in the nest we carefully sewed shut again. Before we had gone three yards the parents were there, and the male had gone inside to the nest-lings. A careful watch proved that for the first four days neither of the parents brought visible food in the bill, and it is fair to record them as feeding by regurgita-tion for that length of time at least. (See Foreword.)

On the sixth day the young Bush-tits were covered with a hairlike grayish white down, and had quadrupled in size. This was the last observation of that family I was able to make. Meanwhile several other broods of Bush-tits had flown and were being cared for in the neighboring shrubbery by the adults, although seem-ing well able to feed themselves. An old nest that I secured measured ten inches in length, four and a half in diameter at the bottom, and the doorway was just the size of a dime; a nickle was too large to pass through it.

The call-note of the Bush-tit is commonly described as "scritt, scritt," very weak and thin. Aside from this, the male gives voice to a conversational warble, quite in keeping with the diminutive size of the bird. This species, like the other Bush-tits found in California, are of untold benefit in destroying eggs, grubs, and adult insects injurious to the trees, especially black scales and caterpillars.

741. CHESTNUT–BACKED CHICKADEE. — *Parus rufescens.*

FAMILY : The Nuthatches and Tits.

Length : 4.50–5.00.

Adults : Throat blackish brown ; crown and nape clear brown ; sides of head white ; line over eye black ; back reddish brown ; under parts white ; sides chestnut.

Young : Crown, nape, and throat dark brown ; back olive-brown.

Geographical Distribution : Alaska to California (Mt. Shasta).

California Breeding Range : Northern humid coast belt in Del Norte, Humboldt, and Mendocino counties.

Breeding Season : April.

Nest : 12 to 40 feet from ground, in dead trees, either in natural cavities or old woodpeckers' holes ; materials cattle hair, fur, wool, feathers, or moss.

Eggs : 5 to 7 ; white, sometimes finely speckled with rusty brown. Size 0.64 × 0.47.

IN the northern humid coast belt along the most northern edge of California the Chestnut-backed Chickadee is a common resident. He keeps to the more open woods along the roadways, and is even more fearless than the common chickadee of the Eastern States. Hanging head downward over a slender twig, searching for bugs under the young leaves, swinging in happy-go-lucky fashion from the tip of a branch, scampering in flocks through the tall trees, he is a most fascinating

little chap. His nestlings are handsome fluffy counterparts of their parents, and present an appealing picture
of innocence as they sit on a concealed perch waiting
to be fed.

After the breeding season these birds unite in flocks,
often in company with the golden-crowned kinglets and
Oregon chickadees.

742 a. COAST WREN–TIT. — *Chamæa fasciata phæa.*

FAMILY : The Nuthatches and Tits.

Length : Wing 2.37, tail 3.41, bill 0.42.
> Upper parts sooty brown, darkest on head; under parts chestnut
> streaked with dusky. Eye pale yellow.

Geographical Distribution : Humid coast region of Oregon and California.
California Breeding Range : Transition zone of the coast region from
> Carmel River, Monterey County, northward through the State, east
> through the San Francisco Bay region.

LIKE the pallid wren-tit, this species belongs exclusively to the Pacific slope and is a characteristic bird
of California. It is a common resident of the humid
coast belt, and its clear ringing song is one of the usual
sounds in a quiet tramp along the San Francisco Bay
meadows. That it is much more frequently heard than
seen is due to the shy dodging and persistent hiding
among the low bushes.

754. TOWNSEND SOLITAIRE. — *Myadestes townsendii.*

FAMILY : The Thrushes, Solitaires, Bluebirds, etc.

Length : 7.80–9.50.

Adults : Upper parts brownish gray, under parts lighter ; two white bars on wing ; tail-feathers edged with white on outer web and across end ; bill short, flattened at base ; legs weak.

Young : Plumage, except wings and tail, spotted with buff; wings and tail brownish gray, marked like those of the adults.

Geographical Distribution : From British Columbia to Mexico and from the Black Hills to the Pacific, chiefly along highest altitudes. South in winter to Southern United States.

California Breeding Range : Local in the high Sierra Nevada from Mt. Shasta to San Bernardino mountains.

Breeding Season : June.

Nest : Bulky ; of twigs, pine needles, and grass or moss ; on the ground, under roots of overturned trees, in crevices, in banks, or among rocks near water.

Eggs : 3 to 6 ; pale ashy or whitish, spotted with rusty. Size 0.93 × 0.67.

AMONG all the forest singers of California, the Townsend Solitaire is without a rival; and were he as easily heard as is the mockingbird or the thrush, he, and not they, would be the theme of the poet's verse. Only in the majestic solitude of rugged mountains, when all the world is silent, will he pour out his soul in music ; and to hear him at his best requires hard climbing and long, patient waiting. In the highest Sierra Nevada his song rings clear morning and evening ; and on a tall, dead tree, sharply outlined against the sky, you may discover the happy singer. As you watch, suddenly, without pausing in his burst of melody, he flies outward and up-ward, higher, higher, singing as he goes, until the silver notes fall like a shower of music which the listening earth drinks eagerly. His song ended, he floats down again, alighting with the easy grace of a mocker, and is at rest all but his quivering wings. He seems to squat rather than perch and is happiest when flying.

It was rare good luck that showed me the only Solitaire's nest I ever found. A rolling stone and a misstep landed me flat on my back directly in front of it and within a foot of the water's edge. At first I did not realize my good fortune, because I did not recognize the nest or the young. It was a bulky affair, under a huge boulder which lay in such a position that only two inches intervened between the earth and the overhanging stone; and in this low-roofed crevice the Solitaire had gathered more than a quart of grass, weed stems, shredded bark, pine needles, rootlets, and dead leaves. These seemed to lie in a thick mat as if driven there by the wind, and, but for the hasty exit of a bird, I should never have looked at them.

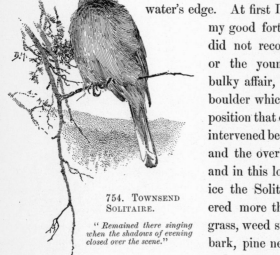

754. TOWNSEND SOLITAIRE.

"*Remained there singing when the shadows of evening closed over the scene.*"

Examination revealed a foundation of larger weed stems and a neatly moulded inner nest. In it were five feathered nestlings. They were much browner in tone than the adults and were beautifully mottled on the breast with light brown. At first they crouched far back in terror, but when I put in my hand to pick up one the others popped out faster than I could catch them. This unexpected début startled me and called the adult male, who had evidently lingered in the neighborhood. He was naturally much distressed and, without coming nearer than fifty feet, lit on a conspicuous perch with many restless turnings and flutterings. Finding that this did not win me from my unfortunate proximity to his brood, he slipped out of sight and began calling to the young in a loud, liquid note more imperative than plaintive. I sat immovable as the rock behind me, and in half an hour was rewarded by seeing both Solitaires come near enough to be recognized without a glass and feed a nestling who was crouching in a heap of stones, thirty feet from the nest site. As the parents were so much alike in form and color, I could not tell which one came to him. The other disappeared behind the stones and probably found the rest of the young to care for. So long as I sat there neither of the adults came into sight again; and, putting back into the nest the young Solitaire I had caught, I withdrew to a distance and hid. More than two hours elapsed before either adult returned to the locality, and then the female was seen slipping silently to the nest. Her mate took up his guard on a high bare tree and after a time tried to sing, but the song lacked the joyous spontaneity of his usual outburst and, cutting it short, he flew down near the old nesting site. In a few moments he reappeared on the bare tree and remained there singing when the shadows of evening

closed over the scene, but the next morning the entire
family of Solitaires had vanished utterly from the vicinity, so far as any trace of them could be found.

758. RUSSET–BACKED THRUSH. — *Hylocichla ustulata.*

FAMILY : The Thrushes, Solitaires, Bluebirds, etc.

Length : 6.70–7.50.

Adults : Upper parts olive-brown, brownest on tail ; conspicuous light
  yellow eye-ring ; sides of head washed with reddish brown ; chest pale
  buff, with wedge-shaped spots of dark brown ; belly white, washed
  with olive on sides.

Geographical Distribution : Pacific coast from California north through
  British Columbia ; south in winter to Lower California, Mexico, and
  Guatemala.

Breeding Range : From Northern California to Alaska, chiefly in Boreal
  zone.

Breeding Season : May and June.

Nest : Compact and bulky ; of plant fibre, shreds of bark, and moss ;
  placed in saplings or bushes.

Eggs : 4 or 5 ; pale turquoise blue.   Size 0.94 × 0.65.

THE Russet-backed Thrush is a common species along
the Pacific coast from latitude 37° northward, remaining
through the summer in the foot-hills and lower mountains, and occurring southward during migration. It is
a lover of dense thickets, retiring and unsociable, protest-
ing against intrusion with a sharp "chuck, chuck," and
dodging into impenetrable tangles when aware that it is
discovered.   Only at twilight and in the earliest dawn
may one hear the rich sweet song of this shy singer.   As
the first full notes float out from the quiet woodland, the
bird-lover knows that a thrush and no other is the songster.   The music is less spirituelle in quality than the

song of the wood thrush, but instantly suggests the latter. A nest of the Russet-backed that was built in a roadside thicket between San José and Alum Rock Cañon contained, May 20, three young Thrushes evidently about a week old. They were sparsely covered with brownish gray down, and pinfeathers were just showing along the feather tracts. Both parents disappeared, and did not come back so long as we remained in the vicinity. Fearing lest any attempt to study the development of the brood at close range

758. RUSSET-BACKED THRUSH.

"*Only at twilight and in the earliest dawn may one hear the rich sweet song of this shy singer.*"

would result in their being deserted by the parents, we allowed the opportunity to pass by and did not visit them again.

759 a. AUDUBON HERMIT THRUSH, OR SIERRA HERMIT THRUSH. — *Hylocichla guttata auduboni.*

FAMILY : The Thrushes, Solitaires, Bluebirds, etc.

Length : 7.50–8.25.

Adults : Upper parts light brownish gray ; tail rufous ; chest thickly marked with broad, wedge-shaped spots.

Geographical Distribution : Rocky Mountain regions, from the northern border of the United States, south to Mexico and Guatemala ; east to Texas; west to the southern Sierra Nevada.

California Breeding Range: Breeds sparingly and locally in the Boreal zone of the Sierra Nevada, from Mt. Shasta south to Owen's Lake.

Breeding Season: May and June.

Nest: Composed of twigs, straws, rootlets, coarse grass, and moss; placed in bushes.

Eggs: Usually 4; greenish blue. Size 0.86 × 0.64.

OF the Sierra Hermit Thrush, Mr. Lyman Belding, who first discovered the subspecies and named it, writes: "It is the finest song bird of the Pacific Coast, breeding in many localities in the sierras on both slopes, usually choosing damp, densely wooded localities for a summer home. It begins to sing about the middle of May at 5,000 feet altitude, below which it is seldom found in summer, and sings until about the first of September, when it leaves for warmer regions. Altogether I have found seven nests of this bird; all of them were within a few feet of paths. They were mostly well concealed, but one was the reverse, having been saddled on a fallen, dead, barkless fir sapling, with nothing to hide it except a few dead and leafless twigs. This nest contained four young, which were quite fit to leave the nest about the middle of June. Three of the nests were in yew trees, one was in a hazel bush, and two were in deer brush. The highest was about ten feet from the ground and the lowest about three feet. There was more or less moss used in all, though the materials used in them varied considerably."

759 c. DWARF HERMIT THRUSH. — *Hylocichla gúttata nana.*

FAMILY : The Thrushes, Solitaires, Bluebirds, etc.

Length : 6.00–7.00.

Adults : Upper parts rich olive-brown, brownest on crown and rump, dullest on tail ; under parts buffy, spotted on chest with wedge-shaped marks of brown.

Geographical Distribution : Pacific slope, north to Washington, south to California.

Breeding Range : Breeds rarely in the Sierra Nevada and northward to British Columbia.

Breeding Season : June.

Nest : In a bush, near the ground.

Eggs : Lighter than a robin's, and unmarked. Size 0.83 × 0.63. (Young Ornithologist, Vol. I. p. 149.)

THIS is an abundant winter visitant to California, occurring in almost all localities west of the Sierra Nevada, but there is only one record of its nest being found within the State. Mr. C. N. Comstock, of Oakland, took a nest of this species containing two eggs, in June, 1883, at the Calaveras Big Trees.

761 a. WESTERN ROBIN. — *Merula migratoria propinqua.*

FAMILY : The Thrushes, Solitaires, Bluebirds, etc.

Length : 10.00–11.00.

Adults : Head, wings, and tail brownish bláck ; back brownish gray ; throat streaked black and white ; breast and belly bright red-brown ; under tail-coverts white.

Young : Under parts yellowish, spotted with brown ; upper parts grayish brown, streaked with light.

Geographical Distribution : Western United States from Rocky Mountains to Pacific.

California Breeding Range : Along the higher Sierra Nevada south as far as the San Bernardino mountains.

Breeding Season : May to August.

Nest : In low trees and bushes, sometimes near or on the ground ; made
of grasses, moss, and rootlets ; plastered with mud, and lined with
fine grass.

Eggs : 4 ; turquoise blue.

THE Western Robin, although like his Eastern representative in coloring, is quite unlike him in habits. Instead of building his nest near the homes of men, he goes up into the lonely Sierra Nevada forests ; there I have found it containing two blue eggs, when snow four feet deep lay a hundred yards away.

All through the spring and summer he remains in the high altitudes of the Sierra Nevada, breeding along the crest of this range as far south as the San Bernardino mountains, but with the cold days of the fall he starts on his vertical migration to the lowlands. In the winter this species occurs nearly throughout the State ; but, as all birds sing best at the mating season, he is almost silent when in the valleys, and seems quite a different bird from the cheery " Robin Redbreast " who picks up crumbs in our dooryards.

The nests also of the Western Robins that I have found have been somewhat different from those of the Eastern bird and very much prettier, being decorated with moss woven in the mud instead of straw, and carefully lined with moss. It is really a beautiful structure, with the mud practically concealed from view. The eggs of the two species are alike, and the newly hatched young are the same naked, wriggling, skinny nestlings in both cases. In both cases, also, I affirm that they are fed by regurgitation for the first four days, the adult swallowing the food before he gives it to the young. By the fifth day earthworms are given the nestlings after being broken into small mouthfuls, and, as the days go by, these worms as well as large insects are given whole. The young Robins are voracious eaters, each one consuming, one authority says, sixty-seven earthworms daily. Certain it is that they double in weight every twenty-four hours at first, and at the end of sixteen days are nearly as heavy as the adults. Usually the eighteenth day witnesses their first flight, but it is a long time after that before they learn to forage for themselves.

All efforts to find a "Robin Roost" in California, such as is common among the Eastern species, have failed and I can obtain no definite information on this subject. It may be this is one of the habits abandoned with their entrance into the Land of Perpetual Summer.

763. VARIED THRUSH. — *Ixoreus nœvius.*

FAMILY : The Thrushes, Solitaires, Bluebirds, etc.

Length : 9.00–10.00.

Adult Male : Upper parts dark slate-color, feathers edged with light gray ; wings banded with dark brown ; side of head black, bordered above with brown line; under parts light red-brown ; breast verging to orange, and divided from throat by a black necklace.

Adult Female : Similar to male, but much duller in coloring.

Young : Like female, but duller and more or less spotted with light brown.

Geographical Distribution : Along Pacific from Alaska to Northern California, south in winter as far as Lower California.

Breeding Range : Recorded at Humboldt, California, during the summer, and may breed there. Breeds northward to Behring Sea.

Breeding Season : July.

Nest: Bulky ; in bushes and low trees.
Eggs: 4 ; pale greenish blue, sparsely marked with brown. Size 1.13
   × 0.80.

From November to March the Varied Thrush, or
Varied Robin, as he is sometimes called, ranges locally
throughout the western part of California and is one

763. VARIED THRUSH.
"Silent and shy."

of the handsomest of our winter visitants.   Wherever there
are holly berries, manzanita, or
mistletoe there are sure to be
flocks of these gayly
colored birds.   Silent
and shy, they take
alarm at first sight of
an intruder and fly up
the cañon, lighting
here and there, but
keeping well ahead of
the observer.   They
are often found, too,
along salt-water
beaches, sometimes in
company with the
Western robin, sometimes alone, but under all circumstances as silent as if they never sang, contenting themselves now and then with a rare chirp that is without
the faintest suggestion of their glorious summer music.

When the first sunny spring days come, the Varied
Thrush starts on his trip northward, taking it by easy
stages, and *en route* he sometimes breaks into a sweet

call-note, but is for the most part as silent as in the winter. By short stages he reaches his nesting ground, in the dark spruce forests from the northern limit of California to Alaska, and here only may one hear him sing. Even here he is the shyest of woodland choristers, seldom seen, though his weird music floats through the silent forest at twilight and dawn like the voice of a spirit bird. It consists of five or six notes in a minor key, each one uttered with a peculiar crescendo of its own, complete and perfect in itself, yet in perfect harmony with the others. In July, when his mate is brooding somewhere among the dense spruces, he chants his evening hymn as full of holy transport as that of the hermit thrush of the Adirondacks, or from the top of some tall pine at daybreak he carols a matin. Never does he seem either enthusiastic or hurried. His spirit is as full of peace as the forest in which he makes his nest.

WITH DUSKY, GRAY, AND SLATE-COLORED PLUMAGE

390. BELTED KINGFISHER. — *Ceryle alcyon.*

FAMILY : The Kingfishers.

Length : 11.00–14.50.
  Head with occipital crest ; bill heavy and longer than head ; wings longer than tail.
Adult Male : Upper parts, crest, and belt across the breast bluish slate-color ; under parts and collar white; wing-quills black, marked with white ; middle tail-feathers slate-color; other tail-feathers black, spotted with white.
Adult Female : Similar to male, but belly partially banded, and sides washed with rufous.
Geographical Distribution : North America.
Breeding Range : United States and British Columbia.

Breeding Season : In California, April and May.
Nest : An excavation 6 to 12 feet long, in a bank, usually over water.
Eggs : 4 to 8 ; white. Size 1.35 × 1.08.

ALONG the streams of the interior valleys of California
the Belted Kingfisher lives, the only requisite for his
happiness being sufficient water to furnish his necessary
supply of small fish. No fresh-water pond or brook is
complete without him. Unsocial and even quarrelsome,
he is usually seen sitting alone on a low perch overhanging the water, waiting in silence for the gleam of a
fin. Suddenly out he dashes, hovers above the waves
a moment, then plunges down to reappear with a struggling fish in his bill and fly to a different perch to devour it. Should he wait long with no success, he flies
to another fishing ground a few yards away, uttering his
harsh rattle ; for he is angry, and wants the world to
know it. This cry of anger rings loud and clear when
he sees you watching him, and all the woodfolk take
warning at it. A deer will stop drinking instantly on
hearing it and break for cover, although you have not
moved an eyelash. Even more than the jay, is the Kingfisher the sentinel of the wooded lakes, and woe to the
luck of the hunter whom his keen eye detects in a
blind.

His nesting place is a steep bank where he can excavate for himself a burrow from six to twelve feet long,
rising at a gentle incline and ending in a dome-shaped
cavity from eight to ten inches in diameter. It usually
takes from one to two weeks of labor to prepare this
subterranean home. In digging, the bird uses his heavy

bill and queer toes with their shovel-shaped nails, two of which have become united half their length through constant service of this sort. His method of starting the hole is similar to that of the bank swallow. Hovering in front of the bank, he strikes again and again as a hummingbird drives his bill into a flower tube, until a small break has been made in the clay or sand of the bank. This is enlarged with bill and claws until he gradually disappears in it, only a shower of sand occasionally testifying to his progress. As in the case of the flickers, both male and female work at the excavating, changing about every twenty minutes. The one who has been resting returns to a perch near by, uttering the characteristic cry, — this time not expressing anger, — and almost instantly the mate leaves the hole and flies off to his or her fishing, taking no notice of the relief guard, who promptly enters the burrow and resumes work. When the nest is completed and the first one of the six or seven white eggs has been laid, the mother bird broods con-

390. BELTED KINGFISHER.

"He strikes again and again."

stantly by day, leaving only early in the morning and late at night.

If she sees her nest being examined she returns at once, uttering her hoarse rattling cry in great excitement, and if possible enters it. The male guards the nest and brings food, rarely if ever brooding the eggs. He sometimes prepares a second and shorter burrow as a sleeping place for himself at a little distance from the original nest.

The Kingfisher's habit of commencing incubation as soon as the first egg is laid causes a great discrepancy in the size of the nestlings, which is doubtless increased by the greater attention paid to the stronger ones, who crowd to the front to be fed. The young are absolutely naked when born, and present a ludicrously top-heavy appearance. Nevertheless, to the eyes of their fond parents they are beauties, and are valiantly defended. I have known the mother to allow herself to be pulled entirely out of the burrow by her hold on a stick thrust in, and then turn back into it, showing fight all the way. The male, meanwhile, was administering a series of well-deserved swooping strikes with his bill on the cap of the tormentor.

Unless disturbed, the pair will occupy the same nest year after year; and if a new one must be excavated, it is usually in the same bank. According to the Kingfisher code of ethics, only one pair can fish in a stream or pond, and their rights are usually respected by all the others.

424. VAUX SWIFT. — *Chætura vauxii.*

FAMILY : The Swifts.

Length : 4.15–4.50.

Adults : Upper parts dusky brown, lighter on rump ; under parts gray, merging to whitish on throat ; tail spined.

Geographical Distribution : Pacific coast region, from British Columbia to Mexico ; east casually to Montana and Arizona. Migrates to Central America.

California Breeding Range : From the Santa Cruz mountains northward through humid coast belt.

Breeding Season : May and June.

Nest : Of small twigs glued together in the shape of a half saucer, and fastened to the inside walls of hollow trees.

Eggs : 3 to 5 ; white. Size 0.72 × 0.50.

THE Vaux Swift, while not very abundant anywhere in California, is found as a migrant in all parts of the State, and breeds in suitable localities from Santa Cruz northward. In a hollow cottonwood tree near the river, and a short distance from the town of Santa Cruz, a colony of several pairs of these small Swifts nest every year. On the fifteenth of June three of the nests contained eggs, and the others were empty but would doubtless be used later. Early every morning, four to five o'clock, the adults could be seen skimming over the river quite near the surface, every now and then darting down as if to sip, and instantly rising again. One that we found on the ground, apparently injured, had very large liquid eyes like the chimney swift and was most appealingly confiding. It was either too stunned or too courageous to be afraid, for it rested contentedly in my

hand, making no effort to escape, not even closing its
eyes as do some birds to feign death. The birds nesting
in the tree were exceedingly timid, and disappeared as
soon as the tree was touched at the base.

447. ARKANSAS KINGBIRD. — *Tyrannus verticalis*.

FAMILY : The Flycatchers.

Length : 8.00–9.50.

Adult Male : Concealed red crown patch ; head, neck, breast, and upper
parts light ashy gray ; throat whitish ; belly lemon-yellow ; wings
brown ; tail black, with inner web of outer feathers white.

Adult Female : Similar, but crown patch smaller.

Young : Like adults, but crown patch wanting, and wing-coverts edged
with buff.

Geographical Distribution : Western North America, south in winter to
Guatemala.

California Breeding Range : Transition and lower Sonoran zones.

Breeding Season : May 1 to June 25.

Nest : In trees, not far from the ground ; woven of twigs, weed stems,
rootlets, hair, string, paper ; lined with wool or hair, and decorated
with feathers.

Eggs : 4 ; creamy pinkish, marked with brown and purple irregularly
over entire surface. Size 0.94 × 0.65.

LOOK for the Arkansas Kingbird in the open country
about the river valleys, rather than in the forests or
mountains ; wherever water and willows are found
throughout the Northwest, you will be sure to find him.
A week or so before their mates come in the early spring,
you may see a company of these gay bachelors in the
tree tops singing with more energy than melody, a queer
conglomeration of the notes of blackbird, blue jay, and

chimney swift, with the cry of a kitten. Far into the night you may hear a soloist, but the chorus is silent after the sun has set. With the earliest peep of dawn they are astir again, down to the water for a bath ; and such a splatter ! Half a dozen in a place like urchins in a swimming pool, and each one trying to make the greatest splashing ! Heads down, tails up ! Heads up, tails down ! Twisting and wriggling, until every little feather stands for itself and the bare skin is plainly visible between them. A shake, a shower of pearly drops flashing in the sunlight, and a very porcupine-like little bird flies up to a sunny perch to preen and shake and preen again. Before his long performance is finished, a lovely golden butterfly flutters by, and, regardless of wet wings, out dashes the hungry little bird after him. Ten to one he gets him, comes back to the perch to breakfast, and flies down to a weed stalk below to hunt for crickets or grasshoppers. After his appetite is appeased he is ready for a scrimmage, and very shortly you may see him tumbling about in midair, the pursued or pursuer of half a dozen of his kind in mock combat.

447. ARKANSAS KINGBIRD.
"*Watching with a great show of alertness.*"

As soon as the demure gray dames arrive from the South, a change comes over the spirit of the bachelor, —

a change of degree rather than kind.   He becomes more noisy, and the combat with his former comrades is no longer for mere fun but for a lady's favor.   If it must be won by war, he is ready; if not — well, he has already selected a snug spot in an oak tree, protected from wind and weather by a broad trunk and heavy foliage, — a charming place for a nest.   Will Madam look at it?   A few days later both are seen bringing twigs, rootlets, paper, rags, — anything in fact that she fancies and can carry and weave into the characteristic structure. Around the top, on the outside, she will, if possible, weave dull-colored but never black feathers in an upright position curving inward over the cradle.   Now, it may be that these are intended for ornament; but as they wave rakishly in the wind, they serve the double purpose of somewhat protecting the eggs and young and rendering it almost impossible for an observer to tell from below whether or not the mother is brooding.   So whenever there is a chicken yard within a hundred yards of the nest tree, feathers will adorn the nest.   Inside it is lined with a felted mat of cow hair, wool, or some warm material or vegetable fibre.   In a week it is completed, and an egg is laid each day thereafter until there are four.   By this time the gay bachelor has become a model benedict, bringing the little mother moths, dragonflies, ants, caterpillars, big black crickets without number, and bees, — the *drones, rarely the workers.*   When she leaves home for a short outing, he sits near the nest watching with a great show of alertness, but not daring in his masculine awkwardness to brood those precious eggs. Even when on guard duty his sex asserts itself, and the sight of a fat moth tempts him to forsake his post long enough to snap it up.

When the mother bird returns, she alights near, preens her feathers carefully, answers his note with a twittering chirp, turns the eggs, and settles herself on the nest with many little fussings to make herself comfortable.

For thirteen days the mother broods while the father bird watches, and then the wonderful bits of bird life in the nest bring another change. Now the male is ever on the wing, catching and bringing food to those hungry pink mouths. At first they are fed by regurgitation, but after the third day large insects are torn apart and given fresh. Fourteen crickets in ten minutes was the record of one busy forager. The watchful male no longer tucks his head under his wings at night, but sleeps with it drawn back between his shoulders, at his post a few feet from the nest. If danger threatens, not only he and the mother bird will defend the nestlings, but their calls will often bring every Kingbird of the neighborhood to the rescue.

In two weeks the babies have grown so that they overflow the nest, and one balances himself outside. And now his lessons begin. As soon as he has learned to use his wings he is taught to catch his food in the same way in which he must obtain it all his life. I have seen the parent bring a dragonfly or other insect, alight with it opposite above the young bird, and call his attention to it in a peculiar low twitter. Then, when quite ready, he releases the prey, which half falls, half flutters, downward. Nearly always the nestling is out after it and back with it in his beak before you can realize how it is done. Many times have we watched them, and the lesson is always given in this way, and always repeated until there can be no fear of missing. Then the young are taken to the meadow and taught to dart down after butterflies or grasshoppers. In some way they learn that the worker bees have stings and must not be caught, but that the drones are delicious morsels. So even at the bee-hive they are a benefit to the farmer, while among the fruit trees and meadows their value can scarcely be overestimated; and the stigma of "Bee-bird," so long unjustly borne by them, is fast becoming a word of praise among intelligent people.

448. CASSIN KINGBIRD. — *Tyrannus vociferans.*

FAMILY : The Flycatchers.

Length : 8.00–9.00.

Adults : Crown with concealed red patch ; upper parts and breast dark gray ; belly lemon-color ; chin white ; tail black, tipped with grayish.

Young : Duller ; wing-coverts margined with buffy, and no crown patch.

Geographical Distribution : From eastern slope of Rocky Mountains to Southern Wyoming, Western Texas, New Mexico, and Arizona ; from Oregon to Lower California.

California Breeding Range : Chiefly in upper and lower Sonoran zones throughout the State ; south into Lower California.

Breeding Season : May 27 to July 30.

Nest : Similar to that of the Arkansas kingbird.

Eggs : 2 to 5 ; similar in color and markings to the Arkansas kingbird's. Size 0.99 × 0.76.

UNLIKE the Arkansas kingbird, the Cassin loves the mountains and the coast. His nest has been taken at

an altitude of twelve thousand feet, yet he is by no
means rare along the lowlands.   Pine, oak, cottonwood,
walnut, hickberry, and sycamore trees are his chosen
nesting sites, and on the horizontal limbs of these the
bulky cradle is constructed.   Twigs, rootlets, weed stalks,
string, rags, and plant fibre form its walls, grotesquely
decorated with feathers, like those of the Arkansas kingbird.   These last, waving rakishly in the wind, are quite
in keeping with the character of the bird.   From two
to five eggs are laid, and incubation lasts fourteen days,
the female alone brooding on the nest, although the
male is always near to defend.   The courage of Cassin
Kingbirds cannot be doubted; and though they are far
less quarrelsome than the Arkansas, they are not a whit
less brave in defence.   In some instances their pluckiness
exceeds that of their relatives, for while the latter are
content to live at peace with hawks and crows, Cassin
Kingbirds drive both these from their neighborhood by
an onslaught both fierce and speedy.   For this they
have good cause, for crows are thieves and cannibals,
feasting on the eggs and young of smaller birds.

The young Kingbirds, although born naked, soon
develop feathers.   They stay in the nest about two
weeks, and are taught to fly and hunt in the same
manner as are the little Arkansas nestlings, and as also
are the young of the Eastern kingbird, called the tyrant.
Of the many broods of the latter that I have watched,
the process has ever been the same.   Nor do they differ
greatly in any of their habits.   The Cassin, sitting on a
fence or a weed stalk, flying out after a passing insect,

chasing a crow, or perched on a dead twig all fluffed
out for a sun-bath, shows the same characteristic traits
that amuse us in his relatives, and we welcome the sight
as of an old friend. His food consists of large insects
and caterpillars, with possibly a peck at the farmer's
fruit. His call is the shrill note of his family, somewhat
modulated.

454. ASH–THROATED FLYCATCHER.— *Myiarchus cinerascens.*

FAMILY : The Flycatchers.

Length : 8.00–8.50.

Adults : Throat and chest light gray, merging to white on the throat ;
belly sulphur-yellow ; upper parts grayish brown ; two white wing-
bars ; tertials edged with white ; outer tail-feathers with outer webs
distinctly white.

Young : Similar to adults, but tail-feathers rufous.

Geographical Distribution : Western United States from Northern Oregon
south to Mexico, east to Colorado, south in winter to Guatemala.

California Breeding Range : Below Transition zone, nearly throughout
the State.

Breeding Season : May 5 to June 24.

Nest : In knot-holes of trees or giant cactuses or in woodpeckers' holes,
and sometimes behind pieces of bark ; lined with hair, snake skin,
grass, and rootlets.

Eggs : 3 to 6 ; buffy, covered with longitudinal scrawls of purple.   Size
0.88 × 0.65.

QUITE different from the noisy kingbirds are these
demure, dignified Flycatchers.   Even in Southern California they are only summer residents, going south to
Guatemala in the winter.   They nest indiscriminately in
the dense thickets of the river bottoms or in the oak
groves of the foot-hills, in the cañons or on the desert
plains, where the cactus and the mesquite are the only

green things. The call may be mistaken for that of the phainopepla, but never were birds more unlike in appearance or habits. This species, more than any other of the flycatcher family, deserves the name of "tyrant" which has been given to its Eastern relative. Not only will it drive all other birds, large or small, away from its nest tree but, it has the reputation of being a "claim-jumper." It has been caught nesting in newly formed cavities prepared by both the Texas and Gairdner woodpeckers, and in one case at least I know the woodpeckers were at work on the hole when driven away by usurpers. The battle raged vigorously at intervals for a whole day. No sooner had the Flycatchers settled the affair and begun to line the nest with rabbit fur, than the woodpeckers returned to the fray; during the temporary absence of the bandits they scratched out every bit of the unwelcome material, and prepared to reoccupy their home themselves. But as always, the fiercer temper of the Flycatchers prevailed over the brave resistance of the woodpeckers, and after repeated defeats they surrendered. Afterwards under the tree was found one broken egg of the little woodpeckers, probably scratched out of the nest cavity in their energetic endeavors to get rid of the rabbit fur, and telling more pathetically than any words the story of their ruined hopes.

This family of Ash-throats were wonderful upholsterers, for the cavity was thickly padded on sides and bottom with short hairs and rabbit fur, until there was little space left. In this were laid three small eggs, and on June 9 incubation began. During the fifteen days

following I did not once see the male enter the nest or
bring food to the female. She seemed a careless mother,
leaving the eggs nearly every day for several hours at a
time. At least once during these absences she had enjoyed a bath, for her feathers seemed quite wet when
she came to the tree. After a short preening she slipped
inside. I presume this was a daily occurrence. When
the nestlings finally broke the shell, it was not necessary
to climb to the nest to discover the fact, for the changed
behavior of the male told the secret. He was all fussiness, and instead of dozing in the sun on an exposed
perch, he came every five minutes or so with bugs for
those small naked babies. At first he swallowed these
and flew almost immediately to feed the young by regurgitation, but as they grew older he carried raw food to
the nest. Often he alighted on the tree near the tiny
doorway and by pulling off the wings and legs prepared
the soft parts of the insect to be eaten by his nestlings.
From the amount of food consumed one would imagine
nothing smaller than young owls inhabited the nursery.
Twenty-two grasshoppers were taken in less than half an
hour, making more than seven apiece. The nestlings
being so small, this seems an appalling amount to be
crammed into those tiny throats ; but it evidently agreed
with them, for they grew at a surprising pace, and on the
sixteenth day they were well prepared for their début.

The first flight was no farther than a sheltering branch
of the same tree, and there the plump little fellows sat
all one day looking out over the green forest world with
wondering baby eyes. On the fourth day, in a lower

tree, the mother gave them a lesson in catching insects. She brought a small butterfly and lit a little above and in front of one of the young. She fluttered out toward him holding the insect in her bill, then she released the latter so that it flew lamely down just in front of the eager baby. He almost lost his balance in his swift darting down after it, and was obliged to alight upon a lower perch to eat it, instead of returning in true fly-catcher fashion to the one just left. This did not suit his fastidious drillmaster, whether because of the low perch or lack of obedience to rules is unknown. She fluttered, scolded, and coaxed; but he finished his meal, shut his eyes tightly after the manner of nestlings, and rested where he was. Later on she had persuaded him to come up higher, and the lesson was repeated with variations at intervals all day. Three days after this he was catching flies for himself, although still following the mother about and begging with quivering wings for the larger insects he saw her seize, and too often getting them.

485. OREGON JAY. — *Perisoreus obscurus.*

FAMILY : The Crows, Jays, Magpies, etc.

Length : 9.50–11.00.

Adults : Forehead and nasal tufts white ; top of head and back of neck sooty black ; back, scapulars, wings, and tail brownish gray ; tail slightly tipped with white ; feathers with white shaft-streaks ; under parts white.

Young : Dull sooty-brown, darkest on head ; under parts brownish.

Geographical Distribution : Northern California, Oregon, and Washington to British Columbia.

California Breeding Range: Higher mountains of Northern California.

Breeding Season: March 15 to May 15.

Nest: Compactly built of fine twigs, interlaced with dry grass, moss, and plant fibre; lined with fine tree moss; placed usually high up in fir trees.

Eggs: 4 or 5; pearl or greenish gray, spotted and flecked quite evenly with lavender and gray. Size 1.04 × 0.79.

WE are accustomed to think of jays as mostly blue, or, at least, having some blue in their plumage, but here is a variety that has not a single blue feather. From the tip of his crestless head to the

tip of his long tail he is sober black, white, and brownish gray. and elegant in are his relatives, fronted, and Cali- some one has much more like chickadee.

Nor is he smooth appearance, as the coast, blue- fornia jays. As said, he looks an overgrown

485. OREGON JAY.

"*Not a single blue feather.*"

Like the chickadee also, he is easily tamed, coming to house or camp for food and becoming so familiar as to be a source of great amusement. It is only necessary to settle oneself quietly and feed him to be overwhelmed with his attentions. Mr. Anthony tells of a funny experience with these birds. He says: "While dressing deer in the thick timber I have been almost covered with

491. CLARKE NUTCRACKER

Nucifraga columbiana

Jays flying down from the neighboring trees. They would settle on my back, head, or shoulders, tugging and pulling at each loose shred of my coat, until one would think that their only object was to help me in all ways possible. At such times their note was a low plaintive cry."

The nest-building commences early in March, and a site upon the horizontal branches high up in a fir tree is commonly chosen. Both birds bring material, — twigs and moss from the sides of the trees, and bits of bark, — and both work at shaping the nest. At least two weeks are occupied in this work and two more in incubation. On account of the high altitude chosen for residence and the lofty site of the nest itself, the breeding habits of these Jays are less frequently observed than those of the jays of the valleys and foot-hills. In California this species occurs only in the northwestern corner and as far south as Mendocino County.

491. CLARKE NUTCRACKER. — *Nucifraga columbiana.*

FAMILY : The Crows, Jays, Magpies, etc.

Length : 12.00–13.00.

Adults : Bill cylindrical ; wings long and pointed ; uniform light gray, becoming whitish on forehead and chin ; wings and middle tail-feathers glossy black ; a patch on wings and outer tail-feathers white.

Young : Similar to adult, but upper parts shaded with brown, and under parts more or less barred with brown.

Geographical Distribution : Higher coniferous forest of Western North America.

Breeding Range : In California the pine regions of the Sierra Nevada from Mt. Shasta to the San Bernardino mountains.

Breeding Season : March 15 to May 15.

Nest: Bulky ; of twigs ; lined with shredded bark, grasses, and pine needles ; placed in coniferous trees, 8 to 40 feet from the ground.

Eggs: 3 to 5 ; light green, irregularly marked with brown, gray, and light purple.　Size 1.22 × 0.95.

"As black as a crow" loses its significance when one looks at the soft gray plumage of the Clarke Crow, or Nutcracker, of the California mountains.　In coloring he is much more like our common shrikes than like the family with which his structure classes him.　And with the change in plumage we find a change of heart, for the Nutcracker has few of the reprehensible traits of his kin. True, if nuts and insects were scarce and eggs or young birds plentiful, his menu would doubtless include the latter ; but his choice is always for vegetable or insect food.　Grasshoppers and the big wingless black crickets he devours in untold numbers, and grows fat on the diet. Butterflies he catches on the wing in flycatcher fashion ; grubs he picks from the bark, clinging to the side of the tree trunks and hammering like a woodpecker ; like a crossbill, he hangs to the under side of a pine cone and probes for seeds ; meat or fish he will steal, if he can, from the camper, after the manner of the Oregon jays. He shares with this bird the epithet of " camp robber." His migrations are always vertical and for the purpose of food supplies.　Breeding commonly in the spruce belt in September when the piñon nuts are ripening, he comes down the mountains in flocks to feast upon them. Farther north, the deep snows drive him toward the valleys until he finds some snow-bound ranchman's or miner's camp, where scraps of the refuse will provide his daily meals.　In the silence and desolation of the winter forest, he is hailed as a welcome bit of life and fed until he becomes very tame and very saucy.

It is on the crests of the Sierra Nevada that these birds are found most abundantly. Here they sun themselves on the highest peaks, frolicking noisily in the clear, bracing air. When hungry or thirsty, out they dart from their lofty perches and, with wings folded, hurl themselves down the cañon with the speed of a bullet. Just as you are sure they will be dashed to pieces, their wings open with an explosive noise and the headlong fall is checked in a moment. Sometimes the descent is finished as lightly as the fall of a bit of thistle down ; sometimes by another series of swift flights ; often by one rocket-like plunge. At the foot a mountain brook furnishes food and drink. As the shadows creep up the sides of the cañon, the Nutcrackers follow the receding sunlight to the summit again, mounting by very short flights from tree to tree, in the same way that a jay climbs to the top of a tree by hopping from one branch to another.

My own records of the nesting habits of this bird as studied in the San Bernardino mountains differ somewhat from those made by observers in more northern regions. The nests were all rather bulky, composed first of a platform of twigs, each one nearly a foot in length, so interlaced that to pull one was to disarrange the mass. Upon this, and held in place by the twigs at the sides, was the nest proper, — a soft, warm hemisphere of fine strips of bark, matted with grasses and pine needles until it was almost like felt. This is stiffened, bound, and made firmer by coarse strips of bark around the outside, these also binding it to the twigs and helping to hold it on the limb. So firmly is the whole put together and fastened to the branch that no storm can move it from its foundations. None of the nests were higher than twelve feet from the ground, and one was only eight feet up. They were in neighboring trees only about fifty yards apart.

On the tenth of March three nests contained two and three eggs respectively; incubation had begun, and silence reigned in Nutcracker Camp. Whichever bird happened to be on the nest was fed by the other, and in one instance I am positive that it was the female who brought food to her mate. I judged this because of her more fluffy, worn plumage and heavier build. Incubation lasted eighteen days. The newly hatched young in these nests were naked and very dark bluish gray. I think those recorded by another observer as "pied black and white" must have been taken at a later date. When two weeks old they do look somewhat mottled, though I should describe it as light and dark dusky rather than black and white; or possibly whitish and dark gray would hit it nearer. They were fed on piñon nuts, which were carried to the nest and hulled by the adult while perched just outside on the branch. I could not discover that any other food was brought them. At first this was given by regurgitation, but when the young were a few days old the food was supplied to them direct.

As soon as they were ready to leave the nest they were coaxed by short flights to the nut pines, and readily learned to shell the nuts and provide for themselves. Then it would seem a complete change of diet was necessary; for they disappeared from these regions entirely, flocking to a locality where berries, fish, and insects abound. By the middle of June not one was left in the old breeding grounds. We missed their harsh "jar-jaar," the flash of their black and white wings in the summer sunlight, and the woods seemed strangely silent bereft of their gay company.

567 a. OREGON JUNCO. — *Junco hyemalis oregonus.*

FAMILY : The Finches, Sparrows, etc.

Length : 6.00–6.50.

Adult Male : Head, neck, and chest black or dark slate-color ; the chest line being convex instead of straight against the white under parts ; middle of back dark brown ; sides deep pinkish brown ; three outer tail-feathers white ; outside pair entirely white.

Adult Female : Similar to male, but slate-color in place of black ; crown and hind-neck washed with brown, remainder of upper parts brownish ; sides and flank dull pinkish brown.

Young : Upper parts brown and streaked ; under parts buffy.

Geographical Distribution : Pacific coast, Alaska to British Columbia ; south in winter to California, east to Eastern Oregon and Nevada.

Breeding Range : From British Columbia northward.

Breeding Season : April to July.

Nest : Of dry grasses loosely put together ; lined with cow hair ; placed generally on or near the ground, in holes among the roots of bushes and trees, and often under wood piles.

Eggs : 4 or 5 ; whitish or greenish white, more or less specked with reddish brown.   Size 0.77 × 0.56.

616. BANK SWALLOW. — *Riparia riparia*.

FAMILY : The Swallows.

Length : 4.75–5.50.

Adults : Upper parts grayish brown or sooty, darker on head and wings, paler on rump and upper tail-coverts ; under parts white, with a broad band of sooty across chest and sides ; usually a sooty spot on breast.

Young : Similar to adults, but feathers of wings and rump with buffy or whitish edgings.

Geographical Distribution : Northern hemisphere in general; in America migrating south in winter to Cuba and Jamaica, Central and Northern South America.

California Breeding Range : In suitable localities throughout the State.

Breeding Season : June and July.

Nest : In horizontal holes or burrows excavated in sand banks and banks of streams ; thinly lined with fine twigs, grasses, and feathers.

Eggs : 3 to 6; white. Size 0.72 × 0.50.

AMONG the birds that I have watched, few have been more timid and more difficult to study than the dull-colored Bank Swallows. Unless you have seen them, as with wings fluttering they strike the first blow into the hard sand or clay of the nesting site, you will be puzzled as to how it is done. Feet and bill divide the toil, and but for the wings you might suppose a small gray mouse at work. The soil must be stiffer than light sand in order to prevent a "cave in," and not infrequently clay or mixed gravel and sand are chosen. These offer a discouraging resistance to the delicate beak and claws, but the persistent little miners keep bravely at work in spite of obstacles, so long as human intruders are out of sight. An attempt to investigate their work or study them at close range, if persisted in, usually results in abandonment of the site.

Like all swallows, these birds are eminently gregarious, nesting in colonies of hundreds. The old birds come back to the same nest year after year, and the young of the colony make homes for themselves near by, until the bank looks as if riddled by cannon balls. The nests are rudely excavated tunnels about two feet long and a little larger at the inner end. In this the Swallows place a lining of grass and feathers. In such a nest we found in one instance six small white eggs resembling those of a chimney swift, but less transparent. In another, lay the naked, newly hatched young, so small and pink that they looked like tiny new-born mice. In another nest there were, on June 2, four fully fledged young, who popped out at the first disturbance. One flew into my hand and died instantly from fright.

Watch from a distance a colony of these Bank Swallows during the morning or evening feeding-time. Every little doorway is filled with eager heads on the *qui vive* for the coming meal. As the adult birds alight at their own nest, the nestlings of the neighborhood whose supper is belated stretch their little necks and watch the feeding with mingled curiosity and longing. A step overhead or a sudden shadow, as of a hawk across the sun, and, as if by magic, the yellow bank presents only rows of empty black holes.

622 a. WHITE–RUMPED SHRIKE. — *Lanius ludovicianus excubitorides.*

FAMILY : The Shrikes.

Length : 8.00–10.00.

Adult : Upper parts pale bluish gray ; bill, lores, and nasal tufts black ; rump whitish, under parts pure white, sometimes very lightly marked.

Young : Similar, but colors less strongly contrasted, tinged with brown and narrowly barred ; wing-coverts tipped with dull light buffy.

Geographical Distribution : Western North America from eastern border of the plains to Lower California, and from Manitoba to Mexico.

California Breeding Range : East side of the Sierra Nevada from Shasta valley, south to Lower California, chiefly below Transition zone.

Breeding Season : April and May.

Nest : Placed in hedges, scrubby, isolated little trees, thorn trees, thickets. The nest is large, loose, and bulky ; composed of weed stems, grasses, cornstalks, rootlets, paper, etc. ; thickly lined with chicken feathers.

Eggs : 4 to 6 ; grayish or yellowish white, marked and spotted with purple, light brown, or olive. Size 0.97 × 0.73.

IT is not easy, at a distance, to distinguish the White-rumped from the more familiar California shrike ; but while the former has pure white under parts, the entire plumage of the latter is tinged more or less with brownish, and the under parts are quite dingy, being covered with wavy hair-lines of brown. The range is different, but the two are likely to overlap somewhat in spite of the dividing line of the Sierra Nevada.

Both species indulge in the much censured habit of impaling their prey on thorns or on the barbs of a wire fence ; but this is largely from necessity when the catch is either mice or small birds, as the habits of the Shrikes in captivity have proved that they must have some such way of fastening raw meat before they can tear it.

He does destroy numbers of small birds each year, and for this we condemn him; but, on the other hand, the good he does may outweigh the evil. Jerusalem crickets, grass-hoppers, field mice, and lizards form the largest part of his diet, and it would be difficult to com-pute his value to the farmer.

622 a. WHITE-RUMPED SHRIKE.

"*Impaling their prey on thorns.*"

Except for the difference in environment, the nesting habits of the White-rumped closely re-semble those of the California Shrike. In fact, but for location, an expert can scarcely distinguish the nest and eggs of the one from those of the other, and the sets of different pairs of birds often differ as much as those of the two species.

622 b. CALIFORNIA SHRIKE. — *Lanius ludovicianus gambeli.*

FAMILY : The Shrikes.

Length : 8.00–10.00.

Adults: Upper parts slate-gray, tinged with brownish ; upper tail-cov-
    erts sometimes abruptly light grayish, or even white, same as the
    white-rumped shrike ; under parts dull white or grayish, darker on
    sides ; breast usually distinctly undulated or narrowly barred with
    grayish, and sometimes tinged with pale brown.

Young: Similar to adults, but colors less distinctly contrasted.

Geographical Distribution : California, especially the coast district.

California Breeding Range : Coast region from Red Bluff to San Diego.

Breeding Season: April and May.

Nest: Usually in a scrubby tree; from 5 to 30 feet from the ground;
  bulky; made of coarse twigs, straws, grass, feathers, cotton, and
  wool.

Eggs: 4 to 7; gray, marked and spotted with purple, light brown, and
  olive. Size 0.97 × 0.73.

IN a scrubby tree or thorny bush the California Shrike
builds her nest of whatever materials may strike her
fancy. Usually the bulk of it consists of weed stems
and rootlets; but an astonishing amount of trash, such
as string, bits of lace, black ribbon, and feathers, were
woven into one that especially interested me. The lace
was recognized as belonging nearly half a mile away, and
had probably been carried by the bird all that distance.
Feathers which waved rakishly on the rim of the structure came from the chicken yard of the same ranch where
the lace was originally owned. In place of the usual
tough rootlets, palm fibre and yucca thread had been
used with a large proportion of shredded bark and
weed stems. The whole was lined with a felted mat of
cow hair nicely padded into place on sides and bottom.
Inasmuch as the bird was seen to bring this hair in
small bunches and all this felting was done by him, the
result was surprisingly smooth and compact. Both sexes
worked busily at the building, being frequently at the
nest together.

On May 17 the first egg was laid, and one each day
thereafter until there were five. Twelve days were required for incubation, and on June 3 five naked nestlings were cuddled in a tangled mass in the soft cup.
And now we had a fine opportunity to watch the hunt-

ing of the so-called "Butcher bird." The favorite perch
was a telegraph wire, and from there swoops were made
downward into the grass with startling swiftness. Not
a movement in the meadow escaped him, not a cricket
could jump but he saw it, even fifty feet away, and
caught it at the first trial. For the first week the food
was swallowed by the adults and given to the young in
a partially digested form by regurgitation. Then came
an intermediate stage in which they received fresh food
bitten up by the adult. After the nestlings were strong
enough to help themselves at all, the insects were held
firmly in the beak of the adult and pulled off, a bit at a
time by the young bird. No food was hung up in the
nest tree.

When the young Shrikes were fully fledged and had
left the nest tree, they still followed the parents about
with open mouths and quivering wings, begging for food
until they were nearly five weeks old. They still tore
bits from insects held in the beak of the adult or impaled on a barbed-wire fence, which was their favorite
perch. When six weeks old, one of the young birds managed to capture a grasshopper, and I saw him trying to
impale it on the fastening of a telegraph wire insulator,
watched by an adult Shrike two feet away.

Although usually silent except for a harsh note of
alarm, both the California and the white-rumped shrike
have a love song strikingly at variance with their reputation for wanton butchery. One can scarcely credit
the shrike with the tenderness expressed by the sweet
warble that comes from the nest tree when the satiny

gray mother bird is brooding the eggs. The harsh voices of both sexes soften to musical gurgles when they are near the young in the nest, and the cruel, bloodthirsty villain of popular bird lore loses the fierceness he is supposed to possess. The young Shrikes inherit the family traits of patience and silence, and even when hungry, cuddle down in unwinking stillness, evidently having fullest confidence that somehow their wants will be relieved.

703 a. WESTERN MOCKINGBIRD. — *Mimus polyglottos leucopterus.*

FAMILY: The Wrens, Thrashers, etc.

Length: 9.00–11.00.

Adults: Upper parts plain gray ; wings and tail blackish ; wings with white patch at base of primaries ; wing-bars, white-tipped wing-quills, and tertials with whitish edgings ; under parts white, tinged with grayish, more brownish in autumn.

Young: Upper parts more brownish, back indistinctly streaked or spotted with darker ; breast spotted with dusky.

Geographical Distribution: United States (rare north of latitude 38°), from the Gulf of Mexico to the Pacific coast, and in Lower California.

California Breeding Range: Chiefly in the San Diegan district, but also throughout the lower Sonoran zone to San Joaquin valley.

Breeding Season: April, May, and June.

Nest: Of small twigs and weeds ; lined with finer material and sometimes horsehair and cotton ; placed from 6 inches to 50 feet high, in thick bushes, hedges, vines, and trees.

Eggs: 4 or 5 ; pale bluish or greenish, spotted with reddish brown. Size 0.94 × 0.71.

THE Western Mockingbird is to Southern California what the American robin is to the Eastern States, — the friendly dweller near the homes of men. From the fruit trees in the orchard, from the shrubs on the lawn, from the tops of the house chimneys, he pours " such a flood of delirious music that the woods and the streams stand silent to listen." No bird has been oftener written about. It would be difficult to say anything original concerning him, but Mrs. Bailey's inimitable description is worth quoting :

" The Mocker almost sings with his wings. He has a pretty trick of lifting them as his song waxes, a gesture that not only serves to show off the white wing-patches, but gives a charming touch of vivacity, an airy, almost sublimated fervor to his love song. His fine frenzies often carry him quite off his feet. From his chimney-top perch he tosses himself up in the air and dances and pirouettes as he sings, till he drops back, it would seem from sheer lack of breath. He sings all day, and often — if we would believe his audiences — he sings down the chimney all night, and when camping in Mockerland in the full of the moon, you can almost credit the con- tention. A Mocker in one tree pipes up, and that wakes his brother Mockers in other trees, and when they have all done their parts every other sleepy little songster in the neighborhood — be he sparrow or wren — rouses enough to give a line of his song."

His nest, placed often in the hedgerows bordering the lawn, is presided over by his more quiet mate, who broods for fourteen days on the mottled blue eggs. There is no need to peek into the nest to ascertain whether those eggs have hatched, for his fussiness pro- claims the event to all who care to know. And now come busy days. Both male and female Mockers flit through the green like silent shadows hunting insects under the leaves, earthworms on the ground, or berries in the garden. These are all swallowed first and delivered to the infant Mockers by regurgitation for the first few days, or until the babies' eyes open. After that, the number of earthworms, butterflies, etc. devoured by those nestlings rivals the story of the young robins who in twelve hours ate forty per cent more than their own weight. There seems to be no limit to their appetite and scarcely any to their capacity. Even after they leave the nest and are nearly as large as the adults, they follow the overworked father about, begging with quivering wings. They are remarkably handsome youngsters, with their soft brownish coats and spotted breasts, well deserving the care and pride their fond parents bestow upon them.

727 a. SLENDER–BILLED NUTHATCH. — *Sitta carolinensis aculeata.*

FAMILY : The Nuthatches and Tits.

Length : 5.00–6.10.

Adult Male : Top of head and nape blue-black ; sides of head and under parts white ; back bluish slate-color ; wings and tail marked with black and white.

Adult Female : Top of head bluish gray ; otherwise like male.

Geographical Distribution : Western North America east through the Rockies, south to Mexico.

California Breeding Range : Transition zone, except in humid coast belt.

Breeding Season : April and May.

Nest : In natural cavities of oak trees or old woodpecker holes ; lined with moss, short hair, and feathers, sometimes grass.

Eggs : 5 to 7 ; buffy white, thinly speckled with rusty and purple. Size 0.74 × 0.53.

PART way up the mountain-sides, on the clearings sparsely covered with large oak trees and surrounded by heavy timber, the Slender-billed Nuthatch makes his home through the long summer days. When the winter storms threaten and food becomes scarce, he sometimes works his way leisurely down to a lower altitude where insect life is more easily found, but usually he remains all the year in the same locality. So protective is the coloring of these slate-colored birds that, but for their nasal "yang, zang, henk-ah, henk-ah" (described by Mrs. Bailey), they might pass unnoticed by the casual observer. They travel head downward round and round the trunks of the oaks, hunting in every crevice for larvæ and clinging to the under side of the large limbs as easily as if right side up.

The pairs remain together all the year round, and their housekeeping commences early in the spring with none of the grotesque demonstration so usual among birds. Quietly a cavity in an oak or a dead pine is selected and filled almost to the brim with feathers, fur, short hair, and moss by the united efforts of both busy workers. By May 1 the nest is complete and the mother bird has begun her cares. She is a close sitter, seldom leaving the nest for food, but depending on the supply brought by her mate and only indulging herself in a wing-stretching once or twice a day. The male is very attentive, going to the nest so often that one wonders when his own meals are eaten. As soon as the young are hatched, which is twelve days after sitting begins, the female assists in the search for food and comes to the nest quite as often as the male. For the first few days the feeding is by regurgitation.

728. RED–BREASTED NUTHATCH. — *Sitta canadensis.*

FAMILY : The Nuthatches and Tits.

Length : 4.12–4.75.

Adult Male : Top of head black ; a white line over the eye and black line through the eye ; upper parts bluish slate-color; tail with white patches on outer feathers ; under parts whitish, washed heavily with bright red-brown.

Adult Female : Entire upper parts bluish slate-color ; under parts paler and duller than male.

Young : Similar to female, but duller.

Geographical Distribution : Mountains of North America, south in winter to Southern United States.

California Breeding Range : Breeds irregularly along the higher Sierra Nevada in the middle and northern parts of the State.

Breeding Season : May and June.

Nest : In an old stub, usually within 6. feet of the ground ; lined with shredded inner bark and vegetable fibre.

Eggs : 4 to 8 ; grayish white, sparsely speckled with red-brown. Size 0.60 × 0.50.

THE Red-breasted Nuthatch is the same familiar slate-gray bird in California that he is in the oak groves of Illinois or the forests of Maine. In California he follows the footsteps of spring up into the mountains, and makes his nest in the natural cavities of dead trees, coming down to milder levels when the snow flies. Yet he is a hardy little fellow and loves the cold, and only the decrease of insect life induces him to seek a fatter larder elsewhere. The nesting habits of this species are essentially like those of the slender-billed nuthatch.

730. PYGMY NUTHATCH. — *Sitta pygmæa.*

FAMILY : The Nuthatches and Tits.

Length : 3.80–4.50.

Adults : Top of head olive-gray; nape and chin white ; line through eye black ; upper parts bluish slate-color ; under parts pale grayish buffy, nearly white on upper breast,

Young : Similar, but wing-coverts edged with buff.

Geographical Distribution : Mountainous regions from British Columbia south to Mt. Orizaba, Mexico ; from the Rockies to the Pacific.

California Breeding Range : Local in Transition zone, chiefly in the southern Sierra Nevada and in the Santa Cruz district.

Breeding Season : June.

Nest : In holes in trees, from 10 to 40 feet up ; lined with wool, cattle hair, and feathers.

Eggs : 6 to 9 ; white, speckled with reddish. Size 0.54 × 0.44.

ABOUT Tallac on Lake Tahoe, as at most points in the Sierra Nevada, these mites in gray scamper up and down the tall pine trees, upside down or right side up, as the case may be, — it is all one to them. In August and September, when the clans gather after nesting time, the trees seem to be literally alive with them. Their shrill " wit-wit " is varied by a whistled trill, and when all the flock is calling at once the combined noise resembles that of a brood of young chickens. They move in crowds from tree to tree, running over the trunks and branches, searching every smallest crevice for bugs, and twittering a low sweet monologue. The flocks keep together all winter, and move down into the valleys as the cold weather comes on and the food supply grows smaller. In March the upward migration is begun again ; but now the flocks separate, numbers dropping out on the way to nest in lower altitudes, and by the time the timber line is reached the birds are scattered into small companies of three or four. By June, nesting sites are chosen, — if, indeed, the same ones are not used each year, — and each little pair is well settled in housekeeping. At Lake Tahoe a hollow post several feet out in the water held a nest of these gray midgets, the entrance being a crevice scarcely large enough for a mouse. Both birds worked busily carrying feathers into this crevice until it seemed there must be at least a peck of them tucked away inside. Although I stood in a boat with hand resting on the post not a foot from their doorway, they came and went as unconcernedly as if no one were within miles of them; and when the young were hatched, the same winsome trust was displayed when an intruder visited the nest.

Another nest found, June 14, ten feet from the ground in a dead pine was also entered through a crevice; the birds displayed the same fearlessness, going inside with food, while the bird-lover stood on her horse's back and tried to make the opening large enough to admit a friendly though curious hand. The brave little bird would light on the trunk just above the nest hole, and, running quickly down, dodge in when the fingers of the investigator were pulling at the crevice. Under such circumstances only a hard-hearted collector would persist in bothering the courageous parents. So, withdrawing to a short distance, she kept watch to learn what food was brought and how often. Both male and female were busy hunting some sort of white larvæ that they obtained from an old stump. The adults did not swallow these, but carried them in their bills, — which convinced me that the nestlings were at least five days old. For my own observation proves that the young of perching birds (as well as *Macrochires* and most *Pici*) are fed by regurgitation for four or five days, the length of time varying in different species and depending on the kind of food brought. Birds eating large insects are fed on raw food sooner than those feeding upon minute insect life, such as ant eggs, gnats, etc., and seed-eaters last of all.

In the case of the Nuthatches the entire brood left the nest, June 16, so that they must have been two weeks old when discovered. They were fed by the parents for some time after their début, and most of the time were kept well up in the thick branches of a live pine tree, where we could hear but could not see them.

730. PYGMY NUTHATCH.

"Both birds worked busily carrying feathers."

733. PLAIN TITMOUSE. — *Parus inornatus.*

FAMILY: The Nuthatches and Tits.

Length : 5.00–5.60.

Adults : Upper parts olive-gray, becoming lighter and grayer on under parts ; belly nearly white.

Young : Upper parts tinged with rusty brown ; under parts whitish.

Geographical Distribution : Pacific coast west of the Sierra Nevada, through California and Oregon.

California Breeding Range : Oak regions of upper Sonoran zone west of the Sierra Nevada.

Breeding Season : March and April.

Nest : In natural cavities of dead trees, or sometimes in old woodpeckers' holes ; lined with rabbit fur or feathers.

Eggs : 6 or 8 ; plain white. Size 0.64 × 0.49.

THE tufted titmouse of the Eastern United States finds its California counterpart in the Plain Titmouse, an independent, aggressive little bird found among the live oaks of the foot-hills. He seldom enters the pine forests, but loves the sunny open slopes, where he wanders with small flocks of others of his species, searching for insect life in a very businesslike way through the tall bushes and oak trees. His common note of "tsee-day-day" is not unlike that of the mountain chickadee, and occasionally he indulges in a whistled "peto, peto" that reminds one of his pretty Eastern cousin. But these are only two of a variety of notes the bird utters under various conditions.

The nest of this species is usually in a cavity of an oak tree limb, the entrance being through a knot hole well sheltered from the rain. To watch the development of the brood it is usually necessary to mutilate the tree, and so I have contented myself with observations made outside the nest. Both sexes share in the fun of nest-building, busily carrying short hair, feathers, and wool, and staying inside long enough to settle a much larger house. They work industriously for five or six days, until it seems as though at least a peck of trash had been tucked into the old oak tree. Then, after a day or so of play, the mother settles down to fourteen days of brooding in the dark nest hole. In a case which I recorded she was fed by her mate at short intervals during all this long incubation, and many were the worms I saw him carry to her. He never entered the nest without first calling from outside, when she would answer and often come up to the door to be fed. We knew at once when the young had come out of the shells, for his exaggerated anxiety and comical airs of business told

733. PLAIN TITMOUSE.
"Busily carrying short hair, feathers, and wool."

his secret. A listening at the doorway further confirmed this three days later. He now scolded at any approach to the nest and tried to win our attention to himself, while the female slipped in and out with food. My theory that most young birds are fed by regurgitation *at first* was confirmed in this case by the fact that, although I was within twelve feet of the nest whenever either bird entered it during that first day, not once was any food visible in the beak of either. After the fourth day the worms and insects carried were frequently projecting on each side of the small beak, but up to that time there had been none seen, though a careful watch was kept with both opera glasses and naked eyes. On the sixteenth day one of the young appeared in the doorway, but dodged back when I advanced a cautious hand. He was very like the adults, but somewhat browner on his head, and the under parts were clouded with light and dark gray. The crest was developing finely, and gave him a pompous look in funny contrast to his timid manner, as he raised it in surprise just before leaving the doorway. As my hand approached, the crest flattened and the little fellow seemed to crouch and slide down backward into the darkness.

738. MOUNTAIN CHICKADEE. — *Parus gambeli.*

FAMILY: The Nuthatches and Tits.

Length: 5.00–5.75.

Adults: Throat and top of head black ; white line over eye, black line through eye ; sides of head white ; upper parts gray ; under parts grayish white, becoming dark gray on sides, washèd with rusty.

Geographical Distribution: Western United States in Boreal and Transition zones from the Rockies to the Pacific coast, and from British Columbia to Lower California.

California Breeding Range: In Transition zone along the whole length of the Sierra Nevada.

Breeding Season: June.

Nest: In an old woodpecker hole or natural cavity, 2½ to 17 feet from the ground ; lined with cattle hair, fur, or wool.

Eggs: 5 to 9 ; white, sometimes spotted with rusty around the larger end. Size 0.60 × 0.41.

" IT was a cheery *chick-a-dee-dee* that gave me my first introduction to this vivacious bird in the sierra, and when I later discovered a nest hidden securely in an old pine stub deep in the forest, I could not resist the impression that here indeed was contentment. Here, far from the habitations of man, and beside an abandoned trail which had long since ceased to re-echo human footsteps, had settled a pair of Mountain Chickadees. No matter how fared their neighbors, and with no time to gossip with the shy warblers of their domain, these little birds seemed unconscious of all else save their piny mansion.

" True, they were not fastidious, and had taken up housekeeping in old quarters ; and their particular stub, with its deep-creased bark and rotten foundation, did not differ from a thousand other stubs which dotted the forest. But this stump, still capped by the winter's snow, was destined to become the arena of intense activity with the advent of spring.

" My first nest was found on June 11, 1898, as Mr. L. E. Taylor and I were walking along the stage road. An old spruce stub, about three feet high and nine inches through, stood near the road, and a two-inch hole in its top led down into the darkness. On scraping the stub a series of hisses came forth denoting young. We tore open one side of the stub and beheld a nest of nine young Chickadees ready to fly. They scrambled up the side of the rough wall and three escaped into the brush. In plumage the young birds were counterparts of the adults. The male bird was calling near by, so we patched up the stub and continued on our way." [1]

The above is the first part of an excellent article on the Chick-adee, too long to be quoted entirely.

The location of the nest of this species is usually less than four feet up; but one en-terprising pair that I myself watched at Mt. Tallac had chosen a deserted wood-pecker excavation in a dead tree, nearly forty feet from the ground. The location was that of the chest-nut-backed chickadee, but I am as positive about the identification as one can be without a gun. In the same grove another pair occupied a hollow stub only two feet up, and so frail that a touch broke open the side. There were three eggs in the nest when discovered, and one was added each day until there were seven, when sitting began. In fourteen days the seven small Chickadees had broken the shells, and lay a wriggling mass of naked bird

738. MOUNTAIN CHICK-ADEE.

"The birds were very fear-less."

[1] Chester A. Barlow, in "The Condor," 1901.

life. We left the side partly open to watch the brood. The birds were very fearless, and allowed me to sit within a few feet of the nest while the young were fed. This enabled me to discover that the nestlings were fed by regurgitation until four days old, when fresh food was given. Whether or not the adult digested the food I do not know; but in every feeding for the first four days the insects were carried to the young in the throat of the adult, and forced up when needed, accompanied by a large amount of saliva.

The young Chickadees were slow in feathering, and remained in the stub nearly three weeks; then a spontaneous exit occurred early one June morning. For fully two weeks longer the young were seen begging to be fed by their indulgent parents, and showed little disposition to become self-supporting. Their plaintive "dee-dee, dee-dee" was uttered continuously when they were not asleep.

741 a. CALIFORNIAN CHICKADEE. — *Parus rufescens neglectus.*

FAMILY : The Nuthatches and Tits.

Length : 4.50–5.00.
Adults : Similar to chestnut-backed chickadee, but sides and flanks pale ashy gray, faintly washed with brownish.
Geographical Distribution : Coast region of California from Sur River northward.
Breeding Range : In redwood belt of coast district, from Monterey to Marin County.
Breeding Season : April.

Nest: In deserted woodpecker hole, or in natural cavity in stub, from 2 to 10 feet from the ground; lined with cow hair, rabbit fur, wool, or moss.

Eggs: 5 to 9; white, sparsely specked with rusty. Size 0.63 × 0.47.

THE Californian Chickadee is confined to the coast region of California, and, Mr. Otto Emerson says, can always be found in the redwood belt. In habits it is similar to the chestnut-backed chickadee, nesting rather higher up in the trees than the mountain variety.

744. LEAD–COLORED BUSH–TIT. — *Psaltriparus plumbeus.*

FAMILY: The Nuthatches and Tits.

Length: 4.12–4.60.

Adults: Upper parts bluish gray; sides of head brown; under parts gray, merging to white on middle of breast; belly washed with light grayish brown.

Geographical Distribution: Rocky Mountain district west to the Sierra Nevada, south to New Mexico and Arizona.

California Breeding Range: Desert ranges southeast of the Sierra Nevada.

Breeding Season: April.

Nest: Pensile; gourdlike in form; of plant down, white sage leaves, spider webs, small bits of lichens and moss; the whole carefully lined with small feathers. Entrance, small round hole in wall of nest near the top. Walls 1½ inches thick at bottom, but ⅔ inch thick at top. Nest placed in low oaks and nut pines, 12 to 15 feet from the ground.

Eggs: 4; white. Size 0.53 × 0.40.

THE Lead-colored Bush-tit is a common resident of the desert ranges southeast of the Sierra Nevada, feeding in the junipers and nut pines, and usually to be seen in flocks.

Their constant twittering, though so faint, reminds one of the chatter of a flock of English sparrows, and the birds themselves, although so small, have all the independent airs of that pest. Some one has very aptly described them as "balls of gray down with a tail stuck in." Fascinatingly fluffy mites they are, busy all day long with their own affairs, ridding the trees of scales, insect eggs, bark lice, and many other injurious forms of insect life. They are constantly in motion, hanging head down under the slender twigs, chickadee-fashion, picking at every crevice in the bark and every fold of a leaf-bud, if perchance a bug lie hidden there, and many a tree owes its good condition to their industry.

The nesting habits of this species are very like those of the Californian bush-tit. Among the underbrush of dry watercourses or on oak-covered hillsides you will find their gourd-like nests, usually pensile but often nestled among the thick twigs of a bunch of mistletoe. Wild blackberry vines, also, are favorite nesting sites. Wherever the pinkish gray cradle may swing, the jolly little housekeepers are friendly and fearless. You may watch them at a distance of three or four yards without producing the slightest interruption in their work. When the young are out of the nest and sitting like wee gray puff-balls in unwinking silence in the bushes, the adult will feed them when you are only two feet away; and fully fledged young may, with infinite patience, be coaxed to perch on twigs held in your hand.

These queer little gray elves endure cold that would kill many a larger bird, and are as lively in the winter as in the summer. Almost as soon as the last brood is reared, they join the flocks of their neighbors and forage fearlessly through the fall woods, until the spring calls them to commence nest-building again.

751 a. WESTERN GNATCATCHER. — *Polioptila cœrulea obscura.*

FAMILY : The Kinglets, Gnatcatchers, etc.

Length : 4.00–5.50.

Adult Male : Upper parts dark bluish slate-color, lightest on rump, bluest on crown. A blackish line over eye ; tail black, outer feathers edged with white ; under parts grayish white.

Adult Female, and Young : Similar to male, but grayer ; no black over eye ; upper parts of young tinged with brownish.

Geographical Distribution : Western Texas, west through Arizona to California and Lower California, south to Mexico.

California Breeding Range : Locally through the Sonoran zone, except the humid coast belt.

Breeding Season : May.

Nest : In bushes, 3 or 4 feet from the ground; made of shreds of bark ; lined with plant fibre and feathers, and covered with lichen.

Eggs : 4 or 5 ; whitish, wreathed and speckled with rusty brown and purplish gray. Size 0.57 × 0.42.

THE Western Gnatcatcher is a common resident of the lower mountain altitudes throughout California, a part of those found here in the winter migrating to more northerly parts in the summer and the rest remaining to breed. Mr. Chamberlin writes of this species in " The Condor," March, 1901, as follows : " The name Gnatcatcher is misleading as regards the diet of this species, for I have repeatedly seen one tackle a butterfly almost as large as himself, and bag his game too. I think, however, his food is largely made up of the eggs and larvæ of insects which are found on the under side of leaves and in the crevices of bark. Of the first few nests I saw being built none were finally occupied on their original sites. One pair near my camping place moved their nest and made it over three times before being satisfied to deposit eggs in it. Each time that the nest was nearly complete, the birds would discover a more suitable site, and then the work of tearing down would begin, and it would be moved piecemeal to the new place. Very thin strips of vegetable vellum and rotten bark-fibre made up the bulk of the nest. The edges at the top were drawn in, making the diameter of the opening less than that of the centre of the cavity. The outside was laced over with cobwebs and spangled over with lichens from the oaks, which were bound on with webs also. The selection of lichens varied considerably with the pairs of birds, some choosing dark brown ones with black backs, while others were paler or brighter, — the usual nest being pale green or silver-gray in color."

Mr. Chamberlin does not record the incubation or development of the broods, so I turn to my own records and find that a nest discovered in a low tree near San José, California, contained four eggs on May 3. The mother was observed on the nest at every visit, and the male near by the tree. She was fearless and let me approach very near, almost near enough to put my hand on her. On May 10 the eggs had hatched and four skinny pink nestlings, no larger than small grasshoppers, lay in the nest, — a helpless mass of wriggling legs, wings, and necks, ending in funny knoblike heads. They were fed by regurgitation until the feathers were well started, and even then the food was often chewed by the adult before it was given to the young.

The nest itself was a fairylike structure, not much larger than that of the hummingbird. When not busy hunting insects for his brood, the father flitted through the trees with a happy little song. It was a silvery warble, eminently in keeping with the tiny singer. His note of protest was a shrill " tzee, tzee, tzee," very like the call of the golden-crowned kinglet.

753. BLACK–TAILED GNATCATCHER. — *Polioptila californica.*

FAMILY : The Kinglets, Gnatcatchers, etc.

Length : 4.15–4.50.

Adult Male : Crown black ; upper parts dark slate-color ; tail black ; outer tail-feathers edged with white ; under parts gray ; belly washed with rusty.

Adult Female : Upper parts slate-color, merging to black on tail ; under parts gray.

Young : Like female, but tinged with brown.

Geographical Distribution : Pacific coast of Southern and Lower California.

California Breeding Range : Local in the San Diegan district, northwest to Ventura.

Breeding Season : March, April, and May.

Nest : A compact, cup-shaped structure ; of vegetable fibre, sage leaves, plant down, and spider webs, lined with plant down and feathers. Placed near the ground in weeds, low bushes, or cactuses.

Eggs : 4 ; pale pea-green, thickly speckled with brownish red or rusty. Size 0.50 × 0.45.

ALTHOUGH this Gnatcatcher is a common resident in most parts of Southern California, its nesting habits are more or less difficult to observe. Only one nest of this species has ever come under my observation, and that was snugly woven in a low bush at San Diego. At first view it was difficult not to believe it the nest of the American redstart of the Eastern States, but closer examination revealed a wideness at the base and ornamentation of tiny curled sage-leaves and bits of lichen bound on with spider webs. It contained, May 10, four nestlings so nearly ready to fly that an attempt to investigate resulted in the sudden departure of the four in different directions. Although the flight of each was short, quick, and fluttering, every one of them succeeded in getting out of sight among the thick green, and search revealed but one of the four. He was a bewitching little gray ball of feathers, with just a promise of the tail that should give him his name. During the hour

753. BLACK-TAILED GNATCATCHER.

"He was a bewitching little gray ball of feathers."

that we were able to watch him, he was fed seven times by the male, the food brought being small flies and green worms. The female was evidently with the rest of the brood, for she did not appear. The male seemed to have no fear of us, and came each time with a little challenging note as if he were tempted to drive us away. A mockingbird, who came near by to drink, was fiercely attacked and driven away by the plucky mite, single-handed.

393 c. HARRIS WOODPECKER. — *Dryobates villosus harrisii.*

FAMILY : The Woodpeckers.

Length : 9.00–10.00.

Adult Male : Nape scarlet ; upper parts black, white stripe down the middle of the back ; wing-coverts lightly spotted with white; outer primaries with white spots ; outer tail-feathers white ; under parts uniform gray, or pale grayish brown.

Adult Female : Similar, but with no scarlet.

Young : Like adult, but forehead spotted with white, and crown scarlet.

Geographical Distribution : Pacific coast from Alaska south in winter as far as Monterey.

Breeding Range : In California, only the extreme northern part of the humid coast belt.

Breeding Season : April 15 to June 15.

Nest : An excavation in a dead tree.

Eggs : 4 to 5 ; glossy white.   Size 0.98 × 0.70.

THE breeding range of this species, according to Major Bendire, is very limited and is co-extensive with its geographical distribution.   It is a bird of the humid coast, Transition, and Canadian zones, only remaining resident in the northern part of California as far south as Humboldt Bay.   In winter it wanders to Monterey along the humid coast belt.   It corresponds in general habits to the hairy woodpecker of the north and east, which rids our orchards and forests of innumerable injurious larvæ, such as those of the boring beetle, etc.   The food of the Harris consists of spiders, ants, other insects, and cocoons, besides larvæ, and sometimes acorns and seeds.

It is one of the earliest of the woodpeckers to breed, the nest being completed in an old stump or dead tree as early as April.   The nesting habits are described as identical with those of the hairy woodpecker ; in the case of the latter, incubation lasts two weeks, the young remaining in the nest three to four weeks. Like all young woodpeckers, the nestlings are fed by regurgitation while in the nest, and are dependent on the parents for several weeks after leaving it.

393 d. CABANIS WOODPECKER. — *Dryobates villosus hyloscopus.*

FAMILY : The Woodpeckers.

Somewhat smaller than the Harris woodpecker, and under parts white instead of gray ; otherwise exactly like the Harris.
Geographical Distribution : Southwestern United States.
Breeding Range : In California in suitable localities almost throughout the State, but chiefly south and east of the north humid coast belt.
Breeding Season : March, April, and May.
Nest : An excavation in a tree, usually 12 to 18 feet from the ground.
Eggs : 3 to 6; glossy white. Size 0.96 × 0.70.

IT would be easy for a beginner to confuse this species with the Harris, and especial care must be taken in noting size, under parts, *and range*, for the Cabanis is rarely met with in the humid coast district.

Breeding in the mountains south and east of the coast belt, it occasionally wanders down to the valleys in midwinter, probably seeking better food supplies. It is one of the earliest to commence nesting, fresh eggs having been taken near San Bernardino late in March. The long breeding season recorded in one locality indicates that two broods are raised. When brooding, it is rather fearless, devoted to nest and young, and refusing to leave until driven away. Then both adults remain near the collector, uttering cries of distress, scolding, and doing all that helpless birds can do for the protection of their young.

Like the Harris, the Cabanis is noisy, particularly during the mating season, when its loud drumming and its "kick-kick, whitoo, whitoo, wit-wi-wi" may be heard all day long in the deep pine woods.

Both sexes share the labors of excavating, brooding the eggs, and feeding the young. Incubation lasts about fifteen days, and the young remain nearly four weeks in the nest, being fed most of that time by regurgitation. After leaving they are fed by the parents for at least two weeks, and usually return to the nest at night to sleep.

393 d. CABANIS WOODPECKER.

"*Both sexes share the labors of excavating.*"

Although the usual height of the excavation is from twelve to eighteen feet from the ground, Major Bendire records one as low as three feet and another as high as fifty feet.

The food of the Cabanis woodpeckers consists of larvæ and eggs of insects, berries, seeds, piñon nuts, pine seeds, and acorns. Major Bendire says he has often seen them pecking at haunches of venison hung in the open air, and picking up bits of fat around slaughter houses.

394 a. GAIRDNER WOODPECKER. — *Dryobates pubescens gairdnerii.*

FAMILY : The Woodpeckers.

Length : 6.00–7.00.

Adult Male : Forehead and stripe down the back white ; nape scarlet ; upper parts black ; wing-coverts lightly spotted with white ; outer tail-feathers white, barred with black ; under parts gray.

Adult Female : Like male, but no scarlet on nape.

Young : Like male, but crown scarlet.

Geographical Distribution : From British Columbia to Southern California, east beyond the eastern slope of the Sierra Nevada.

Breeding Range : Suitable localities as far south as Santa Cruz.

Breeding Season : May and June.

Nest : From 4 to 20 feet above the ground, in old stumps and dead trees.

Eggs : 4 or 5 ; glossy white. Size 0.77 × 0.58.

THE Gairdner Woodpecker is the Western representative of the downy woodpecker of the Eastern States. An attempt has been made to divide this subspecies, restricting the California range of the Gairdner to Del Norte and Siskiyou counties, and calling the species "Willow Woodpecker" south of that locality. But in accordance with Mrs. Bailey's "Hand Book," we shall consider the Gairdner Woodpecker to have a range "from British Columbia to Southern California." The willow woodpecker differs from the Gairdner in being a trifle smaller, with lighter under parts and spotted tertials. (*See* Handbook of Birds of Western United States.)

It is usually resident — and probably breeds — wherever found, although not very numerous in any one locality. Its nesting site is usually in deciduous trees, at a distance from four to twenty feet from the ground. The entrance hole is round, about an inch and a half in diameter; and the cavity excavated is from six to nine inches deep. Both male and female share in the work of excavating, and after the nest is finished, the male sometimes prepares a shallower one for himself in the same tree. Nesting begins as early as the middle of April in Southern California, and four weeks later in Sacramento County. Four to five glossy white eggs are laid, and for fourteen days both male and female share the cares of incubation. After the young are grown, they separate from the parents as soon as they can feed themselves, preparing shallow excavations for their own shelter in dead trees or rotting fence posts. Here they spend not only the nights but the stormy days of winter as well, feeding upon the larvæ of insects in the bark.

The call-notes of the Gairdner vary, being a low "pshir, pshir," when searching for food; a "tchee-tchee-tchee," rapidly repeated, which is its commonest call; and a soft "kick-kick" uttered in the mating season.

397. NUTTALL WOODPECKER. — *Dryobates nuttallii.*

Family : The Woodpeckers.

Length : 7.00.

Adult Male : Crown black, sometimes streaked with white ; occiput scarlet ; hind-neck white ; upper parts barred black and white ; middle tail-feathers black ; outer tail-feathers barred black and white ; under parts white, spotted with black on sides.

Adult Female: Like male, but with no scarlet on head.

Young: Like male, but nape black and crown red ; under parts barred with black.

Geographical Distribution: Southern Oregon and California in Upper Sonoran zone, west of the Sierra Nevada and east of the humid coast belt.

Breeding Range: Same as *Geographical Distribution.*

Breeding Season: April and May.

Nest: In dead branches or beneath the bark of stumps.

Eggs: 3 to 6 ; white. Size 0.94 × 0.69.

THE Nuttall Woodpecker breeds west of the Sierra Nevada throughout the greater portion of California, being most abundant in the southern part of its range. In nesting it prefers the oak trees, digging a cavity eight inches deep, about twenty feet from the ground. Mr. Beck, of Berryessa, California, records it as breeding in the mountains east of Santa Clara County, and in one instance occupying a limb in a sycamore tree where a pair of red-shafted flickers had their nest. Occasionally it chooses elders, willows, and giant cactuses. Nesting commences early in April, and after the pearly white eggs are laid both adults share in the incubation, which lasts fourteen days. The young remain in the nest three to four weeks, and after leaving return each night to sleep in it. Both parents defend their nest and young with great courage, the mother sometimes allowing herself to be taken on the nest rather than leave it. Their food consists of insects, larvæ, berries, and fruit.

The call of the Nuttall Woodpecker is described as a series of loud rattling notes entirely unlike those of any other woodpecker. In habits it resembles Gairdner's woodpecker ; but its choice of locality is quite different, as it prefers a higher altitude and is seldom found along streams.

399. WHITE–HEADED WOODPECKER. — *Xenopicus albolarvatus.*

FAMILY : The Woodpeckers.

Length: 8.90–9.40.

Adult Male: Head, neck, upper part of chest, and patch on the wing, white ; nape bright scarlet ; rest of plumage black.

Adult Female: Similar to male, but with no scarlet.

Young: Similar to male, but scarlet on crown instead of on nape.

Geographical Distribution: Mountains of the Pacific coast, including both slopes of the Sierra Nevada, from Washington to Southern California.

Breeding Range: The Sierra Nevada and Cuyamaca mountains to Mt. Shasta.

Breeding Season: May.

Nest: 4 to 18 feet from the ground, in stumps.

Eggs: 4 to 7 ; crystalline white.   Size 0.96 × 0.75.

THE range of the White-headed Woodpecker in California is restricted to higher mountain ranges from Oregon to Southern California. It is common in the fir forests of the Sierra Nevada from four thousand feet nearly to the summit, seldom descending to a lower altitude than three thousand feet. His conspicuous white head makes him recognized by the veriest tyro in bird lore. One would suppose this feature would make him an easy mark for hunters, but in reality there is an effect of protective coloring in the very sharpness of the contrasting black and white, — the one standing out so strongly in the light as to make the other seem part of the shadow and not of the bird.

This is emphatically a silent bird, particularly in the winter. Even during the breeding season in the Sierra Nevada, I have never heard it utter more than a sharp

" hitt-hitt " as it chases its mate through the wood. The nest is usually in a dead pine or fir, seldom higher than twelve feet from the ground. The entrance is round, about one and a half inches in diameter, and the interior is from eight to thirteen inches deep. From four to seven white eggs are laid on a thin lining of sawdust made by the excavating. Both male and female brood during the fourteen days required for incubation. The young are fed by regurgitation at first, and afterwards upon the large black ants so numerous in all the dead pine stumps. They remain in the nest nearly four weeks and, for at least ten days after leaving it, are fed and cared for by both parents, returning to the old nursery to sleep at night while the adults remain on guard outside.

Dr. Merrill, U. S. A., has studied the habits of this bird thoroughly, and written of it as follows : " I have rarely heard this Woodpecker hammer, and even tapping is rather uncommon. So far as I have observed,

399. WHITE-HEADED
WOODPECKER.

" Where the bark is thickest and roughest."

— and during the winter I watched it carefully, — its principal supply of food is obtained in the bark, most of the pines having a very rough bark, scaly and deeply fissured.

The bird uses its bill as a crowbar, rather than as a hammer or chisel, prying off the successive scales and layers of bark in a very characteristic way. This explains the fact of its being such a quiet worker, and, as would be expected, it is most often seen near the base of the tree, where the bark is thickest and roughest. It must destroy immense numbers of *Scaly tidæ*, whose larvæ tunnel the bark so extensively, and of other insects that crawl beneath the scales of bark for shelter."

400. ARCTIC THREE–TOED WOODPECKER.

Picoides arcticus.

FAMILY : The Woodpeckers.

Length: 9.00–10.00.
 Foot with three toes, two pointing forward and one backward.
Adult Male: Crown patch yellow ; upper parts iridescent bluish black ; wings finely spotted with white; outer tail-feathers white ; under parts white; sides barred with black ; forehead and sides of head black and white.
Adult Female: Like male, but without yellow on crown.
Young: Like adult, but crown patch smaller ; under parts brownish ; upper parts dull black.
Geographical Distribution: Northern North America from the arctic regions through the Northern United States.
California Breeding Range: In the Sierra Nevada as far south as Lake Tahoe.
Breeding Season: May and June.
Nest: Usually in dead trees, 8 to 10 feet from the ground.
Eggs: 3 to 4 ; white. Size 0.95 × 0.71.

" THE Arctic Three-toed Woodpecker is essentially a bird of the pine, spruce, fir, and tamarack forests, and is rarely seen in other localities. It is generally a resident, rarely migrating to any distance, and probably breeds wherever found. . . . Its sharp shrill 'chirk, chirk' can be heard in all directions. It seems to feed entirely on such wood worms as attack spruce, pine, and other soft-wood timber that has been fire-killed. It never attacks a healthy tree, and is far more beneficial than harmful. . . . Like the hairy woodpecker, they are persistent drummers, rattling away for minutes at a time on some dead limb, and are especially active during the mating season in April. I have located more than one specimen by following the sound when it was half a mile away. . . . May 10 I found a male busily at work on a pine stump only two and a half feet high and eighteen inches in diameter, standing within a few feet of the road, and close to a charcoal-burner's camp. On May 25 the cavity was found to be eighteen inches deep and was gradually enlarged toward the bottom. The four eggs it contained had been incubated four days. The female was on the nest, and uttered a hissing sound as she left it, and might easily have been caught, as she remained in the hole until the stump was struck with a hatchet." [1]

Incubation lasts two weeks, and the young remain in the nest four to five weeks according to early or late hatching. They are fed by regurgitation for the first nine days and possibly longer, but adults have been seen carrying insects to the nest on the fifteenth day. When alighting with food the adult gives a low cooing call and is answered by a hissing clatter from the young that can be heard at some distance from the nest tree.

Where this bird occurs in California the local orni-

[1] Bendire.

24

thologists have made it a subspecies of the Arctic Three-toed and call it *Picoides arcticus tenuirostris,* or Sierra Three-toed Woodpecker. It is like the Arctic in color and habits, but has a more slender bill. It is found in the northern Sierra Nevada as far south as Lake Tahoe.

404. WILLIAMSON SAPSUCKER. — *Sphyrapicus thyroideus.*

FAMILY : The Woodpeckers.

Length : 9.00–9.75.

Adult Male : Upper parts, throat, and breast black ; throat with a median stripe of bright red ; rump and patch on wing-coverts white ; quills finely spotted with white ; sides of head striped with white ; belly yellow.

Adult Female : Body barred with brown or black and white ; rump white ; head plain brown ; chest with black patch ; middle of belly yellow.

Geographical Distribution : Western United States, from the Rocky Mountains to the western slope of the Sierra Nevada ; winters in Southern California.

California Breeding Range : Along the Sierra Nevada from Shasta to the San Jacinto mountains.

Breeding Season : May 15 to July 1.

Nest : In large dead pines, 5 to 60 feet from the ground.

Eggs : 5 or 6 ; pure white. Size 0.97 × 0.67.

So unlike are the male and the female of this Wood pecker that for a long time they were listed as different species by ornithologists. The general effect of the male's coloring is black, that of the female brown ; and unless one is forewarned or experienced, he is apt even now to look for another name when he first sees the female.

They nest commonly in the Sierra Nevada near Lake

Tahoe and are not at all difficult to watch. The site chosen for a nest is oftenest in the sheltered woods, where they excavate in the trunk of a dead tree. One that I watched was situated about ten feet from the ground; standing on my saddled horse, I could reach into it but for one obstacle, — the relative size of the door and my hand. I was unwilling to cut away the wood about the door, so contented myself with observing from a distance of fifteen feet. The father bird was especially fearless, and sat most of the time on the top of the nest tree, where he drummed occasionally to reassure his mate in the nest. When I tried to put my hand into the cavity, both birds came within six feet of me, uttering low angry calls, and before I had fairly reseated myself in the saddle, the male had entered the nest. I could hear him reassuring the young, which all this time had kept up a tremendous hissing, after the manner of all birds born in hollow trees. As I sat there just far enough away to see well what was going on, both parents brought insects to the nestlings every ten minutes. These were usually butterflies, grasshoppers, or dragonflies; but the male frequently picked up the large ants that swarmed over a log I had broken open, and carried them to the nest. He was much more fearless than the female, — a trait so rare among birds that it deserves especial mention.

In the same tree with this nest of the Williamson Sapsuckers there were a nest of the pygmy nuthatches on the other side of the tree and another of a bluebird a little lower down. The nuthatches were, if possible, even more courageous than the Sapsuckers, but the blue-birds flew far away.

The young Sapsuckers must have been fledged when I discovered the nest, June 10; for on the twelfth they came out of the nursery and flew away with their brown mother and black and white father into the deeper woods, where I lost sight of them. A plummet dropped into the nest hole told me it was nine inches deep. It was on the sunny south side of the tree, and several degrees hotter inside than the surrounding atmosphere. As is always the case with woodpeckers, every bit of excrement had been carried away while fresh by the parent, and the nest was as clean as if freshly excavated.

405 a. NORTHERN PILEATED WOODPECKER.
Ceophlœus pileatus abieticola.

(Common Names: Cock of the Woods; Log Cock.)

FAMILY: The Woodpeckers.

Length : 16.00–19.00.

Adult Male : Head conspicuously crested; bill longer than head; top of head, crest, and malar stripe scarlet; chin and side of head pale lemon-color or white; a white patch on the wings; under wing-coverts white; rest of plumage dull brownish black; feathers of belly tipped with ashy.

Adult Female : Like male, but crown and malar stripe brown instead of red.

Young : Crest salmon-colored, otherwise like female.

Geographical Distribution : Heavily wooded districts of North America, from the Southern Alleghanies north to latitude 63°, west to the Pacific (Bailey).

California Breeding Range : Timbered areas in the northern part of the Sierra Nevada as far south as King's River Cañon and Eel River.

Breeding Season : May and June.

Nest: Hole excavated in the trunk of a large dead tree, from 20 to 75 feet from the ground.

Eggs: 3 to 5 ; white. Size 1.40 × 0.99.

THROUGHOUT the northern part of California in the forests of the Sierra Nevada, the handsome Pileated Woodpecker may be frequently heard, occasionally seen, but never watched unless you are going to live in his haunts months at a time for the especial purpose of making friends with him. But in the Yosemite Valley he is the most conspicuous of all the birds, as well as one of the least shy. With slight trouble you may find the location of his nest in a tall live cedar fifty feet from the ground, and watch the pair as they care for their young. Here the mating season commences about the first of May, incubation lasts eighteen days, and the young remain in the nest nearly six weeks. It is not uncommon to find these nestlings still in the nursery the first week in July in the Yosemite forests. The parents are very devoted to their treasures whether they be eggs or infant Woodpeckers, and the male rarely fails to stand on guard on a high perch ready to warn and defend should possible danger threaten. The method of feeding is like that of the flickers, by regurgitation for the first two weeks or longer. The adult comes with gular pouch full of food and alights at one side of the nest hole to rest a moment. Though he may have come noiselessly and from the other side of the tree, yet his approach is always heralded by a mowing-machine chorus from the young, plainly heard some yards away. If old enough, the queer-looking little heads are thrust out of the door-

way, and the parent, inserting his long bill into the open
mouth of a youngling, shakes it,vigorously, thereby emptying the food from his throat into that of his offspring.
Each in turn is fed in this odd fashion.

The newly hatched Pileated Woodpeckers are even
homelier than young flickers. They have the same ball-
shaped body with long, help-
lessly weak legs set very far
back on it, and two long
appendages that look like fat
earthworms rather than
like wings. Their in-

ordinately
long necks
end in a giraffe-
like head with
sightless eyes,
large ear-holes,

405 a. NORTHERN
PILEATED WOOD-
PECKER.

"*After a few trials he
learns to hammer right
merrily.*"

and a grotesque bill in which the lower mandible pro-
jects beyond the upper. They roll helplessly about,
unable to squat on account of their round bodies, and
unable to steady themselves with either their legs or
wings; their chief means of support being the neck,
which braces itself by the head as well as it may.

If a finger be offered to their open mouths, they swallow two inches of it, eagerly sucking on it with surprising
strength.

While you have been examining the young, — which, if you are a woman, must be lowered to you, — the parents have ceased to protest and are watching you in silence from behind a tree trunk a hundred feet or so away. After you have replaced the nestlings and left the immediate vicinity, the adult birds will wait an hour or more before they come back to investigate the damage, and then it is the mother who finally ventures into the molested home to brood again, while the " Cock of the Woods " watches, as before, from a neighboring tree.

For a week or two after the young have left the nest, they follow their parents begging for food with ludicrous eagerness ; at this time the provender brought them consists of nuts, berries, ants, and the larvæ of beetles. These, especially the nuts, are often placed in a crevice of the bark, and the youngster is compelled to pick them out. After a few trials he learns to hammer right merrily and is ready to forage for himself. Unlike other woodpeckers, but like the flickers again, the Pileated is often seen eating ants on the ground or on a log; hence his name of " Log Cock."

The call-notes of the Pileated Woodpecker are very like those of the flicker, but louder and flatter in tone, " kac-kac-kac-kac " and " wucker-wucker-wucker " being the most common. When the bird is much excited, the note is a modification of both a loud and harsh " hiker-hiker " rapidly repeated. As it excavates a new nest every year, there are often fresh chips at the foot of the nest tree to the amount of two or three quarts. The cavity is from seven to thirty inches deep and about six inches wide at the bottom, unlined save for a small amount of chip-like sawdust. Like that of the flicker's nest, the doorway is quite as apt to be oval as round, and is from three to four inches in diameter. The eggs are from three to five, glossy, transparent white, and become opaque as incubation advances.

407 a. CALIFORNIAN WOODPECKER. — *Melanerpes formicivorus bairdi.*

FAMILY : The Woodpeckers.

Length : 8.50–9.50.

Adult Male : Upper parts, sides of head and chest iridescent black ; chest streaked with white ; crown red ; feathers around base of bill black, bordered by band of white or yellow ; rump, wing-patch, and belly white.

Adult Female : Like male, but with red crown separated from the white or yellow forehead by a black band.

Young : Like adults, but colors duller.

Geographical Distribution : Mexico and western border of United States from Western Texas to California, and north along Pacific coast to Southern Oregon ; south to Lower California.

California Breeding Range : Suitable localities in lower Transition zone west of the Sierra Nevada.

Breeding Season : April 15 to July 15.

Nest : Cavity or excavation in trees, from 20 to 50 feet from the ground.

Eggs : 4 or 5 ; glossy white. Size 1.00 × 0.75.

THIS is the Woodpecker most uniquely Western in all his ways. He belongs exclusively to the oak belt and can be found only where these trees are abundant. Not at all shy, he seems to the Eastern bird-lover to replace the redhead of the home forests, and his gay " wake-up, wake-up," is a welcome greeting from an old friend. Like the redhead, he is very emphatic in his manner of

407a. Californian Woodpecker

Melanerpes formicivorus bairdi

speech, emphasizing his conversation with ludicrous contortions of his body.

But his uniqueness lies in his habit of storing up food for the winter, according to the advice of King Solomon, — food in this instance meaning the cartridge-like acorns of the live oaks. For each one of these he chisels out a hole which is so exact a fit that once the nut is in, man requires a tool to get it out. Round and round a tree he goes, filling it as full of these acorns as the law allows, and not sparing the limbs until it is honeycombed from top to bottom. In front of the residence of Dr. David Starr Jordan at Palo Alto, stands one of these trees, a living monument to the industry of *Melanerpes formicivorus bairdi*.

Like the redhead again, he is a valiant defender of his property, — be it acorns, eggs, or nestlings. He is universally lord of all he surveys, fearing no bird of his own size and no quadruped of any size. He will fly furiously at a squirrel, and set upon a cat without the least hesitation, aiming directly for its eyes, provided puss is dangerously near his young. Though I have never found him quarrelsome or tyrannical, I have frequently noticed that smaller birds scatter when he alights in their vicinity.

His nest is excavated in a live oak tree, usually on the under side of a large branch at some distance from the trunk, and from fifteen to twenty-five feet from the ground. Both male and female share in the labor of excavating the nest and in the incubation of the eggs. The cavity is usually about eighteen inches deep, five inches wide at the bottom, and one and three-fourths inches in diameter at the entrance. Incubation lasts seventeen days, and the young remain in the nest about three and a half weeks. They are fed upon the larvæ of black beetles, grasshoppers, ants, and fruit. At certain seasons of the year this species is almost exclusively a fruit-eater, and at all times it prefers vegetable to animal food. Its call is a loud, clear two-syllable note, which it usually utters when perched on top of a stump, where it loves to sit and drum. It returns to the same nest tree year after year, but usually excavates a new cavity, frequently utilizing the old one as a shelter for the male on stormy nights.

411. GILA WOODPECKER. — *Melanerpes uropygialis.*

FAMILY : The Woodpeckers.

Length : About 10.00.

Adult Male : Head, neck, and under parts light grayish brown ; middle of crown red ; back, rump, and upper tail-coverts barred with black and white ; middle of belly yellowish ; middle and outer tail-feathers marked with white.

Adult Female : Like male, but no red on crown.

Young : Like adults, with colors duller and markings less distinct.

Geographical Distribution : Southeastern California, southern part of Arizona and New Mexico, south through Lower California.

California Breeding Range : Around the Lower Colorado River, near Fort Yuma.

Breeding Season : May.

Nest : In excavations in trees or in giant cacti.

Eggs : 3 to 5 ; white. Size 0.96 × 0.71.

THE range of the Gila Woodpecker in California is restricted to the southeastern corner, bordering on the Lower Colorado River, in the vicinity of Fort Yuma.

Here it breeds in small numbers, making its nest in cottonwoods, sycamores, and wherever possible in the giant cactus. In fact, Mr. Anthony asserts that its range is governed by the presence or absence of the giant cactus, in which it nests, and on the fruit of which it feeds.

In general habits it is like the Californian wood-pecker, — talkative, noisy, and restless. "When flying from one point to another it usually utters a sharp shrill ' hiut' two or three times, resembling the common call of the phainopepla, and which may readily be mistaken for it. It is also more or less addicted to drumming on the dead tops of cottonwood, sycamore, and mesquite trees. Its flight, like that of most woodpeckers, is undulating rather than swift " (Bendire).

The food of the Gila Woodpecker consists of larvæ, grasshoppers, ants, beetles, the fruit of the giant cactus, and the berries of that species of mistletoe found on oaks and mesquite trees in that region. The same nest excavation is used several years in succession. Major Bendire says that incubation lasts about two weeks, and that both sexes assist in preparing the nest and brooding the eggs.

425. WHITE–THROATED SWIFT. — *Aëronautes melanoleucus.*

FAMILY : The Swifts.

Length : 6.00–7.00.
Adults : Tail about half as long as wing, with stiff narrow feathers ; upper parts blackish ; throat, breast, wing-patch, and rump white ; sides dusky or black.

Geographical Distribution: Western United States, from the Pacific east to Western Nebraska ; from Washington to Lower California.

California Breeding Range: Among the mountainous regions east of the humid coast belt, and along the coast southward from Santa Cruz.

Breeding Season : June and July.

Nest: Glued to crevices of cliffs or walls of caves ; made of short twigs and weed stems and soft vegetable matter ; lined with a few feathers.

Eggs : 4 or 5 ; white. Size 0.88 × 0.53.

THE White-throated Swift is an abundant resident of Southern California, and may be seen in numbers in the vicinity of the Old Mission at San Juan Capistrano, as well as in Los Angeles County and other localities.   Its nesting site is the most inaccessible cliff of the regions where it is resident ; consequently only a few nests have been investigated.   The best account of one is given by Mr. W. B. Judson, of Los Angeles, where the nest was found.   "It was situated about eighty feet from the top of a cliff and one hundred and twenty-five feet from the ground, in a cave about seven feet high, ten feet wide, and extending some seven feet in the face of the cliff.   The nest was placed in a small hole in the roof of the cave, — almost too small to get my hand in without enlarging it, — extending

425. WHITE-THROATED SWIFT.

"*Its nesting site is the most inaccessible cliff.*"

about a foot up in the rock, and then there was a small cleft in which it was placed. It was so firmly glued to the rock that it could not be pulled off without tearing it to pieces. The materials of which it was constructed felt soft and spongy; there were no sticks or twigs in it, and it was lined with a few feathers. Evidently it had been in use during more than one season, as the vegetable matter was quite disintegrated."

458 a. WESTERN BLACK PHŒBE. — *Sayornis nigricans semiatra.*

FAMILY : The Flycatchers.

Length : 6.25–7.00.

Adults : Entire plumage slate-black, except for white belly; outer web of tail-feathers and under tail-coverts white.

Young : Similar to adults, but wing-coverts tipped with light rusty.

Geographical Distribution : Pacific coast from Mexico to Oregon ; eastward nearly to Southern Texas.

California Breeding Range : In lower Sonoran zone from latitude 28° northward.

Breeding Season : April 15 to June 15.

Nest : A compact though bulky mass of mud mixed with dried grass, weed fibre, and hair; lined with soft feathers ; attached to rocks, beams of buildings, or bridges.

Eggs : 3 to 6 ; white, sometimes finely speckled with reddish brown around the larger end.

THE Black Phœbe resembles the Eastern phœbe even more than does the Say. It builds about human habitations near water, and uses mud in the construction of its nest, which is on the same plan, though lacking the beauty, of that of the Eastern variety. Like the latter, it is greatly attached to a locality once used as a nesting site, and returns to it year after year, repairing the old nest or building a new one. The exterior of these nests is made of mud mixed with scraps of vegetable fibre and hair. Inside, it is lined with fine roots, strips of bark, hair, wool, and feathers. For some unexplained reason the nest of this species, like that of Say phœbe and the Eastern phœbe, is infested with innumerable insects, which frequently cause the death of the young. This seems strange in the case of birds that splash in the water so much as do these. One of the first lessons taught the young is the delight of a bath in an irrigation ditch ; to this wholesome recreation they are initiated when about five weeks old.

The food habits are those of all flycatchers, — a restless darting out into the air after a passing butterfly, or down for a grasshopper, and always back to the same perch. Nearly every insect with wings is seized by them with equal alacrity, and their capacity for eating is out of all proportion to their size. Especially is this true of the nestlings, to whom food is brought every two or three minutes and eagerly swallowed with no indications of surfeit. Possibly it is on account of this they develop so rapidly, for in fourteen days the weak naked babies become fully fledged Phœbes, with a pretty call, not unlike that of their parents, but which, to imaginative ears, suggests " feed me, feed me ! " And I may add that this is the interpretation put upon it by the father bird. At first the feeding is done by regurgitation, but when five days old the nestlings are fed on fresh insects.

As soon as they are ready to fly the male takes entire care of them, leaving the patient mother to repair the old nest and undertake the bringing up of a second family. He teaches the young to catch food on the wing, just as the Arkansas and Cassin kingbirds teach theirs, and as I believe all flycatchers do, — by releasing a maimed insect in the air just in front of the hungry little one, who, forgetting fear, instinctively darts out to catch it. At this the father gives a cheery note of triumph, which the nestling soon imitates and unconsciously begins to utter whenever he is successful in seizing his small prey. This and a low twitter during the mating season, and the conventional announcement of his name in a plaintive tone, are all the songs he ever sings.

475. BLACK-BILLED MAGPIE. — *Pica pica hudsonica.*

FAMILY : The Crows, Jays, Magpies, etc.

Length : 17.40–21.75.

Adults : General plumage iridescent black, except belly and wing-patches white ; bill and naked skin of orbital regions black ; tail long and graduated.

Young : Head, neck, etc. dull black, without iridescence on crown.

Geographical Distribution : Middle and Western North America, Alaska and Hudson Bay to Northern Arizona and New Mexico ; east to Eastern Colorado.

Breeding Range : East of the Sierra Nevada, north to Shasta valley, south to Mono Lake.

Breeding Season : April 20 to July 1.

Nest : Globular ; 2 feet in diameter and 3 feet high ; made of sticks, inner walls of mud, lining of fine rootlets ; entrance hole on one side ; placed in small oaks, cottonwoods, and pines, 3 to 20 feet from the ground.

Eggs : 7 ; grayish, heavily and regularly blotched with brown. Size 1.37 × 0.89.

To the tourist or sojourner from the East, the Magpie is one of the most interesting features of Western fauna, ranking with burrowing owls and prairie dogs. From the time one first catches a glimpse of these Magpies until one's face is set homeward, they are a fascinating study. Much handsomer and more intelligent than crows, they are comparatively less known. The average Westerner regards them as a nuisance, and I suspect he is not far wrong in this estimate, but, like their relatives the jays, they yet have something to commend them.

About Lake Tahoe the Black-billed Magpies abound; they build their nests in the young oaks as close to the dooryards as they are allowed. One pair that I watched had nested for six years in the same tree ten feet from a dwelling, and were almost as tame as chickens. They were tolerated on the ground that small rodents will not come where they are. While this theory is not entirely borne out by the facts, there is a grain of truth in it, for a magpie will watch the burrow of a ground squirrel like a terrier at a rat hole and pounce as swiftly on his victim. His curiosity knows no bounds, and any unusual appearance of the neighborhood he must investigate and talk over. An experiment of hanging bits of black, white, red, and yellow cloth on the bushes near the abode of magpies resulted in a curious selection of the yellow and white first and an apparent terror of the red. Repeated experiments seemed to prove that this color was repulsive to the birds, and for a long time I could not guess why, knowing that raw red meat was a favorite dainty. Finally, noticing how excited both birds became at the approach of some little Indian girls who lived in the fishing village and who were dressed in red calico gowns, I was forced to conclude that in some way the wise old birds associated that color with persecution by the children. It seems that the latter had played the old cross-string trick with red flannel, which had been promptly seized again and again by the birds, greatly to the delight of the tricksters, to whom the temptation to snare by this means became too great to be resisted. The feathered playmates learned to shun both the color and the children.

The nest in the oak tree was very bulky, and bore evidence of having been used for several broods. On or in a platform of sticks was a bowl of mud, lined with cattle hair and roofed with a dome-shaped mass of sticks. On opposite sides were entrance and exit, and through the former the tail of the brooding bird usually extended when she was on the nest. For eighteen days her beady black eyes could be seen at the exit, for scarcely ever was she absent, except when she went down to bathe, which was always once and sometimes twice a day. The male fed her devotedly on a great variety of dainties, — crayfish, dead minnows, young squirrels, small snakes or lizards, big black crickets, and, alas! eggs and young of swallows. The latter were nesting in numbers in hollow piles of an abandoned pier near by, and wherever the opening was large enough the Magpie helped himself. Young chickens were also his victims.

On the day the young Magpies emerged from their shells, the mother joined her mate in stealthy journeys to and from the nest. Silently they slipped through the trees, but at the doorway of their home never failed to "talk" in low, gurgling tones as they fed and cared for the little ones. It was wonderful how those harsh voices became modulated for baby ears. Any approach to the nest on my part was received with a chorus of shrieks from both parents, defiant threats directed toward my eyes, and other unpleasantness; but, fortunately, it being only eleven feet from the ground no great climbing was necessary. Surely such homely babies needed no violent defence from kidnapping! They were naked, dark greenish purple, with sightless knobs for eyes and long necks on which the dark skin hung in loose wrinkles. But to the doting parents none were ever more beautiful and none were more closely guarded. Crickets, other insects, and larvæ were crammed down their throats at the rate of forty-three in thirty minutes, — not much for them, but a goodly amount for the hard-working providers to catch and bring. Each one was carefully crushed, the crickets being deprived of their wings and legs before being given to the nestling. To watch these industrious hunters pursue their game in the wet grass near the lake or the dryer wood lots where near the rotting logs they found the huge black crickets, was fully as interesting as to see them feed the young. Though so dignified and stately when walking leisurely on the ground, they became ludicrously excited when in a hurry, and with long tail elevated swooped down upon the unfortunate insect with the air of one doing great deeds.

At the end of two weeks the nestlings were covered with the iridescent sheen of the adults, but their tails were as yet only promises. These developed with surprising rapidity, and when the mature age of three weeks was reached, were as long as babies could manage. For several days there had been restless little heads poking out of the doorways, and on the twenty-second day one youngster, assisted by much clamor on the part of the excited parents, hopped out and sat on a branch. I came too near for his comfort, and away he flew or blew, for his long tail refused to conduct itself in proper magpie fashion and filled with wind like a sail, pushing him helplessly before it. One parent followed his adventures, while the other remained to guard the three left in the nest. These were looking out with longing eyes. Thinking four babies too much for one mother to care for, I resolved to appropriate one of them. It proved a very amusing pet, crossing the continent with me, and eventually became one of the magpie colony at Lincoln Park, Chicago, where it still exists. While with us it learned to say a number of words quite distinctly, as well as to mimic the bark of a dog, the whine of a puppy, and the mew of a kitten; it was far more intelligent than my pet crow and no more mischievous than my blue jay. Family characteristics are prominent in the three.

476. YELLOW–BILLED MAGPIE. — *Pica nuttalli.*

FAMILY: The Crows, Jays, Magpies, etc.

Length: 16.00–18.00.
Adults: Similar to black-billed magpie, but smaller and with bill and naked skin of orbital region bright yellow.

Geographical Distribution: California west of the Sierra Nevada, from Sacramento south to Los Angeles.

Breeding Range: In the Sonoran zone west of the Sierra Nevada mountains, north to Red Bluff, south to Santa Paula.

Breeding Season: April, May, and June.

Nest: Similar to that of the black-billed magpie; placed in oaks, sycamores, and willows, from 25 to 50 feet from the ground.

Eggs: 7; greenish gray, more or less marked with brown over the whole surface. Size 1.25 × 0.86.

THE Yellow-billed Magpie is identical with the preceding species except in the color of the bill, which is yellow, varying from bright straw-color in birds found in central California to dull grayish buff in those inhabiting the northeastern portion. He is nearly two inches shorter than the black-billed, and smaller in proportion. His call-note also is less harsh and loud, being somewhat like "quee-quee-quee" instead of "chack-chack" or "quat-quat" of the larger species. The breeding habits are identical; a full description will be found under the preceding species. Much persecution is rapidly decimating this variety, and where it was abundant twenty years ago it is now scarce. Although much more restricted in its range than that of the black-billed, it is found in more thickly populated portions of the State about Sacramento valley and is a better known bird. It is this species that first arrests the attention of the tourist as the Eastern train pulls slowly into Sacramento.

Eminently social, like all their family, these birds have a certain *esprit de corps* which leads them to forage in bands, making common cause against an enemy or plotting wickedness together, talking incessantly as only they can do.

487. WHITE–NECKED RAVEN. — *Corvus cryptoleucus.*

FAMILY : The Crows, Jays, Magpies, etc.

Length : 18.75–21.00.

Adults : Entire plumage iridescent black, with purplish lights, except the feathers of neck, which are white at base.

Geographical Distribution : Southwestern United States, principally in the lower Sonoran zone, from Texas to Southern California and from Southern Colorado south to Mexico.

California Breeding Range : Southern part of the State in lower Sonoran zone.

Breeding Season : May 6 to July 1.

Nest : Poorly constructed and somewhat larger than those of our common crow ; made of thorny twigs ; lined with cattle hair, rabbit fur, bark, grass, and moss ; placed from 7 to 20 feet from the ground.

Eggs : 3 to 8 ; pale green, with longitudinal streaks and blotches of gray, brown, and lavender, extending from end to end of the egg, and partially hidden by spots and blotches of brown.   Size 1.74 × 1.19.

To the careless observer the White-necked Raven differs from the American raven only in being more slender and slightly smaller, the white of the neck being at the base of the feathers and not conspicuous. In appearance and voice as well as size, they resemble closely the common crows, though more than an inch longer. Their nests are placed in giant yucca, cactus, mesquite, or other low bushes, and occasionally in oaks or willows. In structure they resemble the nest of a crow, being loosely thrown together of twigs and lined with hair from cattle. Old nests are repaired and used year after year, until they become exceedingly offensive from filth.

Incubation begins after the set of eggs is completed, and lasts twenty-one days, only one brood being raised each season.

Like the crows, these Ravens feed upon insects and
animal food as well as grain, coming close to the abodes
of men in their search for it. When their appetite has
been appeased, they will hide the remainder of the feast
under a stone or a piece of bark, in a hole or in the
ground, as do squirrels. By vigorous excavating with
their bills a pit is dug, into which the superfluous
dainties are tucked, and the whole is again covered with
dirt, which looks as if it had never been disturbed. In
some occult way the bird remembers just where each
bit is hidden, and never fails to return for it.

Like the crows, also, they are found in large flocks;
even at breeding season they are somewhat gregarious;
but they are totally unlike the American ravens, in being
easily tamed and in preferring the lowland deserts to
the cliffs. In California they are found only in the
southern and southeastern portions, and are nowhere
very abundant.

494. BOBOLINK. — *Dolichonyx oryzivorus.*

FAMILY : The Blackbirds, Orioles, etc.

Length : 7.00–8.00.

Adult Male in Spring : General plumage black ; patch on hind-neck
cream or buff ; wing and fore part of back lightly streaked ; scapulars
grayish ; rump and upper tail-coverts white.

Adult Female : General plumage yellowish brown, under parts paler ;
upper parts and flanks streaked with blackish ; crown divided by a
median buffy stripe.

Adult Male in Winter : Similar to adult female, but streaks on upper
parts blacker.

Young : Similar to adult female, but more buffy, with necklace of faint
dusky spots ; flanks not streaked.

Geographical Distribution: Generally throughout North America, and seems to be gradually reaching the Pacific coast, migrating to the West Indies and the valley of the Amazon.

Breeding Range: In Transition zone in open prairies locally, throughout its habitat.

Breeding Season: May 15 to July 1.

Nest: Of dried weeds and grasses; hidden on the ground among tall grasses or concealed in a depression.

Eggs: 5 to 7; dull or grayish white to reddish brown, irregularly spotted and blotched with browns and purples. Size 0.85 × 0.64.

ALTHOUGH at present only a rare fall visitant in California, there are evidences that the Bobolink of the East is moving westward with the great tide of civilization, and gradually forsaking the Atlantic coast to become a permanent resident of the Pacific States. There is no other bird quite like him or that can take his place in the heart of one who has heard his tinkling banjo-like song in the meadows east of the Mississippi, —

> "The rollicking, jubilant whistle,
> That flows like a brooklet along."

While his demure brown sweetheart listens in the long meadow grass, Robert of Lincoln flies upward on quivering wings, exploding with melody, and the higher he flies the more joyously he sings. It is a rhapsody on the glory of the June morning and the joy of loving.

His nest is securely hidden in the tangle of clover or wild grass, often placed in the hollow made by a cow's foot, sometimes woven among the clover stems and almost impossible to find. The mother bird broods alone for thirteen days, while Robert frolics gayly over the fields with others of his sex, always within call, but seldom or never feeding her. When the young are hatched, however, he takes charge of them, and I have found him alone with a brood of seven nestlings huddled in a fence corner in Michigan. The young are born naked except for a scanty sprinkling of down, through which their skin is conspicuously visible. When feathered, they resemble the females, and by August first, when even Robert has doffed his gay suit, it is difficult to tell one member of the family from the others. This is their travelling costume, and they start at once on their long journey south to

494. BOBOLINK.

"*While his demure sweetheart listens.*"

winter on the Amazon River.

En route they are known as rice birds, and make havoc of the rice fields of the Southern States, so that farmers and sportsmen alike make war upon them, selling them as "ortolans" in Southern markets. In the spring they come north again, reaching the rice fields in April, when the tender shoots are a few inches high, and stop there a few days to pull them up before coming farther to their breeding grounds. At this season Robert has on his bright new wedding suit of buff, black, and white, and is called the "reed bird."

588 a. SPURRED TOWHEE. — *Pipilo maculatus megalonyx.*

FAMILY : The Finches, Sparrows, etc.

Length : 8.50–8.90.

Adult Male : Head, neck, chest, and upper parts except rump black ; rump grayish ; white patch on outer tail-feathers ; small white patches on wings ; belly white ; flanks chestnut.

Adult Female : Similar to male, but brown in place of black ; back indistinctly streaked.

Young : Upper parts streaked black and brown ; under parts rusty.

Geographical Distribution : Rocky Mountains, west to interior of California ; north through Washington ; south to Lower California and Mexico.

California Breeding Range : Upper Sonoran and Transition zones, east and south of the humid coast belt nearly throughout the State.

Breeding Season : June 1 to July 10.

Nest : Of bark, leaves, and small sticks ; lined with grass ; placed on or near the ground in bushes.

Eggs : 4 or 5 ; pale greenish, finely speckled at the larger end. Size 0.88 × 0.70.

Remark : The San Diego towhee, *P. m. atratus,* is very similar to the Spurred Towhee, but darker and with white markings more restricted.

THE Spurred Towhee is very like the common towhee or chewink of the Eastern United States in coloring, except for the white mixed with the black of his back and wings. He is a common bird in the dense woods of the lower Sierra Nevada mountains, breeding in the edge of the clearings, either on the ground or a few feet up, in cedar saplings and manzanita bushes. Often as I have seen them in a morning's tramp the Spurred Towhee greatly outnumbered other birds, particularly if my way lay through the heavy timber.

His vocal efforts are somewhat different from the bell-like notes of the Eastern species, and have been so well described by Mr. Keyser in " Birds of the Rockies" that I quote his words rather than attempt a description of my own :

" It is a cross between the song of the chewink and that of dickcissel. The opening syllabication is like dickcissel's ; then follows a trill of no specially definable character. There are times when he sings with more than his wonted force, and it is then that his tune bears the strongest likeness to the Eastern towhee's. But his alarm call ! It is no ' chewink ' at all, but almost as close a reproduction of a cat's mew as is the catbird's well known call. Such crosses and anomalies does this country produce !

" On the arid mountain sides among the stunted bushes, cactus plants, sand, and rocks, this quaint bird makes his home, coming down into the valleys to drink at the tinkling brooks and trill his roundelays. Many, many times as I was following a deep fissure in the mountains, his ditty came dripping down to me from a spot far up the steep mountain-side — a little cascade of song mingling with the cascades of the brooks."

588 b. OREGON TOWHEE. — *Pipilo maculatus oregonus.*

FAMILY : The Finches, Sparrows, etc.

Length : 8.00–8.60.

Adult Male : Upper parts black, with white streaks on back concealed, and all white markings much restricted ; small white round spots at tips of wing-coverts ; white patches on outer tail-feathers less than an inch in length ; sides dark reddish brown.

Adult Female: Similar to male, but dark sooty brown in place of black on head, neck, chest, and upper parts ; sides deep reddish brown.

Young : Upper parts almost uniform dark brown ; throat and chest dusky ; neck streaked ; under parts dark buffy.

Geographical Distribution: Pacific coast, from Southern California to British Columbia.

California Breeding Range: Humid coast belt as far south as San Francisco.

Breeding Season : May.

Nest: Of grasses and leaves ; lined with finer grasses ; placed on the ground or in bushes and stumps.

Eggs: 4 or 5 ; pinkish white or pale greenish, thickly speckled with cinnamon-brown. Size 0.94 × 0.70.

THE Oregon Towhee which, south of Mendocino County, Mr. Grinnell has listed as the San Francisco Towhee, differs only slightly from the latter, but has a more restricted range in California. In habits it resembles the common towhee.

The usual nesting site of this species is on the ground, in a tangle of ferns or grasses well shaded under low bushes ; when, however, the proximity of enemies renders a ground nest dangerous, the birds wisely choose the top of a stump hidden among vines, or the thick branches of bushes. The same locality is sought by them year after year.

In the deep woods where the California partridge nests, it is not unusual to find the eggs of that game bird in the nest of the Oregon Towhee. Mr. Cohen, of Alameda, records one Towhee nest four feet from the ground on a live-oak stub and containing four Towhee eggs and fifteen eggs of the partridge. Another recorded by him was on the ground, and contained three eggs of the Towhee and eighteen of the partridge. The Towhee abandoned the nest after six partridge eggs were laid, leaving the partridge to rear the brood. Inasmuch as the Towhee eggs hatch in two weeks, the young being very dark colored and naked, while the partridge eggs require three weeks and the young are lively little balls of down able to run about as soon as dry, the sacrifice of the Towhee's brood is inevitable whenever the two are deposited in the same nest.

Mr. Anthony records finding an egg of this Towhee in the nest of a rusty song sparrow.

605. LARK BUNTING. — *Calamospiza melanocorys.*

FAMILY : The Finches, Sparrows, etc.

Length : 6.12-7.50.

Adult Male in Summer : Entire plumage black or slaty, except for white patch on wings, and sometimes white marks on tail-feathers. Winter adult similar to summer female, except chin, wings, and tail black.

Adult Female : Upper parts brownish gray streaked with dusky ; white wing-patch smaller and tinged with buffy ; tail, except middle feathers, spotted with white ; under parts white, streaked on breast and sides.

Young : Similar to adult female, but more buffy ; feathers of upper parts bordered with buffy white ; streaks on lower parts narrower.

Geographical Distribution : Plains of Dakota and Kansas, west to Rocky Mountains, north to United States boundary, south in winter to Lower California and New Mexico ; occasional west of Rocky Mountains. Irregular in Southern California.

California Breeding Range : In San Diegan district. (Very rare.)

Breeding Season : April and May.

Nest : Of grass and fine rootlets ; lined with finer grasses and vegetable down ; sunk in the ground, or placed under a tuft of grass or weeds.

Eggs : 4 or 5 ; plain pale blue. Size 0.85 × 0.65.

THE Lark Bunting, in form, size, and general habits of song and nesting, resembles the bobolink of the Eastern United States in such a way as to be frequently mistaken for that bird by careless observers. The dark plumage of the male, with his conspicuous white wing-patches and occasional white outlines on the tail, renders him a striking object as he shoots up from the grass like a rocket and whistles his merry song. This he does in true bobolink fashion, never pausing to catch his breath until, sliding downward through the air, he alights within twenty feet of his starting point and finishes the trilling begun in midair. Over and over, all day long, during the nesting time, he repeats this double aërial feat of flight and song. It is as if a sudden explosion of joy within him sent him skyward on wings of music. Its force spent, he flutters down to the quiet gladness of earth once more and soliloquizes sweetly on the wonder of it, as he swings on a low perch.

Like the bobolink, too, he changes his summer plumage to a less striking suit of brown like that of his mate, before he starts on his fall trip to the plateaus of Mexico. His nest is deftly hidden in the weed clumps of a mountain meadow, and neither he nor the demure little mother bird will reveal its whereabouts. In this trait also he resembles the bobolink, for, instead of rising from the nest as the meadowlarks and some sparrows are apt to do, the Lark Bunting slips through the weeds for some distance before reaching her grass-lined cradle.

The baby Buntings are fed exclusively upon insect diet as long as they remain in the nest, and for some time after leaving it. They hide in the cover of the grass and weeds until able to fly well, and at night they cuddle into the thick underbrush, like little quail, with both parents on guard. Even after the first real flight it is not uncommon to find the family keeping together, and by September they have joined bands flitting southward for the winter.

The call-note of this species is a clear, sweet whistle like an interrogative " who-ee ? " and is heard oftenest during spring and fall, when the migrating flocks are feeding along the way. In quality it is not unlike the fall call of the bob-white, but much thinner in tone.

620. PHAINOPEPLA. — *Phainopepla nitens.*

FAMILY : The Waxwings and Phainopeplas.

Length: 7.00–7.75.

Adult Male: Plumage uniform glossy blue-black, except for white patch on inner webs of primaries ; a long thin crest on crown. Winter plumage similar, but many feathers bordered with white.

Adult Female, and Young: Brownish gray, rather pale on under parts.

Geographical Distribution: Arid region of Mexico and contiguous parts of United States from Western Texas to Southern California.

California Breeding Range: Arid lower Sonoran zone.

Breeding Season: May to July.

Nest: Saucer-shaped, rather compact ; of plant fibres, weed stems, twigs, and plant down ; usually in pepper or oak trees, or bunches of mistletoe.

Eggs: 2 or 3 ; dull grayish white, thickly spotted with a neutral tint, dark brown and purple. Size 0.89 × 0.69.

IF, when driving through the streets of Redlands or Riverside, you see a slender bird of iridescent black plumage with a striking black crest, feasting on the rose-colored berries of the pepper trees, or sailing through the air, his conspicuous white wing-patches standing out like sails, be sure that it is the wonderful Phainopepla, one of the most interesting of Western birds. It is a common resident throughout Southern California, and

620. PHAINOPEPLA

Phainopepla nitens

may be studied in almost any locality from Pasadena to San Diego and eastward. Stragglers have been observed as far north as San José, Chico, and Marysville, but their usual haunts are the warmer regions of the southeastern part of the State. Here they nest in the oaks and mesquites, building a loose flat structure which once seen will ever afterward be easily identified. I believe that these birds, like the cedar waxwings, usually remain mated for life, but when the sunny May days come the male performs wonderful aërial gymnastics to win the admiration of the demure brown female. With a not unmusical prelude he springs into the air, performs a somersault much like a long-tailed chat, and comes tumbling back to his perch, where he alights easily and gracefully, not having ceased his song for a moment. The only notice his quiet mate takes of this is a slight elevating of her crest, as a haughty lady might raise her eyebrows. The male's fine crest is constantly erect, cockatoo fashion, as he continues his adulation. In fact, the only time I ever saw it lowered was when one of these handsome birds seemed to be scolding a female, whether his mate or not I do not know. He stood before her with crest down and head stretched out on a level with his body, wings tight to his sides, uttering harsh notes and swaying from side to side in anger. As soon as she flew away he resumed his eating.

One pair which nested in an oak tree near Pasadena appeared suddenly in the neighborhood on the morning of May 16, and a few days later were discovered at work on a nest. A watch was kept from a distance with field glasses, and while it was impossible to see how the weaving was done on account of the thick foliage, it was easy to ascertain that the male bird was the architect. Only once did the female drop down to the nest, and then she remained so long as to make it seem certain an egg was laid. However, the next day she was flying away over the valley with apparently no thought of family cares, and was not observed near the nest tree again until the third day after. Two days later sitting began. In this the male shared to a limited extent only. At least he remained at the nest, but whether or not he actually brooded the eggs I do not know, because a fear of causing the birds to desert prevented a watch at close range.

On the fourteenth day the male was observed visiting the nest very frequently, and an examination revealed two pinkish bits of bird life, naked except for a sprinkling of thin gray down on top of heads and shoulders. There was nothing in their appearance to suggest the elegant form of their parents, and they might as well have been young sparrows. From that time on we obtained an intimate knowledge of their development by keeping watch under the tree. The intervals of feeding varied with the time of day. From four to six A. M. the shortest wait was five minutes and the longest seventeen. During the day as long as one hour sometimes intervened between the meals. Insects and berries were swallowed by the adults, who fed the young by regurgitation. In the case of the wax-wings and Phainopeplas the process of regurgitation lacks the usual violent pumping motion, but consists of a quick eructation of the food from the throat into the bill.

In twelve days the nestlings were growing quite a respectable coat of brownish gray like that of the female, and could be seen stretching their wings in the saucer-shaped nest so near the edge that they were in imminent danger of falling off. Their call was exactly like that of the young cedar waxwings, a prolonged " pee-eet," sweet and plaintive. The song of the adult is more remarkable for enthusiasm than musical quality, and his call-note is a shrill two-syllabled utterance in the harsh tones of a blue jay. Besides this he has a variety of conversational tones which remind one somewhat of the gentle waxwings.

In some localities the Phainopepla is called the black mockingbird, but he has not a single characteristic of the mockingbird family, and certainly his vocal powers do not put him in that list.

665. BLACK–THROATED GRAY WARBLER.
Dendroica nigrescens.

Family : The Wood Warblers.

Length: 4.70–5.40.

Adult Male in Spring and Summer : Head, throat, and chest black, except for broad white stripe above ear-coverts, broad white malar stripe, and a yellow spot over lores ; upper parts bluish gray, the back and sides streaked with black ; breast and belly pure white ; two white wing-bars ; tail with inner web of two outer feathers white.

Adult Female in Spring and Summer : Similar to male, but colors duller ; crown usually grayish, often streaked with black.

Adult Male in Fall and Winter : Similar to summer male, but gray of upper parts tinged with brown, and black markings restricted, sometimes nearly obsolete.

Adult Female in Fall and Winter : Similar to summer female, but plumage softer and streaks on back and upper tail-coverts wanting.

Young Male: Similar to adult winter male, but upper parts browner, crown brownish gray, except in front and sides; streaks on back and upper tail-coverts concealed; black of throat with white tips to feathers; under parts yellowish.

Young Female: Entire upper parts brownish gray, crown bordered with dusky; under parts brownish.

Geographical Distribution: In mountainous parts of Western United States, from Rockies to Pacific; north as far as British Columbia; south in winter to Mexico.

California Breeding Range: Along the Sierra Nevada from San Bernardino mountains to Shasta County.

Breeding Season: May and June.

Nest: Compact and cup-shaped; built of gray plant fibres; lined with hair or feathers; placed in thickets or scrub oaks, or in pines, from 4 to 20 feet from the ground.

Eggs: 3 or 4; white, dotted with reddish brown and purple, chiefly at the larger end. Size 0.66 × 0.52.

AMONG the junipers of the San Bernardino mountains the Black-throated Gray Warbler makes his summer home. The green caterpillars, which some birds refuse and which on some trees seem to be poisonous, are his favorite food. His simple, rather thin little song comes from the sparse stunted growth of the foot-hills where he is busily at work hunting for his dinner, but the bird himself keeps behind the foliage and will not make friends. He seems to be more indifferent than shy, and to prefer the quiet of the thicket rather than gay dashes out into the sunlight. You may know him by the yellow spot in front of and just above the eye. Farther north this species is found frequenting the oak trees almost exclusively, though the nest is usually in a manzanita or hazel bush. In the spring these oaks are particularly infested with the green caterpillars, and the Warblers never seem to tire of devouring the pests. They lean away over to peer under every leaf, or reach up to the twigs overhead, never missing one. Twenty of these worms is an average meal for a Black-throated Gray Warbler, and the total for a day must reach into the hundreds. When several of these busy workers hunt through a tree together, we may feel sure that it must be clean by the time they finish the task.

665. BLACK-THROATED GRAY WARBLER.

"They lean away over to peer under every leaf."

Their common note is a sharp "chip," and their song is rich and very strong during the nesting season. One remarkable trait of these birds is the philosophical calmness which they exhibit over any domestic catastrophe. When their nest is destroyed by jays or other enemies, there is a quiet consulting together over the misfortune, and a beginning again in another bush. A very interesting description of the habits of this species has been given by Mr. Bowles in "The Condor" for July, 1902. The nesting habits resemble those of the yellow warblers.

PLUMAGE BLACK OR IRIDESCENT BLACK

422. BLACK SWIFT. — *Cypseloides niger borealis.*

FAMILY : The Swifts.

Length: 7.00–7.50.
Adults: Tail slightly forked ; entire plumage dusky, and grayish on head and neck ; a black patch in front of the eye.
Young: Similar, but feathers tipped with whitish.
Geographical Distribution: From the Rocky Mountains west to the Pacific, and from British Columbia south to Lower California.
California Breeding Range: Irregular and local.
Breeding Season: June 15 to August 1.
Nest: On inaccessible cliffs ; made of straw, chips, and horsehair ; lined with green leaves and paper.
Eggs: 5 ; white.

THE exact range of the Black Swift, or Cloud Swift, is not definitely known. It is found breeding in various localities in California, but never in places accessible to anything not provided with wings. In the Sierra Nevada and the Coast Range of California it occurs

422. BLACK SWIFT.
"*While flying swiftly through the air.*"

locally in small numbers, nesting in colonies on the high perpendicular cliffs. Dr. Merriam reports it from Inyo County, California, and Dr. A. K. Fisher writes of it in the "Ornithology of the Death Valley Expedition" as follows : "The Black Swift was first observed at Owens Lake near Keeler, California, where a number were seen flying back and forth over the salt meadows. . . . When the flock left the marsh it rose high in the air and went in the direction of the cliffs in the Inyo Mountains, where a colony was evidently breeding."

In flight this species are even more rapid and graceful than the chimney swifts, rarely if ever alighting on the ground or in trees.

Their food consists of small insects caught in their large mouths while flying swiftly through the air.

486. AMERICAN RAVEN. — *Corvus corax sinuatus.*

FAMILY : The Crows, Jays, Magpies, etc.

Length : 21.50–26.00.

Adults : Entire plumage iridescent black, with purple and green lights ; feathers of the throat lanceolate, distinct from one another ; feathers of the neck dull gray at the base.

Geographical Distribution : From the Rocky Mountains to the Pacific; from Canada to Guatemala.

Breeding Range : Southern California and islands adjacent. Recorded north to Red Bluff and Humboldt Bay.

Breeding Season : March 15 to June 1.

Nest : Bulky structure ; of coarse sticks ; lined with bark, wool, or goats' hair ; placed in trees or on cliffs according to locality, which is always inaccessible.

Eggs : 5 to 7 ; thickly spotted with brown, purple, and gray. Size 1.92 × 1.27.

THROUGHOUT the coast district of California, " wherever tall bare cliffs rise from the valleys and deep, steep-

walled cañons cut into the mountain ranges, the hoarse
croaking of the Raven echoes back from cliff and wall."
You may watch him soaring through the cañons or over
the barren valleys with his mate, but to study his nesting habits at close range would require the cunning of a
Mephistopheles. Two or three hundred feet above the
valley, and from thirty to fifty below the top of the cliff,
on a narrow ledge of rock, sheltered by the overhanging
mass, is the place he has chosen to build his nest and
rear his young. More inaccessible than an eagle's eyrie,
few care to investigate it. Thus secure from human
interference, year after year the pair return to it when
the winter rains have given way to spring sunshine and
all the birds of the air are seeking their mates. But the
Raven, having chosen once, remains mated for life; and
the nest, once built, serves for all his broods. A few
more sticks to strengthen it, a little fresh wool or hair
to line it, some strong new rootlets to keep the inner
cup in shape, and the cradle is ready. In it are laid
five, six, or seven large eggs, greenish, mottled with
shades of brown, purple, and pinkish; and both the birds
brood alternately until, in twenty-one days, the nestlings
emerge from the shells. They are not handsome babies,
being naked and of a sickly greenish hue, as if they had
been long dead and had become mummified, but they
are the objects of great devotion on the part of both
parents. One or the other is constantly near them, on
the lookout for danger, and ready to act as a decoy
to any aspiring investigator. Meanwhile the other has
slipped down to the valley or beach for food. It may

be dead fish, or snakes, or lizards, or small mammals.
Or it may be the eggs or nestlings of other birds ; for
the Raven is a cannibal as well as a thief. Young
chickens from the farmyard, young quails from the
valleys, or young gulls from the cliff are equally prized
in the Raven menu. His appearance in any neighborhood creates as much consternation among the feathered
folk as does a hawk, and with even more reason.

In about four weeks the young are ready for flight,
and their depredations begin under the training of the
adults. They learn to sit in watchful silence on the
rock where the cormorant has her nest and at the first
opportunity snatch the eggs or newly hatched young ; to
pick up clams and drop them from a height on the
stones, in order to break the hard shells ; to trace dead
flesh by a sixth sense, and call their brothers to the
banquet. They also learn to splash in the clear, cold
water of the mountain stream or lake until every black
feather stands out for itself like a quill. When they rise
so wet and shiny from this bath in the early morning
sunlight, they look like white birds, and they have fooled
me more than once, until their loud, hoarse croak from
the far distance betrayed them.

Soon after the young are able to forage for themselves,
the family usually disappears from the breeding locality
to some valley where food is more easily obtainable.
Here, after a few weeks, they separate, the youngsters
going about alone and the adult pair remaining together.
Throughout the winter and early spring they haunt the
ranches of the more southern regions and interior valleys,

walking with comical dignity over the ground, chasing each other merrily through the air, tumbling, somersaulting, and even trying to fly on their backs, according to Major Bendire. Their ordinary call is a loud " craack-craack " or a deep grunting " koerr-koerr." Occasionally during the early spring they attempt to sing in low gurgling notes a sort of monologue in monotone, as it were, but evidently expressive of their undying affection, and well understood by the mate for whose ears alone it is intended.

488. AMERICAN CROW. — *Corvus americanus.*

FAMILY : The Crows, Jays, Magpies, etc.

Length : 17.00–21.00.

Adults : Entire plumage glossy black, with purple lights.

Geographical Distribution : North America, except extreme arctic regions.

Breeding Range : In California, interior valleys, also coastwise locally.

Breeding Season : February 20 to June 1.

Nest : In trees, from 6 to 40 feet from the ground ; bulky ; composed of sticks and other coarse material ; lined with fibre, grass, leaves, or hair, the lining being well quilted together.

Eggs : 4 to 8 ; olive-green, irregularly marked with spots and blotches of brown and gray and sometimes lavender. Size 1.65 × 1.15.

NORTH, south, east, or west, wherever found, the Crow is the same jolly black rascal. He may vary somewhat in size ; his plumage may be duller, as claimed, on the Pacific Coast ; he may forsake the tall trees and build on the ground, as he is said to do in British Columbia ; but his well-known " caw, caw," has the same derisive inflection, and rooks present the same weird combination of black forms silhouetted against the evening sky. From these roosts at daylight each morning the entire company scatter over the country in search of food, undoubtedly covering many miles in their flight, but each one finding his way back to spend the hours of darkness in the additional safety that community gives.

As to the economic value of the Crow opinions differ. In California, acorns, beechnuts, berries of various shrubs and trees, seeds and all kinds of fruit, with insects such as locusts, black beetles, crickets, grasshoppers, spiders, cutworms, angleworms, and injurious larvæ form a large part of his daily menu. In addition small mammals and snakes, frogs, lizards, snails, crawfish, fish, all kinds of dead flesh, and the eggs or nestlings of other birds are his victims. It is very disheartening to become interested in watching some brood of song birds develop, and then to find some morning that the crow has made a breakfast on them. And the farmer who finds his cornfield ravaged or his young chicks devoured by a flock of the thieves feels a righteous anger in his heart against the spoilers. The fact that all feathered creatures are arrayed against him is proof to me that, from the bird-lover's standpoint, he does more harm than good.

The California species is said to build much nearer the ground than his Eastern relative, his nest being rarely over twenty feet up and from that down to five or six feet. My own records are, however, that nests lower than thirty feet are rare even in the West. The structure itself is identical with that of the Eastern crow, and is always surprisingly well lined and deeper than would naturally be judged from the side view. Eggs are laid in April most frequently, and, since incubation lasts nineteen or twenty days, the young usually make their appearance about the first of May. They are naked and blind, of an ugly greenish hue, and very repulsive to look at. Only one brood is raised in a season, and the remaining summer months are devoted to the training of these nestlings. At the end of two weeks they appear at the edge of the nest, looking out over the sunny slopes with unwinking blue eyes. From this time until they leave, when three and a half weeks old, they are very restless. Little wings are constantly stretched and flapped, uncertain little legs are trained to balance the heavy body, bills grow strong by tearing the food, and before the day for venturing out into the great unfriendly world has come, they have learned much. What yet remains for them to learn the adults will teach them day by day. Instinct plays a far smaller part in their cunning than we have long been taught to believe, and even in crow education it is the example of the adults that teaches the helpless young what to do and how to do it. Let anyone who doubts this course of training, or is inclined to consider that this opinion is founded on sentiment and not on science, watch the development of a family of young crows.

495. COWBIRD. — *Molothrus ater.*

FAMILY : The Blackbirds, Orioles, etc.

Length: Male 7.75–8.25 ; female 7.25–7.75.

Adult Male: Head, neck, and chest uniform brownish ; rest of plumage glossy black, with a greenish reflection, changing to purplish on back.

Adult Female: Plumage plain brownish gray, darker on upper parts, paler on chin and throat.

Young: Upper parts dull brownish gray, feathers bordered with pale buffy ; under parts dull light buffy, broadly streaked with grayish brown.

Geographical Distribution: United States and more southern British Provinces ; south in winter to Southern Mexico. Irregular winter visitant in California.

Eggs: 8 to 12. Deposited in nests of other birds ; whitish, whole surface covered with brown specks and blotches, usually heaviest at the larger end. Size 0.88 × 0.64.

AMONG the great herds on the plains of the Middle West Cowbirds are found in great abundance. Perched on the backs of cattle, they search industriously for insects, and in the waterless regions may prove a great blessing to the poor creatures tormented with heat and flies. If so, it is the one thing to be said in commendation of a bird universally despised. Unmusical, its only note is a screeching call. It is the sneak of the feathered world and hated by all the rest. Too lazy to build for herself, the female lays her eggs in the most convenient nest whose owners happen to be away. Her ugly nestling is larger and grows faster than his adoptive brothers, and soon succeeds either in hoisting them out of the nest, smothering them in it, or starving them by seizing all the food in spite of the parents' efforts to divide evenly. For every Cowbird reared a brood of song birds or insect-eating birds has been sacrificed, and Californians are to be congratulated that as yet the Cowbird is only an irregular winter visitant to the southeastern corner of their State.

510. BREWER BLACKBIRD. — *Scolecophagus cyanocephalus.*

FAMILY : The Blackbirds, Orioles, etc.

Length : 8.75–10.25.

Adult Male : Uniform glossy greenish black ; head and neck purplish black.

Adult Female : Upper parts brownish slate ; head and neck brownish gray, faintly glossed with purple ; wings and tail glossed with metallic bluish green ; under parts brownish gray faintly glossed with green.

Young : Similar to female, but paler and without gloss.

Geographical Distribution : Western North America, north to British Columbia ; east to Minnesota and Nebraska ; south to Lower California.

California Breeding Range : Below Boreal zone, nearly throughout the State.

Breeding Season : April 15 to July 1.

Nest : Placed in low trees or bushes, not over 8 feet from the ground ; rather bulky ; made of sticks, plant stalks, grass, shreds of bark, dry grass, and moss, generally cemented with earth or manure ; lined with fine rootlets, horsehair, and dry grass.

Eggs : 4 to 6 ; pale gray or greenish white, profusely blotched, marbled, streaked, and spotted with irregularly shaped markings of brown and lavender. Size 0.96 × 0.71.

THE purple grackle of the East is replaced throughout California by the Brewer Blackbird, which closely resembles the Eastern species. It is a trifle smaller, with blue rather than purple iridescence on its black plumage, especially about the head and throat, but has the same conspicuous yellow iris as its kinsfolk. In habits these birds differ from the other California blackbirds in being found less often in the lowland marshes or tule swamps. Abundant throughout the State, they breed chiefly between the highest altitudes and three thousand feet above sea level. Their choice of a building site is varied. In Lower California they have been found nesting in pine; in western Oregon they sometimes choose an old woodpecker's hole one hundred feet from the ground; while in the same State nests have been found on the ground, the rim being flush with the surface. At Del Monte a colony nested in the top of a group of tree yuccas, and at Tallac, on Lake Tahoe, I found them nesting on the rotten piles of an abandoned pier. In company with them were tree swallows; and one pair of fearless feathered mites, known as pygmy nuthatches, had excavated a home in a leaning pile that towered above the rest. In a low, broken post that raised its crumbling top scarcely two feet from the water a mother Blackbird brooded day after day, entirely exposed to view, close to a pier where children played. Strangest of all, the post was the customary mooring place of a rowboat, the loop of rope being removed and replaced several times daily, and always rubbing the nest as it was passed over. Yet the mother bird refused to leave it, and only flattened her body and crouched in terror as the rope was lifted. After the little ones were hatched, June 8, her distress increased, for now a careless move of the boatman might easily overthrow them into the water. One or other of the anxious parents sat on a splintered point of the post just over the nest and scolded from morning until night in loud "chacks," watching all who came and went in the vicinity.

Worms, slugs, black beetles, wingless crickets, grasshoppers, and dragonflies were given to the young at the rate of sixteen in twenty minutes, distributed among the four, — not so large an average as in the case of most young birds, but there was but one parent to forage. For the first three days, at least, the food was first swallowed by the adult and afterwards given to the young by regurgitation, but after that they were fed on the fresh insects.

The nestlings were a soft pinky gray when they first broke their shells, and the second day developed thin mouse-colored down on head and back. In five days their eyes opened, and the lines of submerged pinfeathers were plainly visible. On the twelfth day the little feathered ends had burst through the sheaths. And now began an alarming process of stretching and pecking and wriggling, — alarming because in this case it seemed as though the nestlings must be crowded out into the cold water below. But none of them ever was so crowded, and after nearly three weeks in the nest they flew out into some low bushes on the shore. Here they were fed by both parents for some days longer, being coaxed into the woods near by and cared for devotedly until they had learned to forage for themselves.

As soon as the young are able to take the trip the flocks of Brewer Blackbirds pass on to other feeding grounds. In August and September they are found in the high Sierra Nevada mountains and also on the ocean beach, so it seems to be a mere matter of caprice whether they go to the mountains or the seashore for the hot weather. Later they congregate for the winter in the interior valleys near the farms and stockyards, where they pick up food like so many sparrows. In the spring they forage at the heels of the ploughman or among the herds.

Throughout the summer, fall, and winter their call-note has been a typical Blackbird "tchaak," uttered with a flirt of the tail plainly showing displeasure. But when the rains cease and spring calls them to woo and win their mates, their little black throats ruffle with song. More energetic than musical, it may be; but heard as a chorus it is so full of enthusiasm as to make one forget its lack of harmony. The epithet of "wheelbarrow chorus," applied by Mr. Burroughs to the song of its Eastern kin, is just as appropriate west of the Rockies and fits the case exactly.

611 a. WESTERN MARTIN. — *Progne subis hesperia.*

FAMILY : The Swallows.

Length : 7.25–8.50.

Adult Male : Entire plumage uniform glossy blue-black ; wings and tail black ; tail decidedly forked.

Adult Female : Upper parts duller and color less continuous ; forehead and crown light gray ; feathers of back and rump conspicuously edged with grayish or pale brown ; bend of wing and under coverts mottled profusely with whitish ; anterior under parts and nuchal collar grayish white ; belly and under tail-coverts white.

Young : Similar to adult female.

Geographical Distribution : Pacific coast region, from Oregon south through California and Arizona to Lower California.

California Breeding Range: Chiefly in Transition zone, from latitude 40°
    southward.
Breeding Season: June.
Nest: Generally placed in eaves and cornices of buildings, or in boxes
    specially prepared for them; composed of a large variety of materials,
    — leaves, twigs, straws, string, rags, etc.
Eggs: 4 to 5 ; pure glossy white. Size 0.98 × 0.73.

THE Western Martin is in some ways less progressive
than his Eastern relative, the purple martin, for he still
builds largely in hollow trees. Instead of the familiar
friend we know as circling over our lawns, nesting in
bird boxes, or in holes under the house cornice, and so
tame that we may lift the mother from her nestlings
without frightening her, we find in the Western species
a forest-loving bird. Occasionally these Martins are
abundant about a town or farm building, but it is usually
because some especial pains have been taken to attract
them, and often because the first pair of birds were
taken when young and have become domesticated. They
are the same care-free, merry chatterers as the purple
martin, circling on tireless wings throughout the swarms
of insects in the air, turning, darting, and rising with
marvellous grace and swiftness.

Besides small insects they are fond of beetles and
butterflies, and doubtless they rid the farmer of many
injurious pests wherever the birds can be induced to
colonize. Under whatever circumstances they are found
they are sociable little birds among themselves, never
nesting in single pairs, and when together keeping up a
sweet twittering song.

One looks at the nestling and at the egg in amazement that so much bird could ever have come from so

small a shell. During the first week they double in weight every twenty-four hours, and at the end of four days, although still blind and naked, weigh as much as a canary. Most of the food is given them by regurgitation so long as they remain in the nest. They are slow in developing, and do not fly until nearly four weeks old.

PLUMAGE GREEN, GREENISH GRAY, AND OLIVE

429. BLACK–CHINNED HUMMINGBIRD. — *Trochilus alexandri.*

FAMILY: The Hummingbirds.

Length: Male 3.30–3.75 ; female 3.90–4.10.

Adult Male: Upper parts metallic greenish ; under parts whitish, washed with green on the sides ; chin and throat velvety black, bordered below by a broad band, metallic purple, green, and blue.

Adult Female: Upper parts bronzy ; under parts light grayish ; tail much rounded, with middle feathers green, next two tipped with black, next three tipped with white.

Young: Similar to adult female, but feathers of the upper parts margined with buffy.

Geographical Distribution: Western United States, east to Rocky Mountains, south over table-lands of Mexico.

Breeding Range: From British Columbia south to Lower California, and from the Pacific to the Rocky Mountains, chiefly in the upper Sonoran zone.

Breeding Season: May 1 to August 15.

Nest: In trees or bushes, 4 to 7 feet from the ground; of buffy plant down covered with spider's web.

Eggs: 2 or 3 ; white. Size 0.50 × 0.32.

IN some localities the Black-chinned Hummingbird is known as the Purple-throated Hummer, and this seems to describe him about as well as his more common name, for just below the black chin is a band of iridescent purple that at once attracts attention as he sits sunning himself on a low twig. He is abundant throughout Southern California, but especially so at Tia Juana on the Mexican border and from there to San Diego, among the hills back from the coast. No very definite breeding range can be given him, for he is a capricious little creature, abundant in one locality and rare or unknown in another that seems in climate and surroundings to be identical with the one he has chosen. Whether in the low hot valleys about the Colorado Desert, or in the Sequoia National Park at an altitude of nine thousand feet, he builds his home and rears his young

429. BLACK-CHINNED HUMMINGBIRD.

"Lit daintily a few inches away."

3.7.

in gay indifference to climatic conditions. Nor does he seem to have any especial favorites among the flowers; and this, I believe, is because his food is so largely insects. I have found him hovering over the bells of the Yucca more frequently than anywhere else, though at Tia Juana he was darting into the blossoms of the species of cactus so commonly domesticated by the Mexicans and used to brew a native drink. On one of these low plants a pair had built their nest in a crotch of the prickly leaves. It was composed of buffy plant down and covered with webs and something that looked like the thread of the Yucca. The mother was sitting; the nest was inside the garden fence; a fierce dog guarded the premises, and the Mexican family were away celebrating a church holiday. I could only admire from a distance, and, being unable to drive the mother from her post, did not ascertain whether eggs or young were the objects of her care. There was no question of identification, though Costa's hummingbird is more apt to build on cactus than this species. Another nest, found in the alders of a dry river bed, was quite unlike the first, and but for the father, who, contrary to hummingbird etiquette, sat within two feet of the brooding mother, I would not have attributed it to this species. The male was discovered first, and allowed me to walk up close to him before he took flight. In turning to follow him, I brushed against the branch on which the nest clung, and the female flew off just above my eyes. There were in the nest two newly hatched young, less than an inch long, and a third egg, probably a runt. The tiny cradle was woven of a pithy dark buff material that looked like the punk used by dentists, and was ornamented on the outside with willow buds. The question at once arose as to why this bird, building among the alders, had not used the willow down for its nest, as had the one who built in the cactus. A diligent search failed to reveal the source of the building material, and although I have since found several nests composed of it, I do not know where it is obtained.

Like that of his Eastern cousin, the ruby-throated, as well as four varieties of California hummers, the wooing of the *alexandri* is well worth watching. Should you spy a male, swinging sidewise back and forth through the air, pendulum fashion, look for the dainty little lady on a twig about three feet in front of and a little above him. So absorbed is she in watching and he in performing this curious aërial dance, that neither will notice you. Sometimes at its finish he will drop exhausted on any perch near and pay no further attention to her, but oftener I have seen her dart out into the sunlight as a signal for him to follow, and a merry chase through the blossoms followed. Once, as he sat resting after his graceful and apparently effortless swinging, the female flew toward him, lit daintily a few inches away, and quivered her iridescent wings. Instantly both birds were in the air apparently engaged in a mortal combat, and then he was back upon the perch like a flash of light, while she had disappeared. I have never seen the male Hummer assist at the nest building, and believe all the family cares are left to the female. She is larger and better equipped for labor than the brilliant little sprite who wooes her.

430. COSTA HUMMINGBIRD. — *Calypte costæ.*

FAMILY : The Hummingbirds.

Length: Male 2.75–3.20 ; female 3.55–3.70.

Adult Male: Head and flaring ruff brilliantly burnished metallic amethyst violet, changing to blue and green ; rest of upper parts bronzegreen ; under parts whitish ; belly washed with green.

Adult Female: Upper parts bronzy green ; under parts whitish ; throat spotted with metallic purple.

Young: Similar to female, but duller and with feathers of the upper parts margined with buffy.

Geographical Distribution: Lower California, Southern California, Arizona, and Western Mexico.

Breeding Range: In southern part of California, both east and west of the Sierra Nevada.

Breeding Season: On desert side of mountains, breeds in February; on the coast side, in May.

Nest: Of plant down or fine shreds of vegetable fibre; lined with feathers, and covered with lichen, bark, and leaves; fastened in place by spider web. On bushes, 1 to 6 feet from ground.

Eggs: 2; white. Size 0.48 × 0.31.

THE Costa Hummingbird is a haunter of the desert plains and barren mountain ranges of Southeastern California, where it nests in the branching cactus. On May 16 a nest containing one egg was discovered on a low branch of a willow five feet from the ground. The mother was brooding, and refused to leave until forced to do so. The next morning there were two tiny white eggs. Incubation lasted thirteen days, the young emerging from the shell on the twenty-ninth. At first they were very tiny, naked, grayish bits of bird life with black skinny knobs for eyes, more like worms than hummingbirds; but they grew surprisingly fast, and at the end of the fourth day were covered with yellowish white down on their backs and tops of their heads. By the sixth day this had spread to the wings and rump, the edges of the former began to show dark lines of needle-like points where the pinfeathers were coming through. On the eighth day they had more than quadrupled in size, were darker in color, and were commencing to push pinfeathers through the down. On the twelfth day they seemed like miniature adults, for they were covered with greenish feathers, the hair-like down still sticking out in spots on the crown and back, but the plumage showing some glints of the metallic lustre of the adults. They began to sit up, preen their feathers, and stretch their ludicrously small wings. On the seventeenth day one perched on the edge of the nest an hour, and that night the mother did not attempt to brood them, but clung meekly to the edge as close as they would allow her to come. Evidently they "resented being sat upon," like the ruby-throat described by Mrs. Olive Thorne Miller. They were fed entirely by regurgitation.

During this time the father bird had not once come near the nest, but on the seventeenth day an adult male hovered in the close vicinity and was repeatedly driven off by the mother. Within a week after that both youngsters had flown, but for many days thereafter were often found perching on small twigs in the sunshine, motionless, an hour at a time.

The nest was found to be much flattened from constant perching upon the edges, but was as clean as when newly built. The materials used were plant down ornamented on the outside with tiny bits of gray lichen and small dry leaves, bound with silk from cocoons. Inside it was lined with a few tiny feathers. It measured one and five-eighths inches across the top and three-quarters of an inch deep on the outside, but less than three-eighths on the inside. This was after the brood had flown and, as mentioned before, it was much flattened. As we had not seen it built, we were unable to judge whether or not the male assists in the construction, but he certainly does not share in the incubation or care of the young.

431. ANNA HUMMINGBIRD. — *Calypte anna.*

FAMILY : The Hummingbirds.

Length: Male 3.40–3.60 ; female 3.80–4.15.

Adult Male: Top of head, throat, and ruff metallic pink, bronze, and green ; upper parts and middle tail-feathers iridescent green ; tail forked ; under parts white, washed with green.

Adult Female: Head green, like upper parts ; throat spotted with pink.

Young: Similar to female, but tinged with brownish on upper parts.

Geographical Distribution: Central and Southern California, chiefly west of the mountains, Arizona, and Lower California. North as far as Yreka and Mt. Shasta.

California Breeding Range: Upper Sonoran zone west of the Sierra Nevada.

Breeding Season: January to June.

Nest: From 8 to 30 feet from the ground ; of thistledown and willow cotton ; lined with a few small feathers; covered on the outside with moss, well covered with spider webs, with here and there pieces of lichens.

Eggs: 2 ; white. Size 0.50 × 0.32.

A HUMMINGBIRD with a song would be somewhat of a novelty in the East, but in California it is so commonly met with that one soon forgets to wonder. The first time I heard the male Anna Hummingbird sing, he was perched upon a wire clothes-line and squeaking right merrily, " Te-nit, te-nit, te-wieu, wieu, wieu," repeating it over and over again. This charming performance lasted most of one bright May morning in San José, and when later I discovered a little mate brooding on a nest in a climbing rose, I could but fancy the song was for her benefit. One thing I know, he was " on guard," for whenever I ventured near the rose tree, he flew at me with a harsh little screech, sometimes right into my face. When I found him away from the vicinity of the

nest he would allow me to come very close to him, so
that I could almost touch him while he sat in unwinking
silence like a bud on the moss rose, or a dead bird on a
hat.   The tiny green mother was no less courageous, and
brooded unmoved while I watched not five feet away.
When the little ones appeared they were very like all
the small hummingbirds I had ever seen — naked except
for thin down on back, about three-fourths of an inch
long and with very short bills.   I think our ruby-throat
of the East could have mistaken them for her own but

431. ANNA HUMMINGBIRD.

" Upon a wire clothes-line, and squeaking right merrily."

for the slightly lighter gray hue of the skin.   They were
fed each hour, and oftener, by regurgitation ; the food
given was small gnats and spiders.

It was astonishing how those babies grew ! In two
days they had doubled, and in four days trebled their
original size.   Dark, hair-like down began to show on
crown, spine, and shoulders.   In twelve days feathers
were beginning to replace the down.   In twenty-one
days, just as the wing-stretching and restless wriggling
threatened to upset the wee cradle, they popped out of
the nest one day into the rosebush, sat there an hour

or two, and ventured farther into the world of flowers.
The mother still fed them, but now they seemed to help
themselves from her bill rather than to have the food
pumped or shaken into their throats.   They now called
in the squeaky tones of a young mouse, and the appeal
never failed to bring the mother instantly to their side.
Although I have been interested in several broods from
start to finish, I have never seen one of the eggs hatch
and certainly never incubated one.   Mr. A. W. Anthony
has done both, and has described the process so well that
I quote it entire :

"A nest of this species [Anna Hummingbird] was
found and transferred, eggs and all, to my game bag.
An hour later I was somewhat disgusted to find one of
the eggs pipped, and was about to throw it away, when
a movement on the part of the tiny creature in the shell
suggested that I hatch the egg and find out how baby
hummingbirds come into the world.   So far there was but
a pin point broken, and it was several minutes before the
warmth of my hand produced another movement on
the part of the prospective hummer.   First a squirm and
the point of the bill came into view and was withdrawn ;
after a moment's rest there, a new system was adopted
which consisted of a turning in the shell from right to
left, and cutting a clean, smooth opening with the sharp
horny tip on the upper mandible.   This was hard work
and required all the strength of the little mite, and frequent rests were necessary to recruit.   The cutting was
all done in the same direction, and after about ten minutes
I was obliged to turn the egg over in my hand in order

to watch the proceeding, as by that time the opening had been cut about half-way around, bringing the chick's bill directly underneath and in the palm of my hand. When the shell had been cut four-fifths around, the chick succeeded in getting one claw hooked over the edge of the break, and, by one or two vigorous pushes, broke the remaining space, leaving in my hand two nearly equal parts of what had been a hummingbird's egg, and a squirming something that bore no resemblance whatever to one of the peerless members of the genus *Calypte*. The entire operation of hatching consumed about fifteen minutes."

433. RUFOUS HUMMINGBIRD. — *Selasphorus rufus.*

FAMILY : The Hummingbirds.

Length : Male 3.25–3.70 ; female 3.50–3.90.

Adult Male : Gorget intensely brilliant flame-color, with orange and green lights ; rest of plumage reddish brown, with bronze-green iridescence on crown ; a light band across the breast just below the gorget ; tail-feathers rufous, with dusky mesial streaks.

Adult Female : Upper parts reddish brown and bronze ; under parts whitish, washed with red brown on the sides ; tail-feathers reddish brown for basal half ; middle pair green extending nearly to base ; the three outer feathers tipped with white and banded with blackish ; belly white ; flanks and under tail-coverts light reddish brown.

Young Male : Similar to adult female, but upper parts light reddish brown and darker on rump ; throat with a few bright metallic red feathers.

Young Female : Similar to young male, but rump green and throat dull green.

Geographical Distribution : Western North America, north to Alaska, east to Rocky Mountains, south through Mexico.

California Breeding Range : The Boreal zone of the central and northern Sierra Nevada.

Breeding Season : March to August.

Nest : In ferns, bushes, and vines, overhanging embankments, and some-
    times in trees ; made of plant down, covered with mosses and lichens.
Eggs : 2 ; white.   Size 0.50 × 0.33.

THE Rufous Hummingbird, also known as Cinnamon,
Nootka, and Rufous-backed, is the most widely distributed of all the family in North America. It is found
among the summer flowers of Alaska, and is common
even above the timber line in the southern Sierra Nevada.
Longitudinally it ranges from the east slope of the Rockies to the interior valleys of the sierras and in some places
to the coast.

In Central California nesting begins in March, and the
dainty structure of plant down, lined with cotton down
and decorated profusely with fine mosses and bits of
lichen, is placed on the horizontal limb of a tree or low
bush. Farther north, Mr. Anthony has found it tucked
away in unique places, — on dry roots of upturned trees ;
on the end of a tall fern leaf where other leaves, dropping over it, effectually hid it ; in the long trailing vines
overhanging embankments ; on the sunny side of railroad cuts ; and one little cradle had been built on top
of a last year's nest, " a mere rim being built to raise the
sides, and a flooring being added to cover up a large peb-
ble that could be plainly felt under the cotton lining."

Three years ago this species was not definitely recorded as nesting within the borders of California, but
Mr. Grinnell now gives it as breeding in the Boreal zone
of the central and northern Sierra Nevada mountains. I
have found it in June at Lake Tahoe when there could
be no mistake in identification, as both male and female

were frequently seen in motion and at rest. A unique
courtship that I saw was even more ardent than that of
the Anna hummer. Like a brilliantly polished bronze
pendulum, the gallant little lover swung in an arc of two
yards' extent back and forth for fully three minutes before his coquettish sweetheart. Before he had ceased
she darted out from her perch, and bill to bill they
whirled far up in the air until they looked like big
beetles. I think the flight must have taken them sixty
feet straight up. Then back they came and alighted two
feet apart on the same slender dead twigs. Four days
after this, the nest was discovered on the branch of a
low shrub in a very marshy place. It contained one egg
June 11, and the little bronze mother had begun to brood.
Her favorite feeding ground was twenty feet out on the
marsh, where it was too wet for me to follow, but she
seemed to be licking insects from a small whitish flower
among the reeds. Both sexes were astonishingly fearless, following a little, four-year-old Indian girl back and
forth, and evidently taking her red-gowned figure for an
animated blossom.

Although so tiny, the male courageously attacked and
drove away a Brewer blackbird that had chanced to
alight in the bush containing the wee nest. This blackbird was nesting in a hollow post which stood in four
feet of water fifty feet from the bush. His usual course
in leaving his nest was over the hummer's bush, and the
male seldom failed to dart out at him from his watch
tower near by ; but whether from natural pugnacity or
from a genuine regard for the safety of his own treasures,

I could not decide. The blackbird did not resent the assault, but seemed to endure it complacently, as the big man did his small wife's beating. Unfortunately I was not able to see the end of the matter, as I left the locality on June 16, while the mother was still brooding.

This pair of hummingbirds did what I have seen no others do, — either they really bathed, or, going down to the surface of the water for small insects, they seemed to be bathing. There was no splashing, but they hovered a moment on the surface with rapidly beating wings, wetting their feet and bellies; then they flew away and lit on a sunny perch to preen.

434. ALLEN HUMMINGBIRD. — *Selasphorus alleni.*

FAMILY: The Hummingbirds.

Length: Male 3.25–3.30 ; female 3.40.

Adult Male: Back and crown bright bronzy green ; under parts reddish brown, lightest next to gorget ; gorget brilliant flame-color, changing to orange and green.

Adult Female: Similar to female rufous.

Geographical Distribution: Coast belt from Monterey northward to British Columbia ; migrant through Southern California ; permanent resident on Santa Catalina Island.

California Breeding Range: In the humid coast region from Monterey north through the San Francisco Bay district ; also on Santa Catalina.

Breeding Season: February to August.

Nest: Cup-shaped, small in diameter and deep ; made of plant down ; covered with spider webs and bits of moss ; placed on small twigs, weed stalks, and often on the seed pods of the fine-leaved eucalyptus.

Eggs: 2; white. Size 0.55 × 0.35.

THE Allen Hummingbird is only a summer resident of the United States, spending the winter months over the table-lands of Mexico. It breeds wherever resident, and in California is found oftenest along the coast from

Monterey northward. So far as I can ascertain, it is the only hummingbird resident on Santa Catalina Island, and it was the only species I found there. A nest of this species that I saw was built on the pendent twigs of the fine-leaved eucalyptus. It was placed on top of a bunch of the seed pods and woven to them with fine spider web and silk from cocoons. Deeper and smaller around than any other I have seen, it measured a trifle less than one and a half inches in diameter and the same in outside depth. Inside, the cup was nearly an inch in depth. There was no lining, but the fibre of the white and buffy plant down composing it was more apparent and less compact than is usual in hummingbirds' nests. Outside, it was covered with bits of blossoms and strips of bark of hair-like fineness, making it so nearly the color of the grayish green seed pods that only an accidental discovery was possible.

These hummingbirds are nervous, pugnacious little mites, not tolerating any other species near them, and more or less quarrelsome among themselves; nor will the female allow her mate to come near the nest or feed at the same flower patch where she is feasting. They may be distinguished from the rufous by the bright metallic green of the back as well as by the difference in their breeding range.

Mr. Charles A. Allen, who discovered this species and in whose honor it has been named, writes of it: "Their courage is beyond question. I once saw two of these warriors start after a Western red-tailed hawk, and they attacked it so vigorously that the hawk was glad to get out of their way. And these little scamps were not satisfied even then, but helped him long after he had decided to go. Each male seems to claim a particular range which he occupies for feeding and breeding purposes, and every other bird seen by him encroaching on his preserve is at once determinedly set upon, and is only too glad to beat a hasty retreat. During their quarrels these birds keep up an incessant sharp chirping and a harsh rasping buzzing with their wings, which sounds very different from the low, soft humming they make with these while feeding. . . . During the breeding season the male frequently shoots straight up into the air and nearly out of sight, only to turn suddenly and rush headlong down until within a few feet of the ground. The wings during the downward rushes cut the air and cause a sharp whistling screech as they descend with frightful rapidity, and should they strike anything on their downward course, I believe they would be instantly killed."

436. CALLIOPE HUMMINGBIRD. — *Stellula calliope.*

FAMILY : The Hummingbirds.

Length : Male 3.00 ; female 3.50.

Adult Male : Gorget pinkish purple, streaked with white ; upper parts iridescent green ; under parts white, washed with brown and green on the sides ; tail-feathers dusky.

Adult Female : Upper parts bronzy green ; tail rounded ; tail-feathers, except the middle pair, tipped with white and banded with black ; throat whitish, sometimes spotted centrally with dull metallic purple.

Young : Similar, but under parts washed with reddish brown and throat speckled with darkish.

Geographical Distribution : Mountainous regions of Western North America, east to Rocky Mountains ; south through California, Arizona, and New Mexico to Mexico.

California Breeding Range: In Transition zone along the whole length of
   the Sierra Nevada.
Breeding Season: May to August.
Nest: Willow down, covered with bits of bark, fastened securely with
   cobwebs; built against a dried pine cone.
Eggs: 2; white. Size 0.46 × 0.31.

436. CALLIOPE HUMMING-
BIRD.

*"It feeds upon the painted
cups."*

CALIFORNIA is the land of hummingbirds. Six varieties nest within her borders, and two others are recorded as migrants; while only one species, the ruby-throated, is found anywhere in the East.

Of the eight varieties registered from California the smallest is the Calliope, which is a common summer visitant in the whole length of the Sierra Nevada, breeding in the higher altitudes of the range, rarely below four thousand feet. It loves the mountain meadows and woodlands, where it feeds upon the painted cups, columbine, wild hyacinths, gooseberries, and wild currants. The nests are usually saddled among the small cones of a pine tree and are woven closely to the cones, and so covered with bits of bark and cone as to re-

semble one closely.   In fact, unless the bird be seen to fly
off the nest or to it, the discovery of one of these dainty
homes is almost impossible.   One nest, now in the collection of Mr. William Brewster, at Cambridge, Mass.,
is composed of fine moss and willow down, decorated
with tiny shreds of bark, flakes of wood, and flakes of
whitewash fastened securely with cobwebs; it was placed
on a knot in a rope hanging from the roof of a wood-
shed.   The construction and materials mimicked the
rope and knot on which it was placed.   Mr. Bryant
records another, built on a projecting splinter of a wood-
pile at a height of two feet.   Here, as seemingly under
all circumstances, the bird had tried to imitate the surroundings, and to so place its home that it would be
more or less protected by an overhanging branch, leaf,
or some other object.

459. OLIVE–SIDED FLYCATCHER. — *Contopus borealis.*

FAMILY : The Flycatchers.

Length : 7.10–7.90.
Adults : Upper parts dark-brownish slate, with darker shaft streaks on
　　some of the feathers ; conspicuous tuft of white cottony feathers
　　on each side of rump (generally concealed by wings) ; under parts
　　white through the middle from chin to crissum ; the sides dark and
　　somewhat streaked.
Young : Like adults, but wing-coverts tipped with brownish instead of
　　white.
Geographical Distribution : Through the mountainous regions of North
　　America west of Rocky Mountains to Pacific Coast ; north to Hudson
　　Bay; south in winter as far as Peru.
California Breeding Range : In Transition and lower Boreal zones
　　throughout the State.
Breeding Season : June 1 to August 1.

Nest: Saucer-shaped ; of wiry materials ; fastened to horizontal branches of coniferous trees, 40 to 60 feet from the ground.

Eggs: 3 ; creamy, spotted at large end with brown and lavender. Size 0.90 × 0.65.

ALTHOUGH nowhere very numerous, the Olive-sided Flycatcher is found throughout the forest and mountainous regions of California. It prefers the edge of the timber to the dense wood, and stays along the course of streams or around small lakes in the higher altitudes. Like all flycatchers, it feeds on winged insects caught in the air, — moths, butterflies, dragonflies, June bugs, and beetles. Perched upon a dead branch, one of these birds will catch two dozen insects in as many swift dartings out into the air, always returning to the same lookout to eat them.

About the middle of May the females arrive from the South, and then the call-notes grow louder and merrier. Heard through the quiet hours of dusk or in the silence of a moonlight night, they are singularly like the plaintive notes of our wood pewee. But this is not all the song the little lover can sing, for when he goes a-wooing in the fresh coolness of the morning he trills a right merry lay. What though it be short and of limited range, the glory of the sunrise and the joy of love are in it. It is a beautiful world ! He is glad to be in it, and as you listen you are glad to be in it too. When you hear this warble, you may know that somewhere in the top of a tall spruce tree a wee nest is being woven of fine hair-like rootlets, small twigs, and long green moss. Outside it will likely be covered with lichens, and inside lined with moss. So securely will it be woven to the horizontal limb on which it is saddled that a hard shake will not loosen it. You cannot see it from below, but the nervous little builders are sure to betray its location if you venture near. With tails wagging excitedly and bills snapping with sharp clicks, all the while uttering a shrill "pip-pip-pip," they protest against your presence in their wood. About the middle of June, were you so unmindful of their wishes as to persist in climbing sixty feet to see, you would find three creamy eggs beautifully wreathed with brownish spots in the pretty green nest; but you would meet a warm reception from the furious parents. Were they half as dangerous as they are bold, you would never climb to a second nest.

They are equally intolerant of feathered intruders, especially if they be of their own species. Each pair seems to preëmpt a certain range from a fourth to a half mile in extent near the shore of a lake or along a stream, and on these preserves they allow no poaching. I believe they confine all their excursions to this territory so long as they remain in the same region. Only two things seem to be required in their breeding-ground, — coniferous trees and water. They are extravagantly fond of their morning bath, and are at it when the water is cold almost to freezing. To witness this one must rise with, if not ahead of the sun, for it is the first act of their waking hours. The young also are taught to enjoy a splash almost as soon as they learn to fly.

Only one brood is reared in a season, for they come north very late and leave again by the last of August to winter in the tropics. Incubation lasts about fourteen days, and the young remain in the nest two weeks longer, and in the same tree nearly a week after leaving the nursery. They are faithfully fed by both parents and taught to seize their food in the air, as do all flycatchers; and before the time comes when they must forage for themselves, they have learned the lessons necessary for their safety in the great forest.

464. WESTERN FLYCATCHER. — *Empidonax difficilis.*

FAMILY: The Flycatchers.

Length: 5.50–6.00.

Adults: Upper part grayish olive (more brownish in winter) ; wing-bars buffy ; under parts yellowish, becoming bright sulphur-yellow on belly and under tail-coverts, and shaded with grayish brown across the breast.

Young: Similar, but upper parts browner, with wing-bars rusty buff, the sulphur-yellow of belly replaced by dull white.

Geographical Distribution: Western United States, north to Alaska ; south in winter to Mexico ; east to the east slope of the Rockies ; west to the Pacific.

California Breeding Range: In Transition and upper Sonoran zones throughout the State.

Breeding Season: May 1 to July 15.

Nest: In trees, under banks, in natural cavities, or about buildings, usually near water ; made of rootlets, leaves, and moss ; lined with moss and feathers.

Eggs: 3 or 4 ; white, marked with brown and pale salmon. Size 0.69 × 0.51.

THE breeding range of the Western Yellow-bellied Flycatcher — known also as the Baird Flycatcher, or simply Western Flycatcher — extends through a wide latitude, from Alaska to Lower California. Eastward, it is found through the interior and southwest to the Rockies, but it is most common west of the Sierra

Nevada in California. Throughout this extensive range the breeding season occurs some time between the first of May and the last week in July; and within that period each pair sometimes, but not usually, raises two broods. My own observations lead me to believe that in the same [1] zone there is, in the case of all birds, a difference of about five days in nesting for every degree of latitude. This would make the season north of San Francisco from three to four weeks later than in the San Diegan district.

The Western Flycatcher is even less restricted in his selection of a building site than in choice of climate. On the ground among the roots of trees, up high on a tree branch, in the bottom of a deserted flicker's hole, on a ledge of rock, he seems to follow no law but his own sweet will or that of his wee mate.

The notes on this Flycatcher by Mr. Charles A. Allen, of Nicasio, California, seem to me well worth quoting. He says: "It is a very widely distributed species throughout this part of the State, both among the forests on the highest hills, where there is not a drop of water for long distances, and along the banks of brooks and streams in the lowlands; I have found its nests in all sorts of situations, — sometimes in a small tree, placed in the upright forks of the main stem; again, on the side of the stem where a small stub of a limb or some sprouts grew out; or in a cavity in a tree trunk; against an old stump, or a root which had been washed down during a flood in the middle of a stream; among curled-

[1] See map of life zones, p. xvi.

up roots near the water, etc. I have found a number of nests, when fishing for trout, by flushing the bird from under a bank; and on stooping down and looking, I found the nest nicely concealed by the deep green moss, such as covered the surrounding stones. They always use this particular kind of moss, no matter where the nest is built. Occasionally they nest in deserted wood-cutters' huts, on outbuildings near cover, and a friend of mine has some large water-tanks in the woods back of his house, where for nineteen consecutive years these birds have built under the covered roofs of these tanks. I know of no place in this locality where they do not breed, excepting in very open country. Its song consists of a soft, low note. It shows much distress when its nest is taken, uttering then a low wailing note, like 'pee-eu, pee-eu,' and frequently flutters about the person taking it, snapping its mandibles together."

Mr. H. P. Lawrence gives the call-note as "weet-weet" or "per-teet-weet" uttered in jerky, spiteful accents. My own observations give still a third, "weet-weet-weeter-eet," neither "spiteful" nor "plaintive," but a happy little love song sung early in the morning. The male is remarkably devoted to his mate, feeding her while she is brooding, and caring for her with the same devotion that he afterwards displays for his nestlings. And she receives this with the same pretty coaxing of wings by which the little ones beg for food. After the little ones are hatched, however, she works as hard as he to fill the ever-hungry mouths. Small insects, particularly water insects, are a favorite food, and one writer accuses them of eating newly hatched fish. The food is swallowed by the adults and afterwards given to the young by regurgitation until they are four or five days old.

466. TRAILL FLYCATCHER. — *Empidonax traillii.*

FAMILY: The Flycatchers.

Length: 5.80–6.25.

Adults: Upper parts olive, darkest on head; wing-bars varying from brownish gray to white; eye-ring white; under parts white, shaded with olive grayish on breast, and tinged with bright yellow on posterior parts; under wing-coverts pale yellowish.

Young: Similar to adults, but upper parts browner; under parts more distinctly tinged with yellow; wing-bars yellowish brown.

Geographical Distribution: Western North America, from the Mississippi valley to the Pacific; south in winter to Mexico.

California Breeding Range: In interior valleys, to Sacramento and Honey Lake.

Breeding Season: May 15 to July 15.

Nest: Deep, cup-shaped, bulky; usually built between forks of an upright branch in bushes, near water, 1 to 18 feet from the ground; made of plant down, dry grasses, shreds of bark, etc.; lined with fibre, fur, down, and horsehair.

Eggs: 2 to 4; white or pinkish, spotted mostly at larger end with light brown. Size 0.73 × 0.53.

THE Traill Flycatcher is a common summer resident in all suitable localities throughout the United States, but is distinctly a bird of the open country along the alder thickets of the river lands. It is restless and energetic, flitting about among the bushes but keeping out of sight except when a too enthusiastic sally after a passing insect betrays its whereabouts. But for this and a habit it has of calling out in a fretful tone at the approach of any person, it would never be noticed, so small is it and so well concealed by the waving leaves. Its notes are variously rendered as "pree-pee-deer" and "whuish, whuish," or "huip, huip."

Although so busy, this Flycatcher is never so occupied as to miss a chance of driving another bird, great or small, away from the special clump of alders which the pugnacious mite has preëmpted for his own. When there is no one else within scrapping distance, he contents himself with scolding his mate on the nest. Apparently nothing suits him from the time the nest site is chosen until the brood is reared. Capricious and variable, he places his nest anywhere that strikes his fancy, whether high up in the crotch of a sapling or close to the ground among heavy weed stalks. The materials used are fine, dry grasses, pine needles, plant down ; and for lining, down and horsehair. About the middle of June both sexes may be seen bringing material to the chosen site, and too often one insists on scratching out the foundations laid by the other, until in this way a week is often consumed before the structure is complete. Only the mother bird broods in the beautiful nest ; the male simply straddling the edge in masculine helplessness when left in charge, looking very wise but really quite useless so far as keeping the eggs warm is concerned. In twelve days queer naked bits of bird life fill the cradle, and now the small brown master is full of importance. They are hungry ; away he darts for food, but the demand is ever greater than the supply. To satisfy those four open mouths means a trip every two minutes or oftener. No time has he now for scrapping or bullying his little wife. From early morn he must hustle, snatching time for a hastily swallowed bug *en route* if he can, going hungry if he must. Small wonder that he forgets to sing or even to scold, but becomes for the time a silent, self-absorbed drudge in the workaday world.

468. HAMMOND FLYCATCHER. — *Empidonax hammondi.*

FAMILY : The Flycatchers.

Length : 5.50–5.75.

Adults : Upper parts olive, grayer anteriorly ; wing-bars light grayish or tinged with yellow ; outer tail-feathers edged with whitish ; throat grayish ; breast strongly shaded with olive ; belly and under tail-coverts yellowish.

Geographical Distribution : Western North America, east to the Rocky Mountains ; north to the interior of Alaska ; south in winter to Mexico.

California Breeding Range : Through Transition and lower Boreal zones from Mt. Shasta to San Jacinto mountains.

Breeding Season : June.

Nest : On a horizontal limb of a tree, 2 to 50 feet from the ground ; made of old weed stems, plant fibres, shreds of bark, plant down ; lined with grass, shreds of bark, plant down, hair, and a few feathers.

Eggs : 3 or 4 ; creamy white, sometimes lightly spotted with brown at the larger end. Size 0.70 × 0.53.

THE Hammond Flycatcher is the Western representative of the Chebec of the East. Unlike the latter, however, it is a shy dweller of the mountains, nesting oftenest, in the higher altitudes, from five thousand to ten thousand feet.

Instead of the merry little note which has given the Eastern species its nickname, the Hammond Flycatcher gives only a low, indistinct whistle and a soft " peet." Building in the higher branches of the coniferous trees, it is a most difficult bird to observe during the nesting season.

The food of *hammondi* consists of insects, which it catches by darting from its perch. In sharp contrast to the restless energy so characteristic of its family, it will sit motionless for a long time upon this perch, Micawber-like, waiting for something to turn up. It is comparatively little observed, and is accounted rare, but I believe this is due more to its retiring habits and silence than to any special scarcity of individuals. It is certainly not uncommon in the higher valleys of the Sierra Nevada in June, and would, I believe, allow some investigation of the nesting habits without deserting the brood, for the parents are very devoted.

469. WRIGHT FLYCATCHER. — *Empidonax wrightii.*

Family : The Flycatchers.

Length : 5.75–6.40.

Adults : Similar to Hammond flycatcher, but upper parts grayer ; under parts whiter ; throat often whitish ; outer web of outer tail-feathers abruptly paler than inner web.

Geographical Distribution : Western United States, east to the east slope of the Rocky Mountains ; south to New Mexico ; migrates to Lower California and Mexico.

California Breeding Range : Along the Sierra Nevada, south to Mt. Whitney.

Breeding Season : June 15 to July 15.

Nest : Shaped like an inverted cone ; in hazel, dogwood, or other shrubs ; fastened to the twigs or against the trunk of bush or sapling, 2 to 18 feet from the ground ; made of plant fibre and strips of bark ; lined with feathers and hair.

Eggs : 3 to 5 ; dull white, unspotted. Size 0.65 × 0.50.

Among the pines and aspens that fringe the mountain brooks, this dull-colored Flycatcher hides its nest. As soon as spring fever stirs in his veins, he seeks his favorite haunts and flits about, a gay bachelor, among the buckbush and willows for a week or so before his sweetheart appears on the scene. After her arrival fully two weeks are squandered in the frivolities of courting before the more serious business of housekeeping is begun, but you may be sure he has had his eye on a special cosy fork of a branch, and that he will not allow any other householder to "jump his claim." Then one sunny day about the tenth of June, you will see him bring a bunch of plant fibre and, placing it in the chosen crotch, jump on it and pack it into place with feet and bill. He has worked hard to get it, tugging with all his little strength to loosen some of it, which is the inner bark of the willows, and chewing it back and forth in his beak to render it fine and pliable. After the first bit has been put in place the female does the shaping and weaving, while the male brings the material. When the foundations and walls are completed, a warm lining of feathers is tucked and wadded carefully inside the small structure, and the cradle is ready. The thickness of this lining varies with the altitude and location, being thicker in higher or more exposed localities, while in some instances I have found nests with scarcely any lining and comparatively thin walls, on the sunny side of a cañon. These thinly built nests were invariably in pines and close to the trunk, and further from the ground than the heavier ones. Of the latter, several particularly warm ones were in willows and aspens and were lined with both wool and short hair from cattle or deer. Of four nests in one locality, one was two and a half feet from the ground in a manzanita bush, one four feet in a very exposed crotch of an aspen sapling at the edge of a grove, one was nicely hidden about five feet up in a young pine, and one was eleven feet from the ground, also in a pine tree. All were commenced at about the same time, and the first egg was laid in two of them the same day. In one of the others incubation had begun on the day on which the second egg was laid in the other two. The higher nest was watched less closely, but the brood of two nestlings were seen on the edge of the nest at the same time that those in the lower nest had made up their minds to fly ; so there was not more than three or four days' difference in the ages of the four broods. The nests were all within a radius of a quarter of a mile or less, and were similar in material and construction ; but those in the pines were almost an inch shallower than those in the bushes.

During incubation, which lasted thirteen or fourteen days in two cases, the male was frequently found on the nest, not merely guarding but brooding. When not thus occupied, he flitted restlessly through the bushes, bringing insects to his mate, not spending one moment in idleness except to take a sunbath, and his cheery twitter could be heard all day above the music of his more ambitious neighbors. As soon as the young Flycatchers were out of the shell, he redoubled his efforts and seemed to do much more than half the feeding. For the first few days this was by regurgitation, but later fresh food was given to them. Small wonder that with four such voracious appetites to satisfy he came and went in pre-occupied silence.   In two weeks the babies had filled the nest to overflowing and were fairly crowded out of it.   Then the trials of the father bird really began, for they tagged him from twig to twig with open mouths and quivering wings.   In vain he tried to swallow a bite himself.   Often he seemed to hesitate between the demands of his own hunger and the entreaties of his already too full fledglings, but he usually sacrificed himself to them.   In every instance the mother helped faithfully, and in one case she alone fed a nestling almost as large as herself, at the rate of six bugs in three minutes.   Sometimes she liberated one in front of him, in an effort to teach him to hunt for himself, but he was the only young Flycatcher I have ever seen refuse to try to catch an insect ; he would not budge.   This little comedy was played all one day, and early the next morning the worn and weary little mother was seen alone, no trace of the overgrown youngster could be found, nor did she seem to care.   She called restlessly awhile, but about noon began to enjoy life with the rest of her kin and to forget the cares of yesterday.

615. NORTHERN VIOLET–GREEN SWALLOW.

Tachycineta thalassina lepida.

Family : The Swallows.

Length : 4.75–5.50.

Adult Male : Top of head, hind-neck, back, and scapulars rich green, either the head, neck, or dorsal region, or both, usually tinged with bronze or purple ; rump and upper tail-coverts violet, shaded with purple ; wing-coverts violet, edged with green ; a white patch on each

side of rump, often close enough to form a band ; under parts white ;
ear-coverts and line above posterior half of eye pure white.

Adult Female : Similar to male, but smaller and duller; ear-coverts and
hind-neck dull grayish.

Young : Upper parts entirely dull brownish slate ; feathers of under
parts grayish beneath the surface.

Geographical Distribution : Western United States, east to the Rocky
Mountains, south in winter to Costa Rica, north to Alaska.

California Breeding Range : In Transition zone nearly throughout the
State.

Breeding Season : May and June.

Nest : In cliffs, hollow trees, under eaves of houses, etc.; made of dry
grasses ; lined with feathers.

Eggs : 4 or 5 ; pure white. Size 0.74 × 0.52.

THE Violet-green Swallow is a
strikingly beautiful bird both in form
and coloring. Although its plumage
lacks somewhat of the lustre of
the other swallows, the bright
green-and-violet effects of the
upper parts render it
unique among its kind.
It is a lover of pine
woods and mountain for-
ests, but where these
are scarce, it makes its
home among the bare
cliffs, nesting in crev-
ices in the rocks. In
California all of the nests
I have found have been in deserted woodpecker excavations
which the Swallows had filled
with feathers and bits of grass.

615. NORTHERN VIOLET-
GREEN SWALLOW.

*" It is a lover of pine woods
and mountain forests."*

The young are naked when hatched, but feather into a soft mottled gray with glints of blue and green on the upper parts and the under parts nearly white. They are fed on small insects by regurgitation.

627. WARBLING VIREO. — *Vireo gilvus.*

FAMILY : The Vireos.

Length : 5.00–5.50.

Adults : Upper parts olive grayish ; top of head dull ash-gray ; rump and upper tail-coverts pale olive-green ; white streaks through eye ; wings and tail plain dusky brown ; sides of head pale brownish ; under parts dull white, tinged with olive yellow.

Young : Top of head and hind-neck very pale grayish buff ; lores and superciliary region white ; rest of upper parts buffy, wings with buffy bars ; under parts pure white, except for yellowish under tail-coverts.

Geographical Distribution : North America from Great Slave Lake to Mexico.

California Breeding Range : Through upper Sonoran and Transition zones.

Breeding Season : May and June.

Nest : A strong, durable basket, made of bark strips and fine grasses on the inside ; suspended by the brim from forks of horizontal branches.

Eggs : 4 or 5 ; white, spotted, with reddish brown and lilac around the larger end. Size 0.70 × 0.55.

THE soft green plumage, unstreaked above and merging to greenish white below, is so characteristic of the Vireo family as to win for them the name of Greenlets, which to the non-scientific observer seems quite as appropriate as Vireo. They are small birds, so nearly the color of the leaves as to be observed with difficulty, except for their friendly habit of stopping to chat with you awhile at close range. Each different species has a different remark to make, but whatever is said you are sure to understand and translate into human speech. Mrs. Eckstrom says: "Few birds are easier to tell by their music and harder to tell without it than the Vireos. By all means put their song into words." The song of the Warbling Vireo is a quaint, cheery melody whistled all day long until chill autumn rains drive him to a warmer climate. He is a mountain-lover, choosing the aspens and oaks of the Sierra Nevada rather than the lowland thickets. If he condescends to build in a city park, his nest will swing as near the top of the tallest tree as he can find suitable twigs to hold it. Usually it will be at the edge of a stream or near an open space. In the fall this bird becomes very friendly, coming into the orchards and gardens to hunt busily among the leaves for small caterpillars. At this time he is fond of the cornel berries that grow along mountain brooks, and occasionally condescends to eat mistletoe, though he prefers insect food.

629 a. CASSIN VIREO. — *Vireo solitarius cassinii.*

FAMILY: The Vireos.

Length: 5.00–5.60.

Adults: Top and sides of head dark gray, blending to white on the throat; clearly defined white eye-ring and loral streaks; back dull olive-green; wings with two clear white bands; under parts clear white, tinged with yellow and olive on sides and flanks.

Young: Upper parts dull grayish brown; under parts dull buffy.

Geographical Distribution: Western United States, chiefly on the Pacific coast in summer; east to New Mexico, and south to Mexico in winter.

California Breeding Range: Along the Sierra Nevada.

Breeding Season: May, June, and July.

Nest : Made of dry leaves, cocoons, and spider webs ; lined with grass and
bark ; hung in thickets, bushes, oaks, and alders.

Eggs : 3 or 4 ; white, sparsely speckled with burnt umber.   Size 0.80 ×
0.58.

THE Cassin Vireo is more common along the Sierra
Nevada than through the valleys, and is most abundant
in the coniferous forests half-way up the mountains.
Here its characteristic song, "Mary, Mary, *Mary !* look
up here ! " bears so close a resemblance to that of the
yellow-throated vireo of the Eastern States as to make
it seem like the same bird.

His beautiful basket nest will be swung from the
branches of an oak or spruce, and, so long as the little
green mother is brooding, his happy warble will ring
from the nest tree begging her in tenderest tones to
" look up here ! "   At Slippery Ford on the Lake
Tahoe road, one of these little singers followed me from
tree to tree, whenever I was within fifty feet of his nest,
singing from the lowest twigs a foot or two above my
head and peering down at me curiously as he repeated
his quaint invitation.   His nest was only six feet from
the ground and, June 3, contained four eggs.   Sitting
began that day, and two days later both nest and contents had disappeared and, with them, the happy singer
and his mate, probably into a collecting basket.   I
searched for them day after day, but found no trace of
them in the neighborhood.   Another pair of the same
species were finishing their nest in a tree not far from
the hotel, and it, like the first, was decorated with white
cocoons until it looked almost like a hornet's nest among
the green leaves.   These birds, although building nearer

a dwelling, were less confiding than the first pair, and the male tried many little wiles to coax intruders away from his nest, though there were as yet no eggs in it.

The nest-making of the yellow-throated vireo has been so finely described by Mr. Hutchins in "Bird Lore," August, 1902, and so exactly resembles that of the Cassin Vireo, that I quote from it:

"The birds built the rim of their nest stout and strong, twisting the web about the twigs over and over upon itself where it stretched from twig to twig, till I wondered at their patience and ingenuity. Inside and outside the little heads would reach, with the prettiest turns and curvetings imaginable, till, as the nest grew deeper, the work was done more and more from the inside. Then it was gathered together at the bottom with side joined to side. When this part of the work first took place, the nest seemed to be strangely lacking in depth, and had an unshapely look altogether. But this was the point where the full revelation came to me of how the deepest part is shaped. I saw the bird at this stage inside the nest raise her wings against the upper rim and the twigs which held it, and strain with her wings upward and her feet downward till the nest grew so thin I could see through it in places. Then they began weaving in more material to thicken and strengthen sides and bottom where these had become thin and weak through stretching. This was done many times until proper depth and thickness were both secured."

632. HUTTON VIREO. — *Vireo huttoni.*

FAMILY : The Vireos.

Length : 4.25–4.75.

Adults : Lores and eye-ring dull whitish ; upper parts plain olive-brown ; green on rump, wings, and tail ; narrow white wing-bars ; under parts dull whitish, tinged on sides with olive-yellow.

Young : Similar, but upper parts lighter brown, sides of head buffy brown ; under parts paler.

Geographical Distribution : California.

California Breeding Range : West of the Sierra Nevada in upper Sonoran and Transition zones.

Breeding Season : March to June.

Nest : Neat, compact structure ; made of fine vegetable fibres, bits of paper, and grasses ; covered on the outside with moss, and lined with grasses ; placed in trees, from 8 to 10 feet from the ground.

Eggs : 4 ; white, finely dotted with reddish brown, especially at the larger end.   Size 0.69 × 0.51.

IN the valleys and foot-hills of California the Hutton Vireo builds its nest among the branches of the scrub oaks.   In the materials used it is quite unlike any vireo nest found in the East, for moss forms a large part of its composition.   Sometimes the external adornment alone consists of bits of moss woven in with shreds of spider web ; but occasionally the entire nest will be so draped as to look like a bunch of moss tangled at the fork of a light branch, and will deceive the eyes of an expert collector.   But the bird himself has no talent for misleading you.   His clear, emphatic warble tells you where he is and what he is doing ; for, in the tenderest phrasing of it, there comes an undertone of business, and sure enough he is prosaically hunting his dinner while singing between mouthfuls.   Under every one of the green leaves he peers with unabated interest, searching carefully for the small worms of which he is so fond. His slender bill, with the hook at the end and bristles at the base, reminds one of the flycatchers, but surely this phlegmatic plodder could never belong to the restless, darting, nervous flycatcher family.

Both the male and the female work busily at the building of the nest. Beginning at the top, they weave moss and fibre over and around the supporting twigs, leaving loose ends to be caught into the walls and bottom of the structure. The work is all done from the inside until the walls are firm, and then bits of the external decoration are carefully tucked on.

The brooding is all done by the female, while the devoted master of the household sings early and late from a perch in the same tree. This habit of singing so near the nest is characteristic of all the vireos, but is rare among other birds. He also feeds her very often during the day, and, as soon as the young appear, takes more than his share of the labor of caring for them.

Only ten days are required to incubate the eggs of the vireos, and one of my own records says seven for Hutton Vireo. All vireo nestlings are born naked except for the hair-like down that waves thinly on head and back. In this bird family it is even less perceptible than in most young birds, almost requiring a microscope to discover it. They are fed by regurgitation for five days and, after that, the food is usually reduced to pulp before being given to them. It consists almost entirely of small tree-worms, green and white, the latter sometimes seeming, by their whiteness, to be fruit worms. The intervals between feeding are unusually short, ranging from three minutes to half an hour.

633.1. LEAST VIREO. — *Vireo pusillus.*

FAMILY : The Vireos.

Length: 4.80–5.25.

Adults: Upper parts plain gray, tinged with olive-green on rump, wings, and tail ; wings with one or two narrow bars ; lores gray and white ; under parts white ; sides tinged with olive-gray and pale yellow.

Young: Lores entirely white ; top of head and hind-neck pale brown ; back dull green.

Geographical Distribution: Southern and Central California, Lower California, and Arizona.

California Breeding Range: Northern San Joaquin-Sacramento valley to Sacramento.

Breeding Season: April and May.

Nest: In bushes and thickets ; made similar to that of the other vireos.

Eggs: 3 or 4 ; lightly dotted with brown, especially at the larger end. Size 0.69 × 0.48.

THE Least Vireo is a bird of the warm valleys and foot-hills, frequenting the alder thickets along the wet bottom lands and following the spring into the foot-hills or more northern valleys to nest. It is a tiny mite in grayish green, and scarcely distinguishable from the foliage as it hunts through the bush for insects. Its semi-pensile nest is fastened to the slender twigs of the willows as close to water as it can get. This is not because of its fondness for bathing, but because of the abundant insect life found in wet places. While not a great musician, the Least Vireo calls enthusiastically early and late from the cover of the bushes, showing at times decidedly imitative qualities not possessed by any of its family except the white-eyed vireo.

634. GRAY VIREO. — *Vireo vicinior.*

FAMILY: The Vireos.

Length: 5.60–5.75.

Adults: Similar to least vireo, but lores and eye-ring entirely white; wings brownish, with wing-band indistinct or wanting.

Young: Similar to adults, but upper parts with brownish tinge and wing-bar buffy white.

Geographical Distribution: Southern California, Arizona, New Mexico, Western Texas, and Mexico.

California Breeding Range: Southern California along the San Bernardino mountains.

Breeding Season: March to June.

Nest: Made of coarse dry grasses and shreds of bark; lined with finer grasses; placed in thorny bushes or trees, 4 to 6 feet from the ground.

Eggs: 3 or 4; white, thinly spotted with reddish brown, chiefly at the larger end. Size 0.72 × 0.53.

634. GRAY VIREO.

" *The best songster of all the vireos.*"

THE level mesas and the wide cañons of Southern California are the haunts of the Gray Vireo. Lacking the calm patience of its family, this species hunts nervously among the scant foliage for food, flying restlessly from one clump of the sparse growth of brush to another and singing its quaint roundelay whenever it stops long enough to do so. It is much the best songster of all the vireos, and its melody has a clear, liquid quality, at times melting with a tenderness strangely in contrast with its abrupt motions. Rarely does it wander higher than the tops of the scrubby growth of the rocky hillsides, and it comes fearlessly into view. The basket-shaped nest is swung from a mesquite or thorn bush usually within five feet of the ground, and, except for the overhanging leaves that shelter it from the sun, there is nothing to conceal it from the observation of every passer.

646 a. LUTESCENT WARBLER. — *Helminthophila celata lutescens.*

FAMILY: The Wood Warblers.

Length: 4.20–4.45.

Adult Male: Upper parts bright olive-green, brighter on rump; sometimes tinged with gray, especially on head; orange crown patch concealed by grayish olive tips of feathers, except in midsummer plumage; eye-ring and superciliary yellow; under parts bright greenish yellow, streaked with dull olive.

Adult Female: Crown patch duller and sometimes obsolete.

Young: In first plumage; upper parts olive-green; wing-bars paler or buffy; under parts buffy, shaded with olive on chest, sides, and flanks.

Geographical Distribution: Pacific coast from Alaska to the mountains of Lower California and Western Mexico in winter; migrates eastward to Colorado, Arizona, etc.

California Breeding Range: Southward along the Pacific Coast Range to the mountains of Southern California.

Breeding Season: May 15 to June 15.

Nest: On the ground, often concealed by tall grass or bushes; composed of dry grasses, rootlets, and moss; lined with a few horsehairs and fine fibres.

Eggs: 4 or 5; white or creamy, finely speckled with purplish gray and cinnamon-brown, chiefly at the larger end. Size 0.65 × 0.46.

WITH the spring sunshine comes the Lutescent Warbler on his way from the south to the mountain ranges of California, where he will spend the summer; and as he loiters along the way hunting for insects among the golden tassels of the oaks, we are charmed with his dainty grace and soft sweet twitter.

All day long he flits about through the oak trees, leaning away over the tips of the boughs to investigate a spray of leaves, or stretching up his pretty head to reach a blossom just above him; now clinging head downward underneath a spray, or hovering under the yellow tassels as a bee hovers beneath a flower. But the everlasting hills are calling him, and day by day he goes nearer to them, higher and higher up the range until his own particular thicket is reached, where he can hide his pretty nest and rear his young. And now, from swinging in the tops of the oak trees, he comes down to a snug corner under the thick shrubbery and weaves a cradle of weeds, bark, moss, and grass, lining it with hairs and rootlets. Each one of these rootlets must be pulled off separately, a task as great for his small strength as the uprooting of a sapling would be for a man, yet the average nest requires very many of them. A nest found near Rowardennan, May 26, contained three nearly fledged young and two infertile eggs. It was a typical nest, except that a large amount of moss was used in its construction and only a few rootlets. The location was also somewhat singular, it being squeezed between a stone and a clump of weeds and lying partly under the overhanging stone. There was, of course, no way of determining the age of these nestlings, but the under parts were still somewhat bare when they scrambled out of the nest the next day. Another nest in the locality, half a mile from the first, contained four fresh eggs. This was a foot from the ground, in a bush, and, but for the unmistakable identification, would never have been placed in the same list as the first nest, for there was not a spear of moss in it and it was lined entirely with rootlets. After accidental discovery it was found to be in plain sight from the path.

646 b. DUSKY WARBLER. — *Helminthophila celata sordida.*

FAMILY: The Wood Warblers.

Length: 4.70.

Adults: Similar to the lutescent warbler, but colors much darker.

Geographical Distribution: Santa Barbara Islands, California, and the mainland after the breeding season.

California Breeding Range: San Clemente, Santa Catalina, and other Santa Barbara Islands.

Breeding Season: About June 1.

Nest and Eggs: Similar to those of the lutescent warbler.

THE Dusky Warbler seems to be an island form of the lutescent warbler. It is a common resident of Santa Catalina Island and others of the Santa Barbara group, breeding in the sparse growth of brush on the steep sides of the mountains. On Santa Catalina the nests are commonly on the ground at the foot of a weed stalk, but one was found in a crevice of the cavity left by a small landslide of the preceding winter. They are especially abundant in the vicinity of the Isthmus. Early in the fall flocks of these Warblers fly eastward to the mainland, striking it a little south of San Pedro and continuing east as far as San Bernardino. They are abundant at Los Angeles in August, but disappear entirely in the fall and do not reappear until the next year.

748 a. WESTERN GOLDEN–CROWNED KINGLET.

Regulus satrapa olivaceus.

FAMILY : The Kinglets, Gnatcatchers, etc.

Length : 3.15–4.55.

Adult Male : Crown orange, surrounded with yellow and edged on front and sides with black lines ; upper parts olive, greenest on the rump ; two whitish wing-bars ; under parts buffy whitish.

Adult Female : Similar, but crown lemon-yellow.

Young : No yellow on crown ; under parts tinged with pale brownish gray.

Geographical Distribution : Pacific coast of North America, from California northward ; south in winter to Guatemala.

Breeding Range : Breeds sparingly on the high Sierra Nevada southward nearly to Mt. Whitney.

Breeding Season : July.

Nest : A ball of green tree moss ; fastened to end of pine branch ; lined with feathers and short hair.

Eggs : 5 to 10 ; pale buffy, speckled with buff. Size 0.56 × 0.44.

THE Western Golden-crowned Kinglet is a common winter bird in the coast regions and elsewhere in California west of the Sierra Nevada. He is such a fearless, happy little chap, with his crown of bright orange and his plump green body, that one is instinctively drawn to him and comes to regard his merry " zee-zee-zee " as an attractive sound in the woodland chorus. He will allow you to come within a few feet of him and meets all your friendly advances with charming trustfulness. This sociability is only for the winter, however, when he has the companionship of his fellow-kinglets for moral support and frolics through the oaks in flocks, busily searching under every leaf for insect food. It is quite a different matter in the high forests of the Sierra Nevada where he goes to rear his brood. There he is shyest of the shy, keeping mysteriously in the tops of the tall firs and giving you only a tantalizing glimpse now and then. One female that I watched, or tried to watch, was evidently constructing a nest, for she could be seen fluttering about with her bill filled with nesting material of some sort, and carrying it always to the same tall spruce with a comical air of business. On all these trips she was accompanied by the male, who came and went with her, but never, that I could see, brought any load himself. Whenever she dropped down to where she was building her nest among the thick branches, her mate perched higher in the same tree and warbled in continuous low, sweet song, every now and then darting out, flycatcher fashion, after an insect — which he greedily ate. The song opened with a high-keyed, clear crescendo in tone and volume, diminishing rapidly as it ran down the scale, and was repeated over and over without much variation, like the song of a canary.

749. RUBY–CROWNED KINGLET. — *Regulus calendula.*

FAMILY : The Kinglets, Gnatcatchers, etc.

Length : 4.00–5.00.

Adult Male : Bright crimson crown patch, more or less concealed ; upper parts grayish olive, greener on rump ; two narrow white wing-bars ; under parts grayish white, sometimes tinged with greenish.

Adult Female, and Young : Similar, but lacking the crimson crown patch.

Geographical Distribution : Entire North America.

Breeding Range : Boreal zone, chiefly north of latitude 45°, in Rocky Mountains, Sierra Nevada, and mountains of Arizona.

Breeding Season : May and June.

Nest : Bulky ; semi-pensile ; woven of shreds of bark and moss; lined with hair and feathers ; placed in pine or spruce tree, 15 or 20 feet from ground.

Eggs : 5 or 6 ; buffy, lightly spotted around larger end with pale brown.

ALTHOUGH Mr. Grinnell states that the Ruby-crowned Kinglet breeds "in the Boreal on the sierras south to San Jacinto mountains," he does not say, as he might with truth, that it is rare and very hard to find. The nest is hung so high, usually in the branches of a tall spruce, that only an expert climber can hope to peep into one. Such was Mr. H. F. Bailey, of Santa Cruz, who, May 15, 1901, discovered a Kinglet carrying nest-ing material and watched her, although he could not at first see the nest. June 6, three weeks later, he climbed the tree in which he had seen the bird at work, and found the nest thirty feet up and only six or eight feet from the apex. "It was beautifully made, pyriform in shape, with the small end downward, about six inches long, and five inches through at the thickest part. The cup was very deep and the rim very much contracted, inclosing a spherical space with a small opening at the top. The material used in construction was moss, fur, and silky, fibrous substances woven compactly together. The lining was of hair and feathers. Some of these latter were woven into the rim, the stems firmly secured and the free tips curling inward until they met, thus forming a curtain over the contracted opening and com-pletely inclosing the interior. A very warm house was the result. The number of eggs was seven, incubation slightly advanced, ground color light buff — almost white — with numerous fine, pale, brown spots, so pale as to be indistinguishable, thickest near the larger end. The effect is as if a fine layer of dust had settled on the eggs."

The usual call of a Ruby-crowned is a sharp thin whistle, unmistakable when once heard. On migrations this is his only note, but at nesting time he has a twittering warble of three notes repeated over and over. This cannot be heard so far as his whistle, but is soft and sweet. It is occasionally heard late at night when the wind sweeps through the pine boughs and rouses the little sleepers.

749. RUBY-CROWNED KINGLET.

" Only an expert climber can hope to peep into one."

RED CONSPICUOUS IN PLUMAGE

403.   RED-BREASTED SAPSUCKER. — *Sphyrapicus ruber*.

FAMILY : The Woodpeckers.

Length : 8.50–9.25.

Adults : Entire head, neck, and upper breast red, sometimes lightly striped on sides of head with black and white ; rest of upper parts black, barred with white ; under parts dark gray or yellow.

Young : Duller, head and breast purplish brown instead of red.

Geographical Distribution : Pacific coast district north to Alaska, south to San Bernardino mountains.

Breeding Range : The Transition and Boreal zones throughout its California range.

Breeding Season : May 15 to June 15.

Nest : A gourd-shaped cavity, from 6 to 10 inches deep ; in a live aspen tree, 15 to 25 feet from the ground.

Eggs : 5 or 6 ; white. Size 0.91 × 0.71.

THE Red-breasted Sapsucker is a common summer resident in the Sierra Nevada from Mount Shasta to the San Bernardino mountains. When the cold of winter drives it from the higher altitudes, it migrates irregularly westward through the valleys to the coast.

Among the fir forests of the Sierra Nevada it is conspicuous and frequently met with, and may be heard at a distance of two hundred yards, beating its rattling tattoo for hours at a time. When alone, it is very noisy, but as soon as it suspects your presence, it becomes silent and dodges behind the tree trunk, slipping away as soon as you look in another direction. In the vicinity of Lake Tahoe the mating was arranged and excavation for the nest was begun by May 23. When first observed, the cavity seemed to be about four inches deep, below the first limb of the live aspen tree they had selected for a home, and in six days it was complete.   It was, as I afterwards ascertained, nine and a half inches in depth.

This pair were not so shy as most of those I had watched; after the excavation was partly accomplished, they kept on at their work when I was in full view, though discreetly keeping my distance.   The male was advisory counsel and defender, but candor compels me to admit that he allowed Madam to do more than her share of the hard work.   He was always near, keeping an eye on me and looking into the small doorway to note progress when his mate had flown away for food, but only three times did I catch him making the chips fly himself.

I thought sometimes he seemed stupefied with the sap he had been drinking. This is not an uncommon

403. Red-breasted Sapsucker.

" The mother watched the attempt to drink the sweet syrup."

occurrence with his Eastern cousin, the yellow-bellied sapsucker, who sometimes becomes so intoxicated on the sap of the mountain ash that he will allow himself to be picked up by the hand of a quiet observer. But the Red-breasted is more cautious, and knew instinctively just when my glasses were turned toward him or when I moved hand or foot. I say " instinctively," for often-times I knew he was behind the trunk where he could not see me, and yet the most noiseless movement brought him inquisitively into view. So long as he was on guard the female worked without fear, but when he left on a foraging expedition, she usually became restless and shortly afterwards flew away also.

Incubation began May 30, and lasted fifteen days. The young were fed by regurgitation for the first two weeks. As in the case of most other woodpeckers except the flicker, I know this by closely watching the adults as they come to the nest. As soon as the *bottle* period is over, the food can be seen in their bills. After the first week, some few species, like the flicker, feed by regurgitation, from the doorway, in full view of the world.

The young Sapsuckers left the nest on the seventh of July, and clung to the nest tree for three days. Here they were initiated by both parents into the mysteries of sap-sucking. A hole having been bored in front of each, with grotesque earnestness the mother watched the attempt to drink the sweet syrup. During this time both insects and berries were brought to them by the adults, in one hour one youngster devouring twelve insects that looked like dragonflies.

This species is said never to girdle the trees as does the Eastern variety, and to be far less harmful.

408. LEWIS WOODPECKER. — *Melanerpes torquatus.*

FAMILY: The Woodpeckers.

Length: 10.50–11.50.

Adults: Upper parts, lower tail-coverts and thighs uniform dark metallic greenish; face dark crimson; chest and collar round back of neck grayish; under parts, sides, and flanks pinkish red, with plumage coarse and hair-like.

Young : Like adults, but without red on head and without collar; under parts more grayish than pinkish.

Geographical Distribution: Western United States, from the Black Hills and Rocky Mountains to the Pacific.

California Breeding Range: Along the Sierra Nevada south to Fort Tejon; also in the valleys of the Salinas and the San Benito.

Breeding Season: May and June.

Nest: Excavations made mostly in pines and dead stumps, from 8 to 100 feet from the ground.

Eggs: 5 to 9 ; white. Size 1.03 × 0.80.

THE Lewis Woodpecker, although so handsome, is the most silent and stupid of all its race. Making no attempt to defend its nest, it will sit on a limb of the tree and look on while its home is rifled, uttering no sound and seeming not to care. It uses the same excavation year after year, and will sometimes lay a second set of eggs in the same hole from which the last has just been stolen. The nest is usually high in a tree, and is sometimes thirty inches deep with an entrance two and a half inches in diameter. In summer this Woodpecker is resident in certain localities along the Sierra Nevada south to Fort Tejon, and breeds in the open country along this range. In the winter it may be found nearly throughout the State.

In the summer its food consists of grasshoppers, large black crickets, wood ants, larvæ, wild strawberries and raspberries, cherries, acorns, pine seeds and juniper berries. Where grasshoppers and Mayflies abound, it will gather these insects and stick them into cracks in the bark to be eaten later.

Unlike most woodpeckers, this species have the habits of the flycatcher, darting out to catch an insect on the wing and returning to the perch on the top of a dead pine tree. The young remain in the nest three to four weeks, and are fed upon insects and fruit by the parents for some time after leaving.

After the breeding season is over the Lewis gradually makes his way with his young into the higher mountain forests, where they remain in flocks until the cold weather of late September sends them toward the valleys.

471. VERMILION FLYCATCHER. — *Pyrocephalus rubineus mexicanus.*

Family : The Flycatchers.

Length : 5.50–6.25.

Adult Male : Head of male with crest ; upper parts, except top of head, brownish gray, darker on wings and tail ; crown and under parts bright scarlet.

Adult Female : Upper parts brownish gray ; under parts whitish ; breast streaked with grayish ; belly tinged with pale red or salmon.

Young : Upper parts grayish, feathers edged with whitish ; under parts whitish, streaked across the breast.

Geographical Distribution : Mexico, Southern and Lower California to Central America, north to Southwestern Utah and Nevada.

Breeding Range : If at all in California, this flycatcher breeds in the vicinity of the Colorado River near Fort Yuma. Breeds in Utah, Arizona, New Mexico, and Southwestern Texas.

Breeding Season: April to July 16.

Nest: Shallow and loosely constructed ; saddled on a horizontal fork 6 to 50 feet from the ground ; made of twigs, small weed tops, plant fibre, empty cocoons, spider webs, and plant down ; lined with feathers, hair, wool, fur, and plant down.

Eggs: 2 to 3 ; cream or buff, marked most heavily about the larger end with irregular blotches of brown, drab, and lavender gray. Size 0.71 × 0.53.

IT is most unfortunate that this brilliant bit of bird life occurs in California only as a winter visitor. During the weeks from November to March it is more or less common throughout the southern part of the State, espe-cially that portion along the Lower Colorado River, but it is neither so jubilant nor so fasci-nating as when in its own chosen haunts it wooes its pretty mate. One must cross to the Arizona side of the river and ride some miles eastward, to find it really abun-dant, but the enthu-siast will be well

471. VERMILION FLYCATCHER.
" Pouring out his joy."

repaid. Here, among the mesquite trees, like scarlet blossoms suddenly taken wings, the dashing males chase each other and engage in brilliant combats.

These feathered warriors have tempers as fiery as their breasts. Early in March they arrive from the south or west, and a week later are joined by the females. So

slyly, so quietly do these demure brown ladies slip into
the gay company that, but for the curious antics of their
ardent swains, you might not notice their advent. The
little cavalier can no longer contain his delight. From
a branch where he has been sitting, one will shoot suddenly straight upward, like a fiery spark against the
evening sky. There, high in the air, he poises on vibrating wing, with every feather fluffed out, crest raised,
and tail quirked up over his back, all the time pouring
out his joy in bubbling music. Just as you are sure he
will explode with the rapture of it, down he comes,
lightly as an autumn leaf. It is his wooing, and
somewhere among the green leaves his sweetheart is
watching.

One such aërial serenade had quite an unlooked-for
ending. Evidently the performer had chosen his arena
without properly surveying the neighborhood ; for, as he
hovered in the air only four feet away from an oak tree
limb where sat an Arkansas kingbird, the latter, con-
ceiving this to be a direct challenge and ever ready for
a scrap, darted out at him with indescribable fury.
The result was a kaleidoscopic mingling of yellow, red,
and brown tumbling earthward, the birds fighting as
they fell. The Vermilion had been taken by surprise,
and was no match for his antagonist, but he fought
gallantly. As he landed on his back on the ground,
with feet and bill still eager to finish, the kingbird rose
a few feet above him, poised over him as a hawk over
a field mouse lair, hesitated, and for some occult reason
flew back to his own perch. His honor had been vin-

dicated, his rights enforced, there was no fun in scrapping with a vanquished foe; so magnanimously he withdrew from the field. Left alone, the little Vermilion wriggled over right side up, and sat panting but still full of fight. Evidently he did not know when he was beaten. His beady eyes flashed fire, his crest quivered, his wings were spread and his tail raised, while every individual feather bristled with impotent rage. A small brown bird, evidently his mate, flew down near him uttering low chirps. With the unreasonableness of his sex, he turned like a flash upon her and angrily drove her away. After a few moments of rest he was apparently as gay as ever, and was off again on his wooing, no whit less ardent for his defeat.

His nest was discovered in process of construction nine feet from the ground in the mesquite in which his mate had been hiding. It was a shallow affair of small twigs, fine grasses, vegetable fibre, plant down, and weblike stuff probably from a spider's nest or a cocoon. Inside a thin lining of plant down was matted neatly about. On April 24 the first egg was laid, and one each day thereafter until there were three. Twelve and a half days were required for incubation, and during this time I never saw the male nearer to the nest than six feet. The almost naked nestlings were salmon-pinkish; and, as in the case of most newly hatched birds, the eyes were covered with a membrane. On the fourth day this parted in a slit, giving them a comical, half-awake look, while grayish down stood out thickly on the crown and along the back. On the tenth day they were fairly feathered, but remained in the nest until the fourteenth and sixteenth days, when one and two, respectively, fluttered out on untried wings. The father took charge of the one that left home first, while the patient mother-fed and coaxed the lazy ones. These were finally started into flight by a little judicious jiggling of the nest branch on the part of a less patient observer.

The call of the Vermilion is a characteristic loud and constantly repeated "peet, peet," or "peet-ter-weet." The song is a clear twittering remarkable only for its joyous enthusiasm.

498 e. SAN DIEGO RED–WINGED BLACKBIRD.
Agelaius phœniceus neutralis.

FAMILY : The Blackbirds, Orioles, etc.

Length : 7.85–9.00.

Adults : Similar to Sonoran red-winged, but smaller ; female darker, with upper parts less conspicuously streaked, while under parts are more so.

Geographical Distribution : Great Basin district of United States, south through Southern California.

California Breeding Range : Locally in the interior and southern part of the State, chiefly in San Diegan district.

Breeding Season : April 15 to May 25.

Nest and Eggs : Similar to those of the Sonoran red-wing.

THE Red-winged Blackbird of the East is, in California, divided into three subspecies, — the Sonoran, which occurs only along the Colorado River in the extreme southeastern corner of the State ; the San Diego, which is common locally throughout the interior and southern districts, breeding wherever found, but most abundant in the San Diegan district; and the Northwestern, found in the northern counties. The habits of the species are identical, for all are marsh-loving birds, building their nests among the rushes or bushes along the edge of the water. All the summer, fall, and winter the San Diego Red-wings frolic and feed in large flocks, wandering over the farm lands of the valleys and piping their gay "kon-karee" from all the fruit trees. At this time their food consists of insects that are injurious to fruit trees and the farmers' crops, for they glean alike in the orchard and behind the plough, picking up not only adult insects, but the larvæ and eggs. Grains of all sorts and seeds are also part of their diet, yet the small harm they do is greatly overbalanced by the good they accomplish. When nesting time comes they are off to the marshes and sloughs. Here they nest in large colonies, sometimes numbering hundreds, the nests so close together that the young birds can almost hop from one to the next. After the manner of the yellow-heads, the male Red-wings take small share in nest building or brooding. In the East this bird is not infrequently a victim of the parasitic cowbird egg, and when this happens the brood is abandoned or a second nest is constructed on top of the old one. Occasionally these double-decker affairs are a foot high with one half-incubated brood walled securely into the lower part and a second reared above it. Nests built on the edges of the marsh or near the open water are always much deeper and more securely fastened to the rushes than those placed in more sheltered locations, as if the wise little architects knew the greater strength

necessary to resist the force of wind and wave. The
newly hatched young Red-wings are just the color of a
ripe apricot, and entirely naked. In a few days dark
lines of embryonic pinfeathers show along each side of
the spine and the edge of the
wings; then a soft grayish down
covers throat, breast, and top of
head. By and by brown
feathers push out through
the quills, and the promise
of a tail appears. The eyes
open, the skin grows darker, changing to greenish gray on the forehead, which remains entirely bare
even after they are fully feathered.
When twelve days old the nestlings begin to stand up after the
manner of young birds, stretch legs
and wings, and tease for food with coaxing
chirps. And now the father, who has been
a proud spectator of their progress
as well as a constant attendant on
their wants, has to work harder
than ever. Water bugs of all

498 e. SAN DIEGO RED-
WINGED BLACKBIRD.

"*A spirit of reckless daring.*"

sorts, especially the tiny black beetles that squirm by
hundreds on the surface, dragonflies and butterflies, hairless caterpillars and fat slugs are popped into the ever-
open mouths of those hungry nestlings. The feeding
by regurgitation ceases when the young are four days
old.

There is a spirit of reckless daring inherent in every young blackbird, and the Red-wings are no exception. One of these bald-headed babies balancing himself gingerly on the edge of the swaying nest is a comical sight on a calm day, but funnier still when the wind blows. How tightly his tiny claws grasp the stout rushes, as he bobs this way and that in a desperate struggle to keep right side up! How curiously those in the nest watch his gyrations! Occasionally a second and a third will climb out beside him, and that means that something is sure to happen. Too often it is a tumble for all three back into the nest, or a less lucky tip out into the rushes.

As soon as their wings are strong enough for short flights, the wise parents coax them back to the safer feeding ground of the orchard or farm, where day after day they pick up bugs, and night after night roost side by side with hundreds of other Red-wings in the shelter of the trees.

498 a. SONORAN RED–WINGED BLACKBIRD.

Agelaius phœniceus sonoriensis.

FAMILY : The Blackbirds, Orioles, etc.

Length : Male 8.15–9.35 ; female 6.80–7.86.

Adult Male : Uniform black, except for red and buffy or whitish shoulder patches.

Adult Female : Plumage not so glossy as the male's ; upper parts more or less streaked with dusky ; top of head and fore part of back dark brown, with buffy median crown stripe and superciliary ; shoulders faintly tinged with red ; under parts broadly streaked with dusky and whitish ; chin and throat more or less tinged with buffy or pinkish.

Geographical Distribution : From the Lower Colorado valley in Southern California and Arizona south to Mexico.

Breeding Range: Southeastern portion of State along Lower Colorado River.

Breeding Season : April to June.

Nest : Usually built in reeds or bushes, near the ground, and sometimes in a clump of grass ; made of rushes or sedges ; lined with finer grass.

Eggs : 3 to 5 ; light blue, marbled, blotched, and clouded with light and dark purple and black. Size 1.00 × 0.75.

499. BICOLORED BLACKBIRD. — *Agelaius gubernator californicus.*

FAMILY : The Blackbirds, Orioles, etc.

Length : Male 7.80–8.60 ; female 6.90–7.50.

Adult Male : Plumage black, red shoulder patch ; middle wing-coverts buffy or brownish at the base, but concealed by black tips.

Adult Female : Nearly uniform dusky and streaked ; chin and throat pale buffy or pinkish, the latter marked with triangular spots of dusky.

Geographical Distribution : Valleys of California and Western Oregon, south into Mexico.

California Breeding Range : Locally in the interior valleys west of the Sierra Nevada.

Breeding Season : April to July.

Nest : Placed on tufts of marsh grass or weeds, from 1 to 3 feet above the water ; made of grasses and strips of bark ; lined with grass and sometimes horsehair.

Eggs : 2 to 4 ; light bluish green, generally marbled, spotted and streaked with brown, black, and purple. Size 1.00 × 0.68.

THE Bicolored Blackbird is similar in all his habits to the red-winged. His nest differs only in the bark and horsehair used in construction, and the shallower cup. Like all blackbirds, he loves wet meadows and marshes near open water, and during the breeding season is found in these localities. For the rest of the year he roves in company with the Brewer blackbirds over the valleys of the interior west of the Sierra Nevada mountains.   His call-note is a loud metallic "konkaree" that can scarcely be distinguished from that of the red-wing.

500. TRICOLORED BLACKBIRD. — *Agelaius tricolor.*

FAMILY : The Blackbirds, Orioles, etc.

Length : Male 8.00–9.05 ; female 7.10–7.85.

Adult Male : Glossy blue-black with silky plumage ; shoulder patches dark red, bordered with white (tinged with buff in winter).

Adult Female : Plumage silky texture ; upper parts dusky, with green-ish lustre ; crown streaked ; scapulars and interscapulars with grayish edgings ; wings with grayish and white bands ; throat and chest streaked ; remainder of under parts dusky.

Young : Similar to female, but browner, and under parts finely streaked ; wings with two bands.

Geographical Distribution : Valleys of the Pacific coast from Southern California to Western Oregon.

California Breeding Range : Locally in the interior valleys west of the Sierra Nevada, from Mt. Shasta to San Diego ; east to Lake Tahoe.

Breeding Season : May to July.

Nest and Eggs : Similar to those of the Sonoran red-wing.

THE Tricolored Blackbird is a common resident of the interior valleys west of the Sierra Nevada from Mount Shasta to San Diego. In the vicinity of Lake Tahoe these birds stray across the crest, but not in the numbers in which they are found westward.

They breed in large colonies in the tule marshes and wet meadows, oftentimes placing the nests in trees or bushes after the manner of the red-wing.   " Mr. Hen-shaw found a colony of these birds nesting in a dry pasture in a patch of nettles and briars covering between three and four acres in the Santa Clara valley, Cali-fornia.   The nettles grew so dense and high (twelve feet) that he found it almost impossible to force his way into their midst. Two hundred pair were here congregated to rear their young, and the odor could only be compared to that of a cormorant rookery. Nearly every bush had several nests."[1] This was in 1875. I doubt whether such a patch of wilderness could be found in Santa Clara County at present, but the birds still nest there in smaller numbers. I have never found more than from ten to twenty nests in one place.

The nests can be told from those of the red-wings only by their looser construction and their shallowness. The newly hatched nestlings are exactly like those of the red-wings and are fed and cared for in the same manner; even when a month old they can scarcely be distinguished from their more common Eastern relatives.

515 b. CALIFORNIA PINE GROSBEAK. — *Pinicola enucleator californica.*

FAMILY: The Finches, Sparrows, etc.

Length: Male 7.75 ; female 7.40–7.95.

Adult Male: Upper parts pale vermilion ; head tinged with pinkish and yellow ; scapulars light gray ; wings and tail dusky ; feathers tipped with whitish ; under parts light gray ; entire plumage gray beneath the surface.

Adult Female: General plumage light gray ; top and sides of head, back of neck, and middle of breast bright tan-color ; upper tail-coverts tinged with light yellow.

Young: Similar to female, but brownish gray, with brownish and grayish edgings to wings and tail.

Geographical Distribution: Boreal zone on the central Sierra Nevada ; north to Placer County ; south to Fresno County.

Breeding Range: Coextensive with its habitat.

---

[1] Bendire's "Life Histories," p. 457.

Breeding Season: May and June.
Nest: Flat, thin structure composed of rootlets and twigs, lined with
finer roots, usually placed in coniferous trees.

HIGH in the Sierra Nevada range where, all the year
long, the crevices and sunless nooks hold patches of
snow, where the dark hemlock forests cover the mountain sides with their shad-
ows, the Pine Grosbeak
finds temperature, food,
and breeding grounds ex-
actly to his liking. Nor
when the storms of winter
howl through the pines
does he go far to seek a
warmer climate. He seems
fairly to revel in the swirling
clouds of snow, and, until
driven by hunger to seek food
lower down the mountain,
he will stay in his favorite
haunts. On the edge of a
snowdrift you may see him
picking up the wind-blown
seeds and frozen insect life

515 b. CALIFORNIA PINE
GROSBEAK.

"*He seems fairly to revel in the
swirling clouds of snow.*"

that come there no man knows how. When the summer
suns have warmed the mountains, he whistles most
musical love songs as he frolics through the trees with
his mate. At all times, except the few weeks of the
breeding season, he is found in company with others
of his kind, both male and female. Early in May the

flocks separate, each pair going to its chosen nesting site
in the furry hemlocks, and house-building begins. Both
sexes carry material and weave the walls of the home,
which is well hidden and securely fastened among the
thick branches. It is very difficult to discover even when
you have located the tree, and the birds themselves, although not shy, are wary about disclosing this secret.
So the bird-lover must be content with lying under the
hemlocks and watching the pretty rose-colored male carrying food to his mate through the days of incubation ; and
listening to his liquid trilling, as the setting sun tinges
his breast with a deeper rose, or as at four A. M. he greets
another blue day. He makes a welcome bit of color in
the sombre woods, and delicious music in their silence.
Unless you hear his rival, the Townsend solitaire, who
frequents much the same haunts, you are quite ready to
call him the musician of the mountain tops.

517 a. CALIFORNIA PURPLE FINCH. — *Carpodacus purpureus californicus.*

FAMILY : The Finches, Sparrows, etc.

Length : 5.50–6.25.

Adult Male : Upper parts dark madder-pink, clear on rump, deeper and
brighter on top of head ; back streaked with dusky ; middle of belly
and lower tail-coverts white ; remainder of under parts light rose-
pink with sides and flanks strongly tinged with brownish and streaked
with darker.

Adult Female : Upper parts grayish olive, heavily streaked with brown ;
under parts ashy white, finely streaked ; sides of head with two distinct brownish stripes, one on ear-coverts, the other on each side of
throat, — the two separated by a whitish stripe.

Young: Similar to adult female, but colors duller, markings less distinct, and edgings of wing-feathers more buffy.

Geographical Distribution: Pacific coast of United States, from Southern California to British Columbia.

California Breeding Range: Upper Sonoran and Transition zones west of the Sierra Nevada range.

Breeding Season: May and June.

Nest: A flat thin structure; made of fine rootlets and grasses; placed on the horizontal limbs of trees.

Eggs: 2 to 4; greenish blue, finely speckled on large end with dark brown and black. Size 0.75 × 0.55.

THE California Purple Finch is one of those species which indulge in a semi-annual vertical migration. Spending the winter among the lowlands, feeding through the valleys in small flocks, as soon as the snow begins to melt in the mountains, they work their way slowly to the higher levels. And the fruit-growers are not sorry to see them go, for during their brief stay through the winter months they have eaten the buds of the deciduous trees, doing incalculable harm to the crops.

Half-way up the mountains, at an altitude of from three thousand to five thousand feet, they find suitable breeding grounds in the yellow pines, oaks, and redwoods. The nest is built usually on a horizontal branch, and is composed of wiry grass and fine rootlets woven into a shallow cup and lined with wool or horsehair.

Incubation lasts thirteen days; and, so far as I have observed, the male does not brood upon the eggs, although he does take charge during the absence of the female.

The song of the Purple Finch is a pleasing warble kept up during most of his waking hours in the breeding season. The call-note is a chirp not unlike that of the English sparrow, but somewhat softer.

518. CASSIN PURPLE FINCH. — *Carpodacus cassini.*

FAMILY : The Finches, Sparrows, etc.

Length : 6.50–6.95.

Adult Male : Upper parts pinkish brown, clearly streaked with dark brown ; top of head bright crimson ; rump subdued rose-pink ; throat and breast pale rose-pink ; belly white ; sides tinged with pinkish ; lower tail-coverts conspicuously streaked with dusky ; wing-feathers edged with reddish.

Adult Female : Upper parts olive-gray ; under parts white ; entire plumage conspicuously streaked with dusky.

Young : Similar to adult female, but streaks on lower parts narrower and less conspicuous, and wing-edgings more tawny buff.

Geographical Distribution : Western United States, north to British Columbia, east to Rocky Mountains, south to Mexico.

California Breeding Range : Lower Boreal zone from Mt. Shasta to Los Angeles County ; also Inyo Mountains and White Mountains.

Breeding Season : May and June.

Nest : Flat and thin ; composed mostly of rootlets and grasses; lined with moss and cotton ; placed near the tops of young pines, on horizontal branches.

Eggs : 2 to 4 ; light bluish green, dotted around the larger end with slate, lilac, and dark brown. Size 0.84 × 0.62.

FLOCKS of Cassin Purple Finches are met with along the entire high Sierra Nevada from Mount Shasta southward. The winter storms only drive them a little lower down to the shelter of the brush, or in severe seasons to the foot-hills ; but even then it is not uncommon to find a small flock huddled under a fallen tree for shelter and trying to brave it out in the snow. With the returning spring the flocks go back to their pine-covered haunts in the higher altitudes.

The saucer-shaped nest of this species is placed in the top of a tall fir and is nearly always inaccessible. Twelve days are required for incubation, and as soon as the young are able to care for themselves the brood and adults move higher up the mountain in the wake of summer.

The song of the Cassin Finch is rich and melodious, of a softer quality than that of the California purple finch, but less varied. Its call-note is a clear " cheep."

519. HOUSE FINCH, OR LINNET. — *Carpodacus mexicanus frontalis.*

FAMILY : The Finches, Sparrows, etc.

Length: 5.75–6.25.

Adult Male: Upper parts brownish gray, tinged with carmine; back faintly streaked; forehead, superciliary, and rump rose-pink or carmine; throat and breast reddish; belly whitish, sharply streaked with brown.

Adult Female: Upper parts grayish brown, faintly streaked; under parts white, broadly streaked.

Young: Similar to female; upper parts more distinctly streaked; under parts less distinctly streaked; wing-coverts tipped with buffy.

Geographical Distribution: Western United States from Rocky Mountains to Pacific coast; from Oregon to Mexico.

California Breeding Range: Chiefly below Transition zone, in suitable localities throughout the State.

Breeding Season: April, May, and June.

Nest: A compactly woven cup; composed of grass and vegetable fibre; placed in evergreens, palms, and other trees and shrubs about the house.

Eggs: 3 to 6 ; pale blue, nearly white, thinly speckled with black. Size 0.80 × 0.55.

THE House Finch is popularly known throughout California as the Linnet, and is one bird for whom the residents have little praise. So numerous are these birds and so destructive to fruit that a continual warfare is waged against them by poison and by gun. Hundreds are sold in the bird-stores annually, sometimes at the low price of twenty-five cents each. But to the newcomer and the tourist the pretty pink-breasted songsters are one of the attractive features of the garden, where they take the place of the robin of the East. No bird is more tame or more confiding. In the rose that clambers over your window, or the evergreens on the lawn, he will build his nest, absolutely refusing to believe that he is not wanted. His happy song wakens you in the morning and is the last to cease at night, and when his pretty brown sweetheart is listening, his little pink throat ruffles and swells with the torrent of music. Then he sings on the wing in rocket-like bursts of melody, and executes wonderful gyrations for her sole benefit. A moment later they are off together over the roses looking for a place to hide the tiny home. The choice is varied. A palm tree, a vine at the kitchen door, a nook in the chicken yard, the top of an open-air pantry, the inside of a hat put up for a scarecrow, or a shoe flung into a tree in childish sport, are each and all eligible building sites. After weaving the nest out of grasses usually mixed with pine needles and a few feathers, the little brown mother broods for thirteen days, assisted by her mate at long intervals. The babies are naked, except for a scant bit of down on head and back, and are of a pinkish gray color. Like most young birds, they are born blind and do not open their eyes until the fourth or fifth day. They feather very rapidly, and on the fifteenth day are on the edge of the nest ready for their début. It is at this time that the domestic cat and the small boy collecting for the bird-store get in their deadly work. Were the robins of the East no better protected than are these feathered citizens of California, they would soon become only a legend to tell our grandchildren.

I have watched the Finches feed their young, by regurgitation at first and later with fresh food, and very rarely do they bring fruit to the nest. Seeds of various weeds and small green caterpillars formed the larger part of the diet, at least of the nestlings. In spite of their bad name, I believe they will some day be proved to have accomplished a fair amount of good to offset the evil charged against them, if in no greater way than by eating the seeds of injurious weeds.

521 a. MEXICAN CROSSBILL. — *Loxia curvirostra stricklandi.*

FAMILY: The Finches, Sparrows, etc.

Length: 6.80–7.25.

Adult Male: Plumage dull red; brighter on rump; wings and tail uniform dusky; feathers of back indistinctly streaked.

Adult Female: Plumage olive, varying in shade from a grayish to a yellowish cast.

Young: Plumage light olive; under parts lighter, streaked all over, except on wings and tail, with dusky.

Geographical Distribution: In the mountainous parts of the Southwestern United States from Western Kansas, Colorado, and Arizona, south through highlands of Mexico.

California Breeding Range: Locally in the central Sierra Nevada.

Breeding Season : March and April.

Nest : Of spruce twigs, shreds of soft bark, etc.; lined with horsehair, fine rootlets, etc.; rather flat ; placed in coniferous trees.

Eggs : 3 or 4 ; pale greenish, spotted and dotted about the larger end with shades of brown and lavender.   Size 0.75 × 0.57.

WHEREVER in the Sierra Nevada you find pine cones in plenty, look for the Crossbills.   From Placer County to Mount Whitney they are more or less common dur-

ing the summer.   We use this phrase advisedly, for never were birds more capricious in the choice of feeding and nesting grounds.   If here one season, as likely as not next year will find them miles away.   But because you may not have seen them, do not decide that they are not near.   One hundred feet away a flock of twenty to fifty may be feasting in the tree tops and not one elsewhere.   Or you may have them as neighbors to-day, and to-morrow find no trace of one.   In the winter this is even more true, for they straggle irregularly over the central part of the State even as far south as Pasadena.   At Mon-

521 a. MEXICAN CROSSBILL.

" Head down, chick-adee fashion."

terey they are irregular summer visitants ; and since they are without established laws as to breeding range, they may even be found breeding there.   The nest is placed on the horizontal branch of a coniferous tree, usually about twenty feet from the ground, and both sexes assist in its construction.   From the curiously twisted shape of the bill one would expect them to have some trouble in carrying twigs to it, but they manage very well. Instead of picking up from the ground the twigs needed, they wisely prefer to pull them from the tree, selecting brittle, dead limbs. In procuring the fine rootlets with which the nest is made, their awkward bill is an advantage. It is a great advantage, also, in prying open the pine cones and dexterously extracting the seeds. In doing this they frequently hang, head down, chickadee fashion, or climb over the cones by means of beak and claws. It has been a question how and on what the *very young* Crossbills are fed. Regurgitation would seem to be impossible in their case. Fortune has never favored me in watching a brood develop, for in every instance the eggs were " collected," either by a small boy or a squirrel, before they hatched.

The only sounds I have ever heard a Crossbill utter are the " kimp, kimp," always described in connection with them, which sounds like the crackling of the cones, and a twittering conversation early in the morning when the mate is on the nest. They are fond of water, and bathe early and late.

BLUE OR METALLIC BLUE CONSPICUOUS IN PLUMAGE

478. STELLER JAY. — *Cyanocitta stelleri.*

FAMILY : The Crows, Jays, Magpies, etc.

Length : 12.00–13.00.
Adults : Head (including conspicuous crest), neck, and back dull black ; wings and tail purplish blue, barred with black ; under parts blue.
Young : Similar to adults, but with duller and less conspicuous markings.

Geographical Distribution : Pacific coast from Alaska to Monterey, east to the Cascades.

Breeding Range : Transition zone south through humid coast belt to Monterey.

Breeding Season : April and May (a few rare records in March).

Nest : Usually placed in fir trees 30 to 55 feet from the ground, sometimes in other trees or vines ; made of twigs, moss, and dry grass, well cemented with mud ; lined with fine roots.

Eggs : 3 to 5 ; dull, pale, bluish green, spotted and blotched over the entire surface with brown and lavender. Size 1.24 × 0.92.

" THERE are many handsome blue jays, but the *stelleri* in its numerous forms, with its blue body and high crest, is one of the lords of the race, fittingly associated with the noblest forests of the West " (Mrs. Bailey).

The Steller Jay is variously subdivided in California. The form known as the Coast Jay is usually resident wherever found, and is common in California along the coast from Oregon as far as the southern boundary of Monterey County. In the vicinity of Monterey and Pacific Grove these Jays are very abundant. Some one has called them the "policemen of the woods," but *brigands* would be a much more fitting cognomen. Flying in bands with jolly good fellowship, they are the torment of the more peaceful woodland dwellers. Nowhere are they welcome. The appearance of one is the signal for the more fearless of the small birds to sally out *en masse* and drive them away ; for right well these helpless woodfolk know that here is a monster who will, if he can, devour both their eggs and their nestlings. His mimicry of the notes of various birds of prey strikes terror to the mother birds brooding the young and to the father on guard near by. Small wonder he is hated.

And yet a Blue Jay can be gentle, and few birds are so devoted to mates or young.   Two robins may quarrel, two orioles often do, but Blue Jays never.   If a young Jay is taken from one nest and placed in another, he receives the same treatment from his foster parents that their own young do ; but these same Blue Jays will bring the nestlings of other birds for him to eat.

Their ordinary call-note is very discordant, but I have heard them sing their love songs at four A. M., when no one was supposed to hear but the mother bird on the nest in the tall pine tree. Those critics who write learnedly of bird songs, putting them into notes on a scale, may not speak of this clear, low conversational warbling as "music," but it is the outpouring of a great joy, blessing alike the singer and the one who hears.

478. STELLER JAY.

"*Nowhere are they welcome.*"

In the vicinity of Monterey, nest-building usually begins early in April, and for ten days the male brings twigs, rootlets, moss, and grass, with mud enough to cement them well together.   These the female weaves into a cup-shaped affair quite unlike the flat platform of twigs made by our Eastern jays.   It is oftenest lined with pine needles or rootlets, but occasionally short hair from cattle or deer is found in it.   Incubation lasts sixteen days, and during this time, although the male is frequently left in charge of the nest, I have never seen him attempt to brood the eggs, as the mother does. He will perch on the side of the nest, look at the contents with head cocked sidewise in a comical mixture of pride and masculine helplessness in the care of infants. He knows something is necessary to keep the wonderful treasure warm, but just how to go about it is a puzzle. But when those four dull eggs have become a nest full of queer-looking babies, he knows exactly what to do. They are hungry, and who can feed them so deftly as he? So, from dawn to dusk, he is hustling in true Western fashion for bugs of all sorts and varieties, for fruit and berries. Later he will show these same nestlings how to extract an acorn from the store of the California woodpecker, how to crack a pine nut, how to hold a piece of meat in their strong claws and tear off bits of it, how to dash into the ice-cold water and enjoy the morning plunge, how to shake each little feather and dry and comb it into place again, how to frolic among the tall pine trees or over the sand dunes following the leader, how to hide motionless in the shadows when the hawk flies by, and, alas! how to wait until helpless nestlings are left alone and then sneak up and steal one. All this and more will they learn of the lore of the woods, which every wild creature must know if he would live. That most of these habits are acquired only by imitation is thoroughly proven by the helplessness of those birds which have been taken from the nest when young and raised in captivity. Although liberated as soon as they are fully fledged, they seldom learn to hunt their food until taught patiently and slowly by their captors ; and they never acquire the caution necessary for their self-preservation in a wild life.

478 a. BLUE–FRONTED JAY. — *Cyanocitta stelleri frontalis.*

FAMILY : The Crows, Jays, Magpies, etc.

Length : 11.75–13.00.

Adults : Head, neck, and back brownish slate ; crest blue; forehead streaked with blue ; wings and tail dark blue, and barred ; rump and under parts dull turquoise.

Geographical Distribution : Both slopes of the Sierra Nevada, from Fort Crook south to Lower California. Westward to the interior valleys in winter.

California Breeding Range : Southern coast ranges and Sierra Nevada from Mt. Shasta to Lower California.

Breeding Season : April 20 to July 10.

Nest : Usually in a fir tree, from 6 to 50 feet above the ground, sometimes placed in natural cavities of trees and shrubs ; made loosely of sticks or stems of weeds ; lined with fine roots and grasses.

Eggs : 3 to 5 ; like those of the Steller jay.

THE Blue-fronted Jay constitutes one of the subdivisions of the Steller jay. Along the Sierra Nevada from Mount Shasta south it breeds more or less abundantly, wandering irregularly to the coast in the winter. In general habits it is like the coast jay, and the description of nesting habits will be found under that species. In some localities, however, it is found nesting in cavities in trees. At Julian, California, Colonel Goss obtained a number of nests from hollow trees at a distance from the ground of four to fifty feet. It also builds in snowsheds of the Canadian Pacific Railroad in the Sierra

Nevada. As in the case of the coast jay, eggs and young of other birds form a part of the menu of the Blue-fronted, together with acorns, piñon nuts, insects, and fruit.

481. CALIFORNIA JAY. — *Aphelocoma californica.*

FAMILY : The Crows, Jays, Magpies, etc.

Length : 11.50–12.25.

Adults : Upper parts blue ; back and scapulars brownish gray ; sides of head grayish black ; under parts white, washed with bright blue on sides of chest, middle portion being streaked with blue and brown ; white superciliary stripe very distinct.

Young : Nearly uniform rusty black ; head tinged with blue ; throat white, unstreaked ; chest brownish gray ; belly white.

Geographical Distribution : Pacific coast of United States, from northern Oregon to Lower California ; east to Western Nevada.

California Breeding Range : Upper Sonoran zone, west of Sierra Nevada, south to Lower California.

Breeding Season : April to June 15.

Nest : Usually found in low bushes or thickets, though sometimes in a tree, from 3 to 30 feet from the ground ; a platform of interlaced twigs, moss, and dry grass supports the nest proper, which is made of rootlets mixed with horsehair.

Eggs : 3 to 6 ; buffy or green, varying in shade, blotched with brown. Size 1.08 × 0.80.

To one accustomed to the handsome blue jay of the East or the still more splendid Steller jay of the West, the "flat-headed" California Jay presents a far less attractive appearance. Nor does he improve upon acquaintance ; for, as one becomes aware of all his iniquities, his crestless head seems the typical low forehead of a villain. He is one of the greatest trials a bird-lover must encounter, and I know no reason why the law should protect him to the destruction of our beloved birds of song and beauty. Were he of benefit to the farmer or the fruit-grower, no word of dispraise would I offer ; but he not only robs them, but also destroys annually hundreds of feathered creatures which, living upon the harmful insects, would be of great assist-ance in preserving the crops. No hawk is more de-structive to small birds than is he. Ruthlessly he robs every nest in his vicinity that is left un-guarded long enough for him to carry off eggs or young. Not content with this, he pulls down and breaks up the nest itself. Usually he prefers the newly hatched babies to the raw albumen, and waits for the

481. CALIFORNIA JAY.

"*The colder the better.*"

incubation to be finished. I have seen him sneaking around the nest of a pewee day after day until the eggs hatched, when he at once made a breakfast on the nestlings, — in this case calmly disregarding the frantic cries of the poor little mother. When, how-ever, he must ravage the home of a bird of his own size, he either calls all his kin to help, or comes, like the villain he is, when both the parents are away.

About the farms and henhouses he is even a greater pest, eating the eggs and occasionally killing the newly hatched chicks. Foraging in bands, these Jays destroy quantities of fruit of every variety and pull up the young sprouts of wheat. In short, there seems to be no limit to the Jay's mischief, and nothing too bad to say of him. In addition to all this, every bird-student sooner or later comes to feel a personal grievance against him, for seldom or never does one of these pests fail to discover your presence in a wood and to give warning of it far and wide to everything that flies. As long as you stay, so long will he, perched on the tallest tree-top, sit screaming, " Here she is ! here ! here ! " in open defiance of your wish for quiet or concealment. Every bird in the forest knows and hides. Observation is impossible, and with unspoken maledictions on his little flat blue head you sadly trudge on to another wood. Fortunate indeed are you if he does not collect a band of his fellows and follow you.

There is another side of this story. In spite of ourselves we are forced to admire his dashing courage and gay nonchalance, his devotion to his kind, and his care for his young. There is something uncanny in the wisdom with which these Jays band together for defence or offence. Although so quarrelsome with other birds, they never molest each other, nor do they kill an injured one of their kind, as robins do.

Their nests are placed in low bushes or thickets, or on the horizontal branch of an oak, seldom more than ten feet from the ground, and usually near water. This last requisite seems to be necessary for their existence in other ways than for drinking.   Early every morning every adult Jay takes a cold bath, the colder the better; but the water must be clear.   A tremendous splashing is followed by a long, careful preening of the feathers, which frequently occupies fifteen minutes or longer. Long, close watching has led me to believe that, except where there are young in the nest to be fed, this toilet is made before any hunting is done for breakfast.

The male assists in the nest-building, but not in the incubation.   The latter requires fourteen days.   The mother during the brooding time plunges down to the water once or twice a day, returning to her eggs with feathers still damp, fusses about as if turning them before settling down upon them, and in a moment rises up and fusses again.   This may be only for her own greater comfort, but I have wondered whether the moisture was necessary for the eggs.   As soon as they hatch she ceases to bathe in this way, and, devoting her time to obtaining food, becomes dishevelled and rusty-looking.

One of the first lessons the young Jays learn is to love the water.   It requires some coaxing for the first splash, but they seem to take to their bath as do little ducks, and to find it just as necessary as food.

492. PIÑON JAY. — *Cyanocephalus cyanocephalus.*

Family : The Crows, Jays, Magpies, etc.

Length : 10.00–11.75.

Adults : Entire plumage grayish blue, brighter on head ; throat bright blue, with white streaks ; head not crested ; bill cylindrical.

Young : Uniform dull grayish blue, lighter beneath.

Geographical Distribution : Plateau regions of Western North America, from the Rocky Mountains west to the Pacific coast ranges, north to British Columbia, south to Lower California, Texas, and Mexico.

California Breeding Range : In the piñon belt of the desert ranges, southeast of the Sierra Nevada and locally along the whole length of the Sierra Nevada from Mt. Shasta to the San Bernardino mountains.

Breeding Season : March 15 to May 15.

Nest : 5 to 12 feet from the ground; deep, bulky and compact; composed of piñon, sagebrush, shreds of bark ; lined with fibre, rootlets, and dry grasses thoroughly woven together.

Eggs : 3 to 5; bluish white, entirely covered with fine specks of brown, and sometimes with larger spots and blotches at the larger end. Size 1.19 × 0.87.

THE Piñon Jay is also called Nutcracker, Blue Crow, and Piñario by the Mexicans, in reference to its fondness for the nuts of the variety known as piñon. It is a haunter of the piñon-covered foot-hills, and scarcely ever roves into the higher coniferous forests. Eminently social at all times, it is found in flocks of hundreds feeding upon the ground after the fashion of blackbirds, and like them constantly in motion, — those in the rear flying over those feeding ahead of them and alighting in front of the flock. In this way they progress from place to place, and collectors who know this peculiarity hide along the route to wait for a good shot. Their constant chatter can be heard a long distance, and betrays their approach. They are occasionally seen in company with Clarke nutcrackers in the piñon groves ; but, although they are great rangers, here to-day and gone to-morrow, they do not follow the latter in their vertical migration to the high altitudes, nor are they commonly found north of latitude 40°.

In the summer grasshoppers, insects caught on the wing, and fruit form their bill of fare. They seem to lack the cannibalistic tendencies of their family, and do not, so far as I have observed or can learn, meddle with the broods of other birds.

The call-notes of the Piñon Jay are as varied as those of the Eastern jay and very like them in character. A harsh "j-a-a-h," a guttural chuck, and some soft, low notes uttered at the nest to mate or young are the sounds most characteristic.

Late in March or early in April they commence to build their bulky nests in full view, on the horizontal limbs of a nut pine or a juniper tree, usually within ten feet of the ground. The framework consists of twigs of juniper, nut pine, or sagebrush, and is lined with fine rootlets, bark shredded very fine, and moss or grass. Both sexes share in the incubation, which lasts sixteen days. In devotion to mate and young they rival the nutcrackers, and feed the nestlings long after they are able to provide for themselves. Like young nutcrackers, they are born naked, but are greener in hue. They remain about the same length of time (twenty-two days) in the nest, and learn to extract the sweet kernels of the piñon nuts before they leave it. They are also fed quite as fully on grasshoppers from which legs and wings have been carefully removed. As soon as able to fly they unite with other families in large flocks, and forage from place to place with the roving habits of their species.

597 a. WESTERN BLUE GROSBEAK. — *Guiraca*
cærulea lazula.

FAMILY : The Finches, Sparrows, etc.

Length : 7.00–8.00.

Adult Male : Plumage plain bright blue, with two brownish wing-bands; under tail-coverts with white borders.

Adult Female : Plumage grayish brown, tinged with blue.

Young : Similar to adult female.

Geographical Distribution : Western United States, north to Colorado, California, etc. ; south throughout Mexico.

California Breeding Range : In lower and possibly upper Sonoran zone, recorded from Owens valley, through the San Joaquin-Sacramento basin, to Marysville.

Breeding Season : May 15 to July 15.

Nest : A deep, cup-shaped structure ; compactly built of dried grasses, plant fibre, etc. ; placed in bushes and tall weeds.

Eggs : 3 or 4 ; plain pale greenish blue or bluish white. Size 0.87 × 0.63.

THE Western Blue Grosbeak is a more difficult bird to observe than either the black-headed or the rose-breasted Grosbeak. He loves the thickets and brush of the valleys, seldom going higher than the foot-hills. The male, in plain winter garb, has been mistaken for a female cowbird by amateurs, but one glance at the bill should correct such a mistake. In the glory of his summer blue he is instantly recognized. His song is somewhat misleading, for although the same sweetly whistled turns so characteristic of the Grosbeak song abound in it, the tone quality is thinner and less mellow than that of the black-headed. Nor does he sing so continuously as the latter ; perhaps because the days are shorter in the cañons, where he loves to stay, and he must put in more time eating.

But if not so fine a singer, the Blue Grosbeak is a much better nest-builder than any other member of his family. And this work is well worth patient watching. After much consulting together, the pair agree upon a site, and the foundation of heavy grasses and weed stalks are scratched into place. A pair that I watched, after trying one crotch, deliberately selected another, and removed the material to the new site. Nor could I find out what influenced the choice, unless there was something in the shape that was not quite comfortable to the little mother. Both male and female carried material, and moulded it into form by turning about in it and tucking the unruly ends in with their bills. At the end of the fifth day the compact, rather deep affair, lined with plant fibre and fine grasses, was ready for use; and on the seventh day it contained one egg. An egg was laid each day until there were four; then incubation began.

The Blue-headed Grosbeak is a model father. Day after day found him on the nest. By some mysterious signal he knew when Madam was ready to leave, and never failed to appear just as she flew off, though my dull ears caught no signal between them. Then, pausing a moment on the edge of the nest, he would survey the treasures with a comical air of wisdom. Having satisfied himself that all was as it should be, he settled down, rather awkwardly, but with less fuss than the female ever could succeed in doing.

After fourteen days of waiting, four wriggling, naked nestlings filled the cradle and ate as surely no other young birds ever have done. There was scarcely a moment when one or the other of the parents was not bending over the nest offering food to the wide-open yellow mouths of the offspring. For several days this was given entirely by regurgitation. The adults had a habit of flying down the cañon to their feeding grounds, about a hundred yards away, and I never succeeded in finding out what they brought back. Oftentimes what looked to be the gauzy wings of a dragonfly stuck out on one side of the bill; at other times the food looked like grasshoppers or crickets, but I cannot be sure what it was. When ten days old, the young were feathered in soft tints of grayish brown, with a hint of blue on head and shoulders. But the constant surveillance had made them uneasy; as soon as possible they escaped from it by disappearing from the locality the same day that the little ones flew from the nest, and a diligent search failed to discover their whereabouts.

599. LAZULI BUNTING. — *Cyanospiza amœna.*

FAMILY : The Finches, Sparrows, etc.

Length : 5.00–6.25.

Adult Male : Head, neck, and upper parts turquoise blue; the back darker and duller ; wings with two white bars ; breast and sometimes sides washed with brownish ; remainder of under parts white.

Adult Female : Upper parts grayish brown, with blue on rump; back more or less streaked; wing-bars dull whitish; lower parts pale dull buffy, deeper on chest, and fading to white on belly and lower tail-coverts.

Young : Similar to adult female, but without blue tinge on rump; chest and sides streaked.

Geographical Distribution : Western United States, east to Great Plains and Kansas; south in winter to Western Mexico.

California Breeding Range: Below Boreal zone, nearly throughout the State.

Breeding Season: May and June.

Nest: Of fine strips of bark, small twigs, grasses; lined with hair; placed in trees or bushes a few feet from the ground.

Eggs: 3 or 4; plain bluish white or light bluish green. Size 0.75 × 0.58.

ALTHOUGH the Lazuli Bunting is found on the higher Sierra Nevada, his best loved haunts are the lower mountain thickets and the chaparral-covered foot-hills. While the showily plumaged male flies through the open, from tree-top to tree-top, his little brown mate keeps well within the cover of the bushes, zigzagging her way through the chaparral like a shy sparrow. From the plains to the Pacific this species replaces the indigo bunting of the East.

The song of the Lazuli is loud, sweet, and merry, but is chiefly remarkable for the fine enthusiasm of the singer. Long after the other birds, worn out by family cares, have ceased their music, this blithe " little boy blue" carols his jolly roundelay from the top of a tall tree as gayly as though there were no such thing as work in the world. For this we love him. Yet snugly hidden among the bushes is the cup-shaped nest, where in the June days his mate brooded over the pretty nestlings, and where he was kept busy hunting bugs for the hungry mouths; and there may have been a second brood to be looked after, as there often is in the Bunting family. At any rate, he has had his full share of labor in nest-building, incubating, guarding, and feeding, and has come out of it without losing one iota of enthusiasm in the joy of living.

Baby Buntings are very like their newly hatched sparrow cousins. The thin hair-like down on their heads and shoulders is soon replaced by soft brownish feathers; the broad flat bills take form and comeliness; their funny little elbows become hidden in the wing plumage, and every day sees them stretching up to fly. They usually leave the nest when fifteen days old unless the début is hastened by meddlesome fingers. Up to this time they have been fed on insects, by regurgitation at first, then fresh food is given them, the frequency of meals depending somewhat on the location and the time of day. Early in the morning, after a night of fasting, all young birds are fed as frequently as it is possible for the parents to bring the food; and young reared upon insect diet seem to require more frequent meals than those whose bill of fare consists of seeds. In the case of one brood of young Buntings, the meals were brought every eight minutes from four to five A. M., until their little crops swelled out like marbles. Through the semi-transparent skin I could see enough of the contents to be sure of their menu after they were five days old.

613. BARN SWALLOW. — *Hirundo erythrogastra.*

FAMILY. — The Swallows.

Length: 5.75–7.75.

Adults: Tail forked for about half its length, outside feather tapered to point. Upper parts glossy metallic blue; forehead dark brown; wings and tail changeable purple and green; outer two tail-feathers, marked with large whitish spots; under parts rusty brown, darkest on throat.

Young: Fork of tail shorter; upper parts lighter in color; under parts dull brownish buffy.

Geographical Distribution: Whole of North America, migrating to Central and South America.

California Breeding Range: Chiefly coastwise in more northern portions, but local elsewhere throughout the State.

Breeding Season May and June.

Nest: A cup or bowl-shaped structure ; made of pellets of mud mixed with straws, etc.; lined with feathers ; attached to the side or roof of a cave, or to timbers in barns or other buildings.

Eggs: 3 to 4 ; speckled with brown and lavender.   Size 0.68 × 0.50.

ALTHOUGH choosing to live in a stable loft, the Barn Swallow is an aristocratic-looking bird, his long forked tail giving him an air of elegance unrivalled by any of his comely relatives. Among a family remarkable for their swift, graceful flight he has no superior. Circling low over the earth in search of the insects that live in moist places, or fluttering like a huge butterfly at the edge of a puddle as he gathers mud for his little nest, his is indeed the " poetry of motion."

On the inside of the barn, among the rafters of the roof, is his cup-shaped nest made of alternate layers of mud-pellets and hay. Once during the long afternoons of late spring time I watched these little masons build. Male and female brought mud in their beaks and plastered it to the rough boards. Then long wisps of hay and bits of hair were carried and tucked into place with much poking and patting of the bill. Feathers of all sorts were stuck in promiscuously, until the whole looked as much like a ruffled, headless, Shanghai chicken as like a nest. Some naturalists assert that saliva is mixed with the mud to make it sticky, and it seems to me this must be, for the nest is much firmer than that of the eave swallow and can be taken down intact.

In several nests, May 20, when the watch began, the young were nearly ready to fly, and their little heads were stretched over the edge as if they were trying to gather up courage to make the dive. In other cases the broods were much later. Incubation required twelve days, and in this the male shared equally with the female, seeming fully as much at home on the nest as did she. It was delightful to see them sit side by side on the edge, turning their little blue heads sidewise as they peeked into the cradle and talked it all over together in low sweet twitters. And when the nestlings were finally hatched, one need not climb to discover the fact, for the busy importance of the happy housekeepers told all who had eyes to see. The young were fed by regurgitation until two weeks old, and then the diet was varied by an occasional large insect that looked like a bluebottle fly.

614. WHITE-BELLIED SWALLOW, OR TREE SWALLOW. — *Tachycineta bicolor.*

FAMILY. — The Swallows.

Length: 5.00–6.25.

Adult Male: Upper parts iridescent steel blue ; lores deep black ; wings and tail blackish, slightly tinged with greenish ; under parts pure white.

Adult Female: Similar to male, but upper parts duller.

Young: Upper parts dull brownish slate.

Geographical Distribution: Whole of North America, migrating in winter to the Gulf States and West Indies.

California Breeding Range: Chiefly in upper Sonoran zone, west of the Sierra Nevada.

Breeding Season: May, June, and July.

Nest: In holes, excavations, natural cavities, etc.; made of grasses and straw ; thickly lined with feathers.
Eggs: 4 to 7 ; pure white. Size 0.75 × 0.53.

EARLY in July the Tree Swallows begin to gather in flocks ; and, from that time until they start on their southern migration, innumerable multitudes of them are to be seen flying over the open country. They sit in crowds on telegraph wires or any available perch, gathering late in the afternoon and, when near water, circling over it in an endless game of " Follow the Leader." They dip daintily, each one in turn, rise, circle, and dip again, just brushing the surface with a light splashing, until the shadows of evening fall and it is too dark to watch them longer. In almost any section of the United States they are the swallows best known, at least to city folk, and are, I believe, the ones whose return migration has been celebrated in the old song.

They still adhere to the old habits of nesting in hollow trees, only a small portion having been induced to try the boxes put up for them by bird-lovers. Undoubtedly they will in time accept this substitute and become as changed in their environment as are the eave and barn swallows ; but no one can wonder that they love the forest best and are loath to leave it. At Lake Tahoe we found them nesting in the old piles of the deserted pier, in company with the Brewer blackbirds. They entered the nesting cavities, which were usually two to five feet above the water, by a knot-hole or crevice in the wood. One nest whose brood I watched develop was so filled with feathers that they waved in the doorway, calling the attention of all passers-by. Near this nest a pair of pygmy nuthatches were occupying a small hollow near the top of a pile, entering by a knot-hole too small for a mouse. Both they and the swallows were remarkably fearless.

The incubation of the swallow's eggs lasted thirteen days, both sexes sharing alike in it. We knew this because one would fly in as soon as the other left; but they looked so exactly alike that it was impossible to distinguish one from the other. The newly hatched nestlings were naked, pink, and not unlike a tangle of earthworms. In ten days they were feathered. At this time so fearless were the parents that they did not leave the nest at our approach and, on the last visit, one of the parents allowed herself to be lifted from her brood rather than desert them. This was remarkable in contrast to bank swallows, which are excessively timid; but it was very like the brave little eave swallows and the martins.

For the first ten days of their existence the young Tree Swallows were fed by regurgitation, at intervals varying from five to thirty minutes according to the time of day. During the early morning hours — from four to six — the meals were most frequent. At this sunrise time, also, the adults frolicked over the water, catching insects, skimming the lightest spray of the waves with a splash in the sparkling ripples, and twittering merry greetings as they passed each other.

767. WESTERN BLUEBIRD. — *Sialia mexicana occidentalis.*

FAMILY: The Thrushes, Solitaires, etc.

Length: 6.50–7.12.

Adult Male: Upper parts dark blue and brown; throat purplish blue; breast bright chestnut; under parts brown, washed with purplish blue.

Adult Female: Upper parts brownish gray; blue on rump and tail.

Young: Gray, mottled and streaked with white, darkest on upper parts.

Geographical Distribution: Transition zone of Pacific coast from British Columbia south to New Mexico, east to Nevada.

California Breeding Range: Local in upper Sonoran zone and throughout Transition zone.

Breeding Season: April, May, and June.

Nest: In old woodpecker holes or in cavities of pine trees, usually rather high.

Eggs: 6; light blue. Size 0.81 × 0.67.

In coloring, the Western Bluebird is the counterpart of the bluebird of the East, but he is much more shy, seldom coming close to houses or nesting near the homes of men. He is a resident throughout the foot-hills and lower mountains, coming down to the valleys in winter. I have found him oftenest along country roadsides or in the edge of the woods, and have seldom seen him within the borders of a town even in the winter. This Bluebird, like the mountain species, has the flycatcher habit of darting down from a perch for insects, and often hunting through the grass for them and flying back to the perch to eat. Crickets, moths, grasshoppers, caterpillars, ants, and weevils form the large part of his diet, varied with fruits.

His song is clear and mellow, — three notes repeated

over and over while perching, never on the wing. Except in the location of the nest, this bird is like the mountain bluebird in breeding habits, which have been fully described under that head.

768. MOUNTAIN BLUEBIRD. — *Sialia arctica.*

FAMILY : The Thrushes, Solitaires, etc.

Length : 6.50–7.90.

Adult Male : Upper parts brilliant light-blue ; under parts pale turquoise blue. Winter plumage slightly duller.

Adult Female : Upper parts gray, wings and tail bright turquoise blue ; under parts soft light-brown, washed with blue.

Young : Grayish, indistinctly streaked or mottled with white ; wings and tail blue.

Geographical Distribution : From Great Slave Lake south to New Mexico, and from the Plains to the Pacific.

California Breeding Range : On the higher Sierra Nevada, from Mt. Shasta to the San Bernardino mountains.

Breeding Season : May, June, and July.

Nest : In old woodpecker holes or in natural cavities of dead trees.

Eggs : 5 to 7 ; pale turquoise blue. Size 0.85 × 0.63.

THE exquisite coloring of the Mountain Bluebird renders him easily the most beautiful of all Californian birds. No words can describe his brilliancy in the breeding season, as he flies through the sunny clearings of the higher Sierra Nevada, or sits like a bright blue flower against the dark green of the pines. In the winter the brilliant blue of his plumage is dulled by brownish, but even then he is glorious. All through the State east of the humid coast belt these birds wander during the winter in small flocks, looking like big blue butterflies, as they hover fifty feet above the earth. At this time they have all the habits of flycatchers ; I have seen them at San Diego flying out after insects, or skimming the air like swallows, and hovering like hummingbirds. They have a pretty fashion of quivering their wings a moment as if loath to close them.

Their song is a sweet clear "trually, tru-al-ly," like that of the Eastern species, and a mellow warble. High up in the mountain meadows, where these bits of azure nest, they are usually seen only in pairs, and are frequently the only pair in the neighborhood, and here their feeding habits are those of the thrushes once more.

Both male and female carry material to the old tree which they have selected for a home. Usually the cavity chosen is one excavated the previous year by a woodpecker, but sometimes a natural hole in a dead tree or a crevice about a house is selected. In any case it is nearly filled with dried grass and feathers. Fourteen days are required for incubation, and in this the male often, but not always, shares. When not on the nest himself he brings food to his mate, calling to her in sweetest tones from the outside before entering the doorway. The newly hatched young are of the usual naked pinkish gray type, looking as like tiny new-born mice as birds. On the second day down begins to appear in thin hairs on head and back; on the fourth or fifth day the eyes show signs of opening; on the sixth day they open, and the down is well spread over the bodies.

Up to this time they have been fed by regurgitation, the adult swallowing each bit first to moisten or crush it; but from the fourth day on fresh food is given occasionally, and from the sixth or seventh day all the food given is in the fresh state, not regurgitated. Crickets, grasshoppers, beetles, butterflies, and worms are their menu, with a few berries. The young Bluebirds double in weight every twenty-four hours for the first week, and in twelve days are growing a respectable crop of feathers, though the bare skin is still distressingly visible. Their breasts gradually take on the soft, mottled light and dark, and the upper parts have a hint of blue among the grayish brown on the wings and tail. One would suppose this blue on the upper parts would be too conspicuous, but when the youngsters leave the nest and perch on the soft gray of the dead trees, they become almost invisible in the strong sunlight.

YELLOW OR ORANGE CONSPICUOUS IN PLUMAGE

497. YELLOW–HEADED BLACKBIRD.
Xanthocephalus xanthocephalus.

FAMILY : The Blackbirds, Orioles, etc.

Length : Male 8.60–10.10 ; Female 7.50–8.30.

Adult Male in Summer : Plumage uniform black, except yellow or orange head, neck, and chest, and white patch on wings.

Adult Male in Winter : Similar, but yellow feathers on top of head tipped with brown.

Adult Female : Dark grayish brown, throat and chest dull yellow ; breast mixed with white.

Young Male in First Winter : Similar to female, but larger, and deeper colored.

Young : (Nestling) General color pinkish brown ; upper parts indistinctly streaked with lighter beneath ; wings and tail blackish.

Geographical Distribution : Western North America from British Columbia south to Mexican table-lands ; east to Wisconsin, Indiana, and Texas.

California Breeding Range : Interior valleys, east of the humid coast belt.

Breeding Season: May 15 to July 1.

Nest: Like an inverted cone in shape ; fastened to the upright tules, from 1 to 2 feet above the surface of the water ; the outside is composed of coarse marsh-grass and fine tules woven together ; lined with fine grass and pond weeds and occasionally plant down.

Eggs: 3 to 5 ; greenish white, evenly blotched and speckled with browns and gray.   Size 0.71 × 0.53.

IN suitable localities throughout California, as elsewhere in the United States, the Yellow-headed Blackbird breeds abundantly.   The interior valleys east of the Coast Range are his favorite haunts ; there, except during the nesting season, he may be found picking up insect food in the newly harrowed ground.   Grasshoppers, big black wingless crickets, all sorts of marsh insects, and the larvæ and eggs of beetles form his bill of fare ; and much does the farmer owe to his good services.   When the winter rains have ceased and the warm spring sunshine floods the valleys, the large flocks of these handsome birds leaving the farms and fruit ranches betake themselves to the tule marshes, where their noisy wooing can be heard far and wide.   While the male rocks and sings on the tall reeds, the soberly gowned female is busy building a nest among the swaying rushes.   First she brings heavy, wet pond-weed and marsh-grass, and with it winds several of these together, weaving it in and out and making a firm support for the superstructure.   Bits of dried rushes and last year's tule are twisted in to form the walls, which are then warmly lined with the finer marsh-grass and pond-weed.   No feathers or other animal matter are used in it, but occasionally a little plant down, as if the blossom had ripened after having been caught accidentally in the weaving.

No help has the mother bird had from her mate in this labor, except the encouragement of his cheery song as he swung always in sight of her, ready to join her the moment she left her work. In a few rare instances I have known him to make a pretence of nest-building a few feet away from the real cradle, either to amuse himself or deceive me, for the loosely woven affair was never regarded seriously by the female. She sometimes perched near it, regarding with amusement the masculine attempt at housekeeping, and with a scornful flirt of her tail went back to her own cosey nest. It was often a week or two after the latter was entirely finished before the first egg was laid. For fourteen days the female brooded, hidden by the green tules, hearing only the gay banjo-like song of her mate, the hoarse croaking of the frogs, the "chaacks" of her yellow-head neighbors, and the grunts of the rails. Never, by any chance, does the gay lord of that small household assist her until the wonderful transformation has come, and hungry nestlings are stretching their open mouths beseechingly from the green cradle. Then his paternal instinct awakes, and he hustles for food to fill them.

497. YELLOW-HEADED BLACKBIRD.

"Beseechingly from the cradle."

From the very first they are fascinating, pinkish salmon
babies, without feathers or down, except a very little
patch on the head and shoulders, and a thin dark strip
on either side of the back. Developing very rapidly on
the diet of water-snails, slugs, and slimy water larvæ of
all sorts, on which they are fed by regurgitation at first,
they soon become handsome enough in their soft brown
coats to delight any father's eyes. Their bills change
from buff to black, and the inside of the throat becomes
an exquisite rose-pink. Nor are their heads bare, as is
the case with young red-wings. In two weeks or sixteen
days after hatching they are ready to leave the nest, and
now it is the father who coaxes them step by step back
through the rushes to the safer meadow and teaches
them how to find their own food. As soon as they learn
this they become very independent and, leaving their
parents, join flocks of other young Yellow-heads, who,
with a few adults, keep together the rest of the summer and through the fall and winter. They scatter over
the valleys, wherever the food supply tempts, chattering, frolicking, and gradually donning adult plumage
until, when spring calls again, they are off *en masse* to
marshland.

501 b. WESTERN MEADOWLARK. — *Sturnella magna neglecta.*

FAMILY : The Blackbirds, Orioles, etc.

Length: Male 8.31–10.14 ; Female 7.74–9.00.
Adult Male : Upper parts grayish brown, streaked and barred with buffy,
white, and black ; crown with median buffy white stripe ; lores yel-

low ; superciliary buff; middle of tail heavily marked with black ; tertials, rump, and tail heavily barred; outer tail-feathers white ; under parts bright yellow, with black crescent on breast and black spots on sides; flanks and lower tail-coverts white.

Adult Female : Similar, but lighter colored.

Young : Colors much duller, with less distinct markings ; crescent on chest faintly marked.

Geographical Distribution : Western United States, from Wisconsin, Illinois, and Texas to the Pacific ; north to British Columbia ; south to Lower California and Mexico.

California Breeding Range : Suitable localities throughout the State.

Breeding Season : April.

Nest : On the ground, usually at the foot of a bunch of grass ; made of grass, loosely covered over.

Eggs : 3 to 7 ; white, spotted irregularly over the entire surface with brown and purple. Size 1.10 × 0.90.

THE Western Meadowlark differs from the Eastern species chiefly in the quality of its song, in which it greatly excels the latter. The wild sweet notes have a carrying quality, and at the same time a liquid mellowness that is peculiarly in harmony with the wind-swept prairies of the West. It is also longer, more varied, and more sustained than the song of the Eastern species. Major Bendire compares it to the " matchless, clear, tinkling utterances of the finest of our Western songsters, Townsend's solitaire." Its alarm notes differ somewhat also, being less harsh, more a remonstrance than a scold.

Of a somewhat paler plumage than the lark of the East, it is closely allied in habits, living in the open meadows and clearings along streams. Down among the tangled grass of the lowland prairie it builds its nest, — a snug little hollow in the soil, lined with dried grass and often roofed with the same. Both male and female assist in moulding the nest and in the cares of incubation. This lasts thirteen days, and the young remain in the nursery twelve days longer, leaving it before they are able either to fly or to perch. Yet so protective is their coloring and so jealously does the long grass guard its secret that, search as you may within a circle where you know they are hidden, you will not find one of them. For two weeks longer they remain with their parents, learning to hunt grasshoppers, beetles, and crickets, to hide in the shadow of a green tuft, to bathe in the shallows at the brook's edge, and last of all, to perch in low bushes at night with others of their kind. As soon as they have mastered these things, they are able to provide for themselves and are abandoned by the parents. I have a theory that the young of each year go some distance south in companies guided by one or two adults, returning either the next spring or the second season. Some species of birds do not mature fully until two years old, and this seems to be true of Meadowlarks.

Meanwhile the parents have begun preparations for rearing another brood in the same meadow, but not the same nest. The sun being hotter, this second cradle is more carefully sheltered from its rays by the pulling over of the surrounding grass, and sometimes a runway is made to it, extending four or five feet away. By this the old birds enter and leave the nest proper.

Dr. Coues, in "Birds of the Northwest," writes of some peculiar habits of the Western Meadowlark as follows:

"In April before pairing, hundreds used to frequent daily the parade ground of Fort Randall, where, as the grass was yet scarcely sprouted, good opportunity was offered of observing their characteristic habit — one not so generally known as it should be, since it is related to the peculiar shape of the bill. The birds may be seen scattered all over the ground, busily tugging at something; and on walking over the scene of their operations, the ground, newly softened by the spring thaw, is seen to be riddled with thousands of little holes, which the birds make in search of food. The holes are quite smooth, — not a turning over of the surface of the ground, but clean borings like those made by sinking in the end of a light walking stick, just as if the birds had inserted their bills, and then worked them about till the holes were of sufficient size. Whether they bored at random or were guided by some sense in finding their prey, and what particular object they were searching for, I did not ascertain; but the habit was so fixed and so continually persevered in as to attract general attention."

To this Major Bendire adds his opinion, based on close observation, that they were feeding upon the eggs of the locust, which are deposited just below the surface of the ground.

504. SCOTT ORIOLE. — *Icterus parisorum.*

FAMILY : The Blackbirds, Orioles, etc.

Length : 7.70–8.50.

Adult Male : Uniform black, except white and yellow markings on wings and tail, and bright yellow belly, shoulders, and posterior parts of back ; the rump and upper tail-coverts, usually tinged with olive.

Adult Female : Upper parts olive-green, yellow on rump and outer tail-feathers ; two white wing-bars ; under parts greenish yellow.

Young : Similar to adult female, but under parts less yellow, and breast brownish ; wing-bar yellow, and all wing-feathers tipped with white ; tail tipped with yellow.

Geographical Distribution : Western Texas to California, and from southern parts of Utah and Nevada south to Lower California.

California Breeding Range : In desert regions southeast of the Sierra Nevada.

Breeding Season : May to June 15.

Nest : A pouch-shaped affair ; woven of string, grass, and yucca fibre ; hung under yucca leaves or in other low trees.

Eggs : 2 to 4 ; light blue, marked with brown and gray. Size 0.96 × 0.68.

WHERE the tree yuccas grow, the Scott Oriole makes his home. His brilliant lemon and black plumage and merry song are a welcome bit of life in the arid desert regions of Southeastern California. There, in the cool of the morning, or when the intense heat of noonday beats down from the cloudless sky and up from blistering sand, and all the other birds are still, he pipes his clear, sweet roundelay. Even when worn with the cares of a family of two he sings — less often perhaps and less rapturously than when the spring called him to woo his mate, but still with a bubbling overflow of joy. A little way up the valley is his nest, swung under the sword-like leaves of the yucca and securely fastened with its coarse, thread-like fibre. Here, concealed by the dead leaves, the mother bird sits all day long for two weeks, and keeps the eggs warm, often singing softly to herself the same sweet lullaby. Her devoted mate feeds her and stands guard on a near-by tree, but I have never seen him attempt to get into the nest to take her place when she is absent. He will peer into it with ludicrous

earnestness, evidently not daring to attempt the dangerous task of brooding, lest his bungling should be disastrous. As soon as the naked pink
nestlings have emerged from the
shells and opened their wide bills
for food, his cares begin. And they
know no end until four
weeks later, when all have
learned to care for them-
selves. Oriole nestlings in
general are proverbial cry-
babies, and Scott Orioles are
no exception. Insects of
all sorts in all stages of
development, fruit, and berries are served to them in
such quick succession as to leave
small time for the parent to hunt
any for himself. At first the feeding is by regurgitation, but on the
fourth or fifth day this method gives
place to the more commonly ob-

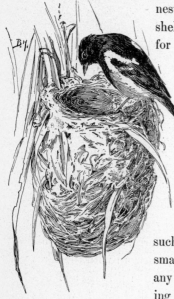

504. SCOTT ORIOLE.
*"He will peer into it with
ludicrous earnestness."*

served one. After this brood is reared, with com-
mendable patience, he is ready to care for another, for
which a new nest in a new tree must be made.

505 a. ARIZONA HOODED ORIOLE. — *Icterus cucullatus nelsoni.*

FAMILY: The Blackbirds, Orioles, etc.

Length: Male 6.90–7.80; female 6.90–7.30.

Adult Male: General plumage saffron-yellow; black patch on throat, extending in front and under the eyes; a band across the fore part of back; tail and wings black, the latter with two white bars and white edgings; tail tipped with white.

Adult Female: Upper parts olive-green, slightly tinged with gray on back; wings olive-brown, with two white bands; under parts plain dull yellow.

Young: Similar to female, but with throat patch as in the male.

Geographical Distribution: Western Mexico and Lower California, north to New Mexico, Arizona, and west of the Sierra Nevada in Southern California; north to Santa Barbara.

Breeding Range: Coast district of Southern California, north as far as Santa Barbara.

Breeding Season: April 20 to July 1.

Nest: Basket-shaped; of green wiry grass and sometimes dry yucca fibres; occasionally lined with willow down, wool, or horsehair; securely fastened with twigs and semi-pensile, at various heights from 12 to 40 feet from the ground.

Eggs: 3 to 5; speckled with brown, and having zigzag markings. Size 0.88 × 0.62.

DODGING about among the dull green, the Arizona Hooded Oriole makes a gay bit of color, like a brilliant blossom in the acres of chaparral that abound in the San Diegan district. His orange breast rivals the poppies in its gorgeous hue, and his song fills the air with music. In all his ways he is much more like the orchard oriole of the East than like any of the Western species. His protest is the same harsh " scraack." His call-note is the same clear whistle, and his song has the same joyous sweetness. Like the orchard oriole, he haunts the heavy

foliage, flitting through the open only *en route* to a fresh
pasture. Restless, shy, ever on the move, searching for
caterpillars on the under sides of the leaves chickadee
fashion, picking in the crevices for larvæ like a nuthatch, and snapping up grasshoppers with a little jump
as do young meadowlarks, he is usually to be found
within twelve feet of the ground.

His wooing is as ardent as the brilliant plumage would
typify. Rivals not a few he fights, and to the victor
belongs the spoil, whether she will or no. With song or
with harsh scolding note he wooes or threatens, giving
her no peace until his suit is accepted. Then both
gather material for the characteristic nest, which the
female weaves. It is hung on the under side of a fan-
palm leaf or in low trees or bushes, sometimes in a
bunch of mistletoe, sometimes in willow or gum trees,
and in one instance, at Monrovia, California, it was hung
to a banana leaf. In material used it differs radically
from all the other oriole nests in California, for instead
of gray or brown plant fibre, horsehair, string, shavings,
and other grotesque accessories, it is built of green grass
and the moss from the trees. It is sometimes stiffened
with yucca fibre, but the prevailing color is invariably
green, as in the nest of the orchard oriole ; hence it is
exceedingly difficult to discover among the green leaves.
By the time it has turned yellow the brood has flown.
Not so deep nor so pensile as that of the other Californian varieties, it swings like a little basket from the
slender support, or is secured by upright twigs to which
its walls are fastened. In Texas the bird often hollows

out a snug nursery for itself in a ball of the tree moss. In this case, or when fastened to the under side of a palm leaf, a small opening is left as an entrance for the female.

Incubation lasts thirteen days, and in this the male takes no part. His duty is to sing from a concealed perch near by and bring tidbits to the mother bird as she broods. If you listen closely and patiently, you may hear her imitate his song in low tones of sweet soliloquy.

The young Orioles are born naked except for flecks of down on the crown and along the back. They are fed by regurgitation for four or five days. The eyes open on the fourth day, and pinfeathers soon begin to darken the skin. In two weeks' time the nestlings are fully fledged, looking much like the mother, and are ready for their début. Nevertheless they are very helpless, and are fed and cared for by both parents for some time after leaving the nest. The food of this species consists almost entirely of insects, and great is the debt of the farmers to their good services.

508. BULLOCK ORIOLE. — *Icterus bullocki.*

FAMILY. — The Blackbirds, Orioles, etc.

Length: 7.50–8.60.

Adult Male: Under parts, sides of neck, whole malar region, forehead, and distinct superciliary stripe yellow or orange ; narrow throat patch, crown, back of neck, back, and stripe through the eye black ; wings with white patch and edgings; tail mostly yellow, but the middle feathers and the tips of others black.

Adult Female: Upper parts olive grayish, streaked with black on back, but changing to live yellow on rump and tail; top of head and hind-

neck yellowish olive, becoming brighter yellow on forehead and superciliary region ; wings with white bands ; under parts lemon-yellow,
fading to gray on belly ; throat usually with more or less of black.

Young : Similar to female, but colors duller ; no black on throat, and
yellow sometimes almost wanting.

Geographical Distribution : Western North America, north to British
Columbia, east to and including the Rocky Mountains ; south in
winter to Mexico.

California Breeding Range : Chiefly in the upper Sonoran zone throughout the State.

Breeding Season : May and June.

Nest : Fastened at sides and rim to branches of the birch, alder, cottonwood, poplar, and often to bunches of mistletoe growing on cottonwood trees ; placed from 6 to 40 feet from the ground ; made of
vegetable fibres, horsehair, and inner bark woven together ; lined
with horsehair, down, and wool.

Eggs : 3 to 6 ; grayish or bluish white, or pale buffy, marked with irregular fine hair lines. Size 0.89 × 0.64.

THE handsome Bullock Oriole fills the same niche in
the country west of the Rocky Mountains that the
equally handsome Baltimore oriole occupies in the
Eastern States. Like the other two species found in California, it is only a summer visitant, arriving in March and
going back to its winter haunts in late September. Like
the Baltimore oriole, it loves the open country of the
interior valleys, and the margins of streams fringed with
alder ; it is never found in the deep forests or the higher
altitudes, and seldom or never strays across the Coast
Range into the humid coast region.

Its call-notes and song resemble those of the Baltimore,
but have less sweetness and variety. Where the latter
whistles half a dozen variations on his original theme of
five notes, the Bullock is content to repeat the same
phrase with few modifications. Nor have I ever heard
him give the love song that is poured out by the Balti-

more with such tenderness just at dawn when his mate is on the nest.

In nesting habits it resembles its Eastern relative, weaving a pensile bag-like affair of wild flax and plant fibre stiffened with horsehair and lined with plant down and fine moss. This is a typical nest, but string, bits of rag, and colored wool are often used also. The whole is fastened securely around the rim to the finer twigs of alder, eucalyptus, oak, juniper, or pepper. About San José, California, I have found it oftenest in pepper trees. In Texas and elsewhere it is said to hang its cradle in the bunches of mistletoe ; it may do this among the foot-hills, also, but it does not choose this site by preference. Most of the nests hang within fifteen feet of the ground, but I have found them forty feet up from the base of a tree on a steep slope. Although this species less fre-quently use the nest a second season than do the Balti-mores, they have a curious habit of building a second close beside the first and often fastened to it. There is no way of ascertaining whether or not it is the same pair who come back to their favorite location and build this addition to their old home, and in bird lore it is never safe to hazard a guess. Never having seen a male oriole of any species attempt to brood either the eggs or the young, I am convinced that in every case the fourteen days of incubation of this species is the task of the female alone. Her mate is always within calling distance, keep-ing a vigilant watch for squirrels, crows, and jays ; and should any one of these enemies appear, not only he but the mother bird, joined by all the orioles and blackbirds within hearing, will fly at the intruder and effectually banish him from the vicinity. When newly hatched, the young orioles are naked, pink babies with little tufts of thin white down on head and back. For nearly a week after they are feathered the down waves rakishly on either side of the crown and about the shoulders, gradually wearing off as they brush about through the bushes.

Like all oriole babies, these demand the constant attention of both parents, crying loudly for more the moment their mouths are emptied of the last mouthful, not in the least trying to help themselves, but following the adults about for a week or two after leaving the nest. No wonder that, worn out by unremitting care of this first brood, the parents have neither the strength nor the time to undertake a second in the same season. I believe the families usually keep together until late in August, when the males join flocks of their own sex for the September migration southward.

In "The Condor" for July, 1901, the following statement with regard to the food habits of this Oriole is worthy of special note: "The chief food of the Orioles consists of insects and injurious caterpillars. . . . They are particularly fond of a small green caterpillar that destroyed the foliage of the prune trees a few years ago. The Orioles are often seen in the berry patches, but they are usually in search of insects, as is proven by an examination of a great number of stomachs." These facts regarding the food habits of our song birds are of great value to the bird-lover, but even more so to the farmer. Naturally he will protect any species which is proven beneficial to his crops.

514 a. WESTERN EVENING GROSBEAK. — *Cocco-thraustes vespertinus montanus.*

FAMILY : The Finches, Sparrows, etc.

Length: Male 6.70–7.30 ; female 6.50–7.30.

Bill: Large and heavy.

Adult Male: Upper parts yellowish olive, shading to yellow on rump ; forehead and superciliary bright yellow ; crown, tail, and wings black, the latter with large white patches ; under parts greenish yellow, shading to lemon-yellow on under wing and tail-coverts.

Adult Female: General plumage yellowish or yellowish brown ; throat bordered on each side by a dusky streak ; whitish patches on wings ; under parts light gray.

Young: Similar to female, but color duller and more brownish, with markings less sharply defined.

Geographical Distribution: Western North America, from the Pacific coast eastward to the Rocky Mountains ; south to Mexico.

California Breeding Range: Local in the high Sierra Nevada from Mt. Shasta to the Yosemite valley.

Breeding Season: May 1 to June 15.

Nest: A comparatively slight structure ; composed of small sticks, roots, and sometimes lichens ; lined with finer roots ; placed in coniferous or willow trees, from 12 to 50 feet from the ground.

Eggs: 3 or 4 ; green, blotched with light brown.

LINED against the dark green of the pine tree in the golden glow of sunset, as he settles for his night's rest, the Evening Grosbeak is a bird of striking beauty. Seen flying across the open when the first rays of the rising sun flash on the yellow of his breast, brightening and deepening its pale lemon to a color like gold, while his clear whistle calls through the dewy air, he is a joy forever. Daintily eating the maple buds or the young shoots of the juniper tree, stopping ever and anon to pipe his wild, free song that has in it the breath of the pine woods and the silver cadence of the mountain brook, he is " an April poem that God has dowered with wings."

He is seldom or never alone, but travels with a merry band of his fellows, from the southern valleys where he feeds in winter to the northern mountain heights. There among the pine forests where the yellow lichen clings to the rugged trunks, he will build his nest and rear his brood. And now you discover the reason for his greenish yellow coloring ; for, as he flits here and there among the lichen tufts, picking up bits to line or decorate his nest, you are struck with the way in which he becomes invisible. So, in cases where the lichens are used in the nest-building, it is difficult to tell whether or not the bird is brooding. The lichens are seldom used, however, unless the nest is placed in a fir or pine tree. When built in a willow, rootlets and finely shredded strips of bark take its place. Whether this material is chosen because of convenience or with an eye to protective coloring no one may say, but I believe it is only a matter of whatever is most easily obtained. Both sexes assist in the nest-building and in gathering material, which is moulded into shape by a turning about of the bird's body after the manner of the black-headed grosbeak. The only nest I have ever seen was entirely inaccessible, in the top of a fir tree at least thirty-five feet from the ground. The tree stood on the side of a cañon, and it was possible from a point above it and a hundred feet away, by means of field glasses, to watch the birds at work. But at this distance one could only observe in a very unsatisfactory degree and could gain few facts that are sufficiently definite to be recorded. I know that the female was on the nest and the male always somewhere in the vicinity every time I looked during a watch of fifteen days. After that, both flew back and forth with food, but I was entirely unable to tell what the menu might be, except in one case, where the male alighted a moment near me with a caterpillar (not the hairy kind) in his beak, and then flew straight to the nest.

On the fifteenth day after I first observed the parents carrying food, the nest-tree was deserted and not a glimpse could I catch of young or old. This was at a height of seven thousand feet in the Sierra Nevada, and I fancied they had gone to the lower altitudes to feed upon the buds of the deciduous trees and in the fruit ranches of the foot-hills. With the solitude of the forests the Grosbeak leaves his quaint, sweet song. Henceforth, until spring calls him back to the breeding grounds, he will utter only the single whistled note, and no one who hears shall guess that he can sing.

529 b. WILLOW GOLDFINCH. — *Astragalinus tristis salicamans.*

FAMILY : The Finches, Sparrows, etc.

Length : 4.08–4.82.

Adult Male : General body plumage yellow, in sharp contrast to black forehead, crown, lores, wings, and tail ; wings with faint white edgings ; tail-feathers with white patches.

Adult Female : Upper parts dark olive-brown, sometimes tinged with olive greenish ; wings and tail dull blackish brown, with markings similar to male ; throat dull greenish yellow, remainder of under parts dull grayish, more or less tinged with yellow.

Young: Plumage darker in tone than that of the adult.

Geographical Distribution: Pacific coast from Washington to Lower California.

California Breeding Range: Chiefly in the upper Sonoran zone, from Shasta valley to San Diego.

Breeding Season: May to July.

Nest: A compactly woven cup-shaped structure; composed of plant fibre; lined with down and other soft materials; placed in tall bushes or low trees.

Eggs: 3 to 5; bluish white. Size 0.65 × 0.52.

THE Willow Goldfinch of California is in form, color, and habits so exactly like the goldfinch or "thistle-bird" of the East that one wonders why Western ornithologists have made a subspecies of him. His shorter wings and tail and his smaller black cap are the only points of difference. Although he is resident wherever found, he changes his bright yellow and black plumage in the fall to a more sober garb of dark olive and black, and in his new suit is not always recognized as an old friend. In the spring, likewise, when the olive has given place to the gold, you hear it said, "The wild canaries have come back again," when they have really been there all the time. His happy call has been interpreted as "per-chic-o-ree, per-chic-o-ree," and fits well with the gay undulating flight of the little songster. In addition to this he has a merry twitter that might be called a song. When the thistles bloom, he commences his housekeeping, building an exquisite cup-shaped nest in the fork of a willow, so low that one may with small exertion peep into it. It is beautifully lined with a compact felting of thistle-down and moulded smoothly on the edges with wonderful skill. The two pale blue eggs are brooded by the mother for ten days, and then the naked pinky nestlings require all the care of both parents. They are beauties, to the eyes of one who loves bird babies, being perfect in form although so tiny. Their eyes open in a few days, and feathers begin to show along each side of the back and on the edges of the elbows. In ten days they have begun to look charmingly like their devoted mother, with coats of soft olive and brown. It is exactly the right color for nestlings, and when they have left the cradle and sit motionless for hours among the green leaves, they are invisible to all eyes but those of the parents.

Like the young of all seed-eating birds, they learn to forage for themselves much sooner than do those whose food requires skill to catch. Almost as soon as they can balance themselves the Goldfinch babies cling to the top of a thistle or a bunch of goldenrod, helping themselves to the seed as independently as any of the adults. But when father or mother alights near, the little wings begin to quiver and the bill opens expectantly, even though the little crop be too full to hold more.

Goldfinch nestlings, like very many others hitherto unsuspected, are fed by regurgitation. The adult comes to the nest with his crop conspicuously loaded, and soon transfers the contents to the empty crops of the young, which at once show the change. The food brought is thistle seed from which the down has been carefully plucked, leaving only the small brown part. When full of this the naked crops are distressingly suggestive of a flaxseed poultice.

530. ARKANSAS GOLDFINCH. — *Astragalinus psaltria.*

FAMILY: The Finches, Sparrows, etc.

Length: 4.00–4.50.

Adult Male: Upper parts olive-green; crown, wings, and tail black, with inner webs of tail-feathers white; under parts entirely deep lemon-yellow.

Adult Female: Upper parts grayish olive-green; under parts light greenish yellow; wings and tail dull black.

Young: Similar to female, but tinged with buffy, and wing-coverts tipped with buff.

Geographical Distribution: Western United States, north to Oregon, east as far as Utah and Colorado, south to Lower California, New Mexico, and Western Texas. In winter to Cape St. Lucas.

California Breeding Range: Chiefly below Transition zone nearly through the State.

Breeding Season: May to August.

Nest: A small, compact felted mass of vegetable fibre, moss, grasses, leaves, and fine bark; lined with plant down and sometimes with thistle-down; placed in trees and bushes, from 3 to 40 feet from the ground.

Eggs: 5 to 6; pale bluish or greenish white. Size 0.63 × 0.45.

THE Arkansas Goldfinch differs from the "willow" chiefly in its habitat, being a bird of the orchard and garden as well as of the wooded highway. It is found in the mountains along the edges of clearings to a height of six thousand feet. In breeding habits it resembles the willow, commencing its nest when the thistle-down is at hand for lining and the seeds for food for the nestlings. Except in the breeding season, it is found in small flocks, feeding upon the seeds of weeds or plants, and to a limited extent upon berries and haws. Along the edge of a country road in the fall, the weed tops blossom with these merry songsters, who fly up as you come near, only

to alight again a few feet farther on, singing the same gay
"perchicoree, per-chic-o-ree" as do their Eastern kinsfolk.

531. LAWRENCE GOLDFINCH. — *Astragalinus
lawrencei.*

FAMILY : The Finches, Sparrows, etc.

Length: 4.50–4.70.

Adult Male: Upper parts brownish gray (the back sometimes tinged
with olive-green), changing to bright greenish yellow on rump and
wings ; crown, face, and throat black ; median under parts yellow ;
lateral under parts light brownish-gray, becoming white on tail-
coverts and middle of belly.

Adult Female: Similar to male, but colors duller, and without black on
head or throat.

Young: Similar to female, but duller and lower parts indistinctly
streaked.

Geographical Distribution: California west of the Sierra Nevada ; south-
eastward in winter to Arizona.

California Breeding Range: Local in upper and lower Sonoran zones
west of the Sierra Nevada, as far north as Chico. Recorded from
Ventura County and San Gorgonia Pass.

Breeding Season: April, May, and June.

Nest: Composed of wool, fine grasses, down, and feathers, closely woven
together ; lined with long hair ; placed on extreme end of the limb
of a live oak tree. Sometimes the nest is composed entirely of
grasses.

Eggs: 4 or 5 ; pure white. Size 0.62 × 0.44.

THE Lawrence Goldfinch is a haunter of the cañons
and the lower range of pine forests. Like the Arkansas
and willow goldfinches, it is found in small flocks feeding on the seeds of weeds and flitting from one foraging
ground to another in the winter days. Early in April it
seeks its breeding places in the foot-hills, where, securely
hidden from prying eyes in the unfrequented cañons, it

rears its brood. By November it comes down to the lowlands, driven probably by lack of food supplies fully as much as by the cold weather.

607. LOUISIANA TANAGER, OR WESTERN TANAGER. — *Piranga ludoviciana.*

FAMILY : The Tanagers.

Length : 6.75–7.75.

Adult Male : Head and neck red, brightest on crown ; back, scapulars, wings, and tail black; the wings with two broad yellow bands; rump, upper tail-coverts, and under parts bright yellow. Winter plumage like female.

Adult Female : Upper parts olive-green ; back and scapulars grayish ; wing-bars dull light yellow ; under parts pale grayish yellow, becoming bright yellow under tail-coverts.

Young : Similar to adult female, but paler beneath ; upper and lower parts indistinctly streaked with dusky.

Geographical Distribution : Western United States ; straggles eastward in migration to the Atlantic States.

California Breeding Range : Chiefly in Transition zone along the entire length of the Sierra Nevada.

Breeding Season : April to July.

Nest : Thin, saucer-shaped structure; made of bark strips and grass stems ; lined with rootlets and horsehair ; usually placed on the horizontal limb of a tree, preferably an evergreen, about 15 to 30 feet from the ground.

Eggs : 3 to 5; light bluish green, lightly speckled with browns and purples, chiefly at the larger end. Size 0.95 × 0.65.

WHEN Louisiana stretched across the continent from the Mississippi River to the Pacific Ocean and north to British America, the most beautiful bird within its borders became known as the Louisiana Tanager. This appellation has long since ceased to be appropriate, for the bird is only a rare migrant in the State whose name it bears, and its centre of abundance is in the Rocky Mountains. Here and in all the Western mountains it breeds in the coniferous forests. In the Sierra Nevada the Tanagers are among the birds most commonly observed, and in May the buffalo berries near Pyramid Lake fairly blossom with them. Early in the morning the rather monotonous song rings clearly from the top of the tall pines, and a dash of yellow tipped with red and black appears against the dark green of the trees or the blue of the sky. The song is very like that of the Eastern tanagers, but less musical, having a shrillness and flatness of tone that are not pleasing to the ear. Its call-note is short and incisive and has been rendered as " pitic, pitictic."

The nest of this brilliantly plumaged bird is commonly placed on a horizontal branch of a fir or pine, and is so concealed by the foliage as to be practically invisible from below. Unlike the scarlet tanager of the East, it constructs a carelessly woven saucer-shaped affair, so shallow in some instances that a hard wind storm would throw the contents out were not the mother brooding over them.

Incubation lasts thirteen days, and is performed by the mother bird alone, the male rarely if ever going to the nest until the brood are hatched. As soon as the nestlings are out of the shell, however, he assumes his full share of the labor of feeding them. In the case of one brood at Slippery Ford in the Sierra Nevada, the male brought fifteen large insects and countless smaller ones in the half hour between half-past four and five one June morning. During most of the day the trips to the nest with food averaged ten minutes apart. The longest period of fasting was twenty-three minutes, and the shortest one and one-half minutes. Usually one can tell what food a nestling has swallowed by looking closely at its distended crop, as the contents are visible through the

607. LOUISIANA TANAGER.

"A dragonfly had been captured for breakfast."

nearly transparent skin. But these young Tanagers were twenty feet from the ground in a slender fir, and I could not examine them; consequently I could judge of the menu only by the foraging of the adult, and by what I saw sticking out of his bill. When he darted out into the air and back again in flycatcher fashion, I knew he was after a small insect. When he came from the bushes with a bunch on either side of his beak, I was sure he had picked up a caterpillar; when wings of gauzy texture projected on one side of the mandibles and a long black body on the other, I made a Yankee guess that a dragonfly had been captured for breakfast.

As soon as the nestlings were able to fly they came down to the cover of the lower brush and fed in company with their parents. We knew this by the anxiety of the adults and by their efforts to lead us away from the immediate vicinity when we stumbled into it, but long and patient search revealed only one of the young birds. He was sitting on a low bush, looking as solemn as a young owl, and allowed us to go close to him. Except for size he looked like a goldfinch nestling and was no more timid than the latter. The adults moved anxiously through the branches over our heads uttering plaintive calls of fear and low purring notes of remonstrance with us or of reassurance to the young. I am convinced that but for their excitement he would have known no fear.

Later, in August, small flocks of young Tanagers were seen, in company with vireos, feeding among the pine trees and evidently gathering for the fall migration. They were following the flycatcher fashion of catching insects on the wing, beginning when the sun touched the tops of the trees and moving downward as the day advanced and the insect life nearer the ground awoke to activity. In like manner they retreated to the tree tops as the shadows fell in the afternoon.

645 a. CALAVERAS WARBLER. — *Helminthophila rubricapilla gutturalis.*

FAMILY : The Wood Warblers.

Length : 4.75.

Adult Male : Top of head gray, with chestnut crown patch ; white eye-ring ; back olive-green, more yellowish on rump and upper tail-coverts ; under parts rich bright yellow.

Adult Female : Similar, but duller ; little or no chestnut on crown.

Young : Upper parts brownish gray ; rump greenish gray ; under parts dull yellow, becoming buffy brown on belly.

Geographical Distribution : Western United States from Pacific coast to Rocky Mountains ; south in winter to Mexico.

California Breeding Range: Along the Sierra Nevada from Mt. Shasta
    south to Mt. Whitney.
Breeding Season: May and June.
Nest: On the ground; composed of leaves, bark strips, and weed stems;
    lined with finer materials of the same kinds.
Eggs: 3 to 5; white, spotted with reddish brown and lavender, in a
    wreath around the larger end. Size 0.64 × 0.45.

THE Calaveras Warbler may be said to correspond to
the Nashville warbler of the Eastern States. In California it is a haunter of the brush-covered hillsides, hiding shyly in the scrubby undergrowth and singing from
the concealment of the deer brush and chaparral. Mr.
Chester A. Barlow writes briefly in "The Condor,"
November, 1901, of its occurrence in the Sierra Nevada:
"Although the species is far from rare in numbers, it
appears that but comparatively few of its nests have
been taken; but this is not strange when we consider
the nature and extent of the country selected for nesting
sites. It is usually by the merest chance that a nest is
discovered, as successful a method as any being to beat
through the ' mountain misery ' in the vicinity of where
the male bird is found singing. On June 9, 1899, I
flushed a Calaveras Warbler from her nest in tarweed
beneath a small cedar at Fyffe, California, at which date
the nest held five half-grown young. On June 10, 1901,
at Slippery Ford, California, a nest was found built
among an accumulation of dry black oak leaves beneath
a deer brush on the side of a gulch. It contained five
eggs, two-thirds advanced in incubation."

652. YELLOW WARBLER. — *Dendroica œstiva.*

Family : The Wood Warblers.

Length: 4.50–5.25.

Adult Male: Upper parts bright yellowish olive-green, brightest on rump; forehead bright yellow; front of crown sometimes tinged with orange; wing-feathers edged with yellow; under parts yellow; breast and belly streaked with rufous.

Adult Female: Upper parts yellowish green, darker than in the male; lighter on forehead and rump; under parts paler and duller, usually unstreaked.

Young: Similar to adult female.

Geographical Distribution: North America, except Alaska and Southwestern United States; migrating to Central America and Northern South America.

California Breeding Range: In upper Sonoran zone chiefly, and elsewhere throughout the State.

Breeding Season: April, May, and June.

Nest: Compact cup-shaped structure; made of grayish plant-fibre, spider webs, etc.; lined with down and feathers; placed in bushes or trees.

Eggs: 2 to 6; bluish white, spotted usually in wreath around the larger end, with brown, black, and lilac gray.   Size 0.66 × 0.48.

THE Yellow Warbler of California is the yellow warbler of the East, the " summer yellow bird " of the Massachusetts farmers, sometimes erroneously called the wild canary, and its " wee-chee-chee-chee-cher-wee " rings as joyously from the chaparral as from the wild rose and the blackberries.   Next to the robin and the bluebird, it is the bird best known to the country children, who find its nest in the hazel bushes on the way to school.   In California it is somewhat more shy and less apt to come into view from every roadside thicket.

The nest is an exquisitely moulded cup lined with plant down that has been felted until it is like shining white satin; even the rim presenting a smoothly rolled appearance. It is placed in an upright crotch of a low bush with little attempt at concealment. One little nest that we found had two of the leaves fastened down over it in the weaving, probably by accident, and they formed a complete shelter and protection from the wind. The female flew in at one side and usually sat facing the opening, perfectly concealed, yet seeing all that occurred around. But the typical Yellow Warbler nest is built with an eye to sunshine and fresh air and recklessly exposed to the gaze of every passer-by.

The small bluish eggs, wreathed with minute brown spots at the larger end, are very like the eggs of the German canaries, and I have placed them under a sitting canary hen for hatching. The only drawback was that they hatched in twelve days, which was two days sooner than those of their adoptive mother, and caused her to throw them out of the nest and go on sitting on her own eggs. Under normal conditions they hatch under their own mother in twelve days, and sitting is never begun until the full complement is laid, so that the whole brood emerge from the shell on the same day. At first, like most young birds, they are naked except for sparse down on the head, but at the end of a week they have pinfeathers on wings and tail and thin down on the other parts of the body. In another week the feathers have burst their sheaths, and the nestlings are the prettiest things in the wood. They are fed upon insects by regurgitation for the first few days, and later upon the fresh food.

655. YELLOW–RUMPED WARBLER, OR MYRTLE
WARBLER. — *Dendroica coronata.*

FAMILY : The Wood Warblers.

Length : 5.65.

Adult Male in Spring and Summer : A yellow patch on the crown,
rump, and either side of the breast ; upper parts bluish gray, streaked
with black; two white wing-bars ; tail black, with gray edgings ;
outer pair of tail-feathers with large spots of white ; throat white ;
breast and upper belly heavily marked with black ; lower belly
white.

Adult Female in Spring and Summer : Similar, but smaller, and colors
duller ; upper parts browner ; breast simply streaked with black.

Adult Male in Fall and Winter : Upper parts grayish brown, streaked
with black on back and scapulars ; yellow crown patch concealed by
brown tips of feathers ; throat and chest buffy brown ; chest streaked
with black ; yellow patches obscured; black patches with white edges
to feathers.

Adult Female in Fall and Winter : Similar to winter male, but smaller ;
upper parts browner, yellow crown patch restricted or obsolete ; under
parts pale buff-brown in front and on sides ; centre of breast and
belly yellowish white ; yellow breast patches indistinct.

Young : Similar to adults, but no yellow anywhere except sometimes on
rump ; whole plumage thickly streaked above and below.

Geographical Distribution : North America, chiefly east and north of
Rocky Mountains ; rare west, except along the Pacific coast ; south
in winter to Middle States, West Indies, and Panama.

Breeding Range : British Columbia and Alaska.

Breeding Season : June 15 to July 15.

Nest : Of vegetable fibres; lined with mosses, feathers, and hair ; placed
in coniferous trees, 5 to 10 feet from the ground.

Eggs : 3 to 6 ; white, spotted chiefly around larger end with brown and
lilac. Size 0.70 × 0.52.

THE Yellow-rumped Warbler differs from the Audubon
warbler in having a white throat. Both species are very
like the Myrtle Warbler of the East, and Mr. Grinnell
lists the Yellow-rumped in California as the " Alaska
Myrtle Warbler," while Mrs. Bailey calls it " the Eastern

representative of the Audubon warbler" because its range is extended eastward to the Rocky Mountains. But it certainly seems more like a Western representative of the Myrtle Warbler, with its white throat and its early migration. East and West it is one of the first of its family to start for the breeding grounds in the spring.

656. AUDUBON WARBLER. — *Dendroica auduboni.*

FAMILY : The Wood Warblers.

Length : 5.12–6.00.

Adult Male in Spring and Summer : Throat and rump yellow ; upper parts bluish slate, streaked with black ; large white patches on wing-coverts ; tail black, with patch of white ; under parts with patches of white, yellow, and black.

Adult Female in Spring and Summer : Similar, but colors duller, and with less black on under parts ; upper parts tinged with brown ; yellow crown patch restricted and partly tipped with brownish gray ; wing-bands narrower ; chest and sides grayish, marked with black ; color-patches restricted.

Adult Male in Fall and Winter : Duller and browner than summer males.

Adult Female in Fall and Winter : Similar to winter male, but smaller and duller.

Young : Upper parts streaked dark and light brownish gray ; under parts light and streaked.

Geographical Distribution : Western North America, north as far as British Columbia ; east to eastern base of Rocky Mountains ; winters in valleys of Western United States, and south to Guatemala.

California Breeding Range : In Transition zone along the Sierra Nevada from the San Bernardino mountains to Shasta County.

Breeding Season : May and June.

Nest : Usually in pines or spruces, 4 to 5 feet from the ground ; composed of shreds of bark, pine needles, and fine rootlets ; lined with hair and feathers.

Eggs : 4 or 5 ; greenish, speckled with black, brown, and purple. Size 0.67 × 0.52.

MRS. BAILEY calls this bird " the whirligig of perpetual motion," and the name fits. A flash of yellow, black, and white flits through the clearings in the Sierra Nevada and you are conscious that an Audubon Warbler has flown by. He has all the tricks and manners of a fly-catcher, darting out after insects or dodging about among the tree tops, always in a hurry, always in a mad chase for something to eat. Unless you go to his summer haunts in the Sierra Nevada you will not see him at his best, for the "winter visitant" of the valleys wears a more sober plumage of dull brown streaked with black and only a little yellow visible. In his breeding grounds among the pines and spruces of the mountains he is a brilliant, happy-go-lucky little chap, not at all shy, but is so absorbed in his own busy life as to care little who watches him. The four nests I have

656. AUDUBON WARBLER.

" Always in a mad chase for something to eat."

found were all near Tallac on Lake Tahoe, and were all in young spruce trees, within five feet of the ground, along a frequented path. On June 15 one contained young a week old, and three held eggs in various stages of incubation. The pair whose young had hatched so early were very friendly, feeding them without much fear while I sat within three or four feet of the nest and on a level with it. They usually came with nothing to be seen in their beaks, but the insect food they had gleaned and carried in their own throats was regurgitated into the throats of the young. When the latter were five days old the mother bird, for the first time, brought an insect large enough to be seen, and crammed it into the open bill of one of the nestlings, and from that time on most of the food brought was eaten by the young while fresh.

In the brood whose incubation was closely watched, I found that twelve days elapsed between the laying of the last egg and the advent of the young. The female did most of the brooding; the male was found on the nest only once, but was usually perched on a neighboring tree warbling his enthusiastic little song, " cheree-cheree-cheree-cheree." After the young were feathered enough to leave the nest, — which occurred when they were two weeks old, — the male forgot to sing and became a veritable family drudge with the brood ever at his heels clamoring for food.

668. TOWNSEND WARBLER. — *Dendroica townsendi.*

FAMILY : The Wood Warblers.

Length : 4.90–5.30.

Adult Male in Spring and Summer : Head and throat black, with bright yellow superciliary and malar stripes ; breast bright yellow ; belly and under tail-coverts white ; the latter, also sides and flanks, broadly streaked with black ; back bright olive-green, with black arrow-point streaks; wings and tail blackish; two white wing-bars, tail with small white spots at end of lateral feathers.

Adult Female in Spring and Summer: Similar to winter male, but black streaking of upper parts and sides restricted or obsolete; crown sometimes blackish; throat often blotched with black.

Adult Male in Fall and Winter: Similar to summer male, but black obscured; crown and hind-neck with olive-green edges to feathers; cheek patch with olive-green tips to feathers; throat lemon-yellow; chest and sides spotted with black.

Adult Female in Fall and Winter: Similar to summer female, but upper parts, sides, and flanks brownish, with streaks of upper parts indistinct.

Young Male: Similar to adult winter male, but streaks on crown and back obsolete, and yellow of throat paler.

Young Female: Similar to adult winter female, but yellow paler and markings less distinct.

Geographical Distribution: Western North America, chiefly near the Pacific coast, north to Alaska; migrating east to Rocky Mountains. and south in winter to Guatemala.

Breeding Range: In the pine forests, from Oregon to Sitka.

Breeding Season: June.

Nest: Compact, cup-shaped; made of gray plant fibres; lined with feathers, placed in bushes or trees.

Eggs: 3 or 4; white, spotted mainly about the larger end with brown and lavender. Size 0.64 × 0.53.

MR. GRINNELL says: " The Townsend Warbler occurs in California as a winter visitant in the Santa Cruz, and sparingly elsewhere west of the Sierra Nevada; occurs more widely during migration."

It is one of those tantalizing Warblers who persist in staying in the tops of tall trees, where they dodge in and out among the foliage in a most exasperating way. But, in spite of all difficulties, if the " Warbler madness " has taken possession of you, a day of neck-breaking study will count for nothing as against the possibility of identifying a species unknown to you, and *townsendi* offers unparalleled opportunities in this line.

The common note of this species is a high-keyed "tseep." The song is very short, and heard from below is scarcely more musical than that of a grasshopper sparrow.

669. HERMIT WARBLER. — *Dendroica occidentalis.*

FAMILY : The Wood Warblers.

Length : 4.70–5.25.

Adult Male in Spring and Summer : Top and sides of head bright yellow, the occiput, and sometimes the crown, spotted with black ; throat black ; under parts white, sometimes streaked on sides ; nape olive-green streaked with black ; rest of upper parts gray, washed with olive-green and streaked with black ; wings and tail black ; two white wing-bands ; tail with the two outer feathers on each side mostly white.

Adult Female in Spring and Summer : Similar to winter male, but forehead and crown more or less mixed with yellow ; body more olive ; dusky patch on throat and chest.

Adult Male in Fall and Winter : Similar to summer male, but the yellow of crown and occiput more or less obscured ; black streaks of back mixed with gray, and black throat patch specked with white.

Adult Female in Fall and Winter : Upper parts olive-gray ; crown with traces of yellow ; under parts brownish white.

Young : Upper parts plain ash-gray ; under parts brownish gray, except that the belly and under tail-coverts are white.

Geographical Distribution : Western United States, chiefly near Pacific coast ; migrating east to Rocky Mountains, and south in winter to Guatemala.

California Breeding Range : In Transition zone along the Sierra Nevada from Mt. Shasta to Mt. Whitney.

Breeding Season : June.

Nest : Of fibrous stalks of plants, fine dead twigs, lichens, and pine needles, bound with cobwebs, and woolly materials ; lined with soft inner bark and hair ; placed in coniferous trees, from 25 to 40 feet from the ground.

Eggs : 3 ; dull white or grayish green, spotted or blotched with lilac, gray, or brown, chiefly around larger end. Size 0.67 × 0.47.

WHILE a fairly common bird along the lower Sierra Nevada from Mount Shasta southward, the Hermit

Warbler is comparatively little known.   Its shyness and
its quiet way of slipping from tree to tree, keeping well
out of reach in the conifers, makes any extensive observation of its habits diffi-
cult.   On the Placer-
ville-Tahoe stage route,

669. HERMIT WARBLER.

" With her beak full of cobwebs."

I heard this bird sing
and caught tantaliz-
ing glimpses of him
in the tops of the
manzanita and deer
brush along the road-
side ; but, seeming
to know intuitively
whenever we made
a stop to study him, he would instantly end his thin
little song and vanish among the green leaves.

On June 8, after quiet hiding and patient watching, we saw a female of this species fly away with her beak full of cobwebs which trailed nearly two inches, and alight on a tall cedar not ten feet from the travelled stage road; but the tree was so difficult to climb that we could not investigate it. In a moment she flew out of it, empty-mouthed, and further waiting for her second visit was fruitless. Meanwhile her mate had devoted himself to hunting for insects under the leaves of the deer brush, and seemed equally oblivious to her presence and her absence. I fancied him a self-centred mite because, when she alighted beside him, coaxing with a pretty chirp as nestlings do, he fed her in a matter-of-fact fashion and resumed his own meal. Long, careful searching in this and other places failed to reveal any nest, although it is certain there was one in process of construction near by. Mr. Barlow found one, and, after " collecting " the female, discovered there were young in the cradle. These were promptly cared for by the male, who fed and brooded them.

Mr. Bowles describes the song of this bird as " zeegle-zeegle-zeegle-zeek," but to me it sounded more like " jiggle-jiggle-jiggle-jig." Although not loud, it has a carrying quality which at once arrests attention. The call-note is a sharp " tseet."

680. MACGILLIVRAY WARBLER. — *Geothlypis tolmiei.*

FAMILY : The Wood Warblers.

Length : 5.00–5.75.

Adult Male : Head, throat, and breast slate-gray ; throat feathers margined with gray ; rest of under parts yellow ; lores black ; a distinct white spot on each eyelid ; back olive-green, sometimes merging to grayish olive.

Adult Female : Similar to male, but crown, hind-neck, and sides of head and neck mouse-gray, fading to grayish white on throat and breast.

Young : Similar to adults, but plumage softer ; throat, chest, and spots on eyelids yellowish ; streak over lores pale yellow.

Geographical Distribution : In the mountainous regions of Western North America, from the east slope of the Rockies to the Pacific, north to British Columbia, south in winter to Panama.

California Breeding Range : Through Transition zone along the Sierra Nevada from Mt. Shasta to the San Bernardino mountains.

Breeding Season : May 15 to June 15.

Nest : Of dried grasses ; lined with finer grasses and horsehair ; placed in weeds, bushes, or low shrubs, 1 to 6 feet from the ground.

Eggs : 3 to 5 ; creamy white, marked near the larger end with spots and pen lines of dark brown and lilac gray. Size 0.72 × 0.52.

IN the chaparral and underbrush ; in ravines where small brooks wind in and out, their borders fringed with thick bracken ; on the scrubby hillsides, — the Macgillivray Warbler hides shyly among the low foliage, or sings an odd little trill as you pass. These are his chosen haunts, and here among the ferns he will build a dainty nest so carefully hidden and so closely guarded that only by accident can you discover it. And if you do chance to locate it and part the ferns the least bit to peer into it, unless the eggs are nearly ready to hatch they will be abandoned by the timid Warblers and your opportunity to see a brood develop will be lost. Under these circumstances it is small wonder that little is known concerning the nesting habits of this species, so far as the time of incubation and the rearing of the young are concerned. One nest, found near San José, June 2, and containing young about six days old, was visited daily with no disastrous results, but this is only a partial success among a long list of failures. In this case the parents were so shy that they refused to go to the nest with food while an observer was in sight, and the field glasses could reveal nothing sufficiently accurate to be recorded. The nest was nicely hidden in a clump of weeds on the edge of a small brook and within five inches of the ground. A jump across the brook almost into it resulted in its discovery. When watched, the adults alighted at some distance from it and dodged from clump to clump and through the weeds until they reached the spot where it lay. Close observation failed to record accurately how often they went with food, so slyly did they slip through tangles and open like small gray mice; the crops of the nestlings, examined immediately after feeding, bulged with insect food dark in color. They left the nest after four days' watching, and were probably less than ten days old.

681 c. PACIFIC YELLOW–THROAT. — *Geothlypis trichas arizela.*

FAMILY : The Wood Warblers.

Length : 4.70–5.75.

Adult Male : Forehead and sides of head black, bordered above with white, sometimes tinged with yellow ; rest of upper parts plain olive-green ; under parts yellow. In winter washed with brown.

Adult Female : Upper parts olive-brown, without black, ashy, or white ;

crown sometimes washed with reddish brown, tail with greenish; under parts yellowish white.

Young : Similar to adult male, but black mask less distinct.

Geographical Distribution : Pacific coast from British Columbia to Lower California; east to the Cascades and Sierra Nevada ; south in winter through Lower California and Mexico.

California Breeding Range : In the San Diegan district, northwest to Santa Barbara, and possibly northward.

Breeding Season : May and June.

Nest : On or near the ground, among weed stalks ; cup-shaped ; of grass.

Eggs : 4 ; white, finely speckled with brown.

MINGLING with the song of the yellow-headed black-birds and the tinkling music of the marsh wrens, the clear "wichity, wichity, wichity," of the Yellow-throat rings from lowland marsh in the warm May sunshine, telling the world that spring and nesting time have come. If you follow the song to its source, you may catch a glimpse of a black-masked little head, flanked by bright yellow, peeking at you with bewitching curiosity, — curiosity mixed with fear, however ; for, as soon as discovered, the head is quickly withdrawn, and only a moving of the leaves tells where the singer has hidden himself. But you have seen enough to make you curious in your turn, and to induce you to attempt to pursue the fascinating flash of yellow and green. In a moment more you see him again, a small greenish bird scrambling for dear life through the tules or underbrush, turning his odd little face constantly to keep watch of you, or flying over a small open space to dive hurriedly into the shelter of the thicket. From clump to clump he flits until, when he has led you far enough from his nest, he dodges down to the thickest tangle of marsh grass and hunts for his dinner of insects while you hunt in vain for him. With all this hiding he is not particularly shy, and you feel inclined to set him down as a clever little tease who has purposely led you a chase for his own amusement. Throughout the long summer days his cheery, energetic song floats over the wet meadows and out from the blackberry tangles or the tule swamp. Neither the heat nor the cares of a family diminish his ardor one whit. He even springs into the air in the exuberance of joy, performing chatlike gymnastics to his own merry music.

On the bulky nest, snugly hidden low in the bushes or long marsh grass, his plain little mate sits brooding for twelve days, unrelieved by the dapper singer. It is possible that he may feed her, but I have never been able to catch him at it. The female slips noiselessly, without protest, away through the underbrush at the first approach to her nest, and scolds at you from a safe distance, while the male, bold enough when danger threatens, comes nearer, calling, " quit, quit, quit."

You are certain to know when the eggs have hatched by the storm of " quits " that greets your approach, for the Yellow-throat is a devoted parent. Tirelessly he hunts through the wet sedge for insects, swallowing them himself first, and feeding the nestlings with the partly digested food until they are able to take it fresh from the field. And long after the young are feathered and out of the nest, they follow the adult about, refusing to help themselves, coaxing to be fed, until you wonder he has any strength left to sing. The female takes a full share of this labor, but is less often seen because more shy.

683 a. LONG–TAILED CHAT. — *Icteria virens longicauda.*

FAMILY : The Wood Warblers.

Length: 7.00–8.00.

Adults: Upper parts olive-gray ; superciliary, eye-ring, and malar stripe white ; lores and line under eye deep black ; throat and breast bright yellow ; belly and under tail-coverts white.

Young: Upper parts plain dull olive-gray ; lores gray ; throat whitish ; chest, sides, and flanks grayish ; rest of under parts white.

Geographical Distribution: Western United States, east to Great Plains ; south into Mexico.

California Breeding Range: Chiefly in upper Sonoran zone, west of the Sierra Nevada.

Breeding Season: May.

Nest: Of dry leaves, grasses, and strips of bark ; lined with finer grasses ; placed in thickets and brambles of low undergrowth, from 2 to 5 feet above the ground.

Eggs: 3 or 4 ; glossy white or pinkish, speckled and spotted with shades of brown, which are heaviest at the larger end.   Size 0.92 × 0.70.

" Is the odd jumble of whistle, chucks, and caws uttered by one bird in that copse yonder, or by half a dozen birds in as many places ? Approach cautiously and perhaps you may see him in the air, — a bunch of feathers twitched downward by queer, jerky notes which animate it. One might suppose so peculiar a performance would occupy his entire attention, but never-

683 a. LONG-TAILED CHAT.

" Where he whistled and sang from dawn until dark."

theless he has seen you. In an instant his manner changes, and the happy-go-lucky clown, who a moment before was turning aërial somersaults, has become a shy, suspicious haunter of the depth of the thicket, whence will come his querulous '*chut, chut*' as long as your presence annoys him."[1]

This perfect description of the tricks and manners of the chat is the best means of identifying the species. Birds with olive-green backs and yellow under parts are common enough, but one that combines the qualities of a Punchinello with the grace of a professional gymnast is rare. To the chat, life is one long joke.

"His coming in the spring is like the arrival of a brass band. . . . When not whistling, or scolding like an oriole, calling like a cuckoo, or piping like a shrill-voiced rock squirrel, he will bark like a dog."[2]

It is hard to believe this of a bird not much larger than a sparrow and belonging to the family of warblers. But no words can describe his antics, though nearly every writer on birds has tried. Mr. Bradford Torrey and Mrs. Bailey have succeeded better than any others in interpreting this eccentric clown of the bird world.

Most of his aërial gymnastics are for the benefit of his demure sweetheart, who rarely indulges in such foolishness herself. He is like the small boy who *must* turn handsprings to show off.

One of these birds that built his nest in a willow thicket near Pasadena took his full share of nest-building, and would bring the material soberly enough, give it to

[1] Chapman. [2] Bailey.

the female, who seemed to do all the weaving, start
out for more, and " straightway forgetting what manner
of man he was," end in one of these curious song
flights. Usually, however, he came with strips of bark
or leaves and looked on with conversational chucks that
I guessed rather than heard, as most of my observing of
him was done through the field glass. After the beginning of incubation, which lasted fourteen days, he paid
little attention to either the mate or the nest during the
middle of the day, but frequented a thicket fifty yards
away, where he whistled and sang from dawn until dark,
but as soon as the eggs had hatched he was all devotion.
At this time it was possible to watch from a concealed
position, and to keep a record of his visits to the nest
with food. On one day, which seemed to be a fair
average, when the young were eight days old, they were
fed twenty times between five and six A. M., eight times
between nine and ten A. M., eleven times between
three and four P. M., and seventeen times between five
and six P. M. For the first four days there was no
visible food in the bill of the adult, and the feeding
seemed to be by regurgitation. After that, parts of
insects could be seen protruding from his bill, and were
given to the young in a fresh state. Beetles, grasshoppers, and butterflies were all in the dietary, and were
brought indiscriminately ; but hairless caterpillars seemed
to be the favorite food. The adults are said to eat
berries, but I saw none brought to the nest for the
young.

685 a. PILEOLATED WARBLER. — *Wilsonia pusilla pileolata.*

FAMILY : The Wood Warblers.

Length : 4.25–5.10.

Adult Male : Upper parts bright yellowish olive-green; crown glossy blue-black ; under parts bright yellow ; forehead sometimes orange-yellow.

Adult Female : Similar to male, but back of crown usually indistinct, being concealed by olive wash.

Geographical Distribution : Western North America, chiefly along or near the Pacific coast; north to Alaska ; south in winter through Mexico to Costa Rica.

Breeding Range : April 15 to July 2.

Nest : Of leaves, bark strips, weed stems, vegetable fibres, and rootlets ; lined with finer grasses ; placed in thickets and blackberry vines, on or near the ground.

Eggs : 2 to 4; white or creamy white, speckled with reddish brown and lilac gray, often in the form of a wreath around the larger end. Size 0.60 × 0.48.

IN the warm spring days comes the handsome little Pileolated Warbler, with his long title of Western Black-capped Flycatching Warbler. He is a common migrant throughout the valleys of California, and flits over the underbrush like a big yellow butterfly ; but, as nesting time approaches, he withdraws to the mountains, and is seen on the lowlands no more until fall. Not shy, he watches you with quite as much interest as you observe him, calling saucily from his low perch, and readily answering to an imitation of his " seep see." If you are motionless and coax long enough, he will even alight on a spray of chaparral held in the hand. In movements he is an odd little mixture of flycatcher and hummingbird, darting out for a passing insect, or hovering on whirring wings to pick one from the under side of a leaf so swiftly the eye can scarcely follow him. His song reminds one of the tinkle of a brooklet in its merry, rather metallic melody, and is a distinct note in the medley of spring music.

Like his Eastern relative, the Wilson warbler, the Pileolated builds his nest close to the ground in a swampy willow thicket, and is not infrequently a victim to the marsh rats and snakes. The first brood is usually hatched early in May, and is fed by regurgitation by both parents until four or five days old, when the usual food of small insects and little green worms is given to them in the fresh state. As soon as their nursery days are over, the male

685 a. PILEOLATED WARBLER.
"*His song reminds one of the tinkle of a brooklet.*"

takes entire charge of the nestlings, feeding them for ten days or two weeks longer.

For the second brood a locality slightly higher up the mountain may be chosen, but oftener the little mother builds her second nest within a hundred yards of the first, commencing it alone, while the male is still occupied with the first series. Incubation lasts twelve days, and is, I think, attended to solely by the female, although the male is frequently at the nest both to feed her and to watch over — but not brood — the eggs.

746. VERDIN. — *Auriparus flaviceps.*

FAMILY: The Nuthatches and Tits.

Length: 4.00–4.60.

Adult Male: Crown bright olive ; forehead sometimes orange ; rest of head, neck, and breast yellow ; upper parts gray, with red-brown patch on shoulders ; under parts whitish.

Adult Female: Similar to male, but coloring duller.

Young: Upper parts gray, tinged with brownish ; no yellow, and no chestnut shoulder patches ; under parts white.

Geographical Distribution: From Southern Texas to the Pacific, and from latitude 38° to Mexico and Lower California.

California Breeding Range: Local in the desert regions of Southeastern California along the Colorado River district.

Nest: Large, retort-shaped or globular ; composed externally of thorny twigs and stems interwoven ; thickly lined with weed stems and feathers ; a small round entrance at one side ; placed in bushes or low trees.

Eggs: 3 to 6 ; pale bluish white, speckled with red-brown. Size 0.59 × 0.43.

THE Yellow-headed Bush-tit, or Verdin, occurs most abundantly in California at the extreme southeastern corner bordering on the Colorado River. He is a tiny mite, not so large as the Rivoli hummingbird, which lives in the same district, across the river, in Arizona. But although so small a bird, the Verdin has most remarkable traits, and is the most fascinating of all the California birds. From his wee yellow throat he pours such a flood of music that you search eagerly for the singer, and can hardly credit your senses when you find

him scarcely bigger than your thumb; you have been
looking for something the size of an oriole at least. But
there he sits, as perky as if he were of respectable size,
and sings the ditty over again to prove that he can do it.
And when you first find his nest, the
wonder grows. Surely such a mite
will build a dainty house like that of
the hummingbird. But not so! A
retort-shaped affair, ludicrously out of
proportion to the
diminutive archi-
tect, is woven of
twigs and stems,
each one a heavy
load for the little
builders, and lined
to bursting with
feathers and flower-
stems. It is at least
twenty times the
size of the mother bird who broods
in it, and we do not wonder that it
is used summer and winter so long
as the walls remain firm. One would
suppose this one nest were large

746. VERDIN.

"*A retort-shaped affair.*"

enough to hold both master and mistress of the household; but, as if his industry knew no bounds, the male
constructs his own apartment in the same neighborhood and occupies it all winter alone. I believe that
the female constructs her own winter nest, and also

the breeding nest in cases where the winter nest is not used for that purpose. The architecture of the two is somewhat different in those I have observed, the nest built by the female being larger, more carefully lined, and with a decided hollow in the centre of the bedding material as if to keep the babies from rolling out. The nest of the male was simply a hollow gourd-shaped affair with little or no lining, and might pass for a dummy nest such as there is reason to believe he does occasionally build. Every nest found had a neck-like entrance extending downward and ending in a round hole. They were all located in mesquite thickets within six feet of the ground, and most of them were easy to watch. In ten days after the last bluish white egg was laid, there were three infinitesimal bits of naked bird life, huddled tightly together in the middle of the feather-lined hollow. A slit carefully cut at this time and fastened shut after each observation enabled me to keep an exact record of the development of the brood. Although I could not watch the mother feeding the young, I am positive it was done by regurgitation, for she would eat as unconcernedly as if merely occupied with her own dinner, and fly at once with apparently empty mouth into the nest, emerging shortly to repeat the performance. During the first five days the male was not seen to go into the nest, but sang right merrily near by. After that time the young began to make themselves heard in hungry cries, and he began to carry food to them, which we could see in his bill. This food consisted almost exclusively of small green worms, and eggs and larvæ of insects. The young Verdins remained in the nest quite three weeks, and long after their début they returned to the nursery every night to sleep. The usual note of the adult Verdins is a chickadee-like "tsee-tu-tu" uttered while hunting, chickadee fashion, among the terminal buds and under the leaves for their insect food, and this the nestlings mimic in two syllables as soon as they leave the nest, — "tsee-tee, tsee-tee." It is a cry of hunger, and never fails to bring the parent with food.

SUPPLEMENTARY LIST OF CALIFORNIA BIRDS

(RARE MIGRANTS AND SUBSPECIES)

The following list contains all species and subspecies which occur, even accidentally, in California, and has been compiled from Mr. Ridgway's "Manual of North American Birds," Mr. Grinnell's "Checklist of California Birds," and Mrs. Bailey's "Handbook of Birds of the Western United States."

2. HOLBŒLL GREBE. *Colymbus holbœlli.* Rare midwinter visitant coastwise.

3. HORNED GREBE. *Colymbus auritus.* Rare midwinter visitant — along the coast and on inland lakes.

17. PAROQUET AUKLET. *Cyclorrhynchus psittaculus.* One record of five specimens.

35. SKUA. *Megalestris skua.* One record by G. N. Lawrence.

36. POMARINE JAEGER. *Stercorarius pomarinus.* Migrant coastwise.

38. LONG-TAILED JAEGER. *Stercorarius longicaudus.* One record by L. M. Loomis.

40a. PACIFIC KITTIWAKE. *Rissa pollicaris.* Rare winter visitant coastwise.

42. GLAUCOUS GULL. *Larus glaucus.* Rare winter visitant along the coast.

55. SHORT-BILLED GULL. *Larus brachyrhynchus.* Winter visitant coastwise.

56. MEW GULL. *Larus canus.* Winter visitant coastwise.

62. SABINE GULL. *Xema sabinii.* Rare migrant.

64. CASPIAN TERN. *Sterna caspia.* Rare winter visitant along the coast.

66. ELEGANT TERN. *Sterna elegans.* Fall and winter visitant.

71. ARCTIC TERN. *Sterna paradisœa.* Rare migrant.

86.1. RODGERS FULMAR. *Fulmarus rodgersi.* Irregular fall and winter visitant.

91. PINK-FOOTED SHEARWATER. *Puffinus creatopus.* Summer and fall visitant along the coast.

96. SLENDER-BILLED SHEARWATER. *Puffinis tenuirostris.* Midwinter visitant.

97. BLACK-TAILED SHEARWATER. *Priofinus cinereus.* One record by G. N. Lawrence.

102. PINTADO PETREL. *Daption capensis.* One record by G. N. Lawrence.

105. FORK-TAILED PETREL. *Oceanodroma furcata.* Irregular visitant.

106. LEACH PETREL. *Oceanodroma leucorhoa.* Records doubtful.

129. AMERICAN MERGANSER. *Merganser americanus.* Fairly common locally in summer.

130. RED-BREASTED MERGANSER. *Merganser serrator.* Common winter visitant coastwise.

131. HOODED MERGANSER. *Lophodytes cucullatus.* Fairly common fall and winter visitant in the interior.

132. MALLARD. *Anas boschas.* Common resident locally.

135. GADWALL. *Chaulelasmus streperus.* Fairly common resident.

136. WIDGEON. *Mareca penelope.* Recorded from Eureka.

137. BALDPATE. *Mareca americana.* Abundant winter visitant locally.

138. EUROPEAN TEAL. *Nettion crecca.* Recorded by J. G. Cooper only.

139. GREEN-WINGED TEAL. *Nettion carolinensis.* Abundant winter visitant locally.

140. BLUE-WINGED TEAL. *Querquedula discors.* Rare.

141. CINNAMON TEAL. *Querquedula cyanoptera.* Summer visitant.

142. SHOVELLER. *Spatula clypeata.* Winter visitant.

143. PINTAIL. *Dafila acuta.* Abundant winter visitant, a few remaining to breed.

144. WOOD DUCK. *Aix sponsa.* Common resident.

146. REDHEAD. *Aythya americana.* Common resident locally.

147. CANVAS-BACK. *Aythya vallisneria.* Common winter visitant locally.

148. SCAUP DUCK. *Aythya marila.* Fairly common winter visitant.

149. LESSER SCAUP DUCK. *Aythya affinis.* Common winter visitant coastwise.

150. RING-NECKED DUCK. *Aythya collaris.* Rare.

151. AMERICAN GOLDEN-EYE. *Clangula americana.* Winter visitant coastwise.

152. BARROW GOLDEN-EYE. *Clangula islandica.* Rare.

153. BUFFLE-HEAD. *Clangula albeola.* Winter visitant.

154. OLD-SQUAW. *Harelda hyemalis.* Rare.

155. HARLEQUIN DUCK. *Histrionicus histrionicus.* Fairly common summer resident.

162. KING EIDER. *Somateria spectabilis.* One record by H. W. Henshaw.

163. AMERICAN SCOTER. *Oidemia americana.* Rare.

165. WHITE-WINGED SCOTER. *Oidemia deglandi.* Winter visitant.

166. SURF SCOTER. *Oidemia perspicillata.* Common winter visitant.

167. RUDDY DUCK. *Erismatura jamaicensis.* Common resident locally in the interior.

169. LESSER SNOW GOOSE. *Chen hyperborea hyperborea.* Common winter visitant.

169.1. BLUE GOOSE. *Chen cærulescens.* One record by Belding.

170. ROSS SNOW GOOSE. *Chen rossi.* Fairly common winter visitant.

171 *a.* AMERICAN WHITE-FRONTED GOOSE. *Anser gambeli.* Common winter visitant.

172. CANADA GOOSE. *Branta canadensis canadensis.* Fairly common midwinter visitant.

172 *a.* HUTCHINS GOOSE. *Branta canadensis hutchinsi.* Winter visitant.

172 *b.* WHITE-CHEEKED GOOSE. *Branta canadensis occidentalis.* Winter visitant, breeding northeast of the Sierras.

172 *c.* CACKLING GOOSE. *Branta canadensis minima.* Winter visitant.

174. BLACK BRANT. *Branta nigricans.* Midwinter visitant coastwise.

176. EMPEROR GOOSE. *Philacte canagica.* Rare.

178. FULVOUS TREE DUCK. *Dendrocygna fulva.* Common summer resident in the San Joaquin-Sacramento valley.

188. WOOD IBIS. *Tantalus loculator.* Irregular visitant.

210 (*part*). SOUTHERN CALIFORNIA CLAPPER RAIL. *Rallus levipes.* Resident throughout Southern California.

215. YELLOW RAIL. *Porzana noveboracensis.* Rare visitant.

222. RED PHALAROPE. *Crymophilus fulicarius.* Migrant coastwise.

223. NORTHERN PHALAROPE. *Phalaropus lobatus.* Migrant coastwise.

234. KNOT. *Tringa canutus.* Casual migrant.

239. PECTORAL SANDPIPER. *Tringa maculata.* One record by J. G. Cooper.

240. WHITE-RUMPED SANDPIPER. *Tringa fuscicollis.* One record by W. E. Bryant.

241. BAIRD SANDPIPER. *Tringa bairdi.* One record by J. Mailliard.

255. YELLOW LEGS. *Totanus flavipes.* Two records.

256 *a.* WESTERN SOLITARY SANDPIPER. *Helodromas solitarius cinnamomeus.* Migrant.

258 *a.* WESTERN WILLET. *Symphemia semipalmata inornata.* Migrant coastwise, occasional winter visitant.

270. BLACK-BELLIED PLOVER. *Squatarola squatarola.* Migrant.

272. AMERICAN GOLDEN PLOVER. *Charadrius dominicus.* Rare migrant.

274. SEMIPALMATED PLOVER. *Ægialitis semipalmata.* Migrant coastwise.

276. LITTLE RING PLOVER. *Ægialitis dubia.* One record by R. Ridgway.

280. WILSON PLOVER. *Ægialitis wilsonia.* One record by A. M. Ingersoll.

282. SURF BIRD. *Aphriza virgata.* Rare migrant.

283.1. RUDDY TURNSTONE. *Arenaria morinella.* Migrant coastwise.

286.1. FRAZAR OYSTER-CATCHER. *Hæmatopus frazari.* Rare.

300 *c.* OREGON RUFFED GROUSE. *Bonesa umbellus sabinei.* Resident from Cape Mendocino northward.

308 *a.* COLUMBIAN SHARP-TAILED GROUSE. *Pediœcetes phasainellus columbianus.* Resident in the northeastern corner of the State.

319. WHITE-WINGED DOVE. *Melopelia leucoptera.* Rare visitant to southeastern portion of California.

320 *a.* MEXICAN GROUND DOVE. *Columbigallina passerina pallescens.* Rare.

334 *a.* WESTERN GOSHAWK. *Accipiter atricapillus striatulus.* Rare resident in northern part of State.

340. Zone-tailed Hawk. *Buteo abbreviatus.* One record by J. G. Cooper.

347 *a.* American Rough-legged Hawk. *Archibuteo sanctijohannis.* Rare winter visitant.

357 *a.* Black Merlin. *Falco columbarius suckleyi.* Rare winter visitant to northern portion of State.

358. Richardson Merlin. *Falco richardsoni.* One record by H. W. Henshaw.

369. Spotted Owl. *Syrnium occidentale.* Fairly common resident of the San Diegan district.

370. Great Gray Owl. *Scotiaptex cinerea.* Rare winter visitant in northern part of State.

372. Saw-whet Owl. *Cryptoglaux acadica acadica.* Eleven records as winter visitant.

374. Flammulated Screech Owl. *Megascops flammeolus flammeolus.* Two records.

374 *a.* Dwarf Screech Owl. *Megascops flammeolus idahoensis.* Three records.

375 *c.* Dusky Horned Owl. *Bubo virginianus saturatus.* Fairly common resident of the humid coast belt north of Monterey.

376. Snowy Owl. *Nyctea nyctea.* Rare winter visitant.

381. Elf Owl. *Micropallas whitneyi.* One record by R. Ridgway and one by L. M. Loomis.

394 *b.* Batchelder Woodpecker. *Dryobates pubescens leucurus.* Rare winter visitant.

394 *a* (*part*). Willow Woodpecker. *Dryobates pubescens turati.* Resident in Upper Sonoran and Transition zones in certain localities.

396. Texas Woodpecker. *Dryobates scalaris bairdi.* Fairly common in desert region southeast of the Sierras.

396 *a.* Saint Lucas Woodpecker. *Dryobates lucasanus.* Two records as breeding in desert region along Colorado River.

402 *a.* Red-naped Sapsucker. *Sphyrapicus varius nuchalis.* Winter visitant to southern part of State.

412 *a.* Northern Flicker. *Colaptes auratus luteus.* Occasional winter visitant.

413 *a.* Northwestern Flicker. *Colaptes cafer saturatior.* Winter visitant in north end of State.

418 *a.* Frosted Poorwill. *Phalænoptilus nuttalli nitidus.* Resident in desert regions of southeastern portion.

420 *a.* Western Nighthawk. *Chordeiles virginianus henryi.* Summer visitant in desert regions.

431.1. FLORESI HUMMINGBIRD. *Selasphorus floresii.* One record by Bryant and one by Emerson.

432. BROAD-TAILED HUMMINGBIRD. *Selasphorus platycercus.* Rare summer visitant along the Sierra Nevada.

444. COMMON KINGBIRD. *Tyrannus tyrannus tyrannus.* Rare summer visitant.

456. PHŒBE. *Sayornis phœbe.* One record by H. S. Swarth.

464.1. SAINT LUCAS FLYCATCHER. *Empidonas cineritius.* One record by A. W. Anthony.

469.1. GRAY FLYCATCHER. *Empidonax griseus.* Summer resident in central portion of State along Boreal Zone; winters in San Diegan district.

474 *g* (*part*). ISLAND HORNED LARK. *Otocoris insularis.* Common resident on the Santa Barbara Islands.

480. WOODHOUSE JAY. *Aphelocoma woodhousei.* Resident along the desert ranges east of the Sierra Nevada.

481.1. SANTA CRUZ ISLAND JAY. *Aphelocoma insularis.* Resident on Santa Cruz Islands.

498 (*part*). NORTHWESTERN RED-WINGED BLACKBIRD. *Agelaius phœniceus caurinus.* Recorded by R. Ridgway at Mendocino County in May.

519 *c.* SAN CLEMENTE HOUSE FINCH. *Carpodacus clementis.* Resident on all the Santa Barbara Islands.

528. REDPOLL. *Acanthis linaria linaria.* One record by J. M. Willard.

540 *b.* OREGON VESPER SPARROW. *Poæcetes gramineus affinis.* Winter visitant.

542. SANDWICH SPARROW. *Ammodramus sandwichensis sandwichensis.* Rare visitant.

549.1. NELSON SPARROW. *Ammodramus caudacutus nelsoni.* Two records.

558. WHITE-THROATED SPARROW. *Zonotrichia albicollis.* Rare visitant.

559 *a.* WESTERN TREE SPARROW. *Spizella monticola ochracea.* One record by Feilner.

567 *b.* SHUFELDT JUNCO. *Junco hyemalis shufeldti.* Occasional winter visitant.

569. GRAY-HEADED JUNCO. *Junco caniceps.* One record by W. B. Judson.

573 *a.* DESERT BLACK-THROATED SPARROW. *Amphispiza bilineata deserticola.* Summer visitant.

581 *k.* MERRILL SONG SPARROW. *Melospiza cinerea merrilli.* Winter visitant.

581 *e* (*part*). OREGON SONG SPARROW. *Melospiza cinerea phœa.* Winter visitant.

581 *d* (*part*). MENDOCINO SONG SPARROW. *Melospiza cinerea cleonensis.* Resident in north humid coast belt.

581 *d* (*part*). MARIN SONG SPARROW. *Melospiza cinerea gouldi.* Resident in Marin and Sonoma counties.

581 *d* (*part*). SANTA CRUZ SONG SPARROW. *Melospiza cinerea santæcrucis.* Resident in the Santa Cruz district.

581 *c* (*part*). SAN DIEGO SONG SPARROW. *Melospiza cinerea cooperi.* Resident in the San Diegan district.

581 *d* (*part*). SALT MARSH SONG SPARROW. *Melospiza pusillula.* Resident in the San Francisco Bay region.

581 *h* SANTA BARBARA SONG SPARROW. *Melospiza graminea.* Resident on Santa Barbara and Santa Cruz Islands.

581 *i.* SAN CLEMENTE SONG SPARROW. *Melospiza clementæ.* Resident on San Clemente, San Miguel, and Santa Rosa Islands.

583 *a.* FORBUSH SPARROW. *Melospiza lincolni striata.* Winter visitant.

585. FOX-COLORED SPARROW. *Passerella iliaca iliaca.* Rare visitant.

585 *a* (*part*). SHUMAGIN FOX SPARROW. *Passerella iliaca unalaschcensis.* Rare winter visitant.

585 *a* (*part*). KADIAK FOX SPARROW. *Passerella iliaca insularis.* Winter visitant.

585 *a* (*part*). YAKUTAT FOX SPARROW. *Passerella iliaca meruloides.* Winter visitant.

585 *a* (*part*). SOOTY FOX SPARROW. *Passerella iliaca fuliginosa.* Winter visitant as far south as San Francisco.

585 *c.* SLATE-COLORED SPARROW. *Passerella iliaca schistacea.* Summer resident.

588 *c.* SAN CLEMENTE TOWHEE. *Pipilo clementæ.* Resident on San Clemente and other Santa Barbara Islands.

594. ARIZONA PYRRHULOXIA. *Pyrrhuloxia sinuata sinuata.* Recorded only at Fort Yuma.

618. BOHEMIAN WAXWING. *Ampelis garrulus.* Recorded as occurring in February, 1892, in northeastern corner of the State.

621 (*part*). NORTHWESTERN SHRIKE. *Lanius borealis invictus.* Midwinter visitant in northern part of State.

622 *c.* ISLAND SHRIKE. *Lanius anthonyi.* Resident on Santa Catalina, San Clemente, and the Santa Cruz Islands.

625. YELLOW-GREEN VIREO. *Vireo flavoviridis.* One record by W. W. Price.

629 *b.* PLUMBEOUS VIREO. *Vireo solitarius plumbeus.* One record by H. W. Henshaw.

636. BLACK-AND-WHITE WARBLER. *Mniotilta varia.* Rare migrant.

646. ORANGE-CROWNED WARBLER. *Helminthophila celata celata.* Recorded only by H. S. Swarth.

647. TENNESSEE WARBLER. *Helminthophila peregrina.* One record by J. Grinnell.

652 *b.* ALASKA YELLOW WARBLER. *Dendroica æstiva rubiginosa.* Migrant.

654. BLACK-THROATED BLUE WARBLER. *Dendroica cærulescens cærulescens.* One record by W. E. Bryant.

657. MAGNOLIA WARBLER. *Dendroica maculosa.* Rare migrant.

672. PALM WARBLER. *Dendroica palmarum palmarum.* One record by W. O. Emerson.

675 *a.* ALASKA WATER THRUSH. *Seiurus noveboracensis notabilis.* One record by L. Belding.

681 *a.* WESTERN YELLOWTHROAT. *Geothlypis trichas occidentalis.* Summer visitant.

681 *c* (*part*). SALT MARSH YELLOWTHROAT. *Geothlypis trichas sinuosa.* Resident at San Francisco Bay.

681 *c* (*part*). TULE YELLOWTHROAT. *Geothlypis trichas scirpicola.* Resident in San Diegan district.

687. AMERICAN REDSTART. *Setophaga ruticilla.* Two records by W. O. Emerson and L. Belding respectively.

704. CATBIRD. *Galeoscoptes carolinensis.* One record by C. H. Townsend.

708. BENDIRE THRASHER. *Toxostoma bendirei.* Occurs only in desert regions of southeastern California.

719 *a* (*part*). SAN JOAQUIN WREN. *Thryomanes bewicki drymœcus.* Resident in central part of State.

719 *d.* SAN DIEGO WREN. *Thryomanes bewicki charienturus.* Resident in San Diegan district.

719 *b* (*part*). DESERT WREN. *Thryomanes bewicki eremophilus.* Resident along desert ranges in southeastern part of State.

719 *a* (*part*). SANTA CRUZ ISLAND WREN. *Thryomanes nesophilus.* Resident on Santa Cruz and Santa Rosa Islands.

719.1. SAN CLEMENTE WREN. *Thryomanes leucophrys.* Resident on San Clemente Island.

733 *a*. GRAY TITMOUSE. *Parus inornatus griseus.* Resident along the desert ranges.

742 (*part*). INTERMEDIATE WREN-TIT. *Chamœa fasciata intermedia.* Resident in humid coast belt from Monterey County northward.

742 (*part*). NORTHERN WREN-TIT. *Chamœ fasciata phœa.* Resident in north humid coast belt.

749 *a*. SITKA KINGLET. *Regulus calendula grinnelli.* Winter visitant.

752. PLUMBEOUS GNATCATCHER. *Polioptila plumbea.* Resident locally in the desert region of southeastern part of State

759 (*part*). COAST HERMIT THRUSH. *Hylocichla aonalaschkœ verecunda.* Winter visitant.

762. SAINT LUCAS ROBIN. *Merula confinis.* One record by W. O. Emerson.

763 (*part*). NORTHERN VARIED THRUSH. *Hesperocichla nœvia meruloides.* Winter visitant.

INDEX

THE YOUNG BIRDS OF ILLINOIS

MRS. WHEELOCK'S EARLIER WORK

NESTLINGS OF
F,OREST *and* MARSH

BY

IRENE GROSVENOR WHEELOCK

Author of " Birds of California"

Beautifully illustrated with twelve full-page photogravures and about fifty delicate half-tones in the text from original photographs.

This volume is a capital one for the lover of things out of, doors, of the woods and the fields, and particularly of the birds, and will furnish abundant suggestions for original field work.

" Her studies have been made in the vicinity of Chicago, and she has evidently had unusually good opportunities to observe certain species — opportunities of which she has availed herself so effectively that her book contains much that is novel."— *Bird-Lore*, New York.

" The numerous illustrations of nests and nestlings add greatly to the realism of her graphically related experiences in the field, and combine with the text to render her book especially attractive as a popular contribution to the life history of some of our commoner birds."— *The Auk*, New York.

" Mrs. Wheelock would seem to have the magic touch in taming the shyest and rarest. She has a host of incidents at command and illustrates her pleasant narrative with many illustrations direct from nature. The volume is a delightful addition to the library of the bird student and lover."— *Philadelphia Public Ledger.*

PRICE, $1.20 net

A. 'C. McCLURG & COMPANY, Publishers

BIRDS *of* THE ROCKIES

WITH CHECK LIST OF COLORADO BIRDS

BY

DR. LEANDER S. KEYSER

Author of " In Bird Land "

With eight full-page bird portraits (four in color) by Louis Agassiz Fuertes; thirty-three text drawings by Bruce Horsfall; eight photographic views of mountain scenery showing the habitats of the birds, and an elaborate index.

In Mr. John Burroughs' recent paper in *The Atlantic Monthly*, on " Real and Sham Natural History," he said : " Mr. Leander S. Keyser's ' Birds of the Rockies ' tells me just what I want to know about the Western birds — their place in the landscape and in the season, and how they agree with and differ from our Eastern species. Mr. Keyser belongs to the noble order of walkers and trampers, and is a true observer and bird-lover."

" The book is beautifully illustrated. . . . Mr. Keyser is an intelligent observer and has a good general knowledge of his subject. . . . A book that is well worthy of extended sale, and which occupies a hitherto somewhat neglected field in the list of popular bird books."— Dr. J. A. Allen, in *The Auk*, New York.

" Mr. Keyser abandoned himself to the fascination of bird-study on plains and foothills, mountain parks and peaks, and his recountal of his experiences cannot fail to arouse the spirit of desire in the minds of those who follow his pages. The book possesses scientific as well as literary value."— Frank M. Chapman, in *Bird-Lore*, New York.

PRICE, $2.50 net

A. C. McCLURG & COMPANY, Publishers